THE ITALIAN SCREWJOB

ALSO BY CHRIS TULLBANE

<u>The Murder of Crows</u>

See These Bones
Red Right Hand
One Tin Soldier

<u>Stories from a Post-Break World</u>

The Stars That Sing
The Storm in Her Smile
A Sure Thing

<u>The Many Travails of John Smith</u>

Investigation, Mediation, Vindication
Blood is Thicker Than Lots of Stuff
Ghost of a Chance
The Italian Screwjob
A Dead Man's Favor *
Godswar *
John Smith Doesn't Work Here Anymore *

*Forthcoming

THE ITALIAN SCREWJOB

CHRIS TULLBANE

GHOST FALLS PRESS

NEVADA

First published by Ghost Falls Press 2022
The Italian Screwjob. Copyright © 2022 by Chris Tullbane.

GHOST FALLS PRESS

Publisher's Cataloging-in-Publication Data
provided by Five Rainbows Cataloging Services

Names: Tullbane, Chris, author.
Title: The Italian screwjob / Chris Tullbane.
Description: Henderson, NV : Ghost Falls Press, 2022. | Series: Many travails of John Smith, bk. 4.
Identifiers: ISBN 978-1-955081-07-8 (paperback) | ISBN 978-1-955081-06-1 (ebook)
Subjects: LCSH: Vampires--Fiction. | Mediators (Persons)--Fiction. | Murder--Fiction. | San Diego (Calif.)--Fiction. | Rome (Italy)--Fiction. | Humorous stories. | Paranormal fiction. | Fantasy fiction | BISAC: FICTION / Fantasy / Urban. | FICTION / Fantasy / Humorous. | FICTION / Occult & Supernatural. | GSAFD: Fantasy fiction. | Humorous fiction.
Classification: LCC PS3620.U45 I83 2022 (print) | LCC PS3620.U45 (ebook) | DDC 813/.6--dc23.

Book cover design by Jake @ jcalebdesign.com

FIRST EDITION

For Nami,
the reason for everything

ACKNOWLEDGMENTS

Thank you to everyone who helped make my seventh book a reality:

My angel-wife, Nami.

The crew: Claudia, Cory, Jamie, Johanna, Keith, Kerri, Mark E., Mark M., Mitch, Montie, Sam, Shawn, Simon, Tom, and Ziggy.

And always last but never least, my parents.

This book would not be what it is without your input and support!

CHAPTER 1

IN WHICH PRIVACY LAWS AND OFFICE HOURS
ARE EQUALLY IGNORED

I read once that there's such a thing as getting too much sleep. Someday, I'd love to have that problem. Four and a half hours after I'd gone to bed, I was awake again, still smelling of beer. The usual nightmare was already fading from my brain, replaced by a grim certainty that something new had gone horribly wrong.

Normally, that would have meant I was naked and chained up in a prison cell or even splayed out on the cracked earth of a hell dimension, but I recognized the lumpy mattress beneath me as the one I'd had since high school, and my arms were wrapped tightly around the pillow I'd nicknamed Anastasia, for reasons both personal and obvious.

I stared up at the ceiling of my bedroom. Barely large enough for a dresser and my twin bed, it was a far cry from my family's old house in Chula Vista. The fact that I was paying rent only added insult to injury. My parents' recent move to Austin had meant I'd finally had to find a place of my own to live in.

Sort of.

A glance at my wonderphone told me it wasn't even ten yet. On a Sunday. With my two-person detective agency currently between cases, there was no reason for me to be up.

Yet here I was, awake and troubled.

With pillow-Ana still whispering sweet nothings in my ear, it took an embarrassingly long time to identify the source of that strange sense of doom, but once I had, I flopped back in my bed with an irritated groan.

At the back of my brain lurked a tiny bundle of *other*, the result of a vampire queen's failed attempt to enslave me almost two years earlier. What had originally been intended as a leash had instead become a sort of mental tether between the two of us, a two-lane highway across which emotions flowed.

It was *Lucia's* worry that had woken me.

I mentally rolled my eyes, fully prepared to go right back to sleep, nightmares and vampire panic attacks be damned, when a second realization struck: it had been literally months since I'd felt the queen this strongly. A combination of the mental walls I'd painstakingly learned to erect and the physical distance between Cardiff and Hillcrest had reduced the femmepire's presence to a muted buzz at the back of my brain. For me to not only feel her concern but be *woken* by it could only mean one thing.

She was nearby.

I pulled on a mostly clean t-shirt and went looking. The door to Juliette's much larger bedroom was open, but neither my business partner nor her blood donors were inside, and the only bathroom was similarly vacant. In a condo as small as ours, that left only the combined kitchen and living room to check.

I crept down the hall.

"Greetings, my thrall." Lucia looked up from a cup of coffee, one eyebrow arched as she took in my bedraggled state. "It is good that you are finally awake. There is much for us to do."

∘∘∘

Lucia looked like she'd come from a week-long spa retreat, glowing with health and vibrancy, from her golden, toned skin to the pristine perfection of her unlined face. The femmepire was one of my least favorite people in the world, but even I had to admit she looked phenomenal for four hundred.

Not that I was going to tell her that.

"You've grown out your hair." What had once been a platinum-blonde angled bob curving around her face now fell in straight lines down to bare shoulders. Both that hair and the usual snow-white outfit set off her million-dollar tan to perfection.

"Your perceptiveness continues to amaze."

I walked past the femmepire to pour my own cup of coffee. Two creams and three sugars later, I took a seat across from my so-called mistress.

"I preferred the old look."

"I will have my stylist whipped and driven from the city." Before I could say anything, she rolled eyes as cold and blue as an arctic sky. "I was being facetious, Mr. Smith. As ever, your opinion is not worth the air used to voice it."

"What are you doing here, Lucia?" I took a long sip of coffee, burned my tongue, and did a terrible job of hiding that fact.

"Your skills are required."

"You don't have me on retainer anymore, and office hours are eight to five." I took another painful sip. "Weekdays only."

"Eight in the morning? Come now, Mr. Smith. Even you are a better liar than that."

"I *wish* it was a lie. Juliette's obsessed with turning the agency around and she doesn't care whose sleep patterns she has to wreck in the process."

"A member of the People *working* for mere humans." Lucia's sneer spoke volumes. "I am pleased that I no longer have to concern myself with how that one's actions reflect upon my House."

"You don't even have a House anymore. And the only reason she's working at all is because you nuked her finances."

"I agreed to unfreeze her accounts and remove the liens on her properties. I made no guarantees regarding the state they would be returned in."

That was Lucia-speak for *I had someone burn down my former subject's houses* and *empty her bank accounts.* The queen's long-held philosophy was to repay all harm three-fold, and her exact definition of harm was… malleable.

"Besides," she continued, "I left her *this* space, did I not?"

"Yeah, you're a real saint. Now, tell me what you want or go away. I have two hours of sleep I'd like to get back to. Maybe three."

"On occasion, I have permitted your illusions of independence, Mr. Smith, but we lack the time for such frivolities. Tonight, a plane will leave this city's airport, and you and I will be on it."

Lucia's voice was buttery smooth, her tone utterly confident, but that undercurrent of worry that had first woken me remained, seeping across our bond. I didn't have to be a detective to know something was wrong.

I wasn't entirely sure I cared though.

"Where is this theoretical plane headed? Aspen? Bora Bora? Should I pack board shorts or ski gear?" Not that I had any of the latter. Even with Big Bear only a couple of hours away, ski trips belonged with booze cruises and three-ply toilet paper on the list of niceties that my budget simply couldn't support.

Board shorts, however, would *not* be a problem.

"We will be traveling to Rome." The femmepire took another sip of coffee, either immune to its scalding temperature, or—

Oh. Right. I tapped a finger against my own mug and concentrated. The ceramic chilled quickly, as if it had been left in the refrigerator, and my next sip of coffee was just about perfect.

A spike of irritation floated across the bond to me, but Lucia's face remained calm and composed. Which was *very* un-Lucia, to be honest. She'd been irate when she first learned the witches had inadvertently given me access to her Talent.

I was still puzzling over the queen's strange behavior when her words finally sank in. "Wait… *Rome? *You mean *Italy? *The place you were banished from on pain of death like a hundred years ago?"

"Yes." Mention of her exile brought back the femmepire I was used to, blue eyes flashing with rage, voice cold and sharp.

"Don't get me wrong," I said. "I'm all in favor of a plan that might get you killed. I just can't see why *I* would join you."

"Lady Dumenyova is in trouble."

That simple statement sucked all the air out of the kitchen.

"What kind of trouble?" I finally asked.

"Without our aid, she will be executed by month's end."

Well, shit.

ooo

Before I could ask any of the questions that had started to bubble up in my brain, we heard the front door open.

"Little bird," Juliette shouted, "are you up?"

"If I wasn't, I would be now."

"Good. You can help Angel with the bags—" Juliette's voice cut off as she came into view. The femmepire I called the Duchess of Snark was clad in her usual riding garb of a motorcycle jacket, t-shirt, and skin-tight jeans. After a narrow-eyed glare at Lucia, she turned on me. "John, when I said you could have house guests, I was thinking desperate divorcees or emotionally stunted coeds. *This*," she said, waving in the direction of the femmepire queen, "is totally unacceptable."

"Distressed that I am witnessing the depths to which you have fallen, child?" Lucia took another sip of coffee, as comfortable as if she were in her own home.

"More like worried that industrial strength bleach won't be enough to remove your stench," the other woman shot back. "Now get the hell out of my house, you overfed, overprivileged, skanky-ass bi—"

Lucia surged to her full—if unimpressive—height, her voice a winter storm that filled the small kitchen. "I will visit my thrall *whenever and wherever* I choose. If you think it is within your power to stop me, do so now or be silent."

"Let's maybe talk about this like rational adults," I suggested in my best mediator voice. While I loved Juliette like a smoking-hot, wildly disturbing stepsister, her propensity for starting trouble had always exceeded her ability to finish it.

"Whatever." Juliette dropped down into a chair, running a hand through her spiky hair. "If you and your thrall want to meet, go do it somewhere else."

"You can both stop calling me a thrall any day now."

"It is what you are," Lucia replied irritably.

"This is what you deserve for opening *our* door to someone like her," growled Juliette at the same time.

"She was already at the table when I woke up!" Which raised the obvious question. "How *did* you get in, Lucia?"

Before the queen could respond, Angel came around the corner, laden down with shopping bags. "Don't everyone get up and help on my account or anything. I can totally carry all the damn groceries—"

She stopped dead at the sight of Lucia, eyes wide and fixed upon the curvaceous femmepire. I rose from my chair, peeled unresponsive fingers away from plastic, and transferred the bags to the counter.

"This would be your other donor?" Lucia stalked over to Angel, a head shorter than the barista despite her snow-white, skyscraper-high heels. The two could not have been more different. Lucia was gorgeous, even for one of the People, with salon-perfect hair, flawless skin, and a wardrobe worth more than my still-new car. Meanwhile, Angel was every bit as human as I was, skinny and casually dressed in a black tee, black jeans, and a brown vest, her only jewelry the silver bangle that Juliette had bought her for Christmas.

Vampire-quick, my partner was between Angel and the queen.

"Rest easy, child." Lucia's teeth flashed in the vague approximation of a smile. "I have no intention of taking her from you. And our tastes are not at all in alignment."

I winced, anticipating an angry retort that never came. Instead, Juliette was frowning.

"Did you say *other* donor?"

"I did. I was given leave to enter by a delightful young man carrying a wetsuit and a six pack of beer. Easy on the eyes, for a monkey, and with barely three brain cells to rub together."

"That sounds like Bobo." The surfer *entrepreneur* had been a dick since the very first night Juliette brought him home. I continued to hold out hope that he would fall beneath the waves and wind up a blood sacrifice to the Mer's watery gods.

Assuming the Mer performed sacrifices. Or worshipped gods, for that matter. I had yet to meet one, given that they didn't breathe oxygen, and even wading into the ocean was enough to get me seasick.

"You know he hates it when you call him Bobo. But it does sound like him," agreed Angel, her gaze still stuck on Lucia.

"Brian." Juliette breathed the name like it had four letters instead of five.

"I didn't ask," replied Lucia with a shrug. "This pathetic shambles you call a life is of no concern to me."

The longer this conversation dragged on, the greater the likelihood of it ending in a fiery apocalypse. Or a wintry one. And I'd had enough of those for three lifetimes. I interposed myself between the two femmepires, aware that even Juliette could tear my arms out of their sockets without the slightest effort. "Was there anything else you needed to tell me, Lucia?"

"Our flight departs at seven. A driver will swing by to collect you at five. See to it that you are on time for once." A small frown marred the beauty of her face as she took in my appearance. "And *try* to look presentable?"

She swept out of the kitchen and the front door banged shut.

"I hate that woman," fumed Juliette.

I shook my head and went to burn some toast.

"Try being her thrall."

CHAPTER 2

IN WHICH PACKING AIN'T EASY

"You're going to *Rome?* With Lucia?" Juliette was looking at me like I'd sprouted a second head. "Have you been drinking the hard stuff again, little bird? You know what tequila does to you…"

"Funny. And I thought we'd pinky sworn to never again mention the *T-word* after last month's debacle." I polished off my second-to-last piece of toast, wishing it had been an Egg McMuffin. "Ana's in trouble."

"Who's Ana?" Angel snagged the remaining piece of toast from my plate, willfully disregarding the sacred laws of breakfast ownership.

"Anastasia Dumenyova, Secundus, Stone Lady, emotionless robot, blah blah blah," recited Juliette. "She's Lucia's assassin and John's would-be girlfriend."

"You're dating an assassin?" Angel gave me a confused look. "How have I never met her?"

"The key word you missed was *would-be,* sweet cheeks."

"She's very busy," I said. "Mainly thanks to Queen Crazy Pants, who you just met. We've been on a couple of dates since I moved in with you guys, but—"

"But little bird wouldn't know how to close the deal if someone gave him an instruction manual and a thirty-minute head start. He has the game of a prepubescent choirboy."

"—but it's hard when she spends so little time here in San Diego," I finished, ignoring Juliette.

"Did Lucia say what Anastasia has been imprisoned for?" The mocking tone had—mostly—left the femmepire's voice.

"Other than breaking her exile? No."

"What was she even doing in Rome?"

"I have no idea."

"And how will the two of you putting yourself in danger help?"

"We… hadn't gotten to that part yet when you walked in."

"And somehow *you're* the senior partner of our agency." She shook her head. "You're going to Rome purely on the say-so of a woman who has consistently lied through her pointy eyeteeth even as she manipulated you from one catastrophe to another?"

When she put it like that…

"Be honest: it's the enormous rack that makes you act like a moron, isn't it?"

I opted not to answer *that* question. "Ana is the closest thing Lucia has to a friend. Also, she'll be breaking her own exile by returning to Rome."

"Unless she plans to slip off the plane before it departs. Or has promised the Italian Court a peek into your funky brain in exchange for clemency. Or is just sick of sharing Anastasia with you."

Angel's eyes went wide at the last comment, but Juliette and I turned to her, speaking in unison.

"Not *that* way."

Juliette's blood donor seemed disappointed.

"Any of that could be true," I admitted, "but Ana *has* been gone for the last few weeks." Sixteen days, two hours, and roughly five minutes, to be precise. "And before she left, she told me where she was going."

Juliette raised one eyebrow. "Rome?"

"It's almost like you're a detective, Duchess." Ana had actually said *Europe*—her willingness to spill secrets about her work for Lucia only went so far—but I wasn't going to let reality get in the way of an awesome burn. "Anyway, I don't know what Ana was doing there, or how she got caught, or how it is that I'm supposed to help," I added, heading off the other questions I saw lurking in Juliette's yellow eyes, "but if my presence can make a difference—"

"Then you're going. Just another empty-headed knight galloping off to rescue the dragon."

I didn't think that was how the fairy tale usually went... but vampires did have their own literature.

"Even if I wasn't in love with her, I owe her for saving my life like half a dozen times."

"You *do* need saving a lot," Juliette mused.

I gave the femmepire a look. "I'm not the only one. Xavier. The Hawthorne house fire. And let's not forget the witches and their summoned demons."

She rolled her eyes. "Fine, she's a paragon of cold-blooded virtue, and I guess I owe her too. But if you really think I'm going to just drop everything to go to Rome with you—"

"I don't."

"Oh. Well, okay then." She chewed on that a little bit, nonplussed. "Are you sure you want to do this alone?"

"Backup would be awesome," I admitted, "but you're still getting your new, post-House life set up here with Angel and Bobo. You need to focus on yourself for a bit."

"That's shockingly considerate of you, little bird."

"Plus..."

"Plus?"

"We're starting the Superchargers investigation tomorrow."

"Oh, right." Juliette started to nod, then froze. "Wait, you're leaving me alone on that? No freaking way!"

"It's a cheating spouse case. You've already done like five of those since joining the agency."

"For *human* clients! Humans that don't have your stupid immunity to compulsion. What the hell am I supposed to do with *goblins?*"

"You could try actually investigating?" I didn't bother hiding my smile. Since inviting herself on as my partner at the agency, Juliette had been using her vampire mojo as a shortcut on investigations that would have otherwise taken weeks. It was bad enough that she could *physically* run laps around me… having her do the same in my primary profession, without any training whatsoever, was totally unfair.

The Superchargers, however, were one of our local goblin tribes, and goblins, like many of the creepy-crawlies of the world, were resistant to vampire mojo. Which meant Juliette was going to have to rely on genuine detective skills for the first time in her brief investigative career.

"You've been working with me for almost a year now. I'm sure you'll be fine." I pretended to give it some serious thought. "Either that or the tribe will eat you."

"You and Lucia deserve each other."

"I'll call and check in every night, assuming I don't get kidnapped, stripped naked, and tortured again."

"Again?" asked Angel.

"It happens more than you'd think," Juliette informed her human chew toy.

"It really does." In the past few years, I'd seen almost as many dungeons as motel rooms. And I'd seen a lot of motel rooms. "Hopefully, Italy will be different."

"Do you even have a passport?"

"We live half an hour north of the Mexican border. Of course I have a passport." A sudden thought wiped the smug smile off my face. "What I don't have is luggage."

"I've got a bag you could use," Angel offered unexpectedly. Maybe she and I were finally turning a corner in our relationship. Or maybe she was still coming down from the overwhelming experience of meeting Lucia for the first time.

"That would be great. It's not… hipster couture, is it?"

"What would *hipster luggage* even look like, asshole?"

"I'm guessing it would be described as a *satchel* and have at least one thoughtfully scrawled Bukowski quote on it."

"If you don't want it…"

"No! I'd be delighted to make use of your hipster satchel," I assured her. "Only…"

"Only?"

"It doesn't have any sentimental value, does it?"

"What?"

"Things have a history of blowing up around John when he's on a case," explained Juliette. "Cars… houses…"

"And you invited him to *live here* with us?!?!"

"He caught me in a moment of weakness."

"She was drunk."

"Plus, his rent covers our groceries."

I was pretty sure *Angel* didn't pay rent. Then again, if the alternative involved having to serve as a juice box for a hungry vampire… I was going to choose rent every time.

"You *will* bring my bag back. Undamaged." Angel's eyes were kind of pretty when they glinted angrily like that. Violent disdain had always been my sexual kryptonite.

"Of course I will!" Unless circumstances beyond my control resulted in that bag getting fed to an angry volcano god, obviously. "Let's go dig it out of your closet, and then I'll… pack."

Juliette sighed. "You don't have any clothes to wear, do you?"

"I have *clothes*. But Lucia said I should be *presentable*. Other than my mediator suit, I'm not sure my wardrobe is particularly appropriate for hobnobbing with vampire nobility. Unless they like Star Wars?"

If Lucia was any indication, they wouldn't even know what Star Wars was. Heathens.

"Screw 'em." Juliette shrugged, not at all self-conscious in her faded t-shirt and scuffed jeans. "What are they going to do, murder you for not wearing a tie?"

"Maybe?"

"Fair. It *is* Europe. Maybe call up Kayla and her morsel and get them to take you shopping?"

"They're out of town, remember? K's taking Darlene to Australia to meet the family." Darlene was one my best friends in the world, and Kayla, her vampire lover, wasn't far behind.

"That sucks. I guess you're on your own then." Juliette turned to her donor, ignoring my pleading expression. She gently plucked Angel's hand off the table and held it in her own, tracing patterns on the other woman's pale skin.

"Do you want to maybe come along—"

"Nope." The replies came in stereo, right on top of one another. Neither woman spared me a glance. It was almost creepy.

"We'll be busy," said Juliette.

"Busy?"

She gave me a pointed look.

"Right." I coughed. Even *baristas* got more action than me.

"If Lucia is sending someone to pick you up at five, that gives you plenty of time to get your shopping done. Why don't you go do your thing until… let's say three?"

"It's barely ten in the morning," I pointed out. "Are you really planning on being 'busy' for five hours?"

That just seemed excessive. And exhausting.

"There's a reason he's still single, isn't there?"

"Dozens of them," confirmed Juliette.

"You both suck."

CHAPTER 3

I returned to our condo at the appointed time to find Juliette alone in the kitchen. The femmepire had her feet on the table, a bottle of beer in her hands, and a satiated smile that spoke volumes about the day's activities.

"Where's Angel?"

"Bedroom." The smile morphed into a grin. "Poor girl is kind of wiped out."

"From feeding you or…?"

"Oh, I'd say it's a little bit of A and a lot of B." Juliette's grin widened. Feet still propped up on the table, she extended both arms above her head in a slow stretch that revealed a wide expanse of taut stomach. "Me? I feel pretty damn fantastic."

"I'm sure you do." She looked it too, bright eyed and glowing like she'd gotten an extra ten hours of sleep. The morning's shirt had been replaced by a white, cropped, Sex Pistols tee, one of her favorites for lounging around the apartment. "Did Bobo ever make it home?"

"Brian is still out. Whenever he gets back, we will have a long talk about opening the door to strange and impossibly obnoxious women."

"It didn't sound like she even needed to compel him." My stealthy campaign to get Bobo evicted was weeks in the making, but swiftly picking up steam.

"If *you're* any indication, all she had to do was shake her oversized breasts in his face. Besides, it's *your* fault she was here at all."

And just like that, my hopes of a quick victory went up in smoke. I retreated to fight another day, nodding at the beer in Juliette's hand.

"Ballast Point?"

"You know it. They make one hell of a red ale."

"And do those ales travel in packs…?"

Juliette smirked and waved in the direction of the cupboard. "Have at it, little bird."

Best. Partner. Ever. I set my shopping bag down and made a detour to grab a beer. Upon returning, I held the bottle out and she casually popped the cap off with one flick of her thumb.

"Sometimes, your species has its uses."

"Pity the same can't be said for humans. Most of them anyway." Yellow eyes flickered in the direction of the master bedroom.

"And here you thought keeping donors of your own would be too much trouble."

"Sixty years ago, the neighbors *freaked* when someone populated their house with unmarried sex objects. These days, nobody gives a crap. I'm not sure the world would care even if they knew the whole truth. It definitely makes things less of a drag." Her eyes drifted to the bag at my feet. "Did you get everything you needed for the trip?"

"Of course." I paused to reconsider. "At least I think so."

"You think so?"

"A pair of gray slacks, some *nice* socks, and two more dress shirts that should work with my suit."

"That's *it?* After five hours of shopping?"

"I got lunch too."

"Of course you did."

"Between this and what I already have, I should be fine."

"John, can we assume that Lucia wants you to mediate on Anastasia's behalf?"

I nodded. While my shining secondary career as San Diego's mediator for the supernatural had been stuck in neutral this past year, a political brouhaha in Rome pretty much demanded my particular set of skills.

"And do we agree that the nobles of my species are always enormous pains in the ass when it comes to matters of politics?"

"I wish it was *just* politics."

"Then shouldn't you expect to be in Rome for *at least* a few weeks? I don't think one suit is going to cut it."

"Weeks? Shit. Mike's getting married on the 7th!"

"That's almost a month away, little bird. You'll either be dead or done with the mediation by then." She paused, the beer halfway to her lips. "I don't still have to go to your so-called best friend's wedding if you're dead, do I? I've never even met him!"

"Given that my parents will be coming back to San Diego to attend, you might be too busy telling them how I died doing something stupid. Besides, you technically weren't even invited; you were just going as my plus-one… and only if Ana was still away."

"And isn't *that* the sort of thing every woman loves to hear?"

"Maybe?"

Her expression told me I'd answered incorrectly.

"Anyway," I continued, "it's not like my budget is unlimited. This pretty much wiped out my reserves."

"Seriously? The agency isn't doing *that* badly. All joking aside… if I'm charging you too much rent, you should tell me. I don't have a clue what you humans pay for things these days."

"Only because you so rarely pay for anything."

"Obviously." Like most vampires, Juliette had no moral issues with using her powers to simply take what she wanted, whether that something was a pair of Louboutin heels or a Ducati. The only reason she paid for groceries was because Angel had given her a long speech about how retail theft hurt the unfortunate employees.

"It's not the rent."

"Then what is it? If you had a drug habit, I'd smell it on you… and I know you're not a gambler."

"I *could* be a gambler." Riverboat John had a certain ring to it.

"You play the nickel slots."

"What's wrong with nickel slots?"

"Which leaves—as usual—Anastasia Dumenyova," she concluded with a sigh.

"Dating is expensive," I admitted. Especially when dating a four-century-old woman with more elegance and sophistication in her little finger than I had in my entire body. The infrequency of those dates had been one of the few things keeping me afloat.

"You do remember that she's filthy rich, right?"

"It's impossible not to, when she picks me up in her Model S." I sighed. "I can't have her pay for everything. That would kind of ruin this whole responsible adult image I'm going for."

"So will going bankrupt. Or," smirked Juliette, "showing up to Rome in flip-flops."

"I do have shoes!"

I made a mental note to pack my shoes.

Juliette eyed her now-empty bottle of beer and shrugged. "Well, it's not like fashion has ever been a key contributor to your success. Clearly. I'm sure everything will be fine."

"I hope so." I finally remembered my own beer and took a sip. "Is this… warm?"

Some people preferred room temperature ale, but I'd been raised to drink it cold, like a civilized human being. Without waiting for a reply, I wrapped a hand around the bottle and concentrated. My next sip was ice cold.

"You're getting better at using Lucia's power," said Juliette, "and it's been a while since you passed out from doing it."

"I only fainted the one time, and I'd just skewered a demon with an ice spear the size of my Corolla. Something minor like this just makes me tired. And hot. Thankfully, nothing cures heat exhaustion like a frosty beer." I took a healthy swallow.

"There's something very wrong with that logic—"

"Says the femmepire drinking warm beer."

"—but you've got more important things to focus on."

"Like what?"

"Like getting packed?"

"Oh. That." I couldn't help but grin. I was flying to Europe on someone else's dime to save the woman I loved.

How freaking cool was that?

ooo

Angel had left her bag out for me, and my predictions of *hipster-satcheltude* proved painfully accurate. If my twin careers as detective and mediator ever finished fizzling out, I could always try my hand as a carnival fortune teller.

To be fair, it was more rucksack than satchel, which was good, since even my limited wardrobe would have been tough to squeeze into a satchel. The bag did scream hipster though, from the distressed brown leather to the unnecessarily long straps and preponderance of buckles. I packed most of my clothes, my toiletries, my well-worn copy of Mediation for Dummies, and… pretty much everything else I owned into the bag, and cinched it shut.

My suit, however, was going to be a problem.

"Duchess," I called out into the hall, "do you have something I can put my suit in? Something that won't end with it looking like it was wadded into a very small ball?"

"Keep your voice down, idiot." I heard the door to the master bedroom she shared with Angel and Bobo creak open as she ducked inside. Moments later, it closed again, and she came back with a long, flat garment bag.

"Thank you." I paused after taking it from her. "Why do *you* have a bag like this?"

"Is that a trick question?"

"I just have a hard time picturing you carrying it with you as you trailed punk bands across America," I explained.

"Times have changed since the 70s, little bird. These days, I travel in style, and with more than one outfit." She nodded to the bag I still held in my hands. "That works as well for dresses as it does suits."

"Dresses?" I eyed the femmepire. In addition to the aforementioned t-shirt, she was wearing cut-off sweats that were the furthest thing from formal.

"I do have dresses, asshole."

"Sure, but all the ones I've seen to this point were handkerchief-sized."

"Are you complaining?"

"Absolutely not." I was dating Anastasia, but only a blind idiot would be unaware that Juliette was dangerously attractive. "But I'm pretty sure you could fit three of those dresses into your *purse*."

"And this is why you're a man, and cannot have nice things," Juliette replied primly. "That is no way to treat silk. Now, do you want the damn bag or not?"

○○○

A very short time later, I carried both bags with me into the kitchen and dropped into a chair next to Juliette. The femmepire had her laptop on the table and was focusing intently on its screen.

"Harry Potter fan fiction?"

"Funny. I prefer Draco anyway."

"Of course you do."

She waved a hand at the screen. "This is info on our local goblin tribes. Since you're dumping the investigation on me, I figured I should brush up on things."

I wasn't the most astute of individuals—something of a career limiting characteristic for my primary profession—but even I could pick up on Juliette's worry. "After I've made a sandwich, why don't we go over the particulars of the case together?"

"Don't you need to head downstairs?"

"Nah." I checked my bond. "From the feel of it, Lucia just left Ana's place in Cardiff. It'll be half an hour at least before she makes it here to pick me up."

"I'm sure I'd be fine without your help, but if you're bored…"

We spent the next twenty minutes reviewing the details of the case. San Diego had three local goblin tribes: the Superchargers, the Padres, and the Clippers. I had no idea why goblin tribes took their names from local sports franchises or why the Clippers had stuck around after the NBA team moved to Los Angeles, but it did make them easy to remember.

My former client, Chief Tikky-Wokka Tomlinson—four and a half feet of foul breath and gray, knobby skin—had hired us to look into the affairs of one of his wives, Rihanna Mariah Kardashian. And by *the affairs*, I meant he wanted us to prove that she was having one.

"I still don't get it," decided Juliette.

"How someone who looks like *that* can have multiple wives?"

"That too," she admitted. "But if he thinks she's sleeping around on him, why doesn't he kick her ass to the curb? Why does he need to hire us?"

"Adultery is a killing offense in goblin society," I reminded her, "and Rihanna was originally part of the Clippers. If he kills her without proof, the other tribe will retaliate. And a blood war between tribes would be bad."

Juliette shivered. Goblins made up for their size through viciousness and sheer numbers, as a pack of Infected had learned to their regret when coming to town to root on their Denver Broncos. If the werehorses had asked permission before intruding, they *might* have made it back to Colorado alive.

Or maybe not. Team affiliation bordered on a religion for goblins. My predecessor, the Rook, had mediated the resulting fallout, and given that the city was still standing, I could only assume he'd been successful.

"So, we just need to find that proof?" Juliette seemed relieved. Despite the supernatural trappings, this really was like one of our usual cases.

"If it exists, yeah." I finished my sandwich and pushed the plate away with a sigh. "Although if you can figure out some way for this to *not* end in someone's death, that would be awesome too. Corporal punishment for a broken marriage is frankly unacceptable."

"So is cannibalism, which goblins also practice."

That was a good point. "Well, just do what you can. At the end of the day, nobody's paying us to modernize goblin society."

"Thank the gods," my partner muttered.

"Remember, I'll be a phone call away if you need anything."

The bond informed me of Lucia's arrival moments before the door buzzer sounded. I spared a glance for my dirty plate.

"I'll take care of it," said Juliette. "This once."

"Thanks." I met her yellow eyes and smiled, trying to appear confident. "I'll be back in a few weeks."

"Are you *sure* you want to do this?"

"Why wouldn't I be?"

"My room is just down the hall from yours, little bird, and I *do* have super hearing. I've heard the nightmares. Every. Single. Night."

I swallowed. "Can we just pretend they're sex dreams and never, ever talk about them again?"

"If they *were* sex dreams, we would *totally* talk about them. You know that, right? I need my entertainment."

"Of course you do." I sighed. "I won't pretend the last few years have been easy. I'm still trying to process everything that happened with the witches and Zorana, but…"

"But?"

"Ana's in trouble."

"Right." The femmepire sagged back in her chair. "And you wouldn't be you if you took the safe way out. I get that. I just want you to know—" She flushed and fell silent.

"I love you too. Just don't tell Angel or she'll stab me in my sleep with one of those latte art pens."

"You are such a moron." She smiled and walked me to the door. "Try not to get yourself killed."

"I'll do my best." Rucksack over one shoulder and garment bag in hand, I exited the apartment.

Juliette's voice, oddly pensive, followed me down the hall.

"That's what worries me."

CHAPTER 4

Juliette's condo sat on the top floor of a nine-story building. I rode the elevator down to the lobby, Lucia's impatient summons reverberating in the back of my brain.

It was going to be a long trip.

Outside, April was doing its best impression of May Gray. At the curb, a gleaming black limo idled directly in front of the "No Parking" sign. Hillcrest was a fancy neighborhood, but that fanciness usually manifested in the form of designer cupcakes and antique wine cabinets—the limo looked absurdly out of place.

The rear passenger door swung open, and this time the queen's irritation was accompanied by an audible voice. "Put your luggage in the trunk and get in, Mr. Smith. We have much to do."

The trunk already contained two oversized suitcases, both white leather, but I found space for Angel's satchel, and laid Juliette's garment bag on top.

"What's the hurry?" I asked, as we pulled away from the curb. "Lindbergh is twenty minutes away. Thirty, tops. Even for an international flight, we should have plenty of time."

The queen's earlier outfit was gone, replaced by a tailored skirt suit in winter white. It would have almost looked corporate, if both the jacket and the pristine white blouse beneath it hadn't been unbuttoned to display a country mile of cleavage.

"I am capable of calculating both time and distance, my thrall. We have an errand to run before departing for the airport."

"Still not your thrall," I reminded her. The privacy glass was up, shielding us from the driver and making it impossible to look out the front window. "So, where are we going then?"

"Have patience. All will reveal itself in time." Lucia crossed her legs in a soft swoosh of silk and turned to look out the window.

In another sign of slow but steady maturation, I bit back a half dozen retorts and focused on counting to ten in my mind.

I'd only made it to six when Lucia spoke again.

"I understand Caleb Van Stahl has begun another mediation."

"Oh yeah?" The subject change caught me off guard.

"Indeed. Your rival mediator continues to flourish."

"He's more colleague than rival," I said. "We hashed things out over coffee last Christmas. He's working the coastlines while I work the interior."

"And how many mediations have you had in the time since?"

"None," I admitted, glossing over the fact that it had been almost a full year since my last mediation. "But I'm sure *someone* will start a blood feud sooner or later."

I just hoped that someone wasn't my firm's junior partner. People would talk.

Lucia said nothing, which was a message all on its own.

"What do you know that I don't?"

"A vast multitude of things, Mr. Smith."

"About my business, I mean."

"Mr. Van Stahl's new mediation is in Ramona, for the chupacabras."

Which meant Caleb was flat out ignoring our agreement: Ramona was a good hour from the beach.

"Well, shit."

"Yes. While you were busy taking the high road, Mr. Van Stahl was taking your position as city mediator."

I frowned. I had stumbled into the whole mediation gig, and still wasn't particularly great at it, but those few cases had provided welcome breaks from my usual investigative work.

The extra source of income hadn't hurt either.

"I'm sure there's an explanation," I finally managed.

"Such as?"

"I don't know."

"As I thought."

"Why do you care anyway?"

"You are my thrall." Lucia cut off my protest with a slash of a well-manicured hand. "However much we both might wish otherwise, it is an indisputable *fact*. Your actions reflect upon me, and with my power base in the Americas effectively crippled, reputation matters now more than ever. As city mediator, you had both status and prestige. As a lowly private investigator, your value is significantly reduced."

"That doesn't mean you get a say in how I run my business." Caleb breaking our deal was a bit of a shock, but I was sure he'd had a good reason for it. Maybe a preexisting professional relationship with the chupacabras or something? That would make sense.

A small groove appeared between her pale eyebrows. "You are ignoring the larger picture. As usual."

"Screw the larger picture and screw your reputation, Lucia. All I care about is Anastasia. And I can't help but notice that we're talking about everything *but* the case you woke me up for."

"The trip to Rome is lengthy, Mr. Smith. There will be ample time for you to review those details later."

I turned in my comfortable seat to face her fully. "Lucia, if this is going to work, you need to stop treating me like an unpaid servant and start thinking of me as a partner. If you can't manage even that much, then we should call this whole thing off right now."

"You would let my Secundus perish over a matter of pride? Is this what passes for human sentiment in the modern era?"

"Rome is thousands of miles away from anyone I would consider an ally and full of people who want one or both of us dead. Including your own brother, the freaking king of the vampires. If we can't work together, *we're going to lose*. And I refuse to go to Italy just to watch Ana die."

In the back of my mind, I was already formulating a contingency plan. Who could I call to form a sort of supernatural commando squad capable of invading Rome and smuggling Anastasia to safety? Unfortunately, I'd cashed in a lot of my favors when dealing with the witches the previous year, and the list of people left basically consisted of an insane demigod, a ghost, and Juliette. And while my friends were all badasses in their own ways, I wasn't sure the four of us could take on every vampire in Europe. As annoying as it was to admit, Lucia was my best shot at rescuing Ana.

Thankfully, the queen appeared to have reached the same conclusion about me.

"Very well, Mr. Smith. But if we are truly to be partners in this, there can be no signs of dissent between us. You will need to let go of your inexplicable anger towards me."

"Inexplicable? You made me a thrall against my will!"

"An action for which I apologized quite adequately last year."

"I'm going to have you stuck in my head for the rest of my life. An apology—adequate or otherwise—doesn't cut it."

Lucia rolled her eyes. "It is unlikely that your life will span more than a few additional decades anyway. Assuming your attitude doesn't get you killed first. In the meantime, you cannot deny that your station has improved in virtually every other facet since Anastasia hired you to mediate for us. Your investigative agency is flourishing, you are no longer living with your parents, and my Secundus, for reasons I cannot fathom, has yet to crush your irrational dreams of a romantic liaison with her."

"None of which had anything to do with you," I reminded her, "except in terms of us reacting to the messes you created."

"The messes I created?" The temperature in the limo plunged and the queen's pale eyes flashed gold. "Are you willfully blind or merely ignorant?"

Neither of those labels seemed accurate, so I stayed silent.

"It was *you* who dragged my House into conflict with one of North America's largest packs of Infected. It was *you* who gave the Temecula coven direct access to my power, who split the focus of the one individual in this world that I can trust, *and* who cost me my House. *Yet you speak to me of messes?*"

I had a whole list of *yeah, but's* ready to go in response—starting with *yeah, but none of that would have happened if you hadn't enslaved me first*—but the enraged femmepire didn't seem open to my particular brand of logic just then. So instead, we simply glared at each other, breath fogging in the now-frigid air, as our limo continued to navigate the pothole-stricken streets.

Finally, someone dared to break the silence. With a shock, I realized it was me, and that I was using my most polished mediator voice, the kind that could talk werewolves into an amicable divorce and—

—well, technically, that was the most impressive thing I'd ever done with it. But still, it *had* been kind of amazing.

"I won't deny that mistakes have been made. On both sides." Even if she *had* started it. "You and I will never be friends, Lucia, but we want the same thing here: Anastasia safe and free. Can we skip past all the usual arguments and discuss the situation at hand?"

"Very well." She sighed and shook her head, hair pouring over one shoulder like liquid platinum. If vampires ever had bad hair days, I'd yet to witness one. "What is it you wish to know?"

"What is she accused of? They don't execute people just for breaking their exile, do they?"

"Not usually. Although," mused the queen, "there have been exceptions in the past."

"Seriously? Then what's to stop Tomasso from putting you in front of a firing squad too?"

"I am returning to Rome with the blessing of its Council. My exile has been temporarily waived due to the circumstances."

"Circumstances that you *still* haven't shared."

Her anger a thing of the past, Lucia's eyes were back to being the color of a crisp, cloudless blue sky. "My Secundus stands accused of a heinous crime. As her liege, I have both the right and obligation to prepare her defense."

Heinous crime sounded bad.

"What have they charged her with?"

"Regicide."

I blinked.

"In truth, you were wrong about one thing, Mr. Smith. I have many enemies in Italy, but my brother, the former king of the Italian Courts, is no longer among them."

"And—"

"And all evidence suggests that Lady Dumenyova killed him."

Maybe *bad* was an understatement.

ooo

Our limo had turned onto Laurel and started down the steep decline by the time I'd finally come to grips with Lucia's little bombshell.

"Tomasso is dead, and they think Anastasia did it."

"Yes."

"Which is actually a fair assumption, given both her skills as an assassin and your brother's sponsorship of Xavier's own plot to kill you just a few years ago."

"Your command of the obvious remains one of your less admirable traits, my thrall."

"Did she do it?"

The silence that filled the limo was profound. And profoundly disturbing.

"I do not know," the queen finally admitted. "Did I send her to kill him? I did not. But… things do happen."

That settled it. None of us were making it out of Rome alive.

"As liege of the defendant, I am, by rights, granted permission to procure my own investigator," Lucia continued. "You will work with the Crown Watch to reconstruct what happened and identify the real killer."

"Right. Assuming Anastasia is not the real killer." So much for my assumptions that I was headed to Rome as a mediator.

"And if she is?"

"It's been five minutes since you dropped this whole mess on me. I haven't thought it through yet. There'll have to be some sort of Plan B, I guess."

"Plan B?"

"Whatever Ana did or didn't do, there's no way in hell I'm going to let them kill her."

"For once, we are in agreement."

On cue, my imagination supplied an intricate Bond-esque action sequence, where I infiltrated the highly guarded dungeon in Rome, disabled the multitude of guards, rescued Anastasia, and then fled the country in a speed boat. Or an F-15.

I couldn't help but notice that the Bond version of me had abs. Lucky bastard.

"You do realize that this isn't something I have any experience in, right? If you're only allowed one investigator, maybe you should hire someone who has actually worked a murder before."

"If such an individual were available, I would have already hired them. I need someone with knowledge of my kind, who is not currently under the employment of a rival faction. Even more damning, I need someone that I can trust."

Given that I would gladly let Lucia fall on her well-rounded ass in every trust exercise ever invented, I found the sudden declaration of faith difficult to swallow.

"While your business sense is abominable, and your professionalism laughable, it is impossible to deny that you do get results... and your delusional fixation upon my Secundus means you will be properly motivated to save her life. On rare occasions, dedication and desire can be of greater value than experience or skill."

"Ah." That last bit at least made sense. Through another superhuman act of restraint, I avoided pointing out that the queen was depending heavily on a relationship she'd done her very best to keep Ana and I from even having.

Our limo turned before we reached the 5 and slowed to a stop near some ratty apartment buildings. Over the past decade or two, Banker's Hill had become a nice and expensive neighborhood, but these residences were still fighting the good fight against urban gentrification. One of the buildings even had an honest-to-God chicken coop by its door.

"*This* was your super-secret, pre-airport stop?"

"As I said, we have an errand to complete."

"And will I ever find out what this errand—"

I stopped. A familiar figure was making his way out of the nearby alley.

"Marcus." Lucia greeted the other vampire warmly as he joined us in the limo.

"Your Majesty." Dark eyes flicked to me and then back away. "Filthy monkey."

Marcus was, to the best of my knowledge, still a member of the San Diego House whose ownership had been wrested from Lucia. He and his thousand-dollar Armani suits should have been busy counting beans for the House's new leader, Duke Barros, instead of… oh for God's sake, was he seriously kissing her ring?

"Jesus, dude… have some self-respect."

Both vampires ignored me with obvious effort. My ability to annoy other species seemed to increase in direct proportion to the number of them present.

Which really made going to Rome a spectacularly stupid idea.

"Is it done?" Lucia's eyes were bright with anticipation.

"It is, Your Majesty." The manpire released her hand and leaned back in his seat, smiling openly.

"Is *what* done?"

Marcus' lips thinned at my interruption, but with Lucia's nod of permission, he deigned to explain.

"Duke Barros will wake up tomorrow to find his traitorous House bereft of funds, Mr. Smith."

"You robbed the House?" I didn't have any love for Barros, and I actively despised his chief thug, Thales, but both Brazilians scared the crap out of me. Robbing them seemed like a fantastic way to get one's ashes dumped into the Pacific.

"Robbed? Don't be ridiculous. I am an operator of skill, not some bandana-wearing, gun-waving fool who seeks to steal from a train on horseback."

There were times I wondered what century Marcus thought we were living in.

"But you just said…"

"It took seven months, three new projects, and substantially inflated ROI before the fool trusted me sufficiently to restore my position on the Council. Even once I had the financial keys to Barros' so-called kingdom, penetrating his private accounts was a task of additional months. Once I had accomplished that much, however, it was a simple matter to funnel those funds through a small credit union in Mexico which—" He pulled out a gold pocket watch and ostentatiously checked the time. "—as of six hours ago, was dissolved by the federal government for suspected ties to the local cartel."

"And the funds in question, Marcus?"

"Safely deposited into your off-shore accounts, my queen, with no trail for our enemies to follow." The smile Marcus turned on me was unabashedly smug. "I would like to see your pistol-waving idols manage that."

"Trail or not, they will know who's responsible. Why bother with the elaborate charade?"

"Deniability, Mr. Smith," Lucia answered coolly. "Without proof of malfeasance, Duke Barros has no official recourse."

"What about *unofficial* recourse?" To me, Marcus looked way too calm for someone with a billion-dollar target on his back. "Thales isn't going to let a little thing like protocol stop him. And he's a Battle Lord, last I checked."

"That would be cause for concern," Marcus admitted, "if Barros and his ilk didn't have larger troubles to occupy their time."

I slumped back in my seat and sighed loudly. "Could someone just tell me what the hell is going on?"

"Very well. I will even use small words, in the desperate pursuit of your comprehension." Marcus brushed imaginary lint off the gray sleeve of his suit jacket. "The funds that I transferred were a combination of House Borghesi's investments, Duke Barros' own personal accounts, and two other accounts. Accounts that originated with the primary House in Brazil."

"A masterstroke, Marcus," murmured Lucia in tones of glowing approval. She turned to me, a triumphant smile transforming her always beautiful face. "Duke Barros was embezzling from his former House. While his actions had gone unnoticed to date, the disappearance of all funds from those two accounts will surely catch someone's attention."

"And the paper trail leads right to the duke, who will find himself unable to return the funds he stole," finished the manpire. He offered Lucia a half bow from his seat in the limo, a gesture that should have looked ridiculous but didn't. "Barros is ruined, and has no choice but to flee, leaving our former House leaderless. The stage has been set for you to resume control."

Part of me wanted to mock the manpire's flowery speech. The rest of me was wrestling with the shocking realization that Marcus—obnoxious, pedantic, accountant Marcus—was, in his narrow area of specialization, kind of a terrifying badass.

The queen tapped her long nails on the leather arm rest, then shook her head decisively. "I will not be reclaiming the House."

Marcus blinked. "I beg your pardon?"

When Lucia spoke, her voice was hard. "Mr. Smith and I leave tonight for Rome. There are more important things at stake than a single, traitorous House full of individuals who surrendered without a murmur during my convalescence."

"You were in a coma and the coup was completed before most of the People even knew it was happening," I argued. "You can't blame them for that."

"Can't I?" Lucia shrugged slim shoulders. "As I said, there are more important matters in play."

"I… see." Marcus had visibly deflated. "Will you need my aid in Rome then, your Majesty?"

"No." Lucia softened her tone, sounding for a moment like she almost cared. "You continue to demonstrate your skill and loyalty, Marcus. It is time you receive your just reward."

In the movies, this was when the femme fatale would have pulled out her ivory-handled derringer and put two slugs into the unsuspecting henchman's face… but Lucia instead pulled an envelope from her purse.

"As you are aware, Borghesi International owns property across the world. Enclosed within are the addresses and deeds of three estates in some of our more tropical locations. They are yours."

Marcus didn't look like a man who'd just been given three houses. Not that I had a lot of experience with that sort of thing… but television had taught me to expect some mixture of cheers and grateful sobbing. The manpire looked almost… morose.

"Am I to be banished once more?"

Lucia's laughter, like her smile, was a thing of uncommon and rarely witnessed beauty. "This is not *exile*, Marcus. It is merely a reward and a much-deserved vacation. When my business in Rome is complete, we will reconvene to discuss the future."

I watched the manpire leave and shook my head. While I was busy trying to prove Anastasia innocent of a crime she very well might have committed, Marcus would be sipping Mai Tais at one of his beach-front properties.

I should have just stayed in bed.

○○○

"Speak, thrall."

"I'm sorry?"

Lucia turned in her seat to regard me. "You have been staring. While that is hardly an uncommon occurrence with you, your gaze has for once been fixed upon my face rather than my breasts, suggesting that your brain might actually be engaged. So, ask whatever question it is that has woken you from your usual mental torpor."

I marveled at the impressively dense array of insults that had just been lobbed in my direction. "It's not really a question. I'm just kind of shocked—pleasantly shocked—that you're putting Ana's life before your own egotistical ambition for once."

"Is that what you think is happening here?"

"Isn't it?"

"Perhaps."

"Perhaps?" Socrates had nothing on *my* interrogation technique.

"Perhaps I am not quite the monster you have long believed me to be. Or perhaps there is more to this situation than your severely limited mental facilities can discern."

"And which of those is the truth?"

"Maybe neither of them. Maybe both."

"Didn't we *just* agree to set aside our differences and work together on this trip? Allies don't keep secrets from one another."

"How delightfully naïve of you." Lucia's laughter was a little bit less wondrous this time around. "If you live long enough, you will eventually learn otherwise."

And that's all she would say on the subject.

This trip was really, really going to suck.

CHAPTER 5

Roughly ten minutes later, our limousine dropped us off at Terminal 2. The nameless chauffeur went to check our bags in, and I followed Lucia toward the security line, shaking my head.

"I can't believe we're flying commercial. Doesn't Borghesi International have a private plane?" I'd seen enough movies to know how lux those corporate jets were and had been looking forward to having my own in-flight suite and bar.

"Several, in fact," the vampire queen replied over her shoulder, "but they are in use, and scattered across the globe. I will not curtail their profitable endeavors simply for your comfort. My resources are not infinite."

"You and Marcus just ripped off your House—"

"Former House," she interjected.

"—for everything it was worth, not to mention however much he took from Brazil."

"A very large sum," she acknowledged, as we reached the interminable security line. "Yet even such a sum remains some distance from infinite."

I didn't remember much from high school, but her math *sounded* correct. Even so, she was missing my point. "That's not what I… uhm, Lucia?"

While I had dutifully shuffled into place at the end of the line—trained by a lifetime of Southern California theme parks—the queen was skirting that line entirely, making her way past the crowd toward the guards. With a muttered curse, I jumped out of line and followed. By the time I reached the front, a heavyset TSA agent was ushering Lucia through. The lack of protest from the crowd told me Lucia was using her vampire mojo to cloud the minds of everyone present.

I scurried after, passport and boarding pass in hand, and almost impaled myself upon the outstretched hand of that same agent.

"Sir," he told me unkindly, "I'm gonna have to ask you to wait in line." He nodded in the direction of the crowd.

"I'm with her," I said, motioning to the vampire queen just behind him.

The agent didn't even glance in Lucia's direction. "You could be with the King of England, for all I care; you gotta go through the line, like everyone else."

"England has a queen," I pointed out helpfully.

The man seemed unimpressed by my knowledge of international politics. Out of the corner of my eye, I could see some of his fellow agents taking note.

"Lucia…!" I called over the guard's shoulder, finding yet again that panic made my voice go high in a distinctly unmanly fashion. "A little help here?"

"Very well." She rolled her eyes with a put-upon sigh. "Captain Daniels, this man is with me. He does not need to wait in line."

The man's face cleared almost instantly, and his eyes drifted slightly out of focus. "Yes, ma'am! Sir, if you would step on through?"

"Absolutely." I tried not to gloat, but it was difficult... and I didn't try all that hard, to be honest. This was one of the few times vampiric compulsion had ever been used on my behalf, and it didn't suck. It was kind of like being a Jedi-by-proxy.

"Actually," said the queen, "perhaps you should make quite certain that he is not carrying any contraband. One can never be too careful about these things."

ooo

Ten minutes later, having been thoroughly searched by a man who lacked the decency to buy me drinks first, I joined a disgustingly smug vampire queen.

"What the hell, Lucia?"

"As you pointed out, Mr. Smith, we are headed into dangerous territories, where a single misstep might kill us both."

"So?"

"So, I decided to lighten the mood."

"*Lighten the mood?* The dude practically had his hands down my pants!"

"You are headed to Rome, my thrall." She arched one blonde eyebrow. "Modesty should be the least of your concerns."

And what the hell did that mean?

"You know," I finally managed, as we headed toward our gate. "I don't think the TSA uses military rank."

"What are you babbling about now?"

"You called him *Captain* Daniels."

"Who?"

"The TSA agent!" Sometimes, I wondered if Lucia took notice of the people around her at all. The rest of the time, I was certain she didn't. "I don't think that's his title."

"Nor is his name Daniels. What does it matter?"

There was surprisingly little I could say to that.

○○○

While Lucia continued to our gate, I made a quick stop at the restroom. If what I had heard about airplane bathrooms was anywhere near close to accurate, I wanted to visit ours as infrequently as possible. With my luck, the in-flight facilities would be occupied by couples happily punching their mile-high club membership cards anyway.

I stepped around some dude's urine puddle, splashed water on my face, and dried my hands beneath a sputtering blower, when another thought struck me.

With Lucia in Rome and Marcus somewhere unfairly tropical, the most logical targets for Barros' wrath would be out of reach. Which might induce him to go after *less* logical targets. Juliette, having left the House before the coup, should be safe, but that still left quite a few possible victims.

I pulled out my wonderphone and made some hurried calls.

○○○

Lucia had found us the two chairs closest to our gate. I walked over and took a seat next to her, flashing an apologetic smile at the two travelers she had clearly just evicted.

"This is for the flight." The femmepire handed me a thick manila folder that she had pulled from a white Louis Vuitton purse worth twice my monthly rent.

"What is it?"

"Background data on the Italian Court—the people of importance, the present political environment, and anything else you might need to know for your investigation."

"Ah." I opened the folder and found a thick stack of printed pages, each white sheet filled from top to bottom in size eight font. "Does it come with a CliffsNotes?" At her confused expression, I remembered that she had never actually attended school. Not in this century anyway. "A summary, I mean."

"If a summary sufficed, I would have given you one."

Nobody had told me that heroically saving the woman I loved would involve *homework*.

"Mr. Smith." Lucia's voice was soft and deadly serious. "Lady Dumenyova is my oldest friend and my most trusted vassal. I need your aid to rescue her. If I must *force* you to read the briefing, I will do so."

"Because that went so well for you last time," I muttered.

"Perhaps Captain Daniels is still available for a strip search."

"No need to get nasty… I'll read it." I hefted the manila folder in my hand, shaking my head. "This just isn't the way I tend to work."

"I am aware of your so-called process. And I admit that, despite your tendency to bumble into situations you are entirely unprepared for, your efforts have proven effective in the past." She met my eyes again. "But Rome is not some provincial town. There are terrors there who walked the earth before your people had even left their caves. Those beings do not grant second chances."

I hadn't noticed the various supernatural entities around San Diego being all that forgiving either, but I didn't think Lucia would appreciate my keen insight.

"Furthermore," the femmepire continued, "as you yourself have already noted, you will be without your usual safety nets. Lady Dumenyova is in no position to save you this time and we will be far beyond the domain of your godling and his ageless ward."

I swallowed as her words struck home. I'd been involved in a truly depressing number of life-or-death situations over the past two years, and my pale, pudgy, and entirely mortal ass had only survived thanks to interventions by Ana and Lord Beel-Kasan—Bill to his friends—our local demi-god of Nightmares and Terror.

"That's a good point."

"Which is why I said it." I could hear the disdain in Lucia's voice. "If you wish to stay alive long enough to help rescue my Secundus, you *will* study the dossier I have provided."

I hated when she was right. With a sigh, I flipped to the first page. It looked boring. "Do we have any of the details on Tomasso's murder?"

"We do not. Once we have been presented to the Council, you will have an opportunity to review the evidence their own investigator has already accrued."

This was the first I'd heard of a rival investigator. Hopefully, he or she wouldn't be too much of an asshole. Maybe we could bond over P.I. war stories. And knock-knock jokes. And beer.

I made it three or four lines down that first page—which appeared to consist entirely of the genealogy of people, places, or minerals I'd never heard of—before my eyes started to glaze over. With a frown, I forced myself to keep reading. I'd been out of college for six years now, but I still remembered how to study.

Five minutes later, I realized three things. First, I'd gone to *community* college, and had dropped out after only a semester. Second, even back then, I'd never been good at studying. And third and most importantly, at some point in the preceding five minutes, I had drifted off into some sort of fugue state and had absolutely no idea what I had just read. As I was trying to find a page I *did* remember, something else Lucia had said finally sank in.

"Ageless ward?"

Lucia looked up from her gleaming phone with a frown. "I beg your pardon?"

"You said *godling and his ageless ward*. But Bill only has one ward, and Jee Sun is anything but ageless."

"And how old would you say the child is?"

That was a subject of much debate between Juliette and me. "I don't know… seven? Ten?"

"I arrived in this city well before your birth, Mr. Smith, but Lord Beel-Kasan preceded my arrival by centuries. According to my sources, he has never left the region—beyond trips to his native dimension—with one notable exception."

She paused as some unintelligible announcement was broadcast through budget speakers.

"Twelve years ago, Lord Beel-Kasan was gone for eight days. When he returned, it was in a houseboat that nobody had seen before. And he had a young Korean girl with him. Not an infant. A girl, aged somewhere between five and ten."

"Twelve years ago…?" Even I could see that math didn't add up. "That's impossible."

"As I said, ageless."

With those words, Lucia gracefully rose to her feet, phone in one hand and expensive bag in the other. Directly in front of us, a small line was forming at the gate.

I shut the folder and rose to join her. "How do you know all of this?" When I'd first met Lucia—and Bill—the vampire queen hadn't even realized that Jee Sun existed.

"After the godling chose to take an interest in both my House and my thrall, I decided it would be wise to research my opponent. Information," she concluded, with a nod to the folder in my hands, "can be the difference between success and agonizing death."

"I already said I'd read the briefing!" I tried to ignore the fact that, from her lips, *agonizing death* sounded kind of sexy.

As Juliette too often told me, I had serious issues.

ooo

Our flight to Rome would be the first time I had ever flown at all, and a lot of the minutiae of what we were doing and why was lost on me. Thankfully, several years of being a P.I. had sharpened my observational skills into finely honed instruments of investigative destruction. As a result, I smartly had my boarding pass ready when it was my turn to be greeted by the attendant.

"I'm sorry, sir." I blinked in confusion as the dark-suited American Airlines employee handed back my pass instead of running it through the scanner. "We haven't called for general boarding yet."

"What?" Ahead of me, Lucia was still walking down the tunnel.

"The current call is for first class and special needs passengers only, sir." She waved my boarding pass at me. "You aren't either."

I took the boarding ticket and looked at it for the first time since Lucia had handed it to me. Sure enough; I was flying economy. "But… but… she…" I waved vaguely in the direction of Lucia's receding back, as words, for once, failed me.

"Yes, your uhm…" The other woman glanced from Lucia to me, and made an accurate, if hurtful, snap judgment. "…*employer* is flying first class with us today."

Of course she was.

○○○

I only had to sit in the boarding area for another twenty or so minutes before my row was called, but it felt a lot longer. The amused looks from passengers who had witnessed my failed boarding attempt didn't help.

Once on the plane, I stalked past the luxurious first-class section where Lucia was already reclining like a miniature Nordic snow princess, pushed through the mid-aircraft galley and found the aviation equivalent of a cubicle farm.

This was why everyone was always complaining about air travel.

At least I'd been assigned a window seat in my row toward the rear of the plane. That was almost cool enough to distract me from the fact that my knees were touching the back of the seat in front of me.

Safely buckled in, in case the pilot decided to do barrel rolls, I scanned the faces of passengers shuffling in my direction, trying to guess which of them would share my row.

The first terrifying candidate—a six-foot-five, well-tanned dude who had either been a football player in college or eaten two of them— passed on by, one brush of his arm rocking the entire row of chairs, and I breathed a sigh of relief. Whoever sat next to that man was going to have an elbow in their ribs for the entirety of the flight.

I dodged a second bullet when the elderly woman who was loudly reciting a list of everything that had been wrong with lunch to her long-suffering husband filed past my row. So it went for dozens of additional passengers. After fifteen minutes, the steady stream of people had slowed to a trickle, and the two seats next to me remained empty. It was a long way from sitting in first class but having a row to myself would still be pretty damn nice.

And then I saw her.

She was small, a few inches taller than Lucia, with long black hair and sparkling brown eyes. Maybe only a couple years older than me, friendly-looking, and the kind of woman a younger me would have tripped over himself to ask out. I was, of course, already in love with a woman who could stop time with a smile, but as far as seatmates went, this stranger was easily a cut above the alternatives I'd seen so far.

Please, I prayed to the anonymous patron demigod of flights to Rome, *please let* her *sit next to me.* The only thing better than having a row to myself would be sharing that row with someone who could distract me from the fact that we were about to hurtle through the air at ten thousand feet in a vehicle I'd seen crash in like every movie ever.

I avoided making eye contact with my unsuspecting savior, so as to not jinx the whole thing, and held my breath as she made her way down the aisle. After a moment's hesitation, she stopped... at my row.

I risked a peek. She was casually dressed in a t-shirt and jeans and seemed totally comfortable with air travel. In short, the perfect woman to sit next to during the flight. I prepared to introduce myself—

—which was when she stepped aside and let a whirling dervish of braids and energy climb into our row and take the middle seat.

Well, shit.

My keen detective senses began to pick up on the handful of clues I'd somehow missed: the weariness in the woman's expression, the band on her left ring finger, and the tall, skinny dude who had followed her down the aisle and was now helping her put a bag in the overhead bin.

Also? The kid. It was pretty hard to miss the little girl when she was squealing at a volume reserved for car accidents and Nine Inch Nails concerts.

When the man had finished stowing his wife's carry-on, he turned to head back up the aisle with something that looked suspiciously like relief. I spoke up before he could escape.

"Mister, I'm happy to switch seats if the three of you want to sit together as a family?"

A look of poorly disguised horror crossed the man's face. "That's kind of you, but it's cool. I paid for an exit row seat and *really* need that extra space to get some work done." He hefted the laptop bag hanging from his left shoulder and offered an apologetic smile that even I recognized as fake.

"That *was* very thoughtful," offered the woman, once her husband had fled for the relative peace of the exit row. "Thank you."

"Family's important," I said blandly. "I'm John."

She looked up from buckling in her wiggling, screeching, flailing daughter and gave me a smile that transformed her face from cute to downright lovely. "Amanda."

I smiled back. Maybe being trapped on a tiny, explosive tin can next to a hyperactive toddler wouldn't be so bad after all.

CHAPTER 6

IN WHICH BEING TRAPPED ON A TINY, EXPLOSIVE
TIN CAN NEXT TO A HYPERACTIVE TODDLER
IS EVERY BIT AS BAD AS IT SOUNDS

The child's name was Taylor, and she had everyone, including her mother, fooled into thinking she was just a little girl. But the first leg of our flight taught me that the cute toddler exterior was little more than a shell for some sort of screaming, drooling hell beast. I had named her the Destroyer, and over the course of our flight, Taylor had lived down to that moniker, demolishing everything from her own fold-down tray to my practically saintly patience.

"I'm sorry again about your pants," said Amanda for the fifth time, as our plane finished its descent into London, and the two prepared to disembark, "and your papers."

"It's okay," I lied. "I'm sure cherry coke, chocolate, and barbecue sauce will wash out of denim just fine." I avoided making eye contact with the Destroyer, so as to not incite further acts of demonic terrorism. If I survived Rome—and I wasn't even sure I'd survive *getting to* Rome at that point—I was going to find some alternate means of transportation home.

Like a cruise ship. Or a jet pack.

CHAPTER 7

IN WHICH A SUITCASE BECOMES
THE LAST LINE OF DEFENSE

"Mr. Smith, you look ragged."

"After almost a full day in the air? Yeah, just a little." I hadn't been seated next to a hell demon for the flight from London to Rome, but that was all I could say for it.

"Perhaps you should have taken some of that time to sleep," suggested the queen, who once again looked like she had stepped out of the salon. Not a hair was out of place, and that white silk suit was pristine. "There are sufficient obstacles in our path already without adding to them needlessly, don't you think?"

I swallowed my immediate response, reminding myself for at least the tenth time since leaving San Diego exactly what—and who—was at stake. "Flying economy isn't very restful," I finally said.

"I wouldn't know." Lucia fished in her bag for a long scarf that matched her suit exactly. Draped around her neck and over her shoulders, it almost managed to hide her cleavage. Which made it a magic scarf, as far as I was concerned. "I suppose I should at least be grateful that you were so dedicated to your research."

It took me a very long moment to figure out what the hell the femmepire was talking about. She thought I hadn't gotten any sleep because I'd been *reading?* Had Lucia ever even *seen* what economy class was like?

In fact, I'd only made it through the first few pages of the briefing before the Destroyer's Lunchables turned the stack of papers into a sticky, sodden, illegible mess... but the queen didn't need to know that. I just nodded agreeably. Either I was getting better at lying or she simply wasn't paying attention.

As we stepped into the terminal, Lucia stiffened. A small crowd of people had gathered to greet returning loved ones, business associates, or family members, but the queen's gaze flitted past them to fixate upon the tall figure lurking just beyond. The man came our way, slicing through the crowd like a shark through still waters. A black coat topped an equally black suit, the slim lines of the tailoring emphasizing his unusual height. The airport was brightly lit, but those lights seemed to shy away from the black-clothed figure, leaving his features shrouded in darkness.

"Who the hell is that?" I whispered.

"That would be the Kingmaker, Denarius Borghesi." Lucia's words were every bit as quiet as mine, but pure, white-hot rage leaked across our bond.

"Kingmaker?" The rest of what she'd said hit me. "Borghesi?"

"My uncle." Cold blue eyes glanced sideways at me, then flicked back to the approaching vampire. "As you would know, had you actually read the dossier."

Busted.

Before I could explain what had happened, and why it wasn't my fault, the manpire reached us. I looked up and then up some more, forced to revise my earlier estimates. Denarius wasn't just tall, he was absurdly so, topping my own six feet by way more than a head. My friend Bill frequently manifested as a seven-foot-tall spear of asparagus, but Denarius wasn't much shorter.

I glanced from the short femmepire at my side to the giant manpire in front of us and shook my head. There was nothing to suggest the two were related. Lucia was curvaceous, blonde, and blue-eyed, while Denarius was lean and chiseled, cropped black hair forming an unflattering skullcap above a humorless face of chiseled stone and dark eyes.

"Lady Borghesi." His greeting was polite, if cool.

"Uncle." I could have shaved with her reply. "Are you here as escort or executioner?"

"That depends entirely upon you, of course." Denarius shook his head. "Despite all past evidence to the contrary, I did not believe you would be so foolish as to return to Rome."

"The law you love so much permits me to defend my Secundus."

"It does. It also states that, in doing so, you bind yourself to your vassal's fate."

Wait... what?

Lucia waved a hand dismissively. "I did not sleep through *all* of your lessons."

"Only the ones that truly mattered." Denarius' eyes were black pits. "In honor of the blood we share, I offer you this chance: return to your place of exile and I will inform the Council that you never arrived. Your Secundus will die for her crimes, but at least you will live to see another decade."

"Charity from the Kingmaker? You must be even less confident of the claims against Lady Dumenyova than I'd anticipated. I will stay and reclaim what is mine."

"So be it. When you are bound and awaiting the headman's axe, remember that you had a choice. Having escaped death once, you will not do so a second time."

Lucia's smile was wintry. "I am as innocent now as I was then."

"You were found *guilty*."

"Due to the ineptitude of the uncle who allegedly attempted to defend me. This time, I have brought my own investigator."

The two vampires turned in unison toward me.

"What's up?" I smiled weakly, well aware of the sort of impression I made with bloodshot eyes, a full day's growth of stubble, and skin that could only charitably be described as *oily*.

"Mr. Smith, this is Denarius. Afford him whatever respect you think he deserves, and not an ounce more."

Given that Denarius was already one of the scariest non-Blood-Witch vampires I'd ever met, I decided to err on the side of *lots of respect.*

"*This* is your thrall?"

"Do not pretend ignorance, old man. I have no doubt your file on him grows thicker with each passing day."

The number of unsettling revelations was skyrocketing at an alarming rate.

"Of course." Denarius' voice remained mild. "Still, I had heard he was fatter."

"Rumors of my obesity have been greatly exaggerated," I said.

"So it seems. Welcome to Rome, Mr. Smith."

"I love what you've done with the place. It's very… airporty."

Denarius didn't crack a smile. The whole damn family was humorless. "It is my understanding that you do not speak Italian?"

"Not a word. Unless spaghetti counts."

"It does not."

If looks could kill, Lucia's would have murdered me.

"Many in the Court speak English," said Denarius, "but I will find a translator to assist you with those who do not."

"That would be awesome." That complication hadn't even occurred to me. This foreign country thing was going to take some getting used to.

"*Awesome.*" Denarius tasted the word like it was some sort of exotic cuisine.

Lucia's death stare intensified.

ooo

As Denarius escorted us to baggage claim, the two Borghesis locked in a death stare duel for the ages, I became aware of the handful of preternaturally handsome men in black mixed into the crowd around us. Way more discreet than the vampire Watch back home, they otherwise looked very similar; uber-fit, hyper-aware, and armed for werebear.

The sheer number of them that had come—I spotted five, which meant there were probably at least ten—spoke volumes about Denarius' prominence… and made me wish I'd made it as far as his bio on the plane. Lucia's father had been king before Tomasso, so what role did Denarius play in the monarchy? More importantly, with Lucia exiled, and Tomasso dead, was it possible that he stood to inherit the throne?

That was one hell of a motive if you asked me.

When our luggage finally appeared on the carousel, vomited up from the airport's depths, Lucia lifted the smaller of her two suitcases and then nodded towards the other.

I stared back at her as the suitcase disappeared around the bend.

"Mr. Smith! My luggage?"

"What about it?" I had my garment bag in one hand, Angel's satchel in the other, and was ready to go. Hopefully somewhere with food.

"For once in your miserable existence," hissed Lucia, "be a gentleman. Fetch my bag."

I looked from my full hands back to the femmepire who could bench press a bus and sighed.

"Fine." I shifted my satchel to one shoulder and picked the garment bag back up with the same hand, leaving my right hand free for Her Royal Majesty's designer luggage when it made its way back around. "But that damn thing better have wheels."

It didn't.

ooo

Laden down with luggage, I didn't see a whole lot of Fiumicino Airport before Denarius led us out into the loading zone.

"Wait here. I will bring the car around." The manpire strode away, vanishing into the night like the shadow he so resembled.

"So that's your uncle?" I set Lucia's bag—which was either packed with military grade hardware or rocks—on the curb with a grateful sigh, adjusting my other burdens to relieve some of the strain.

"So I have been informed." The former queen was flicking through messages or emails on her ultra-slim cellphone.

"Seems like a swell dude."

"Proving yet again how poor your judgment is."

"Any idea why he didn't just send one of the Watch to bring the car around?" The *queen* would never have deigned to do something herself when there was an ample supply of free labor available.

As the suitcase at my feet so aptly demonstrated.

Lucia looked up from her phone, annoyed. "This is not San Diego, Mr. Smith. My kind are the dominant species in Rome."

I puzzled through that non-sequitur with a frown of my own. The manpires I'd glimpsed earlier were weaving through the crowd to form a defensive perimeter around us.

"That didn't answer my question," I finally said. "At all."

She tucked the phone away with an irritated sigh. "The Kingmaker does not travel with a security team. It would be tantamount to a shark trusting his security to a litter of puppies."

I was briefly distracted by the thought of puppies. My room in Juliette's condo was far too small for an animal, but one day, I would have a puppy of my very own, with floppy ears, thick gray fur, and a penchant for biting the ankles of arrogant vampires.

Then, her words sank in.

"Denarius doesn't use the Watch?"

"He does not."

"Then why are they here?"

I started to wave at the manpire stepping up behind Lucia when something heavy knocked me to the ground. Even as I fell, my previously unseen attacker stepped over me in a blur.

Around us, black-clad figures darted forward, and what I had mistaken for a defensive perimeter zeroed in on the femmepire queen, like a noose tightening around a condemned man's neck.

ooo

I had barely hit the ground when the first manpire reached Lucia. I'd never actually seen the queen in a fight, but Anastasia had clearly been teaching her something. She slipped to one side, reaching out with a hand to capture her attacker's wrist. I was just close enough to hear bones being pulverized, as she tugged on that arm and threw the man forward into one of the attackers near me, toppling him like a bowling pin.

Two combatants were down in just as many seconds, but that left a half-dozen more moving forward in silent fury, as screaming travelers scattered in all directions. Lucia's golden fist connected with the next attacker, leaving a dent the size of a softball in his chest, but the man didn't even seem to notice. Before she could lash out again, a pair of manpires had latched onto her from behind.

I struggled back to my feet, using the attacker Lucia had literally disarmed as a convenient step. She was shaking free of her two assailants when another pair joined them, swarming the monarch like ants on a bread crumb. The four manpires held Lucia trapped as the remaining two closed in to attack her.

I grabbed a suitcase—Lucia's heavy white, hard-shelled bag, instead of Angel's comparatively fragile satchel—and swung it with all my strength at the back of one of the vampires holding the queen.

He barely even budged. It was times like this where I really wished I hadn't lost Bill's one-shot hell gun fighting werewolves out in Santee.

Before I could swing again, he stiffened and fell backwards into me, taking me right back down to the pavement. Up close—way, way too close—I could see the layer of frost that now coated his exposed flesh, as well as the three sizable icicles that had been driven into his chest.

A wave of energy-sapping cold exploded out from Lucia, and the attacking vampires fell away. The queen's suit coat was shredded, exposing dark, bloody marks along one arm, but she was free again, her pale blue eyes flashing golden.

Our attackers weren't wielding the weaponry I'd come to expect from the Watch. Instead, their fingers ended in sharp, slightly curved talons. Only four of the original eight were still on their feet, but there was no trace of fear or emotion on their faces.

And then the vampire whose arm the queen had first pulped stood back up, followed by a second enemy I'd presumed dead. Neither seemed inconvenienced by their bone-crushing injuries. Four-on-two was back to six-on-two… and I *still* didn't have a hell gun.

On the other hand, Lucia's display of power had reminded me that I wasn't quite the defenseless monkey my parents had raised on the not-so-mean streets of Chula Vista. As that last vampire stepped past me to rejoin the fight, I pulled on the queen's Talent, lunged to my knees, and stabbed out.

It was a far cry from the Volkswagen-sized icicle I'd used to kill a major demon in the battle against Nepenthe and her coven. Luckily, this vampire was a hell of a lot smaller than the Hound of Tartarus had been. My icy dagger slid neatly into the manpire's side, and he staggered.

Unbidden, an image of the last person I'd stabbed swam before me, her dark eyes sad, peaceful, and more than a little bit insane. I fought back my rising nausea, shaking my head to dispel the unwanted vision.

It was a good thing too. Despite the icy blade stuck in his side, the vampire was still struggling forward. I picked up Lucia's suitcase again and swung it with two hands right at his head.

This time, he went down.

I hit him five or six more times, just to make sure he'd stay there. When I was done, there wasn't much left of his face, and Lucia's suitcase had said a permanent goodbye to its original color scheme.

The already bitter temperature dropped even further as one of the vampires menacing Lucia transformed from professional killing machine into artistic ice sculpture. Just as quickly, the queen lashed out with her fists and shattered what had once been a manpire into bloody shards of ice.

The witches might have inadvertently given me access to Lucia's Talent, but I was a long, long way from being able to wield it the way she did.

Unfortunately, that display of power still left four attackers on their feet, and Lucia was injured and breathing heavily. I stepped up beside her, gore-coated suitcase in hand, feeling her anger, weakness and pain as if they were my own.

Our inevitable victory was feeling a little bit less inevitable.

"Juliette *was* worried I'd get myself killed in Rome," I said, swinging the suitcase back and forth like it was some sort of bladed weapon instead of a blunt instrument growing heavier by the second, "but I don't think even she expected it to happen this quickly."

"Such as these will not stop me, Mr. Smith."

"Maybe you should tell them that?" I turned to menace the vampires behind us, leaving Lucia to face the other two.

Through our bond, I could *feel* the queen go on the attack.

Unfortunately, I was less effective.

The first of the two vampires in front of me brushed my suitcase weapon aside like it was a mere suggestion of a weapon. The world flashed white, and I found myself back on the pavement, pain radiating from my chest.

I hadn't even seen the punch that dropped me.

Which was kind of par for the course when fighting vampires.

I struggled to get back up, but my feet weren't in the mood to listen, and the manpire was already stepping past me, closing in on the queen's unprotected back. His companion, on the other hand, turned to me, clawed hands coming forward to cut my Italian adventure short—

—only to stiffen and collapse, dead before he hit the ground, a look of shock and terror twisting his features. I barely spotted my defender's dark, curly hair before she faded again from view.

I didn't have Bill's hell gun anymore, but I *did* have a handful of allies in San Diego that even vampires feared. I was just glad this one had been able to make the journey.

Unfortunately, that still left the vampire who had made it past me to attack Lucia from behind. Either the queen heard him, or she felt my spike of alarm across our bond. She staggered away, spinning to try to keep the remaining three vampires in front of her.

The pain and anger leaking across our bond had guttered out, leaving only tiredness and ironclad resolve. Eyes that glowed like copper pennies in the dark Italian night flared even brighter, and a snow-capped wind started to blow, the temperature dropping to levels my sluggish brain helpfully informed me were damn near fatal.

Thanks to that snowstorm, I didn't see when the rearmost vampire vanished. One moment, there were three attackers threatening Lucia. The next, there were two. A tall shadow appeared behind the final pair, noticeable only as a darker patch within the swirling wind and snow, and another attacker fell, this time close enough that I could see his torso sliding in one direction, while twitching legs fell in the other. Lucia lunged forward to crush the throat of the last attacker, and just like that, the battle was over.

The snow died out and the Kingmaker stepped from the shadows, a long blade of inky darkness held at one side. Black blood dripped down that blade to splash against the severed remains of the people he'd just vivisected.

And then, as happened way too frequently in these situations, I passed out.

CHAPTER 8

IN WHICH WOUNDS ARE DRESSED AND MISCONCEPTIONS CORRECTED

Denarius was still wrapping Lucia's arm when I returned to consciousness. Without a glance in my direction, the elder manpire tossed me several strips of torn black cloth.

"Bind your wounds, Mr. Smith, lest you pass out again from further blood loss."

Rather than admit that I wasn't bleeding at all, and had, once again, passed out from exertion, or stress, or latent fainting-goat genes, I carefully wrapped the bandages—recognizable as cloth torn from the now-dead Watch members' uniforms—around my midsection. I even added a pained hiss for verisimilitude.

Don't mind John Smith over here… he's just a stoic badass barely deigning to acknowledge yet another life-threatening wound.

I hadn't known Denarius long enough to tell if he bought the act. Especially since he wasn't even looking in my direction. Having finished attending to Lucia, he was now crouched over the upper torso of the manpire he had literally cut in half.

I staggered over to join him. The noises I made in the process probably undercut my badass image just a bit. I might not have been bleeding, but holy hell, was I going to have some bruises. Every step hurt.

Thankfully, my brain was operating at peak efficiency. "I don't think we could have asked for a clearer sign of Lucia's innocence."

That got both vampires' attention.

"What do you mean, Mr. Smith?"

"We barely made it off the plane before someone tried to kill us. Apparently, Tomasso's real murderer is worried about what I'll uncover."

"So worried that they largely focused their efforts upon your mistress, rather than you," said Denarius.

"The law says Lucia gets an investigator. What happens if she dies before the investigation begins? Would I still get the job?"

"A fair point."

I frowned at Denarius. He couldn't *really* be a Borghesi, could he? Lucia would rather lose her entire House—as events had recently demonstrated—than admit that I was correct.

"Well, whoever it was isn't very bright. It should be easy enough to trace these members of the Watch back to their House."

"Unfortunately, there are several flaws in your analysis." The Kingmaker straightened from his crouch. "A great many individuals want Lady Borghesi dead; this assault is hardly proof of her innocence. In fact, it is entirely possible that this assassination attempt was arranged in *retaliation* for the murder of my nephew."

"Furthermore," he continued, nudging the severed torso at his feet without a care for what the blood pool was doing to his expensive dress shoes, "these individuals were not part of any Watch. Nor were they People at all."

I drew closer to see what he was talking about, doing my best to avoid the bloody bits strewn across the asphalt.

"They *look* like manpires."

"Manpires…?"

"Mr. Smith has a colorful manner of speech which I blame entirely upon both his nationality and upbringing." The queen's voice was flat, absent of the weariness I still felt across our bond. "He means People of the male gender."

"Ah." Denarius turned back to me. "What is the first rule of investigation, Mr. Smith?"

"Bros before hos?"

I was winging it, admittedly. My old boss—the guy who had taught me the ropes as a P.I.—hadn't been big on rules. Or paying me, for that matter.

"Perhaps in the Americas. Here, the first rule is to examine every clue, no matter how small."

"Black clothing. Suspiciously good-looking. Thoroughly dead. I still don't see what makes you—" My voice trailed off as I looked from one corpse to another, noticing something that had somehow eluded me during the fight. "Wait, are those two *twins?*"

"Not unless my enemies found and hired a band of octuplet assassins," said Lucia.

Shit. She was right. All the attackers were identical.

How had I missed that?

"There are other clues, of course," rumbled Denarius.

"All that blood." I'd seen vampire blood—more than I ever wanted to, really—and it was both golden and far less prevalent in a vampire's body than grade-A human blood was in mine. In our battle with the witches, both Juliette and Ana had been badly injured, yet neither had bled enough to fill much more than a measuring cup. Yet the eight dead attackers had left blood *everywhere.* Hell, little rivulets of black liquid were making their way down the sidewalk toward me.

I took a careful step away.

"Indeed. And there is also this." Denarius used the toe of his now hopelessly disgusting dress shoe to lift the ribcage of the severed torso. Beneath it was…

Actually, I didn't know what it was. It was black but glittered in the wan streetlights, extending down the length of the creature's spine.

"Black blood. An inner carapace. And identical appearances."

"Someone has hired the Illutu," growled Lucia.

"Yes. Be grateful that the nest mother sent drones instead of her knights. And only eight of them, at that. This was a fishing expedition at most."

"You really think someone would throw away eight of their troops just to gather information?" I was uncomfortably aware of how close the supposed fact-finding expedition had come to killing us.

"She can always breed more, my thrall. It is the Illutu way. One hive per job, with the nest mother spawning whatever forces are required."

Nest mother. Hive. Drones. "They're *bugs*?"

"Of a sort," said Denarius.

"They are a mercenary species from ancient Akkad."

I pretended I had any clue where that was.

"They are also expensive. Someone wants you dead, Niece."

"As you said, Uncle, *many* people want me dead. It appears not everyone is as willing to trust in the legal process as you."

"Speaking of the law…" I nodded past the Kingmaker, where several police cars had just pulled up, lights flashing.

Denarius frowned, and the blade in his hand melted back into darkness. "I will deal with the authorities… and the witnesses."

I was glad the sword had vanished because that phrasing would have been damn ominous otherwise. Bad enough that my first minutes in Italy had been spent fighting for my life, without adding a massacre into the bargain.

"Maybe make sure that nobody took any video of the attack, while you're at it?" Denarius seemed like the kind of manpire who might not have caught up to 2015 technology just yet.

"Smart phones and cloud storage, yes." He nodded in my direction. "Although our disinformation specialists will take care of any footage that does leak."

Or… maybe he had a better grasp on modern tech than I did. I still only had a vague idea of what *the cloud* even was, other than a place from which nude photos were inevitably stolen.

"And in the meantime, what shall Mr. Smith and I be doing? Pining for your company?"

Given that the Kingmaker had just helped saved her life—not to mention cut down two bug-people drones in a matter of seconds—I thought Lucia was being a little harsh. But I also knew better than to get in the middle of family drama.

Except for the many, many times I'd been hired to do just that, of course. A man does have to eat.

"I will requisition a driver to take you to the palace," Denarius acknowledged. "The sooner you are there, the sooner we can be done with this farce."

"For once, we are in complete agreement."

Something told me they were hoping for entirely different outcomes.

CHAPTER 9

The "driver" Denarius managed to procure for us ended up being one of the beret-clad, Italian policemen who had driven out to investigate our massacre. None of his companions seemed to find his sudden decision to drive two civilians into Rome using someone else's car odd, even though it also meant leaving behind the rest of the squad and an active crime scene.

Vampire compulsion was a powerful thing.

Denarius would be using those same powers to nudge the witnesses into believing that they had seen something less nefarious… or at least less supernatural. Maybe a random mugging, or something. Either that or he would just wipe the memories out completely, leaving both police and witnesses none the wiser.

Not for the first time, I was grateful for whatever it was that made me immune to that sort of thing.

I watched the airport disappear through the Audi's rear window. San Diego had never felt so far away.

"Welcome to Italy, Mr. Smith." Lucia's smile was a sliver of ice. "Let us hope we make it out of here alive."

"I'd settle for just getting to our destination alive," I countered. "Especially if there's a bed."

"You have already mentioned your weariness; there is no need to belabor the point further. We will have to complete a small ceremony upon our arrival, but afterwards, you will be free to take your rest."

"What sort of ceremony?"

"The Council must formally acknowledge my rights as Lady Dumenyova's liege and recognize you as my selected investigator."

"That doesn't sound too bad. Maybe in the meantime, you can tell me a little bit more about Ana's case?"

Blue eyes flickered to the privacy screen between us and the brainwashed driver. "I will do so later, when our conversation is less apt to be overheard."

"Why not just order the dude not to listen?"

"And if he shares your resistance to compulsion?"

"Then he probably wouldn't have left his whole squad back at the airport to chauffeur us into Rome."

"Unless he serves Denarius of his own free will. The People have many servants in this city, and not all of them need to be compelled."

I frowned in the darkness of the car's interior. That didn't make a whole lot of sense. How would Denarius know this policeman would have been among the group to show up at the airport? Hell, for that matter, how would he have known *any* police would show? Unless...

"You think your uncle was behind the attack?"

"Anything is possible, and no one is to be trusted. Recognition of those facts might be the difference between life and death."

"But Denarius just saved our lives!"

"Did he? Or did he reappear only when my eventual triumph had become a certainty?"

The queen and I had very different recollections of the battle, but that was one argument I wasn't interested in having. Maybe Denarius *was* responsible. Even so…

"You've been vetting human servants for the better part of two years now and you have yet to find anyone else with my gift."

"I will not risk my life on the assumption that you are unique."

"That wasn't my point. If you were able to vet servants at the House, why can't you do the same for this dude?"

"Very well." Lucia rapped firmly on the glass partition and waited for it to recede, then issued a stream of Italian to the driver.

In reply, he nodded, and pulled the Audi over to the shoulder of the road, bringing it to a full stop. Eyes still staring straight ahead, he pulled his gun from its holster, held it up to his own head, and started to squeeze the trigger.

"Wait!" I lunged forward in a desperate, far too slow, attempt to prevent the inevitable, but Lucia was issuing another command before my butt had even left the seat.

The driver eased his finger off the trigger, still expressionless, and nodded before returning the gun to its holster. Moments later, the partition was up again, and our car was back in motion.

Lucia turned to me. "It appears we may speak freely after all."

ooo

We rode together in silence, the Italian countryside passing by like one of Jee Sun's black-on-black-on-black crayon masterpieces. Part of me was still waiting for the gunshot, while another part wanted to scream at Lucia for her callousness towards my kind. An even bigger part of me was fixated on the fact that I had almost died less than half an hour earlier, and *still* didn't have a clue what was really going on.

That last thought seemed a little more productive than the first two. I took a long breath, pretended my hands weren't shaking, and glanced over at Lucia.

"Why was Anastasia in Rome?"

"Because I sent her here." Lucia caught my expression and rolled her eyes. "You wish to hear the long story, I take it?"

"You *did* just almost kill a policeman so we could speak freely."

"True." Lucia set her bag on the car mat at her feet, leaving nothing but air between the two of us. "As you know, my brother has made a number of attempts to have me assassinated over the years. The last was the unfortunate incident with Xavier, Lady Dumenyova's former lover."

I was pretty sure she'd thrown the lover comment in there just to provoke a reaction, so I didn't give her one. As far as I was concerned, *former* was the only word that counted.

"You are a detective, Mr. Smith, and not immune to the occasional flash of insight. Have you determined yet why Tomasso would hold such animosity towards his older sister?"

"I figured it was because he'd actually met you. That does seem to be the usual result—"

"Either that or abject adulation," Lucia agreed, without missing a beat.

"—but since the two of you grew up together, he was probably used to your... particular brand of charm." I shook my head. "Honestly, I assumed he wanted you dead because you were a threat to his throne. Before you were exiled, you *were* your father's heir, right?"

"I was, and remain, the rightful ruler of this kingdom, yes."

"Maybe statements like *that* are why he kept trying to kill you."

"I thought as you did, for a great many years. But the conditions of my exile ensured I would never regain power in Rome. In that much, Tomasso had nothing to fear from me."

"Right. Your exile." I thought back to the conversation she and Denarius had shared at the airport, full of subtext I'd been entirely incapable of deciphering. "Why *were* you stripped of your crown?"

"I thought this trip would have already made it clear." There was something ugly and painful behind Lucia's perfect smile. "They say that history repeats itself, yet I never expected the cycle to be so swift."

Through my sleep-deprivation, a horrible possibility gnawed at my brain. By history repeating itself, did she mean…?

Lucia nodded at the expression of stunned realization spreading across my face. "Yes, Mr. Smith. Lady Dumenyova stands accused now of the very crime I was exiled for almost a century ago."

"Regicide?"

"Indeed."

Well, shit.

ooo

"You killed your father?"

"I was accused of such and convicted of the crime by the Imperial Council, yes." The emotions leaking across the bond were cold, dark, and entirely too complex for me to unravel.

"But you didn't do it?" When the witches' spell was still active, I had dreamed myself into some of Lucia's memories. Even as a child, her feelings towards her father had been… conflicted.

"I did not. My father was a monster in many ways, yet he was my blood. Whoever did kill him framed me for the act." The words were light, but her pale eyes were hard and dangerous. "And in doing so, removed two Borghesis from the throne in one fell swoop."

"Tomasso, I'm guessing? It's hard to think of anyone who benefited more from what went down."

"Indeed. I too believed him responsible." That frozen slash of a smile flickered again. "A strategic masterstroke that I would have greatly admired, had I not been both target and victim."

"*Believed?* As in past tense? What changed?"

"Shortly after Christmas, my brother contacted me."

"How?"

"By phone." Lucia shook her head, dried clumps of blood marring the careful lines of her hair. "For almost a century, I believed my brother had killed our father and framed me for the act. And for that same length of time, he believed me guilty of the crime I had been convicted of. He sought my death to avenge our father."

"But if neither of you killed your father… who did?"

"That is exactly what Tomasso was trying to determine. He had stumbled upon something that shook his belief in my guilt, something that hinted at a conspiracy against our family. Ironically, even with all the forces of the kingdom at his command, the only person he could trust was the sister he had been trying to kill for decades."

That was all kinds of messed up.

"So, what did he want from you?"

"Aid in uncovering the identity of our mutual enemy."

"And you bought that?" As far as I was concerned, this whole bizarre conspiracy might have simply been an elaborate ruse to get Lucia to send Anastasia to Rome where… she would then be arrested for Tomasso's death.

Huh. That plan kind of hinged on the king *actually* being dead, didn't it? Which made for a pretty horrible plan.

"Not at first; I am hardly a fool. But Tomasso was persistent… and dreadfully earnest. And if the two of us were able to find my father's true killer—"

"Then your exile might be lifted, allowing you to return to Rome," I realized.

"At the very least."

"So, Anastasia…?" We'd taken a lot longer to get to the crux of the matter than I'd expected, but I was starting to see how the pieces fit together.

"Was sent to meet with my brother, and to lend him aid in the investigation. When I last heard from her, she had landed safely in Florence and was making her way to Rome. And then…"

"Then Tomasso turned up dead."

"Yes. An ally from the court contacted me to inform me of both Tomasso's murder and Lady Dumenyova's capture."

"Did this ally say *how* Anastasia was captured? Or why everyone was so convinced she killed your brother?"

"He did not."

"Well, if all of Rome already thinks you killed your father, I guess it's not much of a leap to think you'd do the same to another family member." I shook my head tiredly. "This makes things harder."

"How so?"

"I figured I'd only need to create reasonable doubt as to Anastasia's guilt. But your father's murder taints everything. Nobody will buy Ana's innocence unless I can dig up some ironclad proof."

A brief, utterly incongruous, flicker of amusement carried across the bond. "Precisely. While the Council regards me as a patricide, our hopes of a successful defense are slim."

Even I could read the subtext. "Exactly *which* murder am I supposed to be investigating?"

"Both, of course." Lucia's words were sharp. "Or has the symmetry of the two situations somehow escaped you?"

"You think the same person was behind both killings."

"Of course. I believe Tomasso may have been closer to discovering the identity of our father's murderer than he suspected. And I suspect that murderer arranged his death, and once again, found a way to point the blame in my direction."

"And hired the bug things to kill us?"

"The Illutu? It does seems likely."

"Jesus. Who are we dealing with here, Sun Tzu?" I frowned. If Sun Tzu had been a vampire, he *could* still be both alive and our enemy. Which was more than a little terrifying.

"Whoever they are, Mr. Smith, they are already dead. They simply have yet to realize it."

ooo

"So, our next step is introducing ourselves to the Council?"

"Formally known as the Imperial Council, and yes. As was detailed in the briefing you elected not to read. Tell me; did I somehow fail to impress upon you the importance of that information, or was this simply another regrettable instance of American anti-authoritarianism?"

"This was an instance of your decision to put me in coach coming back to bite you in the over-privileged ass," I countered. "Just text me the file. When we get to the palace, I'll get someone to print out another copy."

Assuming I'd have time to read it while investigating *two* murders. Something told me homicides were a little bit more time-intensive than my usual Motel 6 stakeouts.

"Very well. But I will require something from you as well."

That sounded ominous. I squeezed a little bit farther away from the femmepire and favored her with a suspicious glare. "And what's that?"

Lucia pulled on her scarf, exposing the tattered remains of her left coat sleeve. The black bandages Denarius had wrapped about her arm looked oddly out of place, given her usual color scheme. The queen looked at me expectantly.

"What?" She didn't want me to buy her a new jacket, did she? Because that was a hard no. Even if I hadn't practically bankrupted myself buying my new clothes, I would never have been able to afford her designer.

"I took several wounds in the battle at the airport."

"I know, I was there." I shrugged, still not seeing where she was going. "So did I." I patted the bandage I'd wrapped around my own midsection, only to be met with the queen's scornful glare.

"We are in a car together, Mr. Smith, and you are my thrall. If you had been cut as you claimed, I would smell it."

"Nobody likes a showoff, Lucia." I left the bandage in place anyway. "And stop smelling my blood. It's creepy."

"I must do more than smell it, if I am to be healed."

Oh, *hell* no! "You're *not* feeding on me again."

"No?" Her voice went low and dangerous.

"No. I told you last time that it was… the last time," I finished lamely. "Besides, I've seen how the People heal. Minor gaping wounds like those? You'll be totally fine by tomorrow. Or Tuesday, at the very latest."

"Tomorrow *is* Tuesday, you fool."

Damn it. Apparently, jet lag was a real thing.

"I cannot go before the Council wounded, Mr. Smith. Our position is already tenuous enough without announcing further weakness."

"Why not drink from your suicidal meat-puppet then?" Mentally, I offered the brainwashed policeman an apology for blatantly breaking the bro code. Better him than me though… and it wasn't like he'd remember it anyway.

"Thalassemia."

"Bless you?"

Lucia scowled. "It is a type of anemia common to this country and possessed by the officer in question. While he would likely survive my bite, he would not recover from it for days."

"Since when do *you* care about what happens to your food?"

"The disease also makes his blood less nourishing," she admitted.

Of course it did.

Lucia ran a hand through her hair, unknowingly spreading the gore even further. "What will it be, Mr. Smith? Will you put us at an even greater disadvantage before this investigation can begin, or will you permit me to feed, as is my right?"

"I'm leaning pretty heavily toward option A."

The femmepire regarded me evenly for a long moment. For once, our bond was utterly silent. "So be it. I will not force you."

"Seriously?"

It was like hearing a scorpion promise not to sting.

"As you pointed out before our departure, our only hope of survival is to work together. Threatening you would no doubt incite another short-sighted act of defiance and we haven't the luxury for such things." She shrugged, and I felt the flash of pain that accompanied her motion. "Perhaps the Council will overlook my injuries. Perhaps beginning from a position of obvious weakness will not unduly impact our chances of success."

Damn it. I really hated it when Lucia spoke sense.

"Fine. Drink. But only enough to heal. And," I continued, extending my arm, "you're going to feed from my wrist."

"I know Lady Dumenyova explained the significance of feeding from that location."

"Yep." By vampire rules, it was a show of subservience.

"Then you must understand why it is unacceptable."

"Other than our driver, who you're going to mind-wipe anyway, we're the only ones here. Nobody will know."

Truthfully, I didn't care about the power play angle. As far as I was concerned, vampires over-complicated everything. I simply wanted to keep her fangs away from the other two popular feeding spots, commonly known as my throat and inner thigh. The first was entirely too close to high school make out sessions, and the second… well, that was too close to *post-high school* make out sessions.

Besides, the one time that Lucia had bitten me, post-bond, had left me writhing like a teenager during his first orgasm. If Lucia was going to bite me again, I was damn well going to do everything in my power to make the act as non-sexual as humanly possible.

"That's my offer," I added. "Take it or leave it."

The queen's pale eyes examined me, searching my traditionally horrible poker face for signs that I was bluffing.

She didn't find any because I meant exactly what I'd said.

"So be it. This once. But if you breathe a word of this—"

"You think I want anyone knowing you bit me again?" I shuddered. "Hell, no. I'm going to pretend this never happened."

"As will I." The familiar ring of gold appeared around Lucia's pupils as she caught my arm in a vise-like grip. Fingers scorching hot against my skin, she rolled my arm over to expose the veins in the wrist.

I squeezed my eyes shut.

…and then opened them wide as teeth sliced into my skin. That sharp flash of pain was almost instantly swept away by molten, sugar-coated euphoria. I sagged in my seat, trying desperately not to moan in pleasure.

I failed. Again.

I had a moment of embarrassment, chased by a healthy dose of regret. Then that golden, rapturous tide drowned out coherent thought.

○○○

I came back to myself sometime later, draped across the seat like a used dish rag. Lucia was back on her side of the car, browsing her phone. At some point during or after the feeding, she had removed her tattered suit coat, scarf, and bandages, and both of her golden arms were now perfectly whole.

"Once again, my blood saves the day," I muttered. Sometimes, it felt like my *blood* was the real hero of my life's story, and *John Smith* was little more than a vessel for its greatness.

"We are far from saved, Mr. Smith," the queen replied without looking up from her phone, "but I will not deny that your blood has its uses."

"Just as long as this is the last time you use it."

"We will see." Lucia met my frown with a cool smile. "Tell me; was the experience truly so horrible?"

"No, and yes." I shivered as a minor aftershock of pleasure swept through me. "Is there any chance Ana's bite would have the same... effect?"

"Has no one told you how rude it is to discuss other women during pillow talk?"

"Pillow talk?"

Lucia's laugh was every bit as lovely as it was unexpected, and I felt my body reacting of its own volition.

Stupid post-feeding afterglow.

"It was a joke, my thrall. While feeding can be a pleasurable experience for both parties, the idea of lasting intimacy between us horrifies me as much as it does you. Perhaps more. To answer your question regarding my Secundus... I do not know. We compel our victims to feel pleasure when bitten, Mr. Smith, but you are, as we have discovered, almost entirely immune to compulsion. Were it not for the bond between us, I suspect my bite would be every bit as painful as—"

"Juliette's."

"Yes," growled Lucia. Somehow, her general disdain for everything John Smith didn't prevent her from flights of jealousy.

No, not jealousy... *possessiveness.*

Like I was a toy that only she was allowed to break.

"So, you might be the one femmepire whose bite *doesn't* hurt? That's just fantastic." I didn't even try to hide my sarcasm. If *Lucia's* bite could turn me inside-out, how much better would it be with someone I *didn't* actively despise?

Apparently, I was never going to find out.

CHAPTER 10

Between my post-fight adrenaline dump, an endless succession of dark countryside, and the pre-, mid-, and post-bite wooziness, I don't know if the drive took forty minutes or two hours. Either way, it seemed excessive. In San Diego, Lindbergh field was like two miles from downtown!

A faint whisper of anticipation across the bond was my first clue that we might finally be nearing our destination. I peeked out the window. Same dark sky. Same tree silhouettes. Same disconcerting lack of pizzerias and never-ending spaghetti bowls.

Rome was kind of a disappointment so far.

We paused at a well-lit gate, three or four times larger and far better defended than the one outside Lucia's former House, then our brainwashed policeman driver turned onto a private road. Eventually, our destination came into sight.

ooo

"Holy shit."

To call the building a *mansion* didn't begin to capture its enormity. I'm not sure even *palace* sufficed, but that was clearly what it was, perched atop a hill high above us. The grounds around us were pitch-black, but exterior lights illuminated the long, sweeping flights of stairs which led up to the building itself. That edifice stretched from tree line to tree line; four stories of imposing walls and decorative marble stonework. There were three towers, a stained-glass window roughly the size of an aircraft carrier, and honest-to-God battlements. My night vision had deteriorated back to almost human levels following the end of the witches' spell, but I was pretty sure I could make out the shapes of people on those walls.

My prison break fantasy died a swift and silent death.

"Home sweet home," murmured Lucia.

"You grew up here?" That explained a lot. If I'd been raised in a building twice the size of Petco Park, I'd probably be an elitist jerk too.

"To some extent. At first, this was merely our summer home. We spent the majority of the year in Rome."

"Isn't *this* Rome?"

Lucia gave me her patented *you are too dumb to even live* look and gestured at the woods around us. "Does it *look* like Rome, Mr. Smith?"

Given that it was nighttime, and I had no idea what Rome was supposed to look like, it wasn't an easy question to answer.

"We passed the city some time ago. Welcome to Villa d'Borghesi. Everything here can kill you."

I didn't waste any brain power on wondering how I'd managed to miss driving past one of Europe's greatest cities. Because that might remind me that I'd just had the closest thing to a sexual experience since… well, since the previous freaking time Lucia had bitten me. "The building is named after your family? That's pretty sweet."

"Indeed." She sounded smug, as only a rich, gorgeous, centuries-old aristocrat could be.

"Don't let it go to your head." I brushed imaginary lint from my shoulder. "There are towns, colleges, and even forts named after *my* family."

"By which you mean *Smith*, I presume?"

"Yup."

Lucia sighed.

The scale of the place only magnified as we neared it. It took five minutes to reach the courtyard, weaving in and out between what I assumed were fountains, statues, or automated gun turrets. A phalanx of Watch awaited us when we finally parked.

I made damn sure they weren't all twins.

"Was your family's place in Rome this nice?" It seemed impossible, but then… so had vampires, at one point.

"It was smaller, but that minor inconvenience was outweighed by its location," she agreed.

"Then why did you even *need* a summer home?"

"As young as you are, Mr. Smith, you have never had the pleasure of spending the summer in a medieval city. It is not something you would wish to experience more than once."

"The heat?" I guessed.

"The smell." She wrinkled her perfect nose, and for just a moment, was almost human.

ooo

Between jet lag, stair-induced exhaustion, and the pace set by our Watch escort, I didn't take much note of the palace as we wandered through it. It was big, brightly lit, and crawling with people that hated us. So… kind of like Fiumicino Airport, I guess.

At least this time, our escorts were genuine vampires, and not creepy, bug-drone copycats. Still, I was picking up on some serious hostility from the black-clad vampires whisking us through the palace's endless halls. I hadn't spent nearly enough time in their company to annoy them yet, so I could only assume that the Watch had come to its own conclusions as to Anastasia's guilt.

I kept my eyes fixed on the hall ahead and my mouth carefully shut. One near-death experience—*two*, if you included serving as Lucia's blood buffet, or *three*, if you factored in the first leg of our flight with the Destroyer—was more than enough for the day.

Finally, after what I suspected had been a needlessly circuitous route, we were ushered past another two guards, through a single open door, and into a small, lushly appointed room. Most of our escort remained out in the hall, but two vampires took up position inside, flanking the door we'd just come through.

I looked about in puzzled bemusement. The furniture was nice enough—two long, velvet-wrapped benches along each of the side walls, and gleaming wooden bookcases flanking both the hallway door and the far more impressive double doors in the opposite wall—but it wouldn't have looked out of place in Lucia's former House. Or Anastasia's seaside home in Cardiff. I'd been expecting something more ostentatious from a palace.

"If *this* is where the Council meets, I don't even want to see where the lesser people have to congregate."

Lucia stood in the center of the room, shoulders back, chin high, and icy gaze firmly fixed upon the double-doors. "This is a waiting room. When the Council wishes to receive us, we will be invited into the primary chamber."

We waited.

The doors stayed shut.

"How long do you think that's going to take?"

"It will take however long it takes." Something sharp slipped into the queen's voice, echoing the emotions coming across the bond.

"In that case…" I took three long strides over to the nearest bench, and plopped down with a grateful sigh, flexing my aching feet.

"I don't suppose the People have perfected bionic limbs yet? My human feet don't seem up to wandering all over Italy."

Lucia didn't bother with a reply, but I nodded anyway.

"True. Why would you need bionics when you already have superhuman strength, speed, and regeneration?"

And about nine million other assorted superpowers. The only thing I had over most vampires was my height… and with Denarius around, I couldn't even enjoy that purely superficial advantage anymore.

One of the guards leaned over and murmured something to his colleague, who replied with a nod, a roll of her eyes, and a sneer. I couldn't hear what they were saying, and didn't speak Italian anyway, but mockery was a universal language, and there was no question I was their target. It felt kind of like being in high school all over again. Except that they were both way prettier than I was.

Actually, that part was like high school too.

"Take your rest while you can, Mr. Smith," Lucia finally growled, pale-eyed gaze still trying to drill a hole through the heavy doors to the Council chambers. "We will be admitted shortly."

"Good." I rolled my neck from side to side. "The sooner we get this over with, the sooner I can go to sleep."

After a shower. And something warm and filling. If there was some way to eat dinner in bed while bathing, my life would be complete.

I decided not to ask Lucia whether the People had patented that concept yet. Or if she'd be willing to provide some startup money so I could do so. I even had a name already picked out… The B3: Bath, Bed, and Buffet. It was a stroke of marketing genius.

Just… not the sort of genius Lucia wanted to hear right then.

Somewhere between five and forty minutes passed without any word from the inner chamber. I was stretched out on the bench, admiring the clean lines of the room's architecture… with my eyes closed.

The last time I'd bothered to check, Lucia had still been maintaining her position in front of the door, looking for all the world like a stone depiction of angelic fury. Except short, of course. And wingless. Still, the set of her jaw and the unending flow of fury making its way across the bond had told me she was prepared to hold that position until the end of time, if need be.

So, I was surprised to wake up and find her seated on the bench, a mere two feet from my head, blue-eyed death gaze locked on my face.

I tried to pretend she hadn't just scared the crap out of me. "Still no word? Maybe the Council doesn't want to see us after all."

"They are making a point in the most odious fashion imaginable," Lucia told me flatly. "Welcome to diplomacy in the Old World."

"At least the bench is comfortable. I could really do with a double-double right about now though."

"A what?"

"A double cheeseburger? From In-N-Out?"

Lucia's lovely lips curled derisively. "Lady Dumenyova mentioned that you had taken her there."

"Twice," I agreed proudly. "It's kind of a staple of my existence."

"Of course it is." The femmepire shook her head absently. "When we are done here, you may request food from one of the palace kitchens. Assuming we survive your introduction."

I was very proud of the calm and considered glance I gave the queen, despite the worry her words had sparked. "What does that mean?"

"It means, my thrall," she murmured, the words barely loud enough to reach me despite our nearness, "that the beings behind this door are ancient, capricious, and unlikely to appreciate your particular brand of *amiable stupidity.*"

"It's only stupid if it doesn't work. But I get it. Mouth shut, eyes and ears open, and follow your lead. This isn't my first appearance at court, you know?"

"You have been to a royal court other than this one?" The queen looked mildly interested.

"Sure. I mediated for the Superchargers, remember?"

That spark of interest flickered out like a candle in a tropical storm. "Goblin tribes do not count."

"I don't know about that. Chief Tomlinson was pretty keen on the whole courtly manners thing," I told the queen. "Until the brawl, anyway."

My lack of vampiric super senses once again prevented me from hearing whatever Lucia was muttering under her breath… but I'm pretty sure I recognized the words *huge* and *mistake.*

ooo

"This is getting ridiculous."

"Indeed." Over the past twenty minutes, the temperature in the waiting room had continued to drop, either a sign of shoddy construction or of the queen's growing temper. Most likely the latter. Finally, she rose to her feet, face set in hard lines. "If the Council cannot be bothered to welcome us, there is a surfeit of things to do."

"Like eat," I agreed.

As we turned to go, the two Watch members by the hall door came to attention, like already coiled springs somehow winding even more tightly.

"Assuming these two let us go, that is."

Lucia looked at the other vampires, eyes glittering gold. "You know who I am. You have one chance to live."

The two guards looked at the blood-spattered queen and swiftly stepped aside.

We were almost to the hallway when the doors behind us swung open. A dapperly dressed older man—clearly human, by virtue of both his age and demeanor—stepped through and bowed to Lucia.

"The Council will see you now, Lady Borghesi."

For some reason, Lucia's anger spiked even higher at the man's words, but she nodded regally, letting none of that emotion show on her face. "Come, my thrall. It would appear the Council has made time for us after all."

CHAPTER 11

Lucia marched into the Council chambers like a gladiator headed for battle. I followed behind, like a shabbily dressed, slightly pudgy, out-of-work mediator. To say I was worried was like saying the palace was decently sized. Despite Lucia's high-handed dismissal of my experience, the Superchargers had taught me that dealing with a foreign ruler in the heart of their power base took a cool head… and there was nothing cool at all in what I was picking up from Lucia over the bond.

I really didn't want her getting us both killed.

The room itself was appropriately enormous; polished marble floors, vaulted ceilings, and walls that curved about us to form a circle. Two sets of doors were found to our immediate left and right, identical to those we had just come through, and a glittering chandelier hung suspended on a delicate silver chain ten to fifteen feet above us.

Along the far wall was a raised platform, kind of like a judge's bench in a courtroom, but far larger, stretching along a good forty feet of wall to form an open semi-circle. More guards stood at attention in front of the platform, and a handful of other individuals lurked to one side, but my gaze was reserved for the people seated up on the dais. There were nine chairs arrayed up there, each one unique, with the centermost chair being, by far, the most ornate. It was also empty, presumably because its rightful inhabitant had been murdered—allegedly—by my assassin girlfriend.

Of the remaining eight chairs, only six were occupied. Lucia's dossier had probably detailed each of the people seated there, as well as their respective genealogies, likes, dislikes, and official votes in the eternal cake vs. pie debate. (Exactly *why* that was a debate was something I'd never figured out: cake was obviously superior in every way.) Sadly, the Destroyer's actions on the plane meant I didn't recognize any of them.

Except for the dude seated closest to Tomasso's throne.

Denarius watched Lucia and I make our way into the chamber without comment. The manpire had somehow found time to shower and change clothes, which only made us look more out-of-place. While Lucia somewhat pulled off the whole blood-drenched goddess of war look, I just looked and felt disgusting.

"History does have a way of repeating itself, doesn't it?" Next to Denarius, a cowled figure leaned forward, his voice sharp and malicious. "A king is dead and Lucia Borghesi comes before us covered in blood."

"Come now, Vigo. You can't fault our former queen's appearance, when it was you who argued that she not be granted time to make herself presentable." The second speaker was clearly a manpire, but his species-given good looks were fighting a losing battle with what I could only assume was a ruthless heroin addiction. A tuxedo hung loosely over the narrow lines of his form and colorless hair peeked lifelessly from under a top hat. Even worse than his appearance was his voice. Thick, phlegmy, and somehow moist, it was like hearing broken glass swaddled in wet tissue paper.

"This is a murder trial, not a beauty pageant," shot back Vigo. There was something odd about how his cloak glittered under the light of the chandelier. Even a manpire knew better than to come to a council meeting in sequins… right?

"In point of fact, this is neither a trial nor a pageant." The newest speaker was female, draped in glittering metallic fabric, and seated on the far left.

"Indeed," agreed Denarius, "though the trial will come soon enough. In the meantime, there is much to do in the wake of King Borghesi's death. Perhaps we should begin?"

"We are not all present yet, Kingmaker." The second woman on stage spoke up. Like Vigo, she was cloaked and hooded, but her outfit was in multiple shades of emerald, and the hair that spilled out of her hood was a watery blonde.

"If the others wished to be here, Contessa d'Verde, they would already be present," replied Denarius. "We have a quorum."

"True enough." She waved a hand dripping with jewels. "I withdraw my objection."

"Thank you. Would you do the honors, Lady Manassa?"

The other woman nodded to Denarius and rose from her chair with the kind of sinuous grace you only ever saw in yoginis and the paranormal. Height was difficult to judge, given the stage's elevation, but I didn't think Lady Manassa was much taller than Lucia. She was lightly clothed in a sari of gold and bronze, her exposed skin copper, vaguely iridescent, and rippling with muscle. Beneath silver, shoulder-length hair was a wide face, enormous green eyes, and lips the color of ripe berries. In place of a nose, two small indentations in the flat space above her mouth suggested nostrils.

I mentally shrugged. When you're friends with a seven-foot-tall asparagus demigod, minor facial irregularities don't really register.

Her voice was surprisingly low yet unsurprisingly melodic, with a slight sibilance that had me thinking of snakes. "This meeting of the

Imperial Council is now in order. Let the records show that there is but a single item upon the agenda tonight."

"Gee, I wonder what that could be?" mused the final Council member present. He had his bare feet up on the table in front of him, thick hands combing through the straggly strands of a black beard. All he needed was a mug of mead and a shield with his dwarven clan's coat of arms on it. "Give me a few minutes and an unlimited supply of guesses. I'm sure I'll figure it out!"

I didn't remember Tolkien's creations being quite so sarcastic.

"Hilarious as ever, Dog," said the tuxedo-clad heroin addict, his tone as dry as his voice was wet.

"What can I say? I'm just overjoyed to no longer be the ugliest person at Court."

"Are you going to let him talk to you that way?" I asked Lucia, my voice so quiet that even I could barely hear it.

"Be silent," hissed Lucia through gritted teeth, "and let me speak."

"Yes, do speak, oh exiled Lady of Winter," added Vigo in mocking tones. "Assuming you even remember the invocation."

Lucia's rage pounded across the bond at me like a second heartbeat. Her words were ice cold and needle sharp. "I remember everything, Duke Marte. *Everything.*"

Denarius cut in before things could escalate further. "You requested this audience, Lucia. Say your piece."

She nodded slowly, regal arrogance oozing from every pore, and raised her voice to address the Council. "I am Lucia Borghesi, Lady of Winter, and blood heir to my father, King Aurelius. I come before you tonight in defense of my Secundus, who stands accused of a crime she did not commit."

"*Are* there any crimes the Stone Lady hasn't committed?" asked Dog.

"I invoke my rights as Primus," continued Lucia.

"So, instead of one head for the chopping block, we get two," mused Vigo. "Two and a half, if we count the thrall."

Wait... what?

Next to me, Lucia seemed unruffled by the latest unhappy revelation. Kind of like she'd already known that little detail.

"Who will witness the exile's claim?" asked Lady Manassa.

"I will," said the tuxedo-clad manpire with a shrug. "Neither her bloodline nor her relationship to the accused are in question."

The blonde-haired contessa waved a hand airily. "Seconded."

"Very well. Let the records show that the exile's claim has been witnessed by Caine, the Lord of Bones, and Contessa Adelina Davili d'Verde."

Given the complete lack of introductions so far, I was grateful to finally have names to associate with all of the people on the stage. Lady Manassa was the nose-less woman who sounded like a snake, Contessa d'Verde was the femmepire in green, Dog was the dwarf, Duke Vigo Marte was the sequined menace, and Caine was the heroin addict. Maybe by the end of the night, I wouldn't be feeling like I'd been invited to the wrong ten-year school reunion.

Denarius addressed his niece. "As Primus, you may enlist an investigator to aid you in your defense. Is this he?"

Either the dude was senile and well on his way to the rabid bloodthirst that preceded a vampire's death ... or he was pretending ignorance for the sake of this little ceremony. After a moment's reflection, I decided it had to be the latter; Denarius seemed a lot of things, but *senile* wasn't one of them.

"Yes." Lucia led me forward. "I present to you John Smith, investigator-for-hire, city mediator, and queen's thrall."

"Rome has no queen," snapped Vigo. "The previous one barely outlasted her coronation."

The bond between Lucia and I went ice cold in a flash, an ominous sign of impending violence. At any other time, watching the femmepire throw down with this asshole would have been the very definition of a win-win situation for me. But there were greater things at stake here than an ex-queen's injured pride... or a mediator's entertainment.

I stepped between Lucia and the duke.

"Hey everyone. It's a pleasure." More or less. Mostly less. "Are there any oaths I need to swear before I begin—"

"What *are* you?" interrupted Lady Manassa.

I paused in confusion. Maybe it was the jet lag talking, but I was pretty sure Lucia had *just* told them what I was, even if the queen had fudged the truth a bit on my current mediator status. So, what was this other woman asking?

I went with the obvious answer.

"Caucasian mostly. There's a little bit of Mexican on my mom's side, and an even smaller sampling of Native American on my father's, but we're predominantly white."

"What?" She looked to the Kingmaker for clarification.

"Nobody is concerned with your ethnicity, Mr. Smith." said Denarius. "Lady Manassa was inquiring as to your *species.*"

"Oh." I shrugged. "That one's easy; I'm human."

"No." The single word was infused with iron-clad certainty.

"Are you certain?" Denarius asked her. "He smells human."

"To me as well," agreed the contessa. "Albeit heavy with the sweat and filth of his travels."

Now they were just being mean.

The sari-clad woman remained on her feet, eyeing me with a quizzical expression that was surprisingly difficult to decipher thanks to the lack of nose. "There is human, yes. But it is not the sum of things."

"I'd know if he were one of ours," declared Dog. "We have a secret handshake and everything."

I frowned, not sure what the dwarf was talking about, or how to respond. "My parents are both one hundred percent human, but I *was* bitten by a werewolf about a year and a half ago. You're probably just smelling the leftover virus."

"Contagion from an Infected lasts only a few days, Mr. Smith," Caine informed me in his horrifying voice.

"So everyone keeps telling me."

"Perhaps you should start believing them then?"

"If you were an Infected, Mr. Smith, we would have sensed it," added Denarius.

"Without question," agreed Caine. "Vivisect enough of them and you will never forget the stench."

I took a careful step away from the Lord of Bones.

Lucia was distracted enough that she forgot to yell at me for speaking. "Nagas possess the ability to sample an individual's essence through smell."

"But she doesn't even *have* a nose!" I glanced apologetically at the naga. "Not that there's anything wrong with that, of course."

"What more can you tell us, Lady Manassa?" asked Denarius.

The lady—naga?—in question regarded me without expression. A slim, forked tongue slid out between her lips to taste the air, and she frowned.

"Nothing at all. There is something else beyond just human, but it is impossible to identify it beneath the presence of so many marks."

Which, as far as I was concerned, was a lot like saying she couldn't see the boojum because of the presence of too many woojums. Jet lag or no jet lag, this conversation made no sense.

"*Marks?* He has more than just the thrall-bond?" For the first time, Contessa d'Verde seemed interested.

Next to me, Lucia had gone quiet and still.

"Yes." The naga studied me for a few minutes longer, and then shrugged sculpted shoulders. "Blood and winter, chaos and fire, dust and age. Whoever and whatever Mr. Smith may be, multiple beings have staked their claim."

"That does solve a mystery that has nagged at me since I first became aware of his existence," said Denarius. "How can a human be immune to compulsion and glamour? The answer is that he cannot… unless he is something other than just human."

Of the other Council members, all but the so-called Lord of Bones were visibly surprised.

"This *creature* is immune to compulsion?" asked Vigo.

"He is," Lucia admitted, the glare she sent Denarius making her displeasure clear. Apparently, she'd wanted my little secret to stay just that. "It is one of the reasons I selected him as my investigator."

"How can we be expected to approve the exile's choice of investigator if we do not even know what he is?" asked the contessa.

"Your approval is *irrelevant*," snapped Lucia. "The law gives me the right to procure an investigator, and I have done so. Everything else is but tired and tedious ceremony, and neither I nor my Secundus have the time for such nonsense."

The woman in green rose from her chair in a swish of silk, outrage evident in every line of her body, but Denarius was on his feet first, a sliver of shadow that even the chandelier's light could not breach.

"Peace. Though Lady Borghesi's words and tone remain as ill-considered as ever, her interpretation of the law is correct. There are no provisions for the Council to accept or deny her appointed investigator."

"Great." I stifled a yawn. "Are we done then?"

"One can only hope," grumbled Dog in a voice just loud enough to carry across the room.

"There remains the matter of the Illutu," Lucia pointed out. "They will not relent after a single failed assault, and you all know the nest mother has greater forces at her command than simple drones. Something must be done."

Vigo's laughter was barbed. "The exile kills two of our kings, and then expects the Council to protect her? Typical Borghesi arrogance."

"The Illutu know better than to assault the palace," said Denarius.

I tried not to make my sigh of relief too obvious. I mean… I'd assumed, but it was good to know for sure.

"So, you will do *nothing*. Yet again." Lucia was considerably less relieved, apparently. As much as I disliked the queen, I had to admire her ability to squeeze so much derision into so few words.

"You are no longer a child to be protected, Lucia. Were it up to me, you would be left to face the consequences of your past misdeeds." Denarius shook his head slowly. "However, this is a decision for the Council as a whole. What say you, Lady Manassa?"

The sari-clad naga returned to her seat before speaking. "I have no quarrel with the Illutu. Nor do I believe the matter merits our involvement."

"It sets a rather unfortunate precedence though," argued Caine. "If we allow the Illutu to operate freely in our city, what will be next? Pixies? I vote we send a message."

"Duke Marte?"

"This is the exile's mess. Let her clean it up, if she can. If a message needs to be sent to the mercenaries, we should do so at a time of our choosing and after the trial."

"Dog?"

The dwarf waved a meaty hand dismissively. "No profit in squashing the bugs, is there?"

"If I get murdered, you'll go back to being the ugliest dude at court," I reminded him helpfully.

"Eh." Dog picked something out of his beard and tossed it over one shoulder. "I've had thousands of years to learn to cope."

"Contessa?"

"Your *darling* niece has been here less than a day and already our troubles multiply. I have no interest in fighting her battles."

"And you, Kingmaker? What say you?" asked Lady Manassa.

"I agree that we have difficulties enough without seeking out more," replied the manpire. He turned to Lucia. "Should you and your Secundus survive the trial, I suggest you return to the Americas immediately. Perhaps the Illutu will not follow you there."

"So be it." Lucia's voice was as cold as an arctic wind.

"As the law proscribes, you and your investigator will have until First Rot to gather evidence and prepare your defense," Denarius continued. "At that point, we will reconvene for trial."

"It has taken a century longer than it should have," added Vigo triumphantly, "but you will finally pay for your crimes."

I wasn't the greatest expert on vampire behavior, but my keenly trained investigative instincts were telling me the robed manpire didn't like Lucia. I added his name to my suspect list... right below Denarius.

"If there are no other matters to discuss?" Lady Manassa looked around the table and nodded in satisfaction. "I declare this session of the Council closed."

"About damned time," muttered Dog. Somehow, he actually got shorter when he climbed to his feet.

Unlike his fellow Council members, Vigo didn't stand at all. Instead, he fell. Fell apart, that is. Before my shocked—and thoroughly disgusted—eyes, the man dissolved, robe and all, into a teeming mass of thousands of black shelled beetles. The swarm streamed up the wall and then around towards an exit.

"Did anyone else just see a dude turn into a bunch of bugs and skitter across the room?" I asked faintly.

"Of course."

"Cool. Just wanted to make sure it wasn't me."

"Duke Marte has a Talent for Beastcalling, Mr. Smith," Denarius informed me, "and rarely attends our meetings in the flesh."

A vampire that could summon—and apparently speak through—masses of insects. A mercenary army of humanoid roaches trying to kill Lucia. Was I the only one who saw the obvious connection?

I moved Vigo above Denarius on my suspect list.

Lucia maintained her position as the Council cleared out. Contrary to myth, Lady Manassa had normal, human-shaped legs, even if her grace and lean muscle definition would have given a ballerina a fatal case of envy. Both she and Contessa d'Verde left without a word, but Denarius came to meet us, trailed by the three individuals who had been standing to the side of the platform.

"Lady Borghesi. Investigator Smith." Denarius gestured to the newcomers. "Allow me to introduce you to three of our resident ambassadors. Each represents one of the major domains of the People."

"I am Ambassador Santos of the great kingdom of Brasilia." The vampire was tall, handsome, and arrogant enough for ten normal people. His bow held more mockery than deference, and he made no effort to restrain a sneer when glancing from Lucia to me. "I have heard much about you both. I shall be interested to discover whether reality measures up to the reports."

Next was a slender femmepire with long, dark hair, blade-sharp cheekbones, and eyes that couldn't seem to decide whether they were brown or gray. She was dressed as if for a business meeting in a pale blouse and black pants, her heels leaving her only a few inches shorter than me. Something about the woman seemed familiar, but I couldn't quite place my finger on what it was.

"I am Deanna Middleton, of the free People of North America." Unlike Santos, her voice had no accent whatsoever.

I frowned to myself. How many American vampires had the last name Middleton?

"Yes." She met my gaze with eyes that momentarily flickered copper and gold. "I believe you know my wayward daughter."

It had never occurred to me that my partner's parents might still be alive. It should have, given that Juliette wasn't even a hundred yet, but vampire lifespans were something I was still getting used to. Juliette had never spoken of either of them, other than to say they had agreed with the decision to kick her out of the New York House, and I'd just assumed they had passed away or been slain.

Yet here was Deanna Middleton, clearly still alive, and—disconcertingly—looking every bit the same age as her own daughter. I had known vampires stayed whatever age they first drank blood, but it had never occurred to me how that might muddy the generational gap.

The whole species made my head hurt.

Before I could tack on some actual words to my wide-eyed, gaping response, the final ambassador stepped forward. Small enough to make Lucia look like a giant, she carefully picked her way forward between the other two ambassadors.

For the first time, I felt a new emotion from Lucia: fear.

"Ti An," she said simply in heavily accented tones. She was swaddled in golden robes a shade darker than her own skin, but her head was bare of ornament and decoration. And hair, for that matter... even eyebrows. Somehow, being bald as an egg actually added to her appearance. In an ageless Asian face, her eyes were the only spots of color, a faded green like jade bleached by the sun.

I shivered. All vampires looked somewhere between eighteen and twenty-five—except Zorana, of course—but those eyes, examining me like a riddle waiting to be solved, had seen things I didn't even want to guess at.

"I represent the Endless Empire of the Sun," she said simply, turning to Lucia. "I offer a minor title and lands in our territory in exchange for two days with your thrall."

Having a woman—any woman—offering to pay for the pleasure of my company should have been an ego boost, but something inside of me—the part that had kept me alive through vampires, werewolves, demigods, and witches—quailed, terrified by the femmepire's interest.

"And what would be left of Mr. Smith, at the end of those two days?" Lucia's tone was thoughtful.

"Physically or mentally?"

Yeah. *That* was all I needed to hear. But before I could remind the two vampires that I was a free man, not some sort of possession to be passed around, Lucia shook her head.

"While your offer is generous, I regret that I cannot accept it at this time. As you are aware, Mr. Smith's services are currently needed."

"Of course." Ti An bowed shallowly to the former queen. "If you and he survive the coming trial, we will revisit the matter."

"As you say." Lucia's return nod was the closest thing to a bow I'd ever seen from the arrogant femmepire. Icy blue eyes tracked the ambassador's departure.

"I don't have titles or lands to offer, but I'd also welcome the opportunity to speak with you at some point, John." Deanna seemed as threatening as a kitten next to the femmepire who had just left. "It has been a long time since I heard from Juliette, and a mother does worry."

"Whereas I have no interest in you whatsoever." Ambassador Santos' eyes were dark and empty, two gaping holes in the olive perfection of his face. "However, I do look forward to the next few weeks of spectacle." He extracted a handkerchief from his breast pocket and ostentatiously dabbed one corner of his mouth. "Court life is all too often dull."

"I'll try to keep you entertained," I replied brightly, before turning to Deanna. "And I'm happy to chat, but I'm not sure what my schedule will be like for the next few days." Denarius had said my investigation would go until *First Rot*, but I had no idea what that was. If we were talking about Tomasso's corpse, shouldn't it already be rotting?

"Fair enough," replied Juliette's mom. She nodded to Lucia, and then both she and Santos made for one of the exits.

"That is the other reason I wished to speak with you tonight," replied Denarius. "Now that the introductions are complete, we must discuss how you would like to proceed with your investigation."

As tired as I was, even basic strategy was a stretch. "I figured I would just interview the staff, take a look at Tomasso's murder scene, and get Ana's story."

"There are over three hundred servants here, Mr. Smith, and almost a hundred members of the People in permanent or semi-permanent residence. It may not be a wise expenditure of your time to interview them all."

"What do you suggest then?" I tossed a glance Lucia's way, but the femmepire seemed lost in her own thoughts.

"Tomorrow morning, I will present the evidence that has been accrued. After that, I have scheduled interview sessions with the more pertinent members of Tomasso's personal staff, as well as the head of his Watch and his Secundus."

I nodded. It was a start. "What about his thralls?"

Denarius and Lucia shared a look.

"Come on," I reasoned. "You can't tell me the King of freaking Europe didn't have any."

"You haven't told him, Niece?"

"It never came up."

"*What* never came up?"

"Tomasso's thralls are dead, Mr. Smith." The elder's voice was granite. "The bond does not permit a thrall to outlive their master."

Well, shit.

CHAPTER 12

It's not every day you learn that your life—and death—are literally linked to a person you can't stand. I could have spent a solid two weeks of alone-time recovering from that little truth bomb.

Unfortunately, I didn't have two weeks. I only had until First Rot to prove Anastasia's innocence. Whatever First Rot was.

"Okay," I said. "Evidence, then staff interviews. I also want to look over the murder scene, and talk to the Council—"

"The Council?" Denarius raised one eyebrow.

"Yeah." I shrugged. "I'm guessing you all interacted with the king more than most. And that gives you opportunity, if not motive."

"You intend to defend Lady Dumenyova by casting blame upon the ruling body of this land?"

Denarius didn't sound angry. Just… mildly interested. Either he had nothing to hide, or he was confident in his ability to hide it.

"I intend to find the real killer, so we can all go back to San Diego. And speaking of *Lady Dumenyova*, I still haven't heard when we'll get to see her."

I glanced at Lucia to see if she'd noticed my extreme generosity in including her in that statement.

She hadn't.

"That will be difficult," admitted Denarius.

For the first time, Lucia showed signs of paying attention. "How so?"

"Despite her relatively limited Talent, your Secundus is quite dangerous. There were few prisons we could be confident she would not escape."

"If this story ends with Anastasia in a coma, I'm going to be seriously pissed," I warned.

"And?"

"And you wouldn't like me when I was angry?" I hated it when vampires called my bluffs.

"I am not certain I like you at all, anger or no anger."

That was just plain hurtful.

"Where is she, Kingmaker?" demanded Lucia.

"I cannot and will not disclose that information at this time."

"Unacceptable."

Lucia and I had spoken the words at the same time. For once, we were in perfect agreement.

"I have to hear her side of the story to proceed with this case, Lord Borghesi." I threw in the honorific on the off chance that Denarius cared about such things.

"Visitors of any kind are not permitted. It is this particular prison's policy, not my own."

"Then move her," said Lucia.

"And where would you suggest we move her to? As I said, this institution was one of the few…" He tilted his head as a new thought occurred to him. It was the most human gesture I'd seen from the manpire all night. "There *is* an alternative location. One that would allow visitors without possibility of escape."

Lucia went still in a way only the older vampires could do. An icy rage bubbled up across the bond.

"You cannot be suggesting…"

"I am. We will place her in the Tower."

Yet again, I had no idea what they were talking about. I desperately needed a fresh copy of Lucia's briefing and about three days to read it all.

"The Tower?"

"It is a relatively recent addition to the palace, Mr. Smith," answered Denarius. "Wrapped in spells that render its inhabitant quite harmless."

I barely managed to choke back my snort of disbelief. If Lucia's uncle thought *anything* could render Anastasia harmless, he didn't know her at all.

"My brother had it built for his traitorous consort after her plot to overthrow him was discovered."

"Is it safe for Ana to be held there?"

I saw the manpire take note of my nickname for the femmepire and tried not to wince.

"Lady Dumenyova will, in all likelihood, be executed following the trial, Mr. Smith." Denarius' voice was uncompromising. "But yes, she will be safe until then. The Tower's magic will impact her only while she is within its walls."

"And we can visit her?"

He nodded slowly, dark eyes never leaving my face.

"Sounds like a plan then."

"Very well. I will make arrangements to have her transferred and will schedule time for you both to speak with her sometime on Wednesday."

I wasn't wild about having to wait two more days to see Anastasia—case or no case—but it didn't seem like I had much choice. We needed to get her side of the story.

"In the meantime," Denarius continued, "I have secured someone who can act as both translator and guide for you."

"Already?" Of all the things I'd seen that night—roach mercenaries, bug vampires, and spooky Asian ambassadors—it was Denarius' obvious competence and efficiency that concerned me most. He didn't seem the sort to jump to inaccurate conclusions… which spoke volumes about the evidence against the femmepire I loved.

"Indeed." Denarius nodded to the side, and a young woman crossed the chamber to join us.

No… a young *femmepire*, I corrected myself, after one glimpse of honey blonde ringlets and shockingly violet eyes. There was no way someone *that* cute was merely human.

I replayed that thought in my head and sighed. I'd been around vampires for so long that I was starting to think like them.

"This is Maria Elena. She will show you to your accommodations and accompany you tomorrow."

Maria Elena curtsied, holding the skirts of a long dress the exact shade of her downcast eyes. "Milady, milord. If you would follow me?"

I started to follow, flush with the heady triumph of being called a lord, but Lucia was already shaking her head.

Don't take this from me, I prayed furiously. I'd only been a lord for five seconds, but the thought of being forcibly demoted back to commoner was already more than I could bear.

The former queen frowned in my direction, as if she could hear my thoughts, but spoke to Denarius. "This is my home. I have no need of guides, and much to do before I retire for the night. I assume I will be staying in my former chamber?"

"You will not." If Denarius enjoyed correcting Lucia, he hid that fact with a grace I would never manage. "The royal princess' suite is occupied."

"Ah yes," mused Lucia. "I had forgotten dear Tomasso managed to spawn a daughter."

I highly doubted she'd forgotten anything of the sort.

"Go with this child, my thrall," she instructed me. "I have other matters to take care of."

Again with the thrall name-calling.

"Oui oui, mon capitaine," I replied in my most obnoxious French accent. If I'd been wearing dress shoes, I could have clicked the heels together. Sadly, worn Air Jordans wouldn't have nearly the same effect.

A puzzled expression marred Maria Elena's lovely face as she led me from the room.

"Êtes-vous Français?" Maria Elena asked as we passed through a different waiting room and back into the hall.

"I'm sorry?"

The femmepire rattled off a long stream of incomprehensible babble that had me flashing back to my many failed attempts to win the heart of Aurélie, our high school's French-Canadian exchange student.

"I don't speak French," I told her. "I'm American."

"Oh!" she exclaimed. "Well, that explains your pronunciation."

"That's not the first time I've been told that," I admitted. Three years of French, and I'd never managed to do anything but make Aurélie laugh. *At* me, not *with* me.

Anyone who says that French is the language of love clearly never tried to learn it in high school.

ooo

Maria Elena was very excited to meet me. She was also very interested in my investigation, very curious as to what Lucia would be wearing to the next day's banquet, very uncertain how life in America differed from what she had seen on the television and internet, and… well, very *everything*, as far as I could tell.

I had discerned all of this, in the span of only a few minutes of conversation, thanks to my highly trained and professionally relevant powers of observation.

Also? Because Maria Elena had told me so. Unprompted. I was beginning to think this was one femmepire who was every bit as young as she looked.

In fact, my guide and translator had kept up a steady stream of conversation since we'd left the council room, which was especially impressive given that we'd been meandering through the endless halls of Palace Borghesi for at least half an hour.

"We *are* headed to my room, right?" I managed to ask when she finally stopped speaking long enough to take a breath.

"Of course." She brushed a wayward curl out of her face. "Why? Do you know a faster route?"

"This is my first time here," I reminded her, keeping my tone gentle even though my feet were about to fall off. I'd lost count of the number of halls and stairwells we'd traversed by that point and was halfway convinced we were moving in an enormous circle. How many statues could one building have anyway?

"Oh, that's right." She pursed her lips. "Don't worry; I hardly ever get lost these days."

"These days?" That was less comforting than it sounded.

"My family's House is in Milan. I came here… almost a decade ago? I think?" She chewed on that thought for a little bit, and then nodded. "I guess it has been that long. Madness."

Maria Elena was *definitely* younger than the vampires I normally rubbed elbows with. If I had to guess—and a guess would be all it was—I'd say she wasn't much older than she appeared, putting her in her early-to-mid-twenties.

I studied her out of the corner of my eye. As I'd already noticed, she was very pretty… tall and long-legged in a dress that somehow matched those shockingly violet eyes.

"They're contacts," she said, as we rounded yet another corner.

"I'm sorry?"

"My eyes." She grinned, flashing an honest-to-God set of dimples in my direction. "They're naturally gray, but I wear lenses to match my outfits."

"How did you…" All women were psychic. It was the only possible explanation.

"I noticed you looking," she continued brightly. "You're remarkably unsubtle, even for a human. Does your mistress know you have a wandering eye?"

"I'm sorry?"

"Given your attachments, I'm surprised you'd even notice someone like me."

She was cute but didn't hold a candle to Anastasia. Luckily, my mediator experience kicked in before I told her just that.

"Men always notice beautiful women," I said instead, speaking from a place of great experience and scant sexual fulfillment. "Any dude who says otherwise is lying. Anyway," I continued, "I wasn't—"

"Perving on me?" She grinned again.

"Right. I was trying to figure you out."

"Oh, that's easy. I'm a Pisces."

"Not at all what I meant." I glanced through an open archway as we marched past. Inside were shelves and shelves of leather-bound volumes, old enough to be whatever comes before first editions. "You *are* one of the People, right?"

"Of course." Maria Elena rolled her eyes. "Do you think your mistress would have just let *anyone* wander off with her thrall?"

I didn't know how to answer that. Since when did Lucia get a say in who I wandered off with? And what made a human guide and translator any less acceptable than a vampire one?

"I guess not?"

"Bingo!"

Either I was doing a masterful job of hiding my confusion, or Maria Elena was particularly dense.

"So, how old are you then?" In human society, it was the sort of question I'd learned not to ask, but femmepires felt differently about such things. For a vampire, age equated to power.

Maria Elena's cheeks colored, which was almost unspeakably cute, in a small woodland animal sort of way. "I'll be three in just a few months."

"Three... centuries?" Jesus. I really was terrible at this.

"No, silly. Three *years.*"

"Oh." I walked in silence for a bit, before her words sank in. "Wait... you're *three?*"

"Of course," she replied cheerily. "How old are you?"

"Twenty-seven."

"For real?" For some reason, Maria Elena seemed astonished.

"Yeah." I shook my head. "If you're only three, how have you been at the palace for a decade?"

The femmepire furrowed her brow for a long moment, before once again unleashing her dimples. "Oh, that's right! I forgot your species calculates age from when you're born."

"Well, yeah." And duh. "The People don't?"

"Why would we?"

"Because that's what age means!" For a brief moment, it felt like I was talking with Bill, my insane demigod friend. I was way too tired to deal with this much crazy. Especially in the absence of milkshakes.

"Not for us. Everything before the first feeding is just practice time anyway. Years spent waiting for the Thirst to hit and then for puberty to run its course."

"So, when you say you're three, you mean..."

"My first feeding was two years and nine months ago." She blushed again. "I rounded up."

Well, that at least made a little bit of sense. And explained why she looked so much older than Lucia's ward, Summer, who was barely pushing seven. In *real* years, not post-blood-drinking years.

"You don't keep track of how old you were when you first fed?"

Maria Elena shrugged cutely. "I remember it, sure. It just doesn't mean very much. As long as you're an adult and fully formed, who cares *when* you made the transition?"

"I'd heard there was some sort of benefit to delaying the process." Anastasia had fought off the all-consuming Thirst all the way into her mid-twenties for just that reason, with an eye to maximizing the potential she could offer her queen.

"That's just an old wives' tale," Maria Elena responded. "Besides, we're stuck with the body we had at first feeding. Who wants to go through life as an old maid? Not me!"

I coughed.

"Oh, don't worry," she assured me. "For a human, I'm sure twenty-seven is very nice."

It didn't *feel* very nice. I scanned the endless hall in front of us. Lots of doors, all of them identical and most of them closed, but I highly doubted any of them was mine.

"And here we are!"

I mentally rolled my eyes. If I'd known that was all it took to make my suite magically appear, I'd have tried it ten hallways earlier.

The door opened on a large, gorgeously appointed bedroom. Wide bay windows looked out over the darkened courtyard we had driven through, and a king bed dominated the room itself, stacked almost chest high with comforters and padding. A small door in the left wall led to what looked like an office, and a matching door in the right opened onto a beautifully tiled bathroom.

"I could get used to this." The only thing keeping me from taking a flying leap into the bed's acreage of plush softness was my own filth. I needed a shower in the worst of ways. "Do you know what happened to my luggage?"

"It should have already been delivered." She crossed the room and rolled back a beautifully carved wooden panel in the wall to reveal a walk-in closet. "Yep, here it is!"

"Fantastic." In fact, someone had already unpacked both bags, and my clothes were all on hangers… even the t-shirts. *And* the underwear.

I couldn't decide if that was weird or awesome or both.

"And here are your mistress' bags," continued Maria Elena brightly, opening another hidden closet. "The two of you should be all set!"

I looked from one closet to the other and then to the bed in the middle.

"Oh, hell no!"

○○○

"I don't understand," Maria Elena repeated for the fourth time. "Why are these arrangements unacceptable?"

"It's *not* how we do things," I said, for the fifth time. In a desperate bid to break the cycle of confusion, I decided to elaborate: "Lucia and I don't sleep together."

"Oh!" Her face lifted. "I understand!"

"Thank God." Hopefully, whoever had put Lucia's clothes in *my* closet would still be available to move them to some other suite. I was done carrying her luggage.

"I'll have one of the servants bring in a pallet for you," the femmepire chirped. "I had forgotten that some of the old ones prefer that."

"That's *not* what I meant! We sleep," I told her, as slowly and clearly as possible, "in separate rooms."

"But what if she wakes up hungry?"

"If it's too much trouble, I can move my clothes myself. Just find me an empty room."

"I can't do that. *Lord Borghesi* made these arrangements."

"Then go tell *Lord Borghesi* that I need a new room."

She blinked slowly at me, like I was speaking a language that wasn't English, French, or Italian.

"You know what," I decided, "I'll just go tell him myself."

I headed for the door, but the femmepire was already in front of me. Even the young ones were stupidly fast.

"Why don't we just wait here for your mistress to arrive?"

"She's *not* my—" I swallowed the pointless protest. "Maria Elena, you seem like a really nice person, and I don't want to get you in trouble, but I am going to speak to Denarius. And I'm going to do it now."

The femmepire wrinkled her nose. Even in my irritation, the gesture seemed unfairly cute. "I'm sorry to do this," she said, large eyes earnest, "but this isn't something you or I get to decide. Now, go take a seat and wait for your mistress."

"Why would I do that?"

The lavender contact lenses had masked the gold creeping into the femmepire's eyes, so my first clue that Maria Elena had just tried to compel me was the slack-jawed astonishment on her face when said compulsion failed miserably.

"You really *are* immune?" She took a half-step back from me as if I had just sprouted demonic horns and a spiked tail. Which would have been kind of cool if I hadn't met some demons earlier that year.

Assholes, every last one of them.

Lousy conversationalists, too.

"As you should have been taught, child, it is the height of rudeness to compel someone else's thrall," came a cold voice from the doorway. "Be grateful that Mr. Smith's immunity has saved you from the consequences of your error."

Lucia walked into the room like she owned it, running her gaze over the furnishings. "This is… adequate. Barely. See to it that a pallet is brought for Mr. Smith to sleep in."

"Of course, your… err… Lady Borghesi." Maria Elena curtsied and fled through the door.

"Lucia, what—"

The femmepire queen slashed one hand through the air like it was a sword, and—imaginary spiked tail or not—my protest died instantly.

"Cease your desperate groveling, Mr. Smith," she said aloud, not even looking my way. "Despite your position as my thrall, you remain a long way from earning a place in my bed."

"That's not—" I was going to say *what I meant* although *how I remember it* would have worked almost as well. I didn't get the chance to say either. Instead, the femmepire queen slapped one hand over my mouth, cutting off my words. As easily as if I were a child rather than someone twice her size, she pulled me into the bathroom.

That bathroom was every bit as fancy as I'd assumed, featuring a tub that could easily fit four people and a walk-in shower with the same multiple-nozzle setup I'd enjoyed in Lucia's former House. A marble countertop vanity and two copper pedestal sinks lined the far wall, but the full-length mirror behind that vanity was doing a lousy job of reflecting us.

I peered in confusion at that mirror before noting the film of frost that was forming over its glassy surface. In fact, frost was spreading out over the bathroom's interior walls. I glanced down at the vampire queen, and saw her eyes were golden, one hand outstretched as she turned our bathroom into an icebox.

"This is the weirdest, least effective, form of torture ever." The quick shiver that wracked my body almost immediately undercut my words.

Lucia looked around the room carefully, nodded in satisfaction, and then hoisted me into the air with a growl, her fangs fully extended. "If you ruin this for us, Mr. Smith," she hissed, "I will kill you long before the Council can do so."

"You already tried that," I gasped back. It seemed wrong that someone barely over five feet tall could lift my six-foot frame off the ground. "And I'm still here."

"For the final time, I was not trying to kill you last spring!" The femmepire dropped me back to my feet.

"Because *that* becomes more believable each and every time you attack me." I rolled my eyes and massaged the tender skin of my aching throat. "Why are we in here anyway? And what's with the winter wonderland theme?"

"In *this* place of all places, Mr. Smith, the walls have ears."

"In the *bathroom*?" That made no sense. "Why?"

"I meant the palace, you uneducated, pea-brained moron!"

"Oh. Right. And the ice…?"

"I have momentarily sheltered us from observers. Including the so-called honor guard my uncle has provided to keep us under watch."

That was a pretty damn ingenious usage of her Talent, to be honest, but I wasn't going to give her the satisfaction of saying so.

"We are surrounded by enemies, seen and unseen," Lucia continued. "As you yourself stated in San Diego, we cannot afford to appear divided, or all will be lost before your investigation can even begin. If that means we share a room, we *will* share a room."

"And blood?" I challenged.

"Unlike the child who brought you here, I am four centuries old." Her voice was cool, giving away nothing. "What I took from you tonight will last me for a week or more."

"And if you get injured again?"

"Then you *will* do your duty. I expect you to do what is necessary to maintain a united front. For Lady Dumenyova's sake, as much as our own."

"Fine." I shivered again as the cold seeped into my bones. "Maybe now would be a good time to fill me in on what the hell is going on then? *First Rot? Trial?* More importantly, is there a reason you decided not to inform me that this bond will *freaking kill me if anything ever happens to you?*"

"It didn't seem relevant."

If we hadn't been trapped in a giant ice box, I would have stormed out of the suite to take my chances with the so-called honor guard. As it was, I just fixed her with my most impressively angry glare. "If I hadn't come to Rome with you—"

"Then my chances at proving Lady Dumenyova's innocence would have diminished, and the likelihood of my own execution would have increased."

"An execution I wouldn't have survived, even staying home."

"Precisely." Lucia shrugged irritably. "What does it matter? We are here now, and if you fail, we will no doubt die well before the trial."

"You're going to have to run that by me again."

"I have no intention of going through with a trial that we cannot win. Better to die trying to free Asya than to have my execution serve as a public example for the gathered nobility." For once, her crystal blue eyes were absent of scorn or derision. There was nothing in the femmepire's gaze but resolve.

I was pretty sure she didn't even realize she'd used her old nickname for Anastasia.

"As for your other questions," the queen continued, "we will discuss them tomorrow before meeting with the Kingmaker. For now, I recommend that you shower and sleep. You will need your faculties about you if you are to prove my trust in you well founded."

"And the briefing?"

"I will have it sent to your phone."

The fact that Lucia knew my number ranked surprisingly low on the list of unpleasant surprises that night.

"What are you going to be doing for the next few days while I try to solve *two* murders?"

"I will continue what I have already started: working to restore old alliances and sow dissension and discord among our rivals."

"Could you maybe skip all the Game of Thrones nonsense, and focus instead on helping me prove Anastasia's innocence? A second pair of eyes wouldn't hurt."

"This is not a game, Mr. Smith, whatever some might tell you."

I should have known Lucia didn't watch HBO. No doubt, human entertainment was beneath her. I mentally rolled my eyes.

Judging by the cold light that appeared in the queen's eyes, she'd somehow *felt* my reaction.

Stupid bond.

"My work here is every bit as relevant to a successful defense as your own, Mr. Smith."

"How so?"

"This is not an American court of law. More than reasonable doubt is required. Unless you can conclusively prove Lady Dumenyova's innocence, her fate—and ours—will come to a vote."

"By who?"

"The Council."

I thought of Vigo and his barely contained contempt, the contessa's casual disregard, and Dog's boredom with the whole affair, and felt a cold chill run down my spine.

"Oh."

The femmepire nodded. "You begin to understand. The Lord of Bones is our ally, but he is currently the *only* vote we can be certain of. We need at least three others."

I did the math in my head, which was way harder than it should have been after the flight and subsequent battle. "Caine plus three others means four votes out of eight… assuming the missing Council members participate. A tie goes to the defense?"

"Four votes out of *seven*. Lady Manassa will abstain, as ever."

"That sucks. She seemed like one of the few people up on the platform who didn't actively hate you."

"Yes." Lucia's eyes flashed like tiny stars. "In many ways, my task will be even more difficult than your own."

I hadn't seen Denarius' evidence yet, but something told me the queen was dead wrong.

INTERLUDE

"Do you truly believe this is the right choice?"

I stop peeking around the corner just long enough to give Anastasia a withering look. "You'd rather I stay cooped up in my tiny little suite like Father wishes? I thought we'd already had this discussion."

Without waiting for a reply, I dart across the hall. The guards, a pair of minotaurs whose sense of smell and hearing make up for truly terrible night vision, remain blissfully ignorant of my passage.

Moments later, Anastasia joins me. Whatever else she's been learning from Gaius, I have to admit her skills at stealth far surpass my own. Until she opens her mouth, anyway.

"I wasn't suggesting we stay in your suite," she breathes back.

"Oh?" I fix her with my best imperious look, the one I've spent my first century as a fully blooded adult mastering. "Because that's exactly what it sounded like."

"You know good and well that I'm every bit as bored as you are." She grins. "But the window would have made for an easier exit."

"I can't even imagine what climbing down the exterior wall would do to my dress." I shudder. "And you remember the earful I got from that woman *the last time I ruined a gown.*"

"If I recall," muses Anastasia, who has taken the lead, *"I also suggested that a white, full-skirted gown was going to make this more difficult than it had to be."*

"I am not *going to tryst with the court's most eligible bachelor in* trousers, *Asya!"*

"I don't think he cares what you're wearing, for however long you do continue wearing it, but a darker color dress would have set off your hair and still lent itself to stealth."

"Actually," I tell her archly, *"I've decided that white will be my official color as queen."*

Anastasia waves me across, and we skirt another of the interior guard stations.

"Why white?" she finally asks.

"Because it's the color of sincerity, good, and purity."

"As exhibited by the fact that you're wearing it while we sneak out of the manor, against the king's express wishes, so that you may engage in a liaison with a demon."

I meet her grin with one of my own. *"Precisely! In fact—"*

Anastasia remains frozen, as if waiting for me to speak.

This isn't right.

Something is—

"In fact—" I/She tries again. *"I— We—"*

The scene begins to melt, like snow under a hot summer sun, and I am suddenly airborne, looking down at a gorgeous young woman, whose spectacular cleavage is almost entirely exposed by the snow-white gown she wears. She shudders once, and then looks up at me with crystal blue eyes far too old for her flawless form.

GET. OUT. OF. MY. HEAD.

NOW!

○○○

I shudder awake, my breath harsh in the cold air. It isn't the first time I've inadvertently shared one of Lucia's dreams or memories, but the experience remains as freaky as ever.

I suck in a long, ragged breath, and try to pull the sheet tighter about me... which is when I realize several things: I am lying on the floor instead of a small and uncomfortable cot, I no longer have a sheet or a gut-hiding sleep shirt, and my arms are shackled to the floor on either side of me.

A candle flame appears in the darkness, almost uncomfortably bright, and a small, sharp-chinned face looms above me, eyes filled with blood.

"Hello, pet!" purrs Zorana.

CHAPTER 13

I emerged from a much-needed shower, still feeling like death warmed over, and squinted at my fogged reflection in the mirror. Jet lag and a nearly sleepless night hadn't magically improved my looks any unless deep circles under the eyes were now in fashion. I toyed with the small ring that I'd hung on a chain around my neck after my shower, but—conscious of the femmepire queen just outside my door—let it fall and lie flat against my chest. Wrapping the towel around my waist, I stepped back into my shared bedroom.

Lucia was still asleep. After a horrible night on a cot that had no doubt once served as a torture device, the palatial bed looked depressingly inviting. The queen had found an additional four pillows somewhere and arranged them on the bed about her like some sort of feather-stuffed throne. Her still-surprisingly long hair fanned out around her head like a platinum halo.

Whatever my personal feelings toward Lucia, it was impossible to deny that she was—

"Are you going to continue staring at me like a filthy, mouth-breathing peasant, or am I free to rise and use the shower?"

—a truly awful person, whose superficial beauty couldn't possibly make up for the many obvious deficiencies in her personality.

"And put some clothes on, for the love of all that bleeds. You have the physique of a pre-pubescent boy with a beer fixation."

"And you have the body of a..." I struggled to find an adequately cutting response. It wasn't the first time a vampire had insulted my masculinity, but repeated experience had yet to improve my comeback game.

Lucia rose from the bed. "Did I not just command you to avert your eyes, thrall?" Her words were unamused. "I know that such is a lot to ask of someone with your deep-seated inadequac—"

"Your hair is sticking straight up," I told her.

"I beg your pardon?"

"Like a porcupine."

○○○

The queen took considerably less time in the bathroom and shower than I had, which was undeniable evidence of yet another femmepire superpower. She emerged in a crisp white blouse and knee-length pencil skirt.

"Aren't you a little overdressed for breakfast?" I asked her.

"Appearance is a weapon, when properly wielded," she replied, voice tight with irritation, after casting one final glance in the mirror. "You would be well advised to put on something more appropriate before the servants arrive with our food."

"You care what a servant might think?"

"Don't be tiresome. Each of our attendants is no doubt in the employ of one or more of Rome's noble Houses. What they see will be common knowledge by supper."

Palace life, I was beginning to realize, was not all I'd imagined it to be.

As if on cue, there was a tap at the door. Moments later, several young servants—all of them human, as far as I could tell—entered, each carrying a tray. In short order, the table in our suite's office was covered with dishes.

My stomach rumbled like a miniature avalanche. I was a little fuzzy on exactly how much time had passed since my last real meal back in San Diego… it had been Sunday when we left, and it was now Tuesday, but Rome was some crazy number of hours ahead of the West Coast, and…

I sighed and gave up. Even with a decent night of sleep, I might have still struggled with the math. Besides, there was plenty of food available now and that's what mattered.

Lucia ate with a sort of fastidious care that might have been charming on someone less horrible but instead came off as annoying. Judging by her expression as I shoveled food into my mouth, my own eating habits similarly left much to be desired.

When the hole in my stomach had been mostly filled, I set down my third glass of orange juice and sighed happily. As always, good food had a way of making the impossibly dire future seem a little bit less daunting. Some people eat when they're stressed or heartbroken… I eat when I'm in danger.

I'd been eating a lot since meeting Lucia.

"How long do we have until we're supposed to meet with Denarius?" I'd checked my phone when I first woke up, but it wasn't getting a signal, and I was pretty sure the time displayed was wildly inaccurate.

"We have a little more than an hour," replied the queen, after a glance at her own, apparently functional, phone. "Ample time to discuss your intrusion into my dreams last night and what I will do to you if it happens again."

"Trust me, I wasn't there by choice."

"No? You slipped upon a banana peel and fell into my subconscious?"

Okay, maybe Lucia *did* watch television.

"I went to sleep. The next thing I knew, I was in your head, and we were barely dressed and headed off to sleep with some dude. The last time this happened was when we were staying in neighboring rooms at Ana's house. Months ago. Whatever is going on, distance must play a part." I gave the queen a significant look. "Which is a great argument for me getting my own room, don't you think?"

"There may be something to what you say," the queen finally acknowledged. "We will discuss the matter further at another time."

Between that and the breakfast I'd recently demolished, I was starting to think Tuesday would be a winner of a day.

"In the meantime," she continued, "I believe you had some questions for me about your investigation?"

Luckily, I'd spent some of my overly long shower remembering what those questions were.

"Yeah. But…" I waved a fork at the office we currently found ourselves in. "Don't you want to do the whole icebox thing first?"

"And ruin the day's outfit? I think not. Questions of law will be of little interest to our listeners."

I frowned but took her word for that. "Well, we covered the generalities of how the trial will work last night, but I'm still unclear on the timetable. What exactly *is* First Rot?"

"Precisely what it sounds like."

Which told me absolutely nothing. Unless…

"You mean the trial will occur whenever your brother's body *literally* starts to rot?"

"Indeed."

"That's morbid, even for vampires. Is his body on ice?"

"Tomasso's corpse is at this moment on a stone altar in the bowels of this building."

"You mean in a morgue?"

"I mean on a stone altar, in a large room just outside the catacombs. When a ruler perishes, his or her body is presented to the kingdom, that the public might come say their final farewells."

It was sometimes all too easy to think of vampires as magically gifted, long-lived, blood-drinking humans. Then you learned about some of their creepy weird rituals, and realized they were every bit as alien as anything described in science fiction.

"That's messed up," I finally managed.

"Is it so different from a human wake? The only distinction I see is in the quantity and quality of mourners."

Rather than acknowledge the point, I moved on to the more important issue. "Wasn't Tomasso killed last week?"

"I believe so, yes."

"Then why hasn't the trial already started? It doesn't take that long for a body to rot." Numerous reruns of CSI had taught me that much.

"We are not human, Mr. Smith. Why do you expect us to behave like your kind, even in death? You will have anywhere between two and three weeks to complete your investigation."

I wasn't sure how long most homicide investigations took, but three weeks sounded pretty good. My investigations back in San Diego rarely went that long.

It meant I might actually make it back for Mike's bachelor's party. Assuming I didn't get murdered, of course.

Lucia had already gone back to whatever it was she'd been doing on her phone. I stealthily moved a cinnamon roll onto my plate and fished out my own phone.

Still no signal.

"What's up with the crappy reception?"

"What are you talking about?"

I showed her my phone.

"Did you purchase a new sim card for your phone?"

"No?"

"And are we currently in America, Mr. Smith?"

"Uhm." That had seemed like a trick question.

"Then why would you *expect* to get reception?"

Because it's my wonderphone, I barely managed to avoid saying. Nobody needed to know I was naming my gadgets. Or how clueless I was about international travel. Wasn't Verizon an international carrier?

"Is there somewhere I *can* make a call from then? I need to download the briefing. And check in with Juliette. Especially if I'm going to be gone until almost May."

"If you had shown such diligence with your *other* career as with that undersized agency of yours, you might very well still be San Diego's mediator."

I fixed the queen with my best interpretation of a steely gaze. "I *am* still San Diego's mediator. One of them, anyway. And that didn't answer my question."

Lucia sipped from her glass of water and sighed. "I was banished from Italy long before the telephone made its appearance here, Mr. Smith. You will have to ask Denarius or that irritating waif he has tasked as your guide to a land line or a computer. Provide me an email address and I also will send the briefing on, yet again."

"Can I just use your phone?"

"Not on your increasingly fragile life." Her smile was thin. "Perhaps you can simply invade Ms. Middleton's dreams as you have been doing mine."

I shivered. I loved Juliette like the slightly psychopathic sister I'd never had, but I was pretty sure her dreams would scar me for life.

And speaking of worrisome thoughts… I set the remainder of the cinnamon roll down with a sigh of my own.

"What do you think Lady Manassa meant when she said I wasn't human?"

"I have no idea." Lucia rose from her chair to retrieve another white scarf from her closet. "Perhaps she was detecting what has become of our bond. Or perhaps you have some small strain of lesser species in your DNA. That would at least explain the insanity of multiple generations of John Smiths."

As someone who'd had to live with the name his whole life, I couldn't really argue.

"Or perhaps she was lying," the femmepire continued, "and sees advantage in convincing the rest of the Council that you are more than you seem. Everyone in that room has their own agenda, and her strategies are considered Byzantine even among other naga."

Huh. A devious plotter? I added Lady Manassa's name to my suspect list, right below Vigo. The sad truth was that everyone I had met so far in Italy was now on that list, with the possible exceptions of Maria Elena and the poor, nameless, and brainwashed policeman who had driven us from the airport.

Maybe three weeks was a tighter timeline than I'd thought.

"If you have finished stuffing your face with a child's weight in food, we should go. The Kingmaker does not like to be kept waiting."

"Right." I rose to my feet, brushing some wayward crumbs off my t-shirt. "What's his deal anyway?"

"You would know *his deal* if you had read the briefing."

"Didn't we already cover why that didn't happen?"

Lucia shook her head in frustration. "A refresher then. Denarius Borghesi, elder of the People. Also known as the Kingmaker, brother to my father, and—as you have witnessed—one of the sitting members of the Council."

"Why do they call him Kingmaker?"

"Because that is what he is, Mr. Smith. Denarius slew the Mad King of Paris more than six centuries ago but chose to place the crown at his younger brother's feet. When my father died and I was banished, there were again cries for Denarius to take the crown himself, but he instead gave it to Tomasso and supported his ascension."

The Mad King had forced Zorana, at the time a potential Blood Witch, to feed well before her time, breaking something inside of her in the process. That action had indirectly and painfully impacted me more than once. Denarius might be a stick in the mud, but he clearly wasn't *all* bad.

"He doesn't sound like the sort of guy who would murder his own family members to gain power."

"Not for power, no."

"For what then?" A century as an exile had clearly made Lucia paranoid. Denarius was a humorless, terrifying badass, but I didn't see any real motive that would make him the killer.

"It is your job to discover that, not mine."

Of course it was.

CHAPTER 14

IN WHICH THE VAULT AND THE CASE MIGHT BOTH
BE AIRTIGHT

"Have you ever considered installing moving sidewalks?" I asked Lucia, a good twenty minutes later. "And escalators? This place is ridiculous."

"Perhaps we would make better time if you spent less of your oxygen on complaints," came the retort. As usual, only one of us was desperately sucking wind… and it wasn't the top-heavy, ridiculously short blonde in stiletto heels.

"Maybe some bike carts or something?"

"I did ride my mare from one end of the great hall to another."

"Is that… some sort of euphemism?"

"I will never understand how your species survived to populate the planet," the queen muttered. "Now, quit your dawdling. We are already late."

Despite the Council's vote to do absolutely nothing about the Illutu, Denarius had assigned Lucia an escort anyway… more disturbingly fit vampires in the all-black uniform of the Watch. They followed us down another flight of stairs without complaint. We were well into the bowels of the palace, creamy marble and mahogany wood giving way to simple stone, when we finally reached a security checkpoint.

Our guards shared a steely-eyed look of brotherly commiseration with the vampires waiting at the checkpoint as we were waved through. Just down the hall and around a corner, we finally reached our destination.

The door was massive and metal—like a bank vault, although I was pretty sure the material was something far more exotic than steel. Adamantium, maybe. Or vibranium… assuming either of those existed. Arrayed on either side were even more Watch members. We'd seen more guards on our trip from the bedroom than Lucia's former House had ever fielded during my time there. Assuming there were more of them sprinkled throughout the rest of the palace—training, sleeping, or guarding Council members—even my rudimentary math skills told me that there had to be a small army wandering the premises.

Maybe fighting our way out wasn't such a great idea after all.

The lead guard, a femmepire whose close-cropped hair made her look particularly dangerous, nodded to our four-man escort and eyed us with poorly disguised distaste.

"Lady Borghesi. The Kingmaker awaits you within."

Lucia offered one of those elitist hand gestures that only people with oceans of money ever seem to master, sort of a *by all means then, you have my royal permission to open the door for me so that I might proceed through it in the stately manner by which I do all things.*

For a simple gesture, it was pretty damn wordy.

Whatever that door was made from, it was as thick as I was wide, and ruthlessly heavy, given the way the other guard was struggling just to move it. I glanced at the dude's bulging biceps as we strolled past and shook my head. If we had to open the door from the inside, it was going to be up to Lucia and her uncle to do the deed; *I* didn't even work out.

Denarius was inside, simply dressed in a dark, high-necked tunic and black, wide-legged pants. "Niece. Investigator." He nodded to us both. "I was beginning to think you were not coming."

"Punctuality is the last refuge of the simple-minded, dear Uncle," Lucia replied sweetly.

"Yet order is our only defense against chaos."

"I've found *chaos* works pretty well against chaos," I offered.

Neither vampire paid me any attention, their gazes clashing like lightsabers. Only not nearly as cool.

I waited for a long moment, but the silent Borghesi standoff showed no signs of resolution. With a sigh, I stepped past them and scoped out our surroundings.

In keeping with the theme of its adamantium door, the room screamed bank vault—from the shelves that lined both sides to the set of safe deposit boxes against the far wall—but it wasn't nearly as grandiose as I'd expected. I wandered over to the card table in the center of the room. The presence of three chairs—instead of the even numbers I would have expected—suggested that table had been set up for our benefit.

"I was kind of hoping for something a little cooler," I announced. "Scrooge McDuck oceans of gold coin or something."

"We own *Banca Monte dei Paschi di Siena*, Mr. Smith."

"I don't have any idea what that is." At some point, people were going to start remembering I didn't speak Italian. Until then, we were going to keep having problems.

"It even *says* bank in its title," sighed Lucia.

"Oh. Got it." I shrugged. *Bahnca* didn't sound anything like *bank* to me, but when literally in Rome…

Anyway, owning a bank was cool, but it wasn't *mountains-of-gold* cool.

If nothing else, my most recent display of ignorance had brought an end to the vampiric eyeball war. Lucia followed me deeper into the chamber, and the great door slowly boomed shut behind us. After a brief pause, interior fans somewhere above us began to circulate with a steady hum.

"This vault," Denarius explained, "is its own distinct entity within the larger framework of the palace. With its own generator, vents, and electrical system, it is a closed system separate from the area around it, and the only entrance is the door through which the two of you have arrived. Furthermore, every inch of its interior is monitored by security cameras."

"Sweet," I offered.

"The point I am trying to make," he elaborated, "is that there is no chance that the evidence you are about to see has been tampered with in any way."

"Oh, right." That possibility hadn't even occurred to me. I was reminded, yet again, how little my career had done to prepare me for investigating a murder.

"Additionally, the evidence has been logged and recorded, so if something were to happen to said evidence, it would in no way impede the trial."

"We have no need to destroy your evidence when Lady Dumenyova is so clearly innocent," said Lucia.

"Of course." Denarius did a better job of controlling his expressions and tone than anyone I'd met, up to and including Anastasia herself, but I was reasonably sure he was either amused by his niece's confidence or irritated by it.

Or just bored. Like I said… his poker face was top-notch.

I gestured at the numerous crates that filled the shelves on either side of us. "That's a metric crap ton of evidence, dude. Did you transport the entire murder scene here?"

"Don't be tiresome, Mr. Smith. In his dotage, my uncle fancies himself as something of a policeman. No doubt, this tiny closet contains evidence of a great many petty crimes."

The Kingmaker's voice was butter smooth. "In our culture, it is customary to mete out punishment as a matter of course, without the pomp and pretense of a trial, but there are some transgressions that must be dealt with in a public and official fashion. This chamber contains five centuries of evidence from such incidents."

"What sort of transgressions are we talking about?" I asked, interested despite myself. I was pretty sure it was the *five centuries* thing. I was basically standing in a real-life crime museum and that was kind of cool.

"The only one you need concern yourself with is that of the notorious Secundus who broke her exile to assassinate Europe's king."

"Broke her exile to *allegedly* assassinate Europe's king," I corrected him.

"She did not come back here for the wine, Mr. Smith."

"We don't know that for sure. And my point is that nothing has been proven yet."

"Which is why you are here."

"Yes," answered Lucia sharply, "so perhaps we should proceed to reviewing this so-called evidence?"

"If your mind had only ever been as swift as your tongue, Lucia..." Denarius shook his head sadly.

I eyed the manpire with newfound respect. Dude threw shade pretty well for someone of his advanced years.

"By all means," he continued, "let us begin. It is time you recognized the hopelessness of your case."

"I have experienced firsthand how limited your investigative skills are, Uncle," Lucia retorted. "I have every confidence that the case against Lady Dumenyova will be similarly shoddy."

ooo

"We're *so* screwed," I muttered for at least the fourth time.

"I did warn you." Despite his words, Denarius' voice was matter of fact, as if he took no pleasure in being proven right.

Technically, all the evidence he had presented to us was circumstantial, but there was a lot of it, and every single piece implicated Anastasia. A loose reconstruction of the femmepire's movements since arriving in Rome showed her circling Tomasso's townhouse in the city multiple times before his death, and camera footage placed a woman that at least vaguely matched her description at the building on the day of the assault. There was even a memo requesting additional security, signed by Tomasso himself, less than a week before his demise. When taken together, it painted a picture of a king suddenly worried for his life, and a notorious assassin circling in for the kill.

Still, if there was one thing I'd learned in my years of tracking down the frisky, sexually wayward husbands and wives of San Diego, it was that even the most suspicious of clients needed convincing. While circumstantial evidence was great for setting the scene, it always took hard evidence to close a case.

Unfortunately, Denarius had that too.

"This hair," he said, extracting a small plastic bag from the crate and placing it in front of me, "was found at the murder scene. Once you have examined it, it will undergo DNA testing and fiber analysis."

I eyeballed the bag. It *looked* like Ana's hair, root and all, but there had to be at least a few other vampires with similarly gorgeous, silky, auburn hair, right?

"Even if the hair turns out to be Lady Dumenyova's, it's hardly proof that she killed Tomasso. Or was even there. There are a lot of reasonable explanations for how it got into Tomasso's townhouse."

"Yes. Perhaps it was simply carried into the room through an open window on a cool April breeze. Or spontaneously manifested on the floor because of a weakening in the trans-dimensional walls."

The jet-lagged portion of my brain badly wanted to discuss those suspiciously weak trans-dimensional walls further, but the rest of me recognized sarcasm when I heard it. "My point is that a strand of hair and a blurry still from a budget security camera are hardly enough to convict someone."

"Perhaps not." Denarius slid a thin packet of pages across the table. "This report contains our findings at the crime scene, although I do commend your desire to visit the location in person."

"Assuming it hasn't been tampered with since."

"The Watch guards the exterior entrance. Nobody has been in or out since my own investigators departed."

"We'll see if that's true," I muttered ominously. Not that I had the slightest notion of how to tell if the scene *had* been tampered with. I flipped through the packet absently. I wasn't much of a scientist, but what I was looking at seemed legit, replete with science-y words and colorful charts.

Of greater interest were the handful of photos that accompanied the report. The first few covered the various entrances and exits from the building. The next handful of pictures mapped the interior of a house that, unlike the palace itself, had clearly been redecorated at some point in the past few decades. And the last set of pictures…

Lucia turned away and crossed the room.

I eyed the queen thoughtfully. The emotions coming across the bond were a chaotic mix. Grief. Disgust. Anger. Even a tiny sliver of joy.

I looked down at the images of Rome's last king, lying where he had died.

The lack of blood would have been surprising, were I not already familiar with the difference between our species. If a human—or an Illutu, apparently—had died like that, blood would have been everywhere.

I took a few slow, deep breaths to make sure the French toast I'd had for breakfast didn't come back to haunt me.

"Did they find the head?"

"The next picture, Mr. Smith."

There it was.

Denarius added another stack of paper to my pile. "The autopsy, as performed under my supervision."

I eyed the pages, which looked every bit as impenetrable as the crime scene reports. "Why don't you summarize?"

Denarius glanced at Lucia but the queen still had her back to us. "Very well. It says my nephew died from massive trauma to the chest, decapitation, and exsanguination."

"Because just one of those wasn't enough?"

"We are the People, Mr. Smith. We do not die easily."

"No kidding."

"*Someone,*" continued Denarius, "drove a hard and sharp implement straight through Tomasso's torso multiple times, pulverizing his heart in the process. That same *someone* then tore the head from his body."

I fought very hard to control my reaction.

"Yes. As I can see you remember, that is exactly how Lady Dumenyova executed Xavier Conteh."

"How would you know that? I'm pretty sure you were here in Italy at the time." Hell, I hadn't even known Xavier's last name, and I'd been there! I moved the elder up a few spots on my *People Likely to Kill Lucia's Little Brother and Frame my Almost-Girlfriend* list.

"As you have commented on numerous occasions, my thrall," said Lucia, "my former House was stuffed to its rafters with traitors, malcontents and spies." She stalked back over to us, jaw clenched and eyes hard.

I watched her force herself to examine each of the photographs detailing her brother's death. For once, even the bond told me nothing about what she was thinking.

"In addition," continued Denarius, "these fragments were retrieved from the wreckage of my nephew's chest." He handed me another evidence bag and a heavy magnifying glass. "They are clearly stone, albeit of a composition our technicians had not encountered previously."

The bag held five jagged slivers of stone, the largest roughly as long as my fingernail. It was black and shiny, like polished obsidian or... whatever that volcanic stuff is. Again, I wasn't a scientist.

"Black rock. I'm not sure why they were confused."

"I provided you the magnifying glass for a reason, investigator."

Oh. Right. I took up the magnifying glass and resumed my examination. And that was when I saw what he was talking about; the tiny shards of ebon rock were shot through with threads of gold.

I swallowed convulsively. Denarius might never have seen that stone before, but I had. It formed the walls of Lord Kala's bar, the Bitter End, a place of spectacular drinks and terrifying clientele. Or terrifying drinks and spectacular clientele... it kind of depended on the night.

The Bitter End existed in its own dimensional pocket—and it was unlikely someone could have killed Tomasso with a pub anyway—but Anastasia was known as the Stone Lady for more than just her poker face. The love of my life had a singular Talent: the ability to transform herself into a living statue of animated stone. And the very last time I'd seen her do so, her stone form had been polished ebony, streaked through with veins of gold.

We were *so* screwed.

ooo

Between the crime scene photographs, the strand of hair, and the fragments of a stone that didn't exist on this dimensional plane, I desperately needed some alone-time to regroup. Unfortunately, I was stuck in that vault with two Borghesis, and I was reasonably sure neither one was willing to let me go just yet.

So instead, I carefully laid the stone fragments aside, next to the autopsy and crime scene reports, and then stacked the photographs and turned them face-down… as much for my benefit as for Lucia's. All the while, I was thinking furiously. If Anastasia really was innocent—and my faith had taken a bit of a beating during the manpire's show and tell—then there *had* to be another explanation for those items. All I had to do was figure out what that explanation might be.

Sadly, I ran out of ways to procrastinate long before I could come up with a viable explanation.

"I did warn you both," the manpire said again.

"It's an impressive frame job," I admitted, "but I *will* figure out who was really behind it. Can I get copies of the reports?"

"Of course."

"If my thrall will not ask, I will. How was my Secundus taken?"

Damn it. That *was* a good question

"Exactly what I was wondering," I lied. "I'm sure your soldiers are impressive and all, but I've seen Lady Dumenyova in action. She kicked Xavier's ass. Handily."

"The Stone Lady is a capable opponent, Mr. Smith, but numbers always tell in the end." Denarius frowned. "In this instance, it was less a factor of our numbers, and more a factor of hers."

"I have no idea what that means." I glanced over at Lucia, but she seemed lost in thought.

"Had Lady Dumenyova come with a partner, either she or her companion would have been on watch, resulting in just the sort of melee and bloodbath you described. As it was…" He shrugged. "Even our kind must sleep."

"You *literally* caught her napping?" There were no words for how ridiculous that sounded.

"Perhaps she wanted to be caught," the manpire said thoughtfully. "Killing one's king is no small matter, even for someone like her."

Lucia's laughter was sharp and barbed. "Clearly, you do not know her. Killing Tomasso would never have caused Anastasia grief."

"Lucia… stop helping." I turned back to Denarius. "How did you track her down in the first place?"

For the first time, the manpire looked slightly uncomfortable.

"We received an anonymous tip regarding the presence of a strange vampire where one should not have been."

"An anonymous tip. Because *that* doesn't scream setup." I infused the sentence with as much sarcasm as it could hold.

"There are always those seeking to gain favor with the Court by alerting us to trespassers."

"Where I come from, *gaining favor* and *anonymous tip* are mutually exclusive."

"Well said." For the first time—possibly ever—I felt something like approval coming across the bond from Lucia.

"It is an oddity, I agree, but hardly germane to the matter at hand. Especially when you consider *this*." Denarius placed yet another plastic bag in front of me. Inside was a heavy golden ring with a broad flat surface and what looked like runes surrounding an inset ruby.

"I'm flattered, dude," I told him, "but this is no time for you to propose. We have a murder to solve!"

He and Lucia *both* narrowed their eyes. Nobody in the whole damn family had a sense of humor.

No wonder they kept getting killed or exiled.

"This," said Denarius, voice dry as bone, "is the signet ring of my House. It was Aurelius' until *his* untimely death and was passed to Tomasso upon his coronation. And it was found in Lady Dumenyova's possessions when the Watch captured her."

Hopefully, either Ana or Lucia would be able to explain that coincidence, because I had nothing. At all. Any more of this and Denarius would have *me* convinced of Anastasia's guilt.

"The ring thing is a bit concerning," I admitted, for once unable to find enjoyment in the accidental rhyme, "but isn't it possible she stole it the day before, when she left the trace evidence of her hair? Maybe that was her whole mission in the first place."

Lucia didn't help at all. For the first time, I found myself missing Juliette. As partners went, she was prone to sudden displays of pique, to occasionally wandering off in mid-conversation, and to an incurable case of boredom that—

On second thought, I was glad Juliette was in San Diego.

"So, it is your position that this was a robbery gone bad?" Denarius, at least, was giving my words the attention they deserved.

"Or a robbery gone right. Maybe she snuck in like a ninja, grabbed the ring, left a single strand of hair as some sort of gentlewoman-thief signature… and then someone else killed your king?"

"You will have a difficult time convincing my peers of that."

Unfortunately, he was right.

οοο

Show-and-tell time was over; Denarius began the slow process of returning everything back to the evidence bin.

"I will have copies of the given reports delivered to your suite."

"Pictures too, please." I would have preferred to never look at those grisly photographs again, but they would be helpful when I visited the murder scene. "And I wouldn't mind seeing some more stills from the security footage."

"Of course. For what it's worth, Mr. Smith, I do regret that you have been tasked with an unwinnable defense."

"Every case looks solid," I said easily, "until you start digging into the inconsistencies. I'm *going* to prove Anastasia's innocence."

"I believe you will try." Denarius offered me his hand across the table. "Your devotion to my niece is foolhardy, but respectable."

"My thrall neither requires nor desires your approval, Kingmaker." Lucia rose from her chair and stalked over to the closed vault door. "And the situation is far less bleak than you realize."

I hoped that, for perhaps the first time in our shared history, the femmepire queen would be correct about something. But I wasn't willing to bet our lives on it. I shook Denarius' hand. "Thank you for reviewing the evidence with us."

"Of course. As I mentioned last night, I have arranged a series of interviews with King Tomasso's staff and servants. Maria Elena will come to take you to an office where you may conduct those interviews."

The prosecution was *never* this helpful on television. Or so annoyingly competent. "Tomasso's servants will make for a good start. What about the Council?"

"Their schedules are considerably more difficult to manage, but Dog, at least, has agreed to see you this afternoon." Denarius' voice was grave. "If you wish to be in any shape to attend tonight's banquet, do not partake of food, refreshment, or recreational items while in his chambers."

I was already kind of terrified.

"And Anastasia is being transferred today?"

"Indeed." Denarius' eyes flashed like cold mirrors, and the shadows dripping from his form seemed to shiver. "Duty compels me to remind you both that any attempts to free Lady Dumenyova or to flee the country will be dealt with harshly."

"It never even crossed our minds," lied Lucia. "Why should it, when it will be so much more satisfying to unmask the real killer and clear my name?"

If nothing else, I had to admire her confidence.

CHAPTER 15

"Sorry again about last night's misunderstanding," breezed Maria Elena, guiding me past a convoy of human servants headed in the opposite direction. "I should never have attempted to compel you."

Had that only been last night? Jet lag was severely messing with my brain. "No worries. I guess it's natural to want to see if the stories are true."

"Even so, I shouldn't have done it."

"And I shouldn't have been a dick about the room arrangements," I decided magnanimously. "Let's just call it even and start over."

"Start over?"

"Yeah." I flashed her my second-best smile. Unlike the Dealmaker™, this one hadn't earned a name yet. In fact, I wasn't entirely sure of its effectiveness, having only ever used it on the occasional bartender down in the Gaslamp Quarter. But that was a worry for another day. "Hi. I'm John Smith."

"Maria Elena Giordano." Her eyes were the color of fresh spring grass today, perfectly matching a sleeveless and knee-length dress. In lieu of a formal curtsey, she unleashed her dimples with a smile that put even the Dealmaker™ to shame.

I grinned back. "It's a pleasure to meet you, Maria Elena. Thanks for agreeing to take me around the palace today."

"Trust me, you're doing *me* a favor. It was this or weapons practice."

"Weapons practice?"

"With Gaius and Sabina." She wrinkled her nose. "Three hours in the mud and sun learning how to shift weight and step correctly. I'd rather be dancing. Or sleeping. Or anything else, really."

"Well, I'm happy to have you," I told her honestly. "It hadn't occurred to me that there would be people who didn't speak English."

"In Italy?"

"Well, yes." It was my turn to blush. "I didn't have a lot of time to prepare for the trip. Lucia only told me we were coming to Rome a few hours before our plane ride."

"What's it like?"

"Flying? Kind of horrible, honestly. I'm just grateful we didn't blow up or get hijacked or something."

"I've been on a plane before, Mr. Smith." Soft green eyes danced. "Sabina and I took a tour through Europe last summer."

"Oh." Well, didn't *I* feel provincial? "What were you asking about then?"

"What it's like being Lady Borghesi's thrall. It must be *amazing*."

"It… has some drawbacks," I offered cautiously.

"Really?" the femmepire gushed. "I know it's politically incorrect to say so, given all that she's done, but I have to admit I find your whole relationship so romantic!"

"I'm sorry?"

"A human dedicating his life to a fallen royal, sworn to serve her to his very last drop of blood!" She practically swooned. "Someday, I hope to get permission from the Council to seek a thrall of my own, but I don't know if I'll ever find someone with that sort of love and devotion."

"Wait… what?" I stopped walking in mid-stride and stared at Maria Elena in dismay. "*I don't love Lucia!* Like… at all!"

"You don't?"

"God no."

"Why did you choose to become her thrall then?"

"It's… complicated," I answered, in one of the great understatements in history.

"Weird."

"That's the story of my life." We continued down what was either our third or fourth hallway in silence, and then turned into a stairwell and started up. "So, what have you heard about King Tomasso's murder?"

"Just that it was awful. And that the Stone Lady did it." She glanced over at me and then away just as swiftly. "That's what everyone is saying anyway."

"Hopefully, *everyone* is wrong, since I'm here to prove her innocence."

"Yeah." Despite her heels, Maria Elena had no difficulty at all navigating the narrow stairs. I felt even more like a lumbering water buffalo than usual. "Do you do this sort of thing a lot?"

"Fly across the world to defend someone from murder accusations with my own life hanging in the balance?" I shook my head. "It's less common than you might think."

"I guess so." We reached the bottom of the stairs and Maria Elena held the door for me. Her smile was gone, her eyes sorrowful.

"I'm sorry you're probably going to die for a woman you don't even love."

If she only knew.

○○○

"Are there any tips you can give me for the trial?" I'd been trying, somewhat unsuccessfully, to pump Maria Elena for useful information during our marathon journey to…wherever it was we were headed.

"I wish, but the last one was well before I was born." She wrinkled her nose again, a gesture that hadn't gotten any less cute with repetition. "Our legal system has always been more Sabina's area of interest anyway."

"And what's yours?"

"The usual," she breezed. "Music, boys, blood, and parties. Speaking of which… are you attending tonight's banquet with your mistress?"

"I don't think I have any choice in the matter."

"Fantastic! These events are usually so boring!"

○○○

The room Denarius had set aside for interviewing the human staff reminded me of my own office back in San Diego, albeit on a larger, and vastly more expensive scale. A single large desk dominated the room, with one chair behind the desk and two in front of it. Bookshelves covered the entirety of one wall and a low dresser ran the length of another, its gleaming surface empty of anything but a coffee machine.

Secure in the chair behind the desk, I rubbed my eyes and stared forlornly at that coffee machine. While it was no doubt a marvel of technological aesthetics, we'd quickly discovered that it lacked both the coffee grounds and water to be of any use. Now into our second hour of interviews, it seemed like it was there just to taunt me.

The man seated across the table, Italian by birth, and human by nature, followed my glance, and murmured something to Maria Elena. Warm, dark eyes peered out from under thick brows, but the few hairs left atop his head were steely gray.

"He says he can bring you some coffee if you'd like."

Maria Elena was every bit as energetic as she'd been when we started our interviews, which was both a testament to vampire fortitude and a direct result of her lack of investment in the proceedings. If she'd been anywhere near as desperate to prove Ana's innocence as I was, our lack of progress would have depressed her as much as it had me.

You're just getting started, I reminded myself. *It's not like you expected a servant's testimony to magically clear Anastasia anyway.*

I rubbed my eyes again and focused back on the other man. "That's right… he served as the king's butler, didn't he?"

Maria Elena nodded.

"Tell him thanks for the offer, but I'm fine." With my luck, the bathroom would be seven hallways and five stairwells away. I looked down at my carefully scrawled notes. "So, I'm guessing he wasn't permitted to accompany Tomasso into the city either?"

Maria Elena didn't even bother to confer with the older man before shaking her head. "King Tomasso used the flat in Rome as a sort of… escape from being king. Or so I heard."

"Of course he did." While it was great that the entirety of Tomasso's human staff had been made available for interviews, it was the vampires I really needed to talk to. I leaned across the desk and spoke directly to the butler. "Can you remember anything unusual about the king's behavior in the past few weeks? Anything at all?"

I'd asked the question of each of the many, many servants who had cycled through our interrogation room, and expected the same wide-eyed look of confusion or clueless shake of the head I'd received from them. This time, however, as Maria Elena translated my words, the butler frowned. When she was done, he issued a torrent of Italian in response.

"He says that King Tomasso had been working later than usual in recent weeks, requesting second suppers as late as one or two in the morning."

"Does he know why the king was up so late?"

Another exchange of Italian. I watched the man's face, looking for any hint of deceit or subterfuge, wishing for at least the tenth time that I spoke Italian. The whole language barrier made it difficult to pick up on subtext.

"He doesn't," Maria Elena told me eventually. "Only that he seemed to be looking through old books."

"Ah ha!"

"Ah ha? Is that a good thing?"

"Maybe." I had no idea what it meant, if anything, but a deviation from normal behavior seemed worth investigating. "Does he know where those texts are now?"

"He says that they were gone from King Tomasso's chambers several days before his death."

Of course they were. If this had been a dime-store mystery novel, it would have been titled *John Smith and the Utterly Hopeless and Unwinnable Case*.

Or maybe just *The Last Case of John Smith*.

The butler spoke again.

"He says you might want to speak with Lord Borghesi on the matter, as he believes at least some of what King Tomasso was studying came from the Kingmaker's private collection."

Ah ha! This time, I managed to avoid saying it out loud, but my horrible poker face gave everything away, as usual.

"Is *that* significant?" Maria Elena wanted to know.

"Probably not," I hedged, "but it means we should be able to find out what Tomasso was reading up on. It might help build a picture of his mindset before…"

"Lady Dumenyova killed him."

"Allegedly killed him, but yes." I turned back to the butler. "Thank you very much for your help. If you can think of anything else that was out of the ordinary with the king, please come find me." I looked to Maria Elena. "Does he know where my suite is?"

She nodded absently, already translating the message.

The butler nodded in reply and rose to his feet. He offered us each a short bow and left, as quiet as a vampire.

I pinched the bridge of my nose, cracked my neck, and waited for the next interviewee to enter.

A minute or so later, I was still waiting.

"Is that everyone?"

"Of the human staff, yes." Maria Elena had pulled her phone out of a small, green purse, and was tapping away on its screen, thumbs and fingers moving with a dexterity only found in vampires and teenagers. "Lord Borghesi has an interview scheduled with the king's Secundus, but that was set for after lunch… and we'll be meeting Gaius in his own rooms anyway. I think the Kingmaker expected these interviews to take longer."

I tried not to take that as a criticism of my investigative process. "So far, nobody has seen, heard, or known anything. As I find more evidence, I'm sure I'll come up with new questions to ask, but this initial pass is really just about…"

"Building a picture of King Tomasso's mindset."

"Exactly. Step one to proving Ana's innocence." I sat there in silence for a minute or two, as Maria Elena continued to type away on her screen. "Are you… taking notes?"

"What?" She looked from the phone to me in obvious confusion before her face cleared. "Oh! No… I'm texting with Niccolo."

"Who?"

"He's one of the Kingmaker's lieutenants on the Council Watch. He was part of your escort last night."

I frowned, trying to remember individual faces but coming up instead with a sea of faceless, black-clothed guards. "Which one was he?"

"The totally ripped one, with the perfectly squeezable ass."

I reminded my lumpy, un-squeezable ass that such jealousy was unbecoming, especially when we already had a girlfriend.

"Squeezable, huh? So, are you and Niccolo…?"

"We play occasionally," she said with a smile, "but neither of us is interested in anything too exclusive. Maybe in a century or two. Maybe not."

"Right. A century or two." After several unsuccessful years spending my Fridays and Saturdays in meat market nightclubs with overpriced cover fees, I couldn't even imagine being stuck playing the dating game for that long.

Then again, considering their success at that game, vampires probably enjoyed it a lot more than I did.

Maria Elena sent one or two last texts and then tucked her phone back away, beaming a brilliant smile my way. "So, what do you want to do now? Lunch won't be ready for an hour, but I can ask one of the cooks to prepare something small."

My stomach gurgled appreciatively at the suggestion, but I shook my head. "Actually, I was thinking we might go see Gaius now instead. Assuming you know where he is, that is?"

"He's out on the training fields, but I think he's busy."

"That's okay." I smiled brightly. "He'll make time for us."

○○○

We were walking through another of the endless halls when Maria Elena suddenly stopped in her tracks and spun to face me.

I did my best to hide my flinch.

Thankfully, the young femmepire hadn't seen it. She frowned. "Did you say *Ana?*"

"I beg your pardon?"

"You said step one to proving *Ana's* innocence."

I hastily revised my estimations of Maria Elena's observational skills. And her memory, for that matter.

"Oh… yeah. As in Anastasia. Or Lady Dumenyova, as everyone here prefers to call her."

"You're on a first name basis with the Stone Lady?" Maria Elena's eyes were wide, and she absently chewed on a strand of honey blonde hair. "I mean, I guess she *is* your mistress' Secundus, but…"

It was my turn to frown. "But what?"

"Aren't you worried she'll kill you?"

"Lucia?" Maria Elena really *was* observant.

"No, Lady Dumenyova!"

"Of course not! Why would she even try?"

"From what I hear, she doesn't really need a reason."

My frown morphed into an outright scowl. "Then you've heard wrong. Ana isn't like that."

"John, the Stone Lady has killed more people than you or I have ever even met. Perhaps your position as Lady Borghesi's thrall has sheltered you from that truth, but even in Milan, people spoke in hushed voices of her past deeds." The femmepire shivered. "The Mad King, Vasily's Monster, the Jade Dragons, and the Stone Lady. The stories told about all of them *still* give me nightmares."

"Stories have a way of growing over time."

"Maybe for humans. Most of the People telling those stories were alive when they happened."

There wasn't much I could say to that. I shrugged. "I'm not saying Ana is perfect—" Although she very obviously was. "—or that her past isn't full of violence and blood. But that isn't who she is anymore. Of all the People I've known, she is the bravest, the smartest, and the most noble. There is no one I'd trust more to do the right thing. That's how I know she didn't do this."

I don't know why it was suddenly so important to me convince the young femmepire. Maybe it was the succession of evidence that Denarius had paraded in front of us that morning. Maybe it was the accusatory glares I'd been receiving from every guard in sight. Maybe I just needed someone—anyone—besides me to believe in Anastasia's innocence.

Maria Elena's bright green eyes went wide. "Oh! I see!"

I waited for the femmepire to elaborate, but she pushed open the door to yet another staircase and waved me through.

ooo

By the time we had reached the bottom of those stairs, I remembered one more thing I'd forgotten to do upon our arrival in Rome. I waved at Maria Elena to stop, and then tried to catch my breath.

"Is something wrong, John?"

"Just a little bit more walking than I'm used to," I wheezed back, waving a hand as if to dismiss the whole thing.

Maria Elena smiled. "Well, we're still ahead of schedule. Do you want to stop and recuperate for a bit before we go see Gaius?"

It sounded like the greatest plan ever conceived, but I shrugged nonchalantly and pretended that I could still feel my legs. "A little bit of rest couldn't hurt, but what I really need to do is check in with my partner in San Diego. Is there anywhere around here that we could go to make an international call?"

Maria Elena wrinkled her nose. "Why would you need to go somewhere for that?"

"Because my cell doesn't work in Italy."

"Oh." She passed me the cell phone she'd been texting on earlier. "Use mine!"

"Are you sure? It could be a long call. Which would be expensive," I elaborated in response to the femmepire's confused look.

"Honestly, I'm not even sure who pays my phone bill."

"Well, whoever they are, my thanks to them… and to you," I told her, taking the phone.

I followed the emerald-skirted femmepire down the hall and into a room twice the size of the suite I was being forced to share with Lucia. One wall was entirely covered by the near ubiquitous floor-to-ceiling bookshelves, while the others held a smattering of portraits, many of them old, faded, and slightly dusty. A couch and several overstuffed chairs bracketed a wooden coffee table. I took my seat in one of those chairs, while Maria Elena wandered over to browse the books.

After half a year as partners, and almost as long as roommates, Juliette's number was one of the five I knew by heart. I tapped it in, preceded by the country code Maria Elena told me I needed to enter, and waited for my partner to pick up.

"Anything good over there?" I asked my escort.

"No idea," she said cheerily. "I'm not much of a reader."

"That's a shame."

"Why?" She twisted to look back at me over her shoulder, her expression once again one of honest confusion.

Before I could reply, Juliette picked up.

"Whoever this is, I'm going to rip out your larynx with my teeth."

"Sounds kinky, but I'm taken. Sort of." I reminded her.

"Little bird?"

"The one and only. I just wanted—"

"What the hell time is it?"

"—to let you know that I had—"

"It's almost three in the morning! We made it to bed like forty minutes ago. You'd damn well better be dying."

I frowned and glanced at the display on Maria Elena's phone. "What are you talking about? It's almost noon."

"In Rome, you moron." In the background, I could hear Angel and Bobo exchanging sleepy questions.

"Oh, right. Sorry, Duchess. But as long as I have you on the—"

It took me a few seconds to realize I was talking to myself.

"That wasn't very long at all," said Maria Elena, not even trying to hide her smile.

"I forgot Rome was nine hours ahead of San Diego," I admitted. "This is my first time in Europe."

"Really? That's so cool! Maybe you can get in some sightseeing while you're here."

It didn't seem likely, but I didn't want to rain on her parade.

The phone in my hand buzzed.

"Hello, you've reached Pizza King," I answered brightly. "What can we put on your pie today?"

"I'd like a double helping of *kick my partner's ass when he gets back to San Diego*, please," came the reply. "Plus anchovies."

"We're all out of anchovies. Sorry about the late call, Juliette… you should go back to sleep."

"I'd say that ship has sailed. Why don't you just tell me what's going on, where you are, and why you're calling from some number I've never seen before."

"My phone doesn't work over here, so I'm borrowing Maria Elena's. She's my guide and translator while I'm here in Rome."

"Ah. Is she cute?"

Across the room, Maria Elena blushed bright red.

"Very," I replied, winking at the femmepire, "and also one of the People and in the room with me right now."

"Whatever." Juliette raised her voice slightly, not that it was necessary. "Hello, Maria Elena. I'd ask you to keep John from getting into trouble if I didn't already know how impossible that task was."

Maria Elena just smiled uncertainly.

"How's your case going, little bird?"

"It's only just started. It took us a day to even get here."

"Did they tell you what she's been accused of yet?"

"Yeah. Lucia's brother Tomasso is no longer with the living."

"What?!" I held the phone away from my ear and winced. "Are you telling me that Anastasia murdered the freaking king of the Italian Court?"

"Someone wants it to look like that, at least." I gave Juliette a quick rundown on Denarius' mountain of evidence. Afterward, there was a long moment of silence.

"Is fleeing the country totally out of the question?"

"Totally," I confirmed. "Besides, when Lucia invoked her rights as Primus, she put her own head on the chopping block. If she gets executed—"

"The world will throw a party?" Juliette ventured.

"I'll die with her."

"Oh. Right."

"You knew about that part of the mistress-thrall relationship?"

"Well, yeah."

"A little bit of warning would have been nice!"

"Oh please. Given the way your life has been going, what were the chances of Lucia dying before you did?"

"They're looking pretty good right about now."

"True. My bad."

Juliette didn't sound repentant. In fact, she mostly sounded irritated, with a side serving of *mildly drunk.*

"Anyway, I called to tell you I was in Rome and safe—"

"For the time being, anyway," muttered Juliette.

"—and to see how the Superchargers case was going. Any progress?"

"Oh that." I could practically see Juliette's shrug from four thousand miles away. "I'm done."

"You are?!?" Jesus. Even without her superpowers, Juliette was a better detective than I was.

"Yeah. Chickadee's totally cheating on the chief. Not that I can blame her, given what Tikky-Wokka looks like. Even for a goblin, that many warts is just unacceptable."

I didn't have anything to say to that. Chief Tomlinson *was* pretty damn hideous. Not that the other goblins I'd seen were much better.

"Anyway, I tailed her to the house of one of the Chief's advisors on Monday. She stayed for *three hours.*"

"Okay… and?"

"And what?"

"Did you get any pictures of them in the act? Or something that proves she and the advisor were…" I glanced over at a very interested Maria Elena and tried to think of a useful euphemism.

"Banging like green-skinned bunnies?"

"Yeah. That."

"She was there *for three hours*, little bird. What do you think they were doing? Pictionary?"

"That's kind of my poi—" I stopped as a truly horrible thought occurred to me. "Please tell me you haven't already informed Chief Tomlinson."

"Not yet. I was planning on doing so tomorrow. Which is now today, I guess. Why?"

"Because you really need some actual *proof* before you start a blood feud between San Diego's goblin tribes!"

Juliette chewed on that for a minute and then sighed. "I'm sure there's a gaping hole in your logic, but I'm a little bit drunk and way too tired to find it right now. So, you want me to keep following Lady Cheater McCheater around?"

"Yeah. If Rihanna Mariah Kardashian already met up with her sidepiece once, chances are she'll do so again. And this time, you might want to get some hard proof that she's cheating on the chief."

"Heh. You said *hard.*"

I was starting to wonder if there would be anything left of my agency by the time I returned to San Diego.

Assuming I did return.

"A few photos of the act should be fine, although video would be even better. Just promise me you'll get *some* sort of evidence!"

"Will do, oh pushy, so-called senior partner." Juliette's voice was uncharacteristically waspish. Maybe it was time to extend an olive branch.

"It sounds like you have everything under control though. Just remember, if you need anything, I'm only a phone call away."

"I thought you said your phone wasn't working?"

Oh. Right. "Well, you can always leave a message with Lucia for me to call you back."

"As joyous as the idea of talking to her Royal Snootiness is, I think I'll pass." I could just barely hear the sound of a sleepy voice in the background. "Oh, I almost forgot, someone called the office looking for you yesterday."

"Really? Who was it?"

"No idea."

"What did they want?"

"Can't remember. It sounded urgent though."

"Did you at least get a number?"

The resulting silence was answer enough. I sank back into my chair, looking up at the ceiling in mute appeal to the patron demigod of missed phone calls and wayward junior partners.

"Someone called the office about something urgent, but we don't know who it was, what they wanted, or how to reach them?"

"Pretty much." Juliette's tone sharpened. "I'm your partner, not a freaking receptionist."

"That much is painfully clear." I abandoned my silent prayer. Either there was no such demigod, or they were busy with something more pressing.

"Speaking of which, I think we should get one."

"One what?"

"A receptionist!" Juliette's next words were spoken under her breath and yet perfectly intelligible over the phone. "Gods… I thought *I* was supposed to be the drunk one."

A glance over at Maria Elena showed the young femmepire still hanging on every word. In hindsight, it would have made sense to wait until the afternoon to call Juliette… and to use Lucia's phone to do so.

"We barely have an office. Why do we need a receptionist?"

"To answer phone calls, obviously."

Which made no sense, given that one or both of us was almost always present to answer the office phone on the all-too-rare occasions that it actually rang. "Why would we spend money we don't have to hire someone we don't need…" I had one of those rare flashes of insight. "Angel wants a job, doesn't she?"

"She doesn't want to be a barista forever, John."

"But we don't need a receptionist!"

"Says the guy complaining about my message-taking skills."

I shook my head and tried to ignore Maria Elena's muffled giggles. "Let's talk about it when I get back."

"*If* you get back," Juliette reminded me helpfully.

"Well, if I don't, then the agency is yours, and you can hire whoever the hell you want. But for now, you should get some more sleep while I deal with the minor matter of my impending execution."

Thankfully, Juliette was too tired to argue further. "Sounds like a plan. Call me at a reasonable hour next time."

"Sure thing." I paused for a breath and then added innocently. "In the meantime, I'll say hi to your mother for you."

I ended the call and beamed at my reflection in the cell phone's screen. Somehow, talking to Juliette always made me feel better.

Maria Elena had recovered from her completely inexplicable giggle attack but remained a picture of wide-eyed amusement. "That was your partner?"

"*Junior* partner," I clarified. "Juliette used to be part of Lucia's House, but now we're roommates and business partners."

"And your mistress does not mind that you live with a former member of her House?"

"A former member of her former House," I clarified helpfully. "And no… not that I know of, anyway."

"What about Lady Dumenyova?"

"Lady Dumenyova?"

"Yes. Does she mind? Does she even know?"

"That I live with Juliette? Of course she knows."

"That you love her, I mean."

"I don't love Juliette at all." Not *that* way, anyway.

The femmepire planted both fists on her hips and scowled at me. "Are you being intentionally obtuse?"

I blinked in confusion. "I am so lost."

"Does Lady Dumenyova know you are in love with her?"

"Her?"

"Lady Dumenyova!!" If this had been a cartoon—or one of my non-Lucia dreams—steam would have been coming out of Maria Elena's ears.

"Oh. Yes." I gave her my patented look of surprise. "But how did *you* know?"

"Oh please. She's a terrifying serial killer, and yet you get a dopey smile just thinking about her. It's blindingly obvious."

Maria Elena, I told myself for the second time that day, was not quite as clueless as she appeared.

"So, you're in love with the Stone Lady, although I can't for the life of me figure out why."

"Because God loves strong women, Maria Elena."

"Which God?"

"Mine… the Christian one."

"Huh." She frowned. "I hadn't heard that about him."

I wasn't sure what to say to that.

"Anyway," she continued, "what about Lady Borghesi?"

"Like I said earlier, I *definitely* don't love Lucia."

She stamped her foot. "I know that! Does she know that you're in love with her Secundus?"

"More or less. It's complicated."

"More like amazing," decided Maria Elena. "And here I thought being a guide would suck!"

The phone vibrated in my hand, saving me from further humiliation. To my surprise, it *wasn't* Juliette calling me back demanding to know what the hell my comment about her mother had meant. I handed Maria Elena the phone.

"You just got a text, I think."

"Nope, just a tweet." Emerald eyes glanced up at me through blonde lashes. "Are you on Twitter?"

I shook my head.

"Instagram?"

Another headshake.

"Tindr? Tumblr? Snapchat? Instagram?"

"I'm not really into social networking," I explained. "Although I think I had a Facebook account at one point."

Maria Elena frowned over at me. "How old are you again?"

"Twenty-seven."

"Well, Tindr sounds like a great way to end up murdered by the monster you love, but you at least need a Twitter account," she decided. "That way, we can stay in touch after you leave."

"Assuming I survive."

"Right." Yet again, my possible demise didn't seem to faze the femmepire. Instead, she was focused on her phone, fingers skimming the surface at a pace that made me feel old, slow, and technologically inferior. "One second."

"Sure thing." I got back to my feet and roamed the study. My interest in the bookshelves dropped precipitously as soon I realized none of the books they held were in English. I went to look at the paintings instead.

Most of them were vampire portraits, as far as I could tell, although the artists' inability to truly capture the supernatural beauty of their subjects meant I couldn't be one hundred percent certain. I did find a painting of Denarius, looking tall, scary, and monochromatic next to a dark-haired, cruel-faced Adonis in royal purple.

I'd only seen Lucia's father once, and it had been in one of her dreams—and from the perspective of a child—but I still recognized him right away. He *looked* like a king … and also someone I wouldn't want to encounter in a dark alley.

Or in broad daylight.

Or anywhere at all.

I shivered and moved on. Three paintings to the left, I found something even more interesting.

"Is this…"

"Lady Borghesi and King Tomasso as children?" Maria Elena came over to join me. "I believe so."

In the painting, Lucia couldn't have been more than twelve, swimming in the many layers of the dress she wore. A *blue* dress. She had been a lovely child, but the artist had captured her in a moment of petulance that I still recognized four hundred years later.

At ten, Tomasso was a tiny version of his father, albeit without any of Aurelius' domineering presence. Both brother and sister stood in their own bubble of personal space, ignoring each other's existence. Behind the two children stood King Aurelius, next to a tall femmepire with long, curly hair the color of fire. Like any member of her species, she was beautiful, but the artist had painted her in wan, unflattering colors.

Which seemed kind of like a career limiting move for a portrait painter. If I'd been in his position and possessed of even a shred of artistic talent, I'd have done all I could to make everyone in that painting look like rock stars.

"Lucia doesn't look anything like her mom, does she?" In fact, Lucia's blonde hair and blue eyes set her apart from everyone else in the painting.

"Oh, that's not *Lady Borghesi's* mother," Maria Elena told me. "She died in childbirth. I think this would have been King Tomasso's mother, Jehane."

"You aren't certain?"

"She died more than a century and a half ago." Maria Elena winked. "That's just a bit before my time."

Even more interesting than the previously unknown nugget that Lucia and Tomasso were half-siblings was the fact that both of their parents were dead. Given the vampire lifespan, that seemed… suspect.

"Do you know what happened?"

"Everyone does. She was caught plotting against King Aurelius, but he loved her too much to execute her for it. Instead, he had a special prison built in the palace so he could visit her from time to time."

"The Tower?" So, it had been Tomasso's mother who was imprisoned there, not Lucia's. That knowledge would come in useful if I ever found myself on a Borghesi-themed episode of Jeopardy.

"You've heard of it?"

"In passing."

"Unfortunately, Jehane died only a few decades after her imprisonment began." She blinked away tears. "From a broken heart, no doubt."

Given what I knew of Lucia's father, I suspected that heart had broken because of massive physical trauma, not grief. "Lucia's mother dies, then Tomasso's mother, and then Lucia gets exiled. Why would *anyone* want to be queen?"

"Oh, the other two weren't queens." Maria Elena seemed confused by my assumption. "They were simply the mothers of the king's children. Once King Aurelius established the Borghesi line as royal, only those of his blood could inherit."

Vampire family dynamics were dumb.

"Anyway," Maria Elena continued, "you're all set up now."

"Set up?"

"On Twitter. For some reason, @johnsmith was already taken, so I had to get creative."

I eyed the femmepire for any trace of sarcasm, but she seemed sincere. Maybe John Smiths were rare in Italy?

"Anyway, you're @san_diego_john," she told me brightly. "And I'm already following you!"

"Uhm… thanks. That was very thoughtful of you."

"Just remember to like and retweet all of my tweets! And you might want to follow me on Instagram, too. I'm building a following over there."

"I'll definitely maybe consider it," I replied.

CHAPTER 16

For the first time since our arrival at the palace, I found myself back outside, following Maria Elena down an exterior flight of stairs every bit the equal in size and overstated grandeur to the one Lucia and I climbed the previous night. The sun was high in the sky, but the air was crisp and cool. Where the front grounds—as seen from my suite's windows—had been decorated with statues, fountains, and carefully cultivated topiary, the so-called back yard was flat and open. A football field's worth of freshly mowed grass eventually gave way to a dozen or more corrals of packed dirt. On the far side of those corrals, I could barely make out a series of stables, blending into the tree line.

Maybe Lucia riding a mare *hadn't* been a euphemism.

Or maybe it had; there wasn't a horse in sight. Instead, the nearest corral was ringed by a handful of black-clad Watch members and one very burly minotaur. From our vantage point on the stairs, I could just make out a feminine figure facing off against a guard twice her size.

"Weapons practice?"

"Unfortunately," said Maria Elena, her ever-sunny smile dimming. She glanced from the grassy field to the inordinately expensive sandals she was wearing and then kneeled to take off the latter. I left my own sneakers on and the two of us headed across the field.

We were almost there when the female trainee suddenly went down.

"Again," called the third and final individual inside the circular confines of the corral. He was small but wiry, with thick black hair cut short above a handsome, nondescript face. In lieu of the standard Watch uniform, he wore a dark brown tunic over plain brown pants that could have come straight from the Middle Ages. His eyes were fixed upon the two combatants. "And this time," he continued, in a colorless voice, "remember to actually move your feet, Princess."

This was Tomasso's daughter? I eyed the young femmepire with interest. Beneath multiple layers of mud and dirt, I could just make out black yoga pants, a sports bra, and what had once been a deep red tank top. Beneath that was a young woman who shared virtually no resemblance with Lucia. Her hair, pulled back into a high ponytail, was long, thick, and black, her eyes every bit as dark as Denarius'. She had an olive complexion instead of a golden tan and, even lying in the dirt, was clearly taller than her aunt.

The glare she unleashed on the other two other manpires, however, was one hundred percent pure femme Borghesi.

It was nice to not have it focused on me.

"If this is weapons practice, where are the weapons?" I asked Maria Elena in a low voice, while the princess pulled herself back to her feet.

"Gaius believes we must work our way up to weapons," she replied, just as quietly. "Nobody even gets a stick until their footwork is vaguely competent."

"Huh." All that training seemed like an awful lot of effort to me… but then, *my* lifespan wasn't measured in centuries.

In the corral, the princess was back on her feet and circling, her face of studied concentration a sharp contrast to the other vampire's relaxed demeanor. When she finally attacked, her movements seemed painfully slow. Human slow, almost.

Her opponent, on the other hand, moved like black-clad lightning. In less than a second, the princess was back in the dirt, glaring up at her opponent as she clutched her ribs.

"What the hell, Carlo?"

"You overextended yourself," the small manpire in brown told her, nodding approvingly to Carlo. "For the fourth time in a row."

"He's twice my size, eight times my age, and fully blooded," the princess complained, still sprawled in the dirt. "And if my life were actually in danger, he and the rest of these ghoulish undertakers would be *defending* me, not giving me bruises!"

"Your father believed as you do," the smaller manpire told her mildly, "and it cost him."

"Thanks to one of *your* former students, Gaius," the young femmepire spat. "Don't think I've forgotten that!"

This was Gaius? I'd been expecting someone… taller.

"I have had many students over the years," Gaius was saying. "Scions from prominent families across our kingdom. Each left with some measure of skill and the free will to use that skill as they wished."

"Yeah. Like assassinating my father."

Gaius squatted down next to the angry femmepire, eyes intent upon her face. "No matter how many allies you amass, or how many guards you surround yourself with, there will inevitably come a time when you have only yourself to rely upon. Training, discipline, and will are the keys to your survival."

"I've found running to be pretty effective," I heard myself say.

Gaius seemed unruffled. "Mr. Smith, I presume? Aren't we scheduled to meet this afternoon?"

"We were. I ran through the staff interviews a little bit faster than anticipated, and figured I'd come find you instead."

"I see." Gaius gestured to the princess, her opponent, and the circle of watching Watch. "As you can no doubt deduce, I am otherwise engaged."

"No worries; I'm happy to wait." I smiled sunnily. "It's not every day I get to watch a Borghesi roll around in the mud."

"Tarn," the princess growled, olive cheeks flushed as she climbed to her feet yet again, "rip the human's arms off."

I watched the guards warily, but it was the barrel-chested minotaur who nodded to the princess. With a deep rumble, it headed my way,

I really needed to keep my mouth shut. In the absence of flamethrowers or bazookas, I took one of Maria Elena's shoes and prepared to defend myself.

The minotaur didn't even pretend to be terrified.

"Desist, Tarn." Gaius' words were mild and softly spoken, but they brought the minotaur's murderous advance to a crashing halt even so. Bovine eyes looked from manpire to princess, and then the eight-hundred-pound behemoth retreated to its original position on the other side of the corral.

After a moment's pause, Gaius turned to the princess. "Upon this field, we honor our ancestors and the sacrifices they made for the People. If there is a need for blood to be spilled, we spill it ourselves. We do not dispatch minions to avenge perceived insults. Are we clear?"

The young femmepire nodded sharply and turned her murderous gaze on me.

Ample experience with her aunt had granted me immunity to death gazes, but… I took a careful step away just in case.

"Very well," she told the manpire in a voice that would have been lovely were it not so full of bile. "Provided this human keeps his observations to himself?"

Gaius shrugged. "His delivery lacks polish, but Mr. Smith's original observation was correct. Often, flight *is* the best option."

I was trying to stay objective, but if Gaius kept talking me up like that while saving me from murderous minotaurs… well, I couldn't be held responsible for our eventual bromance.

"However, one cannot always pick their battles. There are times when a man must defend that which he loves. From what I hear, you are no stranger to battle yourself, Mr. Smith. Perhaps you would care to demonstrate the skills that have kept you alive?"

The princess perked up almost immediately, like a shark tasting blood in the water.

"I'm more a lover than a fighter," I said, unaware that I was still waving Maria Elena's sandal in the air like a weapon.

"Given who you love," muttered Maria Elena, "I'm not sure there's really much of a diff—"

"Besides, I wouldn't want to start some sort of international incident or anything by throwing down with the princess."

"I was thinking you could face off with Carlo instead," suggested Gaius.

Yeah. *That* wasn't happening. "Maybe some other time."

"As you wish." Gaius turned back to the princess. "Again."

ooo

Finally, it was over. The princess picked herself up for at least the hundredth time, and this time, there was nobody waiting to put her back down.

"Is weapons practice always like this?" I asked Maria Elena.

"Yeah. If I hadn't been excused to take you around the palace, I'd be out there with Sabina."

"Wait… *she's* Sabina?"

"Under all the mud and still-forming bruises… yeah. Why?"

"For some reason, I hadn't realized that the Sabina you kept mentioning was Tomasso's daughter." Jet lag was harshing my investigator buzz.

Maria Elena kindly refrained from saying anything, but I thought I detected pity lurking behind her emerald-green lenses.

"With Tomasso dead, shouldn't Sabina be queen now, instead of just a princess?"

"Not until she is crowned. Which won't happen until the Council confirms her claim to the throne."

"Confirms her claim? She's Tomasso's daughter! Are they worried that she might have been replaced by a clone or something?" Stranger things *had* happened, after all. Mostly in movies and poorly written fantasy novels, but still…

"Not that I know of." Maria Elena appeared to give the idea serious thought, before continuing. "I think it's just that nobody wants another Mad King on the throne."

"She only lost her temper a handful of times during that hour-long beatdown," I pointed out. "As well as the one time I opened my mouth. She seems pretty sane to me."

I don't know what had possessed me to start defending Sabina. Maybe it was watching her get dumped in the dirt hundreds of times. Or maybe it was remembering that she'd just lost her father. Just because she was related to Lucia didn't mean she was entirely awful.

"I don't think anyone seriously thinks she's a closet psycho or anything… but there isn't any harm in waiting to be sure."

"Waiting for what exactly?" The answer came to me in a rare burst of insight. "Her first feeding?"

"Yeah. Between hormones and the Thirst, being a teenager can suck, but the transition to adulthood can be even more traumatizing. It can take a few years for us to properly… settle. Emotionally, I mean."

"Sounds like the voice of recent experience." I grinned.

"I was a total disaster." She blushed. "But I'm sure you've heard the stories."

I hadn't… and badly wanted to… but somehow, my noncommittal grunt didn't encourage her to elaborate.

"Anyway," she said instead, "I think the Council just wants to make sure that Sabina has grown out of that phase before giving her the crown."

One brief conversation with Maria Elena had taught me more about the vampire growth cycle than I'd gleaned from almost two years with Ana, Juliette, and Lucia. Either my skills as a detective were growing in leaps and bounds or the young femmepire had yet to learn the value of discretion.

"So, the Court has to make do without a king or queen for a few years? Who will make the decisions in the meantime?"

"The Council, I guess?"

If I'd been dealing with humans, that would have been an obvious motivation for someone on the Council to have arranged Tomasso's death. Unfortunately, the timetable didn't work so well with vampires. Who would be dumb enough to risk their centuries-long life for a few years of marginally enhanced authority?

Unless Sabina wasn't meant to survive to her coronation…

I scanned the corral for the princess and found her having a quiet word with two of the Watch and her minotaur muscle. "I don't want to tell you how to do your job or anything, Maria Elena, but maybe you'd be better off guarding your Primus instead of escorting me around."

"My what?" The femmepire wrinkled her nose in momentary confusion before comprehension dawned. "I'm Sabina's *friend*, not her Secundus!"

It was my turn to be confused. Anastasia's parents had sold her to the Borghesis at a young age to be trained as Lucia's Secundus; I'd assumed the same was true for Maria Elena. "If you're not the princess' Secundus, then who is?"

"I have that honor, Mr. Smith," said Gaius, joining Maria Elena and I at the fence of the corral. He was even shorter up close.

"Weren't you King Tomasso's Secundus?"

"I was. And King Aurelius' as well."

"Is it normal for someone to serve in that role for multiple people?"

"Quite the opposite," said the manpire thoughtfully. "The life expectancy of lords or ladies generally far exceeds that of their Secundi."

Using my finely honed investigative skills and one semester of community college English lit classes, I deduced that Secundi was the plural of Secundus.

"And yet…"

"Yes." A frown appeared upon that nondescript face as if by magic. "I would appear to be the exception to the rule."

I tried to figure out a diplomatic way to point out that *both* of Gaius' previous charges had been assassinated but came up empty. It was clearly time for another readthrough of Mediation for Dummies.

"I'm not trying to be a dick," I told the manpire, "but why would the Council appoint you as Sabina's Secundus, given what happened to—"

"Both King Aurelius and King Tomasso?" Gaius nodded, unruffled by my declaration of his incompetence. "The Council has no say in personal appointments. Lord Borghesi asked me to serve as

Sabina's Secundus until such time as someone closer to her age can be found and trained."

"Lord Borghesi, meaning Denarius?"

"Yes."

Maria Elena was literally standing right there, but neither she nor Gaius seemed to even consider her as a possibility. Some people just weren't cut out to be assassins.

"Nor does the Council hold me responsible for either king's death. Mundane security is left to the House or Crown Watch. A Secundus is responsible only for the implementation of their liege's policy."

Implementation of policy was by far the coolest euphemism for murder I'd ever heard.

"However, given the princess' age, and the lack of any policy *to* implement, I have chosen to coordinate her security myself. Any threat to Tomasso's daughter will have to go through me."

"It could come to that," I warned him. "Whoever killed King Tomasso might want to finish off the bloodline."

"I dearly hope they try." The smile he offered then was far colder than anything Lucia could hope to conjure.

I added the small, physically unremarkable Gaius to the list of vampires I never wanted to piss off.

○○○

Sabina arrived moments later, her minotaur thug in tow. Dark eyes scanned me from head to toe, then she sniffed dismissively, and turned to Maria Elena.

"I'm done, 'Lena. *Let's go.*"

Maria Elena looked from the princess to me and then back again. "Lord Borghesi has tasked me with guiding Mr. Smith around, Sabina."

"Which is how you managed to weasel out of weapons practice yet again. I know. But I'm sure my aunt's thrall can spare you for at least a few hours."

"It's not a problem at all."

"Are you sure, John?"

"Totally. Once I've spoken with Gaius, it'll be time for lunch anyway. Maybe we can meet up after that for the rest of the interviews?"

"Of course." Maria Elena flashed her killer dimples in my direction and took back her sandals with a curtsey. "Thanks! I'll swing by the lower mess hall to pick you up at… let's say two?"

"Sounds like a plan." I didn't have a clue where the lower mess hall was… or what time it was, for that matter, but those seemed like minor details.

Gaius picked out five of the Watch members from the crowd that had encircled the corral. "Guard Princess Sabina until she has reached her rooms. The rest of you may return to Lord Borghesi for reassignment."

Sabina waited for the selected guards to form up around her, gave me another sniff for good measure, and then marched across the field toward the palace, Maria Elena and Tarn following in her wake.

"Five guards *and* a minotaur… even in her family's ancestral home." I whistled. "You really are taking her security seriously."

"Someone needs to." Gaius' tone was mild. "And I am not entirely convinced that Tomasso's true killer is under lock and key."

"You aren't?"

"Lady Dumenyova was my pupil for almost two centuries," Gaius replied. "She is remorseless, patient, and exquisitely precise in the kill, yet none of those qualities were evident in Tomasso's murder."

It wasn't a particularly stirring endorsement, but it was still better than what I'd gotten from the rest of the palace.

"You're the first person in Italy who actually believes she's innocent."

"I did not say that she was innocent."

I was pretty sure he *had*, but rather than point that out, I borrowed one of Ana's own tactics, raised an eyebrow, and waited.

"It has been a century since I last saw or spoke with her," Gaius explained. "Even in so short a time, people *can* change, and King Aurelius' daughter was ever a terrible influence on Anastasia."

I ignored the brief and irrational surge of jealousy at hearing the handsome—if nondescript—manpire call Ana by her first name. Either I was getting too accustomed to stuffy vampire formality, or I wasn't quite as secure in my pseudo-relationship as I'd hoped.

"So, the femmepire you knew a hundred years ago wouldn't have been so sloppy, but you're not sure about her present incarnation?"

Gaius' shrug was barely more than a tightening and release of the shoulders. "I am told she nearly lost her arm in battle less than a year ago. The woman I trained would never have let herself be pulled into such a—" He paused, and his face twisted. "Did you say *femmepire?*"

"It's a term we all use back in America," I told him.

"I... see."

I eyed the smaller man. Lucia's description of the People's trials was still fresh in my mind. Gaius wasn't on the Council, but his opinion did seem to carry some weight. If I could convince him of Ana's innocence, it might go a long way to boosting the queen's vote-getting campaign.

"I haven't known Lady Dumenyova for very long—way shorter than a century, in fact—but I'm willing to bet she isn't all that different from the person you knew and trained. She's being framed for this. I guarantee it."

"Given that you are both thrall to her Primus, and tasked with Anastasia's defense, I suspect you might be biased, Mr. Smith."

If he only knew…

My own shrug was not nearly as subdued as the manpire's had been. "Why not talk to her and decide for yourself?"

"I would, had the Kingmaker not spirited Lady Dumenyova away to the sort of prison that does not allow visitors."

"Well, that won't be a problem much longer. Denarius is moving her to the Tower."

"The Tower?" Gaius' surprise was recognizable only by a slight twist to his lips, something I totally would have missed if I hadn't spent so many precious hours around the similarly stoic Anastasia. "How did you manage that, Mr. Smith?"

Before I could speak, he answered his own question. "Of course… as Lucia's investigator, you would need access to the accused."

"Exactly. And as you pointed out, that wasn't possible in her previous location." However bad the Tower might be, it *had* to be better than the sort of prison that didn't allow visitors.

I hoped.

"Well done indeed. I will seek an audience with Anastasia tomorrow then and see if she remains the woman I knew. In the meantime, there is the matter of our appointment. How may I be of service to you?"

I glanced around the now-empty courtyard, searching for something comfortable to sit on, but there wasn't a couch or recliner anywhere in sight. Apparently, fresh air and tired legs would be my penance for having ambushed Gaius during weapons practice.

"Like you said, I've been tasked with Lady Dumenyova's defense. Since I know she didn't kill Tomasso, I'm trying to figure out who did."

"If I knew that, I can assure you they would already be dead."

I waved off the predictable—and predictably bloody—response. "Of course. I'm guessing the only two people who know are Tomasso and the killer himself… and neither of them is talking." Which was too bad, as a full confession from the real killer would have seriously improved our chances at walking out of Rome alive.

"Then what is it you need of me?"

"Information. I'm visiting the crime scene tomorrow to see if I can find anything that Denarius' inspectors missed, but before I do, I'm trying to build a picture of who the king was."

"Because if you know who he was, it will be easier to identify the anomalies in his death," reasoned Gaius.

"Uhm… right." I made a mental note of that phrasing, as it was way better than anything I'd come up with. "At this point, I only know basic details."

"Then I will endeavor to fill in the gaps." Gaius closed his eyes briefly, marshalling his thoughts. "Tomasso spent his youth in the shadow of his older sister. They fought incessantly as children, and only slightly less frequently in adulthood."

"Did they fight over anything in particular?" Given my own experiences with Lucia, I could only assume that whatever it was had been my so-called mistress' fault.

"You would have to ask one of their servants… if they had not all died of old age many human generations ago. For my part, I believe that it was a combination of several things. First, the exceptional closeness of their ages."

I knew from Lucia's dreams that Tomasso had been a few years younger than Lucia. What I didn't know was why that would matter.

"Children are a rarity for our species. Siblings, even step-siblings, are even more so, and it is practically unheard of for them to be born within decades of each other."

I nodded, still confused. "Right; I get that. But what does that have to do with them arguing?"

"For three hundred years, Lucia was the Princess Heir, and Tomasso was simply Aurelius' second child. That only a handful of years kept the situations from being reversed must have eaten away at the boy." Gaius shrugged again.

"Tomasso wanted to be king."

"Yes. Yet when his father was murdered and his sister exiled for the crime, the young king found himself ill-prepared for the role. As the second child, he had been granted far more leeway in his daily activities… and those activities rarely involved study or education."

"So, Lucia gets banished, and Tomasso gets tossed into the deep end."

"The deep end?"

"Of the pool. Or… any body of water, I guess."

Talking to ancient foreign vampires was proving more difficult than I had expected.

"I suppose." Gaius sighed, staring off into the distance. "To his credit, King Tomasso ruled well for much of the past century, yet he was prone to bouts of depression and self-doubt. There were entire weeks when he would remove himself from the Court."

"Which explains why he had a townhouse in Rome."

"One of his many sanctuaries… a place where he could set aside the crown and focus on less weighty concerns."

"Like what? Video games? Movies? When he wasn't trying to be king, what *was* Tomasso like?"

"I wish I could tell you, Mr. Smith." Gaius shook his head. "Despite my position, Tomasso and I were never close. I believe he held me responsible for his father's death, just as Sabina now holds me responsible for hers."

"Tomasso thought you killed his father?" Given Lucia's revelations about the century-old murder, that little nugget immediately caught my attention.

"Don't be ridiculous." For the first time, a touch of scorn colored Gaius' words, but it faded as quickly as it had appeared. "He felt I should have been able to protect him."

If the dude had trained Anastasia, the most badass person I knew, it seemed like a fair assumption for Tomasso to have made.

"How *did* King Aurelius die?"

"We are not certain."

I blinked. Say what?

"While it did exist, forensic science was more primitive a century ago, Mr. Smith. From what I understand, the king's body was found in his locked chambers with multiple body parts missing."

That sounded like a pretty definitive cause of death to me, but I was just a private eye and part-time mediator. "So, why did they suspect Lucia? That doesn't sound like her style at all." She was more the *grab you by the throat, turn you into a Popsicle, and smash you into pieces* type... but I assumed Gaius already knew that.

"Aurelius and his daughter had a... tempestuous relationship from the day of her First Feeding. On the morning of the murder, witnesses heard the two screaming at one another."

"That's it?" Crap. If flimsy non-evidence like that had gotten Lucia convicted a century ago, we were absolutely freaking screwed this time around.

"No. There was also a large quantity of circumstantial evidence. By all accounts, however, it was insufficient to *conclusively* prove your mistress' involvement. In lieu of execution, the Council voted to exile her." He shrugged, face impassive. "Or so I am told."

"You didn't attend the trial?"

"I did not even know there was a trial until long after it had passed. I was away at the time."

"Implementing policy?"

"Indeed. Transportation was not as swift then as it is now, Mr. Smith. I returned to Rome more than three weeks after both Aurelius' death and the subsequent trial."

"But Tomasso…"

"It was his belief that my absence emboldened Lucia… that she would never have dared strike were I present in Rome." The manpire barked a short and utterly humorless laugh. "I suppose his own murder proves otherwise."

CHAPTER 17

An hour later, I found myself hungry, tired, and discouraged. Also? Very lost.

I had yet to find the kitchen. In fact, I had yet to find anyone who spoke enough English to even understand what I was looking for. For all I knew, the few strangers I had encountered were lost too. Maybe they were every bit as frustrated by my inability to speak Italian as I was.

I was heading down my fifth hall in as many minutes when I heard bare feet slapping against marble. An instant later, a small shape in black rounded the corner at a full sprint, and promptly ran right into me.

Given our respective sizes, it was a lesson in what happens when an immovable object is impacted by a highly resistible force; the runner bounced right off of me and went down in a heap. Golden-skinned hands and feet extended out of a mass of filthy black rags, waving feebly.

I took hold of one of those hands and pulled my accidental assailant to their feet. Either my still-latent werewolf virus was granting me super strength or they weighed practically nothing.

"Sorry about—"

"Hssst!" The figure waved me to silence, and cocked its rag-covered head, like a fox listening for the cries of pursuing hounds.

I frowned and waited, surreptitiously wiping my hand on the hip of my jeans. Whoever this person was, they were even shorter than Lucia, slim-hipped and slim-shouldered beneath their layers of rags. A patchwork hood of similar construction cloaked their features in shadow, leaving only hands and bare feet visible. What I could see of those limbs was every bit as filthy as the rags themselves.

I'd run into the world's smallest and dirtiest Ringwraith.

Before I could ask for directions, I heard another sound: additional footsteps. I glanced down at my newest acquaintance. Their entire body was shaking, as they tossed a panicked glance back in the direction of whoever was coming and then at the long, empty hallway behind me. There was no way they'd make it to the end of that hallway before their pursuer came into sight.

I made the sort of instinctive choice that Juliette had long predicted would get me killed, took three steps down the hall, and pushed open a door to an empty, unused room.

"Hide inside," I whispered. "I'll run interference with whoever is chasing you."

Glittering eyes stared up at me from within the confines of that hood, and then the figure disappeared inside.

Whoever else was coming down the hall, their shadow preceded them by a mile: dark, terrible, and enormous. I swallowed hard, reminded myself that pants-crapping fear was unbefitting a Smith, and headed that way.

I'd taken only a single step when Ambassador Ti An rounded the corner.

I think the femmepire was every bit as surprised as I was, but I was still struggling to figure out how someone so small could have so large a shadow when the ambassador spoke.

"Mr. Smith. Fortune graces us both."

"Does it?" I was getting depressingly used to not having a clue what the vampires of Italy were talking about.

"Indeed, although I must admit I am surprised to find you here. And alone." She took small, careful steps in a circle around me, soft slippers whispering along the marble floor. "Is this how your mistress looks after her possessions? In my empire, we are not so careless."

"In my country, people aren't possessions. Not anymore, anyway. The queen trusts me to do my job without need for supervision."

"So it would seem."

We were a minute or so into our conversation, and the femmepire hadn't blinked even once. Her endless circling was starting to feel vaguely predatory.

"However," I added, "she *is* expecting me shortly."

"Is she now?"

"Indeed," I parroted. Whatever had Lucia terrified of this tiny femmepire, I was feeling it too, a shiver down my spine transforming into outright goosebumps, my mouth going dry without explanation. Which meant, according to the laws I lived by, that it was time for me to take the offensive. I pasted on my second-best mediator smile. "What brings you down here, ambassador?"

"I appear to have misplaced something of value." Those old eyes studied my face. "Have you perchance encountered anyone recently?"

"Tons of them," I told her truthfully, "but either the location of the kitchen is one of Italy's great, unsolved mysteries, or there's a severe shortage of servants in the palace who speak English."

"You have seen only servants?"

"And lots of statues and paintings." I smiled brightly, avoiding the outright lie. "Whenever Sabina gets crowned, her first order of business should be modernizing the décor, don't you think? A moving sidewalk or something would be awesome too." Then, as if the thought had just struck me, "Why? I thought you were looking for *something*, not someone?"

"It is of no matter." The femmepire waved a small hand in the air, as if to dismiss the issue, but her smile was bone dry. "I have no doubt the object will turn up again eventually."

"Have you tried looking in your sock drawer? Or behind the laundry hamper? That's usually where I find stuff."

Ti An ignored my helpful suggestions. "In the meantime, perhaps you can escort me back to my suite. I understand that you are interviewing those who knew the king as part of your investigation?"

"Word travels fast. Did you know King Tomasso well?"

"Well enough. Whether what I know is of value to your investigation is a question only you can answer." She motioned back down the hall, her eyes glittering bright silver instead of the usual vampire gold. "Shall we?"

I knew I'd have to interview her eventually, but I had no desire to spend any more time with the golden-robed femmepire. *Especially* alone and in her suite. "Unfortunately, I'm pressed for time right now," I told her. "Like I said, I'm supposed to meet up with Queen Lucia. I wouldn't want to be late."

"Didn't you say you were seeking directions to the kitchen?"

Damn it. That was the problem with mixing lies with truth.

"That's right," I managed feebly. "I've found it easier to deal with the queen's demands on a full stomach."

"I see." Ti An looked me over one final time, as if eyeing a piece of prime horseflesh. Only… not in a sexual way. Thank God. "Tell young Lucia that my offer has changed. I will double the size of the lands we grant her."

"I'll definitely pass that on." I didn't care that the lie was painfully obvious, even to me. There was no way in hell I was going to let Lucia rent me out to this scary little woman.

Ti An's return nod said a lot of things: that she'd recognized my lie, that she smelled my fear, and that she was confident that, ultimately, neither would prove to be an obstacle to her will.

Much, much later, I'd remember to be impressed by the sheer density of information packed into that simple gesture. For the moment though, I was just glad she was leaving.

Unfortunately, she took only one small step before she stopped again, eyes hard. "It appears you have fouled your clothes, Mr. Smith." She nodded to the smudge where I had wiped my hand on my jeans.

"I was out watching weapons practice," I told her, yet again avoiding an outright lie. "Frankly, I'm surprised I'm not even dirtier."

As on-the-spur evasions go, it was pretty damn impressive, especially by my standards. Sadly, it didn't seem to do the trick; Ti An looked past me and down the long hall, then her eyes snapped to the door of the suite just behind me. Without a word, she breezed past. One hand brushed the door, and it flew open as if an NFL linebacker had launched himself through it. Just as quickly, she was inside.

I hurried up behind her, heart in my throat, and looked in.

The room was empty. A thick level of dust coated the room, entirely undisturbed.

It was a very good thing that Ti An wasn't looking my way to see the shock on my face. Instead, she stood still and quiet, taking in the sight.

"I guess the cleaning staff doesn't make it down here," I mused.

"Indeed." The femmepire spun on her heel and swept past me, somehow avoiding any sort of physical contact despite my position in the open doorway. "We will see each other again, Mr. Smith."

"Looking forward to it," I said. It was my second obvious lie in as many minutes, but the ambassador was already back down the hall, her small strides covering impossibly large stretches of floor. In moments, she was gone from sight.

I followed her to the corner and took a peek, verifying that she was truly gone. Then I did a slow count to fifty and peeked again. Still nothing. Either Ti An was way more patient than I was or she had given up her hunt.

I went back to the room the ragamuffin had disappeared into and stepped inside. Ti An's footprints remained the only disturbance in a dust that must have accumulated for weeks. Without furniture, there wasn't anywhere to actually hide in the chamber, but I did a slow circuit anyway until my brain fully agreed with what my eyes were telling it. The person I'd helped hide was nowhere to be found.

"Jet lag is severely messing with my mind," I announced to myself and whatever demigods might be watching. With a confused sigh, I stepped back into the hall, closing the door behind me.

The Ringwraith was waiting.

"How did you—?" I glanced at the door I had just come through, then back again. "Okay, that's a pretty cool trick."

"It took some time to master," admitted the figure in a hushed, heavily accented voice.

"Couldn't have been *that* long. What are you, twelve? Thirteen?" Despite the rags that cloaked his figure, the voice finally gave him away as male, young and foreign. Granted, *everyone* here was foreign, by my standards… but he didn't sound Italian.

"Something like that. Thank you for your assistance. And the distraction."

"Not a problem." In a conflict between terrifying, ancient, Asian vampires and slightly scary ninja beggar pre-teenagers, I was going to side with the pre-teens every time. Which probably said bad things about my chances of making it to forty. "Why was Ti An after you, anyway?"

"She believed I was spying upon her. She was incorrect."

"Ah." That didn't tell me much, but espionage had never been my thing anyway. "I take it you're not from around here?"

"I am not." He shifted within the confines of his robe. "I have come seeking the source of the shadow falling over all worlds."

It was the most original reason for visiting Rome that I'd ever heard, but it didn't make a whole lot of sense. I nodded anyway. "Well, good luck with that, I guess? I'm John Smith."

"The investigator. Yes, I know." The boy nodded. Word traveled fast, if even the palace beggars knew my face. After a long pause, he pushed the patchwork hood back from his face, exposing dusky, gold-skinned features and jet-black hair that was straight as an arrow and as shiny as if it had just been featured in a shampoo commercial. Narrow, almond-shaped eyes, a brown so dark they were almost black, were made even darker by thick eyeliner. A slash of lipstick turned his small mouth a shocking shade of pink.

That makeup almost kept me from noticing the scars. Tiny crescent moons of scar tissue spread in a haphazard pattern across the exposed skin of his face, and neck. For all the world, it looked like someone had once tried to beat him to death with a rose bush.

I tried to keep the pity from my expression. As usual, I failed.

"They are the vestiges of another time," he said, "and no longer trouble me."

"Sorry," I managed. "I didn't mean to make you—" My mouth clicked shut as I heard voices coming our way. The only good news was that they were coming from behind us, in the opposite direction from Ambassador Ti An's departure.

The scarred boy cocked his head, as if listening to those voices. "I must go." Stepping closer, he extended his right hand, ring finger and thumb bent inward to touch each other, and reached up to tap my forehead with the other three extended fingers.

"What was that?" I dropped my voice to a whisper.

"Consider it a blessing," he told me, painted lips curved upward into a small smile, "courtesy of the Rag Lady."

"Who's the Rag Lady?"

"I am."

I looked again at the eyeliner, the lipstick, and what might have been considered a dress instead of a robe and nodded slowly.

"Then I thank you for your blessing," I told her.

She flashed another smile and scampered down the hall in the direction that Ti An had so recently gone, her pace a far cry from when she had been in full flight. As she moved, her dress seemed to merge with the shadows of the hall. Then she was gone.

Which was when I realized I'd forgotten to ask directions.

CHAPTER 18

IN WHICH DOG ISN'T MAN'S BEST FRIEND

Either the Smith family luck had finally changed for the better, or the Rag Lady's blessing had some serious metaphysical mojo. Either way, the voices I'd heard turned out to be a pair of maids. Even better, they spoke English. In no time at all, I was two floors down and in what turned out to be one of the palace's *three* kitchens.

Looking at the chaos around me, where servants streamed in and out while cooks bellowed orders at underlings who were already doing everything humanly possible, I was suddenly glad I'd never considered a job in the food industry. This was a *lot* of effort for a simple banquet… especially one still hours away. Someone needed to introduce the Italians to nachos, carnitas and beer, or as I liked to think of it, the food of champions.

I was seated at a small table just outside the circle of culinary warfare, polishing off the sandwich that a *very* put-upon cook had produced for me, when Maria Elena finally showed up to collect me. I handed another harried servant my empty plate and followed her out into the blessedly cool, blessedly quiet hallway.

As the voices faded behind us, I finally spoke. "Are the kitchens always that crazy, or has our visit made life a living hell for the servants in the palace?"

Maria Elena shrugged. "There's usually some party or another. And the chefs complain of boredom whenever things get too quiet. Did you get enough to eat for lunch?"

I nodded, but my focus was on my guide. She was still wearing the same dress, and still looking as fashionably cute as ever, but her smile lacked both its usual perkiness and the habitual dimple escorts. "Is everything okay?"

"Sabina's not thrilled that I'm the one escorting you around," she admitted, "what with you trying to defend her father's murderer and all."

"Once she realizes that Ana is innocent, I'm sure all will be forgiven, but if you'd like, I can ask Denarius for a new guide?"

"No, it's fine." Maria Elena shook her head, sending her blonde curls bouncing. "It's not the first time we've had a fight, and I'm sure it won't be the last. The great thing about Sabina is she never stays angry for long."

Not *at all* like her aunt then. Interesting.

"Have you known each other long?"

"Since we were children. Well, since she was a child anyway; I was eleven, by human reckoning, when I was brought here to be her companion."

"From Milan, right?"

"Yes, House Giordano's ancestral home."

"Well, at least your parents waited until you were a pre-teen before selling you to the Borghesis."

"I beg your pardon?!?" The femmepire's eyes went wide with astonished outrage. "Nobody sold me to anyone!"

Oops. "I'm sorry. I just assumed."

"Why?"

"Because that's what happened to Anastasia," I reminded her.

Or… make that *informed* her, if Maria Elena's open-mouthed shock was any indication.

"Lady Dumenyova's parents *sold* her? As a child?"

"Yeah."

"No wonder she has so many anger issues."

Anastasia *didn't* have anger issues, especially compared to most of the vampires I knew, but I chose not to argue the point.

"*My* parents are nobility," Maria Elena continued, "but they wanted me to experience life at the Italian Court."

"And an alliance with the ruling family doesn't hurt either."

"I guess not."

"Did you know the king very well?"

"Why would you ask that?" Maria Elena's eyes went wide again.

"You're the best friend of his daughter. You must have seen him fairly regularly."

"Oh." The femmepire shook her head. "He and Sabina are—or were, I guess—close, but not even she saw him all that frequently. Most of the time, King Tomasso was busy doing king stuff."

"And you and Sabina were busy doing… princess stuff?"

"Pretty much. School… defense training… that sort of thing."

"And boys," I teased.

"For me, anyway. Even if she wasn't a princess and saddled with a reputation to uphold, Sabina is still a little young."

"Oh right." I sighed. "Since she hasn't fed yet, she actually *is* as young as she looks."

"Exactly." Maria Elena shrugged, revving her smile back up to its usual wattage. "Anyway, after almost ten years, the occasional argument between Sabina and I is just par for the course. Although you might want to avoid Tarn for a while. Especially when Gaius isn't around."

That sounded like excellent advice, but before I could say so, the kitchen doors opened, and a small army of servants issued forth, carrying linens and other distinctly non-food items.

"Table service?" I hazarded a guess.

"I guess so," came the unhelpful reply. Outside of her narrow areas of focus, Maria Elena seemed to be spectacularly disinterested in whatever happened around her. Then again, curiosity was probably a less useful trait for professional nobles than it was for private investigators.

The stream of servants finally came to an end, but it was clear that, even outside of the kitchen, we were still in the way. And standing there wasn't doing anything to help prove Anastasia's innocence.

"With Gaius already taken care of, I think Denarius' schedule said we're supposed to meet with Dog?"

"Yeah." Maria Elena's smile flickered again.

"I take it you're not a fan?"

"He thinks my breasts being at eye level gives him the right to do nothing but look at them." Spots of color appeared in her cheeks.

"We could stop at your suite and get a jacket or something?"

"It could be a burka for all the good it would do." Maria Elena rolled her eyes. "No, let's just get this over with."

○○○

The door to Dog's suite was every bit as large as the one leading to Denarius' evidence vault, albeit fashioned from simple dark wood instead of space-age, adamantium-vibranium alloy.

Now, this *is mahogany,* I was informed by the part of my mind that remained irrationally convinced it knew anything at all about wood. *Or maybe some kind of black oak.*

Truthfully, it was hard to focus on the wood itself, given that the door's vast expanse was covered in carvings of naked figures engaging in a bewildering array of sexual activities. My highly trained powers of observation quickly noted that the male figures—who were vastly outnumbered by carvings of the opposite gender—were all both shockingly short and grotesquely endowed.

Artistic license only went so far.

I found a space relatively free of pornography and knocked. It was like tapping on a concrete block, impossible to tell whether anyone inside could have even heard me. Conscious of the presence of a young and impressionable femmepire beside me, I put a little bit more muscle into my second knock.

This time, the sound was almost audible. A few seconds later, the door swung inward to reveal a butler, clad in a three-piece suit of unrelieved black.

"John Smith, here by appointment to see Councilman Dog." Maria Elena's voice was colorless.

Without speaking, the man offered me a short bow and motioned for us to enter.

If I'd thought the rooms I had already seen were the height of opulence, my first Council member's chambers quickly dispelled those illusions. Maria Elena and I followed the servant through a large antechamber, down a short hall past several closed doors, and into a living room three times the size of my office in Logan Heights. A bar ran along one wall, while an enormous television somehow looked undersized on another. The far wall held a mirror, twelve feet wide, if it was an inch, and at least two feet taller than I was. There were also two couches, three coffee tables, and a pool table, every damn piece clearly made from hand-carved mahogany. Last but not least was what looked like—but really couldn't be, given that we were *indoors*—a sunken firepit, set dead center in the room, its stone circle looking rough and out of place amidst all that wood.

"This isn't a suite, it's a freaking lair," I said.

"You better believe it." Dog swaggered into view, potbellied, shirtless, and unbathed. "It's also where the magic happens, if you know what I mean."

"I'm guessing you're talking actual spells." I stepped between Dog and Maria Elena, blocking the other man's breast-seeking eye beams.

"You'd be shocked, investigator." With a chuckle, Dog hopped up onto the couch, legs splayed wide, and hands resting on his ample belly. "So, what can I do for you and this little morsel? Looking to blow blue? Want to chase the dragon?"

"I don't know what any of that means." If he was talking about a literal dragon, my answer was *holy shit, they really do exist?* But the phrase *chase the dragon* was kind of familiar. After a moment, it came to me. "Are you talking about *heroin?*"

"Don't be stupid." Dog sneered. "If all you want is heroin, you can drive into the city for it like all the other plebes. I only offer high class merch."

"Merch?"

"Something to help amp up your party," he replied smoothly. "A few tastes of my inventory and the pair of you won't ever come down."

"No thanks." Denarius' earlier warning against eating or drinking anything in Dog's chambers suddenly made a lot more sense.

"Suit yourselves." Dog dumped a small bag of white powder onto an antique table that was probably worth more than my almost-new Corolla, and hoovered it up with one long, disgusting, snort. "But my original question stands. What can I do for you?"

"I'm investigating Tomas—"

"No shit; I was at the Council meeting."

"Right. So… did you kill him?"

Behind me, I heard Maria Elena choke.

"Did I kill him?" Dog hopped back off the couch and waddled over, face dark despite the dusting of powder across his upper lip. "*Did I kill him?!*"

"It's a simple yes or no question," I pointed out, starting to regret my decision to play the bad—and also *only*—cop in this scenario.

"I don't know how you put it together so fast," the other man growled, "but there's no way you're walking out of here alive."

Well, shit.

CHAPTER 19

I was backing away, fumbling for the item that hung around my neck, when Dog's angry sneer split wide into a shit-eating grin.

"Oh man, that was amazing." Black eyes gleamed and he gave one of those full body laughs that seem fake even when they aren't. "The look on your face…" he said, through gasps and wheezes. "Shit, it was perfect!"

I tried to pretend like I hadn't been two seconds from running for the door. Given all the actual, verifiable threats on my life since becoming San Diego's mediator—not to mention the very real possibility that I'd be executed before summer—I couldn't understand why people kept finding *fake threats* so amusing.

"Is that a *no*, then?" I managed stiffly.

"Why would you say that?" Dog's mirth slowly dwindled, and he shook his large head sadly. "I think it's clear to everyone on this mudball that I'm the most obvious candidate for having killed good old Tommy."

Now I was confused again.

"After all, whenever I kill anyone, let alone a king, I *always* bring with me a stone blade, a few pieces of DNA to implicate some bird I barely even remember from a few centuries back, *and* a footstool, so I can reach my target's heart."

"That really *does* sound like a no."

"I need to thank little Lucia for bringing you. This whole investigation is going to be hilarious."

The surge of bone-chilling terror had thrown me off my game, but I wasn't completely out of the fight. "Let's say I believe you."

"Let's."

"Can you account for your whereabouts on the day of King Tomasso's murder?"

"Maybe. What day was that again?"

I would have called it out as an obvious stalling tactic, but… I realized I had no idea.

"Last Wednesday," clarified Maria Elena.

"Thanks, sweet cheeks." Dog leaned forward, his breath foul despite the significant height differential. "So, she's the body *and* the brains of this little operation?"

"It's possible," I admitted. "So where were you Wednesday, between three and seven?"

"Church service." He gave me a look of cherubic innocence.

"Right. And I'm the pope."

"Nah. *That* guy knows how to take a joke. You, on the other hand… I'm not loving."

I dearly hoped the rest of my Council interviews weren't going to be like this one. Then I remembered Vigo. Maybe a foul-mouthed, drug dealing dwarf wasn't all bad. "Even so, I'd appreciate an honest answer."

"I was here," he said, waving one stubby arm to gesture at the room we were standing in, "getting a massage from a pair of gorgeous virgins."

I rolled my eyes. "I'm serious."

"So is he, actually," murmured Maria Elena.

"He is?" I shook my head at her pained nod of confirmation and turned back to the dwarf. "Can your masseuses confirm that you were here the whole time?"

"Oh, hell yeah. It's *good* to be me."

"Fair enough." I abandoned that line of inquiry to focus on the case. Even if Dog wasn't a suspect, he might still have some useful information. That the change of subject lessened the risk of my throwing up in my mouth was just a small side benefit. "What can you tell me about King Tomasso's mood in recent weeks? Did he seem distracted? Worried? Or do you have any thoughts on who might have killed him?"

"I can't say I've ever paid the slightest bit of attention to Tomasso's emotional state," he mused. "He was a moody bastard even at the best of times. Are we sure he didn't just kill himself?"

"By stabbing himself in the heart three times with a stone blade and then tearing off his own head?" It was… a theory, but not one I was prepared to put my investigative muscle behind.

Dog shrugged heavy shoulders. "Guess not."

"You don't seem to care that someone just killed your king." I wondered if that would work for or against us at the trial.

"*My* king?" Another deep belly laugh. "Boy, you had better pray you never meet *my* king. Tomasso was a colleague, at best. An overstuffed pompous popinjay, at his worst, like the rest of these damn nobles."

Maria Elena's offended snort was the first sign of spirit she'd shown since entering Dog's den of iniquity.

"And you don't care what happened to him?"

"Why should I?"

"As a Council member, how could you not?" The drug-snorting bastard wasn't the only one who could answer one question with another.

"Do you really think that's why I'm here? Politics?"

Damn it… he'd gone for the rare double whammy of answering a question with *two* questions. I was clearly out of my league.

"Isn't it?" I offered weakly.

"I'm here because the boss downstairs told me to be. And what the boss wants, the boss gets."

I tried not to gloat too much over having won our little question-off and focused instead on his words. Downstairs, with a very obvious capital D. Not even jet lag could fool me into thinking he was referring to the palace's catacombs. "You're a demon, I take it?" At least he was smaller than the Hound of Tartarus.

"Bite your tongue, human." Dog scowled.

"He's an imp," Maria Elena murmured quietly.

"That's right, peaches and cream. A genuine, grade-A, straight from the Mother's over-ripe breasts, devil." Large black eyes darted to my face to measure my level of awe.

"Devils and demons are different?"

Apparently, that hadn't been the reaction Dog had been looking for. With a disgusted growl, he marched back to his couch.

"Demons are animals, boy. Monsters too dumb to know they should put themselves down."

"As opposed to cocaine-snorting devils… who are merely *named after animals?*"

"Hey, that quip was *almost* funny. Another century or three and you might be worth knowing." Dog licked something off the back of his hand and grinned widely. "Anyway, narcotics are just a hobby, a way to cope with all the species who infest this earth like bleating sheep. Most of my brothers are stuck downstairs. Only a handful of us made it back up here to follow the boss' orders."

"Corrupting people and capturing their souls," I recalled from Sunday school.

"What the ever-loving goat banger do I care about someone's soul? Especially human ones?" Dog rolled his eyes. *Those* are a dime a dozen."

"But then what—"

"Am I doing here? Watching. Waiting. Indulging."

"And maybe killing a few uppity vampire kings when you get the chance?" It was painfully obvious that the imp hadn't done it, but I was still hopeful pressure might turn up something useful.

"Sounds like way too much work." The contents of another bag made it onto the table and then disappeared up the imp's nose in a flash. "You're all gonna burn anyway; nobody needs my help moving it along."

I looked over my shoulder at Maria Elena, but she seemed as mystified as I was. And a lot more scared. "And why exactly are we going to burn?"

"Because," the devil answered, and the mirth was gone from his voice, leaving something dark and dry and barren, "the locks downstairs won't hold forever. Sooner or later, my brothers are getting free, and when they do, we're remaking this shit stain of a universe into something a little more like home."

ooo

"That was… informative," I decided, once Maria Elena and I were far, far away from the crazy little devil's drug emporium.

"Was it?" Maria Elena managed a wan smile.

"Not really."

The femmepire smiled again, but tension was still coming off of her in waves.

"Hey, it's okay. I know he talked a big game," I told her gently, manfully avoiding the obvious size joke, "but he wasn't going to hurt us."

"How can you be sure?"

"I'm an officially appointed investigator, Maria Elena. To kill me would be to break the Toulon Concordat."

"It would?"

"Absolutely." At least, I *assumed* so. The Concordat protected mediators… and regicide investigators were basically just mediators with nonexistent badges and keen analytical skills, right?

Shit. I should probably make sure of that. And soon.

Somehow, Maria Elena didn't look reassured. "So, *you're* protected. But what about me?"

To be honest, I hadn't thought that far ahead. "Well, it's over now, and we both survived. And at least he mostly made sense, in between the rampant drug usage. I've had *worse* conversations."

"Did your mistress know you were insane when she agreed to take you as thrall?"

Again, I let the gross distortion of my enthrallment slide. "I'm not crazy, Maria Elena… although some of the voices might be."

The look of shock on the femmepire's face lasted for barely a second but it was almost as gratifying as the laughter that spilled out of the femmepire moments soon after. "You jerk! I almost believed you! Why would you even lie about something like that?"

I grinned. "Sometimes, a little bit of humor can help a lot."

Her dimples made a triumphant reappearance.

"A *very* little bit of humor."

ooo

We'd traversed two hallways and a stairwell when Maria Elena came to a sudden halt. "Uhm… where did you want to go to next anyway?"

I stared at her. "I assumed you already had a destination in mind. Where have we been headed for the past ten minutes?"

"Nowhere, really." She blushed. "I kind of just wanted to get away from…"

"Got it." I considered for a moment. I was already exhausted—and craving a nap and a burrito, in no particular order—but there was too much on my plate for me to stop now. "I don't suppose Denarius has managed to set up interviews with any of the other Council members?"

The femmepire glanced at her phone and then shook her head. "I think Dog was it for the day. Thank the gods," she added under her breath.

I frowned thoughtfully. Ana was still being moved into the Tower, Lucia was nowhere to be found, and I didn't have nearly enough time before the vampire meet and greet for a trip into the city to visit the crime scene. Maybe the burrito and nap had been the right idea after all?

"You know," Maria Elena added thoughtfully, "King Tomasso's body *is* available for viewing down in the catacombs. Don't detectives always want to see the body?"

In my personal experience, the answer was *not if I can in any way help it*, but primetime television strongly suggested I was an outlier that way. I nodded. "Good call. I'm trying to solve the mystery of his death… I guess it's only fair that I meet the guy first."

"Cool." She smiled cheerily. "I'm excited to see some real detecting!"

Apparently, the past six hours of interrogations hadn't counted.

ooo

It was unlikely that my next home would be a palace—especially given that my *current* "home" was a guest room in someone else's condo—but if it was, I was going to make damn sure it came equipped with elevators. Also? I was going to avoid building catacombs of any sort. Future Smiths—in the also unlikely event that I found someone willing to bear them—would be laid to rest in cemeteries like normal people.

The Borghesi catacombs had been dug deep into the ground beneath the palace itself: narrow pathways of stone winding in haphazard fashion for what felt like miles. After a handful of turns, I was hopelessly lost, mildly claustrophobic, and entertaining worrisome fantasies about my future life as a mole person.

"There are a lot more people buried here than I would have expected, given your species' lifespans," I told my guide. "Just how many Borghesis have there been anyway?"

"I'm not sure," said Maria Elena, "but the grounds house way more than just the one family." She waved at the delicate inscription that had been carved into the stone cap of yet another tomb. "Human servants, retainers, and the family's closest allies are all interred down here. Once the capitol was moved to Rome, it became the official resting place of our noble class."

"That's a lot of dead people. I guess forcing Tomasso's mourners to walk past all of this is a way to remind them of the family's long history?"

"Why would the mourners come this far?"

I came to a full stop, frowning. "So they could see their king?"

"But his body is on display near the catacombs entrance."

"You mean the room that we walked past almost an hour ago?"

"Exactly!" She smiled proudly at me, as if I'd just solved my first algebra equation.

"*Why* did we walk right past it?" I clarified.

"I figured a short detour couldn't hurt. When else are you going to get a chance to see a millennia-old catacombs?"

"If history holds, I'll probably end up imprisoned down here at some point, actually."

"Huh?"

"Never mind." I dredged up a tired smile. "I appreciate the thought *and* the tour. But can we go see King Tomasso's body now?"

"Absolutely!" Maria Elena flashed her dimples and led us back in the direction we'd just come.

ooo

King Tomasso, was, as the femmepire had promised, laid out on a bier in a room right next to the stairs to this level. Inside the chamber, a line of mourners waited to pay their respects. We took our places in that line and slowly inched forward.

In life, Tomasso had been every bit as tall as Lucia was not, but death made him seem smaller, almost lost within the suit he'd be buried in.

"What do you think?" asked Maria Elena in a hushed voice.

"He's either dead, or really, really good at holding his breath." The look I received was scandalized. "Sorry. Gallows humor is part of the investigative process. Honestly, I was hoping to get a look at his wounds. It didn't occur to me that someone would have cleaned him up already."

"Well, they weren't going to just stick him on a table with a hole in his chest!"

Or with his head detached. "Good point."

Behind us, the next vampire in line cleared their throat loudly, and said something in Italian to Maria Elena.

She responded in kind, throwing in a small curtsy for good measure, before turning back to me. "We can't hold up the line, Mr. Smith. If you want to investigate something, can you do it quickly? Only… could you also try not to touch him?"

Given that I was neither a forensic scientist nor a doctor, I wasn't entirely sure what I was supposed to investigate, but I dutifully called upon my many years of watching television and examined Tomasso's hands, arms and fingers for defensive wounds. I also looked for anything the mortician might have missed—such as a signed confession note from the real killer—but there was nothing to be found. It looked like I might actually have to read the autopsy report Denarius had provided. As if I didn't already have nightmares enough.

"I guess we're done here," I told Maria Elena, after a long pause, and yet another pointed look from the impatient mourner next in line.

We left the room in silence and began making our way back up the first of many flights of stairs.

"So? Have you figured out who did it?"

"It's going to take more than just a few minutes with the body."

Maria Elena nodded knowingly. "Time to bring in the psychics, I guess?"

"Why would—" I paused. "Wait; psychics exist?"

"Of course they do! Sabina and I get our palms read every other month or so."

"Oh." Damn it; a genuine psychic would have made a fabulous backup option in case the much hoped-for murder confession never materialized. "Anyway, now that I've met the former King, we should probably go find his uncle and let him know where my investigation is at."

"I don't think we have time for that, John."

"No?"

"No. Your mistress returned to the suite to get ready for the banquet a while ago. You should probably do the same."

"How could you *possibly* know that?" I eyed Maria Elena with fresh respect. Maybe *she* was a psychic? There was no other possible explanation.

"Because Niccolo texted me when she did."

Okay, maybe there'd been a few other explanations.

CHAPTER 20

IN WHICH CLOTHING UNMAKES THE MAN

The suite was a beehive of activity, both bed and cot almost invisible beneath a socialite's yearly allowance of dresses. In the center of the main room, Lucia stood, silent and still, as women in maid uniforms flitted about her, pinning this and arranging that.

Without turning in my direction—and given her current role as femmepire mannequin, I wasn't sure she *could* turn—the queen spoke. "You are *late*, Mr. Smith."

"That's the job, Lucia," I told the older femmepire in my best impression of a real private eye. "We can't all conform to the man's schedule."

"I don't know which man you are referring to, but you will conform to *my* schedule. The banquet is in less than an hour."

"An hour? It'll take me like ten minutes to get ready. Fifteen, tops." I went to retrieve my suit from the closet, and immediately encountered an unexpected obstacle. "Where's my suit?"

"Are you referring to the navy monstrosity that was clearly the work of a drunken and imbecilic tailor?" Lucia twisted slightly as one of the maids began to work on her hair.

"That's the one… and neither it nor I asked for your approval," I dug through the hanging clothes in my closet. The suit remained conspicuously absent. "Seriously; where is it?"

"I had it disposed of. No doubt, it will make a suitable donation for some street urchin with more need than fashion sense."

"You—" Through great force of will, I narrowly managed to avoid banging my head against the wall. "Fine," I said through gritted teeth. "T-shirt and jeans it is."

I couldn't see the femmepire queen's expression, but her annoyance came through the bond loud and clear. "I have procured clothing for you tonight, my thrall. More suitable garb will be crafted for future public events."

A tap on my shoulder interrupted my slow but steady march toward regicide. I turned and found that one of the maids had exited Lucia's orbit and was now holding a garment bag out to me.

"If sir would like some assistance…" she began in heavily accented English. Beneath a small white cap that looked like it came straight out of a Hollywood period piece, her eyes were large and brown.

"Thanks, but I can dress myself. Seriously. I've been doing it for years. More or less," I stammered.

"Are you sure, John?" asked Maria Elena from the doorway, a smile in her voice. "Adela would be more than happy to… help."

I didn't bother replying, mainly because I couldn't think of anything clever to say. Instead, I took the garment bag from the maid and fled to the bathroom.

ooo

The new suit was charcoal gray with subtle pinstripes and clean lines, tailored from some sort of fabric that felt every bit as rich as it looked. It was the kind of suit men might wear to the Oscars, or when accepting lifetime achievement awards for their work in philanthropic medical research. My old suit, on the other hand, had been a polyester and wool blend, purchased at Men's Wearhouse during their spring sale seven years and twenty pounds earlier.

For once, Lucia might have had a point.

There was a matching vest in the same color and style, as well as a long-sleeved white dress shirt that screamed metrosexual but worked surprisingly well with the rest of the outfit. Someone with actual fashion sense must have picked out the ensemble.

My original plan had been to splash some water on my face, make a vague pretense at combing my hair, and call it a day, but the fancy new suit had me reconsidering my options. I'd walked at least four miles already that day, to say nothing of the hour talking to Gaius on the hot and dirty training grounds. Simply splashing water on my face wasn't going to cut it, and a filthy dude in a sweet suit was still a filthy dude. Besides, e*au d'unwashed Smith* was a notoriously foul fragrance, especially when you considered a vampire's superior sense of smell.

I shook my head, hung the suit carefully on the inside of the bathroom door, and shrugged out of my clothes. The shower's multiple nozzles came to life with a hiss, and I stepped into their benevolent spray with a happy sigh. Mindful of the half-dozen women in the bedroom, I managed to refrain from singing.

I may have hummed though.

ooo

Thirty minutes later, I had a new problem.

Two of them, really.

First, the cut of the suit pants made it blindingly obvious that I had on boxers underneath. I'd heard of visible panty lines, but this was ridiculous. Italian tailors needed to realize that it was 2015 and some men in America were still fighting the good fight against skinny pants.

The second problem was still hanging on the bathroom door's hook—a silk tie with shades of deep purple and charcoal that added a splash of color to the suit without being gaudy or over-the-top. The tie itself was a work of art. The problem was that I'd worn a tie maybe five times total in the past decade, and every one of those times, someone else had tied it for me, from my mom to Juliette to Kayla. I didn't have the foggiest idea what the difference between a Windsor and… whatever that other one was… might be, or which of the two was appropriate for the occasion… or how to tie either one, for that matter.

I cracked open the door. The maids were still circling Lucia like bees orbiting a flower patch. "Could I get some help here, please? Just one of you would—"

"—be fine," I grumbled, as both Adela and Maria Elena reached the door at the same time, the latter using her vampire speed to make up for the longer distance. They both trooped through the door into the bathroom.

"No, no, no." Adela shook her head so violently that I expected her hat to go flying through the air like the world's smallest and whitest satellite. "This will not do at all, sir." She motioned to the obvious evidence of my boxers.

"I know," I told her. "It's a disaster. What I was thinki—Wait! Stop that!"

In this case, *that* was the maid unbuttoning my slacks and pulling them to the ground, very narrowly avoiding taking my boxers with them. I'd been pantsed before—mostly in elementary school by sixth grader and known dickhead Tommy Soccareli—but this woman was clearly a professional. There was nothing for me to do but step out of the slacks, even knowing that Maria Elena was taking notes on what would be breathlessly reported to be an *imperfect and utterly non-squeezable ass.*

Accurate but unflattering gluteal assessment aside, I had to admit I was more comfortable out of the pants than I had been in them. But I didn't think Lucia would be cool with me attending the banquet in my underwear. "Do those come in… a relaxed fit?"

Adela gave me the sort of disbelieving and disappointed look I all-too-frequently elicited in the opposite gender. She shook her head again, muttered something in Italian, and reached for my waist.

"Whoa whoa!" I hopped backwards awkwardly, one hand grabbing the waistband of my boxers while the other tried to fend off the maid's attempts to expose the littlest Smith to everyone in the bathroom.

"Sir." With a stomp of her foot, she placed both hands on her hips, and scowled up at me. *"Those* cannot be worn under the suit. And Lady Borghesi has instructed that you wear the suit. The answer is obvious."

"Then we need a new answer."

"Are all Americans such prudes, John?" asked Maria Elena from her perch atop the vanity.

"I'm not a prude," I growled, still focused on keeping my dude-bits from flopping into sight, "but I'm also not going to prance about in skinny pants without any underwear."

The two women—human and femmepire—shared a look, and then turned back toward me in silence, expressions grim and resolved.

"Seriously," I told them, "I'm not going commando!"

○○○

"I hate Italy," I muttered, trying to find some way of walking that didn't make me feel like I was exposing myself to the world.

At least the women had tied my tie for me. A detailed inspection in the mirror, performed after the ladies had finally departed, had convinced me that the suit looked great. Even my unruly brown hair somehow almost worked with the outfit. If I could just forget that I was naked under those pants...

I was pretty sure more than an hour had passed since my return to the suite, which meant that Lucia's criticism had—for once—been distressingly accurate. On the other hand, if she hadn't thrown away my much, much less stylish suit, I'd have been ready with time to spare. So technically, this was all her fault. Again.

I turned to tell her so, when I became aware that the room was far quieter than when I'd left it. Both Maria Elena and the maids were gone, and the suite now held only one other occupant, Lucia herself. And if my suit had done the impossible and made me look vaguely decent, her dress had gone a lot further than that.

"You look... reasonably pretty."

The smugness leaking across the bond made it clear Lucia knew just what an understatement that had been. The femmepire was, as usual, all in white, but I'd never seen her quite like this before: more Hollywood bombshell than voracious sex goddess. A long silken dress hid what had to be five-inch heels. Even without a belt, the dress hewed closely to her figure, showing off a waist which appeared even narrower when contrasted to the curves above. The dress was strapless, but its neckline was understated and almost conservative. Platinum blonde hair had been teased into some sort of elaborate up-do, leaving nothing to obstruct the view of golden skin and glittering diamonds.

There was no denying that Lucia looked like royalty.

"And you look halfway presentable, for once," she said, "which took every bit as much time and effort as I expected. Shall we?"

We were halfway to the door when a phone rang. With a put-upon sigh—as if she were a waitress being asked to take on a second ten-hour shift—Lucia pulled her phone from a white clutch.

"What is it?"

Without vampire hearing, I could hear only one side of the conversation, and the majority of that was in Italian and therefore unintelligible, but even I could see that something was wrong. The femmepire went pale and concern leaked across our bond. A minute or so later, that concern was replaced with relief, just as strong. The queen said a few more words, still in Italian, and then ended the call. She regarded me strangely for a long moment after tucking away her phone.

"What's going on? Is Ana okay?" A lifetime of Catholic guilt prodded me further. "What did I do?"

"That was Teresa."

"Ana's housekeeper?" Teresa and her husband were old-school Italian, with a particular emphasis on *old*… neither would see seventy again. While the dapper Gustavo had taken to me almost from the start, I was still trying to work my way into Teresa's good graces. "Are they okay?"

"As predicted, Duke Barros and his lackey have fled the country. However, they made one stop before departing. Late last night, they mounted an attack upon Anastasia's home." Her eyes remained fixed upon my face. "Only to be thwarted by a congregation of *pixies*."

I permitted myself a very brief but very smug smile.

"This was your doing, Mr. Smith?"

"Thales didn't strike me as the sort to go quietly. With you and Marcus out of the country, Anastasia's house seemed like the most likely target."

Lucia nodded, but the strange expression on her face only deepened. "Teresa and Gustavo owe you their lives. As does Summer, who remains in residence with them."

I shrugged, uncomfortable with what was starting to feel like actual praise from the femmepire queen. "I like Summer. And Gustavo and Teresa mean a lot to Anastasia. I didn't want anything to happen to them."

"Thank you."

Every now and then, Lucia showed glimpses of being an actual person. I found those moments deeply unsettling.

"But why pixies?" she asked. "I would have thought the Pack more suitable for such a task."

"Carolyn hasn't forgiven me for almost getting three of her wolves killed last fall," I admitted. "Plus, I needed security *right away* and—"

"And the Pack have been incapable of swift action ever since you convinced them to transition to a democracy," Lucia concluded.

I didn't deny it. Democracy had seemed like the perfect solution to a particularly nasty succession fight, but its drawbacks had become apparent over the past year.

"Anyway, Kristin owed me, considering that she practically handed me over on a platter to Nepenthe's coven, and I called in the favor at Lindbergh." I shrugged. "I know pixies are way down on the power chart, but there are like a million of them and they can be vicious when the situation calls for it."

Usually, that situation was some sort of copyright infringement or bit of industrial espionage gone awry, but it appeared vampire attacks counted too.

ooo

When we left the suite, we were met by our Watch escort. Two of the manpires proceeded on ahead of us, while the other two trailed behind. None of them seemed any less hostile than our guards from the night before.

"Denarius is taking your security seriously," I said to Lucia.

"Yes. He is most diligent."

I didn't even need the accompanying burst of anger across the bond to pick up on the sarcasm in the queen's voice. Nor did she require any words at all from me to notice my own confusion. She arched one eyebrow, eyes cold as the arctic circle.

"Do you really think the Kingmaker tasked four of the Crown Watch with my protection, Mr. Smith? In my own family's ancestral home?" Lucia shook her head, her dangling diamond earrings glittering like tiny stars. "My dearest uncle is keeping me under observation. These are spies, not soldiers."

Given the width of the shoulders on the guard directly in front of me, I was pretty sure they could be both spies *and* soldiers, but I nodded. It wasn't surprising that the Council would want to keep tabs on the queen. If she *had* been behind Tomasso's death, they had to assume she'd come to Rome to perpetrate something even more diabolical.

I was just glad that they were following Lucia around and not me. I got along well with the Watch back home—or had, before Barros' coup made me *persona non grata* with the House—but the Italians were something else entirely. Maria Elena made for much more pleasant company.

And speaking of Maria Elena... she had said Niccolo was one of the guards on duty, which meant he had to be one of the four steely-eyed spy-soldiers escorting us even now. But which one? I surreptitiously checked out the asses of the manpires in front of me. Did one of them look more squeezable than the other?

"What on earth are you doing?" hissed Lucia.

"My job," I hissed back in what was either an outright lie or a sad commentary on what this case was devolving into. I gave up on my impromptu gluteal reconnaissance with a sigh—I had no clue what made one dude's ass better than another's—and instead just raised my voice. "Which one of you is Niccolo?"

The manpire to Lucia's right cocked his head, pale gray eyes narrowed.

Aha!

"Maria Elena says hi," I told him brightly. "She's been guiding me around the palace."

"I am aware." Niccolo's English was barely intelligible, but he made up for that shortcoming with a surplus of menace. "You will treat her respectfully."

I spread my hands wide and did my best to look harmless. "I'm all about respect, dude. No worries on that front."

"We shall see." With those words, Niccolo went back to pretending I didn't exist.

I reminded myself that most buddy-cop movies started with some level of friction. No doubt, Niccolo and I would be bros by the time this investigation was over.

CHAPTER 21
IN WHICH SPAGHETTI IS NOT ON THE MENU

Predictably, the banquet was being held on the far side of the palatial estate. For the thousandth time in the past day, I thanked every deity I knew of—and the very many I didn't—that I was a dude; walking all that distance in heels would have made me cry. My rarely worn dress shoes were bad enough.

I needed to learn the Italian word for *blister.*

Lucia, being both a femmepire and immune to such petty trivialities as pain or exhaustion, didn't seem to notice the hardship her own feet and ankles must have been enduring. With her head up to my shoulder instead of mid-chest, she was either wearing platforms or dangerously high heels. Despite that fact, she'd had no issue keeping pace with our not-so-merry escort of spy-soldiers.

When our destination finally came into sight, the Watch took up guard positions in the hallway, leaving the two of us to proceed onward alone. Lucia turned to me, her words low but intense. "Remember, Mr. Smith. Follow my lead tonight. Only speak when you are spoken to. And above all—"

"Don't piss off anyone important," I finished. "Yeah, I heard you the first ten times. But you don't need to stress about me; if we get separated, I'm just going to find a corner and eat my spaghetti in peace."

"Your… *spaghetti?*"

"Or pizza, I guess."

The femmepire pursed her lips. "Maybe it would be best if you did not speak at all."

I was saved from responding by the doorman's emergence. He looked to be pushing eighty really, really hard, and he was every bit as human as I was.

And I *was* human, whatever that naga said.

The old man's suit was almost as slick as mine, his dress shoes considerably more so, and the eyes that swept over us in examination were sharp and perceptive. He nodded to me but offered Lucia a deep bow.

I think he knew I wasn't wearing any underwear.

The queen answered with a slight tilt of her head. One hand in the crook of my arm, as if I were her escort—or, God forbid, her date—she spoke. "You may announce us now."

He nodded again and with a creaking of arthritic bones, pivoted to step back through the arched doorway. He stopped at the top of a wide flight of stairs and his voice rang out like some sort of brass instrument, strong and loud over the continuing murmurs of a dozen separate conversations.

"What's he saying?" I asked Lucia, a good fifteen seconds later, when it had become clear that my inability to understand the lengthy monologue had less to do with the man's accent and more to do with the fact that he was speaking Italian.

"He is recounting my lineage and deeds to the audience," she replied coolly.

"Lovely." Hopefully, he'd skip the part about patricide. "How did he know who you were?"

"It is his job to know these things, and in *this* country, at least, your species has not entirely abandoned basic professionalism. Now, be silent."

I sighed and did as instructed, reminding myself that pushing Lucia down the steps would be petty and wrong. Not to mention ineffectual, given vampire superpowers. As the doorman/herald droned on and on, I instead amused myself by constructing my own personalized list of Lucia's deeds. Or misdeeds, really.

The humor faded quickly. I figured prominently in way too many of those misdeeds.

When the man's speech finally ended, Lucia stepped forward to the top of the stairs, bringing me with her. For the first time, I could see the throngs of people assembled below. Before we could descend into that crowd, however, the doorman spoke again.

"I also present to you," he announced in English, presumably for my benefit, "John Smith, son of John and Maria Smith. Chosen of the Winter Lady, mediator for the lesser city of San Diego, and ally to the Lords Beel-Kasan and Kala."

I'd also recently learned to make a badass guacamole, but apparently nobody wanted to hear about that.

"Let it be known," continued the herald, "that he is Pack-friend and ghost-blessed, a breaker of covens, a defender of Houses, and a slayer of demons."

I frowned. I didn't know what half of that even meant, but the line about breaking covens touched a particularly raw nerve. Nepenthe hadn't left me any choice, but that didn't change the fact that the blood of several dozen witches was on my hands.

Literally, in the case of Nepenthe herself.

The recounting of my deeds took significantly less time than Lucia's, but I could feel the weight of more than a few speculative glances from the crowd. It was eerily reminiscent of that recurring dream where I showed up to give a class presentation naked.

Stupid skinny pants.

○○○

"What was that all about?" I asked Lucia when the herald had finally finished.

"At events such as these, Mr. Smith, it is customary that members of the noble class be announced, and our deeds recounted. It lessens the chance of someone accidentally starting a blood feud through unintentional insult."

"And are thralls normally included in that announcement?"

"They are not." She frowned slightly. "Perhaps your role as investigator was seen as sufficient justification for doing so."

"Fantastic."

Something of my feelings must have leaked through the bond, as Lucia's grip on my arm tightened painfully. "Why does it matter?"

"Because one of my only advantages in dealing with the People is that all of you underestimate me. And that advantage has been pretty much shot to hell now that that glorified loudspeaker has painted me as some kind of rock star."

"You are no longer in San Diego, Mr. Smith." The femmepire started down the stairs and I had little choice but to go with her. "In Rome, the weak are devoured and quickly forgotten. If you wish to survive this investigation, you *must* be a person of consequence."

That did sort of make sense. The problem was, I didn't *do* person of consequence very well. Or at all. Southern California casual was a lot more my style. And speaking of California… "Since when is San Diego a *lesser* city anyway? Does that dude not realize we have *multiple* professional sports teams?"

"Believe it or not, the world does not revolve around your city."

"I know that," I told her smugly. "It revolves around the sun." Nothing like dropping a science truth bomb on the woman who'd been born in medieval times.

Lucia just sighed.

ooo

The banquet hall was sizable, despite being—as Maria Elena had informed me earlier—the smallest of three such chambers in the palace. Elaborately carved marble walls soared twenty feet or more into the air before coming together in a series of connecting arches to form a starburst pattern at the ceiling's center. Large tapestries softened the otherwise austere stone, and a second set of double doors were set in the far wall, every bit as large as those we had entered through. These doors, however, were shut. Above them, a bas relief carving depicted some sort of battle scene.

Judging by their inhuman attractiveness, most of my fellow partygoers were vampires: a hundred or more People decked from head to toe in a glittering array of fashion, from full-on tuxedos to artfully draped scraps of diaphanous silk. One femmepire paraded by in a gown with a train so long that six human servants had been tasked to carry it. She wove through the crowd like a crimson and gold serpent... or one of those dragons from Chinese New Year parades. A second femmepire swayed in the opposite direction, as proud as a sultaness and barely clothed in a dress that consisted of three scarves in shades of blue and green. She wore the outfit well, but green and blue were Ana's colors, and I couldn't help but imagine what my maybe-girlfriend would look like wearing it instead.

Now, *that* was the sort of mental image guaranteed to keep me warm at night.

As we were slowly absorbed into the crowd, I had to admit that my Men's Wearhouse suit would have been woefully out of place among all that finery. If nothing else, the new suit clearly identified me as something more than just a servant. It didn't keep me from feeling awkward and pudgy though, especially with all the supernatural beauty on display. Clothes might make the man, but it took a lot more than cufflinks to blur the species divide.

"Lucia my child. You always did struggle with promptness." The Lord of Bones appeared out of the crowd like a specter of death. Once again, a tuxedo with shiny black lapels hung upon his gaunt frame, and the top hat from the previous night was now perched precariously on his desiccated skull.

"At times, my thrall pays too much heed to the idea of being fashionably late." The femmepire had been frowning in my direction for some reason but was all smiles now as she turned to greet the vampire councilor. "Mr. Smith, you remember Caine, our resident Lord of Bones?"

"He's pretty hard to forget," I admitted. "How's it going?"

"It stopped going several centuries ago, my dear boy." The smile directed my way was all teeth, standard-issue vampire attractiveness blunted significantly by the man's almost skeletal form. Black eyes scanned me from head to toe dismissively, and then he turned and gave Lucia the same once-over. "I see you still believe in displaying your wares like a common harlot."

"And I see *you* continue to focus on matters in which your own constitution forbids you from partaking," Lucia retorted. The amusement trickling across our bond was an odd counterpoint to the frosty tone.

If anything, the man's ghastly grin only widened. "It is less a question of constitution than of desire, my dear. Flesh is, after all, but a shell." The smile flickered and vanished, like a candle flame being snuffed. "As our late, dearly departed, King Tomasso discovered."

"Indeed."

"Indeed," the Lord of Bones echoed, chewing on the word as if he could divine its meaning through taste. "Walk with me a moment, if you will. There are several newcomers to our Court who are simply *dying* to meet you." He offered her an overly-long, frighteningly thin arm, and spared me a cold glance. "Your thrall will have to do without the pleasure of your company."

"Somehow, I'll survive," I offered back sweetly.

He laughed, but even that sound was gross, like he was trying to clear the phlegm from his throat… and failing miserably. "We shall see if that is true," he decided finally. With a tip of his top hat in my direction, he whisked Lucia deeper into the chamber.

I watched the two depart with a frown, then shrugged. It was time for spaghetti.

ooo

In our initial descent into the general scrum of the banquet, I'd spied several long tables along the left wall, piled high with a variety of dishes. With Lucia no longer forcibly guiding me around, I headed toward those tables. The unseen watchers appeared to have left with the queen, and the rest of the people there were intent upon ignoring me. That suited me just fine. Alive and ignored was always, always better than dead and notorious.

Although The Notorious John Smith did continue to have a certain ring to it. Maybe Ana and I could be notorious together?

Not everyone at the party was vampire or human. I'd glimpsed the slightly curved horns of a minotaur in the distance—presumably Tarn—and my quest for the spaghetti table took me past several well-dressed, gray-skinned, crimson-eyed members of a species that my *Fables & Mythology* book had somehow missed. They rumbled what were either polite, if disinterested, greetings, or ominous promises to dine upon my liver.

As I had no idea which interpretation was accurate, I nodded politely back and then threw in a baleful glare for good measure. Sort of a *'Yes, it is nice weather today… but don't eat my liver!'* combo platter.

They didn't attack me, so it must have worked. My experience as a mediator was paying off in spades.

Twenty feet past that not-so-educational encounter, the press of the crowd finally started to lessen. I squeezed past the few stragglers on the outer edge of the hall and approached the food-laden tables in triumph. Within seconds of scanning the tables, that triumph turned to tragedy.

There was no spaghetti. Nor was there any pizza. Or garlic bread. In desperation, I searched for the only other Italian food I could think of… but the polished wooden tables, eight feet long if they were an inch, remained hauntingly free of calzones as well.

In place of the Buca-di-Beppo style feast I'd anticipated were a dozen trays and tiny plates, each of them bearing… well, I was reasonably sure that was *supposed* to be food. I eyeballed what looked like a careful stack of tiny sandwiches the size of my thumb. Why were they green? Another tray contained individual, half-sized skewers of cheese, topped with a single miniature tomato, while a round plate offered up an unholy hybrid of mushroom and sea urchin.

Lucia's reaction to my spaghetti comment was finally making sense. Nobody had warned me that the Italian Court hated food. And life.

CHAPTER 22

"You're in a world of trouble, John Smith!"

I'd heard those words, or something similar, way too many times in the past two decades, but this was the first time I could recall the warning being delivered with such bubbly, cheerful enthusiasm. I swallowed a mouthful of bitter ham and smelly cheese and turned to find Maria Elena trying—and failing—to adopt a stern demeanor.

"What did I do now? And… what are you wearing?"

"Do you like it?" She spun slowly about to give me a full view.

"What there is of it is great," I told her honestly. Her emerald dress from the afternoon had been replaced by its much, much more risqué cousin. The fabric hugged every curve of the femmepire's slim body before ending, precipitously, at mid-thigh.

"What there is of it?" Maria Elena shook her head and laughed. "You really *are* a prude!"

"Just… not used to Italian fashion yet, I think. Are you going clubbing later or something?"

"On a Tuesday?" She wrinkled her nose at the idea, then laughed again. "As the youngest of the People here, Sabina and I feel that it's our duty to shake these parties up a bit. Just because our kind lives for centuries doesn't mean we should all dress like dowdy spinsters!"

I mentally reviewed the outfits I'd seen so far that night. Maybe *dowdy spinster* meant something else in Italy.

"As for *why* you're in trouble," she continued, effortlessly picking up the dangling conversation thread, "it's because you spent the whole day letting me believe you were *just* an investigator!"

"Well, technically, I am…" I began.

"*And* a mediator. *And* a demon slayer! And what's this about being a friend of the Pack?"

"*A* pack, not *the* Pack," I clarified. "Werewolves don't buy into the idea of central authority. Anyway, it's not really a big deal. The leaders of the San Diego Pack and I saved each other's lives once. Also, I helped break up their marriage."

"You did *what?*"

"It's okay," I assured her, "they *asked* me to." Hired me to, actually, but that seemed irrelevant to the discussion. "Besides, they're way happier now as boyfriend and girlfriend than they ever were as husband and wife."

Maria Elena's temporarily green eyes were wide and confused. As usual.

"You know what?" I decided. "It's complicated and not super important."

"*Important* is overrated," the femmepire said with a snort. "I'll take interesting, any day!"

I may have preened, just a bit. As much as I would have liked to have a squeezable ass, being considered interesting wasn't a bad consolation prize.

"Anyway," she continued airily, "I wanted to say hi before Sabina arrived." She entwined one arm with mine and effortlessly tugged me away from the food tables. "If you could maybe sweet talk her a little bit," she breathed into my ear, "it would make things a lot easier for me."

"Sweet talk her? How, exactly?" I murmured back, uncomfortably aware of the lovely young woman glued to my side.

"No idea. *I'm* not a mediator! By the way, did you know that your heart rate elevates every time I breathe into your ear?"

"You don't say." Stupid vampire senses.

"Yes." Her voice was a delighted purr. "It almost makes—"

I never got to find out exactly what it made, because her voice suddenly downshifted from twenty-something temptress right back to bubbly cheerleader in a move guaranteed to cause conversational whiplash.

"And here she is! Sabina, John was hoping to have a word with you, if you didn't mind."

My so-called mediator training was the only thing that kept me from shooting Maria Elena a look of surprised betrayal. Another conversation with Tomasso's daughter was the last thing I'd been looking for. Especially on an empty stomach.

"And if I do mind?" Sabina's voice was every bit as cold as her aunt's, but it lacked a certain something. The threat of unstoppable violence, presumably.

"Then I would tell you to enjoy the banquet and head off to do the same," I replied, grasping for the out I'd been unexpectedly provided.

As if she'd picked up on my relief at that possibility, the other femmepire shook her head, dashing my hopes. The smile she gave me was sharp, like a knife. "By all means, let us talk."

Sometimes, my life kind of sucked.

ooo

"First of all," I told Sabina, once the three of us—four if you counted Tarn—had found a quiet space on the edge of the crowd, "I wanted to apologize for being a bit of a dick when you were training this afternoon." When my apology failed to elicit any sort of reaction from the young woman, I hurried on. "Secondly, I wanted to offer my condolences on your father's death."

"My father didn't just *die*, Mr. Smith. He was *murdered*. And given that you are here to defend the monster who did it, you'll have to forgive me if I tell you to take your sympathies and shove them right up your overfed—"

"Sabina!" Maria Elena stepped between the irate femmepire and me. "You said you'd listen to what he had to say!"

"Perhaps I wanted *him* to listen to what *I* had to say instead."

"It's alright," I told Maria Elena. "If I were in Sabina's shoes—"

"You will refer to me as Your Royal Highness, or not at all," growled the princess.

"—I'd be pissed too," I finished. "Except that I know one thing she doesn't."

"And what is that?"

"Lady Dumenyova didn't do it."

"Oh! Well, that changes everything!" sniped Her Royal Highness. "In that case, the three of you are free to go."

Despite their obvious physical differences, I was starting to think Sabina and Lucia were related after all. I bit back a less-than-diplomatic retort and tried again.

"Pretend for just a moment that I'm right." I ignored the disdainful sniff that came in reply. "If Lady Dumenyova is innocent, then your father's true killer is still out there."

"And all five members of *Beton* are waiting for me in my bedroom." Sabina rolled her eyes.

Maria Elena explained: "*Beton* is our version of the Beatles. They're the biggest name in today's music scene. All men, all two hundred or younger, and all drop-dead gorgeous."

Vampire musicians. No wonder some of us never got laid.

"And are they, by any chance, up in Sabina's bedroom?"

"I don't think so?"

Damn it. I *knew* that had been sarcasm.

"I'm not saying you have to believe me," I told the increasingly less likable princess. "I'm just asking you to consider the possibility that I could be right."

"Fine. I've considered it. So what?"

"If your father's killer *is* running free, I could use your help in catching him."

Whatever Sabina had been expecting me to say, that clearly wasn't it. I had a delightful time watching her struggle for words.

"You want *me* to help *you?!?*"

I shrugged. "I've spoken with King Tomasso's servants and his Secundus. I'll interview the members of his Council too—not to mention anyone else who may have interacted with him—but none of them knew him like you did."

The princess cocked her head, dark eyes boring into mine. "Tell me, human… has anyone explained to you yet what will happen should you lose this trial?"

Years of conversation with Bill and Jee Sun enabled me to roll with the unexpected subject change. "Sure. The Council will execute both Lady Dumenyova and your aunt. And when Lucia dies, the bond will kill me too."

"Doesn't that frighten you?"

"A lot of things frighten me: angry Blood Witches, mercenary cockroaches, deep-water fishing trips… but yeah; dying ranks pretty high up there." I shrugged. "The world is what it is."

"That is a very… American expression."

Given that Anastasia was the one who had first said it to me, I doubted that very much.

Sabina's anger had died down to a low burn. She frowned, almost sadly. "You don't seem like an entirely awful human. I'm sorry that your life is being spent so cheaply on a case that cannot be won."

"It's not over yet," I told her optimistically, "but I really could use your help. If Anastasia *is* guilty, the suspiciously large mountain of evidence will convict her no matter what you tell me. But if she's innocent, some tiny scrap of knowledge might be the key to finding your father's real killer."

The princess' frown deepened, but finally she nodded with a sigh. "Tomorrow. My suite. Maria Elena can show you the way."

Holy shit. Sometimes, even I was amazed by my badass mediator skills.

"In another time or place," Sabina continued, "it is possible I might not have utterly despised you, Mr. Smith."

"You wouldn't believe how often I hear that," I muttered.

Maria Elena covered her giggle with a fake cough.

"As it is, even though it comes in service of an obviously doomed cause, I find your devotion to my traitorous aunt almost impressive."

"Lucia isn't the reason I'm here," I said. "Well, I guess *technically*, she is, but only because she told me about the trial. And paid for my ticket to Rome."

It was Sabina's turn to look over to Maria Elena for clarification. "Is he making *any* sense to you, 'Lena?"

"He's in love with her."

"So what? To hear some of the elders talk, Lucia has had monkeys falling at her feet since she was my age." She shook her head. "Though only the gods know why."

"I think it's her giant breasts," mused the other femmepire.

Why did everyone keep saying that?

"Anyway," continued Maria Elena, "it's not your aunt he's in love with. It's Lady Dumenyova."

Sabina's dark eyes went wide with shock. "You're in love with the *Stone Lady?* But… *why?*"

"Because God loves strong women," she quoted.

"Meaning?"

The green-clad femmepire shrugged, honey blonde curls dancing with the motion. "No clue. He says a lot of strange stuff."

"You're not helping as much as you think you are," I told her, getting a mock pout in reply.

"In love with Lady Dumenyova. Now I really have heard it all." The princess turned to her friend. "And what is that he is wearing about his neck? Surely, he knows not to put his faith in religious idolatry?"

"It's a necklace," Maria Elena started to explain, having apparently glimpsed it during our impromptu dressing adventure. She stopped mid-sentence, realization dawning across her face, and then spun to me with a girlish squeal. "Is it for *her?*"

I blinked. What?

"That's so romantic I want to just kill myself!" Maria Elena had gone full-on fan girl.

"What are you talking about, you inane twit?" In contrast to her words, Sabina's tone was mild, almost amused.

"He's wearing a chain with a *ring* on the end," the other femmepire informed her friend, reaching into my shirt to extract the necklace. "A ring with a *diamond solitaire.*"

"A very *small* diamond," Sabina pointed out.

"True." Maria Elena's smile wilted slightly. "Oh, John… whatever her crimes, even Lady Dumenyova deserves something a little grander, don't you think?"

Apparently, size *did* matter. That was disappointing.

"It's not an engagement ring," I said., "and I didn't bring it for Ana."

"What is it then?" Sabina demanded.

I tucked the ring back into my shirt, fumbling for a believable lie.

Maria Elena snickered. "I'm guessing it's complicated, Sabina."

"No doubt. Are all Americans as strange as you, Mr. Smith?"

"Oh, definitely," I lied. "We're a nation of raving lunatics."

"Is that why you opted not to wear underwear to a formal dinner?"

I coughed, cheeks flaming, even as I tossed a glare in Maria Elena's direction. "Like my dad always says, if you've got it, flaunt it."

"And if you don't?"

"Then make damn sure to buy your own clothes," I grumbled. "Which I'll be doing from now on. Assuming I live that long."

"I will be rather put out if you do not, my thrall." The cold words came from the crowd to my left, as Lucia emerged. The Lord of Bones was nowhere in sight.

"Niece." Lucia nodded in the direction of the princess.

"Aunt." Sabina's tone plunged back down to subarctic temperatures. "Are you here to finish the job your hired killer started?"

"Sabina!" Maria Elena stepped to her friend's side, a small hand on the princess' shoulder.

"Be grateful that your accusations are unfounded," the queen told her niece icily. "If I had gone through the trouble of organizing my brother's assassination, I would have made certain your own death was part of the deal."

A low rumble greeted her words, and the minotaur I had spotted earlier stepped up behind Sabina.

"Peace, Tarn." Sabina raised one hand dismissively. "I have little to fear from a woman who couldn't even hold onto her own House."

Watching Lucia and her niece wage conversational war was a lot like watching Godzilla and Mothra destroy Tokyo. Lucia had the edge in pure, ego-driven contempt, but Sabina had the dismissive, soul-crushing sarcasm of a genuine teenager.

When it came to attitude, however, the two were practically twins… which was frankly amazing, given that Sabina had been born almost ninety years *after* Lucia's banishment. To the best of my knowledge, the two had never even met.

"This may finally be definitive proof of nature over nurture," I decided as their verbal battle finally came to a close.

"Does your thrall *ever* make sense, *Aunt?*" sniped Sabina.

"As my brother should have taught you, *dear Niece*," purred Lucia in response, "humans rarely do."

○○○

"Did you learn anything of value from your ill-conceived dialogue with my niece, Mr. Smith?" Lucia asked.

"Beyond the fact that arrogance is a genetic trait?"

"Yes." I could almost hear Lucia's teeth grind.

"Not really. But I did arrange an interview tomorrow with her. Assuming your little intervention back there didn't blow that to hell."

"She is but a child. Why would you want to interview her?"

"She was Tomasso's daughter. She can give me a unique perspective on your brother. And maybe some clues as to who really killed him."

"Your interviews today went poorly, I take it?"

"Progress is always slow at the start of a case," I hedged.

"So be it." Lucia glanced back over one golden shoulder, but the other two femmepires had already melted into the crowd. "I will, however, ask Denarius to find a new guide for you."

"Why?"

"Because your current escort is the companion of my niece. Surely even you can recognize the potential conflict of interest?"

I shrugged. "She seems harmless."

"I believe you felt the same way about Nepenthe."

I tried not to stiffen at the witch's name. "Maria Elena is an even worse liar than I am. Anyone Denarius assigns to me could be a spy or a threat. As far as adult femmepires go, she's got to be the least dangerous."

"I do wish you would find a different word," murmured the queen, "but this once, you are almost making sense. Any day now, you might rise above your species and put two coherent thoughts together in the proper order."

"Don't count on it." Another terrible comeback. It had to be something in the water.

"As you say," Lucia continued, plucking a flute of champagne from the tray of a passing waiter, "a three-year-old child should be the least of your worries."

"Exactly. And honestly, I think she could even be an asset." I was just a little hazy on the *how*…

If only dimples could be weaponized…

CHAPTER 23

"Lucia, my sweetling. We meet again." The voice was deep and rich, and it stopped Lucia in her tracks. She turned to face the owner.

He was, without question, the most handsome man I'd ever seen in my life. Xavier had been the African Brad Pitt, but this man defied comparison to anyone merely human. It wasn't just his chiseled features and strong chest, or the dark curly hair that fell to broad shoulders while somehow not looking feminine, it was how he carried himself. The dude was walking animal magnetism and chocolate-dipped sex-on-a-stick. If I hadn't been firmly hetero, I might…

I shook myself. Chocolate dipped *what?!* Those were *not* normal thoughts for me to be having. Either I was only learning new things about my sexuality now at twenty-seven or…

Oh. Of course. I built up my mental walls around the small knot of *other* in my brain, and the lust that had been pouring into me from Lucia dwindled to a trickle. When I looked at the man again, he was just a dude. Appallingly handsome, sure enough, but nothing more. Additional details began to seep through, like the fact that he was bare chested, wearing only an open vest, as if he was auditioning to be a Hollywood djinn. It would have been ridiculous looking, except that even his abs had abs. His feet were bare, and the pants he wore were black, leather, and tight enough to give the less talented members of my gender serious feelings of inadequacy.

Lucia glanced up at the other man through lowered eye lashes, and let out a delighted, throaty chuckle. "My Lord, I did not expect to see you here tonight!"

"I regret having missed your invocation before the Council. When I received news of your arrival, I hurried back to Rome with all possible speed. And as you know," he said, his smile exposing a perfect set of gleaming white teeth, "that is very swift indeed."

"As I recall," she replied archly, spots of color appearing in her golden cheeks, "you were not *always* so fast."

"Some situations call for speed, while others demand patience and a certain modicum of… care."

It was only when Lucia giggled—and wasn't *that* a horrible sight and sound—that I grasped what they were talking about. I coughed, embarrassed. Maybe I *was* a prude, but this seemed like a terribly inappropriate conversation to have in the middle of a crowded banquet hall.

"This is your thrall then?" the other man asked, smoothly involving me in the conversation.

"Indeed." As she turned to me, Lucia seemed to remember where she was. The silly smile slid off her face, although her pale blue eyes continued to dance. "May I introduce you to John Smith? Mr. Smith, this is our city's most reclusive Council member, known to one and all as the Horned God."

"On account of these," the man added, sweeping hair back from his forehead to reveal two small, ebony horns. For the first time, I also took notice of his crimson, iris-less eyes. "I believe you met one of my fellow denizens earlier this year."

Denizens? I took another glance at the horns and eyes and had a moment of clarity, followed almost instantly by blind, unreasoning fear.

He nodded as the realization swept across my face. "Indeed. The Hound of Tartarus is an unthinking brute, but we demons must stick together."

Well, shit.

ooo

The first rule of dealing with predators, as anyone will tell you, is to not let them see when you're rattled. But given my always lousy poker face and the way the demon's smile was slowly widening, I was pretty sure that ship had already sailed.

Right into an iceberg.

Then, the rest of what he had said intruded upon my maritime metaphor.

"Did you say *is?*"

"Your pardon?"

"The Hound of Tartarus *is* an unthinking brute?" I prompted.

"Indeed. The bodies we wear in your world," he motioned to his own depressingly broad-shouldered and slim-hipped form, "are but temporary vessels. The vessel can be damaged, even destroyed, but the individual remains untouched."

"Like lizards in people suits."

"What was that?"

"Nothing."

Crimson eyes flashed. "The Hound seeks a new vessel, even now. He is quite eager to resume your acquaintance."

Images of the twenty-foot-tall, multi-armed monstrosity came to me unbidden. It would be just my luck to survive Ana's trial only to end up as demon food.

"As for you, little Lucia, I am gratified to find that the centuries have only deepened your bloom." The demon turned back to the femmepire queen, once again all charm and seductive smiles.

And Lucia ate it up. I watched her stroke a golden hand across the demon's chest. "And you remain entirely untouched by time, my lord."

"Only because there are so many better things to be touched by," he replied, covering her hand with his own, and taking a small step closer.

"So, you're immortal then?" I asked brightly.

Crimson eyes narrowed slightly, before the demon turned the force of his personality back onto me. "Dear boy, would you pardon us for a moment? You and I will have ample time to get to know each other later." While the words could very easily have been a threat, his tone made them into a promise.

"Yeah, I'll pass, but thanks. All this," I motioned to my own, far less impressive body, "is already spoken for. Sort of."

"Be that as it may—"

"And is *Horned God* your actual name, or just a title?"

"Mr. Smith…" began Lucia.

"It's a valid question. If God is a surname, that would make his first name Horned. And that's just silly." I eyed the demon, who was starting to seethe. "Do you have any brothers? Is there a Potato God running around the demon realms?"

"It is a title," the demon hissed. He closed his eyes briefly and exhaled. When he spoke again, his debonair air had returned. "My true name is known only to a select few. Individuals I hold in the highest esteem. You, my dear boy, will likely never qualify."

"I can live with that."

"For a while longer, perhaps." His smile was chilling. "Now, if you will excuse your mistress and I…"

The demon turned to Lucia and offered her his arm, but the femmepire was frowning, in the closest thing to normal behavior since the demon had oozed his way into our presence.

"You never told *me* your name," she told the Horned God, flawless brow furrowed.

"It is not the sort of information my kind gives out—"

"Except to individuals you hold in the highest esteem," I reminded him. "As the Winter Lady's thrall, I'm frankly *shocked* to hear that you don't include her in that group."

"It is of little import," decided the femmepire in question, taking a careful step out of the demon's personal space. "Your species may stand outside the passage of time, my Lord, but *mine* is strengthened by it." Her voice grew cold and hard. "It has been centuries since I was the woman you knew."

"To my eternal delight. I look forward with great anticipation to discovering the new you." He swept into a graceful bow, eyes sparkling with invitation.

Jesus. The dude should have been named the Horny God.

Lucia was about to speak when the unseen orchestra came to a stop. In the sudden silence, a chorus of bells could be heard.

"It appears we will need to catch up at a later time," the demon told Lucia, brushing her hand with his gross demony lips.

I pretended not to see the delighted shiver that went through her, but inwardly, I was rolling my eyes. I waited for the horny demon to make his exit and turned to the queen.

"What an asshole."

Lucia shook herself slightly, as if awaking from a dream. "What was that, my thrall?"

"Nothing." The double-doors in the far wall had swung open and the crowd around us was slowly migrating in that direction. "Where is everyone headed?"

"Into the dining hall, of course. The bells signify that supper is ready to be served."

"Isn't *this* the dining hall?"

"Do you see any tables? Please do try to exercise that walnut you call a brain, Mr. Smith."

"Welcome back," I told her, as we joined the flow of inhumanity. "I was starting to think you'd been replaced by aliens. Or that someone had spiked the champagne."

"Do you have something to say?" Her voice warned me against doing so.

"Is *that* dude seriously your type?"

"Are you telling me you did not feel the pull?" For once, there was no contempt in Lucia's voice. "The overwhelming attraction?"

"To the red-eyed, black-horned, walking innuendo?" I shrugged. "You were feeling enough of it for both of us. And thanks for making me briefly question my sexuality, by the way."

"He is an incubus, Mr. Smith. That is—"

"The dude version of a succubus," I supplied. I'd had a few years to read up on mythology. "And you had a relationship with him?"

"Something like that. A very, very long time ago."

The pieces finally clicked into place. "Wait, was *he* the demon you were heading to meet with in my dream?"

I imagined I could hear Lucia grinding her teeth. "Your dream, Mr. Smith. My memory."

"Gross." I shook my head slowly. "Seems like an awful lot of effort just to sleep with a dude. Especially that dude."

"The Horned God has forgotten more about the art of lovemaking than you will ever know."

"Like that's difficult?"

Damn it; Italy really was ruining my comeback game.

CHAPTER 24

IN WHICH A PIRATE, A SULTANESS AND A FRATMAN
SIT DOWN FOR DINNER

The dining chamber was a lot like the room we'd just been milling about in, except the extravagant tapestries were replaced with extravagant statuary. On the far side of the room, atop a raised platform, was an ornate table with eight equally ornate chairs tucked behind it. In front of and below the dais, additional tables had been arrayed in a series of concentric semi-circles radiating out like ripples on a pond.

I'd seen something similar at Lucia's former House, albeit on a much smaller scale. Vampires seemed particularly keen on declaring their exalted status through physical elevation. Maybe because so many of the old ones were short? Regardless, the individuals up on the dais would have an excellent view of the peons who were sitting, rather literally, below them.

It came as no surprise that I was one of those peons. My dual positions as San Diego's (mostly out-of-work) mediator and deposed queen's thrall clearly didn't count for much in the political hierarchy. Lucia herself fared significantly better; while she was not up on the dais, she shared one of the tables closest to it with the three ambassadors, an empty chair, and Sabina.

Queen and princess, aunt and niece, both femmepires were doing a phenomenal job of ignoring each other. Tarn, the princess' minotaur bodyguard lurked between two absurdly endowed statues along the side wall, a good twenty feet away from his charge. Given how fast vampires were, I had no idea what good he thought he would be all the way over there. Either Sabina wasn't in any danger, or Tarn wasn't all that interested in long-term employment as her bodyguard.

"Why isn't Sabina sitting with the cool kids?" I finally asked.

"Do you mean us?" Maria Elena had been seated—quite by chance, no doubt—to my right. Two of the chairs at our table remained empty, but the vampires occupying the other two were studiously ignoring me. Including, sadly, the femmepire in the blue and green scarf dress, who I'd privately nicknamed the Sultaness of Scarves. My polite requests for the name of her designer—I *seriously* wanted to see Anastasia in a dress like that—had fallen on suspiciously deaf ears. In fact, Maria Elena was the only person willing to acknowledge my existence.

"No; I meant up on the platform." I watched Denarius ascended the short flight of stairs to join Dog, the Horny God, and the Lord of Bones.

"That's the Council table," Maria Elena explained. "All seating is arranged by rank. The higher the rank, the closer you are to the front."

Our table was within steps of the doors we'd come through.

"So, Sabina won't get to sit up there until she's crowned queen?" It had taken me a while, but I felt like I was starting to get a grasp on vampire politics.

"Exactly." Maria Elena watched me scan the crowd for a while, before asking the obvious question. "What are you looking for anyway?"

"Tomasso's murderer."

"Lady Dumenyova isn't here…"

"I mean the *real* murderer."

"Oh. Right." The femmepire looked worried. When she spoke, her voice was a whisper. "You think they're here?"

"It seems likely. The people with the most to gain from his death are all in this room." As far as I knew anyway. Without an actual motive, it was kind of hard to build any sort of profile for the killer.

My comment earned a mild glare from the scarf-clad femmepire. She leaned over and said something to her companion in lilting Italian. The manpire cocked a delicate eyebrow—if he hadn't been a blood-sucking creature of the night, I'd have accused him of overdoing the manscaping—and his eyes darted in my direction. Both vampires laughed.

It wasn't difficult to guess who they were laughing at.

"Do I want to know what our incredibly rude tablemates are saying, Maria Elena?" If the Italians thought they could out-rude me, they were in for a serious wake-up call.

"Probably not—"

"I was wondering what barn your mistress discovered you in," the other femmepire informed me in heavily accented English, "and how many generations of inbreeding it took to attain your level of stupidity. I always find it amusing when monkeys try to think for themselves."

On cue, her companion laughed again.

"I'm picking up on some serious anti-human hostility here."

"Sorry, John. Don't let it—" Maria Elena's comforting words faltered under the withering stares of the other two vampires.

"No worries; I get it. After all, we monkeys are renowned for being impossibly stupid—"

"Indeed you are," put in the manpire.

"—not to mention completely lacking in grace and manners. In fact, even as Queen Lucia's thrall, I'm guessing I must rank about as low as any individual in this room."

"Even lower."

"Even lower." I nodded as I chewed that over. "So that explains why I'm seated all the way in the back. What's *your* excuse?"

The resulting silence lasted for only a moment, but it was a glorious damn moment.

Then, the manpire surged to his feet, and I remembered the adage about poking the bear.

○○○

I was still processing my instinctive flight-or-flight response—*fight* had wisely never even entered the picture—when the snobbish vampire lunged at me in a blur of speed. There wasn't even time for my usual squeak of terror before he was on me.

Make that *almost* on me. I cracked open an eye to see that someone had stepped between us, restraining my attacker without any visible signs of strain.

The newcomer was short—not Lucia short, but close—and built like a brick wall. A tunic in eye-searing red topped a wide belt, loose black pants and knee-high leather boots. Paired with a bushy blonde beard, the bandana on his shaved head, and the eyepatch over his left eye, that outfit could only possibly mean one thing.

"Vampire pirates are a thing? *Seriously?*" How could so much cool be squeezed into any one individual? "Where the hell do I sign up?"

Maria Elena's gulp was audible, but nobody seemed inclined to respond.

"We eat before fight." The pirate's voice was heavily accented by something other than Italian. As he spoke, his teeth flashed gold.

I had never wanted gold fillings so badly in my life.

"This isn't your affair," argued the other manpire, squirming uselessly in the pirate's grasp.

"No?" The pirate dumped my attacker back into his seat, like an ogre manhandling a brownie, and then straddled one of our table's empty chairs. "I am here and hungry. This makes it my affair, no?"

"Don't get your hopes up, dude," I told him. "I don't think these people have even heard of spaghetti."

Next to me, Maria Elena sighed.

"Shut your face, *obez'yana*," the pirate told me, never losing his smile. "In my country, you would eat in back with dogs, where nobody is forced to smell you."

Well, that was just rude.

The manscaping manpire seemed disinclined to cross our newest tablemate, but the Sultaness of Scarves was made of sterner stuff. Eyes flashing, she turned to her companion. "Aimon, what is the matter with you? Why are you allowing this reprobate to order you about?"

Aimon turned to his date. "My apologies, Dulcinea. I forget that you have been absent from court these past hundred years. You have the *pleasure* of now sharing your table with a genuine legend of the People."

A *vampire pirate* legend. I nodded appreciatively. Mad respect.

Dulcinea turned a curious eye on the newcomer. "And what legend is that?"

"You have heard of Vasily's Monster?"

Given the way the color fled from Dulcinea's lovely face, she had.

"I always like that one," mused the pirate. "As if Vasily was not monster enough on his own."

"Vasily?" I had to ask.

"My brother." The pirate's one eye, blue as a robin's egg, narrowed. "Khan of the Steppes."

I managed to hide my frown. Khan was a term I recognized, but steps? The palace had a boatload of staircases, but I wasn't sure even they could rightly qualify as their own territory.

Aimon dredged up a tight smile, polish oozing back into his voice now that the danger had passed. "Shouldn't you be sitting with the other ambassadors, Sergei?"

"I sit where I sit. If anyone has problem with this, they speak to Vasily," said the other vampire, grunting as a waiter handed him a goblet of something dark and steaming. "No doubt, he will welcome distraction. Perhaps, he will only take one of your eyes."

I glanced at Sergei's eyepatch and shivered. I was damn sure going to avoid the staircase kingdom on all future trips across the palace.

ooo

"So, your brother is the king of his territory?" I asked Sergei, desperate for something to focus on other than the bowl in front of me. In place of pasta, we'd been served some sort of soup. My first spoonful had included clams, tomatoes, and something that looked distressingly like eel. A second spoonful was never, ever going to happen.

On the bright side, Maria Elena had explained to me that Sergei was from the steppes of Russia and Eastern Europe, leaving me moderately less terrified of my return trip across the palace.

After two or three full goblets, the pirate manpire seemed happy to talk, gesturing with a roll in his hand, even as he drained his bowl of its contents.

"Fah. Not king. We do not have king in my homeland. Vasily is Khan."

"What's the difference?"

The obvious answer was *everything after the k*, but thankfully Sergei didn't go there.

"We do not consider right to rule a matter of blood. When old khan dies, any can challenge to take his place."

"Who was khan before Vasily?"

"Our father." He slurped the last bits of soup down with a satisfied sigh.

I paused, frowning. Either the manpire's accent was thicker than I'd realized, or he was contradicting himself. "Didn't you just say your people *don't* believe in inheritance?"

"Yah. But by the time our father died, there were none left to challenge Vasily or I."

"And of the two of you, he's older?" I guessed.

Sergei's pale blue eye hardened beneath a bushy blonde eyebrow. "Don't be fool. I am eldest."

"But then why…"

"When funeral was done, and smoke from fire gone, Vasily and I fought, as tradition demands."

"Oh." I suppressed a wince. Nobody likes being reminded of past failures. It was clearly time for some mediator magic. "Well, I'm sure you made a good showing at least."

"Good showing? Fah!" Sergei's teeth gleamed golden. "I was victor."

"You… won?"

"Yah. Vasily take eye, but I break back. And when he heal, Vasily was forced to be Khan, while I roam free."

"Oh," I said yet again. One day, I was going to figure vampires out, and on that day, I was going to write the greatest tell-all book that Hollywood had ever seen.

After which, I'd no doubt be murdered. Possibly by my pseudo-girlfriend, at the express command of my mistress.

God, life was weird.

"But Vasily has last laugh," Sergei continued, beard hiding his deep frown. "He send me here as ambassador. No snow. No bear. Weak vodka. Nothing but peacock fledglings stumbling around like *afh-tsah*."

I didn't have any clue what that last word was, but the miracle of context—and the expressions on Aimon and the Sultaness' faces—told me it wasn't good.

Sergei really was my favorite manpire ever.

CHAPTER 25

I had finally run out of questions to ask Sergei, who as a legendary vampire-pirate-ambassador-brother-to-the-khan had thoroughly wrecked the curve for coolness, when the manpire gestured across the room at the table where Lucia, Sabina, and the other ambassadors sat.

"You are thrall to Winter Lady, yes?" His one good eye was far too intent upon the form of the femmepire queen.

"Yeah. And here as her investigator, to clear Lady Dumenyova's name." Saying the words reminded me that I was in Rome for more than just pasta. "How well did you know King Tomasso?"

"Fah." Sergei spat on the floor, heedless of the scandalized looks from nearby tables. "What sort of man does not like vodka?"

The correct answer was *a man smart enough to prefer rum*, but I didn't think Vasily's Monster was looking for my brand of insight.

"Well, if you remember anything off or different about the king over the last few months, I'd appreciate you letting me know."

Sergei's eye still hadn't left Lucia. Between the pirate and the Horny God, there were a few too many people obsessed with the former queen for my taste. All that attention might complicate matters if we did have to break Ana out and flee Rome.

"How is investigation going?" the pirate wanted to know.

"Not bad at all," I lied, conscious of the fact that at least four nearby tables could hear us. "These things always start a little slow, but I'm confident that justice will prevail in the end."

Aimon and Dulcinea had remained blessedly quiet through the entire first course, but the metrosexual manpire couldn't help interjecting. "From what I am told, there is a mountain of evidence proving Lady Dumenyova did it."

"You can't believe everything you hear," I replied with a lightness I didn't feel.

"So, they *don't* have video of her entering the king's retreat? And they *didn't* retrieve his signet ring from her possession?"

"Well…"

"That's what I thought." Aimon rolled his eyes. "You, your mistress, and the Stone Lady are headed for a date with the executioner."

"What is this?" For the first time, Sergei seemed concerned. Dude really did have a crush on Lucia. At least he wasn't creepy about it like the sex demon.

"In order to defend Ana—err, Lady Dumenyova, Lucia had to invoke her rights as Primus," I explained to the pirate. "Which means she shares her Secundus' fate. It's vampire law."

"Is stupid," growled Sergei. "In my homeland, we settle matter like men."

"By fighting?" I guessed.

"Or drinking. It depends on situation."

"I like your rules better," I decided. "They would certainly make my job easier." While I couldn't speak to her drinking prowess, I had yet to see the vampire who could stop Ana in a fight.

"Yes, the trappings of civilization are a truly terrible burden on the unjust," sniped Aimon.

"A *proper* Secundus would have simply ended her life days ago," added Dulcinea. "Instead, the Stone Lady has allowed her liege to be dragged down by her own inaction."

Sergei rumbled something in reply, but I wasn't listening.

"What do you mean?" I asked the femmepire, speaking right over a manpire that even other vampires called a monster. "About Lady Dumenyova, I mean?"

For the first time, Dulcinea deigned to look at me. She was beautiful, even with the derisive curl of her lip—maybe *because* of the derisive curve of her lip—but at that moment, I didn't care in the slightest.

"A Secundus exists to provide their liege plausible deniability."

"Yeah, I've heard the speech. But what did you mean—"

"If the Stone Lady had died before your mistress intervened, there would be no trial. The Winter Lady would bear no legal responsibility for her Secundus' actions. Your life, pitiful though it may be, would be spared."

"Is stupid," grumbled Sergei a second time.

"Is that common knowledge?" I wanted to know.

"Only to those of us with brains," said Dulcinea.

"Shit." I found myself on my feet without even deciding to stand. And then I was running for the door.

○○○

If anyone in that room had wanted to stop me, they could have. I was moving pretty fast for a twenty-seven-year-old, out-of-shape, beer-loving human, but that was still glacially slow to a near-immortal creature of the night. Or a demon. Or whatever those gray-skinned dudes had been.

So, the fact that I made it to the hall and then past our guard escort meant one of two things; either nobody had noticed me leave—which seemed spectacularly unlikely—or nobody had seen any reason to stop me.

Forty strides later, Lucia's anger roared across the bond at me like a meteor, telling me that the first possibility was a non-starter. I lost my balance in mid-stride, bounced off the wall, but kept going. For once, I had actually paid attention to our path on the way to the banquet hall, and I took the first three turns correctly on the way towards what I believed to be Ana's new tower prison.

The fourth turn… I'm pretty sure that's the one that got me lost.

I eventually found myself in an intersection of two halls, without a familiar landmark in sight. One of those halls was decorated with tapestries and statues, the other with portraits and potted plants. I had absolutely no idea which, if either, led to my destination.

Lucia's ire continued to swell in the back of my brain, until I could almost hear the queen's angry words, echoing down our bond.

I paused. Actually, I *could* hear her words. There was no way my imagination would have come up with some of the names she was calling me.

And that gave me an idea.

I closed my eyes, focused on that small knot of *other* that was my bond, and pushed words back.

Lucia.

Nothing.

At least nobody was around to see the faces I was making in mental concentration. I had it on good authority that I tended to look like a drooling moron.

Undeterred, I tried again.

Lucia.

Mr. Smith? Lucia's voice lost anger quickly. *How are you doing this?*

We know our bond is screwed up, I replied, a*nd that—between my gift and whatever the witches did—it goes both* ways. (Not unlike a certain femmepire detective I'd left back in San Diego, I thought to myself with a snicker.) *It seemed worth a try.*

Indeed. Lucia was silent—mentally, that is—for a long moment. *When I gave you instructions for how to behave in tonight's banquet, did I at any point suggest that it was permissible for you to depart before dinner was concluded? Come back to the hall* now *before your absence is—*

Lucia, I interrupted her in mid-mental-rant, *I need to reach Anastasia. Fast.*

Why?

One day, with tons of practice and mental voice lessons, I hoped I too would be able to squeeze that much irritation, frustration, and anger into a single syllable.

I didn't bother telling the queen about Dulcinea's comments, or that—to the best of my knowledge—Ana didn't know we were in Rome at all, let alone that Lucia had invoked the rite of Primus. I didn't point out that, of all the vampires I knew, Ana was the only one loyal enough to actually seek out death to ensure her liege's safety. I didn't even tell her that the soup had been epically awful.

All I cared about was reaching Ana in time to stop her.

Besides, mental conversation with the queen was every bit as annoying as the real thing.

I'll tell you later, I managed. *But it's important… and I'm lost.*

The bond was silent.

Lucia? I asked again.

Nothing.

Well, shit. I eyed the two halls and tried to figure out which direction I was facing, and where the Tower might be in relation to my present location.

Which was difficult, on account of being lost.

Lucia?!? Of all the times I had wished for the femmepire queen to stay out of my head, this was definitely not one of them.

Be silent, my thrall. I had a faint impression of movement… which couldn't have been my own, given that I was standing still in the intersection, a human statue in the middle of vastly better-looking figures of stone. A moment passed, and Lucia's voice sounded again in my head. *Where are you now?*

Uhm… in the palace? I frowned. *Can't you just use the bond to track me down?*

I may not depart until the banquet is finished, she told me, *however I may be able to guide you on your path. Provided that you give me a better idea of your current location than 'in the palace.'*

Right. I diligently described the two halls, calling upon my highly trained private investigator skills, but my hopes were fading quickly. It had been almost a century since Lucia's banishment. The chances of her recognizing a location from my mental description, let alone—

Very well, she told me. *Take the southward arm of the Sala dei Re down three intersections, then make a left. Then, look for…*

Hold up. I cut off the stream of directions. *The salad d'what?*

The Hall of Kings, you monolingual mongrel.

My next question was so obvious I didn't even have to voice it.

The hallway with the royal portraits. And the plants.

Right. The Saladuray. I nodded helpfully, even though she couldn't see me. *So, which way is southward?*

Yes, my cell phone had a compass app, like pretty much every smart phone in existence.

No, I didn't have my cell phone with me. The skinny pants the queen had forced on me barely provided sufficient breathing room for *a single* package, and I was kind of attached to the one I'd brought with me.

If you know what I mean.

ooo

Whatever else might be said about the femmepire queen—and I was pretty sure that, between Juliette and I, we'd said all of it—there was no denying that her sense of direction was impeccable, and her memory for places even better. I found myself sprinting down halls, cutting through empty chambers, and sprinting up other halls, directions being fed to me as fast as I could follow them.

Ten minutes later, I had followed Lucia's directions to a heavy wooden door, bound in iron, and guarded by two more of the seemingly endless palace Watch. Sadly, neither one was Niccolo, which meant our bromance would have to wait for a future time.

"If you guys are here, I'm guessing the prisoner transfer was completed. I need to see Anastasia Dumenyova immediately."

Neither vampire responded. On any other night, I might have helpfully explained that the whole silent-and-deadly-demeanor thing was almost as played out as wearing all black… but this once, I had better things to do. I stepped between them to open the door.

Moments later, I picked myself up off the ground, rubbing my ribs where something—a sledgehammer most likely—had struck me. The two manpires had closed ranks in front of the door, one of them now holding a machete at his side, while the other pointed a snub-nosed revolver in my direction.

"Uhm… I think we're having a language problem." I made large, sweeping gestures, pantomiming one of them opening the door so I could climb the Tower. "I'm John Smith. The official investigator. I need to get in to see Lady Dumenyova."

"Visiting hours are over, sir." The gun-wielding vampire spoke flawless English.

The number of times I'd been called sir by someone who wasn't a panhandler or telemarketer remained depressingly small, but I ignored the brief wave of pleasure that came from the manpire's show of respect.

"I know that," I lied. "But I need to make sure she is alright."

"Visiting hours are over."

He had dropped the sir. His gun, on the other hand, remained perfectly level. And pointed at my eye.

"You already said that." Knowing that I had zero chance of physically pushing past the two, I settled for raising my voice. "Ana, are you in there? Are you okay?"

No reply.

"Something is clearly wrong," I told the two guards in frustration. "As thrall to Queen Borghesi, I *must* verify that her Secundus has not come to harm on your watch."

"Visiting hours—"

My traitorous mind was feeding me mental images of Anastasia sprawled across a bed, bleeding from self-inflicted wounds. The woman I loved might be dead or dying, and these dickheads wanted to talk visitor's hours? "This is your last chance, dude. Move or I will move you."

Apparently, the second vampire spoke English sufficiently to understand my threat, but I paid no attention to the bastard's laughter. I was busy reaching into myself, through the bond, to the pool of Lucia's power.

The first time I'd used that power for anything sudden and violent, it had damn near killed me. Even now, turning two vampires into popsicles was still way, way past the levels of power I could handle safely, but I didn't care. I'd bring a blizzard into Hell before I let Ana die.

Not that I planned to actually go to Hell. Especially if everyone there was like Dog. But the point stood.

Lucia's power flooded into me like ice water in my soul. My body's temperature spiked in an attempt to combat the rising cold and sweat broke out on my forehead even as an arctic gale sprang up about us. The one manpire had stopped laughing, and was now watching frost crystallize on his machete, but the other's gaze remained fixed on my own, dark eyes starting to bleed into vampiric gold.

I closed my eyes, offered up a small prayer to any god that might be listening, and began to exhale.

"Stop!"

The word echoed, which didn't make a whole lot of sense even in the face of the micro-winter I was preparing to unleash.

It wasn't until Lucia repeated herself that I realized she had shouted into my mind at the same time as someone else spoke aloud. My grip on her power loosened, and just like that, the cold wind ceased.

I cracked open one eye and looked into the dark countenance of the Kingmaker.

Denarius had appeared from nowhere, wrapped in shadow, with that same night-black blade dripping darkness onto the palace's marble floor. Behind him, the two guards had lowered their weapons.

"Mr. Smith." For the first time since I had met him, Denarius appeared genuinely angry. "You have ten words to explain what you are doing here."

Trying not to be obvious about it, I counted the words.

"Ana may be in danger. I need to see her."

Boom. Ten words exactly.

"She is in the Tower, investigator. No harm will come to her there."

"I'm not so sure of that," I told him stubbornly. "She doesn't know Lucia and I are even here yet, does she?"

"She does not."

"Then there's every possibility that she'll do something stupid, like killing herself to preserve Lucia's innocence."

"I assure you, Mr. Smith; that cannot happen."

"Are you going to bet her life on that? *And* your niece's?"

Denarius was silent for long enough that I thought he might have fallen asleep. All the while, the scene in my head continued to worsen. Vampires had far less blood in their bodies than humans, but my imagination covered the entirety of her cell's floor with the stuff.

Finally, the elder manpire stirred. "You have one hour. Use it wisely, as it is replacing tomorrow's scheduled visit."

That seemed colossally unfair, but then… I *had* just come within a breath of unleashing winter in the palace. I nodded, trying to look properly repentant.

At the Kingmaker's gesture, one of the two manpire guards unlocked the door, and pushed it open, while the other spoke quietly into a comm unit. I slipped through and started up the spiral staircase. Thankfully, Denarius stayed behind. The last thing I wanted was that man at my back. Especially when he was pissed.

If Sergei's brother ever wanted to expand his kingdom, I was pretty sure the steps in the Tower would more than suffice as a duchy all on their own. I climbed for what seemed like an eternity, stopped at every third landing by another pair of guards and another closed door. They had all been instructed to let me pass, but I could feel their eyes as I walked past, like an itch—or a target—between my shoulder blades.

At the top was one final landing, with yet another pair of guards. Wordlessly, they unlocked the door.

I pushed past them and rushed inside.

CHAPTER 26

IN WHICH AN INTRUSION REVEALS THE
UNEXPECTED

I stopped short, not even noticing when the door closed behind me. Whatever I had expected a centuries-old, enchanted prison to be like, this wasn't it. Instead, it was… nice? Larger than the suite Lucia and I had been gifted, even. A massive, ornately carved table was set against the far wall, three chairs along its length. Bookshelves lined the other walls, and a couch, coffee table, and recliner completed the luxurious picture.

What I didn't see was the auburn-haired femmepire I loved. If she had already escaped, I would… well, I'd be happy for her, of course. And impressed. As usual. But it would make the next few days difficult for Lucia and me.

Before my mind could continue down that track, plotting byzantine schemes for how the queen and I would sneak out of the palace, meet up with Anastasia, flee Europe, and somehow keep the vampires of Italy from following us in search of vengeance, I noticed three things.

One; the room I stood in lacked a bed.

Two; there was a door to my left.

And three, and most importantly, the sound of running water was coming from that door.

My morbid visions of Ana bleeding out in bed were swiftly replaced with the equally grim picture of her motionless in a bathtub. But it didn't sound like the tub was overflowing yet, which meant I might still have time!

I burst into the bathroom, keenly trained investigative senses taking in the large square floor tiles, the wall-length mirror, the second door leading to a bedroom, the deep tub filling with hot water, and the elegant femmepire standing at the tub's edge. Very much alive and very much naked, save for a copper bangle on one ankle.

"Anastasia!"

She turned to me, hair sweeping over one shoulder like a wave, and I was treated to the very rare experience of seeing her surprised, eyes wide and mouth dropping open.

I crossed the space between us in two steps, wrapped my arms around her and dropped a kiss onto that lovely mouth.

Anastasia stayed frozen for a moment, stiff as a statue in my arms, and then her mouth warmed against mine, and she was returning the kiss with interest.

However long that kiss lasted—a minute, an hour, a year—it wasn't nearly long enough. Couldn't possibly have been long enough. As our lips parted, I leaned my forehead against the top of her head and held her even more tightly. The skin under my hands was cool and silky soft, a delicate exterior camouflaging the steel-coils of muscles just beneath.

"You're alive." I took what felt like my first full breath since leaving the banquet. Adrenaline drained out of me, leaving me giddy and slightly buzzed.

"Indeed I am." Wide jade eyes looked up at me through thick eyelashes. Eyes like Anastasia's just weren't supposed to exist outside of comic books.

"And… naked." My mind finally clued into the fact that I was holding the femmepire I loved in my arms, and she was completely, spectacularly nude.

"Your powers of observation do you credit, as ever." I could hear her smile, even if I couldn't see it, but it was gone by her next words. "But what are you *doing* here, John?"

For a moment, I thought she meant in the bathroom, for which the answer seemed obvious: I was holding the most beautiful—and naked!—woman in the world. Sadly, the tiny piece of my brain that was still functioning decided she probably meant in Rome.

"We're here to clear you of Tomasso's murder," I murmured into hair that shouldn't have smelled so sweet after several days in a dungeon.

"We?" I could feel her sag in my arms. "You and Lucia?"

"Yeah. She brought me in as her investigator."

"Meaning she invoked the right of Primus." Anastasia stepped out of my arms, pinching the bridge of her nose as if she were fighting the mother of all oncoming headaches. "And thus waived all legal protection in the matter. Fantastic."

"Given that her other option was letting you die, I'm going to have to side with Lucia," I said. "This one time."

"The entire point of a Secundus is that we are expendable."

"You're *not* expendable. Not to her, and not to me."

Anastasia lowered her head for a moment. When she looked back up at me, her large eyes were sad. "If Lucia is executed…"

"Yeah." I shrugged. "Either we all go home or none of us do."

The femmepire stepped back into my personal space—a welcome invasion, if ever there was one—and brushed her lips against mine. "You are utterly mad, Mr. Smith, and both you and my queen should have stayed in San Diego where you were safe."

"But?" This close, I couldn't resist stealing another kiss.

"But I am glad to see you, selfish though that thought might be." She stepped away a second time and nudged me in the direction of the door. "And if you are to defend me, then we have much to talk about. Give me a moment to put something on—"

"Do you have to?" Much like the kisses, the words bubbled out of me before I could stop them. Ironically, our closeness was actually limiting my view, but I'd gotten an eyeful when I rushed into the room. My memory was delighting in visions of toned muscle, long, strong legs, and the greatest ass the world had ever—

"I truly do." Anastasia took hold of my arms and spun me about. A second push between my shoulder blades sent me back towards the living room. "And then you can tell me how you gained entry to the Tower and why it was that you charged in to interrupt my evening bath."

"Right. That." My giddiness was already fading slightly, just enough for awkwardness to make its triumphant return. I started to scurry into the other room.

"John?"

"Yes?" I peeked back over one shoulder. Yes, she was still gloriously, fabulously, unashamedly nude. Somehow, she'd gotten even prettier in the last minute.

"I like the suit," she told me, and this time the smile in her voice was echoed by the upward curve of her soft, just-kissed lips.

Maybe these pants weren't all bad.

ooo

Anastasia emerged from the bathroom a few minutes later in a robe. And not the thigh-length, ultra-thin, kimono-style "robe" that late night cable television had trained me to expect; this was a plush white thing that completely covered her all the way down to the ankles. Her face was set in the all-too-familiar expressionless mask.

I held back a sigh and followed her to the table. Apparently, it was time for us to behave like responsible adults, not hormone-stricken teenagers.

"So, what was it that had you so worried about my health, Mr. Smith?" Ana had pulled her hair into a loose bun and was using what looked like a lacquered chopstick to keep it from unraveling. It was one of those weird tricks of physics that I'd never understood, but which women were clearly born knowing. "If you are to defend me, surely someone has explained the schedule for the proceedings? Executions will occur only after the trial."

"Someone said something at the banquet tonight, about Secundi committing suicide to keep their lieges from… well, doing exactly what Lucia just did." I shook my head. "It's kind of ludicrous, now that I think about it."

Anastasia was silent. Worryingly silent.

"It *is* ludicrous, right?"

"Tradition frequently is."

"That's not quite the reassurance I was hoping for."

"I have expected to die in service to the queen from the moment I was made Secundus, Mr. Smith. My life is unimportant."

"Not to me. Not ever."

When Ana spoke next, her words were soft. "And so, you stormed in here, thinking that I might already have taken my own life?"

"Pretty much." I shut my eyes against the succession of bloody images that made one last parade through my brain.

"If the opportunity for suicide had arisen while I was interred in prison, I might have taken it," she admitted. "But now that I have been relocated, opportunity alone is insufficient."

"What do you mean?"

"The spells woven into the very stone of the Tower prevent me from doing harm. Even to myself."

I was relieved to hear that, but… "That's kind of a weird enchantment to put on a prison, isn't it?"

"There are times when keeping a prisoner alive is far greater punishment than simple execution, Mr. Smith."

Given that we all potentially had a date with an executioner in just a few weeks, I knew she wasn't talking about herself. "You mean Tomasso's mother? Jehane, was it?"

"Indeed."

"But… didn't she die here?"

"She did, but not by her own hand. Or any hand at all for that matter. I believe she died of pneumonia."

That threw me for another loop. "I thought she was a femmepire?" Vampires didn't get sick. Well… not unless a coven of witches was sucking the vampire's energy through the link to their very gullible thrall, anyway.

"She was."

"Then how…?"

"The spells on this Tower do more than prevent suicide, Mr. Smith. They also prevent a vampire from calling upon their power."

"Their Talent, you mean?"

"Not just their Talent." She paused for a moment, a rare expression of frustration crossing her face as she thought about how to explain. "Every member of our species is born with some quantity of untapped energy within. Our first feeding gives us a channel to that energy, a channel which widens as we age. Our Talent, should we develop one, is accessed in that same way. Within the walls of this Tower, that channel is obstructed."

"You mean you're *human* in here?"

"Very nearly." Ana rose to her feet, wrapped both hands under the lip of the table and lifted. Several hundred pounds of table rose almost an inch off the ground… but *only* an inch, and the strain of doing even that much was evident on the femmepire's face. Given that she could normally bench press a car without even blinking, the difference was stark. "I have only what my species' natural physiology grants me."

"Shit." That was sufficiently bad news that I didn't even swoon over her science-y words. Instead, I rolled back one sleeve. "Have you tried fresh blood? If it worked to open the channel once…" Thanks to my stupid, potentially non-human gift, Ana's bite would probably hurt every bit as much as Lucia's hadn't but having the femmepire at one hundred percent was worth a little bit of pain. Or even a lot of it.

"I wish it were so simple. The channel has already been opened; further blood will be of no use other than sustenance. The only way to regain my power is to leave the Tower."

"Oh." I frowned thoughtfully. None of the Watch I'd passed on the way up had seemed any less deadly than usual. "Why aren't the guards affected?"

"Because none of them bear the prisoner's shackle." Anastasia nodded at the bangle I had seen earlier. Up close, I could see what appeared to be a spider web of blood, somewhere below the shining metal surface. "One prisoner, one prison, one shackle."

"And only one way to get it off?"

"Indeed. Removal requires the paired key."

Which was no doubt guarded by some kind of spirit dragon.

"Worse." It wasn't until Ana replied that I realized I'd voiced my thought. "The Kingmaker holds it."

"That guy again." I frowned. If Lucia's uncle hadn't personally prevented my murder twice in the past few days, he would really be starting to piss me off. "Well, he's waiting for me downstairs. Maybe if I ask really nicely…"

"Why is Denarius Borghesi here and not at the queen's welcome banquet?" Ana's eyes and voice sharpened in eerie synchrony. "And for that matter, how is it that you convinced him to grant you access to my cell?"

I winced. "That's… a bit of a story."

She waited expectantly, as motionless as the statue she could normally become, jade gaze intent upon my face.

"Actually," I decided, "maybe I should start at the beginning."

ooo

"I do wish you had not threatened the Crown Watch."

"In my defense, I kind of thought you were dying."

"I know. Your willingness to throw yourself into danger at the slightest provocation is at once both your most endearing and most frustrating quality." Anastasia shook her head. "But those guards—and by extension, the entire Crown Watch—now have some knowledge of your capabilities, and that is dangerous knowledge indeed."

It was my turn to shrug. "I don't think it's that big of a deal, especially since Lady Manassa already told the Council I wasn't human."

"She did *what?*"

"Did I not mention that?" Oops. I told her of the naga's declaration and the discussion that had followed. "Lucia thinks she's lying in the service of some inexplicable plot."

"Perhaps. The nagas' strategies can be as serpentine as the gods they worship. If she is not lying, however, it might explain your immunity to mind magic."

"If I wasn't human, wouldn't Zorana's blood scan way back when have shown it?" I managed to say the Blood Witch's name without whimpering. That seemed like progress.

"It should have," she admitted.

"So, unless it's some residual werewolf virus," I said, waving off the almost inevitable objection, "then the naga must have been lying."

"Perhaps." Anastasia drummed slender fingers on the table, her eyes distant.

I was happy to sit and watch her puzzle it through. Partly because I was tired, partly because I was lazy, and partly because Ana's mind was one of the sexiest things about her.

Which was kind of saying a lot.

Finally, she came back from wherever her thoughts had taken her. "You said you sprinted here?"

I nodded.

"The entire way?"

"Well, not quite. Like I said, I had to stop in the Saladuray to get directions."

"The Sala dei Re," she corrected.

I shrugged, not hearing any difference between her words and my own.

"But beyond that…"

"Yeah; I ran." I shrugged, slightly uncomfortable under the intensity of her gaze. "Like I said, I thought you were in danger. That's enough to get even me to exert myself. Why?"

"The banquet hall is slightly less than two miles away by the shortest route, which you did not take. And the Tower itself has two hundred and seventy-eight stairs."

The fact that she knew exactly how many stairs there were didn't surprise me in the slightest. But I still didn't get where she was going with this.

"And?"

"And you sprinted the entirety of that path, and then up those stairs after having drawn upon an unhealthy quantity of the queen's power—"

When she said it like that, I did kind of sound like a badass.

"—and were not even the slightest bit out of breath when you burst into the bathroom."

"Not until I saw you, anyway."

"Flattery is appreciated, Mr. Smith, but ultimately irrelevant to the matter at hand." Anastasia's eyes danced.

I frowned. I could remember sucking wind at various points during my day with Maria Elena and Lucia, but the race to the Tower *had* been fairly wheeze-free.

"Adrenaline can do crazy things to humans," I finally said. "Moms lift cars off their kids, and dads snatch baseballs out of the air, one-handed. I thought I was going to lose you."

That earned me the sort of smile that could brighten a continent. "Perhaps that is it," she acknowledged, "or perhaps the bond you share with Lucia is allowing you to draw upon more than just her Talent."

I blinked slowly, trying to digest that idea. A single question forced its way out of my brain.

"Are you saying I can dodge bullets?"

"That seems optimistic," she cautioned, "and my theory is as of yet unproven. As you said, this could merely be a matter of adrenaline."

"Or werewolf virus."

"John…" She looked up to find me grinning, and shook her head, unable to squelch an answering smile. "All I ask is that you *not* invite assault upon your person in order to test my hypothesis."

"I'll do my best, but…"

"But?"

"But a surprising number of people seem to want to hurt me at any given moment."

"It is one of your many, many gifts," she assured me.

CHAPTER 27

IN WHICH AN HOUR IS NOT ENOUGH

As nice as it would have been to flirt the night away, Denarius' promised hour was swiftly passing. We spent the next few minutes discussing the case itself, our words hopefully muffled from eavesdroppers by the water that continued to run in the bathroom.

"I definitely have my work cut out for me," I admitted. "But I'm not leaving until I've proven your innocence."

Technically, I *couldn't* leave unless I proved her innocence, but saying so would undercut the heroic boyfriend thing I was trying for.

"You have yet to ask."

"Ask… what?"

"Whether or not I did it."

I met her eyes and shrugged. "There was a lot of evidence."

"Enough to convince you of my guilt?"

"Just the opposite." I grinned again. "I don't doubt you could have killed Tomasso… and would have, if Lucia gave the word, but anyone who thinks you'd leave a trail of breadcrumbs behind in the process is a total moron."

"I am innocent because there is too *much* evidence?"

"Exactly. Either you're totally incompetent or someone went overboard trying to frame you. And you're *definitely* not incompetent."

Anastasia shook her head slowly. "I have missed you, John."

"Ditto."

"The evidence?" she finally prompted, when my silent appraisal had tiptoed across the invisible and poorly defined boundary between love-struck fanboy and creepy stalker.

"Right." I coughed, shifting uncomfortably in my skinny pants. "Well, the good news is that a lot of it is circumstantial."

"And the rest?"

"Is problematic." My tired brain protested loudly at being pressed into service yet again. "Assuming the hair Denarius has *is* yours, there's no guarantee that it was collected at the murder scene rather than during your capture." I looked curiously at Anastasia. "About that… did they really catch you napping?"

"They did." Where a less secure person would have sounded defensive, or maybe even irritated, Anastasia sounded… concerned. "And I would pay a great deal of money to learn how such a thing was possible."

"Even the People have to sleep," I told her, unconsciously parroting Denarius.

"True enough. However, I was taught to sleep lightly, and to wake at the slightest noise."

I raised an eyebrow.

"Part of my training as a Secundus. If a Watch member was ever able to sneak up on me while I was asleep, they were paid twenty-five florins, and I was given a week of confinement." She shrugged. "I learned quickly."

"That sounds horrible. How old were you?"

"Nine."

Maria Elena's revelation about how vampires calculated their age came back to me. "That's post-feeding, right?" Which would have made her… I tiredly did the math in my head. About thirty-four, in human years.

"No. It would be another sixteen years before I became an adult in our society."

"Jesus." I shook my head. "That's worse than horrible."

"It was extreme but effective. I have no regrets."

"When *I* was nine, I snuck a bottle of tequila out of my dad's liquor cabinet and passed out in my underwear on the front lawn." I coughed as what I'd just said sank in. "But… you know… learning to stop assassins is cool too."

"I am glad you think so." I could hear the laughter in her voice.

"All the same," I continued thoughtfully, "that training seems better suited for a bodyguard than for a Secundus."

"For the first century or so, the roles were largely the same. While Queen Lucia had a security team, they were ultimately loyal to her father, not her. I was the exception."

"That's a lot of responsibility for a nine-year-old."

"To be fair, I wasn't expected to do much more than slow an assassin until after my first feeding."

Because *that* made it better. "What changed?"

"King Aurelius gave his daughter permission to form her own Watch, and my services as personal security became superfluous. At the same time, the threats facing her began to grow in number and sophistication. As Secundus, it became my duty to remove those threats before they could be acted upon."

"Pre-emptive *policy implementations?*"

"You *have* been talking to Gaius, I see." Ana permitted herself a small smile. "But yes. While a security detail is the last line of defense, it is also the least efficient, as failure risks harm to the individual being protected. Far better to neutralize those threats before then."

"I guess that makes sense." I wasn't sure how to feel about it though. I vaguely recalled the U.S. government using similar language as a rationale for snooping on the nation's email. And for invading foreign countries for that matter. "It doesn't sound like much fun."

"Once, I might have disagreed with you. The travel… the thrill of violence… the careful execution of a plan…"

"And now?"

"Some things no longer hold my interest as they once did."

For a moment, she sounded even older than her years. If the past few years were any indication, my almost-girlfriend's body count might very easily extend into the thousands. Just thinking about that made me kind of queasy.

No… wait; that was the soup. I breathed out a sigh of relief and returned to the original subject.

"So then, as a professionally trained bodyguard, assassin, and spy, it's really unlikely that anyone should have been able to sneak up on you."

"Indeed."

"Is it possible that someone drugged you?"

"Anything is possible, but there are very few drugs that can affect a vampire's constitution," she reminded me. "Outside of these premises, at least."

"Maybe they had some sort of noise cancellation technology or something. Or a sleep spell potent enough to affect one of the People." Or any of a million other conceivable explanations. The riddle of Ana's capture was just one more mystery to add to the existing pile. Assuming *pile* was the correct word for something twice my height and liable to topple over and crush me at any moment. "I keep thinking that if we can figure out the *how*, we might get some sort of line on the *who*."

"The Kingmaker said the tip regarding my location came from an anonymous source?"

"Yeah. Even he seemed willing to admit that was kind of shady." I frowned. "If you *were* drugged somehow, whoever did so could have called in the tip and planted Tomasso's signet ring in your bag."

"They didn't plant the ring. I already had it on me."

I blinked. If I were to make a list of people I could potentially see as thieves, Anastasia would be near the bottom of that list, just above Gandhi and Mother Theresa.

"Tomasso sent it to Queen Lucia earlier this year," Ana explained, "as a sign of his willingness to work with her in finding Aurelius' true killer. I had intended to return it to him when we met."

"Except someone got to him first."

"Yes."

"Well, unless we can prove any of that…?" The femmepire's slow headshake dashed *that* hope. "Then it doesn't help much. But at least it's one less mystery to solve. Unfortunately, it still leaves the most problematic piece of evidence of all."

"The stone fragments."

"Yeah. There are so many issues there that I almost don't know where to start." I glanced over at the femmepire hopefully. "I don't suppose your Talent is a common one?"

"It is not. My father had it, although he could never manifest fully. There are two brothers in Kenya who showed signs of the Talent a decade or so ago. Beyond that…" The femmepire shook her head. "It is possible the Endless Empire has legions of Stonefists, but only their ambassadors are permitted beyond that land's borders."

That did raise a completely tangential question. "Do you know Ambassador Ti An?"

"Only by reputation." Ana's words were soft. "Tread lightly around that one, John. You do not want to attract her attention."

"Yeah."

Anastasia frowned. "Is there something you forgot to tell me?"

"Ti An may have tried to… uhm… rent me from Lucia."

Anastasia went perfectly still. "That would not be advisable."

"No kidding. For once, you, Lucia, and I are all on the same page. But I think it would be a good idea to prove your innocence and get the hell back to San Diego as quickly as possible, just in case."

"I concur." The femmepire drummed her slender fingers on the table's wooden surface. "To return to your original question, the number of individuals known to have my Talent is quite small. As one of the lesser Talents, it was not considered worth preserving, so none of the noble families bred it into their bloodlines."

Lesser Talents? Bloodlines? I was learning more about vampires in this single conversation than I had managed over two years of working with them.

"What about the brothers you mentioned? Could they have left those fragments behind?"

"Not for centuries, if then." Anastasia sounded almost embarrassed as she continued. "Until I took that form against the Hound, I did not know it was even possible."

"Have I ever told you how sexy overachievers are?"

"I do not believe you have."

"Then consider it said." My grin was short-lived. "If nobody else can do what you can, that only leaves two possibilities. First, we missed some fragments when we were gathering up the pieces of your arm—" I spared a glance for that arm, but it was successfully hidden behind a wall of fluffy fabric… and had long since healed, regardless. "—or they went straight to the source."

"The Bitter End."

"Yeah. Which doesn't seem likely. I can't see Lord Kala just letting someone leave his domain with a pocketful of souvenirs."

"Unless he is a part of this."

Now there was a thought to add to my nightmares. I shook my head. "I don't buy it. Dude has helped me on more than one occasion. And he and Bill are practically BFFs. Err, best friends forever," I clarified.

"I am familiar with the term."

Of course she was. As much time as we'd spent together, I still wasn't quite sure how well-versed Anastasia was in modern pop culture. I mean… *I'd* had to introduce her to In-N-Out!

"You are missing one vital question, Mr. Smith."

"I'm probably missing a dozen," I admitted. "Which one did you have in mind?"

"I have manifested in this form only once. How would our unknown enemy even know to use this stone? Why not something more common to Stonefists, like granite or marble?"

That was actually a pretty good point. Only a few people other than me had witnessed Ana's transformation: Juliette, Bill, Jee Sun, a few dozen ghosts, and the witches' coven. The coven had been wiped out and everyone else was either a friend or an ally, and therefore unlikely to intentionally spread Ana's secret.

Either Bill had gotten drunk again and spilled the beans—and given the fact that the demigod had trouble remembering events from hour to hour, let alone month to month, it seemed unlikely—or…

My tired brain had an epiphany.

"You know, the Horny God said the Hound of Tartarus is back demoning things up in their realm. I have to imagine your battle is the talk of the pit. Maybe Horny spread the story to Rome?"

Anastasia's lips quirked, but she somehow resisted the urge to praise my truly ingenious nickname for the incubus.

"The real murderer would still have had to travel to San Diego shortly afterwards," I continued, riding the brief surge of excitement that came with puzzle solving, "either to search the warehouse where we freed Graciela and her ghosts, or to mount their "Mission: Impossible" heist on Kala's domain."

I needed to put together a list of attendees here at court around that time. Whoever had mysteriously gone on sabbatical for a few days would get an express elevator ride to the very top of my suspect list.

Especially if their name was Denarius. Or Vigo.

"Not necessarily." Ana's response took the wind out of my sails. "If they did somehow acquire the stone from The Bitter End, they could have done so without ever leaving Rome."

"Say what now?"

"San Diego is not the sole city with a portal to Lord Kala's bar, Mr. Smith. Nor could it be, given how young your city is."

"Rome has a portal?"

"As do several of the major cities in Europe."

"Well, that makes thing more difficult. But also easier. I'll swing by the bar after I tour the murder scene and see if Kala has any insight into the matter." The demigod had been helpful in the past. Cryptic and scary as hell, but helpful. As a demigod of death and time, he seemed rather impressed by the carnage that seemed to follow in my wake. "I'll also get Lucia to check in with the Horny one to see if he is the reason the real killer heard your story."

This time, Anastasia did smile. "You do not like the incubus."

"Not a fan, no."

"Nor I. But he has been enamored of the queen for centuries."

"Yeah. And she seems to return the sentiment, in a purely physical, totally disturbing sort of way." I shivered. On an aesthetic level, that pairing was the sort of sight to give artists heart palpitations, but I found it kind of gross. "I can't believe the two of you snuck through the palace just so she could sleep with the dude."

For the third time in one night, Anastasia's eyes widened. Either I was getting good at reading her expressions, or my own horrible poker face was contagious. "How did…?" Realization set in. "You are still dreaming her memories?"

"Now that we're back in close quarters? Yeah. Much to our mutual displeasure."

A small smile made its way onto her face. "I remember that night well. We were almost caught multiple times, largely because of the queen's insistence upon wearing a white dress."

"Yeah. A symbol of purity, for a vampire princess sneaking out to have sex with a demon." I snickered.

"Precisely." Anastasia's eyes sparkled. "Had their liaison been discovered when Aurelius was still alive… the fallout would have been significant."

"I can imagine. Not that I *want* to imagine it. Or any of the rest of that night, really." God help me if my dream had started an hour or so later, while the femmepire and demon had been in the act. "What I can't figure out is why she would take a risk like that."

"We were both young, Mr. Smith, and the forbidden has a certain appeal. Given the councilor's notoriety, I believe my queen saw him as both a challenge and a conquest. No doubt, he felt the same about her."

"Did you and he ever…?" Halfway through the question, I wanted to kick myself. Was this *really* something I wanted to know?

"The Horned God keeps his gaze fixed upon the cream of our society, Mr. Smith. Neither my bloodline nor social standing met his standards."

"Then he's an idiot."

"Perhaps." Her voice was soft and contemplative. "It is just as well. In my first century, I might have been foolish enough to say yes."

And *there* was the mental image I hadn't wanted in my head.

"Well, he's an incubus," I reasoned awkwardly. "If I were even a little bit gay, I would totally…" I trailed off. Where had I been going with that thought, and why had it seemed like a good idea to voice it? "Anyway, he's pretty good-looking."

"Your species puts far too much stock in appearance."

"We do?" If she'd been human, I would have dismissed that pronouncement as exactly the sort of thing only a spectacularly gorgeous person would ever say. Those of us living on the *lower end* of the beauty scale faced constant reminders of how important physical attractiveness could be.

"The standards for beauty change almost as frequently as the seasons," she explained. "In my own lifetime, I have been considered too tall, too slender, too broad-shouldered, too dark-haired, too pale skinned…"

"Do we need to go back into the bathroom, so you can get a good look in the mirror? Because trust me… you're not too *anything*, unless it's amazing."

"I would like to someday meet this woman you have imagined into existence. She sounds admirable."

"More like awe-inspiring." I grinned again. "But surely you know that already."

"I know my worth." Her answering smile was wan. "I know also that I am not this perfect individual you have built up in your head."

"I never said you were perfect. Just… perfect for me. I'm sure you have tons of flaws, like…" For once, my tired brain completely failed me. "Well, I'm sure I'll think of one eventually."

"I cannot cook. Even a little bit."

"Why would you need to, with In-N-Out available?"

The look I received was halfway between affection and irritation. I raised my hands in defeat.

"Fine, you've got a crazy number of incredibly well-hidden flaws." I held one hand to my heart dramatically. "I will do my best not to feel too smugly superior."

Ana's laugh was as lovely as it was unexpected. "Somehow, I do not feel like I won this debate, Mr. Smith."

"Strange." I hadn't smiled this much in weeks. "You are right about one thing."

"Just one?"

I nodded solemnly. "You really *aren't* perfect." I waited for a long pause, and then continued. "If you were, you'd remember to call me John."

Jade eyes danced. "But who could say where such reckless familiarity might lead us?"

My brain fumbled in vain for a brilliant reply.

"Are you okay, John?" Anastasia leaned forward, all traces of mirth gone.

"Sorry." I manfully struggled back to the present. "You can't say stuff like that and not expect my brain to explode."

"I will take that as a compliment." She brushed her fingers, soft and cool, across the back of my hand in a lightning-swift caress. "Regardless, we have traveled far from my original point."

"That the Horny God's abs of steel are wildly overrated?"

"That all the beauty in the world does not compensate for ugliness of character." She looked me in the face, jade eyes suddenly solemn. "And a truly good person is beautiful regardless of their appearance."

"That's a cool way of looking at the world," I said, tossing out another grin to hide my sudden awkwardness. "But abs don't hurt either, am I right?"

○○○

"Anyway, vague threats and stripper outfit notwithstanding, the Horny One could be the closest thing we have to an ally, other than Gaius and the Lord of Bones."

Anastasia shook her head slowly. "Beware of demons, Mr. Smith, for they have many faces and a propensity for bloody betrayals."

I thought of the Hound of Tartarus and winced. "Point taken."

"Nor would I put a great deal of faith in the Lord of Bones," she continued. "Caine has ever played the long game."

"Lucia seemed pretty sure he was in our corner."

"My queen has a blind spot for the Council necromancer, as he is one of the few members of your gender who never treated her like an object to be acquired."

"So, we have a grand total of three allies in the court, but two of them aren't particularly trustworthy." Even I could tell that math sucked. "Are we sure about Gaius?"

"He is the one individual in this court that you can trust without reservation."

That was surprisingly definitive. Once again, jealousy raised its ugly head, and this time, it resisted my efforts to squash it back down.

"He trained you?"

"As a Secundus, yes. For multiple centuries." She smiled. "He taught me that what mattered was not birth or blood or even Talent, but will, dedication, and skill."

I didn't want to ask what their relationship had been like, but my traitorous mouth kept running. "Sounds like a swell guy…"

"Indeed. With my parents back in Romania, he became a surrogate father to me. Gaius' lessons have kept me alive all these years."

The envy snake slithered its way back into the dark, unpleasant regions of my subconscious. If Gaius was even indirectly responsible for

Anastasia's presence in my life, the dude was a freaking hero. When this was over, maybe he, Niccolo and I could all go out for beers.

"What's his Talent anyway? Laser eye beams?"

"He has no Talent." Ana read the confusion in my face and explained. "We do not all develop them, Mr. Smith. Nevertheless, I assure you that Gaius is one of the most capable individuals you will ever encounter."

From Ana, that meant a lot. Even so… "How does a guy with no Talent end up as the king's Secundus?"

"Through skill and dedication, as ever." Ana shrugged. "It is not as unusual as you might think. Talent runs most strongly in the noble Houses, and few Secundi come from noble blood."

"Because no aristocrat wants to spend their life in service to someone else?"

"Because a Secundus is expendable. Which is why," she reminded me, "you and my queen should have stayed in San Diego."

Ah yes. That again.

We spoke for a while longer, discussing the details of the case, and how I planned to spend the few weeks I'd been granted to mount a defense, but eventually even that conversation petered out. Afterward, we sat in comfortable silence, as the bath faucet continued its low, burbling roar.

"I should probably turn that off," I finally said, trained by years of San Diego drought. "Or put the stopper back in so you can have the bath I interrupted."

"Bide a little bit longer, please, Mr. Smith." Ana's voice was suddenly whisper quiet.

"Of course." I sank back into my seat. "What's up?"

Anastasia looked away, suddenly uncomfortable.

Uh oh.

"Is everything okay?" The look she gave me was both direct and eloquent enough for even my limited non-verbal skills to interpret. "Outside of the whole murder trial thing, I mean."

"Yes."

I was glad to hear it, because her sudden demeanor reminded me uncomfortably of when she'd first told me she didn't love me and that our relationship had no possibility of a future.

What an awesome breakfast that had been.

I still wasn't sure what had changed her mind, but the few outings we'd managed to squeeze in together, post-witch, had been some of the best evenings of my life.

If we were headed for a reprisal of *that* conversation...

"During my incarceration, I have had all too much time for introspection."

My heart dropped down into my feet with a dull, moist thud.

"Is this about... us?"

"It is. And about the feasibility of there being an us."

I was *not* going to play the *I'm here putting my life on the line to save yours* card, no matter how attractive it seemed as an option.

"I have enjoyed what little time we have spent together, in between your job and my own, but this is not a state that can be maintained indefinitely."

"I knew from the beginning that you had other responsibilities," I said. Even if Lucia had been taking the out-of-state Secundus missions to an all-time extreme, as of late.

"Be that as it may, it is not fair to you."

God save me from people trying to save me.

"What are you suggesting then?"

"It is less a suggestion than a question."

I frowned. This was new. "Ask away."

"Do you want something more?"

"With you?"

"Yes."

I still wasn't sure where she was going with this—it was already the weirdest breakup I'd ever endured, surpassing the ex who had spelled out a breakup note in barely cooked pasta—but my answer was quick and heartfelt. "I do. I'm sorry if that causes—"

"Then I—"

A loud knocking on the hallway door drowned out whatever it was that Anastasia had just said.

"Mr. Smith." Denarius' voice carried easily through the closed door and across the room to us. "Your hour is up."

"Got it. Just give me a second," I called back, turning to Ana. "I'm sorry… I didn't quite hear that."

"Now, investigator."

Holy mother of God, the Borghesis were a pushy bunch. "All I need is ONE FREAKING SECOND, dude!"

"You should go, John." Anastasia was already on her feet.

"Just finish your sentence," I pleaded. "Or I'm going to stay awake all night trying to guess what you wanted to say."

The door banged open, and Denarius was at my side in an instant, fingers wrapped around my arm like an iron manacle. Without a word—and without even pretending that it was an effort for him—he physically dragged me into the hallway.

Anastasia's voice followed us into the stairwell even though the femmepire herself could not. "Tell my queen that I seek her blessing."

I had no clue what those words meant, but Denarius missed a step. Only vampiric reflexes kept us both from tumbling down the remaining two-hundred-and-seventy-five stairs.

The door banged shut.

Goodbye, woman I loved.

Hello, sleepless night wondering what the hell was going on.

CHAPTER 28

IN WHICH A RING IS THE THING

The suite I shared with Lucia didn't have any imprisonment spells on it, but it felt as much like a cell as Ana's had. Part of that was the small cot I was stuck sleeping in. A larger part was the pair of vampires that Denarius had stationed outside my door with strict orders to keep me inside until morning.

I'd tried introducing myself to the guards, but they were pulling the old *we don't speak English* trick. Neither of them seemed to care that I'd missed dinner. Finally, I gave up and went into the bathroom to brush my teeth. Once I was minty fresh, I eyed the still-running faucet. Ana's usage of the bathtub to muffle our conversation was too clever a trick not to repeat. Especially with Lucia conveniently still away at the banquet.

I fished out the chain around my neck and the wedding ring that both Maria Elena and Sabina had thought so little of. That ring was every bit as small as the femmepires had noted, but its value far outstripped its appearance.

And not just to me.

"Valentina," I breathed as quietly as I could, "are you here?"

A woman coalesced next to me, dark, curly hair hanging like an unkempt curtain in front of her pale face. Her nightgown, pure white against the darkness of that hair, left only her hands and feet bare. Before she had even finished materializing, a spot of red appeared in the center of her chest. Within moments, blood had soaked through the front of her nightgown, running in rivulets down skinny bare legs. Just as quickly, the blood faded, leaving nightgown and woman unblemished once more.

That was the wound that had killed Valentina, decades before I was even born. I still didn't know the story of her murder or how she had come back as a ghost, but she was a power, even among the White Ladies of San Diego. Far more importantly, she was my friend.

She was also, to the best of my knowledge, the first of her kind to take a trans-Atlantic flight after death. And the reason one of the two Illutu attacking me had fallen over and died all on his own back at the airport.

"Are you okay?" One of Valentina's legs was hidden by the vanity she had materialized inside, and the fingers of her right hand were phasing in and out of the granite counter, but that was par for the course with ghosts. Far more worrying was the fact that I could see right through her to my own reflection in the mirror. The White Ladies could control their own visibility, of course, but Valentina usually appeared as a solid, if mostly intangible being, not this faded, translucent image of a woman.

She brushed hair out of her face long enough to offer a black-gummed smile, and then stuck her hand out in the air and wiggled it a bit.

"You're *sort of* okay?" I looked to the ring around my neck. In life, it had been Valentina's. In death, it served as her node, the tether that bound her to a particular location. For more than a year, it had been buried in front of my childhood home, making her the unseen fourth member of family Smith, but my parents' move to Austin had changed all of that. At Valentina's urging, I'd scrounged up an old chain from my white-suburban-pretend-rapper days, slid the ring onto it, and hung the whole ensemble around my neck.

In an odd sense, *I* had become her home.

Which made her current state all the more troubling.

"Is it the distance from San Diego?" I asked. Nothing I'd read suggested there was any risk in moving a ghost's node so far from the place of their demise, but it's not like there was a ton of literature on the subject, even in Anastasia's library. "Should I FedEx your node back?"

Valentina shook her head and hopped up to sit on the countertop. As she swung her legs back and forth, large portions of her lower body continued to pass in and out of the vanity. I'd yet to understand how a ghost could simultaneously be solid enough to be supported by furniture yet insubstantial enough to move through it.

"If it's not the distance," I pressed, "then what's wrong?"

She made a sweeping gesture with both hands.

"It's… where we are? Italy?"

Valentina wiggled one of her hands again, and then brought both hands slowly together, palms facing one another, until only an inch or so of space remained.

"Smaller than Italy," I translated. "Just Rome?"

Valentina shook her head again and brought her hands even closer together.

"Even smaller." I glanced around us. "You don't mean this bathroom, do you?"

I couldn't see them through all that hair, but I could *feel* Valentina's eyes rolling at me.

"The palace then," I decided. "Villa d'Borghesi."

Valentina pressed the index finger of one hand to the tip of her nose and pointed the other in my direction, in a gesture that charades players around the world would have recognized.

"Weird. Any idea what's causing it?"

She shrugged expressively, legs still swinging back and forth.

"Okay. Well, tell me if whatever it is gets any worse, okay?"

She looked away and shrugged.

"Please, V? I don't want anything to happen to you."

Valentina chewed on that request, her feet momentarily still. Then she hopped down from the counter to offer a picture-perfect salute, black-gummed smile belying the gesture's military precision. She darted forward, lips brushing my cheek in a brief contact of bone-chilling cold, and then faded through the wall and out of sight.

She liked to wander, especially during the night-time hours, but I had no doubt that Valentina would be at my side if and when I needed her. Anastasia's guards would never know how close they'd come to a catastrophic ending.

I still sucked at poker, but I was learning a hell of a lot about stacking the deck.

INTERLUDE

His fingers are liquid fire against my flesh, strong body bucking underneath me like a prized stallion. I plant one hand on his sculpted chest and roll my hips until he groans.

"Little Lucia," he murmurs, gazing up through impossibly long eyelashes, "you are every bit as sweet as I believed you would be."

He drives his own hips upward, and a moan slips out of me, making me grateful for the closed door and the presence of Asya, standing guard on the other side. She will let us know if anyone is coming.

That is what a Secundus is for, is it not?

I turn back to the Horned God, giving myself over to the pleasure pulsing through me. In unison, our motions begin to accelerate, his hard length—

Oh, HELL no.

—I don't know how I do it, but I am suddenly floating off to the side of Lucia's body, rather than sharing it with the queen. Unfortunately, that just gives me a courtside seat for the enthusiastic and… vigorous… sex taking place between two gorgeous people I really, really dislike. I don't have eyes to shut, or even hands to cover my ears with. Pornography is all well and good—I've been celibate for damn near six years, after all—but this is *totally* unacceptable.

Lucia's cries begin to peak a second time and I panic, imagining myself leaping away, hurtling down the bond and into my own brain.

The good news is that it works.

That is also the bad news.

ooo

"You have a visitor, pet," Zorana says brightly, rocking back and forth in her seat astride my abdomen, in a position that is even more disturbing for its twisted similarity to what I've just seen in Lucia's dream. "Won't this be fun?"

I frown at the Blood Witch's words. This didn't happen the first time, did it?

"Yes," the tiny femmepire decides, digging her fingertips more deeply into two of the many wounds she's made in my fleshy chest. Above and beyond her, my blood floats in the air, spinning like a zero-gravity sculpture. "We do like visitors."

Something shifts noisily in the darkness; something monstrous and reeking of death. I struggle against my bonds, succeeding only in grinding steel manacles deeper into torn skin.

The noise resolves into the staccato echo of heeled shoes. Atop a heartbeat that isn't mine, the sound of shallow breathing fills the cell.

Then she steps into the light.

She had once been attractive, if not quite beautiful; trim and fit and glowing with the self-confidence and resolve that came with middle age. Even now, she could be a yoga instructor or particularly well-adjusted soccer mom… if it weren't for the deep, bloody gash in her torso, where someone has driven a knife in and up to pierce her heart.

Someone.

"Mr. Smith," says Nepenthe, holding the bloody dagger pulled from her own body. "I believe this is yours."

I try to shrink back from the dead woman, but both my bonds and the Blood Witch atop me make escape impossible. Her expression serene—and maybe the tiniest bit friendly—Nepenthe kneels next to me, extends the bloody dagger, and begins carving runes into my arm.

At the sound of my screams, Zorana cackles and redoubles her own efforts. Blood fountains from my wounds like I'm an extra in a Tarantino flick, splashing down around us in an unceasing torrent. Scarlet waves rise like the ocean's tide, washing across my bare chest, funneling into my ears, and sweeping toward my open, screaming mouth.

"WHAT IS THIS MADNESS?"

Everything stops: Zorana's laughter, Nepenthe's dagger, even the rhythmic movement of the ocean of blood. The darkness splits wide to reveal Lucia as I last saw her in her own dream, a sheet twisted around her naked body. Arctic blue eyes are wide, revulsion and horror warring for primacy in her expression.

Those eyes pass over Zorana and Nepenthe, fall upon my face, and widen even further.

"Mr. Smith? What is the meaning of this?"

I try to speak, but the words refuse to come through a throat worn raw by screams. I blink tears from my eyes and shake my head.

She looks again at the bloody tableau of my dream and her face twists. Eyes like blue ice fill my vision, and a hand of golden fire touches my forehead.

"Sleep, my thrall. Sleep and do not dream."

Either our bond is stronger in the dream, or my gift is weaker. Either way, there is no resisting Lucia's command.

I close my eyes and the world disappears.

CHAPTER 29

I wiped a film of steam from the mirror and looked groggily at my reflection. Another lousy night of sleep had done my already dismal appearance no favors, but forty minutes of near-scalding shower had at least left me clean. I pulled on a fresh set of clothes—t-shirt, boxers, and fabulously loose jeans—and set my ear to the bathroom door. Twenty seconds of silence from the other room told me that Lucia was still asleep, despite all the noise I'd been making. Apparently, her childhood training had been a lot less hardcore than Anastasia's.

Lucia still being asleep was a-okay with me. Considering what I'd seen in her dream—not to mention what she had seen in mine—I wasn't ready to interact with the queen just yet. I needed food, space, and time to regain my equilibrium.

Moving like a ninja, I exited the bathroom… and ran smack into a pair of frosty blue eyes.

Well, shit.

Lucia was very much awake, seated on the side of her bed and wrapped in a robe just like the one Anastasia had worn the previous night. Even on the queen's vastly curvier frame, it remained a garment expressly designed to pacify libidos. Not that I needed its help. Between my dreams of torture porn and… well… *porn* porn, my libido was curled up in a ball somewhere in the recesses of my brain, refusing to come out until I offered it ironclad assurances that the coast was clear.

Clear of *what* was a question I hadn't answered yet.

"The bathroom's all yours."

Lucia said nothing.

I dumped my dirty clothes into the hamper, trying to ignore the sounds of my empty stomach reminding me yet again that I'd skipped most of dinner.

"Food will be delivered shortly." Lucia sounded almost as tired as I was. She still hadn't moved from her spot on the bed.

"You're not getting sick again, are you?"

"Have you made another fool's bargain with a witch coven?"

I coughed. "Not this year."

"Then I am not sick."

Clearly, we had *both* woken up on the wrong side of bed. Or in my case, cot. I flopped into one of the chairs at the small table, determined to stay safely silent until breakfast had arrived.

My resolution lasted almost fifteen seconds.

"They're bringing bacon, right? And eggs?" After the banquet's so-called soup, I was no longer taking anything for granted.

"Bacon will be the least of your worries, Mr. Smith, if you do not provide me with an explanation for your behavior last night."

I winced. "Like I told you, I don't have any control over when I dream my way into your head. If I did, I damn sure wouldn't have picked *that* memory. Trust me, I have *never* wanted to know what it feels like to—"

"We will discuss our dreams in a moment," Lucia said, blessedly interrupting whatever the hell I'd been about to say. "I was speaking of your departure from the banquet."

Oh. That. I glanced from the queen to the hallway door and lowered my voice. "Are you sure you want to talk about it here?"

"I have little doubt that the Watch listening outside our door have already been briefed on your idiotic flight through the palace."

"Maybe so, but that's no reason to be sloppy about it." I made a second trip to the bathroom. In moments, the sound of splashing water was doing its best to cover our voices. "Now then… what did you want to talk about?"

"Why you took it upon yourself to leave the banquet, run halfway across the palace, and attempt to force your way past the Crown Watch."

"I already told you: I thought Ana was in danger."

"Astonishingly enough, I am well capable of remembering as far back as last night. I also remember that your explanation was sorely lacking in detail. The time for explanations is upon us."

And so, for the third time in ten or so hours, I explained the circumstances behind my cross-palace sprint.

ooo

"As it turned out, she was fine," I concluded. "Apparently, the enchantments binding her there don't allow stuff like suicide."

"As I would have told you, had you bothered to ask." Lucia shook her head. "The Tower housed Tomasso's mother for the final decades of her traitorous life. My father had no intention of giving her so easy an escape as suicide."

Aurelius sounded like he'd been an enormous asshole. "Maybe he should have enchanted it to prevent pneumonia as well?"

"Perhaps. Although such an ignoble death is a punishment all its own."

"You know, it would have been nice to know ahead of time that you and Tomasso were half-siblings."

"Does it have any bearing on the case?"

"Maybe?"

Lucia rolled her eyes. "My family tree was clearly outlined in the briefing you elected not to read. From a legal standpoint, however, it had little importance. We were both children of Aurelius, and thus eligible for the throne."

"And your mothers were… what, exactly?"

"Irrelevant."

"That's a pretty cold thing to say about your own mom."

"Why should I feel anything for a woman I never met?"

The obvious response was *because she carried you in her womb for nine months.* Unfortunately, I didn't know much about vampire pregnancies. Maybe they only lasted two months. Or maybe vampires didn't even have wombs. Maybe their babies hatched from eggs or were delivered by vampire storks.

And honestly, maybe a dude with two alive and awesome parents didn't have any grounds for telling Lucia how she should feel about her own.

"So, mothers don't count in vampire culture?" I asked. "What if *you* had children?"

"Unlike my father's dead consorts, I am of his bloodline. My children would also be of that bloodline and therefore rightfully considered princes or princesses."

"And the dude who got you pregnant?"

"Would occupy whatever role I granted him. It is a moot point, however."

"Because nobody wants to sleep with you anymore?"

"I beg your pardon?"

"On account of you not being queen," I explained.

Rage leapt across the bond. "I am, and will always be, the true queen of this land."

"Then why is it a moot point?" And even more importantly, when was our breakfast getting here?

"I am nearing the end of my potential childbearing years."

I frowned. "The People can live to like a thousand! By that scale, you're barely middle-aged."

"As I have said a truly wearying number of times, we are not human. On a superficial level, our biology may be similar, but below that surface, the differences are stark."

"Meaning what? Vampire menopause hits early?"

"For a woman of the People, fertility is a fleeting thing. Three centuries, maybe four. A scant few have borne children even later in their lives, but those children rarely survive to adulthood."

"But wasn't your dad like four or five hundred—"

"Our men remain potent until the point of death." Lucia's voice was cold and indifferent, but the bond told me of some other emotion swimming just beneath the surface. "Nature is, as they say, a vengeful bitch."

I couldn't remember anyone saying that, but Lucia had traveled a hell of a lot more than me. "It does seem unfair."

"The world is as it is, Mr. Smith."

That phrase sure came up a lot these days.

"But enough about matters that do not concern you," continued the queen. "Let us instead discuss the mess you left behind in your ill-conceived flight to save my Secundus from a night of peace and solitude."

"What mess? If you mean the business with Sergei and the Sultaness of Scarves, don't worry about it."

"I mean the—" the femmepire began heatedly, only to fall into silence. A deep line appeared between her perfect eyebrows. *What business?*

"Like I said, don't worry about it."

For a moment, it seemed like Lucia would keep digging for details, but she finally shook her head and pressed on. "The mess I was referring to is the political disaster of our appointed investigator disappearing before he could be introduced to the assembled nobility."

"If they didn't want me leaving, they shouldn't have parked me by the door. Besides, you can't honestly think any of them were all that enthused about meeting a mere human."

Without even the decency of a motion blur effect, Lucia was next to the table, hand hot around my throat as she loomed over me. "I will explain this one last time. Our survival requires a great quantity of political capital. Such capital is difficult to come by in the best of times, let alone when operating from a position as weak as ours. And your actions last night demonstrated a level of disrespect that thoroughly undercuts whatever limited authority my lineage affords me!"

By the end of her rant, she was almost yelling.

Even with the running water, the vampires outside our door had to be getting an earful.

I tried to rise to my feet, but Lucia's other hand kept me pinned me to the chair.

"Look," I growled up at her from my position of vertical disadvantage, "we've already established that you can't kill me until after the trial is over—not that your last attempt went so well anyway—so I'm not sure what physically threatening me is supposed to accomplish. Unless you're just enjoying being taller than someone for once?"

Murder flashed across Lucia's face like the headlights of a passing car. It said something that I was able to recognize the emotion so easily.

Mostly, it said I had poorly developed survival instincts.

The queen closed her eyes, released my shoulder, and breathed out slowly, her breath annoyingly minty and fresh despite the fact only one of us had made it into the bathroom that morning. "Mr. Smith, at future functions, I would greatly appreciate it if you spoke with me before electing to depart."

I goggled up at her. "*What?*" I finally managed.

"I would greatly…" she began, a hard light appearing in her large crystal eyes.

"No, I heard you. I just wasn't—"

"If we are to survive my homecoming, Mr. Smith, one of us must behave like an adult. As you seem incapable of doing so, I will assume that role." A rare burst of humor leaked across the bond. "Though it is not one I am accustomed to either."

"Right." As odd as Rome had already been, nothing could have prepared me for *Lucia* suddenly being almost reasonable. And cracking half-decent jokes. "For what it's worth, I'm sorry if me leaving caused any issues last night. I don't always think clearly where Ana is involved."

"Far too frequently, you have a similar effect upon her," said the queen. "When this farce of a trial is over, I will hire a shaman to examine you both for curses."

"Hilarious. If there's something I can do to help smooth things over with the Council—"

"I will let you know. For now, you should focus your attention upon the investigation." She paused, and another flash of unidentifiable emotion filtered across the bond.

"What's up?"

Lucia took her seat on the other side of our small table, her pale eyes strangely free of contempt or rage. "As you mentioned earlier, there remains the matter of last night's dream walking."

"Like I said, I wasn't trying to spy on you and—"

"I am not speaking of *that*, Mr. Smith." Lucia's shrug was almost lost within the folds of her heavy robe. "I am a woman of healthy appetites. That truth does not shame me. What do I care if you should bear witness to it?"

I frowned. It had sure bothered the hell out of me.

"It is your dream that I am more concerned by," she continued. "The one that you somehow pulled me into."

"Well, we know the bond goes both ways… I guess we should have realized the dream thing could too."

"Clearly," said Lucia. "Yet I am more interested in the *content* of your dream."

"Oh." I tried and failed to hide my flinch.

"That was not a nightmare, was it?" She read the answer on my face, and her voice actually softened, like frost melting slightly in the morning sun. "How much of what I saw happened?"

"The Nepenthe part was new," I admitted. "I guess my subconscious mind thinks I should have found a way to stop the witches without—"

"By killing her, you prevented greater catastrophe and saved your own life."

I shrugged. I'd told myself the same thing on multiple occasions, but it hadn't done a damn thing for my conscience.

"And the rest of the scene? With Zorana?"

"That part was pretty accurate." I'd healed astonishingly quickly, probably as an unexpected side effect of the witches pulling Lucia's power through me, but a few scars stubbornly remained.

An awkward silence fell between us.

"I knew that Zorana had questioned you after my fall," said Lucia finally, "but what I saw last night was not…"

"It started with questions. By the end…" I closed my eyes against the sudden image of the little Blood Witch's gleeful smile. "I was lucky that Anastasia got me away."

"So it seems." Another awkward silence was interrupted by the queen reaching across the table to take my hand in hers. As always, her skin was soft as silk and overly warm to the touch. "I apologize for the pain you suffered at Zorana's hands, Mr. Smith. Despite your rampant insubordination, you did not deserve that. Were it within my power, I would see the Blood Witch punished for her actions."

I… didn't know how to respond to that. Especially since I was the primary reason it *wasn't* within her power to do so. I shook my head. "Zorana is broken. That's not entirely on you."

"Be that as it may." To our mutual relief, Lucia released my hand, but her gaze remained fixed upon mine. "Within your dreams, if nowhere else, our bond appears to work as intended."

Meaning she had power over me there that she lacked in the waking world. I nodded, having also noticed that unfortunate truth.

"Then I will visit your dreams each night and ensure that your sleep is free of nightmares."

I didn't like the idea of the queen in my head any more than she already was, but I'd been dealing with this particular nightmare for far too long. A full night of peaceful sleep sounded kind of like a miracle.

"I would appreciate that," I said honestly. "Thank you."

"You are of little use to us asleep on your feet," she explained briskly, "and I have no intention of dying in Rome."

ooo

As I polished off my third plate of breakfast, finally filling the painful void in my stomach, I filled Lucia in on the relevant parts of my meeting with Anastasia. "She wasn't very happy that we came to Rome to rescue her."

"If she truly believed I would stand by and let her die…" Lucia shook her head. "I will discuss the matter further with her today."

"They're still letting us meet with Ana?"

"Not us. Me." The queen waved a hand dismissively. "Your visitation privileges will be restored tomorrow."

"Oh." Any irritation I might feel over that fact was completely wiped away by the memory of Anastasia's body against my own. *So, so worth it.* "You know, Denarius is supposed to be sending over copies of all the autopsy and crime scene reports today."

"Yes. I was in the room when he told you so," Lucia reminded me, a hint of ice finally creeping back into her voice.

"Right. Could you take them to Ana when you go see her?"

"Shouldn't you be reviewing the reports yourself?"

"I already have a full day scheduled, between the rest of the interviews Denarius set up and my trip into Rome to see the crime scene. Also…"

"Yes?"

"I didn't understand half the words I read in the autopsy. I'm not a forensic scientist."

"Nor is Lady Dumenyova."

"No, but she's a hell of a lot smarter than me. And *her* job kind of makes her an expert on the subject matter." I shrugged. "If anyone is going to find something of value in those reports, it's her."

"As you say. I will take her the autopsy findings. However, you should bring the crime scene report with you into Rome."

"Right. To match the report's findings against the scene itself." I nodded slowly. That made sense.

Lucia and I had not only just gone thirty or so minutes without trying to murder each other, the queen had also apologized *and* offered to help stop my nightmares. And now she was making intelligent, helpful suggestions?

This was officially the weirdest morning ever.

"Did Lady Dumenyova have any insights into the matter of my brother's murder?"

"Not really," I admitted. "When Denarius gives someone an hour, he seriously means *one* hour." I frowned as I remembered being dragged down the stairs by the overly tall elder. "Although she did want me to pass on a message to you."

"And you waited this long to—" With a visible effort, she caught herself, smoothing her tone. "What was the message?"

I shrugged. "Just that she wanted your blessing."

The femmepire stiffened. "She *what?*"

"Said she wanted your blessing," I repeated.

"Why now? And with—?" Icy blue eyes widened, and the blood drained from her face. "I will see you dead before I allow that to happen, Mr. Smith."

"Wait… what?"

The hallway door slamming shut behind the departing queen was my only reply.

I was still seated at the table, eyeing what was left of breakfast on the queen's side of our tiny table, when the door swung back open. Lucia marched in, chin high and back stiff, all that regal dignity spoiled somewhat by the fact that she was still in her bath robe.

"Nothing like giving the Watch a show, huh?"

Cold eyes zeroed in on me like precision snipers, but the queen stayed silent as she marched to the closet and pulled out an outfit. Moments later, the bathroom door slammed shut, and the noise of the still-running sink faucet was drowned out by the much louder sound of the shower's six cleverly placed nozzles.

I shook my head. Having Lucia pissed off at me was an almost comforting return to normality… but I still wished I knew what the hell had caused it.

CHAPTER 30

IN WHICH THERE'S NO I IN MYSTERY

For the third time in the past hour, I rolled my neck, feeling the small bones of my neck crack and grind against one another. "This must be what having a real job feels like."

"What's that?" Maria Elena glanced up from her phone.

"Longest. Morning. Ever."

"It's still better than weapons practice." The young femmepire beamed, as cheerful as when she'd first showed up at my suite to take me for more interviews. Between the bright yellow sundress and her own curls, it had been like opening my door onto an unexpectedly sunny day.

After three hours of annoying, tedious, and—worst of all—fruitless interviews, that unrelenting perkiness was inching its way from cute to borderline annoying. Even so, when she flashed her dimples in my direction, I couldn't help but return the smile.

"Alright, who's next?"

Maria Elena checked her phone and shrugged. "I think we've actually talked to all of the king's staff and servants now."

"But they were all human."

"Right."

I eyed the femmepire, but she didn't seem to have grasped my unspoken question. "Tomasso didn't have any vampire staff?"

"Well, he had councilors," she admitted, "and the Crown Watch, of course."

"Exactly."

Her eyes—green today, to contrast, rather than match, her sundress—were wide and confused.

"So why haven't we interviewed any of them yet?" I elaborated.

"That's a good question!" Maria Elena checked her phone a second time. "It looks like Lord Borghesi has arranged for those interviews to start tomorrow." The sudden frown looked out of place on her sunny face. "They all speak English, so I guess you won't need me as a translator."

"That's where you're wrong. As a stranger in a strange land, I don't want to *ever* be without my translator."

"Are you sure?" A smile started to peek through again.

"Where I come from," I told her nobly, "no gentleman would condemn a woman to the horrible tedium of weapons practice."

"California sounds positively amazing!"

"Besides, I do still need a guide."

"From what I hear, you found your way just fine last night." Her indignant look was ruined by the still-present dimples. *"After* ditching me at the banquet!"

"Yeah… sorry about that."

Maria Elena shrugged. "I get it; you were worried about your serial killer love. In a weird way, it's super romantic."

Technically, Ana was a mass murderer, not a serial killer, but that didn't seem like a battle worth fighting.

"Besides," she continued, "since you were gone, I got to have your dessert."

My stomach rumbled loudly, reminding me that breakfast, as refreshingly non-weird as it had been, was now many hours in the past. "Speaking of food, if we're all done with our interviews, should we go find some lunch?"

"We could, but…"

"But?"

"But you wanted to meet with Sabina. And she'll be returning to her chambers right around now. We could maybe see if she wants to talk to you?"

I wasn't looking forward to seeing the young princess again—even before factoring in how Lucia had pissed her off at the banquet—but beggars couldn't be choosers, and neither could private investigators.

I sighed. "Good call. Let's go chat with the princess."

ooo

Weapons practice had apparently gone long, as we ran into the princess on the way to her suite. At least, I assumed it was her, given the escort of Crown Watch and minotaur. The woman herself was completely unrecognizable beneath several layers of dirt and mud.

The anonymous mud-girl certainly *acted* like Sabina. Upon seeing me, she pointed her nose up in their air, squared her shoulders, and marched on past us like we didn't even exist. I stopped Maria Elena before she could follow.

"Maybe we should let her go on ahead first?" I suggested. "It looks like today's training was even more disastrous than yesterday's."

Unfortunately, Sabina chose that moment to stop pretending she couldn't hear us, spinning on one sneaker-clad foot, and driving a muddy index finger into my chest. She might not have had her first feeding yet, but I was pretty sure that poke was still going to leave a bruise.

"Stop acting like this is a joke, you asshole!"

I took a half step back, mindful of the princess' many armed protectors. "I was trying to be *nice*. I figured you'd want to clean up before we talk."

"Oh."

"I meant what I said last night," I continued, trying not to make eye contact with the hairy, horned beast looming behind her in the hall. "I really am sorry for your loss. If it had been my father, I would be a total wreck."

"*My* father," she snapped at me, "was the king of the Italian courts. He had centuries of life left to him. Your father is a common human—no doubt a garbage man or construction worker—with at most decades left on this earth. *How dare you equate the two?*"

I reminded myself that she'd had a rough week, but sympathy was rapidly slipping away.

"First of all," I said, "my dad is an accountant. Not that there's anything wrong with construction workers *or* sanitation engineers."

"Accounting is," she surprised me by saying, "a surprisingly respectable profession."

Nothing about the princess' expression suggested she was mocking me. God, vampires were weird.

"Second," I finally added, "my dad being human doesn't change the fact that I love him, and I don't think your dad being king did either. I'm not equating the two, or trying to say I know how you feel… I'm just offering my condolences."

"Fine. Whatever." Sabina spun away, sending mud in all directions, and resumed her march. After a dozen steps, she glanced back over one shoulder. "Are you two coming or what? I badly need a shower and refuse to converse in this hallway like some sort of beggar."

If Dale, the homeless man who lived outside my agency's office, had been there, he might have had a few things to tell the vampire princess about *beggars*. And aliens. And lizard communists. But Dale was back in San Diego, in the city I found myself suddenly homesick for, so I just nodded and followed behind.

ooo

The suite the femmepire led us to was every bit as large as Dog's, but the luxurious furnishings were largely hidden under a veneer of teenage decor.

"Beton?" I asked Maria Elena quietly, nodding to one large poster of shirtless, olive-skinned men all doing their best to out-smolder each other.

"That's them," she agreed. "Yum."

I scowled. They weren't *that* good-looking.

"I'm going to wash this mess off and have yet another outfit burned," announced Sabina. "Wait here. Make sure he doesn't break anything, 'Lena."

She vanished into a neighboring room before I could reply. A few seconds later, the sound of running water could be heard.

"She does know I'm an adult human and not a hyperactive Chihuahua, right?" I dropped onto a massive, overstuffed couch upholstered in a truly ludicrous shade of red velvet.

"Outside of servants, Sabina hasn't had much contact with your species." Maria Elena perched elegantly on the other end of the sofa, her yellow sundress clashing horribly with the furniture.

"And you have?"

"I'm almost three years older," she pointed out. "In the long run, that doesn't mean much, but at our age—"

"It's the difference between a teenager and a fully blooded adult. Which is significant."

"Exactly." Maria Elena beamed approvingly at me. "You're very quick. I can see why your mistress brought you to Rome!"

The reference to Lucia stole some of the shine from her compliment, but I nodded my thanks anyway. Praise came way too infrequently for me to be picky about it.

"I'm guessing Sabina being royalty doesn't help either."

"How so?"

"Well, her father probably wanted to keep her sheltered and under control," I reasoned, thinking of the few dreams I'd had of Lucia's own childhood, "which would lessen the chances of her spending time with my kind."

"Oh… not so much." The femmepire shook her head. "We've been partying in Rome for years now! But human men can be pests, so we always go glamoured. And with a healthy Watch contingent."

"Including Niccolo?"

"The man dances like a dream," she confirmed brightly. "Anyway, outside of drunk, sweaty club-goers, Sabina hasn't spent a whole lot of time with your species."

"That explains a lot." To the vast shock of literally everyone who met me, I liked to dance, but I still avoided the San Diego club scene as much as possible. Too many drunk Marines, too few unattached women. Being one of those unattached women had to be even worse.

○○○

Half an hour later, Sabina reappeared, fresh-faced and mud free, her workout gear swapped out for a beaded white blouse and layered blue skirt. She took a careful seat on the edge of one of the overstuffed chairs opposite my couch, back ramrod stiff. After a long moment of uncomfortable silence, she shot me a displeased glare.

"It's almost lunchtime. Ask your questions or go away."

"Right." I took a moment to consider how I should begin. My dry run with Dog had exposed a handful of flaws in my YouTube-given interrogation techniques, and the last thing I needed to do was piss the princess off even further. Tarn was standing guard in Sabina's foyer, but I was pretty sure a sharply worded command would have him here in seconds… and Gaius wasn't around to save me this time.

"How close were you to your father?" I finally asked.

"How is that *any* of your business?"

"Sabina…" Maria Elena's voice was soft, but she shook her head at the princess from across the room. "You agreed to cooperate, remember?"

"It's fine," I assured both femmepires, bravely falling on the conversational grenade. "I should have been more specific. As a king, he must have been busy a lot of the time. Did you see him much over the past few weeks?"

"Of course. I *am* his only daughter."

"Right. So, did he seem… worried? Or stressed?"

"Of course not," she informed me tightly. "We Borghesis are made of sterner stuff than—"

I waited for Sabina to finish, but she had fallen quiet.

"You just thought of something?"

"Now that you mention it," she admitted, "he did seem distracted. But not just for the past few weeks."

"Can you recall when you first noticed his distraction?"

Sabina rattled off a stream of Italian, and Maria Elena responded in kind, after a moment of brow-wrinkling thought.

"It was after New Year's," the princess finally said. "At first, I thought he was just upset that I'd gotten drunk in public again, but it never went away."

"Huh. That actually fits."

"With what?" The two femmepires asked in unison.

"With… an alternate theory I'm working on," I hedged, not quite ready to spill the beans about Lucia's recent transatlantic communications with Tomasso.

Sabina's lovely mouth turned downward. "A theory you don't want to share with us."

"If I find further evidence to support it, you'll be one of the first to know. But right now, it really *is* just a theory."

She drummed her fingers on the arm of her easy chair before finally giving a stiff nod that was clearly as much a product of genetics as training.

"Did you ever ask him about it? Why he was distracted?"

"Once or twice, sure. But he just said it was nothing." She shrugged. "Papa didn't like to bring his work home with him. He said he'd seen how that sort of thing could ruin a childhood."

I blinked slowly. Tomasso's parenting techniques were night and day from what I knew of Aurelius'. I'd spent so much time thinking of Lucia's brother as a faceless, shadowy figure bent on destroying us all that the revelation that he might have been a decent father was difficult to accept. Unfortunately, it also did nothing to help my case. "Can you think of someone he might have confided in?"

"Uncle Denarius, maybe? Have you already talked to Gaius?"

"Yeah, after weapons practice yesterday." I shrugged. "Nice enough guy, but I got the feeling his relationship with Tomasso was all business."

"That's true. He was my father's Secundus, not his friend."

"Someone can't be both?"

I received a teenage look of utter scorn. "It defeats the whole purpose of a Secundus if friendship makes you value them too greatly. One of the many reasons 'Lena won't be mine."

"Plus, I suck at fighting," agreed Maria Elena cheerily.

"So, you're okay with Gaius taking the position?"

"Why wouldn't I be? Because he's stodgy and old? Papa didn't care for him either, but Gaius' support was instrumental in his ascension to the throne following your mistress' banishment."

"Gotcha. So, King Tomasso was distracted or worried for the last few months, but nobody is certain why."

"Maybe he'd received word that your stone-hearted lady love was coming to kill him."

I shook my head. "If he thought his life was in danger from Ana—or anyone else—he would have stepped up his security instead of heading off to make himself a target in his townhouse in Rome."

"Are you saying my father *deserved* to be murdered? Do they believe in blaming the victim back in San Francisco?"

"San Diego," I corrected her, "but that's not what I meant."

"King Tomasso didn't increase security, so he must not have thought he was in danger," reasoned Maria Elena.

"Bingo."

"Then what does it have to do with his murder?" demanded Sabina.

Once again, I opted not to share what little knowledge I had of the situation. It wasn't that I distrusted Sabina, but—

Actually, that was *exactly* it. Anything I told her might make its way to the ears of the real killer, ending my investigation before it even began.

"I'm trying to build a picture of the events leading up that day," I told the irritated princess instead. "The more complete the picture is, the easier it will be to identify whatever pieces don't fit."

"That's… not entirely stupid," she allowed. "Is that all you wanted to know?"

"Almost," I promised. "Did you see your father last Wednesday? Before he…"

"Was killed?" Sabina shook her head, eyes shimmering. "Papa liked to focus on business in the morning hours. By the time I finished lunch, he had already left the palace."

"Heading to Rome?"

The princess shrugged. "I would assume so, given that's where he was found. He sometimes went into the city to get away from all of this, or when he needed to think, or when he…" Olive cheeks flooded with color.

"When he…?"

"You know."

I really didn't, as my confused stare no doubt made clear.

"That's where he went for casual sex—" said Maria Elena.

"'Lena!" Sabina's voice cracked like a whip.

"What? It's not a big deal!" exclaimed the other femmepire.

"Inner-city booty calls… got it." Nothing like having a love den in the middle of Rome.

"Yes, *that*. Now, are we done?" Sabina demanded, turning her sharp gaze on me instead of her clueless friend.

"Just one more question. Why do you think your father needed to get away from all of *this*…?" I waved at the luxury surrounding us.

"Ruling a kingdom isn't as fun as it looks, human. When I was younger, Papa would take me on field trips whenever he needed to get away. These days… he had his flat in Rome." Her voice had a strange mélange of wistfulness and outrage.

"What about the Crown Watch? Did they just let him wander off unprotected whenever he felt like it?"

"You'd have to ask Denarius about that. I have enough trouble keeping track of my own guardsmen, especially the ones my best friend keeps sleeping with."

Maria Elena's lovely face was a picture of innocence.

A clatter came from the foyer, and soon after, a small platoon of servants entered, pushing in shining meal carts. There was, yet again, a disturbing lack of spaghetti, but the food that had been arrayed on those carts smelled heavenly anyway.

"Finally," sighed Sabina. "This interview is over."

"Of course. Thank you for answering my questions." I stayed where I was, in the hopes that I might be invited to share the meal.

"You may leave now."

So much for that.

"Can you find your way back to your room on your own, John?" Maria Elena's own eyes were glued to the plates of food. A woman after my own heart, clearly.

"Of course he can," Sabina answered on my behalf, as servants set the table for two. "Didn't he make it all the way from the banquet hall to the Tower on his own last night?"

I opened my mouth to explain, but the words refused to come. My bond with Lucia remained one of Team Anastasia's only strategic advantages, and I couldn't afford to squander it just because I was hungry. Besides, between Lucia's telepathic directions and a full day following Maria Elena about the palace, I was starting to finally get a grasp on the building's layout.

"I'll be fine," I said.

Either I was getting better at lying, or neither of the femmepires really cared.

CHAPTER 31
IN WHICH NOTHING IS AS IT SEEMS

Based on recent history, one could be forgiven for assuming that I promptly got lost yet again. A younger and dumber John Smith no doubt would have done so, willfully and ignorantly repeating past mistakes. I, on the other hand, waited outside Sabina's suite for the servants to emerge, found one that spoke some semblance of English, and followed the whole posse back to the kitchen.

I'd always said that hunger was the *true* mother of invention.

The kitchen was far less busy than it had been before the banquet, and it was simple enough to convince one of the small army of cooks to prepare me another sandwich. This one even came with a separate plate of artisanal cheeses. I thanked the cook and ate my lunch at my designated table in the corner. In place of real ham, I'd gotten some sort of darker, saltier meat, but it went well with the bread and assortment of cheeses.

As I ate, I reviewed what progress I'd made so far. That took me all of three bites, leaving me to ponder my next move as I polished off the remainder of my lunch. If Dog was representative of his peers, then trying to get any answers at all would be a difficult and potentially dangerous affair... but I was running out of other options. Someone, somewhere had to have some insight into the king's recent behavior, and the other councilors seemed like a great place to start.

I also still needed to visit the murder scene. And check the king's quarters here in the palace, for that matter. Tomasso's butler had mentioned that the king had been doing some late-night reading… if I could find the missing texts, I might also find whatever had tipped the king off to Lucia's innocence in Aurelius' murder. And *that* might point me to the real killer.

Assuming that the two regicides were linked, anyway.

Progress had been hard to come by to this point, but if nothing else, I had a plan. I really *was* growing up.

I couldn't wait to rub that fact in Juliette's face when she called.

ооо

After finishing my lunch, I got directions back to the guest quarters and set out on my long, cross-palace sojourn.

This time, I *did* get lost. Again.

For the third time in two days, I found myself wandering down one hall after the other—at least three of which looked like the fabled Saladuray—in search of someone who spoke English, didn't hate me, and might be willing to escort me to Lucia's suite.

For a while, things looked grim. As grim as polished marble floors, and gleaming white stone walls hung with artwork older than my own country could be anyway. Just when I had started to despair, hope arrived in the form of a drab gray dress.

Despite the lack of uniform, the woman's shabby clothing clearly identified her as a servant of some sort. Maybe a thrall for a vampire who had stopped caring about personal hygiene. Ragged brown hair fell limply to bony shoulders that jutted like icebergs under the surface of that shapeless gray dress.

"Excuse me?" I stepped in front of her shuffling stride. "Do you have a second?"

Faded gray eyes met mine, slightly puzzled. The woman stepped around me and continued on.

On any other day, I would have just chalked the whole thing up to *Europeans* and looked for someone more helpful. But between Lucia's inexplicable bouts of kindness and rage that morning, the long hours behind an interview table, and the joys of trying to extract information from Tomasso's only daughter, I was entirely out of patience.

"Seriously?" I called after the woman. "You're just going to ignore me? Would it kill you to show some simple freaking human courtesy?"

The woman stopped in her tracks.

"Oh, thank God… you *do* speak English." I headed to catch up with her. "I just need directions and—"

"You dare?" That voice didn't fit the shabbily dressed servant at all, each syllable ringing like a thousand swords meeting on the field of battle.

I skidded to a sudden and precipitous halt. "I just—"

She spun before I could finish my sentence and there was nothing soft or human in those flat gray eyes. "Your species spills across the earth, befouling all that it touches, and you dare to speak to *me* of courtesy?"

I'm sure I had some sort of brilliant rebuttal ready to go, but the woman didn't give me the chance to reply.

"The lesser races have made for themselves a virtue out of disrespect, but I tell you this: There. Are. Limits." As she spoke, the hallway around us shivered. It wasn't an earthquake—as a Californian, I was more than familiar with those. This was more like… reality itself was trembling.

The air behind her hardened then split, like a window shattering in utter silence, and I found myself looking onto a broken city. Even ruined, there was enough evidence of the beauty that had once existed there to steal my breath. Above toppled statues and shattered walls, a dark and starless sky spread, as far as the eye could see.

Oh, shit.

My eyes darted from the devastated cityscape back to the woman I had stupidly mistaken for human. I had a friend who could open portals like that, but not even Gehenna's endless storms had evoked this level of terror in me.

A slight motion brought my eye back to the ruined city. Behind the largest broken building, something stirred, something with four legs and fur the color of blood.

I blinked in confusion as it rose to its feet to loom over the shattered cityscape. It was a wolf, but a wolf the size of a mountain, with eyes that glowed like golden bonfires. Around its enormous neck, something shimmered: a silver leash, delicate as a spider's web against the beast's bulk.

What the hell had I just stumbled into?

The woman's empty gray eyes met mine, and she nodded at whatever she saw in my face. "You begin to comprehend the magnitude of your error," she hissed, her voice every bit as sharp as the swords it suggested. "Too little. Too late."

I desperately reached for Lucia's power, only to feel it slipping through my fingers. The woman stretched her hand out toward me...

And Valentina made her appearance.

My ghost was barely even visible, but her presence was a cold blast of wind in the hallway. Dark tangles of hair streamed out behind her, and that same invisible wind tugged at her bloody nightgown. I couldn't see her face, but I heard her wordless scream of rage. For the first time in what felt like hours, I remembered to take a breath.

On the other side of Valentina, the strange woman paused, her face still expressionless, her eyes still vacant, even in the face of a White Lady's anger. Then, she brushed her own limp hair aside, took in a single, sharp breath, and exhaled.

Valentina was hurtled backwards, straight through me in a flash of icy coldness. I spun on one foot and watched the ghost tumble head over heel down the long corridor, and then through the far wall, disappearing from sight.

For the first time since I'd pissed off this creature, I felt something other than confusion and terror.

"If you hurt her…" I began in a rough voice. This time, Lucia's power came easily to my will, and I felt the arctic storm gather within me.

My plan was simple. Step one: popsicle this wench of a demigoddess or demon. Step two: run like hell. Step three: find Valentina and make sure she was okay. Step four: if she wasn't… come back and repeat step one.

Unfortunately, before I could put that plan into action, the woman in the gray dress spoke one word.

"No."

Just like that, Lucia's power was gone, pulled from my body like it had been sucked through a hose, leaving only hot, stagnant, emptiness behind. I staggered and nearly fell.

My plan clearly needed more steps, but my feet were deaf to my brain's increasingly frantic commands. I found myself frozen as the woman drew closer, reaching out once again with a half-clenched hand.

"Exalted One!"

For just a moment, I thought Juliette had somehow flown all the way from San Diego to save me. But that didn't make even a little bit of sense. So who—?

"Ambassador Middleton." My attacker glanced past me at the femmepire. "This will only be a moment."

Juliette's mom swept forward into the deepest curtsy I had ever seen, her knees almost touching the ground.

"Your pardon, Exalted One, but I have need of Mr. Smith."

For the first time, the other woman's gray eyes flickered with something approaching interest. *"This* is the Borghesi child's investigator?"

My body regained sufficient mobility for me to manage a shaky bow. "At your service."

She shook her head slowly. "This one time, I will forgive your trespass, human. Never speak to me again."

Both woman and broken cityscape disappeared, and the hallway in front of me reasserted itself with an audible snap.

"I had heard," Lady Middleton said into the hushed silence, "that you were quite mad, but this exceeds even the worst of those tales. What did you to do to anger Minerva?"

Minerva? Something about the name seemed familiar, but I couldn't quite place it. "I just asked her for directions."

The femmepire's reaction was an odd mix of humor and horror. "You risked the ire of a goddess to get directions?"

"Well, yeah…" I paused. "Goddess? As in, capital-G Goddess?"

"Indeed. Are you telling me you didn't know what she was? Are eight-foot-tall women in gowns of golden light so common on the West Coast?"

Eight-foot-ta…. what?

"Most people see someone like that coming and get the hell out of the way." She sighed, looking oddly wistful for just a moment. "Why am I not surprised that my daughter's human companion does just the opposite?"

Before I could reply, two thoughts pushed their way to the front of my confused and terrified brain.

First, I remembered where I had seen the name Minerva: in one of the many mythologies I'd read in a desperate attempt to acclimatize to this strange new world I found myself in. Minerva was the Roman name given to a goddess known more commonly by her Greek incarnation. A goddess of wisdom and battle who had reportedly sprung, fully formed, from the head of her own father.

Athena. Who I had somehow just pissed off something fierce.

I was still grappling with *that* horrifying realization when the second thought knocked me onto my metaphorical ass. It wasn't about how close I had come to death. It wasn't even about wondering why Athena would go by the name of one of her lesser-known incarnations.

No, the thought that hit me with the force of a sledgehammer to my pudgy midsection was simple:

I had just met a goddess. And if Deanna Middleton was to be believed, I had seen right through that goddess' illusion.

○○○

"Thanks for saving my life," I told the femmepire, surreptitiously looking for any sign of Valentina as we walked down the hall. "The immortals I know in San Diego are a lot less… touchy."

"I find that difficult to fathom," said Juliette's mom, "but you're welcome."

"Was that Minerva's home plane we caught a glimpse of?"

"Olympus, yes." Deanna looked so much like her daughter that her relatively strait-laced personality kept taking me by surprise.

"What happened to it?"

"Did you see the wolf?"

"It was hard not to."

"There's your answer. The Fenris wolf came to Olympus, and not even the combined might of their pantheon could destroy him."

"Isn't the Fenris wolf from *Norse* mythology? Shouldn't it have gone after Asgard instead?"

Deanna gave me a considering glance out of lovely golden eyes. "Surely, someone has explained to you the distinction between mythology and reality when it comes to the gods?"

In fact, Juliette herself had said something of that sort back when we were first getting to know each other. "That there's a crossover between various mythologies… and a single god might show up in half a dozen pantheons?"

"Exactly. It's anyone's guess as to whether there are Asgardians and Olympians… or Egyptian or Aztec deities, for that matter. Just as Minerva represented herself as Athena to the Greeks, she might have taken on different personas or forms for other cultures."

"But the Fenris wolf is real." I shivered, remembering the legend of Ragnarök and how the wolf was supposed to swallow the moon. "And the other gods of Olympus? Zeus and Ares and…" I fumbled for other names, drawing a curious and inconvenient blank. "…the rest? Where are they?"

"I don't know," the femmepire told me quietly. "Olympus' fall was a long, long time before I was born. Only Minerva and the Fenris wolf remain, and she serves as the wolf's jailor. If it broke free…"

We shivered in unison.

○○○

"How did you happen to be walking by anyway?" I asked, as we reached a hallway that looked halfway familiar. "Not that I'm complaining, of course…"

"I was actually looking for you."

That brought me to a halt. "You were?"

"I was. One of the kitchen staff remembered you leaving, but you'd wandered quite a ways in the wrong direction. I was hoping that you and I might talk."

I was still having a hard time dealing with someone who looked like Juliette, dressed like Anastasia, and spoke like someone else entirely, but I nodded anyway. "About King Tomasso's murder?"

"No, although I'm happy to speak with you on the subject, of course." Thick brown hair curved about her face, softening the knife-edged cheekbones she shared with my junior partner. "I was hoping you'd have time to talk about Juliette."

My shock must have been evident, as a dark, sculpted eyebrow arched elegantly in reply. "That surprises you?" A sliver of sharpness intruded upon her polished voice, making the resemblance to Juliette that much stronger.

"*You* surprise me," I admitted. "Juliette doesn't really talk about you… or her dad. The last thing I expected was to find one of you in Rome."

"A little over a century ago, the People of North America, deciding that sufficient time had elapsed since our departure from Europe, sought and claimed an ambassadorship to the Italian Court. Each decade, someone is chosen from the pool of Elders in Manhattan and Chicago to serve in that role. It was my turn." She shrugged, momentarily flippant. "It's not New York, but Rome has its merits."

"I'm lucky it was your turn then," I said. "So, what do you want to know about Juliette?"

"How is she doing? She may have been thrown out of our House—and trust me, Mr. Smith, that punishment was richly deserved—but Juliette will always be my daughter." Wistfulness looked odd on her otherwise fierce features. "News from San Diego is sparse and frequently misleading. I have been alternately told that she is a titled Council member, that she leads her own flock, and even that she is… *working*… in the service industry."

"That's pretty accurate, actually. From what I was told, she led a flock in San Diego for at least a decade or two. When Queen Lucia and her entourage arrived, she won herself a spot on the Council of the newly formed House."

"And then?"

"And then she quit the Council."

Deanna's golden eyes glinted dangerously. "And did she give a reason for committing political suicide?"

"She didn't like the paperwork."

The elder Middleton's laughter was every bit as enchanting as her daughter's.

"That does sound like my Juliette," she admitted. "Was this before or after your mistress lost her House?"

"Before. Although I don't think Juliette would have stuck around under Barros' reign, regardless. Dude's kind of a dick." I shrugged. "I think she's happier now anyway. Especially now that she has Angel."

"Angel is… my daughter's pet?"

"Her girlfriend," I corrected.

"Ah." The femmepire pursed her lips thoughtfully, inadvertently reminding me of the disastrous kisses Juliette and I had shared once. "And you accepted the addition of this Angel?"

"Why would I have any say in the matter?"

"As her partner, I think who she lures into your bed would be of great significance."

I coughed. "Juliette and I are *business* partners. We're not involved romantically."

I was pretty sure I could hear Deanna murmur *thank the gods* under her breath, but my recent brush with a goddess had me diplomatically ignoring it.

"She does have a boyfriend too though."

"That *is* excellent news." Deanna smiled. "Are you aware of his lineage?"

"I think he's one-part seaweed and two-parts beefcake."

"I… beg your pardon? She's dating a Mer?"

"Even worse: a human surfer bro," I told her.

"I see." The femmepire sighed and shook her head. "Well, she is young yet. There is still ample time."

"For what?"

"For her to give me a grandchild, of course." Once again, that note of wistfulness had entered her voice.

"You and your husband didn't have any other children?"

"My husband?" Deanna looked startled for a moment, but her features swiftly softened in realization. "Juliette's father and I never wed. Marriage is a largely human sacrament."

"Oh."

"When you live as long as we do," she explained, "the desire to remain with one person all that time is practically unheard of. Thomas and I had a lovely few decades together, but Juliette was the only child to come of our partnership."

For some reason, that thought had never occurred to me. Divorce rates were bad enough among humans… what would they be for creatures that lived millennia?

"You said the two of you are… business partners?" Deanna's eyes sparkled suddenly. "You can't seriously tell me that she is working as a mediator?"

I winced at the thought. Juliette was scary, hot, and competent in a handful of surprising fields, but it was hard to imagine anyone *less* suited to be a mediator than the Duchess of Snark.

Unless it was Lucia herself.

"Thankfully, no. Which is probably why San Diego hasn't vanished into the hellmouth just yet," I replied, grinning. "She's working as a private investigator."

"One of the People, serving as a private dick." Deanna shook her head again. "What an exceedingly ridiculous thought. Is she any good?"

"She's not bad," I admitted. "A little bit inexperienced, but she's picking things up way faster than I did. In fact, she's in the middle of a fairly complica—"

I was interrupted by the delicate chimes of the femmepire's cell phone. She fished it out of her purse, glanced at the screen, and then back at me.

"I apologize, Mr. Smith. Ambassador Santos has requested a meeting with myself and the other dignitaries." She paused, looking uncharacteristically pensive. "If I have time later, would you be amenable to another conversation? I would love to hear more about Juliette's... adventures."

"Absolutely," I told her. After less than half an hour, I was pretty sure I liked Juliette's mom more than I did Juliette herself.

Okay... that was overstating it. But she was *definitely* nicer.

Deanna handed over a sleek business card, with only her name and a telephone number on it. "Call me when you are available."

I agreed before remembering that I didn't have a working phone. Oh well, I could always borrow Lucia's... or Maria Elena's, for that matter.

Of greater importance was the fact that I was *still* lost.

"Before you go, ambassador," I heard myself saying, "could you direct me to Queen Lucia's suite? Between the showdown with Minerva and our own stroll, I'm not entirely sure where we are."

"The palace is a bit of a maze for the uninitiated," she agreed. "It took me ages to find my own way around, but it's quite simple once you get the hang of it. The top floor is reserved for the royal suites and the rooms of those Council members who choose to reside here. One level down, you will find visiting dignitaries to the north, and offices and the Council meeting chambers to the south. And the ground floor consists of guest suites—again, found to the north—and the foyer and banquet halls to the south."

"And below that?" I was confident that I had gone up and down way more than three flights of stairs.

Reasonably confident.

"Below ground are the servant quarters, the primary kitchen, the laundry room and other areas of little note. And below even that level are the catacombs themselves."

"I wish someone had told me all of that two days ago. So, my suite should be on the ground floor then?"

"Precisely." Deanna's smile was a lot more polished than her daughter's. "If there is nothing else…?"

"Actually, I do still have two questions." I was well past the point of being embarrassed about these things.

"Yes?"

"What floor are we on now? Also… which way is north?"

CHAPTER 32

After saying goodbye to Juliette's mom, I had only two immediate goals: get back to my suite and see if Valentina was okay. Surprisingly, the former was proving easier than the latter. After a mere ten minutes, I was almost to the room Lucia and I shared… but Valentina still had yet to reappear.

I found myself unconsciously rubbing Valentina's ring between my thumb and index finger. If Valentina remained… well, whatever the ghost version of *alive* was… she would eventually come back to her node. But the fact that she hadn't done so yet was more than a little concerning. If Minerva had sent her to her final death…

I shook my head firmly. She was fine. She had to be.

I turned the corner and found my suite right where it was supposed to be. The absence of guards at the door meant Lucia was still out working her political mojo, so I would at least have the suite to myself. Step one: try to contact Valentina… presumably by standing in the bathroom and calling her name like she was Candyman. Step two: take a quick nap before my trip into Rome. Step three? Eh. I'd worry about that one later.

I nudged the door open and slipped inside.

The Kingmaker was waiting.

○○○

Denarius was reading from a leather-bound book, his ridiculous length folded neatly into a chair at the small table where Lucia and I had eaten breakfast. Upon my entry, he marked his place with a long finger, closed the book softly, and slipped it onto the table beside him.

"Mr. Smith. Well met."

"Denarius. What are you doing here?" I tried—and failed—to keep the edge out of my voice. Between Lucia and Sabina, I was already heartily tired of the Borghesi family.

"I am here to speak with you, of course."

"Of course." I grabbed a seat across the table from the manpire, noting that his corner was darker than it should have been with multiple lights on. "What about?"

"The only matter of significance: your investigation. Have you progress to report?"

"Are you—?" I took a deep breath and tried again. "With all due respect, why I would tell you? Aren't you the opposition here?"

My years as an occasional mediator had me smoothly substituting *opposition* for *enemy*. I did not want Lucia's ancient detective/lawyer/guardsman uncle thinking of me as an enemy. Especially when I was running around pissing off goddesses.

"Lucia truly has sent you in blind, hasn't she?"

That was a rhetorical question if I'd ever heard one.

"I am not your enemy in this, Mr. Smith."

"Aren't you the guy who amassed the evidence against Lady Dumenyova?" I couldn't help but notice that the manpire had gone straight for the e-word.

"I am."

"And aren't you the guy who will be arguing for our executions?"

"In that you are mistaken."

"How so?"

"This is not a human trial."

"Everyone keeps saying that."

"That is because it is true. There is no opposing counsel. When the first sign of decay appears upon King Tomasso's shell, you and you alone will be addressing the Council."

That sounded suspiciously good for Team Anastasia. "You're not going to present the evidence to them at all?"

"Everyone involved has already been briefed, of course."

Well, shit.

"So, before the trial even starts, everyone is going to be convinced of Anastasia's guilt."

"Indeed. It will be your job to change their minds."

"*Their* minds? Aren't you on the Council?"

Denarius stirred in his chair, like a crow ruffling its feathers. "I have been recused from judgment. Because I argued for leniency in Lucia's last trial, there are those who now hold me culpable in Tomasso's death."

So, our voter pool had been reduced to six, which meant… Actually, I didn't know what that meant. "Tie votes don't go to the defendant, do they?"

"They do not."

Then we still needed four votes.

"And if you had gotten a vote…"

"I would have voted for execution." Denarius' eyes were hard as polished gems. "Lucia is my blood, but justice will be served."

So, it was a *good* thing that he'd lost his vote. I hoped Lucia was doing a better job of keeping track of all this stuff than me.

"However," continued the manpire, "it remains within my power to make your investigation easier, as I believe the past two days have already demonstrated. I ask again: how is your investigation proceeding?"

"Slowly," I admitted. "Tomasso's human servants didn't have much of value to offer."

"And Dog and Princess Sabina?"

I blinked. I knew Maria Elena was keeping Denarius apprised of my schedule, but I didn't realize the manpire would be quite so on top of things. "Rome's resident drug-dealing imp was less than helpful. And a little terrifying."

"Did he inform you of the apocalyptic future where his kind will overrun the planet?"

"Actually, yeah." I glanced at the manpire. "You don't seem concerned."

"When I first arrived at the Mad King's court in the Kingdom of France, Dog was already a fixture. He has been among us for well over a thousand years, Mr. Smith, and yet the world continues to spin."

"Is that why he's on the Council? Seniority?" It sure as hell wasn't his personality.

"In part. When we moved the court to Rome, we were obligated to make certain concessions. One of those was that the Council include representatives of other species."

"I'm surprised you guys didn't just roll into the city and kick everyone else out." That's what Lucia would have done… assuming she had the manpower of the entire European kingdom behind her anyway.

"Even we know better than to anger the Guardian of Rome, Mr. Smith."

"Minerva?" Okay, that made a bit more sense. Not even vampires were dumb enough to piss off full-fledged deities. That honor was reserved for twenty-seven-year-old fratmen.

"Indeed. Ours is the only council in the world to count a goddess as one of its members."

"Minerva's on the council?" I had a truly horrible thought. "Does she get a vote in the trial?"

"Yes. You can be assured of one impartial ear for your defense."

Lucia was going to murder me, again, unless I could somehow smooth things over with Athena. Did florists deliver to Olympus?

"Anyway," I managed weakly, "Dog was a bust."

"And my grand-niece?"

"Marginally better. She said the king had been distracted for several months."

"Even after a century, the crown remained a burden. My nephew was not immune to the pressures of his position."

Gaius had said the same thing. "And whenever he got stressed, he took a mini-vacation in Rome?"

"Yes. As a child, Tomasso had hiding places throughout the palace that he would escape to when times were difficult. The flat in Rome serves—" He caught himself with a grimace. "Served much the same purpose."

"What sort of security did he have for these trips?"

"Tomasso was always accompanied by a pair of the Crown Watch. They did not join him in his flat but stood guard at the building's only entrance."

I frowned over at the manila folder still on my dresser. "There were guards there when Tomasso was killed? What did they see? Why weren't their accounts included in the documents you sent over?"

"Both Isabella and Klaus are missing and presumed dead."

"Dead… or bought off by the real killer." It would help my case immeasurably if I could instead focus on finding the missing guards. Especially since I had actual experience finding missing people, whereas I remained distressingly inexperienced with murder mysteries.

"We are the People, Mr. Smith. Our lifespans measure centuries, if not millennia. Coin is of little value when weighed against being hunted for the remainder of those years." Denarius shook his head.

Unless they'd been offered something more than money, as had been the case with Xavier. But I could tell I wasn't going to convince the manpire of that. Not yet, anyway.

"Let's say they *are* dead." I gave it some thought but it was my turn to shake my head. "It still doesn't make sense. Why dispose of two bodies only to leave the third out for all to see?"

"Perhaps Lady Dumenyova wished to make a statement. Or perhaps she had to flee the scene before she could finish cleaning up after herself."

"Or perhaps she didn't do it." Either Denarius didn't remember Anastasia at all, or his grief was making him stupid. "As far as I can tell, the only statement Tomasso's corpse makes is *Hey everyone, I was totally killed by Anastasia—*"

"You might not want to begin your defense with that sentence," murmured Denarius.

"—and there's no reason the lady herself would want to make that statement."

To his credit, the Kingmaker conceded that point. "And the second possibility? That she was interrupted in the act? It would explain the preponderance of evidence left behind."

I kept shaking my head. "That doesn't make sense either. Whoever this killer is, they'd just killed two of the Crown Watch *and* the king. Who's going to scare someone like *that* off? And for that matter, do you really think they killed the Watch, took the time to dispose of their bodies, and only then made a play for the king? That seems like a fantastic way to bungle an assassination."

"You have an alternate explanation?"

"Yeah. Maybe something about their deaths contradicted the *Lady Dumenyova did it* storyline the murderer wants us to believe." I shrugged. "It's a lot more likely than Ana being both illogical *and* incompetent. Trust me."

"It is possible," conceded Denarius, "but it will take more than words to convince my fellow Councilmembers of such."

I sighed. "That's why I'm heading into Rome tonight."

"And that is the other reason I wanted to see you. When do you wish to depart? I will assign someone from the Watch to take you into the city."

An hour or more in a car with one of the black-clad vampires that clearly loathed me sounded like a terrible idea. Thankfully, I'd already given the matter some thought. "Actually, I had a different escort in mind."

"Mr. Smith, if you are thinking to flee town with my niece, I must inform you that the time for doing so has already passed."

"Not Lucia." The last thing the queen and I needed was more time in an enclosed space together. "Sergei."

Denarius went still within his cocoon of shadows. That alone told me that my half-formed suspicions about the ambassador had merit. "Ambassador Sergei?"

"I figure he has as much invested in the matter as anyone."

The manpire was quiet. "You continue to surprise me, Mr. Smith."

"Meaning I'm not quite as dumb as I look?"

"Meaning I begin to think not all of the stories about you are gross exaggerations."

There were *stories* about me? I hoped some of them ended with me getting the girl.

"If there is nothing else," said the manpire, "I will leave you to make your preparations."

"Actually, I did have a question. One of Tomasso's servants mentioned that the king had been studying some texts or journals in the weeks before he died?"

"Studying might be an exaggeration, but yes, he was finally showing interest in the kingdom's history. I loaned him several volumes from my personal collection."

Ah ha! "Any idea what happened to those books?"

"He returned them to me several days before his death." Dark eyes narrowed. "What does this have to do with his murder?"

"I'm still trying to figure that out," I hedged. "If you wouldn't mind, I'd love to review the books in question."

"As you wish. I will have them sent over." Denarius unfolded himself from the chair. "Are we done?"

"One more thing." I coughed. "About last night—"

"Your actions were ill-considered and potentially suicidal. However, no lasting harm was done," interrupted the manpire, "and I am willing to put it behind us. I trust you are now fully aware of the consequences of further confrontations with the Watch?"

"No worries on that front, dude," I assured him. "I'm a lover, not a fighter. Only..."

His eyes narrowed. "Only?"

"Only that wasn't actually what I wanted to talk about."

Denarius waited for me to continue.

"When we were leaving, Ana said something about asking Lucia for her blessing?"

"Yes."

"So, what does that mean, exactly?"

"It means a few days of imprisonment have utterly unhinged my Secundus." Lucia stood in the doorway. The fluffy robe I'd last seen her in had been replaced by a simple white dress, knotted at the waist by a belt of woven gold cord, but her eyes still blazed a bright and angry blue.

"Kingmaker." She nodded stiffly to the manpire.

"Niece. I trust your visit with Lady Dumenyova was illuminating?"

"How ironic that *you* would speak to me of trust."

"An odd thing for the woman who broke that trust to say."

These two literally never stopped. "Your family dinners must have been a thrill a minute."

Both vampires turned to regard me, and in their shared irritation, I caught my first true whiff of familial resemblance.

"Thrall, I wish to speak with my uncle."

"Sure thing. There's plenty of room in this conversation for three."

"Alone." Lucia's voice was hard.

I sighed and rose to my feet. "I guess I'll go talk to Sergei then."

"The ambassador from the Steppes?" Lucia scowled at me. "Whatever for?"

I glanced at Denarius. "She doesn't know?"

"Know what?" growled the queen, anger rolling across our bond.

"I guess you two really *do* have a lot to talk about."

ooo

The ambassador quarters were precisely where Deanna had said they would be, further cementing her position as my favorite Middleton. The hallway terminated in a large, circular, common room almost like a cul-de-sac, featuring some sort of faded mosaic in the floor, five doors evenly spaced along the exterior wall, and four benches to fill the space between doors.

Wait... *five* doors? A quick recount showed my ability to do basic math had not deserted me. But who was the fifth ambassador?

There was only one way to find out, I decided, and since I had no idea which room was Sergei's, there was apparently no time like the present to do so. I walked up to the first door on the right and knocked.

No answer.

I gave it thirty seconds, knocked again, and then waited a solid two or three minutes, just in case the ambassadors' suites were as ridiculously large as Dog's and Sabina's had been.

Nobody came.

I struck out at the second door too, and the smile I'd worn all the way from my suite finally started to slip. Deanna had been invited by Ambassador Santos to a meeting… what if he'd summoned all the ambassadors? If Sergei was away at a function—having tea or burning down large villages—it was going to seriously screw up my plans for the day. Plus, I didn't want to ruin what had been an awesome exit by slinking back to both Lucia and Denarius in failure.

I tested the nearby bench, and found it hard, cold, and ass-bruisingly uncomfortable. Not good.

Thankfully, my keenly trained investigative skills finally noted one tiny, but relevant, detail; the third door off the cul-de-sac was wide open. *Someone* was home. I headed over and peeked in.

I don't know what I'd expected to find—although nude and terrifyingly over-endowed male statuary was pretty high on my list—but the vast expanse of furniture-free space, enclosed in rough, unfinished stone, wasn't it. What sort of a madman built a cave inside of a palace… and why? Around the cave's perimeter stood tall candelabras, each holding four lit candles and doing surprisingly little to brighten the gloom.

On the bare stone floor, barely brushed by the flickering candlelight, sat Ambassador Ti An, robes spread about her like the golden petals of an alien flower.

The femmepire must have heard me knocking at the other two doors—hell, given vampire senses, she'd probably listened to my heartbeat as I came down the hallway—but her ancient, terrifying eyes remained shut. Her back was stiff, her legs crossed, hands resting, palms upward, on fabric-draped knees.

She looked almost peaceful in that meditative pose... until I noticed another detail almost lost in the uncertain light: her robes were moving of their own volition. Golden fabric undulated through the air, weaving in and around itself with a dull rasp of heavy cloth before coming briefly to rest in a new position.

Someone way smarter than me would probably have been able to interpret the patterns being formed... *I* felt vaguely proud that I recognized them for patterns at all.

I swallowed and took a careful step backwards. Then a second one, until the femmepire was out of sight. Something about that room reminded me uncomfortably of the videos I'd seen of snake pits, filled to the brim with writhing, hungry serpents.

If Ti An was going to pretend she hadn't heard me, I was totally cool with that.

Thankfully, for both my pride and my blood pressure, the fourth try was the charm. In place of a servant or thrall, Sergei himself opened the door, barely clothed in a pair of loose crimson pants and the ever-present eyepatch. Without his shirt, the heavy slab-like muscles of his chest and arms were even more apparent, transforming him from a pirate to a swashbuckling romance novel cover model. A very *short* cover model—without his thick-soled boots, he was at most an inch or two taller than Lucia herself.

In his right hand was an open, unlabeled bottle of dark green glass. He took a long swallow of the bottle's contents, and then peered warily up at me through one crystal blue eye. "Da?"

"I'm headed into Rome," I told him brightly. "Want to come?"

○○○

Sergei's rooms were more like what I'd come to expect from the palace, although both statues and boy-band posters were thankfully in short supply. The manpire himself was leaning against the island of his suite's small kitchen, arms folded across his chest.

"Rome?" he finally asked.

"Yeah. I need to go check out the murder scene."

"Talk to Kingmaker. He give you Watch."

"He already offered," I admitted, "but I'm not convinced I can trust them. Especially when most of them already hate me."

Sergei barked a laugh and muttered something in a guttural tongue. "And you trust me? Because I slap down arrogant peacock?" The solitary blue eye hardened into ice. "What care I if you die?"

This was going swimmingly.

"I doubt you do." I tried to hide my pain at his grunt of affirmation. "But I'm good at what I do—" A drastic overstatement, but I was in the moment. "—and if I die, I'm pretty sure this investigation dies with me."

His face was as blank as the walls of Ti An's cave. For the first time, I started to worry my intuition had led me astray.

"And if the investigation fails," I elaborated, "Lucia will die."

The silence held for another distressingly long time before Sergei finally grunted again. "Who tells you?"

"That you and Lucia are related?"

"Yes."

I felt muscles I didn't even know I had unclench. "Nobody, although Denarius' reaction helped confirm it." I shrugged. "Since I've known Lucia, everything has been about her father or her brother. It wasn't until I came to Rome and saw how little she looked like them that I thought to wonder about her mother."

"Ilyana," offered Sergei, unprompted.

I nodded in acknowledgement, stashing that bit of information away. "So, if Lucia didn't get her height and color from her father, it stood to reason she got them from her mother's side of the family. Imagine my surprise when the only other vampire I've seen in Rome with those attributes decides to take a seat at my table."

"Hrm." Sergei's smile came and went like lightning in a night sky. "Is good guess, I suppose. But only guess. Short and blonde is not so rare."

"Well, yeah." And if I'd been wrong and Denarius' acknowledgement had meant something else entirely, the ambassador would have no doubt tossed me out on what Lucia called my overfed ass. But I hadn't been wrong. "When defending a woman whose guilt is considered a foregone conclusion, you sometimes have to take risks. So, what are you? Lucia's grandfather? Cousin? Half-brother twice-removed?"

"Ilyana was sister to Vasily and I."

"Oh." I winced. "I'm sorry for your loss."

Sergei's shrug looked false even to my undiscerning eye. "It was long time ago."

"And Lucia doesn't know you're her uncle?"

"How could she? Ilyana die in childbirth, and news travel slowly back then. By time we even hear, Aurelius had made daughter Borghesi, from head to toe. There was no purpose in coming to meet."

"But you're the ambassador."

"New ambassador. Father died one-hundred-and-fifty years ago. Seventy years for Vasily to be crowned. Ambassador now for almost eighty."

He had arrived after Lucia's banishment. That explained a lot.

"Does that mean Lucia is effectively royalty from *two* kingdoms?"

"Yes."

Jesus. Maybe I wouldn't tell her that. Her ego was already massive enough as it was.

"Is part of why she was only banished after killing Aurelius," Sergei continued. "Rome did not want war with Steppes."

"And now?"

This time, his shrug was genuine. "She had chance. And Vasily has child and cares little what happen to distant girl he never knew."

"That's Vasily. What about you?"

"I had one sister." The manpire's voice was a low growl that made the hair on my neck stand up, even as my testicles tried to climb up and into my body. "Tiny and perfect, like jewel. Now, she is gone."

"But something of her could live on."

"Yes." Sergei nodded. "I will get car."

CHAPTER 33

IN WHICH ONE GOOD MONSTER
DESERVES ANOTHER

Before our flight to Rome, I'd never been east of Arizona. In fact, I could count the number of large cities I'd been to on two hands, and still have ample fingers left over for flashing a peace sign at ex-hippies in Ocean Beach. San Diego was the coolest of those cities, of course, but I'd taken the occasional road trip to Las Vegas and Phoenix. I'd also driven through the sprawling mess of Los Angeles and on up the 5 to San Francisco. Add the touristy parts of Tijuana to the mix, and I felt like I had a pretty good handle on the variety of cities our world had to offer.

Rome taught me otherwise. By the time we reached the city, in the fume-belching Renault that Sergei called a car, the sun was setting ahead of us, painting the skyline with tongues of fire. I'd never been much of a history buff, but high school lessons resurfaced as we entered the city. Julius Caesar. The Colosseum. Vatican City. Russell Crowe's character from *Gladiator*. Los Angeles was the city of dreams—to people who'd never actually had to live there, at least—but Rome was magic, ancient and pure.

It was also surprisingly modern, judging by the traffic. It had taken us an hour and a half to reach the city's eastern edge, coming in on a two-lane highway that was as picturesque as it was congested. From there, it was another hour to Tomasso's townhouse. Long before we reached it, the sun had truly set, and only the surplus of lights to our north told me when we passed some of Rome's biggest tourist destinations.

We made our way down narrow winding roads, many of them one-way. Mopeds zipped about us in every direction with zero regard for laws or personal safety. I'd been driving since I was fifteen, but I was involved in more near-accidents on that single trip than I'd seen in twelve years in the car-obsessed land of Southern California.

"Is it always like this?"

"Is worse sometimes," decided Sergei, in the first three words he'd bothered to share since leaving the palace. "Is better sometimes too. Once, they ban cars so smog can clear." His teeth flashed in the sharp grin I was starting to recognize. "Was much better driving those days."

"No doubt." As I'd learned from Juliette, being a vampire meant never having to pay a ticket. Or obey human laws. Lucky bastards. I rubbernecked as Sergei careened into oncoming traffic just long enough to bypass someone who had opted to *triple* park. "Is there any chance we can stop by the Bitter End after seeing Tomasso's place? I need to talk to Lord Kala about a thing."

Sergei yanked the steering wheel one way and then the other with casual speed. "Is across river, to south, but not far." He grunted with what sounded like approval. "Good vodka. Never meet Kala."

"He's... different. Nice enough though, and he's helped me out in the past." Mainly because he found me amusing and appreciated the way people tended to die on my cases. I was hoping Kala would be able to explain the stone that had been retrieved from Tomasso's chest.

"Is demigod. Nice… not nice… dangerous either way."

Well, yeah.

ooo

Tomasso's townhome was in what I assumed had to be an affluent area of Rome, but the cars parked along the narrow little one-way were anything but flashy. In place of the Ferraris I'd been anticipating were hatchback BMWs, Smart cars, and the very occasional Mini Cooper look-alike. The Corolla Lucia had given me, now almost a year old, and still blessedly free of dings, would have fit right in.

Sergei's Renault, on the other hand, still stood out as a particularly ugly piece of crap.

The manpire didn't seem troubled by that fact. Nor did he think twice about parking in front of a garage, blocking anyone that might have wanted to exit. He nodded to our right. "Is Tomasso's place. I think."

"You think?"

He shrugged heavy shoulders. "Is first time. Asked directions when get car."

Jesus. If Sergei's Italian was anywhere as broken as his English, we could be half a city away from our actual destination.

"There is Watch," he said, nodding a second time at two black-clad shadows detaching themselves from the building in question. "Hope you have permission to come."

"I do." I eyed the ambassador and made my tone as droll as possible. "I think."

Sergei's bark of laughter followed me into the street.

I was saddened to see that neither of the Watch was Niccolo. Apparently, our beer bro-down would have to wait for some other night. I did recognize the dude on the left as having been part of the original group that escorted a bloody Lucia and me to the Council chambers. He was wearing almost the exact same expression now as he watched me approach—somewhere between disdain, contempt, and hatred. Then, his eyes darted over my shoulder to Sergei. Contempt and disdain beat a hasty retreat.

As I always told Juliette, if you're heading into enemy territory, it pays to surround yourself with badasses.

Okay, so maybe I'd never *actually* said that to Juliette. But I'd be sure to do so when I made it back to San Diego. In the past, the designated badass had been Anastasia. Sergei was a far cry from the femmepire I loved, but his presence had the same effect.

The other Watch member stepped forward and offered a short bow—to Sergei, not me. She was small, although still taller than Vasily's Monster, with rich brown skin and dark eyes that were probably spectacular on the all-too-rare occasions she smiled.

In yet another sign of my obvious growth and maturity, I elected *not* to inform her of that fact. Unfortunately, I was so busy being mature that I completely missed whatever else she had said.

"I'm sorry…" I smiled helplessly, as if I hadn't understood her flawless English. "Do you mind repeating that?"

"I said," she told me coolly, "that we have been instructed to allow you access to the crime scene."

"Yeah, I heard the same from the Big D himself." I looked from her to the blank-faced manpire, then waved the manila folder I'd brought from the palace. "After we're done here, the ambassador and I are going to hit the Bitter End for drinks. If you guys are off duty, I'd love to buy you beers."

The manpire stared straight ahead, steadfastly refusing to acknowledge my existence. I turned back to the woman, flashing a slightly scaled-down version of the Dealmaker™ smile that I would hopefully one day be famous for.

"I like my alcohol as I like my men," the femmepire replied, a smirk on her otherwise severe face. "Aged and strong."

"Tequila it is," I agreed happily.

It had taken longer than expected, but I was making friends.

ooo

After dropping out of community college, I had been desperate to find some sort of job that didn't involve an internship at my dad's accounting firm. For a brief, not-so-shining moment, I'd latched onto the idea of getting my realtor's license so I could sell houses. I was pretty good with people—except for the assholes who didn't like me—and figured that selling a house in San Diego would be easy and profitable work.

One trip tailing Mike's mom around properties in El Cajon taught me otherwise. Buyers were *crazy*, and being a realtor required way more than canned patter, a blinding smile, and a brilliantly designed business card. I dropped that career idea like a bad habit, found an advertisement for a private investigator apprenticeship in the Union Tribune, and the rest was, as they say, somewhat painful history.

As a result, I had no clue how much a townhome like Tomasso's was worth. All I knew was that it was big, had hardwood floors and high ceilings, and both the second and third floors featured a lot of windows and natural light. It was also far more modern than the palace, not just in construction but in furnishing. Gone were the ego-deflating nude statues, replaced by black-and-white photographs, usually of buildings or landscapes. On the top floor, where Tomasso's study and bedroom were located, those pictures gave way to canvases of decidedly amateur art in bright, primary colors.

Sergei grunted as we passed a particularly terrible rendition of the Roman skyline in canary yellow and candy apple red. "Didn't know Tomasso was painter."

"Based on these paintings, I'm not sure he was."

We continued down the hall of terrible art to the study.

"What are we look for?"

"I have no idea. Let's see..." I thumbed through the crime report I'd brought with me. "There were signs of forced entry at the front door, but it looks like Tomasso was killed up here in his study." I frowned. "Shouldn't he have heard them coming up? Especially if they killed the Watch on the way in?"

That part still didn't make any sense to me.

"Maybe killer use magic. Or Tomasso expect company."

"If he expected company, they wouldn't have had to break in."

"True. What do cameras say?" The manpire nodded to the impressive array of security cameras that had monitored our progress through the house.

"Not a damn thing. The killer wiped the feed before they left." As modern as the house was, its security system was still too old to utilize offsite storage for its surveillance footage. "The only video Denarius found was from a building across the street, and its field of vision didn't include Tomasso's house." I passed the video stills to Sergei.

"Is woman, I think?"

"Maybe. Between the blurriness, the low light, the trenchcoat, and the hat, it's kind of hard to tell... and the position of the camera means we don't even know if she went into Tomasso's house." I tucked the stills back into the folder. "But the timestamp puts it around the time of death, so Denarius' people think this is the murderer. And he or she is close to Anastasia's height."

"So, she kill guards, then break in, sneak up, and kill king?"

"That's the story we're here to disprove." I nudged open the study door and found a scene of relative harmony: a large desk, a couch and loveseat that looked as fashionable as they were uncomfortable, and bookshelves along both walls. Only the toppled easel and bloodstains on the large white rug and polished wooden coffee table gave any sign that someone had been murdered. The Watch hadn't even bothered with a chalk outline.

"Did someone clean room?"

I glanced through the crime scene photos and shook my head. "No; it was like this when they got here… except with the king's body, of course."

"Not much struggle."

"Yeah." Broken English or not, Sergei was sharp. "Either the king was too surprised to react, or the killer was just that good."

"Stone Lady is *very* good."

"Yeah." I couldn't quite mask the pride in my voice. Her reputation might end up getting us all executed, but it was still kind of cool to hear someone called the Monster giving my pseudo-girlfriend mad respect. "But not *this* good, I don't think. And you guys are ridiculously hard to kill."

"Take head. Crush heart. Kills everyone."

"There still should have been time for him to fight back." I looked over at the burly manpire. "What was Tomasso's Talent?"

"Lightbringer, like father."

"He… made light?" And Anastasia thought *her* Talent was one of the lesser ones!

"Yes. Aurelius conjure sun in assault on Mad King's castle. Melt stone walls like *masla*."

Okay, I wasn't sure what *masla* was, but that sounded badass. "So… why didn't Tomasso do that to his attacker?"

"Maybe killer take head first?" Sergei frowned even as he spoke. "Is much difficult to do."

"Yeah. Even Anastasia had to chop Xavier down *before* she took his head." I revisited the crime scene report, focusing on the areas I'd previously skimmed. "Huh. Denarius' team thinks the chest wounds happened *first.* According to their timeline, Tomasso would have been painting when the killer entered." I nodded to the fallen easel.

"He then turned and was stabbed in the chest by some sort of stone implement here." *Here* was the site of the primary bloodstain. It was a far cry from the lakes of blood that television—and Tarantino movies—had programmed me to look for, partly because vampires had less blood in their bodies than humans and partly because Hollywood was all about ridiculous excess.

"It was only then that they think the attacker decapitated him. Tomasso toppled over, and his head was placed… there." *There* being the coffee table, a detail that seemed a lot weirder now that I was standing in Tomasso's townhouse. "Why carry it all the way over?"

I dug back into the folder for the crime scene photo of the coffee table. The head had been found lying on its side on the table, dead eyes staring at the entryway. I showed the photo to Sergei. "The positioning has to be deliberate, but I'm not sure what message it was intended to convey. Or why it was lying on its side."

"Maybe it fall over?" Sergei shrugged. "Head was torn from body, yes? Not cut by axe. Stump jagged, not smooth. Hard to balance without spike."

There was the sort of graphic detail my brain didn't need, especially with all the garbage already giving me nightmares. For the first time in a long while, I felt nostalgic for the days when my job just meant taking pictures of half-naked cheating spouses.

"So, the killer put it upright, but it had fallen over by the time the body was found?"

"Yes."

"Maybe. That still leaves the question of what message the killer intended." I eyed the manpire. "What would you do if you walked in on Vasily's decapitated head arranged like that?"

"Laugh."

I blinked.

"Then burn town," the manpire continued thoughtfully. "Kill Dmitri the Younger and clan so they not challenge Vasily's daughter." He paused, then nodded firmly. "Drink vodka."

Apparently, Lucia's bloodthirstiness wasn't *all* from the Borghesi side of the family tree. "And what if the head had just been left next to the body?"

"Same."

That was no help at all. I made a mental note to discuss the head with Ana and Lucia later. Maybe they'd know what it meant. Assuming it meant anything at all… the killer *could* have just been some sort of neat-freak nutcase. Either way, it was a minor mystery next to the still-pressing concern of Tomasso's struggle-free murder.

Wait a minute…

Tomasso had been painting?

"Do you paint, Sergei?"

"No. Write poems."

I grinned. "Ask a stupid question…"

Sergei arched a pale blonde eyebrow.

"You're serious?"

"Is problem?"

"No. It's just that you're not…" Miraculously, I caught myself before going any further down the road to conversational oblivion. "Never mind. I don't paint either, but I had a friend in high school who did." As I spoke, my eyes darted around the room. "He would spend hours in the art room randomly tossing paint at a canvas. Mostly, he just made a mess. But you know what always played a big part in his creative process?"

"Paint?"

"Well… sure."

"And brush. And canvas. And—"

"Music." I interrupted, nodding to the wireless speakers placed around the room, and the small stereo almost hidden on the near bookshelf. "If Tomasso was rocking out to death metal at the time, even his vampire ears would have been useless. The killer would have been able to sneak right up to him, and make sure that first strike caused enough damage to incapacitate the king."

Damn. I was *so* good at this job!

My moment of self-congratulation ended when Sergei crossed to the stereo in question and hit play. The quiet, soothing sounds of some sort of classical piece filled the room. Even my purely human ears could pick out a multitude of sounds over that gentle musical backdrop: Sergei's dismissive grunt, a car driving by on the street outside, and the whoosh of air as all the wind went out of my 'death metal' theory.

So, how the hell did someone sneak up on a vampire, especially one as paranoid as Tomasso had become? And for that matter, why did that question seem so familiar?

"What we do now?"

"I don't know. Can you check the windows up here for any signs of forced entry that Denarius' team might have missed? The front door could have been a red herring." I spread the crime scene photos out on Tomasso's large desk. "I'll canvas the study itself. Maybe we'll find something that didn't make it into these pictures or the report."

Like a motive.

Or an explanation for the impossible.

Or a killer not named Anastasia.

ooo

There is no such thing as a perfect crime. That's one of the many lessons I'd picked up from first reading, then watching, Sherlock Holmes. There would inevitably be some piece of the puzzle that just needed to be recognized, some dangling thread that, when pulled, would unravel the tapestry of deception.

Sadly, that knowledge didn't do me a damn bit of good.

The murder of Tomasso was as imperfect as they came. Anyone with a brain would recognize that someone swift and precise enough to kill Tomasso without a struggle would hardly be stupid enough to leave a mountain of physical evidence behind. *Especially* when they took the trouble to wipe the security logs. The frame job was almost painfully obvious.

But as everyone insisted on telling me, I needed more than reasonable doubt to survive the vampire trial. I needed actual proof, and the only tangible evidence found so far had been carefully—if obviously—planted.

There had to be something I was missing. For at least the sixth time, I ran through the chronology of events, as we knew them:

One: Anastasia arrives in Rome and makes her way to a safehouse.

Two: Security footage shows a vaguely feminine someone crossing the road toward Tomasso's townhome.

Three: Tomasso is killed.

Four: Several hours later, Tomasso's body is found.

Five: An anonymous tip leads to Anastasia's safehouse, where the Secundus is somehow caught napping.

Wait… caught napping. "Aha!"

"Yes?" Sergei stomped back into the room. "You solve murder?"

"Well, no. Just realized something that might help."

I was a poor judge of ancient manpire facial expressions, but Sergei *seemed* unimpressed.

"When Denarius and the Watch went after Anastasia," I continued, "they caught her napping."

"And?"

"And given her training, that shouldn't have been possible. Which means *both* King Tomasso and Anastasia were caught unaware. That's what people in my business call a suspicious pattern."

"Fah." Sergei shook his head. "Magic then?"

"Seems like it. We need to make a list of spells or Talents that would help mask someone's presence, and who in Rome might have access to them."

"Palace will have information."

"Sounds good. I think we're done here anyway." I tucked the photos and report back into their folder. "Let's go hit the Bitter End and call it a night."

We left Tomasso's sad study and the hall of even sadder paintings to take the stairs down and out to the street. In the hour or so we'd spent inside, the temperature had dropped precipitously. I was glad I'd thought to bring the leather jacket I'd… inherited… from the previous San Diego city mediator.

The femmepire Watch member was still standing in the same spot, but her companion was nowhere in sight.

"Where's medium-height, dark, and scowly?" I asked.

"It was his turn to make the rounds." Apparently, vampire eyesight was sufficient for making out my perplexed expression, as she elaborated. "Checking the perimeter? We don't spend all of our time standing in front of doors."

"Well, we're done here and heading over to the Bitter End. We'll be there for an hour or so, if you get off duty and still feel like tequila."

For just a moment, her dark eyes sparkled with something like consideration, but she shook her head. "I don't know how such things work in America, but here it takes more than a pretty smile and AB-negative blood."

"For you to drink tequila?" I asked, confused. After two years, I was no longer freaked out that vampires could smell my blood type.

Sergei mercifully stepped in. "He is not looking for date."

Oh. Yeah, that hadn't been what I was doing. "He's right—" I started to say, but Sergei was continuing.

"Is in love with Stone Lady."

"How the hell did you figure *that* out?"

"Is obvious every time you say name," he told me. "And you say name far too much on endless drive from palace."

"Well, *someone* had to make conversation," I muttered, turning back to the femmepire. "He's right though. I'm just offering free booze, nothing more."

"In that case—" The femmepire's words cut off. "Did you hear that, ambassador?"

Before the burly pirate manpire could reply, something flew out of the darkness, crashing into the concrete sidewalk with a wet thump. In the soft streetlights, I could barely make out the crumpled remains of the missing Watch member.

"That's not good."

From the darkness came a sound like a half-dozen angry women marching their way across the street in stiletto heels, but what came toward us was even scarier than that. It was like some mad deity had fused a scorpion, a roach, and a Tyrannosaurus. Whatever this thing was, it was at least eight feet tall and half again as long, with multi-faceted eyes set in a face otherwise dominated by serrated mandibles. Its chitinous body was supported by four sets of barbed claws, and pincers extended outward from the armored torso. Trailing behind it, casually smashing aside a parked car, was a segmented tail and stinger.

"What the hell is that?" I wanted to know.

"Is Illutu," came the response.

Well, shit.

○○○

The remaining Watch member started to interpose herself between the giant bug monster and us, but Sergei stopped her with an outstretched arm.

"Is mine," he said as he began a slow, rolling walk toward the nightmarish creature. "Take human to safety." The closer Sergei got to the bug, the larger it looked, but the manpire seemed unconcerned.

For a moment, the Illutu was frozen, nonplussed by its opponent's confidence. Then it flowed forward at liquid speed, its many legs, mandibles, and pincers stabbing and slashing like a one-creature medieval army.

Sergei didn't have Anastasia's breathtaking blend of speed and control. He didn't have Denarius' trick of blending into the shadows and striking wherever the opponent was weakest. What he had was strength. In abundance. The manpire batted aside two lance-like limbs, stepped over a third, and caught the claws crashing down upon him from above without any sign of effort. Even so, the bug loomed over him like—

I frowned. Either the Illutu was shrinking or… no, Sergei was definitely growing. From one breath to the next, the manpire doubled in size, exploding out of his romance-novel outfit like Bruce Banner bidding bon voyage to yet another pair of pants. If the manpire had been buff in his normal form, he was almost grotesquely so now, corded arms abnormally long, knots of muscles shifting across his back like tectonic plates. He released the Illutu's claws and hammered a lawnmower-sized fist into the creature's chest, sending it skidding ten feet back across the street and into another ill-fated BMW.

Jesus. Lucia's uncles were *both* badasses. *My* uncle taught kindergarten.

Despite the strength of Sergei's blow, the Illutu seemed unharmed. It crawled out of the wreckage of automobile and rushed back in, pouring over the cobblestones like an avalanche. Super-sized manpire though he was, Sergei was forced to give ground before its furious assault.

"Shouldn't we be helping him?" I asked the femmepire guard.

"The ambassador told me to keep you safe, so I will do so," she growled, taking me by the arm. "My car is just around the corner."

"That corner?" In the darkness to our left, another enormous shape stirred, though the clacking of its pincers was lost beneath Sergei's battle roars.

"Shit. A nest only has three knights. What is so important to send two of them here?"

"It's possible I pissed someone off."

The femmepire spun me in the other direction. "We have to run for it."

"Can Sergei take *two* of those things?"

"He is the Monster. If anyone could—"

Her reply didn't fill me with confidence. "I'm not a fan of the whole *people-dying-bravely-for-me* thing. Between the three of us, we can finish off that first bug, and make it an even fight for Sergei and the second."

She finally nodded. "Use whatever gifts your non-human heritage grants you but stay at a distance if you can."

Non-human heritage? Word really *did* get around at the palace. I nodded, but she was already charging in to face Sergei's opponent, a pistol materializing in one hand and what looked like a pickaxe in the other.

I took a deep breath and reached down for Lucia's power.

There was absolutely nothing to grab onto.

Still.

"Damn it, Minerva!" Whatever the goddess had done to me in the hallway remained in effect, leaving me with only my imaginary werewolf virus and even less reliable combat skills. I looked for some sort of weapon, but there was a surprising dearth of rocket launchers and tanks available on the deserted streets of Rome. "I guess I'll be moral support this time around?"

Then the second Illutu took even that option away from me. Instead of joining in the battle against the two vampires, it bypassed the melee entirely to make a beeline straight toward me.

Only mild dehydration kept me from peeing myself. I tried to run, knowing it was futile.

The femmepire stopped on a dime and turned to hurl herself at the second Illutu like a tiny missile. She bounced off without causing any damage, but the impact altered the bug's charge just enough that the claw I hadn't even seen thundered past my face instead of through it. Rolling to her feet, the femmepire moved back in, gun spitting fire and bullets, pickaxe flashing out to strike at weak points in the bug's armored carapace.

Neither weapon had any effect. In fact, a car window shattering was my first indicator that bullets were ricocheting off the Illutu in all directions. Moments later, the gun clicked empty. The femmepire hurled it at the bug's face, grabbed the pickaxe with both hands, and struck even more fiercely.

It wasn't anywhere near enough to break through the creature's armor, but her frenzied strikes did finally get its attention. Lightning-fast, it curled the length of its body about her like a centipede. Then, it struck from every direction, pincers flashing down, clawed legs stabbing inward. Even the tail snaked its way through like a venom-tipped jackhammer.

The femmepire was brave and she was undoubtedly skilled, but either she didn't have a Talent yet or the one she had couldn't save her.

Three legs struck home, followed by that terrible tail. She was still twitching when the tail unfolded to its full height, lifting her body fifteen feet into the air. Then her body flew through the air to crash heavily into a nearby car.

The Illutu continued its spin until its head was again facing me. Its body slowly straightened out behind it, tail waving like a rattlesnake's. Once again, it started scuttling toward me.

When a second, far larger, form struck the charging bug, I didn't even have it in me to be surprised. I just stared dumbly at what had become a jumble of far too many legs. By the time the two Illutu had sorted themselves out, Sergei was on them, wielding a torn claw in one hand like a whaling harpoon. One of his enormous hands flicked something small and metal in my direction, and the one part of my brain not gibbering with fear recognized the objects as they landed nearby.

Car keys.

"Run away like little rabbit, Smith," Sergei roared, even his voice wildly different in this form. "I show creatures what real monster is."

My protestations of bravery to the now-dead femmepire were long forgotten. I scooped up the car keys, and sprinted for the Renault—

—only to realize exactly *which* car the femmepire had been hurled into. The roof of Sergei's Renault was caved in and two of its tires had blown out from the impact. That car would need thousands of dollars of bodywork and the blessing of at least two automotive-focused demigods if it was ever going to drive again.

I turned back to Sergei just in time to see the manpire take a heavy claw to his head. He dropped to one knee, and it was pure chance that his raised forearm deflected what might have been a killing blow. With a cry that shook the buildings around us, he surged back to his feet, bloodied, but not yet dead.

"Run!" he shouted a second time.

Feeling like a coward, I did just that.

I wasn't even two blocks away when something lunged at me from an alleyway. My head snapped forward from an unseen blow, and pain sent me spiraling into darkness.

CHAPTER 34

IN WHICH ITALY FEELS A LOT LIKE HOME

I came to slowly, conscious first of the sound of voices, then of the cold cement beneath my body, and finally, of all that had transpired in my flight from the apocalypse-sized roaches of doom. That last thought was enough to force my eyes open, but despite the presence of nearby lights, the world they revealed was blurry and indistinct.

Either I'd been taken to another dimension and my eyes were struggling to adjust or—

I winced as the next sensation made itself known: pain. Underneath the pain was nausea, swelling like the ocean I did my very best to avoid. It said something about the depths my life had sunk to that I immediately recognized the symptoms of a concussion. I'd started to lose count of the number of times I'd woken up in a cell, head ringing…

Which hopefully was strictly a factor of how many times I'd gotten captured, and *not* a consequence of those concussions themselves.

Even doubled and blurry, my confines slowly started to make sense. I was in some sort of a prison cell—three walls and a barred gate.

The voices I'd first heard were coming from the other side of that gate, down what must have been a hall and out of sight.

Whoever had captured me, they weren't speaking English, but I listened anyway as the conversation swiftly devolved into a shouting match, the echoes of angry voices bouncing around my cell like a marching band on parade. There was the loud slam of a door, followed by silence and a few muttered words that, even to my ears, were clearly curses. Soon after, footsteps came my way.

He was no vampire, given the heavy jowls and twice-broken nose. Beneath a tangle of quickly graying hair, his face was worn and leathery, a scar cutting through the left side of his upper lip.

At least I thought it was a scar. With the way my vision was wobbling in and out, it could have been a toothpick. Or a cigarette. Or nothing at all.

The man wore a long-sleeved shirt—top two buttons undone to expose even more gray hair—a pair of jeans and an expression that was one-part pissed off and two-parts scared.

Pissed off, I understood. I tended to have that effect on people, through absolutely no fault of my own. But *scared?* That was a new one.

Staying a step away from the bars, as if concerned that I would miraculously heal, leap to my feet, and lunge at him, the man stared at me, saying nothing.

I stared back, trying to project an aura of cool competence despite my position of undeniable weakness on the floor. At least I was clothed this time. When you spent as much time getting captured as I did, you learned to treasure the small victories.

Finally, he spoke. I shook my head.

"I'm sorry. I don't speak Italian."

More words, this time, accompanied by angry gestures.

I repeated myself, but he clearly didn't speak English, and my words set off another, even angrier monologue. I sat back, wiped away the drool that had dried on my chin, and waited.

Eventually, he wore himself out. With a frustrated growl, he pawed half-heartedly at the bars and stalked away, pulling a phone from his pocket. The unseen door slammed again.

If there was ever a time to make my escape, this was it. I eyed the bars. If I could get over to them, I might be able to put my lockpicking skills to good use. The tools I'd used in times past were by my bed back in San Diego, and my captors had emptied my pockets of everything of value, but those were just details. I'd figure it out. Hunger might be the mother of invention, but imprisonment had to at least be an aunt.

I pulled my legs under me, dropped my hands to the floor and started crawling toward the door.

I passed out again about halfway there.

ooo

This time, I woke quickly. One moment, I was blissfully unaware, the next I was fully alert, eyes open, with the cell wall cool against my back.

Wait… what? Hadn't I been almost to the bars when I passed out? How was I back against the far wall? For a brief moment, I flirted with the possibility that my whole failed escape had been a hallucination.

The pool of vomit in the center of the cell, right near where I remembered collapsing, put that fantasy to rest.

Given that the past month had included the-freaking-goddess-Athena, bug mercenaries, and a twenty-nine-scoop sundae with ice cream that Bill swore was from a dimension built out of the stuff, finding myself a handful of feet away from where I'd passed out didn't merit much thought, but my brain didn't want to let it go. How the hell had I gotten from there back to here?

"I moved you."

I looked to my right. Seated in her ragged black dress, looking like the world's most malnourished reaper, was the Rag Lady.

"What?"

"You asked how you got from over there to here," she said simply. "I moved you."

I frowned. Had I said that out loud?

"Yes."

Damn it. I really needed to stop doing that.

I shook my head, then frowned a second time when the motion failed to bring on the expected nausea. In fact, my vision was mostly okay now too. "I really thought I had a concussion."

"You did."

"Did you—?"

"Oh, no." Her smile was sharp and gone in an instance. "Healing is not my forte."

"What *is* your forte?"

"Secrets, mostly."

And that explained exactly what we were doing here. I nodded to the bars of the cell. "If you wanted to talk, we could have just met for coffee or something. Kidnapping me seems a little bit much."

"Kidnapping? You think I did this?"

"You didn't?"

"You helped me, Investigator Smith. Why would I repay your kindness with treachery?"

Because that's how it always goes. This time, I managed to not speak the words aloud. Instead, I forced my brain into action. If she wasn't one of my captors, then she had gotten in here all on her own. And if she could do that…

"I'm not entirely sure you needed my help."

The Rag Lady shrugged. "You'd be surprised. None of the Jade Dragons should be taken lightly. Ti An, least of all."

That raised a myriad of fascinating conversation topics, but for once, I had more important things on my mind. "Do you know who *did* kidnap me then? There was a guy—"

"In this country, they call themselves *Vita Unica*. One life."

"Isn't that a shoe company?"

"You know actual shoe brands?" The Rag Lady glanced down at my own scuffed Air Jordans but let the matter slide. "There's no relation between the company and those who have imprisoned you. That I know of, anyway."

"One Life." I shook my head. "What are they? Demons? Chupacabras? Lizards in people suits?"

"They are human, much like you used to be, Mr. Smith."

"Like I *used* to be?"

"Yes."

"What does that mean?!"

"I'm sorry. Some secrets must be discovered on their own." Her Adam's apple bobbed up and down as she swallowed. "*Vita Unica* is one of many organizations slowly mobilizing across the world."

"Mobilizing? To do what?"

"Expose their supernatural neighbors, of course." She cocked her head. "You didn't think you and the vampires' blood donors were the only humans who knew the truth of this world, did you?"

I *had* thought that, but in fairness, I'd spent very little time or brainpower on the subject. In my experience, vamps just mindwiped anyone who stumbled onto a truth they weren't prepared to see. "If other people know, why hasn't the truth spread? This is the sort of news TMZ would love to break."

"Most people don't want to know. They're not ready for that truth and forcing them to face it might do more harm to the human world than good. For now, organizations like *Vita Unica* are focused on gathering information."

"For now?"

This time, her smile held no humor at all. "Eventually, there will be sufficient evidence to convince even the most strident of doubters. I weep for the carnage that will follow."

Silence fell in my small cell. I could imagine the public outcry that would occur if the truth was known. Humanity was used to thinking of itself as the dominant form of life on our planet; what would happen when it learned it was far closer to the bottom of the ladder than the top?

If our history was any indication, it would mean war. And based on my own experiences, it seemed unlikely our planet would survive that war.

Suddenly, my own problems seemed less urgent. "We can't let it get that far. When my jailers come back, will you act as a translator?"

"For what purpose?"

"Peace... and the survival of all our species."

"You believe you can convince them that creatures of legend and nightmare—many of whom view humans as a food source—should be left in peace?"

"Yeah." I met her incredulous look and shrugged. "I'm a mediator."

"I would like to see you try," she murmured. "Sadly, you will not get the opportunity to do so today."

That sounded definitive. "Why not? Or is this another secret I have to discover on my own?"

"This one I freely share." She cocked her head, listening to something my own senses couldn't perceive. "Each Illutu nest can support only a specific number of creatures at one time, Investigator Smith. A nest mother, of course, followed by a dozen drones—"

"And the two bus-sized warriors I ran into tonight."

"Knights," she corrected. "And there are not two, but three."

Finally, I heard it too: the sound of screams and people dying.

ooo

I scrambled to my feet without so much as a twinge from my formally concussed brain. A cursory examination showed that the barred door was still locked. I spun back to the Rag Lady.

"Can you save them?"

"The humans?" She rose to her feet, drawing up her hood so that it once more hid her scarred features. "Why would I do that?"

"They're just people. They don't deserve to die to a giant cockroach."

"Nobody deserves to die to a giant cockroach, but I cannot interfere without revealing myself."

"To Ti An? How?" I waved off what I already knew was going to be some sort of evasion. "Never mind. It doesn't matter. Can you at least get me out of here, so *I* can help?"

"No," she admitted, "but I brought you someone who can."

Before I could ask the obvious question, a cool wind swept through me, resolving into the shape of Valentina. She was translucent almost to the point of invisibility, but the black-gummed smile on her face filled me with relief.

"You're okay!" I went to hug her, stopped as the impossibility of the action sank in, and settled for my own happy smile and a wave.

"I found this one wandering down paths without end," added the Rag Lady. "Nudging her away from those paths was a small enough thing, and one that appears to have gone unnoticed."

"I don't know why you did it, and I doubt you'll tell me anyway, but thank you for helping my friend."

"That you call a White Lady friend is reason enough." The Rag Lady nodded to both Valentina and me. "Take him as far as you can, my dear."

"We need to save these people," I reminded them both.

"You are a brave soul, investigator, but you are not a fighter."

I shrugged, not willing to give up the argument just yet. "Let's get my stuff, and then we'll see what's what."

"What will be will be." The Rag Lady folded in on herself until there was nothing but rags. Then, even the rags faded.

I looked at the spot where she had been for a long moment, a myriad of questions running through my mind. Unfortunately, whoever she was, whatever she was, the Rag Lady was gone, and we were running out of time.

Valentina's ghostly hand found mine. She took the first breath I could ever remember seeing and tugged me forward through the barred door.

I'd only gone ghost walking once before with Valentina, but it had been one of the scariest yet also coolest trips of my life. This one was quite a bit shorter… we rematerialized just on the other side of the gate, with Valentina somehow even less visible than she'd been minutes before.

"Are you sure you're okay?"

She waggled a hand in the air but waved me down the hall. We passed a second cell—empty, thankfully—and found ourselves in a small room. Against the near wall was a desk with a computer, a printer, and a stack of papers and photos. My possessions—and the keys to Sergei's pulverized Renault—were on a table along the far wall. I hurried over, scooping up the necklace with Valentina's ring and draping it back around my neck. Sergei's keys went into one pocket and my mostly useless phone and mostly empty wallet went into the other.

A closed door to the left was the only visible exit from the room other than the hall we'd just come down. The screams had died off, but through that door, I could still hear the distant whimper of someone in pain.

"We need to help them," I told Valentina again. "The Illutu wouldn't be here if it wasn't for me."

Valentina shook dark curls out of her face and frowned, but she squared her slim shoulders, and turned to face the exterior door. The wind that rose about her was barely more than a breeze, too weak to even stir her hair or nightgown. Before my eyes, she faded even further.

"Stop! I think the Rag Lady was right, V. Neither of us is in any condition to fight." I winced as the whimper choked off with a gurgle. Something large tore through a distant wall, coming closer. "As much as I want to help…"

Valentina nodded, but before she could take my hand a second time, I crossed over to the desk, and scooped up the papers and photos lying there. Whatever surveillance *Vita Unica* had been doing, I didn't want to leave it behind for the police to find when they came to investigate this massacre.

"Okay. Let's get the hell out of here."

Something exploded through the wall in front of us in a rush of sound and terrifying motion, but we were already ghost-walking, and the knight's mandibles closed on empty air.

○○○

Any lingering questions regarding Valentina's weakness were answered by that desperate flight. We barely made it a block before we winked back into existence. Valentina was so translucent that I could barely see her silent scream of frustration.

"It's okay," I assured her. "You got us out. Now it's my turn to get us to safety."

I ran down the street in the same direction we'd already been traveling, taking a quick turn on the first cross street we came to, followed by another turn three blocks down. I had a vague idea of looking for Sergei, in the hopes that he had somehow survived the first two Illutu knights. Unfortunately, none of these streets looked familiar. For all I knew, *Vita Unica's* secret base was on the other side of the city from Tomasso's townhouse.

Even worse, my knowledge of Rome's geography came entirely from the movies and was unsurprisingly useless for navigating the actual city. The lights on the horizon told me I was still within a few miles of one of the city's tourist attractions, but I had no way of knowing whether it was the Colosseum, Vatican City, or one of half a dozen other locations whose cultural value were undeniable even if their names were escaping me.

I kept running… away from those lights and the potential for massive casualties.

It was only when I crossed a small bridge and heard the rush of water beneath me that I remembered something; Tomasso's townhouse wasn't the *only* place in Rome I knew.

I came to a dead stop at the end of the bridge. What had Sergei said about the Bitter End? South of the river?

Again, my lack of basic geography failed me. Did Rome have more than one river, and if so, what were the chances of this being the one Sergei had mentioned. And for that matter, which way was south?

The last question, at least, was easily answered. I pulled out my phone. It might be useless for making calls, but the apps still worked. The compass showed that I had been going west. I stepped off the bridge and took a left. Now what?

Valentina floated in front of me, clearly wondering why I wasn't running anymore.

"That thing will catch us, eventually," I explained, "unless we can steal a car and drive it back to the palace. That seems unlikely, since I skipped the class on hot-wiring and don't really know where the palace is, anyway. Our only other option is to find a place to hide."

A stray thought burst into my head. Lord Kala had once told me that the White Ladies were not truly dead anymore, and that something about their half-life made them incompatible with his domain. Was that the sort of thing that Valentina might sense, and if so, could she guide us to the Bitter End?

When I asked her just that, the ghost paused, cocking her head.

I recognized focus when I saw it, and gave her space, glancing around for signs of the remaining knight. On the east side of the bridge, a figure appeared, but it was human-sized, and walking at a casual pace. The pedestrian's sense of timing couldn't have been worse. I was stepping forward to warn him away when he passed under a streetlamp, revealing the carefully anonymous face of an Illutu drone.

Shit. "We've got to go, V!"

Valentina nodded, and was instantly in motion, streaming out in front of me like a white-winged angel.

Behind us, two footsteps became four, then eight. An even louder noise told me that the Illutu knight had joined the drones in pursuit.

As we fled, I fumbled for whatever it was that had let me sprint across the palace to save Anastasia from her night-time bath, but there was nothing in me other than adrenaline. After a dozen blocks, even that started to fade. My lungs were blocks of ice, my legs numb except for a growing pain in my feet and knees. Maybe I should have joined Kayla and Darlene's running club after all.

I struggled on, fighting for air as another stray thought tried to force its way out of my subconscious. Something about the Bitter End maybe? Like smoke, it slipped through my fingers.

I kept running, hoping like hell that Valentina knew where she was going.

There are limits to what the human body can endure. As a late-twenties, beer-loving, couch potato, my limits were significantly less impressive. I was eyeballing cars as we ran past, hoping against hope that someone had left one unlocked, engine running and keys in the ignition, when a glorious sight came into view. The building itself was completely unfamiliar—a bistro, closed for the night, instead of San Diego's cigar bar—but the staircase attached to that building and leading down below the street was instantly recognizable.

I hurtled the chain link barrier at the top of the staircase and failed to stick my landing on the second or third stair down. By pure luck, my flailing arm caught hold of the stair rail in time to prevent an untimely and thoroughly humiliating demise, but the papers I'd taken from *Vita Unica* went everywhere.

I made my way quickly down the stairs, scooping up photos and documents as I went. When I reached the bottom, I was alone.

Valentina had stopped halfway down the stairs. As I watched, she stepped forward again, only to impact what appeared to be an invisible wall. Kala had been totally underselling that whole incompatibility thing.

"It's okay," I told her. "I'm safe now… get yourself someplace where you can rest and recover."

She nodded, waved, and faded away completely.

One person safe, one to go. I turned and faced the blank stone wall that hid the portal to Kala's domain. It was only then that the thought which had been nagging at me for most of my flight finally came into focus.

The Bitter End's portal didn't open for humans.

I was really starting to hate Italy.

CHAPTER 35

I stood at the base of the stairwell for a solid twenty seconds, staring at the wall that wasn't really a wall, even as the Illutu drones and knight closed in on my location. Both Lady Manassa and the Rag Lady had suggested I was something other than human. If they were wrong, I'd just boxed myself in.

I reached toward the wall.

Nothing happened… not until the tips of my fingers were almost brushing the stone. Then there was a shimmer, and light poured through the mortar, growing in strength and brilliance until the wall itself disappeared, and a simple golden portal hung in the air.

Holy shit. It was true. *What the hell was happening to me?*

Urgent footsteps closing in on the stairwell interrupted my moment of introspection. Survive now, cogitate later. I offered up a quick prayer to whatever deities might still be listening and stepped through the portal.

As ever, the transition to the Bitter End was almost disappointing. As my rear foot lifted from the streets of Rome, its partner came down on a floor of black stone threaded with gold. That same stone formed the walls and ceiling around me. At the bottom of another flight of stairs, the pathway lit by tiki torches that gave off light but no heat, was the bar's front door.

Barry, the world's oldest wereboar, was standing in front of that door, looking very much like someone had dropped a gray-skinned head onto a brick wall, and then squeezed the whole ensemble into a suit. Small, reddish eyes widened as I approached.

"Smith? How did you get through the portal?"

I shrugged. "Werewolf blood, I guess."

For the first time in our multi-year acquaintance, Barry looked halfway interested. "You've been killing wolves?"

"What? No!" I paused. "Well, yes, actually, but that was a while ago, and it was just the one and… you know what? Never mind." I glanced over my shoulder at the portal hanging behind me. "Just so you know, there might be a couple of mercenary cockroaches coming through that. You probably want to armor up… or whatever it is you do."

"Illutu?" Barry scowled. "Why the hell would I get between them and their prey?"

"Because you're a bouncer, and they might be coming to murder one of this establishment's honored guests?"

Barry grunted. "I'm not sure you're technically even allowed in here without a chaperone."

"The portal apparently feels otherwise. Are you saying you're smarter than it is?"

"Are you saying I'm not?"

This was why Barry and I rarely chatted. After all this time, I still didn't know what Steve—mohawked ninja vampire badass that he was—saw in the bouncer.

"Well, if you want, I can just sit out here, but when the bugs come and murder me, there's a high chance of my blood and bodily fluids getting all over your shoes." I eyed the footwear in question. "And size twenty-eight dress shoes can't be cheap."

I knew I'd scored a point when Barry changed topics. "Who sicced the Illutu on you, anyway? And since when is there a nest in San Diego? Does Steven know? Is he okay?"

"I'm not in San Diego. I entered from Rome. Speaking of which… why are you awake? It's like eight in the morning back home."

I was pretty proud of doing *that* math in my head, even if I had no idea whether it was correct.

"I'm awake because I'm working."

"I have to imagine Lord Kala can afford *two* bouncers."

"Lord Kala does what he wishes, human."

I didn't bother to correct him on my species.

"Besides," he continued, "I don't sleep."

"You can't sleep?"

"Don't have to." Barry rolled one massive shoulder back and then the next, each motion accompanied by the ominous sound of muscle fibers stretching. "Given what this extra time has cost me, why would I waste any of it sleeping?"

The obvious answer was *to snuggle with your pillow in the hopes that it will one day become a real woman* but given both Barry's gayness and his already low opinion of me, I didn't bother supplying that answer. Instead, I nodded at the open door just past the wereboar.

"So, are you going to let me in or not? Any moment now, a bug's going to come through that makes *you* look like a toddler, and I'd rather not be here when it does."

Barry yawned. "Sorry, Smith. No chaperone, no entry."

"Fine." I took a seat on the bottom step, placing the papers I'd taken from *Vita Unica* next to me. "I guess I'll just sit here, and we'll see what happens."

"Guess so."

Barry had always been kind of an asshole and my newly strained friendship with Steve hadn't helped matters in the slightest. If he wasn't willing to help me, or at least get out of my way, it was time to appeal to a higher authority.

"Actually, is your boss in? I need to chat with him."

"Sorry, Lord Kala isn't taking visitors."

"Dude, it's one thing to be a dick to me on your own time, but it's a whole other thing when your shitty attitude interferes with Lord Kala's business."

Barry took one long stride to loom over me, gray face hard and tusks quivering with poorly suppressed rage. "If Steven didn't still harbor some faint trace of affection for you, I'd squash you right now like a—"

"Bug?" Knowing that the world hated to pass up straight lines like that, I checked the portal, but there were still no Illutu to be seen.

"I'm giving you the word, straight from the boss himself. He ain't taking visitors."

"Oh." I gave him an apologetic nod, one very manly dude to another, but the angry wereboar just grunted and returned to his post. "Any idea why?"

"He doesn't tell me these things, and I don't ask." Barry cracked the knuckles on his meaty left hand, one after the other, like a kid popping bubble wrap. "Maybe you should go find somewhere else to hide out from the bugs."

"That's not actually why I'm here."

"Do tell."

"It's a bit of a long story, but I'm investigating a murder. At the crime scene, they recovered fragments of stone." I waved at the natural rock surrounding us. "Stone exactly like this."

"Did you seriously come here to accuse Lord Kala of murder?"

"What? No!" Kala was a demigod of death and time, which put simple murder—even a king's murder—far beneath him. Even more importantly, he never left his home dimension. "But I've never seen this stone anywhere else, so I was wondering if the killer came here first and took a few samples when they left."

"Yeah, because Lord Kala is going to stand for some idiot chipping the walls of his domain." Barry rolled his eyes. "So, what was your plan?"

"I wanted to ask if he'd seen or felt anything. Since he's unavailable…" I shrugged. "I don't know. Maybe I can look around or something?"

I could see the word *No* forming on the wereboar's lips, but I spoke again before he could. "Please? It's really important, dude."

He sighed. "I have no idea what Steven sees in you. Are you always this much of a pain in the ass?"

"Probably," I admitted, "but I've got a little bit of extra incentive this time."

"A fat bonus if you crack the case early?"

"The woman I love dies if I don't."

The enormous wereboar fell silent, or at least as silent as someone with lungs the size of garbage bags could be. He glanced at the door and then back at me, broad face conflicted. Finally, he sighed, sending a wave of garlic in my direction. "You're lucky I'm such a romantic, Smith."

"You'll let me search the place?"

"As long as you stay out of Lord Kala's rooms, I guess so."

"And the Illutu?"

"If they haven't showed yet, they ain't going to. Humans aren't the only species unwelcome here, you know."

I met his eyes, trying to let the gratitude shine through my own. "Thank you."

"Soon as one customer complains, you're out on your fat ass."

I was starting to think Barry just didn't like me.

ooo

It was anyone's guess how long searching The Bitter End would take. *Literally* anyone's guess, given that the bar seemed to grow and shrink of its own accord and time was a malleable thing, as Barry's continued existence—many decades after any other were would have gone mad and died—demonstrated.

The wereboar watched me without comment. *Mostly* without comment: every time the portal brought someone new to the bar, I flinched, and every flinch triggered a baritone chuckle from Steve's jerk of a boyfriend.

A full half-hour passed before I finally started to accept that the Illutu weren't coming in after me, and by then, I was still only halfway through the entrance chamber. Even with my search limited to surfaces with visible gold—like in the fragments Denarius had shown me—there were acres of area to cover. Whatever talents I possessed—and I was sure I had some, no matter what Juliette might say to the contrary—there had to be better uses for them than this.

With the Illutu threat at least partially allayed, I had expanded my search area back up the stairs toward the portal. Halfway there, the smooth walls gave way to rough-hewn rock of the same material, and an already difficult task became damn near impossible. How was I supposed to tell the difference between stone that had chipped when Lord Kala carved out his bar and stone that had been purposefully extracted by Tomasso's killer, thousands of years later?

You're a Smith, I reminded myself. *Smith men aren't quitters.*

Unless you counted that whole community college thing.

And my ill-fated attempts to learn to play the guitar.

"Got to be honest, Smith," rumbled Barry, "if I *did* need to sleep, watching you work would do the trick."

I spun to give the bouncer a piece of my mind, my arm inadvertently passing right through the heatless flame of a nearby tiki torch. Thankfully, the flame didn't burn my leather coat. In fact, it didn't burn anything at all. Instead, it extinguished… and in the resulting patch of darkness, the gold thread in the stone around me let off its own dim glow.

"Huh. Never seen that before."

I ignored my gray-skinned and tusked peanut gallery, my mind flashing back to when Anastasia had taken on this stone's form to battle the Hound of Tartarus. The warehouse we'd fought in had been dim, lit primarily by the runes of the witches' evil ghost trap… but Anastasia hadn't glowed. I pulled out my phone and took a video of the phenomenon. If the stone in Denarius' airtight evidence locker of doom also glowed… we could prove it hadn't come from Anastasia.

I panned the phone across the stone wall, grateful that this latest version of my wonderphone had a decent camera. The gold thread continued down the stairs, its illumination fading as it approached the next tiki torch, but right at the boundary between darkness and light…

I took the five steps down to the next torch and extinguished it as well.

"Smith, not all of our customers can see in the dark. If someone falls, it's on you. Meaning, I'll point them in your direction, and let them do whatever the hell they want."

Again, I ignored the wereboar's warnings. In the greater swath of darkness, more of the gold vein glowed, but there were a couple of tiny spots where that river of light was broken. I'd already searched this stretch of wall once, but… I reached up and traced my finger along the nearest spot.

And found an honest-to-God divot, as long as my pinky finger, and less than an inch deep.

Maybe that video wasn't going to be necessary after all.

"What are you—"

Now that I'd found something, I was more than happy to gloat over it to Barry, but when I turned to him, he was motionless, mouth opened in mid-speech. Through the bar's open door, the bar's patrons were likewise still. Even the Mistborn—sentient globes of light that floated about the bar's interior—were frozen.

I looked away and Lord Kala was in front of me.

"Mr. Smith."

People tell me that Lord Beel-Kasan manifests as their deepest fear and judging by the reactions whenever Bill walks into a room, it's hard not to believe them. But to me, he's always appeared as a seven-foot-tall spear of asparagus, and there's nothing scary about vegetables. For my money, Kala is a thousand times freakier.

The demigod wore his usual hooded robe, the candle flames of his eyes barely illuminating the lines of a grinning skull face. The hands extending from his robe's tattered sleeves were fleshless bone, long and delicate. I'd watched a wave of those hands age an ogre centuries in less than a second, from life to death to dust dissipating on the barroom floor.

That said, he'd always been cool to me.

"Hey Kala," I told him brightly. "I thought you weren't receiving visitors."

"I was not." The skull turned to regard me, and those candle flames flared briefly into tiny bonfires. "As Lord Beel-Kasan has no doubt told you, our time is scarce these days."

Bill… hadn't said anything of the sort, but Bill told time with a Mickey Mouse watch, so I wasn't going to sweat the omission. Especially when I could ask Kala what he was talking about and get an answer that wasn't totally insane.

Before I could do just that, Kala continued. "However, when someone begins extinguishing the lights that line my stairwell, I cannot help but take an interest."

"Oops. Sorry about that." I spared another glance for the frozen bar interior. "Why do you bother with torches out here anyway? Couldn't you just get some of the Mistborn to light the way?"

"Like you, the Mistborn are customers, Mr. Smith. They are here to converse, to feed, and to mate. The illumination their presence provides is merely a fringe benefit."

"That makes sense." I paused, mid-nod. "Wait... did you say *mate?*"

"Perhaps we will discuss such matters another time. Of interest to me right now is why you are here and what you are doing."

Right. I gave him the same quick spiel I'd given Barry.

"The entirety of this place is my domain, much as Gehenna is Lord Beel-Kasan's." The demigod's voice echoed hollowly, as if from a great distance. "Nothing happens unless I allow it to, and I can tell you with absolute certainty that I would never permit someone to extract fragments of this realm's essence and then depart." A bony hand waved and the two tiki torches sprang back to life. "I am sorry that you wasted your time in the search. I know how little of it your species has."

Before he could leave—and given his ability to simply step out of time, catching him was a trick in itself—I pointed at the wall. "What are these divots then?"

Kala's sigh was long and surprisingly weary. He reached up a hand and ran his bony fingers across the wall in the direction I'd indicated. "There are no divots—" The hood turned back to me, and the candle flames in Kala's empty sockets flared and then guttered out. "This cannot be."

"—looking at?" finished Barry, as if no time had passed at all.

Lord Kala was nowhere to be found.

If Kala spoke to Barry, I didn't hear it, but the next thing I knew, the wereboar was turning his bulk to the bar, raising his voice so that it carried throughout the Bitter End's uncharted depths. "Bar's closed by Lord Kala's orders. Everybody out. Now."

Some of the creatures that filed past me could have mopped the floor with Barry—not to mention the entirety of a werewolf-infected Seal Team 6—but Kala's name meant the order was followed without a word of protest. In less than five minutes, the only people left in sight were Barry and myself.

"I didn't think the Bitter End ever closed," I said.

"It doesn't." Barry shook his head, bewildered. "Not once since I've worked here. What the hell did you do this time?" He waved off my protests of unfair accusation and pointed a thick finger toward the portal. "When Lord Kala says everybody out, Smith, he means *everyone.*"

"There's a nest of Illutu waiting to kill me out there, dude."

"Doubtful. Some of the customers that just left were headed back to Rome, like you… and they aren't the sort of creatures those bugs would want to mess with. Go."

I gave the bouncer one last pleading look, but my puppy eyes didn't appear to have any effect. "If they do kill me, my ghost is going to float on in and haunt you for the rest of forever."

"Doubtful," he repeated. "No body, no service. That's bar policy."

With that winner of an exit line, he turned around, stepped through the Bitter End's front door, and closed it behind him. The tiki torches around me guttered out, all at once, and the air turned stale.

"Shit." I turned on my phone's flash, took a hurried picture of the divots I'd found and then raced up and through the pulsating portal. Living in The Bitter End might protect Barry from ghosts, but I could totally still haunt Steve. Either way, the wereboar would regret sending me to my doom.

○○○

Rome seemed almost mundane after the Bitter End. I crept forward like a ninja to the bottom of the human stairwell and listened. The street above me was silent. Either the Illutu were gone, or the small army of bugs was clustered around the stairs, entirely motionless and waiting for me to emerge.

If it was the latter, I was screwed. Until whatever Minerva had done finally wore off, I was just an out-of-shape, late-twenties fratman… far from the second coming of Iceman I'd started to believe I could be.

I stopped in mid-step at that thought. Iceman? Really? One tiny taste of power and I was seeing myself as a superhero? Even *with* access to Lucia's Talent, the creatures I was rubbing elbows—or mandibles—with were way out of my league. If I wanted to survive Rome, I needed to stop pretending I was some kind of badass. I climbed the stairs, one hand on the railing, and risked a peek.

Barry—and Steve—could rest easy a while longer; the Illutu were gone. The street was empty, with only the crushed remnants of a car—what was it with the knights and cars?—to show that the bugs had ever been there. Now all I needed was a way back to the palace.

I swallowed a curse. I could have asked one of the exiting customers for their phone. Instead, I'd just watched everyone leave, like a total idiot.

With a shake of my head, I climbed the last few stairs.

A trio of dark-clad figures materialized about me.

I was already throwing myself to the side in a desperate and incredibly clumsy attempt to escape, when I realized something: the figures surrounding me, though dressed in black, were *not* spooky carbon copies of each other. In fact, two were women, and the third was every bit as black as his own outfit.

Relief almost made up for the pain of diving shoulder-first into cobblestone. The Watch had found me.

As I picked myself back up, the manpire touched his Bluetooth earpiece, and said something in Italian. The only word I recognized was my own name. He nodded at the reply I couldn't hear and the two femmepires came to flank me, one almost as tall as I was, the other as short as Lucia and as slim as Darlene. The short one cleared her throat and spoke in heavily accented English.

"Investigator Smith? Wait here, we have transportation arriving shortly."

Shortly was an understatement. As soon as she had finished speaking, a limousine rounded the corner, windows heavily tinted to hide the occupants. Trailed by a small fleet of dark Mercedes, the vehicle rolled to a stop at the nearby curb.

"How did you find me?" I asked the femmepire. "Did Sergei send word?"

Before the femmepire could reply, the rear door to the limo opened. Lucia's particular blend of rage and impatience crackled in my brain, a counterpoint to the cold voice that issued from the car's interior. "Get in, Mr. Smith. You've already wasted enough of my time tonight."

I paused, half-hoping that the Illutu would choose that moment to make their return, but the street remained empty of everything but the limo and its escort. With a sigh, I climbed into the back seat to join my not-so-beloved mistress.

CHAPTER 36

I was barely inside when the car pulled away with a squeal of rubber and the throaty growl of a souped-up engine. Thankfully, the seat I toppled into with a muffled groan was unoccupied. In fact, the entire rear of the stretch limo was empty save for Lucia herself.

At some point in my field trip into Rome, I'd gotten used to the distance between us muting the queen's presence. Now, her emotions—anger and irritation spiked with something I couldn't identify—swept across the bond like a tidal wave, washing away whatever limited mental walls I'd managed to erect. Just like that, my headache was back. I pinched the bridge of my nose, swallowed my sigh, and turned to face Lucia. Then blinked.

"What are you wearing?"

"It is called a dress, Mr. Smith."

That was one way of looking at it, though gown might have been more accurate. White, like everything else in the queen's expansive wardrobe, tonight's dress had long skirts, some sort of hard-boned corset or waist cincher and glittering beading framing a precipitously plunging neckline. Her shoulders, chest and back were almost entirely bare, but a diamond choker around her neck matched the stones dangling from her ears. Her hair was, once again, up in some sort of complicated style, and long evening gloves—also white—covered her arms all the way past the elbow.

All she needed was a crown and a whip, and her cosplay as a fantasy princess would be complete.

"Aren't you kind of overdressed for a rescue mission? Not that I'm complaining, of course."

"You like the dress?"

"I like not dying to the Illutu," I told her honestly. "The dress is strictly okay."

That last part was slightly less honest.

"I am relieved to hear of your ambivalence." She gifted me with a wintry smile. "Had you expressed appreciation, I would have burned it upon our return."

I sighed and sank back into the limo's comfortable seats. "It's not entirely horrible to see you too, Lucia. Thanks for coming."

"What choice did I have?" she asked. "There I was at another formal dinner, working to secure the votes necessary to save my Secundus when word arrived that my thrall had, yet again, gotten himself into trouble." Pale blue eyes flashed. "What were you thinking, coming to Rome with a single vampire escort? Had our experience at the airport already fled your fragile human mind?"

"*Vasily's Monster* is not your average manpire," I reminded her.

"No? Then where is he now?"

That stopped me cold. "I assumed he had called this in."

"No." Lucia's lips thinned. "*That* was one of the Watch assigned to secure my brother's townhome. There is a separate detachment working to extricate her from the remains of a car."

"She survived?" Two emotions shot through me. First was elation… that there was one less person's death to lay at my door, and that I might still have the chance to buy the femmepire tequila in thanks. That elation was quickly replaced by guilt. I hadn't even thought to see if she was breathing before I ran like the rabbit Sergei named me.

Lucia's reply didn't help with the guilt. "For the moment, yes. Whether she lives long enough to receive medical care remains in question."

My body ached everywhere. My feet felt like someone had spent the last few hours smashing them with a wooden mallet. I wanted nothing more than a shower and two to seven years of sleep… but I refused to let the unnamed tequila drinker die on my watch. I met the queen's still-angry eyes. "Tell the driver to take us there."

"Are you giving me orders now, thrall?"

"If she's going to make it, she needs blood," I insisted. "I can give that." And maybe I could find some clue as to what had happened to Sergei in the process.

"Your blood is *mine*, Mr. Smith." Lucia's voice cracked like a whip.

I opened my mouth, but the usual angry words wouldn't come. Could I possibly be *too tired* to fight with her?

If so, Hell was having one hell of a snowball fight.

I kept my voice level. "The Crown Watch hates us, Lucia. Me helping to save the life of one of their own could change that."

"An insightful and strategic motivation," she said, "which I do not for a moment believe to be the reason for your demand."

It really sucked that even someone I loathed could see right through me. "Three vampires fought to protect me tonight. One is dead. One is missing. If I can save her…" My voice trailed off. "I have to try."

The queen's expression softened minutely. "You are not the only human in the world, Mr. Smith. The team dispatched to her location brought donors with them."

I sagged back in my chair with relief. "I hope she makes it."

"And I hope your trip tonight was worth it." Lucia was still watching me, eyes aglow in the limo's dimly lit interior. "What progress did you make?"

"Can it wait until after my shower?"

"We are eighty minutes from the palace, Mr. Smith. How did *you* wish to pass the time?"

Something told me *peaceful, blessed silence* wasn't going to fly as a response.

This was my penance for talking her uncle's ear off, wasn't it?

○○○

"So, I should be able to prove that the stone fragments in Denarius' evidence vault were taken from The Bitter End," I concluded hoarsely, somewhere between five and twenty minutes later.

"Provided that the gold striations in those fragments glow."

"Yeah. The photo of the divots should help too." I paused, tired thoughts racing. "Although having Kala testify would *really* help."

Lucia's laugh was still distressingly beautiful, but she paused in mid-peal. "I'm sorry, were you being serious?"

"The word of a demigod has to hold some weight."

"Lord Kala does not leave his domain, my thrall. Not ever. And if he did, it would certainly not be in this city."

"I'm not the only one irritated by the lack of spaghetti?"

"I was speaking of Minerva."

"*Minerva* likes spaghetti?" I frowned. "Can't she just wave her hand and summon pasta by the bowlful or something?"

For a moment, Lucia's sigh was every bit as tired as mine. "How did I find myself bound to an imbecile?"

"I vaguely recall it having something to do with enthralling me against my will."

"The question was rhetorical, Mr. Smith." The femmepire shook her head slowly. "It has been centuries since Minerva allowed another deity access to this city. It is one of the reasons the People moved our capitol here, despite the concessions we had to make."

"Yeah, your uncle said something about that when explaining why the Council here is only half bloodsucker." I frowned. "I just didn't realize it applied to other gods too."

"Olympus fell when the Fenris wolf came calling," murmured Lucia. "Though she has leashed the wolf, the question of who sent it remains."

"Another god?"

"That would appear to be her suspicion. Thus, she forbids all deities from trespassing upon her land."

"So no Lord Kala, even though his bar plays a part in this case."

"Correct."

A new thought occurred to me, far too late. I'd been treating Kala as nothing more than the ultra-scary owner of a trans-dimensional bar, but he was a demigod of time and—more importantly—death. Why hadn't I asked him to seek out Tomasso's ghost and find the truth from the king's own spectral lips?

There was no way of knowing when—or even if—Kala would re-open the bar, which meant I'd missed my golden opportunity.

Worst. Homicide. Detective. Ever.

Lucia saw the expressions racing across my face but misidentified the source of my dismay. "Yes. Despite the holes you have found in my uncle's case against Anastasia, you have not made any progress in identifying the true killer. We need a viable suspect, Mr. Smith, and sufficient proof to sway at least one or two votes on the Council."

"I'm doing what I can. At least we know they were able to kill Tomasso without your brother putting up any sort of fight. Not to mention remove a piece of Kala's domain without the demigod even noticing. That's got to narrow the suspect pool."

"Presumably, they also had something to do with why my Secundus was so easily captured."

"You didn't buy the whole *captured-while-asleep* thing either?"

Lucia shot me a look of pure, upper-class scorn. "Lady Dumenyova slept outside my door for her first century. Not once during that time was I able to slip past her."

"Probably because you were wearing skyscraper high heels."

She rolled her eyes. "It will no doubt shock you to learn that I have not always worn heels."

It kind of did.

"They fell out of human fashion for a century or two," she explained. "There are times when I question the value of blending in with your species, but we do as we must."

"Right. Anyway, if Anastasia was incapacitated, Sergei and I were thinking Tomasso might have been too."

"You believe he did not struggle because he was asleep?"

"It doesn't explain the missing guards, but it's a start. We look for people with motive and we compare it to a list of people with applicable Talents."

"Thank the gods we have multiple weeks yet," muttered Lucia.

"Tell me about it. Hopefully, Ana can narrow things down further. You did give her the autopsy report, right?"

Whatever rapport we'd inadvertently forged vanished in the blink of an ice-cold blue eye. "I did. She will review the data before our visit tomorrow."

"Cool." I wasn't sure what I'd said or done *this* time to piss the queen off. It hadn't been the shoe comment, which meant it had to do with either the autopsy or, more likely, Anastasia. "So, did she say anything—"

"She told me that she was tired," Lucia cut in. *"Tired!"*

"Well, I doubt she's sleeping well, given where they've put her."

"Are you *intentionally obtuse*, Mr. Smith?"

The anger surging across our bond touched off my own temper, but I struggled to keep it restrained. "Two years ago, I didn't know the People existed. Is it so hard to believe that I might not understand every single facet of your screwed up society yet?"

Lucia's voice was bitter. "It has felt like decades."

"Try walking in my shoes," I told her.

"Given that those shoes should have been consigned to the waste dump years ago, I would rather not."

I shrugged. She'd replaced my old Corolla with a newer model, but I was keeping my shoes until the soles fell off completely.

Lucia's next words were quiet. "I take it then that you remain ignorant as to the nature of the blessing Lady Dumenyova has requested?"

"Yeah, but I'm all ears."

"If only that were true." The queen looked out her side window at the dark countryside. "There was a time, in my species' vast and glorious history, when a vow of fealty was considered all-consuming. A sworn vassal was meant to devote every moment of their waking lives in furthering the aims of their liege. They were permitted neither hobby nor ambition, neither dream nor relation."

"Sounds kind of like being a thrall."

"Perhaps it was. It took some time for the flaws in such a system to be exposed."

"You mean that even the People aren't robots? Seems kind of obvious to me."

"You are American. You know little of loyalty or service."

"So, vassals actually lived up to those impossible standards?"

"Not all, admittedly. Only the most loyal or fervent."

"What *was* the problem then?"

"Only the gods live forever, Mr. Smith. And when those loyal vassals aged and died, who was there to replace them?"

I started to shrug, stopping as realization struck. "The less-loyal vampires."

"Or their progeny." She nodded, still gazing out the window. "By forbidding relations amongst the faithful, the ancients were breeding out the very quality they so prized."

"And the blessing?"

"Was implemented to lessen the system's effects upon our population. In the end, even that measure was judged insufficient, and that system itself was abandoned long before my birth. Only Asya would dredge up such ancient history and then adhere to it as a matter of principle."

I already had a vague suspicion as to where this was going, but I had to know for sure. "Lucia, what exactly was she asking?"

"Is it not obvious?" The queen's voice was soft as silk, but the eyes she turned in my direction were jewel hard. "She seeks my permission to take you as her consort."

My mind blanked. "Meaning…"

"Even you cannot possibly be this stupid."

I swallowed my retort. Somewhere deep inside of me, giddy joy was trying to bubble up through a blanket of confusion and the frosted rage of Lucia's own emotions. "So, this request isn't… typical?"

"Is anything about my Secundus typical?" Lucia shook her head. "I do not know what the traditions are like in the other realms, but to the best of my knowledge, this is the first time a blessing has been requested in over a thousand years."

"What about Xavier?"

"What about him?"

"She didn't request your blessing with him?"

"A consort is not…" Lucia swallowed whatever she had been intending to say, and simply shook her head, the diamonds in her ears sparkling like tiny stars. "No."

"Then why me?"

The words slipped out, barely louder than my own breath.

"That is precisely the question I asked."

"And her answer?"

"I have already given it to you."

"That she was tired. Tired of what?"

"I do not know."

"She didn't say?"

"I chose not to stay to listen."

Wow. Lucia was almost as shitty a friend as she was a queen.

"Tired of killing, maybe," I decided. "Or… of being alone?"

"Either way, one truth is evident."

"Oh?" I was pretty sure her truth and mine were different.

"You have broken my Secundus, Mr. Smith, and in doing so, completed your cycle of vengeance."

I was so busy coming to grips with the idea that Anastasia, the woman I loved, the woman who was so far out of my league that she was playing a different sport entirely, had formally asked her maniacal boss for permission to date me that it took a long time for Lucia's words to sink in.

"My what?"

"I took you as my thrall against your will, and you have responded by shredding my reputation, siphoning my Talent, and breaking my House. Now, at long last, you will take from me the only person I have left." The queen's voice was as cold as ever, but it was also hollow. "I would murder you now with my bare hands and to every hell with this case, except…"

"Except?" I had already slid as far away from the queen as possible, but not even the limo's cavernous interior offered safety if the femmepire decided to make good on her threat.

"Except then she would be gone for good."

I studied the silent queen. My lie detector was notoriously buggy, but that statement had had the ring of truth to it. All the same, I couldn't help but think she'd originally intended to say something else.

"And your blessing? Did you give it?"

"I have yet to decide if I will even consider the matter."

"Humans have a saying: if you love someone, set them free."

"I am already quite aware of your species' rampant stupidity."

I let the comment slide right off my newly love-armored skin and tried a different tack. "These ancient vassals who asked their lieges for a blessing…"

"What of them?"

"When the blessing was granted, did they cease to serve? Or did they continue to do so despite also being permitted lives of their own?"

For the first time since this conversation had begun, the waves of fury and bitterness slowed, as Lucia considered my question. "They continued to serve."

"That seems relevant, don't you think?"

The rest of the ride passed in blessed, peaceful silence.

INTERLUDE

Flickering torches paint the room in shifting territories of light and darkness. A small form huddles in the chamber's center, curled in upon itself like a ball. From that shape come muffled, wordless sobs, each sound cutting off before it can carry.

I try to move closer, but don't have legs to walk on. That realization should trouble me. Instead, it tells me that I am dreaming.

Ten feet away, the huddled form shifts again. Platinum blonde hair shimmers in the wavering torchlight.

Right. I'm not just dreaming… I'm dreaming one of Lucia's memories. Again.

Either I'm getting better at this or she is. I've managed to avoid the usual disorientation of sharing Lucia's form, instead entering the dream as a disembodied spectator.

The door to my right opens, and Lucia's sobs choke off instantly. Red-rimmed eyes, barely visible through a curtain of hair, dart to the door. Moments later, a slim shadow slips inside.

This is only the second time I've seen Anastasia as a child. She is older than she was in that first dream, but little else has changed. Still small, still serious, and still shoddily dressed. She lets the door swing shut behind her and crosses to Lucia in a rush, kneeling to put her arms around the princess.

Of their own volition, Lucia's arms come up to return the hug, her heavy, ornately beaded robes a sharp contrast to the other girl's coarse gray smock. She ducks her head against Anastasia's shoulder, small body shaking as she continues to weep.

"This must stop, your Highness." In the way of dreams, I'm not at all surprised to suddenly understand Ana's words, even though they are in Italian.

Lucia looks up at Anastasia, and the curtain of hair falls away to expose a mottled series of bruises from temple to jawline. Her button nose is swollen and almost as red as her eyes. "It was my fault. If I had paid more attention in my lessons…"

"King Aurelius would have found another excuse." Anastasia's voice reflects the fury that lights her eyes. "He always does."

"His word is law, Asya. When you and I are grown, we can leave this place, but until then—"

The princess' words die out, and both she and Anastasia spin to face the door. A moment later, I hear it too; the heavy tread of someone approaching. Golden light slithers through the cracks in the doorway, growing brighter with each footstep.

Lucia shrinks inward upon herself, pale eyes wide in renewed terror.

In the non-dreaming present, Anastasia's poker face is legendary, but as a child, her emotions are all too easy to read as they flicker across her face. Anger and fear mix in equal measure, but beneath those conflicting sentiments, something resolute and unwavering begins to form. She rises to her feet, bare legs sticking out from under the worn smock, and turns to face the doorway. "It stops today, your Highness."

The door bursts open and light floods the room as if the sun has risen in the hallway. At the center of that impossible radiance is a figure, almost as tall as Denarius and twice as broad. The air around us thickens, crackling with Aurelius' power.

Hands shaking, breath coming in uneven gasps, Anastasia steps forward to block the king's entry.

The scene freezes, and in that sudden stillness, Lucia turns to face me. "My father destroyed her." Though she still wears the shape of a little girl, I recognize the adult Lucia's voice. "It was a month before Anastasia was able to walk again, but when she emerged from the infirmary, she found Gaius waiting. By my father's order, her training as Secundus began that very day. She was eight."

Jesus. No wonder everyone thinks Lucia killed her dad.

"She was right though."

"About what?" I hadn't known I could talk in this dream until the words escape my nonexistent lips.

"That was the day the beatings stopped." Something in Lucia's young face twists, gaining maturity if not age. "As a child, Asya faced down the king of Europe to protect me. That is the measure of the woman you are attempting to steal away."

Before I can protest, Lucia is standing in front of me, her pale eyes flashing gold. "No more words, thrall. Not tonight. Not after dredging up this memory."

Once again, my normal immunity to compulsion is nowhere to be found. I open my mouth, but nothing comes out.

She turns back to the frozen scene and shakes her head. Her voice is quiet, but the words carry in the stillness of the dream.

"Asya was anything but stupid, even as a child. She knew she would be punished, maybe even killed, but she did it anyway. For me." Her voice trails off, and small hands clench into even smaller fists. Her next words are a whisper. "It is time for you to go, Mr. Smith. Go—"

A cold wind strikes my ethereal form and drives me backward through the wall of her dream, down the channel of our bond, and into my own mind. There, Zorana waits for me in silent anticipation, but the queen's final words follow me into that darkness.

"—and sleep a sleep without dreams."

My nightmare dissolves into a different kind of darkness.

I fall into blessed oblivion.

CHAPTER 37

IN WHICH A PICTURE IS WORTH AT LEAST A FEW
DOZEN WORDS

Lucia was gone when I woke. Either her command to sleep had packed some extra mojo, or the whole almost-dying-to-bugs-then-being-kidnapped-by-humans-then-almost-dying-*again*-to-bugs thing had wiped me out. Either way, my phone informed me it was almost nine in the morning.

I raced through my shower, threw on a clean t-shirt and my backup pair of jeans—the first pair having been thoroughly thrashed by the previous night's adventure—and sat down to eat the breakfast that had been left on our table.

As rough as my trip into Rome had been, the memory I'd dreamed afterward was almost worse. Lucia had seemed to think it a lesson on the sort of person Anastasia was… but I already *knew* the sort of person she was. That's why I loved her, after all. The larger revelation had been about Lucia herself. I was glad the queen was off… doing whatever it was she was doing… as it saved me from a potentially very awkward morning. Our bond seemed intent on breaking every rule of basic human privacy.

At least, the memory transfer only seemed to be flowing in one direction so far. I had way too many memories that *I'd* be embarrassed to relive—starting and ending with that weekend in Tijuana. Having Lucia along as a silent voyeur? No, thank you. Her witnessing my Zorana nightmare had been bad enough.

Still, the image of a young, physically beaten Lucia haunted me through breakfast, leaving everything I ate tasting vaguely of ash. I knew parenting had changed in the past four centuries, but some things would always be bullshit, regardless of the era.

Desperate for distraction, I went and fetched the folder I'd brought back from Rome. I pushed aside my plate of partially eaten food and spread the folder's contents across the table. I'd already reviewed the report and photos of Tomasso's murder scene, of course, so they went into a neat stack to my far left. The autopsy report was with Anastasia, so there was nothing to review there either. That left the papers I'd taken from *Vita Unica's* safehouse.

There were several dozen scraps of paper, all torn from some sort of spiral notebook, and covered in text—sometimes pencil, sometimes blue or black ink. The handwriting varied from page to page, and sometimes even more frequently than that, suggesting multiple people had taken turns writing. As for what they were writing about… well, yet again, that would have to wait for someone who understood Italian. The formatting, however, with a recognizable header and date above each wall of text, suggested that this was some sort of journal or log.

The dates threw me for a moment before I remembered Europeans formatted their dates with the day first instead of the month like I was used to. The pages I'd liberated dated back to the first of the month. I added those pages to the crime report stack, in the hopes that Lucia or Anastasia would translate them at our joint strategy session later that day. If *Vita Unica* was truly aware of the supernatural beings in the city, they might have recorded something of value.

As I cleared the pages away, I found that the journal wasn't the only thing I'd recovered from the safehouse. A slim stack of glossy eight-by-elevens spilled onto the table. The top picture showcased a sun-dappled street, and a familiar building; Tomasso's townhouse.

Vita Unica had been staking out Tomasso's getaway home? This was way better than Denarius' grainy video footage. I laid the photos neatly out on the table in front of me, retrieved a notepad and pen from the room's small desk, and got to work.

ooo

Sometime later, a knock came at the hallway door. I opened it to find a smiling Maria Elena.

"Good morning, John! Are you ready for another day of interviews? Duke Vigo Marte awaits!" Today, she was wearing a soft blue dress, colored lenses a match for the slightly darker blue belt and heeled sandals that completed the ensemble. Her smile was as bright and cheerful as ever.

I had trouble matching that smile. "Actually, I'm not quite ready yet," I lied. "Do you mind helping me with something first?"

"Sure!" She followed me into the suite, and over to the table where I'd been doing my investigative research. "What do you need?"

"I've heard a lot from various people about Tomasso the king, but I'm still trying to get a read on Tomasso the person."

"You think his murder might have been personal, not political?" At my nod, Maria Elena gave it some consideration, twirling a honey blonde curl around her slender index finger. "I guess anything's possible. But how can I help? Like I've told you, I didn't know the king very well."

"Yeah, I remember." I frowned back, recalling our earlier conversation. "You only ever saw him when he came to visit Sabina."

"Exactly!"

"Have you ever heard of *Vita Unica*?"

Maria Elena's smile dimmed, but she rolled with the apparent non sequitur. "Are they some sort of band?"

"No. They're a group of humans who know your kind—and others—exist."

"Oh wow. That's crazy." She frowned for the first time. "Do you think they killed—"

"That was my first thought… although the how of it escaped me." Killing a single vampire would be hard enough for regular humans, let alone three vampires, one of them a king. "But apparently, they were content to just run surveillance."

"Surveillance?"

"On Tomasso's townhome. Every day, for at least a month." I slid four photos across the table to her.

The color left Maria Elena's lovely face.

"It's not what you think," Maria Elena stammered.

"No?" My voice sounded hard, even to my own ears. "Because it looks to me like you were visiting Tomasso on at least a weekly basis."

Each photo featured the front door to Tomasso's townhouse. Each showed a solitary female entering the building. The angle was poor, but the resolution was superb, and that woman was clearly identifiable as the femmepire seated across from me, all the way down to eyes whose color changed in each picture to match the day's outfit.

"Go ahead," I told her. "Tell me again how you never interacted with the king."

Maria Elena shrank in upon herself. "Who… who have you shown these to?"

For the first time, it occurred to me that I'd confronted a vampire with evidence implicating her in regicide without any sort of backup or safeguards. She was young for one of her kind, but still stronger than me… and I didn't have Lucia's Talent to fall back on.

"Queen Lucia," I lied. "And Ambassador Sergei."

"Not Sabina?" The femmepire's relief was obvious. Which made no sense.

"Not yet. But I'm pretty sure she'll figure it out when you're executed for her father's murder."

"Executed…" Maria Elena's eyes went wide. "But I didn't kill anyone!"

"It's a little late for that story, don't you think?" I nodded to the pictures. "Those show you entering Tomasso' townhouse on multiple occasions. Denarius has video of someone approaching the building on the night of the king's murder… and that someone looks an awful lot like you."

Or Anastasia. Or pretty much any woman not named Lucia. But admitting so seemed like a poor way to get a confession.

Maria Elena shook her head, sending curls dancing in both directions. She scanned the pictures, then picked one up and waved it at me. "This was the last time I was there, but it was more than a week ago. Days before he was killed! You have to believe me!"

"Given that you've been lying to me since I arrived, I don't know why I would."

"I didn't kill him!" For the first time, she looked angry.

"No? Prove it."

"I… I'm not sure how to do that."

"You can start by telling me what you were doing visiting the king on a weekly basis." Given my usual business, I could think of one possibility. "Were you and he…"

"Ew! No!"

"Ew?"

"He was my best friend's father! I don't know what things are like in San Francisco—"

"San Diego."

"—but here, that sort of thing is *not* okay!"

"Then what…?"

"I was spying on her, okay?!"

"On who?"

"On Sabina! For the past five years, I've given the king weekly reports on his daughter's activities."

"Why?"

"Because he would have sent me back to Milan, if I didn't!"

"No, I mean… why did he want you to spy on his own daughter?"

"How should I know?"

"You didn't ask?"

The look she sent me was pure scorn. It was one I was overly familiar with from the women in my life, past and present. "I come from a minor family and was still more than a year from my first Feeding when he ordered me to become his spy. Exactly which part of that entitled me to interrogate the king as to his motives?"

"The part where you were Sabina's friend, maybe?"

"That's *not* how things work here." The femmepire took a deep breath. As she let it out, her eyes searched my face. "You're not going to tell her, are you?"

"Sabina? Why would I? I'm not even convinced that you're telling the truth yet."

"You think I made this up? Seriously? Why would I do that?"

"Because you needed a reason for showing up in those pictures. One that absolved you from Tomasso's murder?"

"I. Didn't. Kill. Anyone." Maria Elena smacked the table with an open palm, and every paper and picture on it bounced almost an inch into the air from the impact. "I was with Sabina the day King Tomasso died. The *entire* time."

"I'm going to verify that with her, you know." I added a reminder in my notebook.

"Good." The femmepire ran the back of one hand across her eyes, wiping away unshed tears. "And when she confirms it... you won't tell her about the other stuff, right?"

"Not unless it becomes relevant to the case."

"Thank you, John." Again, her relief was apparent. She swallowed a few times, then spoke again. "I'm sorry I didn't tell you. Are we... are we okay?"

My natural inclination, the part of me that Juliette called my idiotic white knight complex, was to say yes, if only to ward off the possibility of future tears. But I'd been through a lot over the past few years, and that little voice in my head wasn't half as strong as it had once been.

"I don't know," I said instead. "You lied to me. To my face, and multiple times. In and of itself, that's not such a big deal, but I'm here trying to save the life of the woman I love. I don't have time for people I can't trust."

"I see." Maria Elena looked down. "Do you want a new guide?"

"I think the need for a guide is over with, actually." I rose to my feet. "I'll verify your story with Sabina. Don't leave the palace until then."

I'd thrown the last part in, just because it was the sort of line I'd heard in every police procedural ever. In truth, I had no way to keep her from leaving, or even to know if she had gone.

Either Maria Elena didn't realize that detail, or she didn't want me to know that she had. She nodded, eyes still downcast, and rose from her chair with a whisper of fabric. "Okay. I'll... be around, I guess."

Then, she swept out of the room at vampire speed.

I reminded myself that the femmepire had lied to me, and that any misstep in this investigation would cost Anastasia her life. Not to mention Lucia's and my own. Even if she'd had nothing to do with Tomasso's murder, she'd wasted time I couldn't afford to lose. Sending her away just made sense.

So why did I feel like total crap?

ooo

In my limited experience, there were bad ideas and then there were *bad* ideas. The first tended to just leave you feeling like a dumbass—trying to find parking in the Gaslamp Quarter on a Friday night or deciding to ask out the cute French-Canadian exchange student in front of the entire cafeteria. The second though? Those were the ideas you prayed you might survive long enough to regret.

I was starting to think that visiting Vigo without an escort fell into the latter category.

The door to the councilor's suites wasn't all that different than Sabina's or even Dog's, but the thing that met me at that door was a whole new breed of servant. Vaguely human-shaped at best, it was utterly featureless, and the low light was sufficient to reveal that its "body" was little more than a mass of squirming, wriggling insects. A thousand carapaces glittered in the low light, as even more legs twitched and waved in unison.

When I stepped into the parlor, the construct collapsed back into a teeming mass of creepy crawlies. The army of insects poured back across the floor and around the corner into the main room. In moments, I was alone.

"Come or go, investigator." The voice was thin and reedy, like a smoker on his last lung, but it came from deeper in the suite. "But make your choice quickly."

Go was sounding pretty good right then, but I had a case to solve; I followed the vanished insects into the next room.

I didn't even see Vigo at first. It was hard to focus on anything but the bugs.

The floors, walls, and ceilings gleamed like they had been carved from polished obsidian, but the way those surfaces shifted gave away the lie. If a thousand beetles, ants, and other insects had met me at the door, this single room held millions. The sight of that teeming mass was bad enough, but it was the sound that gnawed at me; a low, pulsing hum—of wings, of legs rubbing together, of mandibles clicking.

I'd never had a bug phobia, but Italy was threatening to give me one.

On the floor before me, the mass shifted, parting like black waters in a biblical ocean until a path forward emerged. With each step I took, the path extended a little bit further. Eventually, I was at the room's center, surrounded and wishing desperately for weapons-grade insecticide.

It was only then that I saw Vigo.

I'd met a lot of vampires over the past two years, and they were almost as varied as humans; short and tall, slender and curvaceous, Asian to African, Latino to Caucasian. But even with those variances, every vampire I'd ever seen was both disgustingly fit and depressingly attractive. There was no such thing as a fat vampire or an ugly one.

Or so I'd thought.

Vigo was enormous. Actually, *enormous* was an understatement. The manpire didn't sit on the couch; he enveloped it, rolls of pale flesh spilling over the couch's arms. Legs wider than my own still-pudgy mid-section tapered sharply to tiny, weirdly delicate feet, and his arms were so short as to be almost vestigial.

Within a pale, fleshy, and perfectly round face, dark eyes narrowed at my obvious shock.

"You have something to say, investigator?"

I had a *lot* of things to say, but I didn't think Vigo or any of his twenty million insect attendants wanted to hear them. So instead, I tried to pretend I hadn't been staring and launched into my usual spiel.

"Yes. Thank you for seeing me, Duke Marte. I'm hoping with your help that we might be able to catch Tomasso's real killer."

"*King* Tomasso," the manpire corrected, each word escaping him like air from a leaky tire. "And both the king's killer *and* the creature whose orders sent her here have already been quite neatly caught."

By which he meant Anastasia and Lucia, I was guessing. "That's clearly what someone wants us to believe," I argued, "but the evidence doesn't hold up to scrutiny. Already in my investigation, I've found—"

"A likely story." Vigo waved one stubby arm dismissively. "It was my understanding that you were here to ask questions, not insult my intelligence."

"Right." Whatever Lucia had been doing since we reached Rome, her efforts to curry favor didn't seem to be working with Vigo. "Where were you on the night of the king's murder?"

The smile the manpire gave me was oily. "Right here, of course."

"Why *of course?*"

He cocked his head, and those sharp eyes narrowed again. "As you might surmise from its physical appearance, this shell rarely goes anywhere. I believe the last such occurrence came in what your pitiful species calls the nineteenth century."

I looked at the teeming mass of insect life that surrounded me. Other than the couch, there wasn't a scrap of furniture in the room.

"Doesn't that get boring? Or lonely? You don't even have a television, dude."

"I am a Beastcaller, investigator." He nodded to the bugs, as if I had somehow missed them. "I see what they see. I hear what they hear. And when they feed, I too am nourished. I have little need to leave these suites, and even less desire to do so."

That was almost as fascinating as it was disgusting, but I was here to clear Ana's name, not learn new and horrifying things about her species.

"Did you ever meet the king in person then, or did you interact with him purely through… uhm… intermediaries?"

"He did visit, upon occasion—perhaps once a year—but the majority of our conversations over the centuries occurred by proxy."

"And what did you talk about in those conversations, if you don't mind my asking?"

"Matters far beyond your ken, I assure you."

"No need to bring my family into this. And nobody says kin anymore, anyway," I muttered. "Did King Tomasso seem distracted in recent months? Or worried?"

"The life of a king is fraught with distractions, investigator. It is why I have never sought such a position for myself."

"That sounds like a yes," I decided at length. "Do you know *what* he was concerned about?"

"I would not tell you even if I did."

"Even if it helped catch the real killer?"

"As I've already told you—"

"Yeah, yeah." I watched color surge into the manpire's cheeks ay my interruption. "Let's pretend for a moment that Lady Dumenyova didn't kill King Tomasso."

"If you wish to ignore reality, the imp has any number of illicit goods to aid you in your quest." Vigo's smile oozed. "However, I will not partake at this time. This shell is, after all, a temple."

If so, I didn't ever want to meet the deity worshipped there.

"It's just a thought exercise," I explained. "If Anastasia didn't kill the king, who would top your list of suspects."

"The Winter Lady herself."

I sighed. "Other than Lucia, I mean." As he opened his mouth again, I cut in. "Or Marcus or anyone else working for the queen."

"She has not been a queen for a century, boy."

"Whatever. My question stands."

"So it does." He shifted ponderously in his seat, eliciting groans and squeaks from the couch. "Sadly, I am done with hypotheticals for the day."

"I can come back tomorrow."

"I think not." The smile slid off Vigo's face, replaced by a snarl. "Your so-called queen murdered Aurelius in cold blood, human, and then sent her half-tamed dog to do the same to his son. I will watch both of their executions through a thousand eyes and take great satisfaction in the view my Talent affords me."

"Maybe you're right," I acknowledged, "or maybe I'll convince the Council of Anastasia's innocence, even without your help."

"It is possible." The manpire eyed me speculatively. "I admit that I knew nothing of you before your arrival at the palace, but details of your recent history have been surprisingly easy to come by."

I didn't like the sound of that but covered my nervousness with a lazy shrug. "And?"

"And one truth becomes apparent, beyond the falsehood of your supposedly adversarial relationship with Lucia."

If Vigo thought Lucia and I were faking our mutual animosity, I had to question the validity of his so-called research. "What truth is that?"

"You are far more capable than you would have others believe."

I frowned at what appeared to be a genuine compliment. "I've had my share of successes," I admitted, "although not everyone sees it that way."

"Fools, all of them."

My frown deepened. Moments earlier, it had seemed like Vigo was throwing me out, but now... were we having a moment?

"That is why I agreed to this interview."

"So, you *do* have information for me?" Could vampires be bipolar? Or had the strain of one hundred and fifty years with only bugs for company driven the manpire completely insane? Either way, I felt a sudden stirring of hope that this interview hadn't been a complete waste of my time.

His next words crushed that hope.

"I have nothing for you, investigator, but death."

"Uhm... what?" I made to back up, only to find that the path had closed behind me.

"Despite your mistress' undeniable guilt, there remains a chance of you convincing the Council otherwise." Vigo shook his head, eyes flashing golden from across the room. "I will not allow her to evade justice once more."

"Seriously, dude... the rumors of my effectiveness have been greatly exaggerated," I told the manpire as the open space about me started to shrink.

"Be that as it may, I will not leave the matter to chance."

"People know where I am," I argued, shrinking back from a rising tide of many-limbed monstrosities. "The *Kingmaker* knows."

"He knows only that you were scheduled to meet with me," Vigo corrected, spreading both arms wide and adopting an expression of mock concern. "I was quite distraught when you failed to show."

"What about when they find my body?"

"What body? A few thousand dermestid beetles can strip a body of flesh in no time at all. Those same beetles will bore through solid bone, if instructed to do so. There will be nothing left of you, no evidence at all that you were ever here."

Okay, visiting Vigo alone *definitely* belonged to that second category of bad ideas. I'd escaped giant roaches only to hand myself over to their diminutive—but far more numerous—cousins. If any deities were watching, I hoped they appreciated the irony.

The mass of insects cinched tighter around me at a glacial pace; a clear sign that Vigo planned to prolong and enjoy my death. I scanned the room in desperation. The hallway door was way too far for me to make a run for it, but Vigo, himself… he was only fifteen or so feet away. Five long strides and an adrenaline-and-werewolf-virus-fueled leap might get me to the couch. And once there, the threat of physical violence to the duke's shell might force the manpire to call off his minions.

I tried to ignore the fact that those fifteen feet were covered by insects, so thickly layered that they put the world's deepest shag carpet to shame. Between the poisonous creatures and the merely hungry ones, I'd be lucky to make it five feet. Especially since, as everyone kept telling me, I didn't *have* any werewolf virus left in my system…

I watched clear floor slowly disappear around me and pushed those defeatist thoughts away. I could do this.

A loud knocking from the distant foyer came just as I was about to leap. I pinwheeled my arms desperately to keep from toppling over into the mass of creeping death. The insect mass had come to a halt several inches from my feet.

Another knock sounded, and Vigo frowned in irritation. A small swath of bugs piled atop one another to form a humanoid construct that flowed around the corner to the hallway door.

I revised my earlier estimates on the number of critters in the room. The ten thousand or so that had just left to answer the door hadn't made a visible dent in the numbers surrounding me.

"Duke Marte." The voice was strong, young, and female. I was pretty sure I'd never heard it before. "My Lady requests a moment of Investigator Smith's time."

"Investigator Smith can no doubt manage his own schedule." Vigo's voice—the strong, confident tones I remembered from the Council chamber, rather than the asthmatic wheezing of his physical form—issued forth from the doorkeeper in reply. "Why bring the matter to me?"

"Because she saw him enter your chambers less than twenty minutes ago."

I still didn't recognize the voice, but the slight sibilance of her words told me who she served. Lady Manassa was officially my favorite naga ever.

Bright spots of color appeared in Vigo's egg white cheeks. He spoke through his doorkeeper once again. "My servants are everywhere, child. I would know if your lady had eyes on—"

"I'll be right out," I interrupted, speaking loudly enough to make damn certain that my voice carried to the door. I glanced over at the furious manpire. "Vigo and I were just about done here anyway."

"This is far from finished, investigator." This time, the manpire used his own mouth to speak, but the wheezing words echoed around me, repeated by the writhing masses I would no doubt see in my next Zorana-starring nightmare.

"If you do think of anything that might help my investigation," I told the councilor brightly, "feel free to schedule another appointment through the Kingmaker."

An appointment which I would happily and unapologetically refuse. I left that part unsaid, but I was pretty sure he knew it as well as I did.

A smile oozed back onto the manpire's face. "I look forward to your misguided and ultimately futile defense at the trial, and the *three* executions that will no doubt follow soon after."

The black-bodied waters finally parted, providing a clear path back to the foyer. I beat a hasty retreat, pausing only when I reached the safety of the hallway.

"You never know," I said, directing my words at the faceless doorkeeper that was Vigo's proxy, "I might win. I've been told I'm far more capable than others believe."

Thousands of mandibles clicked loudly in reply, sounding for just one moment like a single individual grinding his teeth.

ooo

I waited until we were safely away from Vigo's suite—assuming any place in the palace was safe from the duke's chitinous hordes—before turning to my unexpected savior.

As I'd suspected, she was clearly a naga, bearing the same strong cheekbones, wide eyes, and lack of a nose that I'd observed in the Lady Manassa. Her hair was copper instead of silver though, and piled carelessly atop her head in a messy style I just couldn't see the more elegant councilor adopting.

"I'm John," I told her, offering my hand.

She stared at my hand for a long moment, puzzled, and then shrugged and raised it to her lips. Her mouth was cool and dry against the back of my hand. I had goosebumps by the time she released it.

Well, *that* was different.

"I am Aasha."

"You couldn't have come by at a better time," I told her honestly. "I have a few minutes until my next appointment, and I'm more than happy to spend all of that time speaking with your lady."

"The Lady Manassa is unavailable at this time," said Aasha, "and requests the pleasure of your company this afternoon when you have finished meeting with the Winter Lady and her Secundus."

I blinked. The nagas were remarkably well informed about my schedule, considering that the latter half of that schedule had only been determined on the drive back from Rome the previous night. "If the Lady Manassa doesn't want to see me until the afternoon, why were you—"

"When word came that you had attended Duke Marte on your own, she suspected you might find yourself in need of assistance. The rest of the pit was busy, so I came to speak on your behalf."

"It was not one of my better plans," I admitted, "and that's saying something, considering the disasters I usually stumble into."

Silver eyes gleamed with humor. In a futile attempt to hide her smile, she swept into an elegant curtsey, the hem of her blue and silver threaded sari almost brushing the palace floors. "It was my honor to serve."

"It was *my* honor to not get eaten by Vigo's bug army." I offered a bow in return, with considerably less elegance and grace. "My thanks to you and the Lady Manassa both. Please tell her that I happily accept her invitation and look forward to speaking with her later today."

"I will do so at once." She curtseyed again, then turned to go, only to pause in mid-step. She glanced back at me over one shoulder. "When you do meet her..."

"Yes?"

"In our culture, it is customary for the male to kiss the female's hand, and not the other way around."

Note to self: nagas didn't do handshakes.

With another poorly concealed smile, she made her way down the hallway and out of sight.

Once Aasha was gone, I checked the time again. Five past eleven. I was scheduled to meet with Ana and Lucia at noon, which was when the Tower ban that Denarius had so arbitrarily imposed upon me finally expired. That gave me half an hour before I needed to return to the suite to grab the case files and head over. That wasn't enough time for a nap, and it was still too early to give Juliette another call… even if I'd had a working phone.

But what to do?

As I wandered down the hall, lost in thought, I passed a handful of vampires headed in the opposite direction, each of them clothed in the all-black of the Watch uniform. Before they could leave, I grabbed the closest one's arm.

Pain radiated up through my shoulder, and I found myself on one knee, the arm I'd touched the vampire with pointing straight up in the air even as my hand was rotated to put pressure on the wrist.

"Never touch me again, human."

"Noted," I squeaked. "I just wanted to ask a question."

"You haven't earned the right to ask questions."

One of the other vampires said something in Italian, and my attacker laughed, but the pressure on my arm and shoulder never waned.

"This once, however, I will ignore the slight. Speak."

"Can you… you know… let me up first?"

"No."

God, vampires were assholes. Most of them anyway. "Has anyone heard from Ambassador Sergei?"

"No."

Damn it. "Then can I get directions to the infirmary?"

"The infirmary? I have yet to truly injure you, human, but if you wish that to change…?" He torqued my arm a little bit further.

"Not for me," I gasped. "I wanted to check in on the woman brought in last night."

"Yovanna? Why?"

So *that* was her name. "She got hurt protecting me. I wanted to see if there was anything I could do."

The pressure on my arm disappeared. I staggered upright to find the manpire frowning in confusion. "What could one such as you do to help?"

"I don't know. Bring her water, give her someone to talk to… whatever might help."

He turned to his companions and then back to me, shaking his head. "You will not be permitted to visit her."

"Oh."

"However, I will tell Yovanna that you offered," he continued, his voice now lacking its original aggression. "It is the best that I can do."

"Thank you. I would appreciate it."

"I believe you actually would." With one last strange look, he rejoined his fellow Watch. The three of them were gone well before the ache in my arm had subsided.

Screw it, I decided.

I was going to go hide in my suite until it was time to visit Ana.

CHAPTER 38
IN WHICH LUNCH HAS A COST

I reached the Tower early. In San Diego, five minutes here or there was hardly worth comment. However, in the palace, the Crown Watch took great pains to block my entry until the exact moment the clock ticked over to noon. Which meant that, with all the stairs I had to climb to reach Anastasia's prison, I ended up being late for our appointment. And for lunch, if the scent of grilled chicken was anything to go by.

Lucia was already there, seated at the long table against the far wall, a plate of food before her and a glass of red wine in one hand. Without even looking in my direction, she raised her voice.

"You are late, Mr. Smith. Again."

Already irritated by the wait *and* the climb, I was a breath away from firing back with something less than polite. Fortunately, my first sight of Anastasia in more than a day stole that breath away.

The Secundus was seated across the table from Lucia, her own plate untouched, her glass full of water instead of wine. She was dressed uncharacteristically in black instead of her usual blues and greens and her jade eyes were large and serious.

"Mr. Smith." She flashed a short-lived smile, then nodded to Lucia. "My queen tells me you are continuing to put yourself in harm's way."

I crossed the room, and took the remaining chair at the table, in the hopes that a plate laden with food would magically manifest in front of me. "Word really *does* travel fast in the palace."

Both women went still.

"We were speaking of your trip into the city last night."

"Oh. That. Yeah, that wasn't fun."

Lunch still hadn't appeared.

"What did you *think* she was speaking of, thrall?"

I put on my very best innocent smile, but neither woman seemed to buy it. Like the Dealmaker™, that smile clearly needed work.

"I *may* have just narrowly survived another attack on my life," I admitted. "And almost had my arm torn off by the Watch."

Lucia sighed. "And what did you to do to incite the Watch into trying to kill you this time, Mr. Smith?"

"What?" My frown cleared as I realized her misunderstanding. "Sorry, those were two totally separate events. *First*, I evaded a murder attempt, and *then* I got beat up by the Watch."

"Who tried to kill you, John?"

"Vigo," I told Anastasia. "He seemed concerned that I might actually win the trial."

"What does Duke Marte know that we do not?" asked Lucia.

"With his Talent? Probably a metric shit ton." I glanced around the room. "In fact, do we know he doesn't have spies here, right now?"

"The Tower was intentionally constructed on the far side of the palace from the councilors' chambers, Mr. Smith. The duke's sphere of influence does not reach this far."

Which put Tomasso's distant townhouse in Rome entirely out of Vigo's reach. I shrugged and moved on. "Anyway, I would have been bug food if one of the Lady Manassa's nagas hadn't come along and saved me."

Neither femmepire blinked at the news. In fact, I wasn't sure Anastasia had blinked since I mentioned the attempt on my life.

"In the future," suggested Lucia, "perhaps you should contact me instead of relying upon the providence of passing strangers."

"I was surrounded by the world's scariest ant farm," I pointed out. "How exactly was I supposed to—" My voice trailed off as realization set in.

"Yes." Lucia's eyes blazed brilliant blue. "Our bond."

"I didn't think of that."

"Of course not. Instead, you use it merely to demand directions or invade my dreams."

"Not by choice!" Except for the whole directions thing, which had actually been kind of useful.

Anastasia's voice, deep and rich like cheesecake drizzled in chocolate, cut through our bickering. "Why was Maria Elena not with you when you went to meet Duke Marte?"

Oh. That. I started to explain, then stopped.

"It might be better if I just recap the whole morning…"

ooo

By the time I finished my tale, Lucia was on her third glass of wine. "I left you alone for a single morning, my thrall. How can any individual find so much trouble in so short a time?"

"Juliette says I have a gift."

"That is not the word I would choose." She shook her head, sending platinum blonde strands spilling over the shoulder of yet another pristine white suit.

"Do you believe Maria Elena's story?" Anastasia had finally started blinking again, somewhere around the three-minute mark of my story. She'd also put down the dinner knife she'd somehow palmed without any of us noticing. I tried not to look at the mess she'd made of its handle.

"I don't know," I admitted. "She's probably telling the truth about spying on Sabina, but that doesn't mean she's telling the truth about everything. I'm starting to realize my lie detecting skills leave a lot to be desired." Neither woman seemed inclined to dispute that last statement. I tried to hide how much that stung... and failed, because my poker face *also* still sucked. "Regardless, I think we can assume she isn't Tomasso's murderer."

"On account of being a mere child?"

"Yeah. Even if she was able to overpower Tomasso, we're working under the assumption that both his murder and Aurelius' were linked. And she definitely wasn't around back then."

"She could still have had a hand in my brother's death," Lucia pointed out. "As an aide, if not the principal actor."

"I guess so." It didn't feel right, but my hunches had spent the last few years getting me into trouble, so I wasn't giving them much say in the matter. "I need to question her again, I think."

"Bring her here," suggested Anastasia. "Between the two of us, we should be able to unravel the truth of her testimony."

"I'm... not entirely sure she'll be able to give any testimony at all with you in the room." I glanced over at the lovely femmepire. "She's kind of terrified of you."

"All the better. Fear can be a useful tool in such matters."

The door to the stairs cracked open, saving me from responding. A human servant brought in a tray with a fresh plate of steaming food and placed it on the table before me. Silverware, a cloth napkin, and a crystal glass—filled with water, not wine—swiftly followed.

"The matter of the child can wait," Lucia decided once the servant had left. "And the matter of Vigo's clumsy attack will *have* to wait, as we are in no position to strike back at him yet."

"Why do we even need to?" I was already working on my first bite of delightfully seasoned chicken. "Dude broke the Concordat by trying to kill me. Shouldn't the gods smite him now or something?"

"The Concordat does not apply in this instance," Anastasia told me. "You are not here under the auspices of a mediation."

"Murder investigators don't get protection?"

"Beyond what they can arrange for themselves? No. Furthermore—"

"The Concordat only applies to cross-species conflicts," interrupted Lucia. "Though you are human, you are here as my representative, making this an internal matter for the People."

"Which means everyone gets to take a shot at me."

"Which means," corrected Anastasia, her voice momentarily every bit as hard as the queen's, "that your days of wandering the palace without security *must* end. And any future trips into Rome should involve no fewer than a dozen Watch."

Lucia seemed as startled by Ana's burst of anger as I was, but she gave the other femmepire a firm nod of agreement.

"I didn't go into the city alone, Ana. I'm not a complete idiot."

Some of the harshness left Anastasia's face as her eyes refocused upon me. "I would never suggest you were. And if you were going to bring only a single guard with you, it is difficult to argue against the choice of Vasily's Monster."

"I just hope he's okay."

"It will take more than an Illutu knight to end that one."

I very carefully didn't point out that there had been *two* knights. I was already feeling badly enough about essentially abandoning Sergei in the middle of Rome. Even if he'd told me to.

"How did you convince him to escort you?" asked Ana.

The floored me. "You mean you don't know either?"

"Know what?"

I glanced at Lucia, but she seemed as clueless as her Secundus. Apparently, Denarius hadn't opted to give her an explanation after my departure.

"Ambassador Sergei has one brother, Vasily. But a long time ago, they had a sister, who was sent to Rome to bear the European king an heir." I met Lucia's pale blue eyes and saw the first stirrings of realization. "Sergei is your uncle."

There was a sharp snap, and then the cup of Lucia's glass slid free of its shattered stem, spilling wine across the tablecloth.

○○○

One of the guards outside Ana's door poked his head in to see what the noise was, but no servant ever came by to replace Lucia's glass. Which was just as well, really... a drunk Juliette was hilarious, but a drunk Lucia wasn't something I ever wanted to see.

I expected follow-up questions on the blood-relations truth bomb I'd just detonated, but when the queen had regained her composure, she instead pulled a small object from the inner pocket of her snow-white blazer. Murmuring something in Italian, she placed the object in the center of the table.

"Is that... a bird skull?"

As a reasonable, non-serial-killer sort of human, I wasn't all that familiar with animal remains, but this certainly *looked* like the skull of a small bird—maybe a sparrow or a pigeon. The bleached white bone had been carved with small, unreadable runes. Its empty eye sockets, on the other hand, glittered with sparkling color, like someone had attacked them with a bedazzler.

Anastasia turned to Lucia and something passed between them.

"This was..."

"Freely given, my Secundus, for the duration of our stay."

I waved my hand to get their attention. "Ignorant human here. Does anyone want to explain what's going on, and why it has Lucia grinning like a canary-eating cat?"

I frowned. Maybe the bird-related metaphor had been a bad choice, given the item on the table.

"It is a relic, Mr. Smith," explained Lucia. "One of the few that Caine has ever made."

A bird skull. The Lord of Bones. I probably should have made that connection, but it had been a long week. "And what does it do?"

"It allows us to speak freely. When activated, as I have just done, those within its sphere of power cannot be heard by those without."

"How do we know it works?" I remembered Ana's own words about Caine's trustworthiness.

Without a word, Lucia plucked the water glass right out of my hand and dashed it to the floor.

"I was drinking that!"

"I do have to live here for the next few weeks." Anastasia's words were mild.

Lucia rolled her eyes and motioned to the door.

This time, nobody had come to investigate the noise.

"Okay, so maybe it works," I admitted. "And maybe next time, we could just try shouting or something, instead of spreading broken glass all over the floor of Ana's prison."

"Maybe next time, you will choose to accept what I am saying, instead of challenging me at every turn."

Don't bet on it, I managed to avoid saying. "Fine. So, if the recap of my morning wasn't a reason to use the sparrow skull, why activate it now?"

"Anyone with ears and a brain could divine what you did this morning, my thrall. But I would prefer that our enemies *not* know where we are in the investigation."

That was… actually a pretty good answer. I took another bite of marinated chicken, lamenting the loss of my water.

"Should we talk about this whole Sergei and Vasily thing?"

"That I have two previously unknown uncles and you may have gotten one of them killed last night? Is that what you wish to spend our time discussing?"

I winced. The last thing I needed was Lucia adding to my guilt trip. "On second thought, we should focus on the investigation."

"Indeed. Before we begin, however, there is the matter of the request Lady Dumenyova made two nights ago."

The chicken turned to ash in my mouth. I straightened out of my habitual slouch and shared a glance with Anastasia.

"My lady, perhaps this should wait until I have been given an opportunity to explain to Mr. Smith what my request actually entailed," Anastasia began, her voice uncharacteristically nervous.

"I have already had the dubious privilege of providing that explanation," Lucia answered, lips curled downward.

"I see." Anastasia turned to me, but as usual, I wasn't sure what nonverbal message she was sending my way. I answered with a smile, trying to let my feelings for her shine through.

"Mr. Smith is not who or what I would have chosen for you, Anastasia, and I admit to serious doubts regarding both his worthiness and his ability to provide you with even a miniscule amount of happiness."

This was going well.

"*Everything* he touches turns to dust," the queen continued, "including the House we shared. I would save you from that fate."

"My queen—" began Ana, her voice strained.

"However," Lucia continued, overriding the other woman's protest, "I was reminded last night of the many sacrifices you have made for me since we were children. If you are truly certain that *this* is what you want…?"

"I am." There was nothing but iron certainty in Anastasia's voice. Which was as gratifying as it was surprising.

Lucia nodded. "So be it. In that case, I will consent—"

Holy shit!

"—to serve as your second in this matter."

Wait… what?

Anastasia's eyes had gone wide with the confusion I felt. "My second, your Majesty?"

"Come now, Asya… surely, a woman who digs up the ancient practice of a liege's blessing is familiar with the concept of seconds?"

"I'm not," I pointed out helpfully.

The queen turned to me, her smile anything but sweet. "It means that I have accepted the responsibility of evaluating your suitability as a match for my vassal."

"Evaluating *how*, exactly?" Because if this involved some sort of freaky sex thing, I'd… I glanced between femmepires… well, I'd muddle through, I supposed.

"The process is not dissimilar from that which you have been undertaking with the members of the palace," Lucia told me sweetly. "I have known Asya for almost four centuries, but you for only a scattering of months across a span of scant years. A series of interviews will help me determine if you are worthy of being paired with my Secundus."

This close, the queen's feelings leaked across our bond unbidden, scorn and malevolent delight. And beneath both sentiments, something that felt like grief. None of those emotions showed on a flawless face that was, for just that moment, as inscrutable as Anastasia's.

"Think of it as a job interview, Mr. Smith, for a position I suspect you are spectacularly unqualified for."

"I'm a P.I.," I muttered. "I've never *had* a job interview."

"Then this will be your first."

Well, shit.

CHAPTER 39

Between our bond and my nonexistent poker face, Lucia had
no difficulty picking up on the surge of fear and worry that her words
had caused. I felt an answering flicker of satisfaction across the bond,
but her lovely face remained serene.

"With that unpleasantness out of the way, perhaps we should
turn our attention to my brother's murder?"

I'd never thought there would be a day when I was *happy* to
discuss a homicide, but anything was preferable to thinking about
Lucia overseeing my love life.

"I have apprised Lady Dumenyova of what progress you made
in Rome," the queen continued. "How do you wish to proceed from
this point?"

"I'll get Denarius to schedule an official interview with Maria
Elena. Hopefully, she or Lady Manassa will have more insight into
what Tomasso was doing prior to his death."

"We already *know* what he was doing! He was investigating our
father's murder. Why are you wasting time verifying this fact when you
could instead be seeking out the killer?"

Either my mid-morning, near-death experience had taught me restraint or Anastasia's presence had a mollifying effect. Either way, I managed to swallow my initial, poorly considered reply. After a count to ten, I tried again.

"Shockingly, your word is unlikely to be accepted as fact unless I can find corroboration. So, I'm trying to get confirmation from someone who *hasn't* been directly or indirectly accused of murdering Tomasso."

Lucia drew herself up in her chair, spine going ramrod stiff. "A queen's word—"

I cut her off. "The only people in Rome who still see you as a queen are the ones we *don't* need to convince. And they're very much the minority. We need at least two more votes, remember?"

"How will finding someone who supports our story help with this case?" asked Anastasia.

"For starters, it gives you a reason to have been in Rome."

Lucia's open palm slapped the table surface like a cannon shot. "How many times must I tell you this, Mr. Smith? It is not enough to provide plausible deniability. We need a suspect!"

I gritted my teeth. If she told me that one more time, I was going to throw myself out the damn window. Once I found a room with windows.

"I suspect Mr. Smith is aware of that fact, my queen. Perhaps, we should allow him to finish."

I nodded my gratitude to the auburn-haired femmepire. "Yeah, our need for a suspect sank in somewhere around the twentieth time you told me so, Lucia. But a suspect alone is useless without evidence."

"And your line of inquiry will help in that goal?"

"Whoever framed Ana for this murder had to know she was in Rome. And the only way they could have known that is if they knew Tomasso had reached out to you."

"Unless I was spotted entering Italy," countered Anastasia.

"Were you?" asked Lucia.

"I do not believe so, but anything is possible."

Lucia considered the other femmepire for a long moment, then nodded stiffly. "True enough." She turned back to me. "Even if your line of reasoning proves correct, the murderer is unlikely to admit to being aware of my brother's actions."

"Exactly." I beamed.

"Perhaps you might explain your thought process a little bit further," Ana suggested diplomatically, overriding whatever Lucia was starting to say.

"As king, Tomasso dealt with a lot of people on a daily basis, right? Even when he went to Rome, he had guards with him."

"Guards who are now missing."

"My point is that there must have been people who had some clue what he was doing. If we can find any of those people, they might help us identify others."

"Which would give us another dataset for identifying the murderer," concluded Anastasia.

"Yeah. Obviously, we need hard evidence as well, but the murder scene was days old by the time Lucia and I arrived in Rome. If there was something the photographers missed, it had already been cleaned up long before my visit. Did you see anything odd in the autopsy?"

"Forensics are not my area of specialization, but no. While the toxicology report has not yet been completed, the rest of the data supports Lord Borghesi's narrative. Tomasso suffered multiple blows to the chest, but the actual cause of death was decapitation."

"Which helps us not at all," said Lucia.

"If the fragments of stone were placed to implicate Ana, I think it's a reasonable assumption that the way in which he was killed was also significant," I argued. "Whoever killed Tomasso knew precisely how Anastasia killed Xavier. That's yet another dataset for us."

"One that encompasses the entirety of the palace."

I blinked. "Say what?"

"I sent the traitorous captain's corpse back to Rome shortly after his failed coup," explained the queen, "as a message to those who would dare to conspire against me."

"Of course you did." I sighed. "Maybe we should approach this from a different angle."

"I believe I suggested that not even five minutes ago."

I ignored Lucia, like the mature, responsible adult I occasionally pretended to be. "We don't have any evidence that points to the real killer, and the likelihood of finding any is pretty damn low as long as the suspect pool remains *everyone in Rome*. So maybe our first step should be trying to narrow it down based on what little we do know?" I turned to Ana. "Do you have a pen and paper?"

"I believe so." She made a careful detour around the shards of shattered glass and returned with a notepad and pen.

I put the manila folder containing Denarius' crime report to one side and drew three horizontal lines on the top page of the notepad. Above the first line, I wrote the word Motive. Above the second, Means. And above the last, Opportunity. I was pretty sure I'd stolen this idea from television, but it seemed worth a shot.

"Let's start with motive. Why kill Tomasso?"

"Why kill any royal?"

"Other than their personalities, you mean? No clue. I grew up in a democracy," I reminded the queen.

"Generally, the rationale is either political or personal," answered Anastasia.

"That's a start." I added the first name to the list.

"Sabina? You believe my un-blooded *niece* killed her father?"

"Not particularly, no, but this isn't a list of people we think killed him, it's just a list of everyone who might have had motive to do so. If she found out that he'd enlisted Maria Elena to spy on her…"

"By that logic, you should add Maria Elena to the list as well," reasoned Anastasia. "Perhaps Tomasso planned to tell his daughter the truth about Maria Elena's role."

"And she killed him to keep the secret?"

"And to avoid being sent back to her House in shame. It is as viable a motive as any."

"Good point." I added the young femmepire's name to the list. "Who else? Was there any bad blood between Tomasso and the rest of the nobility? Unpopular rulings? Public slights?"

Lucia plucked the pen from my hand and added three new names to the list. I didn't recognize any of them.

"Minor Houses," she told me. "Two of them sought to provide Tomasso with a consort and were rejected."

"And the third?"

"Was not rejected." She met my eyes. "Though she bore him a child, my spies tell me there was little love between the two. Her House has not gained the prestige it anticipated."

"Sabina's mother?" I frowned. "I didn't even realize she was alive. Why isn't she on my interview schedule?"

"She returned to Ibiza more than a decade ago." Lucia shrugged. "But you wanted anyone who might have motive."

"Fair. And that brings us to the Council. I know they all gain a little bit more decision-making power for the handful of years until Sabina is crowned, but that doesn't seem like a motive in and of itself. Did any of them have other reasons to want Tomasso—and Aurelius—dead?"

Both femmepires frowned.

Anastasia shook her head. "Minerva has no need for earthly authority and Dog cares only about his bacchanalian pursuits."

"And the others? Duke Bugs-a-lot?"

"He and the contessa were both vigorous supporters of my father," said Lucia, "and transferred that support to Tomasso. They argued for capital punishment at my own trial."

"So even though they might hate you enough to frame you, they liked Tomasso too much to kill him." Unfortunately, that really did mesh with the impression I'd gotten from Vigo. "Not to mention, the duke would have had to actually go into Rome for his swarm to reach Tomasso. Who does that leave?"

"Caine and the Horned God," said Anastasia.

"Our two strongest supporters in Rome."

"The Horned God is a demon, your Majesty, and Mr. Smith and I sent several of his kind back to the depths just last year."

"And what of it? If you had spent as much time with the incubus as I have, you would know how little he cares about his fellow denizens."

I shivered. Lucia's full-motion memory of her time with the demon had scarred me for life.

"What of Caine? It was his word that brought you here, my queen. He is the very reason your life hangs in the balance of this trial."

"I make my own decisions, Secundus." Lucia's voice was ice cold. "As you should well remember."

I didn't know what *that* was about, but Anastasia had gone still, so I was guessing it wasn't good. I hurried to fill the sudden ensuing silence.

"Is that everyone then?"

"There is still the Lady Manassa and the Kingmaker, thrall. I do not have reason to suspect the naga, but you may recall that I identified my uncle as a suspect from the start."

"But didn't he refuse the crown on multiple occasions? Why would Denarius kill Tomasso? *And* his brother?"

"They were family, Mr. Smith."

"That's... a horrifying answer," I replied.

"Family conflicts are rarely rational. If you aren't yet aware of the fact, I despair for your agency's future."

"I've met the surviving members of the Borghesi clan, and trust me, Denarius is the closest thing to rational you people have." I added the manpire's name to the list anyway, purely as an excuse to avoid the queen's suddenly blazing eyes. "So basically, we have three minor Houses, two super-young femmepires, and a dude who doesn't want a crown *and* saved both our lives at the airport? That's it?"

"Motive is sometimes apparent only after the fact," reasoned Anastasia. "Perhaps we should focus on your other lists instead?"

We both ignored Lucia's impatient sigh.

"Alright; let's go with means then. Who could have managed to sneak up on both Tomasso and a fully trained Secundus?"

In reply, Anastasia passed me a separate sheet of paper covered in ink. "When Queen Lucia mentioned the need this morning, I took some time to put together a list of Talents that seemed applicable, as well as the known possessors of those Talents."

There had to be several dozen names on that list, neatly subdivided into categories as she'd said. The Talents listed ranged from things like invisibility (*so* badass) to teleportation (even cooler, but the only vampire with that Talent was nine hundred years old and living somewhere in Asia) to something called...

"Shadecasting?"

"It is the Talent of manipulating shadows, Mr. Smith. For concealment, for weaponry, and—if the practitioner is strong enough—for egress."

"They can walk through shadows?"

"Yes."

Teleportation was no longer the coolest Talent on the board.

"And Denarius is a Shadecaster," I noted.

"He is." It was Lucia's turn to beam brightly in my direction. "Motive *and* means. Imagine that."

I looked away from her smug smile. Denarius was scary as hell, but I didn't buy *family* as a viable motive, and the manpire seemed like a stand-up dude. Frankly, I trusted him more than our supposed allies...

My eyes turned to the bird skull on the table. A device that could mute sound, preventing eavesdropping... or perhaps preventing anyone from hearing the bearer approach.

"What about that?" I asked, nodding to the skull.

"What of it?"

"Well, we're talking about Talents that would allow someone to sneak up on someone, right? What about devices?"

Lucia looked to Anastasia who frowned in consideration before shaking her head. "I woke only when the Watch already had me pinned. Had they been using this device it would only have covered their approach within a few feet."

"Because then you'd have been inside its sphere of power, and able to hear them," I realized.

"Exactly."

"Perhaps I should remind you both *yet again,* that the Lord of Bones is our ally in this matter," hissed Lucia.

It was my turn to shrug. "All our lives are on the line here, Lucia. You can't blame me for being thorough."

"For being thorough? No. For wasting time and energy? I very much can."

"My queen..." began Anastasia.

"Enough! As my chosen investigator in the matter, you are granted latitude in how you conduct your investigation." Lucia's voice dropped to a threatening purr. "But we currently have only two Council votes that can be relied upon. Take great care, thrall, that you do not cost us either of those votes."

I shook my head. Obnoxious as she was, the queen kind of had a point. "I take it your efforts to sway some of the neutral votes have yet to pan out?"

"We will discuss my work momentarily," she replied. "For the time being, let us continue with your own exercise."

"I'm sorry?"

"There is one more list, John," Anastasia pointed out.

"Oh. Right. Opportunity." I put my wayward thoughts back into some semblance of order.

"By opportunity, you mean what, exactly? If it merely involves access to Rome, this will be a long list…"

"More than just that, Lucia. As you've mentioned a few times, we're not just investigating one murder, we're investigating two. I'd love to have more information on Aurelius' murder—"

"Then why haven't you asked?"

"Asked?"

"About my father's murder. It was only a century ago, and I was falsely accused, convicted, and exiled for the act. I can promise you the details remain fresh in my mind."

I… wished I had a good answer for that. The truth was, I'd fallen back into a purely human mindset. A century was a very, very long time ago for my species. About halfway down my sheet of paper, I added two more lists. The left one had all the details we knew about for Tomasso's murder. The right list was blank. I nodded to Lucia. "Go ahead."

Five minutes later, I put the pen back down and examined the lists. The good news was that Lucia hadn't been lying; she'd remembered every detail presented at the trial for her father's murder. The bad news was that none of those details were very helpful. The truly terrible news was that there didn't seem to be any overlap between the manner of Aurelius' murder and Tomasso's.

"So, King Aurelius was found dead in his suite here in the palace, with his eyes and hands missing, and no signs of either forced entry or a murder weapon." The fact that I'd been able to listen to and recount the gruesome details of the murder without losing my lunch said bad things about what the last few years had done to me. "What made them think you were responsible?"

"When found," Anastasia explained, "the king's body was ice cold."

"Presumably because it was winter," muttered Lucia, "though the windows in his room were shuttered."

"That's it? His body was cold?" I'd been right way back when; if this was all it took to convict a queen, we were utterly screwed.

"And numerous witnesses recalled an argument between my father and I that morning," admitted Lucia. "One that ended with him telling me that the next time he laid eyes upon me, I would have changed my position."

An argument was troubling, but I didn't really see the connection.

"To which I replied," continued the queen, "that he was more likely to lose those eyes than I was to change to suit him."

Oh.

"I was speaking figuratively, of course, but the manner of his death suggested otherwise."

"It's still kind of iffy. I know these aren't human trials, but shouldn't it take more evidence to accuse a queen?"

"There was also an eyewitness," added Anastasia. "Who saw a hooded woman fitting Queen Lucia's description entering and leaving the king's suite around the time of his death."

"An eyewitness who disappeared shortly after the trial, no doubt sent to live out their human life in luxury somewhere far away from Rome," added Lucia.

"So, their story was made up?"

"Of course it was. I had no desire to see my father again that day… or even that month. However, Anastasia and I were alone at the time of the murder, with nobody to vouch for our location."

"Couldn't the guards have discredited the witness' report?"

"What guards? My father was secure in his power and preferred not to spend his life shadowed by the Watch."

"Given what I've heard about his assault on the Mad King's palace, I guess that confidence was at least somewhat understandable. He was a Lightbringer, like Tomasso, right?"

"He was."

"Were there any signs that he had used his Talent to defend himself?"

Anastasia and Lucia traded looks, before the love of my life shook her head. "There were not."

"Interesting."

"If they were able to reach Tomasso and myself without being detected, it stands to reason that they might have done the same with Aurelius," reasoned Anastasia.

"Sure, although the killer's first strike would still have to have incapacitated both kings to the point of them not being able to use their Talent. Regardless, it's one of the only two things these murders have in common."

"What is the second?" Lucia asked.

"They both implicated you, directly or indirectly."

"Yes. It would appear I make an all-too-convenient scapegoat where my family is concerned." She pointed back to the paper. "How do these details help in completing your logic exercise?"

Logic exercise. Was *that* what I was doing? Not bad for a community college dropout. Unfortunately…

"They don't, really."

The queen's sigh was audible and heartfelt.

"They do support our assumption that the same person killed both of your family members though," I pointed out, thinking through the situation out loud. "And if that's the case, then it limits who we place on the opportunity list."

"How so?"

"They would have to have been present in Rome at the time of both murders," pointed out Anastasia.

"Exactly. And alive for that matter. Which rules out both Sabina and Maria Elena."

"And leaves virtually everyone else at Court, not to mention the entirety of the Council."

"Does it though?" I met Lucia's icy blue-eyed gaze. "We know the Horned God was away when your brother was murdered. And the American ambassadors rotate every decade; I doubt Juliette's mother was serving here during Aurelius' death."

"Juliette's mother?"

I nodded at Anastasia. "Deanna Middleton is the current ambassador. She's kind of amazing."

"I see." Ana's tone was light, but…

"In a totally platonic, mother-of-my-business-partner sort of way," I assured her.

"John…" The femmepire's eyes danced. "If I truly were concerned that you were going to throw yourself at the feet of another woman, I would not have sought my queen's blessing."

I grinned back. "Good. Because there's only one woman's feet I'm interested in…"

"Spare us the stomach-turning details of your aberrant sexual fetishes, Mr. Smith," interrupted Lucia. "We have two murders still to solve."

"Right." I coughed, aware that my cheeks were burning. That wasn't what I'd meant *at all.* Not that there was anything *wrong* with foot fetishes, but… "Anyway, my point is that we should figure out who was here for both murders and exclude everyone who wasn't."

"Few of the Noble Houses spend all of their time at the Court."

"True," agreed Lucia, "and the representatives they do send tend to change based upon the House's need."

"Their need?" I asked.

"If the noble family has someone of age, they might be sent with a guardian to find a suitable match with another House. If there is open conflict between two Houses, the representative would more likely be a senior diplomat."

"Or a warlord," murmured Anastasia.

"Indeed. It depends upon the desired outcome." The queen gave me a thoughtful look. "Perhaps this line of inquiry is not a complete waste of time."

"I'll alert the media." I rolled my eyes. "Anyway, can you put together a list of which nobles were present at the time of Aurelius' murder, and compare it to those here last week?"

"Of course. Court records are extensive, and our memories of that time remain sharp."

"Because it wasn't all that long ago for the People."

"Precisely."

That took care of the noble families, leaving the Council, assorted functionaries, and the handful of individuals who didn't fit neatly into any category. People like… "What about Gaius? Was he really away at the time of your father's death?"

Lucia nodded. "On a mission to India, I believe, though neither he nor my father ever told me the goal of that mission."

"And the Council?"

"I can tell you who was present at the time of my father's murder, but as for Tomasso's…"

It was Anastasia's turn to lean forward. "That is something I can assist with. As I was to travel to Rome, I made it a point to identify possible threats."

"Save for the one that saw you captured."

Anastasia met her queen's gaze without blinking. "Yes."

Another awkward silence fell. I was still thinking about how best to end it when Lucia beat me to the punch. With a sigh, she took Anastasia's hand in her own.

"I apologize, Asya. I am not myself."

Her apology was, in my informed and unbiased opinion, the sole example of Lucia not being herself since I'd arrived, but something in Anastasia's demeanor softened anyway. She squeezed the other woman's hand. "Nor I, your Majesty. This place…"

"Yes." Lucia nodded again. "Prolonged exposure to the Tower would wear on anyone."

For some reason, I didn't think Ana had been referring to the Tower. But she nodded anyway and bowed to the other femmepire. Still holding Lucia's hand, she turned back to me.

"While the Horned God was the only councilor away from court last week, two of the ambassadors here at that time have since been replaced. Ambassadors Santos and Ti An arrived separately, just before the two of you."

"Is that common? Ambassadors swapping in at the same time?"

"It is not," answered Lucia. "However, Santos' predecessor was a close friend of Duke Barros. When Barros' financial malfeasance was uncovered, his allies must have all fallen under suspicion."

"Marcus' plan was a success then?" asked Anastasia.

"It was. The San Diego House is leaderless."

"Surely, Marcus holds the House for your return?"

"Marcus is hiding out in some island village that he now owns," I told her, "and Lucia has opted to abandon the vampires who remain as some sort of petty revenge."

"Vengeance was but one factor in my decision, Mr. Smith," murmured the queen. "As I told you in California, there are a multitude of considerations at play in every strategy."

Her words didn't make any more sense to me now than they had in the limo, but Anastasia's eyes widened in sudden realization. Once again, I was the odd person out.

"As for Ti An," continued Lucia, "I suspect she was sent here once word of my brother's death reached the Endless Empire. If anyone can turn chaos into an advantage for the empire, it would be she."

"How did she get here before we did?"

"Ti An travels quickly, my thrall, and you do not."

That was kind of hurtful, considering she'd made the travel arrangements. "It doesn't sound like their predecessors had anything to do with Tomasso's murder, but can we find out where they were on the day in question anyway? Just in case?"

"I will see what can be done."

"For what it is worth," said Ana, "neither the current ambassadors nor their predecessors possess Talents that would lend themselves to the sort of assassinations we are investigating."

"Not that we know of, at least," murmured Lucia. "After all, none of us knew that Xavier had developed a second Talent. Somehow."

Anastasia nodded. "It *is* possible that someone else repeated his feat and has managed to keep it a secret for over a century, but Xavier was only the second instance of multiple Talents that even Zorana had heard of. To think that there could be two such individuals within a century, and that they would have both been members of this Court and involved in plots against your family..."

"It does seem pretty unlikely," I agreed. "Not to mention that it would kind of ruin our chances of narrowing down the suspect pool. If you're going to operate under the assumption of secret, hidden second Talents, you might as well also include people with applicable Talents who have since died. After all, they could conceivably have faked their own deaths to plot revenge."

I grinned, but I was the only one. Lucia glanced at her Secundus, who nodded slowly.

"I was making a joke, guys."

"And yet it is an avenue worth investigating," replied Lucia.

"And far more likely than a second Talent," agreed Anastasia.

"It's not like we're hurting for suspects. Living ones, I mean."

"Be that as it may, I will put together a list." Anastasia offered me a bleak smile. "I might as well put my enforced free time to use."

Lucia finally released Anastasia's hand and rose to her feet. "Very well then. We will reconvene once we have the necessary information. Should we identify those who had both the means and opportunity to kill my father and brother, we will then be able to focus our investigation upon those individuals. Perhaps then, the motive of the killer will become clear."

I wasn't sure who she was explaining this to, given that it had been *my* idea, and Anastasia had probably figured out the point of the three lists the moment I made them, but before I could comment on that fact, Lucia turned to me.

"You and I will have a private supper tonight. See that you are back at our suite by no later than seven."

"I was thinking about just grabbing something from the kitchen instead—"

"I have agreed to serve as Lady Dumenyova's second," she reminded me. "Allowances must be made for the present situation, but I will *see my duty done*."

"Dinner sounds good." Trust Lucia to take turn a meal into an interrogation. I started to stand, but Ana's hand on my arm stopped me cold.

"My queen, I would speak to Mr. Smith."

Lucia's regal nod almost made up for her eye roll. "Of course you would. I will leave the two of you to your… discussion, then."

"Thank you," Anastasia said without any tangible trace of mockery. "May we also retain the Lord of Bones' artifact for our conversation?"

Lucia threw up her hands. "So be it. My meetings this afternoon will be public anyway. My thrall, I will expect you to return the artifact tonight."

Which meant I was going to need some sort of bag, as there was no way in hell I was touching a bird skull—even one that had been decorated by a hyperactive adolescent—with my bare hands.

Lucia nodded as if she'd heard my unvoiced consent—and given our bond, maybe she had—and left, splinters of broken glass crunching beneath her expensive heels.

CHAPTER 40

IN WHICH MATTERS OF THE HEART
ARE RARELY UNDERSTOOD

I waited for the hall door to swing shut. Then, I waited for the sharp staccato of Lucia's heels to fade away. Finally, I waited for Anastasia to say something. When that didn't happen, I eventually decided it was my duty to break the silence.

"Is that shirt new?"

Jesus. No wonder I was single. Mostly single.

As inane as the question had been, it did seem to serve its purpose. Ana stirred from her contemplation and nodded. "The few outfits I brought to Rome have been confiscated. Clothing, such as it is, is being provided during my stay."

"Well, it's not very *you*, but..." I shrugged. "You pull off the all-black look way better than any of the goths I knew in high school." To say nothing of the goths I'd met *since* high school.

"And here I thought you preferred leather," she teased, referencing the warrior Valkyrie costumes she and Lucia had worn to the mediation with Bill.

"Leather is admittedly awesome, but mostly..."

"Mostly?" One delicate eyebrow arched.

"Mostly I just prefer you," I admitted.

"Oh."

Another silence fell. "Are you okay?" I finally asked. "You look…"

That same eyebrow rose again.

"Beautiful," I hastily ad-libbed, "but… also tired."

"Yes."

"Because of the Tower?"

"Not in the way you are thinking. As the prior occupant showed, one can live here for some time with no ill effects."

I considered death by pneumonia an *ill effect* but understood her point. "Then what…?"

"When my parents sold me to King Aurelius," she finally told me, "I was young, afraid, and innocent. As I aged, I swore I would never be so helpless again. Yet here I am, unable to act *at all* even as my queen is forced to treat with those who wish her dead, even as you struggle to survive attacks from every direction."

"Not every direction," I joked. "So far, the floor has been pretty—"

"John." Her voice, quiet but iron-hard, cut through my babble. "It is not a laughing matter. Since I met you, I have tried to protect you."

"And you've done a great job," I reminded her.

"Have I?"

"Yeah." I didn't even hesitate. "Admittedly, I *do* tend to get kidnapped a lot, but every time you've been there to save me."

Which, I realized far too late, was kind of the point. Because Ana wasn't going to be saving anyone while she was stuck in the Tower.

"I'm not entirely helpless myself," I told her, in one of the world's great lies.

"I know." Anastasia looked away, and for a moment, I thought those two syllables were all I'd be getting. "But to sit here and do nothing…"

It was my turn to reach across the table and take her hand.

"I get it." I squeezed her cold fingers. "But maybe it's time for Lucia and me to save you for a change."

Not that we were making a particularly good showing of it so far. Thank God the trial was still a few weeks away. And speaking of that trial… I glanced over at the bird skull on the table and lowered my voice, just to be sure.

"Besides, you and I both know that even if we lose the trial, there's no way in hell Lucia will march meekly to her own execution. She will fight."

"She will lose."

"Obviously, because she won't have bothered to figure out a plan of escape beforehand. Because, as far as I can tell, she never thinks *anything* out beforehand." I beamed a smile at the woman I loved. "So, I guess it's a good thing she has you to come up with that plan on her behalf."

"A plan to fight our way free of a gathering of some of the most powerful beings in Europe, to escape a palace that is swarming with guards, and to navigate a city currently patrolled by the Illutu, so that we might somehow return to San Diego unscathed?" Anastasia's answering smile was considerably less sunny. "Once again, I think you overestimate me."

"I never said it would be easy. But between an obnoxious, egotistical queen, a brave but ultimately clueless human, and *you*… I'd say you've got the best chance of coming up with something that even has a miniscule chance of success." I shrugged. "It's something to do, anyway. Hopefully, it won't come to that. Maybe Lucia will magically transform into a diplomat for the ages."

"Should the Lord of Bones and Horned God both side with my queen as she expects, we will only need another two votes," Ana pointed out.

"Yeah. I'm just not sure where those votes are coming from. Vigo clearly hates her, and it sounds like the contessa isn't much better. Denarius doesn't get a vote, Lady Manassa always abstains, and Dog could go either way, depending on what drug he's on at the time."

"Do not forget Minerva. She is a goddess of wisdom, after all, and has always been regarded as rational and temperate."

"Unless you ask her for directions," I muttered. "At which point, she goes ape shit."

"I beg your pardon?"

"Didn't I tell you I'd run into Minerva in the halls?"

Judging by the femmepire's flinty expression, I had not.

ooo

"There are times," Anastasia said wearily, when I had finished yet another recap of yet another life-threatening event, "when I am not certain whether to laugh or to cry."

I was a great believer in laughter, myself, but given the mess the femmepire had made of yet another piece of silverware during my brief tale, I decided to treat the question as rhetorical. One thing Juliette had taught me over the past half year was that there was a time for John Smith, and there was a time for blessed silence.

"Is Ms. Zhukova okay?"

"Valentina? Yeah, thanks to the Rag Lady." I shook my head slowly. "Otherwise, I might still be held by *Vita Unica*. Or have died to the Illutu when they came calling."

Anastasia's jade eyes narrowed.

"Hey, I'm *positive* I told Lucia about *Vita Unica*."

"I am aware of both the human organization, and the fact that they briefly held you last night. But I have never heard of this Rag

Lady. Who is she, and how did she manage to rescue both Ms. Zhukova and yourself?"

"All good questions," I admitted, "which I don't have the answers to."

I gave a quick summary of my encounters with the World's Smallest Ringwraith.

Anastasia's poker face was in full effect, but her voice was rueful. "Only you would throw yourself into opposition with one of the most dangerous People in the world for a complete stranger—"

"It seemed like the thing to do," I began.

"—only to have that stranger turn out to be uniquely qualified to rescue your ghost, and in doing so, indirectly save you from the Illutu."

"I know it sounds ridiculous…"

"Ridiculous? I suppose. Yet strikingly familiar to we who know you." Ana's eyes danced. "What am I to do with you, Mr. Smith?"

I had some pretty good ideas, at least one of which involved the removal of that black t-shirt. "Once I've had my interview with the queen, maybe we can find out."

It was the femmepire's turn to lean across the table. She brushed my lips with hers in an all-too-brief kiss, but when she settled back into her seat, the poker face was gone and her expression was… pensive.

"What is it?"

"The blessing."

I nodded. "Yeah. I'm not sure how to convince Lucia I'm a suitable match for you. The trial seems less daunting, honestly."

"That was not what I meant." Ana looked away. "I should not have made the request—"

My heart sank into my shoes.

"—without consulting you in the manner. You have every right to reject the proposition."

I looked across the table at her. Warm lamplight picked out the red highlights in her hair, tracing the graceful sweep of her long neck to shoulders strong enough to bear the problems of three people. She thought *I* might have second thoughts?

"I may not have understood the question when you asked it the night before last, but my answer remains the same."

"It does?"

"Of course!" I rounded the table to kneel by her chair. "Ana, you're the best thing that has ever happened to me! How could you doubt that?"

"It has been almost a year now since we began dating," she murmured, "yet you have never broached the subject."

"Of Lucia's blessing? I didn't even know that was a thing."

"Of *us*."

Oh. That.

I fumbled for the proper words. "The last time we talked about our relationship…"

"Yes?"

"You told me that you didn't love me, and that we couldn't be together." It had been the worst breakfast ever, even worse than that morning after Tijuana. "I guess I didn't want to risk a repeat of that conversation."

"And you believed that was what would occur?" Ana's tone was guarded, giving away nothing, but I took the fact that she hadn't moved away—or karate chopped me into oblivion—as a good sign.

"Maybe? I don't know. After you rescued me from Zorana, things between us changed, but… I was afraid to find out exactly how. Or why." The idea that this astonishing creature could care about me even half as much as I did her still seemed utterly ludicrous.

Ana reached down to cup my cheek, tilting my head up until our eyes met. "Last year, I killed and buried my father. It is our way, and things between he and I were barely cordial, but he was the only family I had left. The act itself was easy, but the emotional aftermath was not. Yet when I returned to San Diego, there you were—"

"Completely ignorant of the tragedy you'd just endured and selfishly fixated on my own issues."

The hand cupping my cheek tightened. "Do not put words into my mouth, Mr. Smith."

In the Tower, without access to her species' true might, I knew Anastasia couldn't *really* pulp my skull like an overripe peach, but it kind of *felt* that way. I nodded again and stayed quiet.

"There you were," she said again, "so young and bright and full of life. I told myself that I was protecting you by pushing you away, that I was making a sacrifice so that you could live the life you deserved." Anastasia shook her head, her eyes never leaving my face. "In truth, I was protecting myself."

"From what?"

"From watching someone else I love grow old and die."

A very small part of me noticed that the femmepire had used the *L word*, but the majority of my brain was fixated on what she was actually trying to tell me.

"It was cowardice," she concluded, "but I convinced myself that it was a selfless act. You would be free to live your life, and I would maintain the life I had become accustomed to."

"What changed?"

"You nearly died at Zorana's hand. Three days later, still far from whole, you agreed to rescue a woman you despise simply because I asked it of you." Her eyes glistened. "Even then, it wasn't until your subsequent showdown with Nepenthe's coven that I recognized the truth."

"What truth?"

"There is very little chance that either of us will survive the century," she said, "and I would rather spend what time we have together than apart."

"That was the most romantic yet disturbing declaration of love I've ever heard." I couldn't help but grin. "And ditto."

Her hand fell away from my face to grab a fistful of shirt, and she pulled me off my knees and against her, our mouths coming together almost by magic. By the time that kiss ended, my breath was short, my heart was beating a thousand times a second, and all the blood in my body had taken an express elevator ride to somewhere below my waist.

Soft eyes gazed into mine across the distance of a few inches, Anastasia's breath cool against my suddenly overheated flesh.

"Win this trial, John, and convince the queen to grant us her blessing."

Somehow, I mustered the brainpower to put words together. "Yes, ma'am."

CHAPTER 41

The Lady Manassa's chambers were in the same wing as Vigo's and Dog's but reached via a smaller hallway and tucked into what my still-slightly-befuddled mind insisted had to be the back corner of the palace. I wasn't sure what that said about her ranking on the Council. It did, however, mean that she couldn't possibly have seen or heard me enter Vigo's suite that morning. So how had she known to send someone to intervene?

From the hall, there was little to distinguish the naga's suite from every other oversized room in the wing, but when Aasha opened the door to admit me, a wave of humid air rushed out past her. The air in the foyer was damp and sticky, like a Florida swamp in mid-afternoon. In place of the usual hardwood floors were wide stone tiles in pale gray and ivory.

My shirt was already sticking to my back, but Aasha didn't seem troubled by the sauna-like environment. She offered a liquid curtsey. "John Smith. The Lady Manassa awaits your presence." She hesitated, breaking from the script to nod at my feet. "If you wish to remove your shoes, I promise that they will remain undisturbed."

Given where my battered Nikes had been in the past twenty-four hours, it was an understandable request. I stacked my shoes by the door. Even through my socks, the tiles were warm and slightly damp.

As I rose, Aasha eyed my socks. Her own feet, I saw, were bare—small and delicate with a slight dusting of scales. Finally, she shrugged and took me deeper into the suite.

As soon as we left the foyer, the source of the humidity became apparent. Dog's suite had been a '70s style drug emporium. Vigo's had been the gathering place for the world's bug-centric nightmares.

Lady Manassa's was a grotto.

Several steps from the foyer, the tiled floor descended into dark water. Lanterns hung from ivy-covered walls, light filtering through the thick foliage that divided the single, enormous room into smaller sections.

The young naga followed those steps down to the water's edge. A series of individual stones, each protruding just barely above the water, formed a path leading deeper into the room. Aasha nodded to that pathway.

"Watch your step, Mr. Smith."

Maybe I *should* have removed my socks.

I was halfway into the room when I saw the first snake. It was six feet long, as thick as my arm, and dangling like a fisherman's hook from a branch directly in front of us. I stopped so suddenly that even Aasha's inhuman grace couldn't keep her from running into me. We were teetering together on a single stone when I made the mistake of looking down.

The water around our feet was teeming with serpents.

That was all it took for me to lose my balance completely and plunge into the pool.

ooo

I didn't have a fear of snakes, any more than I had one of bugs, but plunging headfirst into a dark watered pool full of them?

It's possible I panicked.

I don't remember anything after I went into the water, so technically, it's *also* possible that I reacted like a stone cold badass with ice in his veins, warding the snakes away with steely resolve and calmly swimming back to the stone path.

But I'm pretty sure I panicked.

Either way, when I came back to myself, I was on solid ground, t-shirt and jeans plastered to my body and smelling vaguely swampy. Something that felt a lot like seaweed was wrapped around my ankle under the leg of my jeans.

"My apologies, Investigator Smith," someone was saying. I was pretty sure they'd been talking to me for a while now, but their voice was only now starting to seep through. "I forget sometimes that your species has an aversion to serpents. Rest assured that neither they nor my people mean you harm."

I looked up from the tiled floor and the puddle slowly forming around me to find the Lady Manassa, seated calmly at an ornately carved table. Silver hair was piled artfully atop her head, and today's sari was pale green with gold threading, complementing both her eyes and skin.

She nodded to one of the available chairs. "Would you care to have a seat?"

I eyed that chair. It was every bit as beautifully carved as the table, with a soft cushion—also in green—atop its seat. It was also probably worth more than I was, and I was sopping wet. Ruining something that valuable seemed like a terrible first step in this relationship.

Either I said the words aloud or my reservations came through on my face. Either way, Lady Manassa nodded again. "Of course, you should be made comfortable first." She raised her voice just enough for it to carry over the sound of softly shifting water. "Nyah. Please bring Mr. Smith a towel and change of clothes."

Nyah was another naga, similar enough in appearance to Aasha to be sisters, if not twins. She emerged from one of the hidden regions of the grotto with a white fluffy towel on one arm, and something in pale blue silk on the other.

I toweled off my face, head, and arms, but the problem was *all* of me was soaked. I didn't want to ruin the nice chair, but I also had no intention of stripping down with an audience. If the nagas were allies, I needed to impress them, and pudgy, naked human was unlikely to do the job. And if they weren't allies... well, showing my soft underbelly to the enemy sounded like a terrible idea.

Again, Lady Manassa read my mind with a facility I was used to only from my mom. Or Anastasia. Or the damned femmepire queen who had a direct path into my brain.

"There are few places within our grotto that can be considered truly private, Mr. Smith, but Nyah will take you someplace slightly more secluded so that you may change."

Thank God. I followed the young naga down another path of stones, doing my damnedest to ignore the snakes above and below me. Twenty or thirty harrowing steps later, we reached another tiled platform along the chamber's edge. The circular room was ringed with thick vegetation, walling it away from the rest of the grotto. Furniture—a narrow bed, wardrobe, and dresser—reinforced the idea that this was a separate room, even if the sound of water, and the occasional hiss of what were probably John-eating snakes made that illusion difficult to maintain.

With a curtsey—slightly less polished than Aasha's—Nyah handed me the blue silk and retreated back down the path.

I waited a few moments then stripped out of my sopping wet t-shirt. My jeans took a lot more effort, and it was only when I had finally removed them that I realized the seaweed around my left ankle wasn't seaweed at all.

I think my yelp—high-pitched as a terrified, pre-pubescent boy's—startled the snake as much as it did me. Either way, it uncoiled, and made a beeline for the pool. I took a calming breath and waited for my testicles to climb back down out of my throat.

"Is everything okay—? Oh!"

And there was Nyah, drawn back by my squeak of terror and promptly exposed to just the sort of white pudge I'd been trying to hide.

I sucked in my stomach—a slightly easier task than it had once been—and thanked the deities of indecent exposure that I at least still had my boxers on. And that those boxers weren't the ones with animals and rocket ships that a past girlfriend had bought me as a joke.

"Sorry," I told her, trying in vain to deepen my voice so as to make up for the soprano squeal. "Just startled by one of the inhabitants."

Amazingly, the young naga's gaze was directed neither at my mid-section nor my boxers. Instead, she glided closer, pale eyes fixed on my chest.

There's a certain hardwired response men have when a pretty woman—even a pretty snake woman—checks us out, but before I could puff out said chest and mutter inanities about the sheer amount of weight I benched, Nyah was speaking.

"I had no idea investigation was such a dangerous profession."

Even my under-developed man-child brain had trouble taking that comment as some sort of allusion to the sleek, strongly muscled, and deadly physique I didn't have. I looked down to see what on earth she was talking about.

My scars were showing.

Usually invisible against my pale skin, some combination of the grotto's lamplight and the water still dripping down my chest had caused the scar tissue to shine a muted silver.

"It's been a rough few years," I admitted. Thanks to a handful of factors—Davis Hawthorne's werewolf virus, the bond I shared with Lucia, and the witches who had subverted that bond—I had survived wounds that should have killed me, but the evidence remained, painted across my shoulders and chest.

At least Zorana's bite marks were gone. If I had to see those in the mirror every day…

I shivered. The nightmares were bad enough.

○○○

The blue silk turned out to be a robe. It would have looked unbelievable on Anastasia. On me, it looked ridiculous. Still, it was dry. Even more importantly, it was light. Given the humid air of the grotto, a heavier robe would probably have killed me.

Assuming the snakes didn't.

Seated across from me, Lady Manassa placed both of her hands atop the table, palms facing skyward. The bow she offered was little more than a head nod, her eyes still fixed upon me through long lashes.

What little I knew of nagas had come from human mythology books and—given that she and the others *weren't* just human heads atop snake bodies—most of it had been wrong. I had no idea if her gesture had any significance, but I did my best to copy it, feeling awkward and ungainly.

"Thank you for seeing me, Lady Manassa, and for the change of clothes… and for Aasha's timely intervention this morning. As I'm sure you are already aware, I needed to speak with you and the other Council members about the late king's murder."

She nodded in regal acknowledgement, and then spoke before I could push on. "I invited you here for just such a purpose, Mr. Smith, and will be happy to tell you what little I know. However, among my kind, it is customary that matters of business be dealt with only after tea."

"After… tea?"

"Yes. Will you indulge an old woman's traditions?"

The thought of the Lady Manassa—who looked thirty and had the skin and muscle tone of someone barely in her twenties—as an old woman would have once made me laugh, but a few years around vampires had taught me better. Appearances were all too often deceiving.

At my nod, she lifted one hand from the table and motioned to the side. Aasha and Nyah reappeared, the former carrying two delicate china cups, the latter an equally delicate teapot. Four people, but only two cups?

Again, Lady Manassa read my mind. "My daughters will not be joining us, investigator. The tea ceremony is for those whose actions prove them to be adults." Her liquid voice had a small measure of censure to it.

The young nagas were still distant, but over the grotto's trickling water, I heard Aasha mutter, "I'm not the one who walked in on the human while he was naked."

"No," her sister hissed back. "You're the clumsy idiot who knocked him into the water in the first place."

Lady Manassa shook her head slightly, as if to herself, and cast me a glance across the table. "Do you have children, Mr. Smith?"

"Not yet."

"They are a blessing," she replied, humor leaking into her words. "Or so I am told."

That surprised a grin out of me. "My mom uses other words."

"Your nest mother is still alive?" That was from Nyah, whose wide-eyed look made her seem, for one moment, every bit as young as she appeared.

"Both my mom and my dad are," I replied. "Why? What had you heard?"

"It's just that your kind live such short lives," she offered. "And with you already so old, I had assumed your nest mother—"

"Nyah." There was no humor at all in Lady Manassa's voice this time. "Place the pot as you have been taught and leave us."

With a huff, the young naga did just that. Her mother turned back to me once she had gone.

"Again, I apologize, Mr. Smith. She is only a century old, but that is no excuse for her rudeness."

Only a century old. I really needed to start hanging out with humans again.

"It's not a big deal," I replied. "We're pretty informal in San Diego. In fact, I'd appreciate it if you just called me John."

Without moving at all, the Lady Manassa somehow managed to convey both gratitude and acceptance. "You do me honor. Within these walls, you may call me Divya."

"So Manassa is your last name?"

"My title. As the Lady Manassa, I am the chosen voice of my people."

We paused for Aasha to pour the tea, the young naga's graceful motions weaving together like steps in a dance. When that dance had reached completion, her mother nodded and raised a cup.

A handful of awkward moments passed before I realized I was supposed to do the same. I scooped up my cup, trying not to start an international incident by spilling tea all over the table.

I'd expected a toast—or maybe even some sort of tea guzzling competition—but Divya seemed content to study the contents of her cup. If she'd had a nose, I'd have said she was smelling it, but… With a mental shrug, I looked into the depths of my own cup.

It looked like tea. It smelled like tea too.

Finally, the naga murmured something that sounded almost like a benediction and raised the cup to her lips to take a sip. I did the same.

It also tasted like tea. I let the liquid roll around my mouth before swallowing it down, wishing that it had been coffee instead. Or an ice-cold Coke. Or even a beer… preferably something dark and chewy.

"It's very good," I finally offered, once again cementing my status as a diplomat beyond compare.

"The drinking of tea," Lady Manassa told me, "is meant to offer us time to reflect upon our place in the world. Where we have come from. Where we hope to travel in the future."

I'd come from San Diego… and I really hoped I'd be going back there sooner rather than later, but I didn't think that was what she was talking about.

She savored another sip and then eyed me across the copper lip of her china cup. "I was relieved to hear that you had returned safely from Rome last night."

"Me too," I told her, rolling with the subject change. "I just wish my safety hadn't come with such a price."

"The Watch guarding Tomasso's townhouse?"

"And Ambassador Sergei."

Divya nodded. "If it is any consolation, I believe one of the two younglings survived. As for Vasily's Monster… that one is not so easily destroyed, I assure you."

"Nobody's seen him since I left him fighting two of the Illutu knights. If he's alive, what could he possibly be doing?"

"Given his reputation, I suspect it involves either drinking or killing." The naga nodded to the teapot. "More tea, Mr. Smith?"

"No, thank you." If the whole tea thing was a plot to keep me off my game, it was working splendidly. Between the quick subject shifts, the elaborate drinking ceremony, and the very real fear that my nipples were poking through my robe, I was having a difficult time keeping up.

"Perhaps later," mused the Lady Manassa. "In the meantime, now that tradition and our ancestors have been satisfied, we should turn our attention towards the reason for your presence in Rome."

By which, I assumed, she meant the investigation.

"That would be great. But first, I do want to say thanks again for your help with Duke Marte. I'm not quite sure how you knew I was visiting him—"

"If the palace were a living creature, John, it would subsist entirely upon gossip and rumor. For the past few days, the majority of that gossip has centered upon the activities of you and your mistress. There is very little that you do which is not immediately discernable to those paying attention."

I tried not to react to the thought of my every move being studied by beings of great power and possibly greater malice. It was like being a freshman in high school all over again.

"Well, I'm glad you were paying attention. Aasha came at the perfect time."

"It was our pleasure to be of assistance in the matter," Divya told me smoothly.

"She said you wanted to see me?"

"Yes." The naga's fingernails were painted with some sort of opalescent polish. She drummed those fingers on the table as she pondered her words. "One of the many rumors I mentioned is that you truly believe Lady Dumenyova to be innocent of King Tomasso's murder."

"It's not just a rumor," I told her. "It's fact. Anastasia didn't do it."

"But of course you would say so, with your own life depending upon her innocence."

"From what everyone keeps telling me, her innocence isn't all that relevant to the outcome of the trial."

"True enough. At this level of government, politics always come into play." Her gaze sharpened. "Be that as it may, I would have your word on the matter."

"That Ana is innocent?"

"Indeed."

"I didn't realize a human's word counted around here."

"For some, it does not. For many, humans are simply one more species, neither more nor less trustworthy than the rest of us. But then," she reminded me, "you are not quite human, are you?"

That again. "I guess it's possible that there's some strain of something in my blood, but if so, it's news to me. And my parents. On *that*, you have my word."

"And on the other matter?"

"She didn't do it," I confirmed.

"How can you be certain?"

"Because she told me so."

"Even in a human court, that would not be a winning argument, John. People lie."

"Not Anastasia. More importantly, if she *had* killed the king, I can guarantee she would have been gone long before anyone even knew the deed was done. And she sure as hell wouldn't have left behind a trail of painfully obvious clues to implicate herself."

"A valid point." For a second time, she drummed her fingernails against the table's surface. "Is it true that you care for her?"

"This palace needs a new hobby," I decided. "One that doesn't include theorizing about my love life."

"Does the vampire return your sentiment?" Ageless eyes watched me closely.

"Yes. We're… working through some stuff. Kind of." I breathed out a long sigh. "Please tell me you didn't invite me over to tell me what a bad idea the relationship is?"

"Two individuals in love, one of them the People's infamous Stone Lady?" She shook her head, eyes distant. "We are not oracles, Mr. Smith, able to predict the outcome of our choices. We are left to roll the dice and pray for a happiness that is ephemeral by its very nature." Those green eyes refocused on me. "There are times when even a bad idea is worth pursuing."

I was, as Juliette was all too happy to point out, clueless when it came to women, but over time, I'd developed a single, barely perceptible chink in my armor of ignorance. In the years since I'd opened my own agency, I'd had any number of unhappy men and women show up on my doorstep. Heartache, it seemed, looked the same on a balding, mid-fifties man as it did a thirty-eight-year-old blonde with dark roots… or an ancient being out of myth.

We were talking about something more than just my relationship with Ana.

"That sounds like the voice of experience."

"Yes."

"Does it have anything to do with why you wanted to see me?"

"It does."

One of the most important lessons I'd learned from Anastasia was that there were times to speak and times to wait. This was the latter.

Eventually, she spoke again. "From all accounts, you are conducting a reasonably thorough investigation of King Tomasso's death… and his life. At some point, you will learn that he and I once had a relationship."

Whoa. Lucia's brother had game. "Once?"

"Yes. It ended badly several months ago." Green eyes narrowed, she cut off my next question. "I did not kill him."

"He was the one who broke things off?"

"Yes."

Crap. Jilted lovers made for *awesome* suspects.

On the other hand, jilted lovers who freely admitted their relationships and seemed more sad than angry made for slightly *less* awesome suspects.

Unless said admission had been made to throw me off the scent…

Television, I decided, did a shitty job of capturing how difficult homicide investigations really were.

"I understand that this admission makes me a suspect," Divya continued, "regardless of whatever else I might tell you."

"It kind of does," I admitted. "Where were you on the day of Tomasso's death?"

"I was here, as my daughters can attest."

"Can anyone less—"

"Familial?"

"Yeah. Can anyone not related to you confirm that?"

"There are roughly a thousand other witnesses," she said tightly, "but you do not speak their tongue, and I suspect you would consider their testimony biased as well."

I would have preferred *not* knowing that there were a freaking thousand snakes in the grotto with us, but I did my best not to show

how that revelation had rattled me. "It's nothing personal," I told the naga. "These are questions I'm asking everyone."

"Understood." She unbent slightly, again without moving at all. "Please continue."

"Assuming that you are innocent—" Kind of a huge assumption, and one that I was only committing to for the sake of this question. "—and that Anastasia is likewise innocent, who do you think might have killed Tomasso?"

"I don't know. My time with him may have colored my perception, but I believe he was generally well liked."

"He was a king. He couldn't have gotten along with *everyone*." If HBO had taught me anything, it was that every king had haters. And that the life of a king involved a large quantity of bare breasts and random violence.

Divya gave it a moment's consideration. "On the Council, Duke Marte and Contessa d'Verde were his strongest supporters next to the Kingmaker and me. The ambassadors all kept a professional distance, of course. The imp despised him, but the imp despises everyone. The Horned God is ever-focused upon his own pleasures, while Minerva operates on levels far beyond our petty political machine."

"And Caine?"

"He was Tomasso's strongest opposition on the Council," she admitted. "I had always suspected it was due to loyalty to your mistress, but perhaps there was something more."

"Huh." Given that the necromancer was our main ally, we were screwed if Lucia's trust in him had been misplaced. "Well, that's helpful. If you think of anyone or anything else…"

"Actually, that is the other reason I requested your presence."

I perked up.

She paused to unravel a brightly striped snake from the leg of our table, transferring it to the tiled floor with a soft murmur. In moments, it had slithered away, disappearing into the increasingly terrifying foliage. "I will understand should you wish to continue treating me as a suspect, Mr. Smith, but if you choose instead to trust in my innocence, I believe I can be of assistance in your investigation."

"How so?"

"My relationship with the king lasted multiple decades. Even for those such as we, that time adds up. Should you have further questions about who he was, I might be able to offer answers... and insight."

"That's very generous." Suspiciously generous, as my old boss used to say.

"Is it? Either I killed Tomasso and seek to ingratiate myself into your investigation to remain free of suspicion, or I loved a man who was killed before his time and seek vengeance on his behalf. Neither motive reeks of generosity."

"Maybe generous was the wrong word." I hated it when the suspects were smarter than I was.

"Regardless, I am a resource should you care to use me."

"I'll definitely consider it. Actually, I do have a question."

"Ask and I shall try to answer."

"Why did Tomasso break up with you?"

"I beg your pardon?"

"You're smart, you're a babe, and you seem spectacularly sane compared to most of your fellow Council members. What's not to like?" Hell, half an hour in her presence, and her lack of a nose seemed *right* instead of weird. Still, as another snake slithered by, I stumbled onto the obvious explanation. "Did he have a problem with your... pets?"

"They are less pets than vassals, but no. Tomasso was never troubled by their presence."

"Even the poisonous ones?"

"They are all poisonous, John." Divya shook her head again. "But the People have little to fear from a serpent's bite. It is one of the reasons they make good consorts for our kind."

Ordinary, fat-assed human detectives, on the other hand, made terrible consorts and had absolutely everything to fear from snakes. Especially poisonous ones.

I shivered, despite the heat.

"I guess he wouldn't have dated you for decades unless he was cool with snakes. But that just leaves us back at square one. Why did he break up with you?"

"I wish I knew."

"He didn't tell you?"

"He did not. Over the past year, our time together began to dwindle. When we did meet, he was distant and distracted, his ardor significantly diminished." She offered a shrug and self-deprecating smile. "When you live as long as our species do, you learn to recognize the signs of a relationship's end, but I was not ready to move on. When I pressed the issue, Tomasso simply told me that he lacked the time, the energy, or the interest to continue our romance."

Dick move, Tomasso.

"At the time, I believed there was more to it than that… some secret he would not divulge." Her smile turned wan. "But perhaps that was simply the fantasy of an old woman unwilling to face the truth."

Shit. Beautiful, angry women were sort of my kryptonite, but beautiful, *sad* women were worse. My mouth was moving before my brain even realized I was going to speak. "You're not wrong. There *was* something Tomasso wasn't telling you. And if I'm right, the breakup didn't have anything to do with you at all."

"I cannot decide whether that makes me feel better or worse."
She folded her hands together and hit me with a look that was one part
command, three parts plea, and one hundred percent devastating. "Can
you tell me what it was that was so much more important to him than
our relationship?"

And because I was both an idiot and a sucker for doomed
romances, I told her.

By the time I was done, the enormity of that decision had
finally caught up with me. If I was wrong about the Lady Manassa, if
the naga was involved in one or both of the regicides, then I'd just
royally screwed our investigation.

Lucia was going to kill me.

○○○

"So, you believe that the murders of Aurelius and Tomasso
were perpetuated by the same individual, yet that individual was *not*
Lucia Borghesi?"

"Pretty much."

The Lady Manassa shook her head slowly. "It seems a great deal
of trouble for someone to go through simply to rid themselves of your
mistress. There are easier ways."

As far as I could tell, Lucia had already survived many of those
easier ways, but I just nodded. "I don't think the murders were actually
about Lucia at all."

"Oh?"

"Yeah. I'm guessing whoever killed Aurelius had their own
reasons for doing so. Lucia was just a convenient person to frame."

She frowned. "I was here during that time. The only person
who would seem to have profited from Aurelius' murder and Lucia's
banishment is Tomasso himself."

"I know. We're missing something, but I'm not sure what it is.
After Aurelius' death, Tomasso ruled peacefully for a century. It wasn't

until he started revisiting his father's murder that he himself was targeted."

"His investigation into the matter may have made him a threat to the killer."

"That's what it seems like. He *did* tell Lucia that he'd found something."

"But not what."

"Well, no. But it had to be something fairly convincing for him to do a complete one-eighty with regards to his sister. If I can find out what that information was—"

"You will be able to unmask the real killer and clear the names of both the queen and your lover."

My lover. God, I liked how that sounded.

"I wish I could be of help—" Divya's voice trailed off.

"What is it?"

"It could very well be nothing."

"Sometimes, even the most minor detail can crack a case wide open."

She nodded. "A few years ago, Tomasso became interested in the historical records of his family's time in Rome."

"Denarius said something similar. Was that odd?"

"It was. While the king's interests were varied, history was not one of them."

"What was he looking for?"

"At the time, he said he wanted to grow as a king by learning more about his father's own reign. Could his suspicions date back so far?"

"I'm not sure." The image I'd so far built of Tomasso was that of a young—for a vampire—man thrust into a position he wasn't prepared for. Looking to the lessons of his ancestors seemed a fairly reasonable thing to do. "He helped orchestrate an attempted coup in

Lucia's House right around that time. I can't see him doing that if he was starting to suspect her innocence."

"A fair point. But in the course of that research…"

"He may have stumbled onto something that made him take a second look at his father's murder."

"Or the research had nothing at all to do with his revelation."

"That's also possible," I admitted.

"I was closer to him than anyone but his daughter and the Kingmaker," the naga said, her voice strained, "Why would he not confide in me on this matter?"

I didn't want to give the obvious answer to a woman so clearly grieving, especially when that woman had telepathic control over an entire grotto of venomous snakes. Fortunately—or unfortunately—she reached the conclusion all on her own. The drumbeat of opalescent fingernails came to a ragged halt.

"He didn't trust me."

I called upon my mediator training to avoid looking at where her nails had dug deep into the lacquered surface of the extremely expensive and ornately carved table. Regrettably, I'd never actually been trained as a mediator. The Lady Manassa took one look at my face, followed my gaze to her own hand, and sighed.

"I do apologize, Mr. Smith. While Tomasso was not the first man I have loved, and will not be the last, I believed what we had merited at least a modicum of trust."

The trees behind her rustled, disgorging a half dozen snakes onto the tiled floor. Those snakes slithered over to coil around the naga's legs like creepy scaled legwarmers. It's possible that was how snakes offered comfort, but I'd seen way too many National Geographic specials—including one where a Florida python squeezed a swamp alligator to death—to be comfortable with the sight.

"If I think of anything else, I will communicate it to you," Divya continued, her voice small, "but in the meantime, I would appreciate time alone to reflect. Aasha will see you to the door."

When a heartbroken snake queen tells you to go, you go. I rose from my chair and offered Divya another bow, still awkward in my silk robe.

"We *will* find Tomasso's killer, Lady Manassa."

I just hoped it wasn't her.

∘∘∘

The trip across the grotto went smoothly this time, and I reached the entry room without a second tumble into snake-infested waters. Aasha stopped at the tile's edge, curtseyed, and then motioned to the door. When I didn't move, she rolled her eyes and took my hand in hers to brush her lips across the back of it. "There. Now will you go?"

At some point, I was going to have to correct the young naga about the whole hand-kissing thing. Maybe in a few days. Or before I left Rome. Or when I was old and gray. For now, I let the misconception slide, and plucked at the silk robe I still wore. "Actually, I was hoping to get—"

"Your clothing!" I'd never seen someone with Aasha's coloring blush before. She dropped another curtsey. "If you stay here, I will fetch it at once."

It was a matter of minutes before Aasha returned, my clothes over one arm, and my socks in hand. My shirt and pants were surprisingly dry.

My socks were anything but.

"If there is nothing else, I will leave you to get clothed and depart."

Aasha was already halfway back to the grotto when my voice stopped her. "Actually, there *is* one thing I need. Since you asked."

Any question that the naga was inhuman was answered by the swift, virtually boneless manner in which she spun on me. "I am not kissing your hand again!"

I raised my pile of clothes in a placating manner. "I wasn't asking you to."

"Oh. Then what is it?"

"Do you have a phone I can borrow?"

CHAPTER 42

The good news was that Aasha did, in fact, have a phone. The better news was that it was a spare, and she told me to keep it. The best news of all was that I was able to find my way back to the suite I shared with Lucia without getting lost… or killed by bugs, snakes, or giant mercenary roaches.

Everything was coming up roses.

Except for that whole matter of two still-unsolved murders and the three lives hanging in the balance.

Whatever. When the outlook was this bleak, even small victories became worth celebrating. Victories like my suite being empty of a certain blonde, busty, and bit—err, *belligerent*—queen.

I made myself comfortable on the bed I never got to sleep in, and dialed Juliette's cell.

It rang a half dozen times before going to voicemail.

With a frown, I checked the phone's clock. It was after eight in San Diego, which meant Juliette was definitely up. Her early morning ways had been one of the most difficult adjustments for me when I moved in with her. I'd naturally assumed that someone who worshipped at the altar of the punk rock gods would sleep to a decent hour like the rest of us, but not even punk had been a match for a vampire's physiology. If the sun was up, so was my junior partner.

It was unnatural.

With a shrug, I tried the number for our office instead. The phone was on its fourth ring—and I was starting to imagine all the very many ways Juliette's goblin surveillance could have gone horribly awry—when a woman answered.

"Middleton & Smith Investigations. This is Angel. How may I help you?"

Son of a bitch!

"Angel, this is John."

I heard a cough, a muttered *shit*, and suddenly Juliette was on the line.

"Little bird, how the hell am I supposed to know it's you if you keep switching phones?"

"I already told you my wonderphone doesn't work out here. Maybe you could try *not* screening calls from Italy?"

"Maybe *you* could try leaving a voicemail for once?"

I swallowed my retort, refusing to go any further down that rabbit hole when a far bigger issue was at stake. "Juliette, *why is Angel answering our office phone?*"

I heard her say something to Angel, followed swiftly by the distant slam of a door. Moments later, Juliette came back on, her voice entirely too cheerful. "She's our new receptionist, just like we agreed!"

"We didn't agree on that! In fact, I remember giving a pretty damn definitive no."

"Eh. Once you get that six-years-of-abstinence stick out of your ass, you'll realize what a spectacular idea this is."

I closed my eyes and counted to ten. It didn't help at all.

"Duchess, we don't have the money for a third employee. Hell, we don't even have the space!" Between my desk and hers, the office barely had room for clients.

"I'm way ahead of you on that front. Once we knock down the wall between us and 2C, we'll have room to spare."

"*What?*"

"It turns out Carl's one-man accounting firm next door wasn't doing so hot. The space opened up yesterday, and I snatched it for a song. You can thank me when you get back to San Diego!"

I listened to a low grinding sound for a good five seconds before realizing it was coming from my own teeth. "I've been gone for less than a week and you've hired a third employee that we don't need, doubled our office space—and more importantly, our rent—*and* requested tenant improvements? How the hell can we afford—" The answer was painstakingly obvious. "Who did you compel?"

"Just some asshole executive. He had more money than sense, so I helped him resolve that imbalance. It won't be a problem! Don't worry about it."

When Anastasia told me not to worry about something, I didn't. When it was Juliette saying it... I worried. I worried hard.

"What happened to being cautious about when and how you flexed your vampiric muscle?"

"Well, let's see. Lucia's out of the country, so no worries there. And Barros and Thales have run for the hills—" When I failed to respond with the appropriate level of shock or surprise, her voice sharpened. "—which apparently you already knew about and decided not to share. Anyway, anyone with the authority to give a crap about my activities is at least temporarily out of the picture."

"And when the cat's away, the mice will play."

"Screw playing. I'm taking this business to the next level."

Of course she was. I couldn't decide if I was pissed that she'd gone over my head or that she'd accomplished more with the agency in one week than I had in years.

"So anyway," she said, "how's Rome? Solve any murders?"

"Not yet, but there's plenty of time. At least I hope so."

"You *hope* so? I thought the timeline for the trial was fixed?"

"It is. We have a few weeks until the rot starts to show and the trial begins."

"Then what's wrong?" Before I could say anything, her voice changed a second time. "If you tell me you've managed to get attacked *again* since our last conversation, I am literally going to punch you through this phone."

I didn't think Juliette understood what literally meant… but on the off chance that I was wrong, and she really did have phone punching powers, I opted not to correct her.

Sadly, my silence just served as confirmation.

"Gods, little bird. Who was it?"

"Which time?"

Juliette had always been quick to rant and rave. It was only when her voice got quiet and sharp that you really needed to worry. I could have shaved with her next words.

"Start at the beginning and tell me what the hell is going on."

ooo

By the time I had finished, Angel was back in the office with Juliette, and the femmepire's voice had lost its edge, replaced by weary disbelief.

"The Illutu again? *And* human death squads?"

"Don't forget Vigo's bug hordes."

"And a whole swamp of venomous snakes."

"I don't think that one counts. The Lady Manassa has been nothing but helpful."

"Sure she has."

"I'm serious."

"Tell me something… does this naga have breasts?"

"Uhm… obviously?"

"Then I'm not trusting your opinion of her. At all." I heard a rustle of papers, and a low exchange of voices between her and Angel. "I can be in Italy by Friday night… Saturday morning at the latest."

"Juliette, we've talked about this. You *have* a case." Caution and several years of knowing her forced me to ask the obvious question. "You… didn't tell Chief Tomlinson that his wife was sleeping around yet, right?"

"You told me to wait on that until I had proof, remember?"

"Of course, *I* remember… I'm just glad to hear you do too."

"Anyway, I don't think she's having an affair anymore. Or not just *one*, anyway."

"I beg your pardon?"

"I tailed her again. Different house, different goblin guy. She's got lousy taste in men—and cheating's a damn stupid idea given goblin society—but you kind of have to appreciate her sex drive."

"Did you get any proof this time?"

"No. This goblin had some muscle standing guard outside. The whole species being immune to compulsion is total bullshit."

"Welcome to what life is like for an *actual* P.I."

"Yeah, yeah. Anyway, I can have Angel take over stakeout duties while I fly to Rome to save your lily-white ass."

I was oddly touched… partly by the offer, but mostly because she'd chosen to describe my ass as lily-white rather than fat. All the comments I'd received since arriving in Rome had left my ego seriously bruised.

"Maybe we should let Angel spend more than a day or two as a receptionist before bumping her to full-fledged detective?" I suggested, giving in to the unexpected yet now entirely unavoidable expansion of my agency. "I don't plan to leave the palace anymore, and I'm pretty sure Ana and Lucia are going to stick me with a security detachment."

"I hope they come loaded for bear," she muttered. "Demon bear."

So did I, to be honest.

"So, outside of nearly dying on multiple occasions, have you made *any* progress?"

"I can prove that some of the evidence pointing to Ana is fake. I'm going to need a lot more than that though to win the trial."

"Maybe it's time to subject everyone to another retelling of the one thing you learned from Journalism class?"

By which she meant the five W's. "We're kind of past that point already. Ana is putting together a list of possible suspects, and I'm digging into Tomasso's last days in the hopes of finding whatever evidence convinced him Lucia was innocent of their father's murder."

"And what *is* her high and mightiness doing? Besides flashing cleavage at everyone in sight?"

"I'm told it's called diplomacy."

"Sure it is." She sighed and I heard a distinctive squeak, like someone had just leaned back in a comfortable, fake-leather executive chair. *My* comfortable, fake-leather executive chair.

"Tell me you're not sitting in my chair."

"Do you really want me to lie?" The smile left her voice as quickly as it had come. "Seriously, little bird... is there anything I can do?"

"Just keep on doing what you're doing."

"Expand our office into yet another suite? Well, I could probably convince the tenants in 2A to relocate..."

"I meant with the goblin investigation. It sounds like you're making progress. With any luck, you'll have it wrapped by the weekend."

"And *then* I'm flying out to save your fat ass."

So much for lily-white. "Deal."

"Good. Now, is there anything else, or can I get back to making our agency look good?"

"That's all I had. If you need anything, call this number. Otherwise, I'll check back in a day or two."

"Wait! I almost forgot!" Juliette's voice caught me with my finger hovering above the end call button.

"Yeah?"

"I was dead to the world the last time we talked—because you're a moron with no concept of time zones—but… did you say something about my *mother*? Or was that just a nightmare?"

"It definitely wasn't a nightmare," I told her smugly, ending the call with a tap of one finger.

Almost immediately, the phone buzzed with an incoming call. I sent Juliette to voicemail and turned off the phone. Then I made my fat, lily-white ass a little bit more comfortable in Lucia's ridiculously soft bed. Given the night I'd had, to say nothing of the morning and afternoon that had followed it, I was beat.

A nap sounded like a great idea.

CHAPTER 43

IN WHICH BLESSINGS SHOULDN'T BE COUNTED

In retrospect, going to sleep in Lucia's bed probably wasn't a great idea. If the queen had found me there, I wouldn't have lived long enough for the Council to have me executed… or for Juliette to murder me once I got back to San Diego, for that matter.

Thankfully, my nap was short-lived. I woke back up to find seven missed calls and one text message, all from Juliette's number. None of the calls had been more than a second long, so I pulled up the text instead. It was short and to the point.

One funny joke deserves another. Say goodbye to your bed, little bird.

I'd had that lumpy bed since I was a pre-teen, and Juliette knew how sentimental I was about stuff like that. Not even the Duchess of Snark would destroy a genuine Smith heirloom, would she?

Yes. Yes, she sure as hell would. I sent back a quick text:

Not a joke. Will fill you in later. Promise. Please don't destroy my bed!

I figured that raised the chances of my bed's short-term survival from five percent to at least twenty. Twenty-five, if the femmepire remembered how I'd just magnanimously offered employment to her chew toy girlfriend.

When no reply came back, I shrugged, banished the matter from my still-sleepy brain, and went to take a shower. I desperately needed to scrub off whatever weird bacteria I might have collected in the nagas' snake-infested waters.

I probably should have done that *before* napping in Lucia's bed, but… I'd been pretty tired. And better her bed than my cot.

ooo

I had just finished getting dressed when the bond warned me of Lucia's impending arrival. I hurriedly ran a comb through my hair—with the usual lack of results—and went out into the bedroom to wait.

Less than a minute later, the femmepire queen swept in. She stopped dead at the sight of me. "Thrall."

"Lucia."

"Is *that* what you're wearing for our dinner?"

I looked down at my fresh t-shirt and jeans. "That was the plan."

"I see. I had thought you might care enough about Lady Dumenyova to put forth a modicum of effort."

"I'm here in Rome trying to save her life. Why should my outfit matter?"

"Perhaps it doesn't. Perhaps I will choose to grant my blessing even though you are dressed like a shoeless vagrant." The femmepire queen's voice hardened. "The decision is yours."

With a sigh, I headed to the closet.

ooo

Ten minutes later, I emerged from the bathroom in a button-down and one of the few pairs of dress pants I'd brought from San

Diego. I'd even put on a belt, which seemed counter-intuitive given that we were about to have dinner. "Happy now?"

"Do you often parade about without shoes?"

"If we actually leave the suite, I'll put on my dress shoes. But those things give me blisters."

"Try wearing heels."

"Been there. Never again." I'd been five at the time and the resulting trip to the emergency room had not been fun. Weak ankles were one of the many things—including my own name—that I'd inherited from my dad.

Lucia let the comment slide in a way that Juliette never would have, giving my outfit another frank, disapproving glance. "I simply do not understand what she sees in you."

The feeling was mutual, but that seemed a dumb thing to say right before my interview. I shrugged. "Life's a mystery, I guess. So, what now? Is there an application I have to fill out or something?"

"Once our food arrives, we will eat our meal, like civilized beings," she told me. "I will then ask you a series of questions. Your answers will determine whether or not I find you to be a suitable match for my Secundus."

I was guessing these questions wouldn't be multiple choice.

"Could we bring in an impartial third party or something?"

"I beg your pardon?"

"You hate me." The feeling was mutual, but again, I wasn't going to point that out while she had veto power over my relationship with Anastasia. "I can't imagine anything I could say will convince you to give us your blessing."

"Perhaps not. But it is my blessing that was sought. I will not abdicate my responsibility in the matter."

"So, you're the only one who can say yes or no, and you're definitely going to say no. Why are we even going through the hassle?" And why had she forced me to change out of my t-shirt and jeans?

"Give the word and we will call this entire thing off, Mr. Smith. I will even leave the suite to you for the remainder of the evening so that you may relax and eat in peace."

That sounded generous to me… which meant, given the source, I couldn't trust it. "Just like that?"

She fixed me with an imperious eye. "I am not going to give you my blessing. We both know this, but as Lady Dumenyova's second in the matter, I am honor-bound to grant the interview. You, on the other hand, are free to end this farce at any time."

"By giving up."

"By accepting the inevitable. Why should we have to suffer through each other's company when the outcome is already certain?"

I frowned. That was a pretty good question. An even better question was why the queen would be dangling this possibility in front of me like a plateful of tiramisu. Lucia never did anything unless it benefited her… and I had to imagine she was looking for something more than an escape from dinner. Even a dinner with me.

"If I backed out of this, I'd lose any chance of gaining your blessing," I reasoned.

Lucia rolled her eyes. "A blessing we have already determined you will never receive."

"Right. But calling off the interview makes it *my* fault. Whereas if we go through this interview, and you then decide I'm unsuitable—"

"Which I will."

"—then *you're* on the hook for explaining to Ana why you rejected her request." I met the queen's pale blue eyes. "I don't think that's a conversation you're excited to have."

Lucia blinked and looked away. It was quite possibly the first time I had ever won a staring contest with a vampire.

"I know Anastasia is important to you," I continued. "I think you want her happy every bit as much as I do."

Actually, I was pretty sure Lucia was ninety-five percent hell beast, five percent evil incarnate, and largely incapable of emotions other than anger, spite, and derision. But if my brief and moderately successful career as a mediator had taught me anything, it was that appeals to someone's better nature—even someone without a better nature—could prove successful in the most unexpected of situations.

And Lucia having a heart would *definitely* be an unexpected situation.

The bond had gone quiet, but Lucia shook her head, her words faint but still distinct. "If only you were as capable at your job as you are at destroying my life."

"We all have our talents." I shrugged. "Maybe this whole thing is a waste of time and effort, like you said. But Anastasia is worth that time and that effort. If she thinks your blessing is important, then I'm going to do everything I can to get it."

"So be it." The queen mirrored my shrug, then waved one hand dismissively, her many rings catching the lamplight. "The farce will proceed as planned."

As if in reply, a knock sounded at the door.

Dinner had arrived.

ooo

It wasn't spaghetti. After four days without even a glimpse of the fabled pasta, I was starting to think Italy was suffering an undocumented noodle shortage. It was deeply troubling. If I hadn't already been busy with the whole murder thing, I would have opened an investigation into the issue.

Or gone back to San Diego, where spaghetti was only slightly less common than burritos, fish tacos, and smoothies.

On the bright side, whatever it was we'd been served instead was pretty awesome. I was clearing my plate at record speeds when the queen spoke again.

"What progress did you make this afternoon with the Lady Manassa?"

Despite—or because of—my nap, I still hadn't figured out a way to reframe my decision to tell the naga all our secrets as some sort of strategic masterstroke. And I really didn't want to piss Lucia off—more than I did just by breathing—before she made an official decision on the whole blessing thing. "It's hard to say, really."

One pale eyebrow rose. "How so?"

My efforts at vagueness having proven to be a complete failure, I changed tactics, and opted to stall instead. "Do you really want to talk about that now? Here?"

"A fair point. We should activate the Lord of Bones' trinket first." She held one hand out, palm upward.

I'd meant we should wait until our next meeting with Anastasia… but going to fetch the bird skull at least gave me a few more seconds to come up with something meaningful yet non-incriminating regarding my visit with the nagas. I made a detour to the bathroom for a paper towel, carefully wrapped the skull in that towel, and then handed both towel and device to the femmepire queen.

"Why, pray tell, is it wet?" Lucia did whatever it was that was necessary to activate the device, and then set it on the table between us.

"It was in my pocket when I fell into the nagas' pool."

"When you *what?*"

"It's okay," I said, "I survived. Obviously."

"You survived. Your dignity did not. No wonder you were reluctant to tell me of your visit."

That was both true and an awesomely convenient excuse to hopefully table the whole discussion. I nodded. "Yeah. It sucked. Anyway, should we move on to the—"

"When the meal is done, Mr. Smith." Lucia took another bite of her own entrée, made a face as if it was somehow not to her liking, and continued. "Did you get anything of value from the Lady Manassa? Why did she request an earlier audience?"

Damn it. There really wasn't any way to avoid this conversation, was there? I sighed. "She wanted to tell me she didn't have anything to do with Tomasso's murder."

"How… proactive of her." Lucia's tone was puzzled.

"Yeah. Apparently, the two of them were an item … until your brother dumped her just a few months ago."

The femmepire queen froze. "My brother had relations with the voice of the nagas?"

"Had relations?" Sometimes, I forgot how old Lucia really was. "That's one way of putting it, I guess. They were dating for several decades."

"Making her the most likely suspect in his death."

"Just because she spent the most time with him?"

"Of course not. Although it does make me question her taste."

Even with Tomasso dead, Lucia seemed to have a hard time letting go of the whole sibling rivalry thing. A century of assassination attempts had clearly left their mark.

"Then why…?"

"Use that underdeveloped organ you call a brain for a moment. Someone murdered my father and framed me for the act. The only person we've identified who profited from that murder was my own brother."

"Who has now also been murdered," I pointed out.

"Exactly."

Usually, I was the one with the crazy theories that nobody could follow. Having the shoe be on the other foot kind of sucked.

"Don't you see?" she continued. "What if the goal of my father's death *was* to give Tomasso the crown he would never otherwise wear? A plot implemented not by my brother himself, but by someone who cared for him. Someone who took the opportunity to then begin a relationship with him soon after."

"And then killed him when he broke up with her?"

"Or when he began to suspect what she had done. Presumably the one event preceded the other."

"That's a reach." Even by my admittedly loose standards.

"Is it? Recall that a woman was spotted at both murder scenes."

"Even if everything you say was true, how would Divya have been able to kill…" I stopped in mid-sentence. "Her snakes."

"Precisely. The People are immune to most poisons, but not even we are immune to everything. And a serpent would certainly be stealthy enough, particularly under naga supervision—" Her voice went ice-cold. "Did you just call her *Divya?*"

"Yeah. That's her name, right?"

"Why, pray tell, are you and the naga on a first name basis after a single conversation?"

"I guess people just tend to like me."

"Not in my all-too-extensive experience." The emotions coming across the bond were a jumbled mess, impossible to interpret. "For some reason, she sought a more casual setting for your conversation. But why?"

"Maybe she's just as sick of all this pointless formality as I am?"

Glacial blue eyes flickered down to the table that hid my still-shoeless feet. "Or she wanted to put you at ease, making it a chat between acquaintances rather than the formal interrogation of a murder suspect."

Lucia might not have a heart, but for the first time in our shared history, I was starting to think she did have a brain… even if that brain worked in singularly bizarre—and entirely incorrect—ways.

"So, you trade first names," she continued, "and no doubt share some manner of food and drink, and by the time you reach the question-and-answer stage, she has you convinced that she is trustworthy, someone who could be an ally in the investigation. And having been convinced of such, you likely pull back from asking the more difficult questions. In fact, you might even elect to offer a few answers of your own."

Okay, now *that* was just spooky. I'm not sure even a poker face like Ana's would have hidden my wince.

Lucia was out of her chair in a flash, looming over me—to the extent that she could loom over anyone—and my half-eaten supper. "What did you tell her?!"

"Pretty much everything." This had gone exactly as horribly as I'd expected. Maybe that nap had been a terrible idea after all. "That Tomasso was investigating his father's death. That we thought the two murders were connected. All of it."

"Then we are doomed. You have killed us all."

"Don't you think you're being a little bit dramatic?" Those were words I wanted back as soon as I'd said them. When, in the history of humankind, had that particular phrase ever produced a positive reaction?

"Dramatic?" Blue eyes sparked with fury. "Our only ace card in this investigation was that we knew the person who killed my brother had also killed my father… and that individual did not know that we knew. Yet not only did you elect to share this information—despite strict orders not to—you shared it with the woman who has now become our prime suspect!"

"I don't think she did it," I said, ignoring the scathing look that came my way. "She seemed genuinely sad that Tomasso was dead… not to mention surprised when I told her *why* he had been killed. My gut tells me she didn't have anything to do with his murder."

"Tell me," Lucia pressed, her voice bitterly cold, "is this the same gut that led you to give a vial of your own blood to Nepenthe?"

"Well—"

"Who then used that blood to siphon my power, imprison the White Ladies of San Diego, and nearly destroy us all? Is *that* the vaunted gut you've again entrusted our lives to?"

"The Nepenthe thing was a mistake, but I've learned from it."

"Have you? From where I am sitting, you appear to have learned nothing at all."

I could see her point, not that I would ever admit it. But what Lucia didn't understand—couldn't understand—was that being a detective *meant* trusting your gut. In the absence of signed confessions or indisputable video evidence, intuition was too often all we had to go on. If I couldn't trust my own instincts, then I wasn't any good to anyone. And those instincts told me one thing.

"I don't think she did it," I insisted again.

"And if she did?"

"Then she already knew the murders were linked… and that Tomasso was investigating the matter. What did telling her cost us?"

"The element of surprise, you imbecile!"

"Well, yeah. Obviously." I stared down at my still half-full plate, thinking furiously. After a moment, I shrugged. "I think that was going to happen anyway."

"How so?" There was no give in Lucia's voice, but at least she wasn't trying to murder me. As impossible as it might have been for an outsider to believe, this was one of our more civilized disagreements.

"I have a few weeks to solve two murders, one of them a hundred years old," I reminded her. "Unless the killer is a total moron, that's nowhere near enough time."

"I thought you were supposed to be an investigator?"

"I'm the closest thing to one you have available," I shot back, in another of my conspicuously poor retorts, "but it takes time to interview people, and the truth is, there's way too much ground for me to cover. If Ana weren't being held in the Tower, maybe she and I could handle it together. But she's stuck there, and you're busy doing whatever the hell it is you're doing, and I'm left running around trying to talk to everyone who ever met Tomasso, while also canvassing his home, talking to demigods, and being attacked by Illutu and pro-human terrorists!"

"And giving our primary suspect forewarning helps this situation *how*, exactly?"

The answer was, of course, that it didn't. But even I could see that was a losing argument. "If I'm right and Divya is innocent, then we get a fresh set of eyes on the case, not to mention someone who knew Tomasso better than anyone over the last few decades."

"And if she did kill both my brother and my father?"

"Then maybe we've given her enough rope to hang herself? Before I spoke to her, she was barely on our radar at all as a suspect. At least now we know we should focus some of the investigation more closely on her."

"And *she* knows that she needs to find and destroy whatever evidence Tomasso had acquired of her involvement in the murder before we can use it against her! Which means..." Lucia's voice trailed off. "Which means she might lead us directly to it."

"Exactly." I hadn't thought of that *at all*, but I went with it. "Who do you trust to put on her as a tail? Denarius? One of the Crown Watch?"

"Don't be absurd. The Watch answers to my uncle, and *he* remains as much a suspect as the naga."

"Who *isn't* a suspect?"

Instead of answering, Lucia fished her own phone out of her purse, and tapped in a number. "Caine? It's Lucia."

I couldn't hear the Lord of Bones' reply, but Lucia smiled politely. "Yes, thank you. I need eyes on the Lady Manassa. Yes, immediately."

Another pause as she listened to Caine, and then Lucia rolled her eyes. "Of *course* I know she and Tomasso were dating. You are not the only source I have here at the palace. Regardless, Mr. Smith thinks she might be responsible, and she may either have, or soon be looking for, the evidence that implicates her in my father's murder as well."

A look of satisfaction crossed her beautiful face. "Excellent. As ever, I value your continued assistance in this matter."

She ended the call and gave me a smug look.

"Done."

"So, now we have yet another suspect watching the other?"

"As I told you and Lady Dumenyova earlier, the Lord of Bones is *not* a suspect."

"Is that why you *already told him* all the details we were *both* supposed to keep secret?"

"Obviously. While you have been taking leisurely runs around Rome, I have been attempting to curry favor with the voting members of the Council. I could not do so alone, and my allies most certainly needed to be fully briefed on the matter, were they to be of any help whatsoever."

"Allies? As in plural?!"

"Of course. The Lord of Bones and the Horned God are both fully in our corner."

"You're telling me you'd already done the very thing you've been riding me about for the past ten minutes? And not just once, but twice?"

"The difference, Mr. Smith," the queen told me, every line of her fabulous form stiff with regal arrogance, "is that neither of the individuals I elected to tell are viable suspects."

"According to you. And only you."

"Yes. According to me. Someone who has been making this sort of judgment for a great number of human lifetimes and is considerably better at it than you."

I coughed twice to cover the laugh that startled out of me. And if my coughs sounded suspiciously like the names *Barros* or *Xavier*…well, that's only because they were two of the many, many recent examples of Lucia's poor judgment.

Hell, she was sitting across the table from a third such example.

"Caine's minions will keep a close watch on the nagas," continued the queen, either unable to interpret my coughs or magnanimously choosing to ignore them. "This may not end up the debacle I had feared it would be."

"Fabulous. Can I finish my food then?"

"By all means." Lucia waved a golden hand. "Eat. It is what you do best."

My non-spaghetti didn't taste nearly as good cold.

○○○

I finished off my meal, because I hadn't been raised to be a barbarian. Also, because my parents had taught me that I wouldn't get dessert unless I cleaned my plate.

Lucia, on the other hand, simply picked at her supper. Nevertheless, when the servants came in to remove my plate, she motioned to have them remove hers as well. "That will be all."

Apparently, dessert would have to wait.

The femmepire queen eyed me for a long moment, saying nothing. I did my best to return that gaze. I vaguely recalled reading a blog post about interviews that said it was important to not show fear. Or… had that been a Natural Geographic special about predatory species?

Either way, it was kind of apt.

Our standoff continued for another minute before Lucia finally nodded, but as she opened her mouth to speak, my borrowed phone buzzed.

It was another text. Just like the last one, it was from Juliette. There were no words, just a GIF that slowly resolved itself into the image of a dumpster in some alleyway. In that dumpster was a mattress, its shape barely visible behind curtains of smoke and flame.

Holy shit.

Before I could fully freak out, another text followed.

It isn't yours… but it could be!

Murder trials were one thing, but *this* was a whole new level of crisis. I tapped out a quick reply.

DON'T BURN MY BED!

Then tell me wtf you meant about my mom, asshole.

She's the ambassador to Rome. She's nice… unlike her bed-burning fiend of a daughter. Seems to miss you.

Whatever you do, DON'T tell her anything personal about me!

I winced.

What am I saying, Juliette followed up with, *even Mom has breasts. You gave her my whole damn life story, didn't you?*

I really didn't know where I had gotten this reputation from. Or why it was so depressingly accurate.

Would you rather I let her think you and I were dating?

Oh HELL no.

Well, there you go.

"Mr. Smith," said Lucia, still sitting across the table, "I all too frequently make allowances for your species, your gender, and your limited intellectual capabilities, but there are limits. Put the phone away or I will be forced to give you a lesson in table etiquette."

"Didn't you just call the Lord of Bones while we were eating?"

"Only to ameliorate the consequences of your own idiocy."

No dessert was worth this. But something far more important than dessert was at stake. I tapped out one last message.

Got to go, Juliette. Lucia has a stick up her ass. Might be a tree.

"Sorry. There was an emergency in San Diego that I had to deal with." I tucked the phone back into my pocket and gave the queen a scaled-down version of the Dealmaker™. "But now I'm all yours."

"Yes. In a strange way, you are. Which is, at least in part, what tonight's meeting is all about."

"Say what?"

"Lady Dumenyova seeks my blessing to begin a formal courtship with you. As both her second in this matter and your bonded mistress, only I can ascertain whether the match is viable." From her purse, she extracted several sheets of paper, carefully folded in half, and flattened them out on the table before her.

"Did you seriously print out a list of questions?"

"I did. While dalliances between our two species do occasionally occur, official courtships are exceedingly rare. I had to dig through the palace archives to find a valid template for this examination."

"That's a lot of trouble to go through considering you've already made up your mind."

"The more detailed the rationale for my rejection, the less likely it is to cause additional friction down the line. I am, as lawyers sometimes say, intent upon crossing the t's and dotting the i's."

"Of course you are," I muttered, quietly enough that a human wouldn't have heard it.

"It is also my hope that, during this process, you will similarly come to an understanding as to why the match cannot be." Lucia spread her hands wide, lush lips curving into what someone who didn't know her would describe as a *warm and inviting* smile. "At which point, all will be as it should."

"You've never been in love, have you?"

"You are the subject of this interview, Mr. Smith, not I."

Which was answer enough.

"Let us begin with the obvious," she continued. "What are your intentions regarding my Secundus?"

"The usual, I guess?"

"Elaborate."

"I just want to make her happy."

"So self-sacrificing!" mocked Lucia. "You want nothing for yourself?"

"That's not what I'm saying." I paused to marshal my thoughts. "I want to spend my life with her. To wake up with her each morning, to share new experiences with her, to be there when she needs me, and to grow old with her."

"Only you would be growing old," the queen pointed out.

"Yeah, well… there's not much I can do about that, right?"

"And when you are seventy and incontinent, and Anastasia remains young and able, what then? Shall she follow you about with a wet cloth and your allotment of daily medications?"

It was distressing to realize that Lucia's view of old age mirrored mine almost exactly.

"Honestly," I said. "I'm not sure I'll even make it to thirty."

"While I agree that death from old age seems unlikely, you should spare a thought for that eventuality anyway. I have seen your species when you are old and infirm. It is not a pretty sight."

"At least *we* don't all go psychotic."

Lucia pretended I hadn't said anything. "And if you *should* make it to thirty, or even forty… where do you see yourself then?"

"In San Diego?"

"In life, you cretin."

Jesus. This interview stuff was actually hard. "Well, I assume I'll be still working as a P.I. with Juliette. Hopefully, I'll still have my hair."

"And children? Have you ever thought about raising a family?"

"Sure. There has to be at least one boy if I'm going to continue my family's insane naming tradition, right?"

There was a moment of silence. When Lucia finally spoke, her voice was almost gentle. "Your kind and ours are not genetically compatible, Mr. Smith."

"Meaning?"

"Anastasia will never bear children of your seed."

"Oh." I vaguely recalled Juliette saying something to that extent, way back in the early days of my vampire education, but I'd never really applied it to my own situation. "Well, it's not a dealbreaker—"

"No? It is my understanding that humanity is hardwired to spawn offspring at every opportunity."

"You have some strange ideas about humans."

"So, you find the prospect of going through life without children acceptable?"

"I'm only twenty-seven," I reminded her. "Children wouldn't have been in the plans for years anyway. If it comes to it, we could always adopt. If Ana even wants children."

"She does not."

"How do you know?"

"Because she, too, is four hundred years old, my thrall, and likely past the point of fertility. If Lady Dumenyova had wanted children, she would have had them when she was young."

Lucia had just recently covered the whole vampire fertility timelines, but again I hadn't really made the connection with Ana. "So, our genetic incompatibility doesn't really matter anyway."

"For *her,* it makes no difference," she agreed. "But *you* need to think long and hard on the subject of children. Would you give up your species' limited facsimile of immortality for her?"

"I don't know about *immortality,* but I'm here in Rome, risking my *mortality* to save her. Anastasia is worth it."

"You say so now." Lucia moved on to the next card. "And how many sheep will you offer for the honor of—" She frowned. "I think we can skip that question, given the modern era we find ourselves in."

Exactly how far back had she gone to find these questions?

"What is it that draws you to Lady Dumenyova," she asked instead, "beyond the disconcerting manner in which she treats you like someone of actual consequence."

Lucia's insult game was as potent as ever. But at least *this* question was easy.

"Everything, really. She's smart, she's beautiful, she's incredibly competent, she's a badass..."

"Reasons to admire her, to be sure. Is that all your so-called love is? Admiration?"

Okay; maybe it wasn't going to be so easy. "I'd really rather be telling her this than you."

"And I would rather you had never come into our lives at all. Answer the question."

Right.

"I love that someone so strong is also considerate and patient," I said eventually. "I love that every smile from her seems special and miraculous. I love hearing her laugh and watching her move. I love that she takes things like duty and honor so seriously, even when it has made our dating almost impossible. And yes, I love that she treats other people *as* people, regardless of species. I've met hundreds of your kind, and she is far and away the best of you."

To my surprise, it was Lucia's turn to nod. "On this one matter, we are in agreement." Her smile turned sharp. "And if we turn that question upon its head? What does she see in you?"

"Shouldn't you ask her that?"

"I am asking you." The ice in her words made me shiver.

"Well..." I paused. "I suppose she..."

"Yes?"

"I don't know," I admitted. "Maybe it's because I treat her like a person? Beneath all that awesomeness, I think she's also incredibly lonely."

"And you represent a convenient and warm body to temporarily fill that void?" Despite her words, Lucia's tone was considering. "Perhaps. Yet if that were the case, she could have simply taken you as a lover, as she has done in the past."

"Excuse me?"

Pale blue eyes glittered. "Surely, you did not think Lady Dumenyova had remained celibate since her relationship with Xavier?"

"I... guess I didn't really think about it." After all, *I'd* gone without for the last six or so years. At that point, what was another few decades?

Answer: a really long freaking time.

Lucia's smile turned victorious as she watched the emotions scroll across my face. "Yes," she continued, "perhaps you should ask her of the long line of partners that she has taken to her bed."

For the first time, a little bit of heat entered my voice. "Aren't you supposed to be her *friend?*"

"I am and have been since well before the birth of your fledgling country."

"Then why are you fighting to keep her from being happy?"

"Perhaps I am doing just the opposite, in saving her from making a terrible error."

"Right. Because of your expert judgement in these things." I rolled my eyes. "Let me ask *you* something; did she ask your blessing for any of those lovers?" I read the answer on her face and pushed on. "And she didn't ask your blessing for Xavier either."

"I suspect she knew such a blessing was unnecessary. I needed a Captain of the Watch. Lady Dumenyova brought him to me."

"Yeah, and then dumped his traitorous ass."

"Seventy years later."

"Which is hardly any time at all to you people." I shook my head. "Ana was alive centuries before I was even born. She'll be alive centuries after I'm gone. You want me to be jealous of her past and future relationships—"

"Are you not?"

Of course I was, but I sure as hell wasn't going to admit it. Instead, I said, "Sex is sex. She could have slept with me at any time in the past two years. All she had to do was even vaguely hint at the idea. You think I'd have said no?"

"I think you would say yes to anything with a pulse."

"Instead, she chose to seek your blessing for a formal courtship. With me. For the first time in her already long life." I locked eyes with the femmepire. "So, you tell me, what do I have to be jealous of?"

Sometimes, I impressed even myself. No wonder I'd been moderately successful as a mediator.

"As for your original question," I continued, flushed with heady triumph, "I have no clue what she sees in me. Maybe it's the way I treat her. Maybe it's that I can speak in-depth about the Star Wars extended universe. Maybe she just has a secret fetish for dudes who will take her to In-n-Out. Frankly," I admitted, "I think she could do better. I'm sure you agree. But what we think doesn't really matter, does it?"

"The fact that we are having this conversation suggests otherwise."

"Does it?" I shook my head again. "Maybe. Or maybe she's just—in her distinctly old-fashioned and insanely honorable way—giving you a chance to do the right thing for once. The choice is yours. Refuse to give your blessing and maybe everything will go back to the way it was, as you're so clearly hoping. Because history is full of examples where standing in the way of love worked out for everyone involved."

"And the alternative?"

"*Say yes.* As you've already pointed out, I'll be lucky to die of old age… and even if I do, that'd still be just a blip in your lifetimes. Sooner or later, I'll be gone. Maybe a few decades are a small price to pay for her continued friendship?"

"To this point, you have spent less than three years in my service, yet those were the longest years of my life. The thought of decades more is almost too great a tragedy to bear."

"You've got decades more of me, regardless of what you decide," I pointed out, tapping my head, "and through absolutely no fault of my own. Maybe you should focus on not driving away the one vampire who still gives a damn."

Across the table, Lucia was silent, spine ramrod straight and pale eyes glittering as she mulled over my words.

"There may be some merit to your words," she finally said.

Holy shit. I was a rock star.

"Win the trial. Solve my brother's murder. Should we survive the next few weeks, we will revisit this conversation."

"That… sounds almost like a qualified yes?"

"Does it? Allow me to correct your misunderstanding then. It was instead an unqualified *do your damn job so that we all live long enough for me to decide one way or the other.* I make no promises as to what that decision will be."

Since I couldn't trust her promises, I was okay with that.

"If that's what it takes," I said, "I'll have this whole damn thing wrapped up in a week."

In the movies, that was when lightning would have flickered outside the window, accompanied by a peal of rolling thunder as various deities took note of my sudden hubris.

In the real world, there was instead a knock at the door.

In retrospect, I'd have preferred the thunder.

CHAPTER 44

IN WHICH SOMETHING IS DEFINITELY ROTTEN…
BUT NOT IN DENMARK

I wasn't too worried when I went to open the door, given that whoever was knocking had passed through the small army of Watch that shepherded Lucia from location to location on Denarius' orders. If I was lucky, one of the servants had just come to slip me a pastry or something. If the gods truly loved me, there'd be a whole plateful of them.

There were, in hindsight, two problems with that little fantasy.

First, the only deity for miles around was Minerva, and she had seemed more inclined to give me a painful death than some sort of delicious, flaky, and chocolate-filled confection. And second, the person standing in front of the door wasn't a servant at all.

"Maria Elena?" If I'd had time to properly prepare myself, I might have been able to summon up the irritation I'd felt toward the young femmepire earlier that day. As it was, I took note of her pale face, puffy nose, and red-rimmed eyes, and couldn't help but ask, "Are you okay?"

"John… can we talk?"

"Absolutely. Only…" I added, remembering where we were and who else was present, "I'm kind of in the middle of something. Can it wait until tomorrow?"

Maria Elena glanced at the Watch members who flanked her in the hallway and shook her head. "I don't think it can."

That sounded serious. More serious than a follow-up apology for her earlier lie should have warranted. Against my better judgement, I found myself letting her into the room.

As the door swung shut behind her, she stopped dead at the sight of Lucia. "Lady Borghesi… I…"

"Have spent much of the past week hindering my thrall's investigation by withholding vital information? Yes, I am aware."

Jesus, Lucia. I packaged up my appalled reaction and fired it at the queen across our bond. Unfortunately, Lucia was already getting pretty good at ignoring that sort of thing.

"What is it you wished to tell us, child?" she continued, her voice still hard.

"It's…" Maria Elena turned back to me, her large eyes wide. "I think I'd better show you instead, John."

"Show me what, exactly? You found something that might impact our case?" That might be *better* than a plateful of pastries.

"Sort of." She glanced around and then dropped her voice to a whisper. "It's not something you want me mentioning where others can hear."

"Actually, you don't have to worry about—"

"Convincing my thrall to accompany you," Lucia interrupted smoothly. "You should instead be worried about convincing me."

"You wish to accompany me, Lady Borghesi?"

"Don't be ridiculous. I am far too busy for such things. However, I am Mr. Smith's mistress. Requests for his time should go through me."

I knew from experience that if I gave Lucia an inch, she'd take the whole damn continent. Before she could continue, I jumped in.

"If it will help the case, I'm in." I ignored Lucia's cold glare. "Where are we headed, Maria Elena?"

The young femmepire spared a glance for the closed door, and then mouthed something at me to avoid saying it out loud.

I… had no idea what she was trying to tell me.

With a frown, she tried again and then just rolled her eyes and pointed down.

Downstairs. Well, that was spectacularly vague.

"Still here in the palace though?"

She nodded.

"Fair enough. Let me get my shoes."

"Your security contingent will not be in place until tomorrow, Mr. Smith," Lucia reminded me, "and I will not have you foolishly follow this child anywhere without protection."

Given that she had let me wander the palace by myself that afternoon, Lucia's sudden concern for my health rang false, but I shrugged. "Fine. We can take one of your guards." I turned to Maria Elena, who seemed concerned by that development. "How about Niccolo? You like him, right?"

"I think it would be best if we went alone."

"Go with the Watch or without my thrall," commanded Lucia.

Maria Elena bit back a sigh. "Fine. Niccolo it is."

○○○

A few months earlier, Mike and I had met up with his fiancée, Susan, for a dinner down in the Gaslamp Quarter. Mike and I had hit a bar or three beforehand and were already well into the *talk loudly and laugh at everything* phase of our night by the time we showed up. Susan hadn't been happy, not with me, and not with her future husband. Before that night, I'd never realized silent glares could be so loud… or that a simple meal could become a multi-hour ordeal.

The walk with Maria Elena and Niccolo was kind of like that. Niccolo seemed irritated—even more than usual—to have been tasked with my security. Maria Elena seemed irritated—an emotion I'd thought her incapable of—to be stuck with the manpire's company.

I wasn't irritated at all, but I *was* hoping we reached our destination sooner rather than later. And that a stop by one of the kitchens afterward would be possible. I never had gotten any dessert.

As Maria Elena had suggested with her pantomime, we went down. It wasn't until we'd reached our third stairwell, that I realized just how far we were going. The only things on this level were the catacombs… and Tomasso's body. On cue, the femmepire stopped just outside the room where Tomasso was on display. The line of mourners we'd previously encountered had dried up and we were, as far as I could tell, the only three living creatures on the entire level.

"Niccolo, would you please watch the door for us?"

Niccolo roused himself from his snit just enough to bow to Maria Elena, right hand held to his heart in some form of vampire-player salute. "It is the least of what I would do for you, 'Lena."

A line like that from me would have gotten an eyeroll, at best, but *I* didn't have a perfect and squeezable ass; Maria Elena blushed prettily and smiled her thanks.

That smile dropped away as soon as the manpire's back had turned. She pulled me deeper into the room, all the way to the altar that held Tomasso's corpse. She then nodded significantly at the king's form.

I followed the direction of her nod but didn't see anything out of the ordinary. And the fact that vampire corpses on oversized tables *didn't* qualify as out of the ordinary said all that needed to be said about my recent history.

"What am I looking at?"

With a sideways glance at Niccolo—whose back was still turned to us—Maria Elena leaned forward, extended one index finger, and pointed.

I frowned and crowded in to see. Tomasso was clothed—and thank God for that—but at the point his right wrist extended from the cuff of his sleeve there was a minor… discoloration.

"Is that… a bruise? Like from some sort of needle or puncture?" Shit. Maybe Lucia's snake theory wasn't as crazy as I'd thought.

Or maybe, given the way Maria Elena was looking at me, *I* was crazy. Maybe it's because she'd been lying to me for days, but I was finding the femmepire's mannerisms significantly less cute than I had previously.

With another glance in Niccolo's direction, she took hold of the king's sleeve and pulled it up the arm a quarter of an inch or so.

Tomasso's forearm was mottled. Even more telling, a few flakes of tissue had fallen away when she tugged on the shirt. Add in the tiniest whiff of putrescence when I leaned in to take a closer look and the conclusion was unmistakable.

Tomasso's body was somehow already starting to rot.

And Lucia, Anastasia and I were officially out of time.

○○○

Maria Elena carefully pulled the shirt cuff back down, hiding the evidence of the king's deterioration, her worried eyes meeting mine.

"How long until someone notices?" I asked her, my voice barely audible even to my own ears.

"I've done my best to hide what there is. If we're lucky, and the spread is slow, you might have a few days. At most."

Well, shit. I'd just finished telling Lucia that we had way too little time to adequately investigate her family's murders. Now, I was finding even that had been overly optimistic.

"Do what you can, please. We need all the time we can get."

"I'll try. The smell is a bigger problem though, especially for my kind." She chewed her lip, thinking. "Maybe I can bring down a scented candle or some sort of incense. But any delay I manage is going to be strictly temporary."

"I know. But it might make all the difference in this case." It seemed unlikely, to be honest, but delaying our inevitable executions even for an extra day or two seemed like a worthwhile goal. "What were you even doing down here?"

"After you and I… talked… I found Sabina and told her."

"About this?" If so, we were screwed. More screwed.

"About the work I had done for the king."

"Oh." That was an odd non-sequitur, but I nodded anyway. "How did she take it?"

"Once she finished yelling at me, she came to yell at her dad."

I winced.

"That's when I saw the rot."

"Did Sabina see it too?"

"I don't think so. She was kind of dialed in on her own drama."

That seemed to be another family trait. For once, I was glad. "So, nobody knows but the two of us?"

"I believe you mean the three of us."

Damn it.

In unison, Maria Elena and I turned to the door. Niccolo was no longer watching the hall. Dark eyes flicked between Maria Elena, Tomasso, and I.

"First Rot signifies the end of your investigation, human."

"It doesn't *have* to. Give me two days… maybe three. I'll find the real killer."

"The real killer currently resides in the Tower," he replied, "and three days will not change that fact."

"Ana didn't do it, dude," I pleaded. "I just need enough time to prove that."

"Time is something you no longer have."

For a brief moment, I thought about killing the manpire, stashing his body somewhere in the catacombs, and pretending the whole thing had never happened. Unfortunately, without Lucia's Talent, my chances of killing anyone, let alone one of the vampire ninjas on the Crown Watch, were nonexistent.

Also? My parents had raised me to *not* be a murderer… and there were already way too many corpses haunting my dreams.

"Niccolo…" Maria Elena brushed past me to stand before the other vampire. "I believe Mr. Smith. I know this would be a minor bending of the rules, but it's only a few days. Would you do that? For me?"

I couldn't see her face, but judging by Niccolo's reaction, Maria Elena was hitting him with the most potent puppy dog eyes known to man or vampire. I watched the hard lines of his face soften.

"For you. This once." He shot me a glance. "Two days."

Whatever minor harm Maria Elena had done to my investigation was completely eclipsed by the two days of grace she had just single-handedly gifted us.

Now, I just needed to make the most of our literal, if temporary, stay of execution.

ooo

"Lucia, we have a big—"

Without even glancing my way, the femmepire queen held up one finger in the universally recognized gesture for *give me a moment.* As opposed to that second, even more popular, one-fingered gesture. Her other hand held a slim, silvery phone to one ear.

"Whoever that is, I really, really hope they're confessing to both murders," I muttered, walking over to my recently vacated chair and dropping into it. The table was now empty of everything but the glittering bird skull, and I couldn't escape the sense that dead, bedazzled Tweety was staring accusingly in my direction.

"I… see."

Those were the first words Lucia had spoken since my return. Her tone banished thoughts of vengeful sparrow spirits from my mind altogether. In the past few years, I'd heard and seen Lucia in a variety of emotional states, from smug satisfaction to weary contempt to—most frequently—icy rage. But this was the first time I'd ever heard something that could be described as… heartbroken.

My keenly trained powers of observation started filling in some of the details I'd missed initially. Lucia's face—usually a shade of gold that spoke to both fabulous genetics and the wealth to manage a year-round tan—was pale and drawn. Cold blue eyes had gone distant, her back was stiff and rigid, and the emotion rolling across the bond was…

Either she was sick—for the second time in her entire life—or whoever was on the phone was giving her really bad news. And given that I hadn't loaned my blood out to any witch covens recently, I was betting on the latter.

"I understand. Thank you for keeping me informed." She ended the call and tossed the cell, underhand, across the room to land on her bed.

"Who was that?"

"Teresa."

"Crap." One of Anastasia's two blood donors. "There's been another incident?"

"There has."

I frowned. "Kristin and the pixies promised they'd watch the house until we came back. Even if Barros and Thales managed to scrape up reinforcements, I don't see—"

"It wasn't Duke Barros. Or Thales." Lucia met my confused gaze. "Summer's parents have reclaimed their daughter."

"You mean…?"

"Yes. She has returned to Brazil."

Summer, also known as Princess Tea Leaf, was one of the few individuals in the world that Lucia and I adored equally. "Lucia, I'm sorry."

"I should have expected it. They sent Summer to be my ward when I had a House and aspirations of empire building. Now, I am a queen without even the dream of a kingdom. My Secundus is on trial for murder, both my personal power and my inherited authority are in tatters, and San Diego itself has dissolved back into lawlessness. What sort of guardian can I be to the child?"

"If we win the trial, there's nothing to prevent you from going back to San Diego and reclaiming the House. Barros and Thales are out of the picture, and your brother is gone. There's no reason you couldn't start fresh."

"That dream is dead, Mr. Smith." Lucia shook her head.

"But what about—"

"I will *not* debate the matter further, thrall!" The femmepire's voice cracked like a whip.

"Fine. But Jee Sun is going to miss her playmate."

"As will we all." I watched Lucia rebuild her composure. Even the dark-watered grief flooding across our bond slowed to a trickle. "Let us focus instead on the matter at hand. All else is immaterial. What did my niece's lying friend have to tell you?"

"Mainly that we're screwed." I described what I'd seen with Tomasso's body, and that both Maria Elena and Niccolo had agreed to keep the secret. "Even assuming she's able to keep evidence of the rot hidden in the short term, our timetable's been shot to hell."

I didn't speak any languages other than English—unless you counted Pig Latin—but the words out of Lucia's mouth sounded suspiciously like curses, and in more than just Italian. When she finally ran out of steam, I asked the question that had been bothering me since the catacombs.

"I thought vampire corpses took several weeks to deteriorate. How is it that Tomasso is already visibly rotting?"

"It would seem that our enemy wishes to accelerate the timing of the trial." I received a cold look from my supposed mistress. "How strange that this should happen so soon after you decided to tell the Lady Manassa the full details of our investigation."

I didn't have any snappy comebacks for that one. "The timing *could* be coincidental."

"Yes. And you *could* be a credit to your profession."

"Real nice. So, what do we do now? My next Council interview isn't until tomorrow, but I could try to find the contessa and interview her tonight instead…"

"And in doing so, risk having her question why you had abandoned my uncle's careful schedule? I think not."

"That schedule was based on the assumption that we had weeks to investigate, not days," I protested. "We're going to *have* to abandon it at some point."

"Yes, but only after we have taken steps to avoid alerting our enemies." Lucia nodded to the nearby dresser. "In the meantime, you have a small mountain of documents over there. Can you say with certainty that your review of those documents is both complete and comprehensive?"

"No."

"Then you have your task for the night. Tomorrow, we will reconvene with Lady Dumenyova, and devise a more comprehensive plan of attack."

"Can't you get us in to see her tonight?"

Lucia's next words were slow and condescending, as if she was addressing a four-year-old. "A late-night impromptu meeting with Anastasia would draw unnecessary attention, my thrall. Attention which, *as I have already explained*, we cannot yet afford." Lucia pulled on her suit jacket and took up her purse. "Review the case files. Find something you and my uncle both missed. When I return, I expect results."

"And where are you going?"

"To rally what few allies we have."

"Won't *that* attract attention?"

"I am a peer of the court, Mr. Smith. A rendezvous with the Horned God will hardly merit comment."

Images of her long-ago sexual encounter with the incubus flashed through my mind. "Are you looking for help or just making a booty call?"

Surprisingly, the four-hundred-year-old femmepire knew exactly what a booty call was. She arched one pale eyebrow. "Focus on your responsibilities, Mr. Smith, and permit me to focus on mine."

Which…wasn't a very satisfying answer at all.

CHAPTER 45

IN WHICH DAWN BRINGS NO RELIEF

"Wake up, Mr. Smith."

I cracked open one—probably bloodshot—eye, found Lucia standing over me, and groaned. "What time is it?"

"Time for you to stop pretending to do work," she answered, gesturing at the paper-strewn table I'd fallen asleep on, "and actually do some."

"What?"

"We meet with Lady Dumenyova in half an hour."

"Oh." I yawned and stretched. Passing out mid-cram session had been one of the few college experiences I'd been happy to miss out on. The fact that I'd traveled halfway around the world to rectify that gap in my life experience was not lost on me.

My bleary eyes focused on Lucia, who looked fresh as a daisy. Even though…

"Is that the same suit you were wearing last night?"

"It is." She stripped out of the jacket, tossed it in the general direction of her bed, and headed for the bathroom. "While you were sleeping the night away, some of us were at work."

"Yeah, I just *bet* you were," I said to the queen's retreating back.

The bathroom door closed between us without further reply. I heard the sound of rushing water as Lucia turned on the shower.

"Don't take too long," I called out. "I need to shower too!"

ooo

Roughly forty-five minutes later, we were escorted up the last few steps in the Tower. The guards outside Anastasia's cell ushered us in and shut the door behind us.

"My queen. Mr. Smith." Anastasia was awake and alert. She'd traded her black t-shirt for a deep blue one but was otherwise dressed much the same as she'd been the day before. Only her hair—slightly darker than normal—suggested that she too had showered not too long before.

"Lady Dumenyova. You will have to forgive our tardiness, but it seems Mr. Smith is incapable of haste." Lucia had swapped her suit for a sleeveless camisole and knee-length skirt, accompanied by the requisite skyscraper-high heels.

"Next time, try leaving me more than ten minutes to shower," I muttered back. "It takes time for me to get pretty."

"There isn't enough time in the world for such a thing."

"I see the two of you continue to get along splendidly." There was amusement buried somewhere deep beneath Anastasia's diplomatic tones, but that humor faded away as she continued. "I was surprised to hear that you would be visiting so early. Weren't you supposed to be meeting with the Lord of Bones, John?"

"Yeah. Officially, Caine requested that the meeting be rescheduled for tomorrow."

"And unofficially?"

"I told him that the three of us needed to meet posthaste." Lucia crossed the room to take her usual seat at the head of Anastasia's table, placing the still-creepy bird skull in front of her.

"Something has happened?"

"Time has grown unexpectedly short."

"On account of Tomasso already beginning to rot days ahead of schedule," I elaborated, joining the two at the table. My stack of papers went next to the reports I'd left behind on our previous meeting.

"Ah." Ana nodded, already deep in thought. "I take it from the Lord of Bones' subterfuge that the condition of the king's body is not yet public knowledge?"

"Yeah. We're sitting on that info for as long as we can, but—"

"But there are concrete limits as to how long it can be hidden."

"Exactly."

"Mr. Smith will still attend his interview with the contessa later today, but it seemed more efficient to use this morning to formulate our new strategy, rather than have him investigate one of the two Council members whose innocence we are certain of."

Anastasia's frown, little more than a slight downward twitch of the lips, reminded me that the Secundus had her own doubts about Caine, but she exhibited the restraint four centuries sharing space with Lucia must have instilled. "Do we know if someone tampered with the body? I have read about instances where a body rotted early, but a single week badly strains the boundaries of possibility."

"Unfortunately, it would take a thorough examination to answer that question, and such a procedure—"

"Would alert the Kingmaker and others to the truth we are trying to hide," concluded Ana.

"Precisely. We must assume one of two things: either the body was tampered with, or my brother was killed at least a few days prior to his discovery."

"I don't see how that last one is possible," I said. "Some of the servants I interviewed mentioned seeing Tomasso at the palace that week."

"And Denarius himself indicates that the Watch who went missing accompanied Tomasso out to Rome that morning," agreed Anastasia.

"You've spoken to Denarius?"

"It was in his notes on the murder scene, John."

"Right. Must have missed that." I rolled my neck around, feeling far older than my age. "I don't suppose you found anything else I missed? We could use a breakthrough right about now."

"I'm afraid not." For the second day in a row, Anastasia looked almost as tired as I felt. Still heart-stoppingly lovely, but tired. If there was any benefit at all to Tomasso rotting ahead of schedule, it was that it would cut her imprisonment in the Tower short. "Were you able to meet with the Lady Manassa?"

"He was," answered Lucia, apparently on my behalf, "and promptly told her everything."

"It wasn't *quite* like that." I recounted the conversation for a second time. By the time I'd finished, Lucia was irritated with me all over again, while Anastasia was—

I shook my head. There were times when Ana's poker face hid her emotions far too well.

"On one hand," I finished, "I get why Lucia thinks it looks bad. On the other, I'm pretty sure Divya was telling the truth."

"Something you are hardly qualified to determine," said Lucia.

I waited for Ana to defend me, but she was silent. The bottom fell out of my stomach.

"You agree with Lucia?"

"I did not say that," she replied, choosing her words with care, "but John, you must admit that there have been times—"

"When his bleeding heart and substandard powers of perception have caused him—and through him, us—untold troubles?" Lucia interjected. "Quite right."

I didn't even spare the queen a glance, my eyes locked with Ana's own. "You don't think the naga was being honest with me?"

"It is possible," she replied at length. "Certainly, I was aware that she and Lucia's brother once had a relationship of some sort—"

"You were?" Lucia seemed as surprised as me.

"One of a Secundus' many duties is keeping track of her liege's enemies, my queen." For a single instant, a smile danced across Ana's face. That smile faded as she turned back to me. "It is not that I doubt you, John. Your insight has proven invaluable in the past."

"But...?"

"But the Lady Manassa is older than Rome itself. On the tongue of someone so old, truth and lie can be impossible to distinguish."

It was my turn to frown. Divya hadn't *looked* two thousand years old... and she and her daughters had all had a refreshing sort of frankness to them, completely at odds with the rest of the Court. "I still think she was telling the truth."

Lucia's sigh was harsh and loud. "Now you see what I have had to deal with these past few days, Asya. Are you certain that *this* is the man you wish to be courted by?"

Anastasia continued to hold my gaze as she replied, her voice soft and firm at the same time. "I am certain, my queen."

Just like that, my defensiveness fled.

"I might be wrong," I admitted, "but as I told Lucia, I don't think it cost us anything."

"Unless your disclosure of sensitive information is the reason for Tomasso's sudden change in condition."

I ignored the queen. "Divya's story about her breakup with Tomasso fits our narrative. If she was telling the truth about his research, it also gives us a place to keep looking."

"Didn't Lord Borghesi say that Tomasso had returned his borrowed texts?"

"*Those* books, sure. But that just means they weren't the ones that mattered."

"We have mere days to identify the killer, and you want to spend them trying to duplicate my brother's research?"

I shook my head. "Not duplicate. As far as we know, Tomasso spent months hunting the identity of Aurelius' killer. We don't have that sort of time. But if we can get an idea where that research took him, we could potentially jump to the end."

As Lucia and I sniped back and forth at each other, Anastasia had been digging through the documents I'd left her. She placed one of the crime scene photos on the table, face up.

"This might help."

It was one of the many shots that had been taken of the king's murder scene. In the foreground was Tomasso's headless body, sprawled out on the floor.

"What are we looking at? Something with my brother's body?"

Anastasia tapped the photo, redirecting our gazes. "Not his body, my queen. The bookshelves behind it."

I'd seen those shelves when Sergei and I investigated the crime scene in person, but between the blurriness of the photo and my own still sleepy eyes, I still wasn't sure what she was getting at.

Lucia saw it first. "The fourth shelf, on the left. There's a gap between volumes."

"Yes."

After a moment, I saw it too. But... it wasn't the only gap on the shelves. What made this one noteworthy?

"Look at the bindings, Mr. Smith."

I sighed. "Can we pretend for a second that I don't have vampire eyes?"

Anastasia winced. "Of course. I wasn't thinking." She pointed to the other books on that shelf. "These books are a series of texts detailing the history of the Borghesi family, John. Volumes one, two, four and five."

I was going to have to take her word for it. To me, the text on the bindings was nothing but a blur of indistinguishable chicken scratches. "So, what happened to volume three?"

"Exactly."

"I am familiar with this history series," interjected Lucia. "My father's murder was the endpoint of the *fourth* volume, not the third. If Tomasso was researching our father's death, why would he be looking in volume three?"

Both femmepires looked to me, but I could only answer with a shrug. "I have no idea. It might not be anything… Divya *did* say he started out researching Aurelius' reign to become a better king."

"Assuming we can believe anything that woman told you." Lucia tossed the photo back down. "This is pointless."

"Welcome to my world, Lucia. Cases are solved a piece at a time. Maybe this is relevant, and maybe it isn't, but it's another potential lead to pursue."

The queen gave a grudging nod. "My father had multiple printings of these histories commissioned. I should be able to acquire a copy of the volume in question."

"Awesome. In the meantime, we should probably—"

A heavy knock at the door interrupted me. Before the echoes of that knock could even fade, the door crashed open.

Denarius stood in the hall, shadows thick about his tall frame.

"Mr. Smith. Niece. Lady Dumenyova." He didn't move an inch, but his shadow poured past him into the room, plunging the interior into twilight. "There are developments we must discuss."

ooo

Lucia arched a pale eyebrow. "Uncle, I know that, given your march to senility, simple concepts like privacy and courtesy may now escape you—"

"Be silent, child. It is courtesy and courtesy alone that forces me to pretend you do not already know what I am about to tell you." Now, Denarius *did* enter the room. "The king's body has begun the initial stages of decomposition. First Rot is upon us."

In the hallway behind the Kingmaker, several Watch milled about, but I could clearly pick out Niccolo's face. Maria Elena was going to be *pissed.*

"The trial begins tomorrow morning," Denarius continued. "Prepare yourselves accordingly."

Before he could leave, I found myself out of my chair, braving his shadow to cross the room.

"Do you have something to add, Mr. Smith? Or perhaps to confess?"

I ignored the latter question on the grounds that anything I said would incriminate me. "Don't you think it's kind of suspicious that Tomasso's body started rotting so far ahead of schedule?"

"There is no schedule for this sort of thing, investigator. Merely a range of acceptable possibilities."

"And where does First Rot starting less than a week after death rank on that range of possibilities?"

"It is admittedly unusual," he concluded, "yet not entirely unheard of."

"Which do you think is more likely? That Tomasso's body should set a speed record for decomp all on its own or that someone gave that process a little push?"

"Mr. Smith's query has merit," said Lucia. "As liege of the accused, I demand a formal examination of my brother's body for signs of tampering."

"Have no fear. I have already put in an order for such an examination to be performed."

"Excellent. We should further delay the trial until said examination is complete."

"The law makes no provision for a trial's delay once First Rot has been found, regardless of the circumstances involved."

"How remarkably shortsighted," said Lucia. "Tell me, do you *enjoy* having someone make fools of both you and your precious law? Or is this your own play to do away with us before the truth can emerge?"

The elder manpire's face was carved from stone, eyes every bit as dark as the shadows surrounding him. "Tomorrow morning, Lucia. Attend or forfeit your only chance to present a defense."

Just like that, his shadow was gone from the room. Moments later, so was Denarius.

Lucia eyed the now-closed door with a scowl, and then turned on me. "And so, two weeks becomes three days becomes less than twenty-four hours. What now, my thrall?"

That was a *really* good question.

○○○

I walked back to my seat in a bid to buy time for my brain—never the swiftest of tools, even without pulling an all-nighter—to come up with a solution. Unfortunately, seven steps proved insufficient for that task. I took a seat, looked from femmepire to femmepire, racked my brains, and still had nothing. Finally, I just did what I'd always done in similar situations; I opened my mouth and waited to see what came out.

"One day isn't enough time to solve either murder."

Okay…so *that* wasn't helpful at all.

"Thank you for belaboring the obvious, Mr. Smith."

"You're very welcome, Lucia."

"Are you suggesting that we abandon the investigation entirely, John?" As ever, Anastasia was, quite literally, the voice of cool reason.

"Sort of." I put my jumbled thoughts into some semblance of order. "What all do we need before the trial?"

"A signed confession from the true killer that also absolves my Secundus and I of responsibility?"

"Yeah, that'd be fantastic." I rolled my eyes. "And if we don't get that?"

"An equally viable suspect," supplied Ana.

"Right. As everyone keeps telling me, this isn't a human trial, so there is no presumption of innocence. Which is bad for us. On the other hand, that means we need less proof to support our own accusations, right? We can't solve the murder—either murder—but what we *can* do is come up with a viable suspect and enough ammunition to sway one or two of the neutral Council votes."

"And how are we supposed to get either?"

I had no clue, but I wasn't going to tell them that.

"He has no idea," growled Lucia. "I have entrusted our defense to a moron."

Damn it. I really needed to work on my poker face… and on *not* transmitting my thoughts and emotions across the bond. The crazy thing was that as soon as the words left Lucia's royal mouth, I realized I actually *did* have a clue.

All hail the great and powerful deities of contrariness!

"That's not true, Lucia. There are a ton of leads to pursue. The problem is we don't have time for me to pursue all of them."

"Now, you are merely speaking in circles. Or tongues."

"For *me* to pursue all of them," I repeated. "But if we take the high priority leads and split them up between the three of us, we might make some progress." Enough progress to convince the Council of Anastasia's innocence? Unlikely. But I didn't have any better ideas.

"Need I remind you that Lady Dumenyova is unable to leave this Tower and that I already have my own part to play in winning the necessary votes?"

"Do you think more wining and dining is going to make any difference? Are you going to be able to convince Vigo or the contessa to stop hating you in less than a day?"

Lucia's silence was all the response I needed.

"By the same token," I continued, "there isn't enough time to approach our suspect pool the way we've been doing it so far."

"What is your suggestion then, Mr. Smith?" asked Anastasia.

"If we can narrow down our suspect pool to three or four possible killers then Lucia and I will focus our efforts on those people. Maybe we'll find something that helps us."

"And what will I be doing?"

"Pretty much everything else. Finish the list of People with relevant Talents, on the off chance that one of them jumps out at us. Figure out how all of this nonsense fits together. Come up with *something* I can use in the trial tomorrow."

"Is that all?" Ana offered one of her rare smiles.

"It seems as if you want my Secundus to do your job for you."

"She's the smartest person in the room, Lucia. Someone near and dear to my heart once told me that I needed to learn to better utilize the assets available to me."

"A wise someone, no doubt," murmured Anastasia, her smile widening.

"Smoking hot too," I agreed.

Lucia looked between us and rolled her eyes, the emotions leaking across the bond a mix of annoyance and amusement.

"But to answer your question… no, that's *not* all," I realized. "If Lucia can get you a copy of the book missing from Tomasso's shelf, I need you to go through that as well. Maybe you can figure out what he was looking for?"

"I will do what I can," she promised.

I shook my head in sudden bemusement. "I can't believe I'm saying this, but it's actually too bad Juliette didn't come with me to Rome. An extra pair of eyes would be really helpful."

"You could always enlist the services of Ms. Giordano," suggested Anastasia. "Assuming we now believe her to be trustworthy?"

"Maria Elena?" I nodded. "I think she proved that last night."

"For all the good it did us," muttered Lucia, "given that the secret of my brother's condition lasted less than a day."

"Because of the guard *you* forced us to bring along. And when Maria Elena finds that out, I'm pretty sure Niccolo is a dead man."

Not *literally* dead; Niccolo was a member of the Watch after all, and Maria Elena was a three-year-old with limited combat skills. But I suspected the manpire would find himself blacklisted from the booty call phone directory for the foreseeable future.

"Perhaps Maria Elena can also retrieve the book in question, freeing you and Queen Lucia to focus upon your suspects."

"Good idea. With Sabina pissed off at her, I'm sure she'll be happy to have something to do."

"Very well then." Lucia took back control of the conversation. "Where do we start?"

My stomach growled, answering that question more eloquently than I ever could.

○○○

After four crepes, two glasses of orange juice, and a blueberry scone, my stomach was finally appeased. I pushed aside the empty plate and mentally prepared myself for the difficult task of whittling our enormous suspect list down to a bare handful.

It was… easier than expected.

Golden bangles clinked together as Lucia counted off her primary suspects on two fingers. "The Lady Manassa. My beloved, king-making uncle. Both had the means. Both had the opportunity. One of them is surely the killer."

My traitorous, easily duped gut disagreed, but I hadn't come up with any viable suspects of my own. I sighed. "So that's it? Two suspects?"

"You would prefer fifty?"

"I'd prefer someone with an intelligible motive," I shot back.

Anastasia shook her head. "I'm not certain we have the time for motives."

"I know." I shrugged helplessly. "Alright, fine. If you take one of them, Lucia, I'll take the other. Any preferences?"

"Given your inherent fallibility when it comes to women, I suppose I have no choice but to speak with the naga."

"Leaving me Denarius."

"Yes. Try not to let his *rakish good looks* and *scintillating charm* interfere with your objectivity." Lucia's sarcasm was thick, aimed at me as much as her own uncle.

"Not a problem. I'm genetically hardwired to despise him." I smiled. "After all, he's a Borghesi."

CHAPTER 46

Much of investigative work is tiresome and repetitive. There's a reason so many of us drink heavily, and it's not because of prolonged exposure to the very many lousy things people do to each other. Not *just* because of that anyway.

Burnout is a real thing.

But every now and then, there are days that remind me why I love the profession, days where the inscrutable magically becomes scrutable, where a single discovery sets off a chain reaction, and suddenly, the answer assembles itself, like a puzzle being pieced together, or a stained-glass window taking shape.

This was not one of those days.

CHAPTER 47

IN WHICH THERE ARE NO GOOD NIGHTS

"Twelve freaking hours and nothing to show for it. This case officially sucks."

Not even my incidental usage of the word *sucks* to describe a case about vampires lifted my spirits. Eleven hours to go until the trial, and I'd spent my day getting absolutely nowhere.

"You learned nothing at all?" asked Anastasia. The three of us had reconvened in Ana's Tower cell.

"Nothing that helps." I sighed. "I have multiple witnesses who report seeing Denarius in the palace at the time of Tomasso's death, but—"

"As a Shadecaster, he could have crossed to the city and back with none the wiser," growled Lucia.

"Exactly. Still, according to the people I spoke with, he and Tomasso got along pretty well. Nothing like the relationship *you* had with your family."

"At any point in your useless flailing about to prove or disprove his alibi, did you actually speak to the man himself, or have I yet again overestimated your dubious professional skills?"

"Yeah, I interviewed Denarius… for all of about five minutes."

"And? Did he do it?"

"What part of *five minutes* was unclear? I have no idea if he did it. As soon as he realized I was investigating him as a suspect, he pulled out that shadow sword he'd used at the airport, told me I was a fool for wasting both of our time, and gave me ten seconds to get the hell out of his office."

If my internal clock was at all accurate, I'd managed my exit in roughly seven. But that didn't seem like the sort of accomplishment Lucia or Ana wanted to hear about.

"You failed," Lucia concluded.

"Yeah, pretty much." I ignored the queen's glare, almost too dispirited to fight with her. "What about you? Did you have any luck with the Lady Manassa?"

That question wiped the look right off her lovely face. "I do not like that woman," she growled.

"Given that she dated your brother for decades—during which you were his personal bogeyman… err, woman—I assume the feeling is mutual. Why? What did she say?"

"She sat there in silence, sipping from a cup of tea, and paying my words only the barest modicum of attention!"

I frowned. "That's surprising. She was super polite to me."

"Perhaps Lady Dumenyova is not the only woman addled enough to fall for your dubious charms."

Anastasia cleared her throat meaningfully.

"Or maybe you did something to piss Divya off." Some emotion sparked across our bond, and I groaned. "Why do I suddenly have a mental image of you storming into the grotto, and throwing out accusations like rice at a wedding?"

The bond went silent. "It is bad enough having you invade my memories when we sleep. To do so when I am awake…"

"Wait; you actually *did* that? And she *still* offered you tea?" The Lady Manassa was a saint.

"I said the naga drank tea," Lucia corrected me sharply. "It was not offered to me."

"Well, no wonder."

"Nor would I have partaken of it, had it been," she continued. "The fact that you did so while in the midst of a small army of venomous serpents says all that needs to be said about your mental state."

"Says the woman who pissed off a naga in the midst of that same army!"

"My queen… Mr. Smith… this bickering gets us nowhere."

Anastasia was right. And as much as I disliked Lucia, the truth was, I wasn't really angry at her. No more than usual, anyway.

"Sorry," I told both femmepires. "I'm just frustrated. This was the last full day we had, and we're back right where we started."

"Not entirely."

Both Lucia and I perked up, but the expression on Anastasia's face was a long way from optimistic.

"You made some progress on your end, Asya?"

"To an extent." Anastasia passed me a sheet of paper. "As requested, I have added in the individuals who possessed Talents of note but died at some point in the past few centuries."

I scanned the page. Two dozen names had grown to almost fifty. "There were an awful lot of deaths, weren't there? Are all of these from old age?"

"Very few." Anastasia shrugged. "We were not always as civilized as we are now, and Aurelius' reign in particular was a bloody one."

"Though preferable by far to his predecessor's," put in Lucia. "Indeed."

Which didn't say much, since his predecessor had been known as the Mad King and was the reason Paris was no longer the seat of the European kingdom.

I glanced through the completed list of vampires, but nothing new jumped out at me. If only one of them had been named Vampire Killer McKillsALot—

Lucia plucked the page from my hand, scanned the names, and sighed. "Well done, Lady Dumenyova, but as Mr. Smith has pointed out, we lack the time to investigate the names on this list."

"I know." Anastasia shook her head. "I took the liberty of providing Ms. Giordano a copy of this list, and she has promised to do what she can to verify their deceased states, as well as return a list of any descendants I might have missed…"

"Descendants? You think one of them has been posing as their own offspring?"

"That seems… unlikely," said Anastasia.

After a moment, I nodded. It was a little too close to the plot of Highlander for comfort. "Then why do we care about their children?"

"Bloodlines, you fool," Lucia answered tiredly. "Talent is often inherited, as I have told you on more than one occasion."

"But if they shared the Talent of their parent, wouldn't they already have been on Ana's list?"

"Only had they revealed that Talent publicly."

"So, our killer might be the child of one of these dead vampires who… what? Hid their Talent for more than a century? Why would anyone do that?"

"Perhaps to avoid suspicion after killing my father and brother?"

"It seems like a reach."

"You are not wrong, and as my queen has pointed out, we lack the time to investigate the matter further anyway. By the time young Maria Elena completes her task, our trial will likely be over."

"So much for progress," grumped Lucia.

"It's still more than either of us accomplished." Not that *that* was saying much. I eyed Anastasia. "You spoke to Maria Elena?"

"I did. As requested, she brought by a copy of the volume missing from Tomasso's study."

Now we were getting somewhere. "And? What was he looking for?"

"I do not know." The femmepire pushed aside a stack of papers, and handed me a small, leather-clad book. "I read through it twice while awaiting your return. It chronicles King Aurelius' first few centuries as king in Rome; his ascension to the throne, the birth of his children and the deaths of his consorts."

"But there's nothing about his own murder?" I flipped open the book but found only pages upon pages of handwritten Italian. I passed it over to Lucia.

"Aurelius' assassination occurred a good seventy years later and was detailed in the subsequent volume."

"One of the books that *wasn't* missing from Tomasso's shelf."

"Yes." Anastasia's voice was soft, considering. "Either the killer took this book to throw us off the scent or there is something in its pages that I am not seeing."

"Or Tomasso really was just reading through it to find lessons on how to be a king and the missing book is lying on a table somewhere in one of the many, many rooms in his townhouse."

"That is also possible." Ana shook her head again. "I fear this is yet another dead end in your investigation."

"You *still* made more progress than either of us. Not bad for someone who's been stuck in an anti-vampire cell the whole time."

"For all the good it has done us." Ana's jade eyes met mine. "Have you given any thought to tomorrow's trial?"

I'd had a ruthlessly hard time doing anything else, but I got the feeling that wasn't what Ana meant. "Mostly just in an abstract *oh god, oh god we're going to die* sort of way."

The femmepire's smile was there and gone in a flash. "You might want to spare some time to plan your remarks."

My... remarks? Oh crap. This wasn't a human trial, as everyone kept telling me, but I was still going to have to address the Council. Which meant I needed some sort of speech... not to mention a plan for how I was going to string together all this non-evidence into something that would convince a collection of terrifying psychotics that Ana should go free.

This was going to be high school debate class all over again. Except this time, a C- would get us killed.

"That's a really good point. Do you have any more paper? And a pen? I should get started on that immediately."

Lucia closed the book with a snap of her wrists. "While you do so, I will make one final effort to rally support to our cause... as I should have been doing instead of wasting time with tea-drinking nagas."

"You wouldn't have said it was a waste if we'd caught the killer," I muttered under my breath.

The queen opened her mouth to reply—in as unflattering a way as possible, I assumed—but caught herself. She took a deep breath, and I could almost hear her counting to ten across our bond. I assume that's what she was doing anyway ... despite her century in the United States, Lucia all too frequently still thought in Italian.

Finally, she glanced from Anastasia to me. "Should the trial go poorly, we might find ourselves in cells awaiting execution by this time tomorrow. When you have finished preparing for the trial, you may take this time for yourselves."

I had no idea what she was talking about, but Anastasia caught her breath. "Are you certain, your Majesty?"

"I will go to my grave spitting defiance into the wind, Secundus, but there are some battles not worth fighting, and others lost before the first strike."

I was still wondering what the hell *that* meant when Lucia turned to me, blue eyes cold and clear as a winter sky. "I will meet you both here tomorrow morning, thrall."

And then she was out the door.

"Was that...? Did she just...?"

"She did," Ana confirmed.

"Lucia just gave us her blessing?"

"This was not her blessing. Not yet. Think of it more as a... temporary dispensation."

To do what? As tired as my brain was at that moment, the answer took a while come to me. But once it had, I sat straight up, my eyes going wide. "Seriously?"

"Indeed." Ana's slow smile sent my hormones into overdrive. "So, tell me, Mr. Smith, would you like to stay the night?"

When I finally spoke, my voice came out as a croak.

"Yes."

"I am glad." Her gaze was almost tangible, like the lightest of caresses along my cheek.

"So... uhm... should we go back to the bedroom?" Jesus. It had been a while—a really, really long while—but that was no excuse for acting like a fourteen-year-old virgin.

Anastasia laughed softly. "As much as I would like that, perhaps we should first finish our preparations for the trial, in the hopes that this night does not end up our last?"

I found myself nodding, overcome with the thought of twenty, thirty, or even fifty more years with this woman. A future I had never fully believed in was suddenly almost attainable.

All I needed to do was win a piddling little murder trial.

I picked up the pen and started to write.

CHAPTER 48
IN WHICH THE DROUGHT CONTINUES

"This is not what I expected." Lucia's voice, cold and clear like expensive crystal, roused me from sleep.

From sleep but *not* from bed, judging by the hard surface below my cheek and the painful crick in my neck. I blinked my eyes open, and an object swam into shape on the table next to my head.

A pen. And a notepad.

"He worked on his opening statements well into the night," Anastasia replied, somewhere behind me. "When he finally fell asleep, mid-word, I lacked the heart to wake him."

I bolted upright, every muscle in my back and neck screaming in protest. "It's morning already?"

"It is." Behind me, both Lucia and Anastasia were fully dressed, the former in another pristine white suit, the latter in black slacks and a green blouse that bore passing familiarity with her usual attire. "I have taken the liberty of ordering us breakfast."

"Did we…?" Part of me clung to the hope that the sex had been so mind-blowing that it had short circuited my memory.

"We did not."

That settled it. God officially hated me. "You could have woken me up."

"John, when a man falls asleep even with the promise of sexual relations dangled in front of him, it is a sure sign that he needs his rest."

"Or that he's an utter imbecile."

For once, I agreed with Lucia.

Anastasia watched me slowly stretch with concern. "Perhaps I should have moved you to a more comfortable location though."

"What is wrong with him?"

"I'm human," I groaned. "Our muscles don't magically heal like yours do, which means we get cold and stiff if we stay in the same position for too long." I waved off Ana's apologetic look. "It's my fault, not yours. Anyway, I'm more pissed off that I wasted our one night together."

"If your work last night helps us win the case, it will be worth it," she reminded me.

Six years of abstinence was telling me otherwise.

"Well, hopefully, it all pays off then," I decided. "Is it okay if I grab a shower before breakfast arrives?"

"Please do." Lucia nodded to a hanger. "I took the liberty of bringing you a change of clothes for the trial."

On the hanger was a very familiar, new suit. With skinny pants.

As if my morning couldn't get any worse.

○○○

A long shower did a lot to help me wake up, and even more to soothe my sore, cramped muscles. It did nothing to make me feel better about literally falling asleep instead of finally *having relations* with Anastasia.

A glance through what I'd written the night before didn't improve matters. Constructing a defense when you have a multitude of suspects—no matter what Lucia said—and a dearth of actual evidence was not a skill I'd learned in my one semester of community college. Or while interning for private investigator, for that matter. What I had in the notebook was little more than a random assortment of facts, along with an opening statement that I'd rewritten at least a dozen times.

"How does this trial thing work, anyway?" I asked. "Obviously, I give an opening statement of some sort, but then...?"

"You present the evidence you have gathered to the Council, along with viable alternatives to the prevailing theory of Lady Dumenyova's guilt. The Council is then free to ask you questions. When they are finished, they vote."

"That's it?" Jesus. So much for my vague hopes of stalling until some sort of key clue could magically appear; it sounded like we'd be convicted by lunchtime.

"Not quite," answered Lucia. "Once the Council has made their preliminary votes public, you will be given an opportunity to sway those who voted against us."

Because *that* was going to go well. "What about witnesses?"

"You have a witness that can clear Lady Dumenyova?" For a moment, Lucia was almost as impressed as she was surprised.

"Obviously not, or last night would have gone way differently," I grumbled. "I was thinking I could call some of the people I interviewed to testify in support of our alternate theory. People *did* recall him being distracted, after all."

Lucia nodded. "You can present said witnesses at the same time as your other evidence. Be aware, however, that the Council will likely have a Truthfinder present."

"Is that what it sounds like?"

"Someone who can smell deception? Yes."

I tossed the notepad aside. "Then why are we even bothering with this? Just put Ana on the stand, have her state that she didn't kill Tomasso, and we can call it a day!"

"A Truthfinder's role is to find deception outside of the People," Anastasia replied gently. "The Talent does not work on our own species. Or most elder species, for that matter."

I shrugged. "Well, I don't expect any of my witnesses to lie anyway, so that shouldn't be an issue." A sudden, mildly horrific thought occurred to me. "Will they use their Talent on me?"

"Only if you present yourself as a witness." The queen waved a hand dismissively. "As investigator, it is widely accepted that you will lie whenever possible to convince the Council. Clearly, they remain unaware of how terrible a liar you truly are."

"Honesty is a virtue."

"The fact that you actually believe that says everything." Lucia sighed. "Stick to the truth whenever possible. Make your lies small and employ them only when they will be most effective."

That had been my plan all along, so I just nodded.

○○○

I was in the bathroom struggling to put on the tie that Lucia insisted I wear when nerves really started to set in. What in God's name was I doing? I wasn't a lawyer. I wasn't even a homicide detective. Maybe with a full month and a team of carefully trained assistants, I could have accomplished something. As it was, I was headed to a murder trial—one where the burden of proof was on the defense, not the prosecution—with little more than a notebook of random theories and a collection of witnesses who could only testify that the former king had 'been weird' for the past few months.

I reminded myself that I hadn't been prepared to mediate between vampires and an asparagus demigod either, and I'd come out of that one alright... enslaved by an egomaniacal queen, yeah, but otherwise alright. But the Council scared me way more than Lucia ever had and the one person who had always managed to pull my ass out of the fire was now depending upon *me* to save *her.*

There was no way this ended well.

Either my poker face gave me away, or Anastasia just got tired of watching me fumble at my tie from the living room. The next thing I knew, she was in the bathroom with me, slender fingers accomplishing in seconds what I hadn't managed in multiple minutes. She finished, patted the tight knot of the tie, and then looked up at me, jade green barely visible through dark lashes.

"Be calm, Mr. Smith. Be calm and have faith."

"Do you know something I don't?"

"Only that we are both survivors," I could hear her smile, even if I couldn't see it, "and that you are often at your best when things are at their worst."

"Then I should be primed for superstardom," I murmured, "because this time, I think we're totally screwed."

"If all else fails," she suggested, her voice dropping even lower, "stall for time."

"I'm sorry?"

"While I would prefer you prove our innocence, we are not entirely out of options should the trial go poorly. I have been preparing something of a fallback plan, but the accelerated timetable poses issues."

That sounded promising. "How much time do you need?"

"A day, at minimum. Two would be better, but I suspect that is beyond even your considerable abilities. And John…" Ana spared a glance at the door to the living room. "Tell Queen Lucia nothing for now."

"You don't trust her?" When the hell had *that* happened?

"I trust her with my life, if not yours," she replied, "yet I do not trust her allies. If she should let something slip to one of them…"

"Got it." I took a long breath and then exhaled, trying to expel my tension with it. "I'll do what I can to win the trial or lose it as slowly as possible."

"I know you will." Anastasia took a step away, pulled my suit coat off the hanger, and helped me slip into it, tugging at the fabric to ensure it fell in clean lines.

"About last night—"

"You needed your rest. Survival first, Mr. Smith. Then, we will celebrate."

"Deal."

A knock sounded at the exterior doorway. I took one last second to examine myself in the mirror. My hair was, as usual, a disaster, but I otherwise looked presentable in the elegant suit and dress shirt Lucia had given me.

You almost couldn't tell that I had, once again, been forced to go commando.

CHAPTER 49

IN WHICH JOHN SMITH GOES TO TRIAL

Denarius was waiting just outside. The four of us made a slow, somewhat strange procession down the endless array of steps, only to stop again when we reached the bottom and the final guard post within the Tower itself.

Denarius looked to Anastasia. "Lady Dumenyova, do I have your word that you will not attempt to escape once we leave the confines of the Tower?"

Anastasia's voice was cool and impenetrable. "Would you trust the word of an alleged murderer, Lord Borghesi?"

"This one, I might."

Ana smiled thinly but said nothing.

"For you to leave the Tower, child, I must remove your leash," he continued, "but I will not do so without your pledge on this matter."

"You have no choice *but* to do so, Uncle," hissed Lucia. "The law you love so much states that the accused has a right to be present at her trial."

"Of all the minutiae of law and justice, why am I not surprised that *this* is the one piece you actually bothered to learn?"

"Because you are not an entirely stupid man. Or so they tell me." Lucia arched one golden eyebrow. "Stop stalling."

"Very well." Denarius nodded to one of the Watch manning the guard post, who brought forward an armful of heavy iron shackles. "I had hoped to avoid this, but since you insist…" He bent to bind Anastasia's ankles, then rose and bound her wrists behind her back.

I gave the shackles a professional once-over. Vampires were strong, and Anastasia in her stone form was even stronger, but the iron bands looked like they could restrain a giant. The pin holding them locked was as thick as my wrist, and the chains between each band were thicker still. Breaking out of those was going to be a problem.

Walking wasn't going to be a picnic either. The bands around Ana's ankles had only a few links between them, and a heavy length of chain linked her ankle cuffs to those around her wrists. At best, she would be restricted to a slow shuffle.

With the prisoner safely bound, Denarius extracted a small copper penny from his pocket. Dropping back to one knee, he found the golden chain that had almost been entirely covered by Ana's new leg irons and pressed the penny against it.

In the movies, that's where some sort of ruthlessly expensive special effect would have occurred. Maybe a sudden nimbus of light, or a crackle of static energy to tell the audience that the Tower's leash had been lifted. Sadly, I'd learned that magic in the real world was all too often a disappointment in the effects department. There was nothing at all to suggest that something had changed. Even so, the manpire rose back to his feet.

"Lady Borghesi. Lady Dumenyova. Mr. Smith. The trial awaits."

He offered a short bow and swung open the Tower door.

The hall in front of us was packed with the Crown Watch. I counted at least fifteen guards, and every one of them had their weapons—axes, truncheons, swords, and even guns—drawn and ready. All eyes were on Anastasia as she stepped outside the confines of the Tower for the first time in days. She closed her eyes and as she took in a breath, I could practically see the energy seeping back into her.

I could also hear the clenching of at least a dozen Watch sphincters, even though Ana was thoroughly shackled, and even more thoroughly outgunned. Tension choked the hallway, and beneath that tension was something that smelled like fear.

Only Denarius seemed unaffected. He waited for the rest of us to exit the Tower, and then barked an order. The Watch formed up around us in a wall of ninja death machines, and I started to reassess my original estimates. Not counting Denarius himself, we now had four guards in front of us, two each on either side, and another four behind… and yet the hall ahead was still awash with black uniforms.

"How many freaking guards did you bring, dude?"

"All of them, Mr. Smith. Today, the Crown Watch has but a single duty."

"An impressive display," offered Lucia. "A pity you did not provide my brother similar protection."

A handful of the nearby Watch shifted their hard-eyed gazes to the femmepire queen. The rest maintained their wary vigil around Anastasia.

As a monkey, I didn't merit much more than the occasional glance. For once, I was cool with the species-specific disrespect.

ooo

When Denarius said he'd summoned all of the Crown Watch, he really meant *all* of them. We passed at least five choke points in our slow march across the palace, each of them teeming with black-clad guards, and when we finally wound to a stop, there were another half-dozen vampires flanking a large pair of double-doors.

I frowned at those doors. I'd been half asleep when we arrived in Rome, but this didn't *look* like the entrance to the Council chambers. "I thought we were headed to see the Council?"

"We are. They will join us within."

"The palace has a whole separate room for murder trials?" That seemed excessive. Kind of cool, but mostly excessive.

"This is one of the other banquet halls, Mr. Smith," Lucia informed me, spiking a warning of some kind across our bond.

"Indeed," confirmed Denarius. "There are too many points of egress from the Council chamber for it to be properly secured."

"Because nine million screaming ninjas just isn't enough."

"Security was admittedly not the only concern. The banquet hall offers us something that the Council chamber lacks."

"Which is?"

Denarius nodded to the guards near the doors, and they hastened to pull them open. Inside was the sort of crowd Disneyland only *wished* they could attract.

"Standing room for the audience, Mr. Smith."

ooo

Like a lot of people, I'd had the stereotypical dream where I was standing in front of a class without any clothes on. In *my* version of the dream, that class had consisted of cartoon characters and every girl I'd ever asked out and been rejected by in high school… but fundamentally, it was the same basic experience: a blend of uncomfortableness, inadequacy, and humiliation.

This was worse. Even before adding in the skinny pants.

A table had been set up in the center of the room and a long, dais—reminiscent of the one in the Council chamber, albeit temporary in nature—curved in front of the far wall. A human man in a suit stood on one side of the dais—presumably the translator Lucia had requested—but the space between platform and table, and table and door, was clear.

The rest of the room was packed. Here and there, I saw more black-clothed Watch, but Denarius' guards were outnumbered ten to one inside the banquet hall by vampire nobility and their House members. Placed further back in the crowd were the servants; I spotted at least a dozen people I'd interviewed over the past week.

Even as my heart rate was tripling, some small part of my mind—for once, not the piece that Lucia had forcibly inserted—was kicking into its own brand of overdrive. This was a zoo, and a disaster in the making… but it was also an opportunity, if I could figure out how to take advantage of it. If I'd learned anything from history— mostly historical movies, but still—it was that crowds were collectively dumber than the individuals involved. And if there was one thing I understood, it was dumb people. Surely, there was some way to use the mob to our advantage.

The crowd was too large to react instantaneously to our arrival, but as Denarius escorted us forward, silence spread in fits and starts. Soon, all eyes were fixed upon us.

On Lucia and Anastasia, really. With Denarius in the mix, I wasn't even the tallest person in the group, and that was traditionally my only claim to fame at vampire parties. Nobody spared me more than a glance, and I couldn't blame them for that. If I'd been in the crowd, instead of serving as its potential entertainment, I'd have been transfixed by the two femmepires too.

Lucia stalked forward like a woman on the warpath, golden skin, platinum hair, and gleaming white outfit combining to make her look like heaven's shortest and bustiest angel. Anastasia came more slowly, but even hampered by shackles, her movements were graceful, strong, and elegant.

Next to the two of them, I felt like the world's grubbiest troglodyte. I kept my eyes fixed ahead and offered a little prayer that the God of People-Who-Tripped-and-Fell-on-Their-Faces-at-the-Worst-Possible-Time was busy elsewhere having a beer.

By the time we reached our chairs—hard, wooden stools that looked like they'd been pulled straight from the set of a television show on early pioneer lifestyles—there was no sound at all in the chamber. We took our seats, flanked by a semi-circle of Watch, and the crowd finally took a breath, like some sort of multi-headed organism remembering it needed oxygen to survive.

With her arms and feet shackled and linked together by a length of chain, there was no way for Anastasia to sit comfortably, but she offered no complaint as I helped her onto the centermost stool. Lucia sat to the left, and I took the stool on the right. The table that had been placed in front of us matched our Little House on the Prairie chairs, the rough furniture contrasting unflatteringly with the richness of our surroundings.

"Someone's working overtime to make us look bad. Is anyone else worried that this table is going to collapse?" I held my breath as I placed the notes I'd brought with me onto the surface in question, relieved that the slight weight of a notebook and a few dozen pictures proved insufficient to send the table crashing to the floor.

"It will last long enough to serve its purpose, Investigator Smith." Despite his words, I thought I detected a note of irritation in Denarius' tone as he regarded the shabbiness of our seating arrangements.

Or maybe I was just projecting.

"Only if the Council ever shows up," I replied. The dais in front of us remained empty. "If today doesn't work for them, we can always do this another time. How does August sound?"

Between the acoustics of the room and the supernatural hearing of many of its inhabitants, my words carried further than I'd intended, prompting a few scattered chuckles, and a far greater number of angry expressions.

"I understand your need for constant babble, Mr. Smith," said Lucia softly, "but perhaps you should instead devote your efforts to preparing our defense."

That sounded like a pretty good idea, but I was as prepared as I was going to get without an extra week of time and the president's speech writers. So, I scanned the crowd instead. Positioned at the very front were Princess Sabina and two of the city's four ambassadors. Sabina ignored me completely, but Deanna—still looking far too much like a civilized Juliette for my comfort—offered up an encouraging smile. Next to her was Ti An, resplendent in her usual golden robes, and watching me with an intensity that only accelerated my testicles' northward journey.

Sergei was still missing.

Behind the ambassadors were the ranks of vampire nobility. Several rows back. I spotted the Sultaness of Scarves, now far more sedately—and consequently, less interestingly—attired. Her sneer did terrible things for the lovely lines of her face. Moments later, that sneer disappeared, as her eyes focused on someone next to me. Blood drained from her face, and she hurriedly—and awkwardly—dropped her gaze, turning to engage her nearest neighbor in conversation.

"Do you know her?" Anastasia murmured in my ear.

Ah. That explained the Sultaness' reaction.

"Sort of. She was my tablemate at Lucia's disastrous welcome home banquet," I breathed back.

"The one with the dress you liked so much? The so-called Sultaness of Scarves?"

"That's her."

"She is far from a sultaness, John. It would be a stretch to even call Dulcinea a lady."

I coughed to hide my laugh. "I take it you two have a history?"

"A single interaction only."

"It must have left quite the impression."

"Several, to be precise. It is a pity that she has since healed."

This time, my laugh came through loud and clear.

God, I loved that woman!

○○○

When the Council finally deigned to arrive, they did so individually and in manners as varied as the beings themselves.

First was Vigo, or at least Vigo's bug proxies. A thousand or more insects scuttled through the door in formation, splitting to stream across opposing walls until they met once more atop the dais in a seething mass. As more and more insects fed into that writhing pile, it swiftly grew to take the shape of a hooded and cloaked man.

"Given that the real Vigo is like five hundred pounds, at least… who exactly is that supposed to be?" I asked Anastasia.

"The duke as he once was. Or perhaps as he wishes to be."

The Lady Manassa was escorted to the dais by Aasha, both nagas draped in elegant, embroidered saris and overrobes, and each bearing a crimson, jeweled serpent coiled about their right arms. From her seat, Divya met my gaze evenly, her expression giving nothing away. Aasha was less circumspect; the glare she shot first Lucia then me made it clear both how she had taken Lucia's accusations and who she blamed for them.

If Lucia was full of herself—and dear God, was she ever—then the Contessa d'Verde took things to absurd new heights. Four men, bare-chested, heavily oiled, and distressingly similar in appearance to Juliette's surfer meathead blood donor, carried the contessa in on an honest-to-God palanquin, its base sculpted into the shape of golden flames, rising to frame the passenger. The femmepire herself reclined on a handful of plush cushions, legs drawn up under her emerald gown. Light caught on the golden threads in that dress, and the hooded cape she again wore atop it.

"What's with the fire motif?" Before Anastasia could reply, I came up with the answer myself. "Firestarter?"

"Indeed. Her duels with Andrés were the stuff of legend."

I had yet to speak with the contessa, but I couldn't help regard her a little bit more favorably for that. Anyone who had fought with Andrés couldn't be *too* bad. The manpire Firestarter—dead two years earlier in Xavier's failed coup—had made even Marcus seem cool by comparison.

No pun intended, of course.

After the contessa was Dog, sprawled on his back in the belly of a wheelbarrow pushed by his own bare-chested servant, this one, a young woman with comically large breasts. Given Dog's stubby legs, some form of transportation was eminently practical, but the vehicle he'd chosen, and the fact that he was entering so soon after the stately contessa, made it clear his entrance was as much about mocking his fellow councilor as it was about reaching the dais in a timely fashion.

The flames he'd cut out of colored paper and taped to the sides of the wheelbarrow were also a pretty solid indicator.

The Horned God came next, not from the door, but from deep within the crowd, the mass of people surging up against him and then breaking away in what was either a facsimile of a human ocean or intended to suggest something more sexual. Given that every individual who had managed to actually touch the demon soon fell to the ground in moaning ecstasy, my money was on the latter. He too, was shirtless, putting the rippling muscles of the contessa's servants to shame, and his leather pants were tight enough that you could actually see the muscles in his legs shift as he prowled forward.

They also gave way more of a view of his dude parts than I was comfortable with. I had no idea how the dude could even walk with that thing.

"He has changed not at all," murmured Anastasia.

After the incubus, Caine's arrival was almost dull. The gaunt manpire wore his habitual tux, eyes looking sunken and fever bright under the brim of the ridiculous top hat. He marched slowly forward, the clack of his heeled dress shoes a counterpoint to the heavier thump of his polished ebony cane. That cane was carved into the elongated shape of a woman, and topped with a shrunken, heavily fanged skull.

"What's the deal with the walking stick?"

"They say the woman was a lover who dared to cheat upon the Lord of Bones. Caine slew her, took her soul, and imprisoned it within the staff of his cane."

"And the skull?"

"All that remains of her former lover."

"That's just a story though. Right?"

Anastasia shrugged minutely. "It happened before my time, but I have spoken to those who swear it to be true. Certainly, it would explain Caine's personal crusade against the Infected."

"How so?"

"Note the fangs." She nodded to the skull as the manpire took his seat with a dusty creak of bones. "Werejaguar, I believe, though Caine's antipathy has grown to encompass all of the many species of Infected. There are no packs or prides left in southern Europe, and the few solitary individuals who remain head for safer territory whenever the Lord of Bones takes the field."

That got a frown out of me. Some of my friends and former clients were werewolves, after all.

Last to enter was the goddess Minerva, and judging by the reactions of those around me, she appeared in pyrotechnic glory, at the center seat of the dais. I didn't see either the manifestation or the fireworks. Instead, I watched the tired, shabbily dressed older woman, slowly walk from door to platform, unnoticed by those around her. She paused at the base of the dais, and slowly turned. Eyes gray as sun-faded cement met mine, then narrowed.

I unfocused my eyes and let them drift past her, pretending I was every bit as blind as everyone else.

The Goddess of Wisdom wasn't fooled. Thin and colorless lips twisted in disgust, then she turned and shuffled onward. A minute or so later, she reached her seat, and the room erupted in awed amazement at her sudden, no doubt impressive, manifestation. She waved a wrinkled hand and Denarius, now stationed behind the translator on the left side of the dais, took that as his cue to speak.

"Mr. Smith, you may begin your opening remarks."

"Just like that? I assumed there would be some sort of long, painfully involved ceremony to start things off." The more elaborate the better, given Ana's request that I drag the trial out for as long as possible.

"You assumed incorrectly."

Well, shit. I shuffled the papers before me and tried to order my thoughts.

"Is he going to speak or is this some new type of defense I've never heard of?" asked Dog. "Because I have to tell you, I don't think it's going well so far."

"If you wish to make any opening remarks, Mr. Smith, now is the time," repeated Denarius. "Otherwise, the Council will proceed directly to a vote on the matter."

"No... I'm ready. Totally." Heart in my throat and dude parts swinging uncomfortably free, I rose to address the Council.

"Since coming to Rome, people have been telling me that this isn't a human trial... that the laws of my kind don't apply. I get that.

Our two species are different, so it's no shock that our cultures and legal systems are too. But there are a few tenets that I think are, or at least should be, universal. Justice means punishing the guilty instead of the innocent, and Lady Dumenyova *is* innocent. That is the unavoidable truth. The evidence gathered against her is circumstantial, and over the course of the next few days—"

Someone in the audience coughed. Up on the dais, I saw Dog mouth the word *days* with a look of abject horror.

"—I will disprove each piece of evidence in turn." I looked from the Council to the crowd and back. "An innocent defendant and an absence of hard proof. In a human court, that's all that would be required for a verdict of not guilty. But those same people have been telling me that innocence alone might not be enough, that some or all of you could choose to ignore reality in pursuit of your own vendettas. Please, don't let it come to that. Show those gathered here that the law matters. That the People remain superior to my own species in all things, even justice."

As far as opening speeches go, it wasn't going to win any awards. As far as I could tell, it hadn't even fazed the Council. But maybe it had planted some seeds of doubt in the crowd at least. If evidence wasn't enough to sway a vote or two, I hoped public opinion would be.

All I had to do now was not screw the rest of the trial up.

ooo

"For my next witness, I'd like to call upon—"

"Investigator Smith," sighed Contessa d'Verde, pinching the bridge of her unseen nose as if to fight off a headache, "exactly how many witnesses do you intend to call?"

I checked my notes. "Just four more."

"Unholy shit! *Days* might have been an understatement," groaned Dog.

"You have called eleven witnesses to the stand, Investigator Smith, and to this point, the only information you have produced from them is that King Tomasso was, and I quote, 'distracted for some months prior to his death.' Will witness number twelve have something new to tell us, or is this all an exercise in wasting our time?"

"I believe it is important to convey Tomasso's mood in the weeks leading up to his death."

"I can't imagine why it matters," said the contessa, "but you may consider that information successfully conveyed. Now, assuming that there is a point to any of this, can we *please* move on?"

"Absolutely." I glanced back down at my sheet of paper. "For my *final* witness, I call upon the Lady Manassa."

That sent a buzz through both crowd and Council. Aasha sent me another glare over her mother's shoulder, but Divya herself showed no expression.

"Lady Manassa," said Minerva, in the first words she'd uttered all day, "you are not bound to testify. You may refuse if you wish to do so."

"I am willing to speak, Exalted One, though I am uncertain as to what purpose it will serve." She turned to me. "Ask your questions, investigator."

To think… only a day ago, I'd been John. Letting Lucia go talk to the naga had been incredibly stupid. I just hoped like hell it wasn't about to come back to haunt us.

"Thank you." I took a long sip of water to soothe a throat that was already raw and aching from way too much talking. "Can you tell the Council what your relationship was with King Tomasso at the time of his death?"

"At the time of his death?" She frowned slightly. "I would say we had very little relationship at all."

"And why is that?"

"Several months before he was killed, Tomasso ended our relationship."

Dog rocked forward in his chair. "Wait… what? You and little Tommy were bumping uglies?"

Something very like disgust flickered over the naga's face. "That is not how I would phrase it, but we were involved romantically for some time, as I believe many of our fellow Council members were already aware."

The contessa, Caine, and the Horned God all nodded.

"How the hells did *I* not know this?" complained Dog.

"It might have something to do with centuries of heavy drug usage," mused the incubus to his right.

"Good point." Dog subsided back in his chair and waved a stubby hand. "Carry on."

I nodded. "I am sorry to bring up bad memories, but prior to your breakup, had you noticed the signs of distraction that King Tomasso's human servants have testified to?"

"Yes." Divya's poker face was almost as good as Ana's, but I thought I detected a note of confusion in her beautiful, if alien, features. "At the time, I believed it was because he was beginning to pull away from me."

"And now?"

"Now, I suspect that our breakup may have been a symptom of something else, rather than the cause."

I breathed a sigh of relief. Until that point, I honestly hadn't been sure if she was going to be a hostile witness. Since I had no authority whatsoever to force her to talk, that would have been problematic.

"Thank you," I said, trying to communicate my gratitude with both voice and eyes. "When did you first sense that he was becoming distracted?"

"A month or two before our breakup."

"Which puts it somewhere around five to seven months before his death?"

"Yes."

"I suppose it's my turn to ask," sighed Vigo. "Are you going somewhere with this, monkey?"

"Show some respect, Duke Marte," snapped the contessa. "It cannot be easy for the Lady Manassa to discuss such a painful time."

That was help from an unexpected corner; I gave the hooded woman a nod of gratitude and turned back to Divya. "You and I have already talked about this, but could you tell the rest of the Council what it was that had begun to occupy King Tomasso's time in the past year, even before he became distracted?"

The small line appearing between Lady Manassa's eyebrows and above what should have been her nose suggested the naga had no idea where I was going with this. Still, she answered readily enough. "Tomasso had been looking into the details of his father's reign. I believe he was hoping to gain insight into how to better himself as a king."

"A laudable goal," murmured the Lord of Bones.

"Totally." I agreed. "Whatever his faults, I think King Tomasso was trying to be a stand-up guy. Unfortunately, I am fairly confident that it was that research which got him killed."

That got everyone's attention. Even the Horned God took a momentary break from flirting with half the women (and a quarter of the men) in the audience.

"How so?" asked Dog.

"I can only assume he found something of sufficient import that our exiled former queen felt called upon to have him killed for it," said Vigo.

"Sure, which is why I'm featuring it as a cornerstone of my defense." I rolled my eyes. "Come on, dude."

The duke's avatar rose halfway out of his seat, many tiny wings whirring. "I will say this one final time, monkey. Get to the point."

Thankfully, I was pretty sure the duke killing me mid-trial would be frowned upon, so I was free to reply in kind. "Don't get your carapaces in a bunch. I'm getting there. I just have a few final questions for the Lady Manassa first." I turned back to the naga. "This research King Tomasso was doing… can you recall what it entailed?"

"He spent several hours each day reading through old journals, as well as histories from that time frame," she replied.

"And can you recall what book he was reading, if any, at the time of your unfortunate breakup?"

She shook her head, a small frown on her face. I tried again.

"Is it possible that you would at least recognize it, if it was presented to you?"

This was another pivotal point. In our conversation at the grotto, Lady Manassa hadn't had a lot of information on Tomasso's research. Unless she was actively trying to help my investigation, her answer was going to be no, and I was going to have to figure out some other way to get to where I needed to be.

"I might," she allowed.

I tried not to make my sigh of relief too obvious. I took a quick moment to write a note on my top sheet of paper, making certain that Anastasia could see it, and then reached beneath those papers to withdraw the book Maria Elena had acquired for us.

"And is this the book Tomasso was reading at the time of his unexplained change in behavior, the sudden distance that led to your breakup and ultimately persisted until his death?"

Divya met my eyes from across the room. "It is," she lied.

Holy crap. The nagas were still on our side.

○○○

"And?" demanded Vigo into the sudden silence. "What is in this book you've so carefully identified?"

"I'll get to that too," I told him, carefully *not* enjoying his growl of irritation, "but first I wanted to thank Lady Manassa for her testimony." I offered Divya another completely graceless bow and turned back to the rest of the Council. "Now, with your permission, I'd like to tell you all a story."

"Oh goody," said Dog with a smirk. "I love story time." Something gold and glittering disappeared up the imp's nose, and he rocked back in his chair in a moment of boneless delight.

"Once Upon a Time," I began, sparking more than a few laughs from the crowd, "there was a king. And that king had two children, a boy and a girl."

"I believe we know how this story ends, Investigator Smith," warned Minerva.

"I think you might be surprised," I told the goddess, in another of many moments that could easily have gotten me fed to the Fenris wolf. "Some time after his children had grown to adulthood, the king was killed. His daughter was convicted of the horrible crime, and exiled as punishment, and the son succeeded his father as king."

"Only to be killed when his sister sent her assassin to finish the deed," concluded Vigo. "We are aware."

"That's *a* story, I guess," I said, "but it's not the story I'm telling. Nor is it the story of what *actually* happened. You see, some months before the second king's murder, he reached out to his estranged sister, looking to mend their relationship."

"Now I *know* this is just bullshit," muttered Dog.

"Why on earth would this fictional king seek peace with his father's murderer?" asked the contessa.

"Because," I told her, "he realized she hadn't killed his father after all. Even more importantly, he realized his father's true killer was still at court. In fact, they're in this room right now."

For a moment, my words cast a spell of silence over the entire room. Then, that moment ended, and everyone was yelling at once.

CHAPTER 50

Before I knew it, Lucia was at my side, fingers digging into my arm, and voice harsh in my ear. "What are you doing?"

"I may have gotten carried away," I admitted, for once not worried about eavesdroppers. "Sometimes, I think I should have majored in drama instead of English lit."

"It has at least bought us time, my queen," said Anastasia who, despite her shackles, seemed prepared to defend us both.

"Has it truly? When this chaos is quashed—and it *will* be quashed—the Council will expect my thrall to not only name the true killer but provide proof of their involvement!"

"Wasn't your whole plan to name either Denarius or Divya?" I hissed back. "How is this any different?"

That gave the femmepire queen a moment's pause. When she spoke again, her voice was warmer by at least a degree. "Since when do you *ever* follow my plans?"

That… was a good point.

"Recriminations are pointless," decided Lucia, conveniently ignoring the fact that she'd been recriminating pretty damn hard just a moment before. "What's done is done. Which of the two will you accuse?"

"Not the Lady Manassa, I think," murmured Anastasia. "Not after that testimony."

"I figured you'd catch that."

"Catch what?" demanded Lucia.

"The naga supported Mr. Smith when she had every opportunity to do otherwise."

"Not to mention every *reason* to do so." I eyed the lovely Secundus. "Were you watching the Council during the reveal of the book?"

"As your note requested, yes." She frowned slightly. "Dog was oblivious, and the Horned God wasn't even looking in your direction. The Lord of Bones and Contessa d'Verde seemed surprised, while Minerva, Denarius and Vigo gave away nothing."

I mirrored her frown. So much for my cunning plan to expose the killer by springing Tomasso's missing book on them. "What about during story time?"

"It was much the same, I'm afraid." Anastasia looked apologetic. "They are each elders of their kind, John, and well-versed at hiding their true feelings when they so desire."

"And so, we have nothing," decided Lucia, her expression cool even as emotions rolled across the bond, "save for vague thoughts that the Lady Manassa is on your side. Which is no doubt what the naga wants us to believe. So again, I ask… who will you name as the killer?"

I gave it a moment's thought, and then shrugged. "I'll try to stall. Maybe request a recess so everyone can settle down or something."

"What difference could that possibly make?"

"I don't know, but it couldn't hurt."

Lucia scowled and was about to reply when the entire room fell silent.

Minerva had risen from her chair, face hard. I have no idea what the rest of the room saw or heard, but every eye was fixed upon the goddess.

When she finally spoke, her voice was granite. "There is a time and a place for chaos, but this is not that time, and my domain will never be that place. Control yourselves, or you will be controlled."

That settled the crowd down faster than I would have believed possible. Even the Council returned to their seats, though none of *them* had the grace to look sheepish.

"You have had your fun, investigator," continued Minerva, "but I will hold you directly responsible for any further outbursts."

That sounded ominous. And colossally unfair.

"All I did was tell a true story—"

"My thrall hears and obeys, Exalted One," cut in Lucia.

I frowned, momentarily torn between being angry at Minerva telling me what to do and at Lucia accepting orders on my behalf. Then, the rational part of my brain—small as it was—reminded me that this was the freaking goddess Athena giving out orders. Disobeying her was a good way to end up as wolf chow.

Minerva waited for my nod before returning to her seat.

"So… uhm… where was I?" I finally asked.

"You were somehow trying to prove that the ladies Dumenyova and Borghesi were innocent of not only King Tomasso's murder, but that of King Aurelius as well," the contessa helpfully reminded me.

"*Prove* being the operative word," added Vigo. "I have yet to hear a single word discrediting the accusations against Lady Dumenyova. Nor have you produced even a shred of evidence supporting this new fable of yours."

"Given the riot that erupted before he could even finish speaking, there was hardly time for Mr. Smith to present his proof," said Caine. "Perhaps we should allow him to do so before dismissing his words out of hand."

Considering I didn't *have* a suspect, let alone evidence to implicate that suspect, the Lord of Bones' interjection was less helpful than it might have been. Still, one thing mediation had taught me was how to roll with the punches.

Conversationally, anyway.

"Absolutely. However, Duke Marte has a point. We should first discuss the evidence in Tomasso's murder."

"Hell's fiery asshole," complained Dog, "this is the most incoherent defense ever."

The Horned God rolled his eyes at the grumpy devil and offered an aside to the crowd. "This is why drugs are bad, my sweetlings."

I ignored both incubus and imp. "By the time I'm done, I think you'll all properly understand why I opened with the ten-megaton truth bomb."

"The what?" Even Lady Manassa looked confused.

"Never mind." I checked my notes again—a gesture which was, by this point, more nervous tic than anything. "When seen as a whole, the evidence against Anastasia *is* substantial. But when examined piece by piece, I think you'll see that it doesn't add up. Take the security footage. All it gives is a brief glimpse of a tall woman crossing the road toward Tomasso's townhouse in Rome. There is nothing to say that woman is Lady Dumenyova. There is nothing to say that the individual in question even entered Tomasso's townhouse. It's entirely possible that whoever she was, she was visiting a friend—maybe a relative, or a secret lover—in one of the neighboring townhomes." I took a carefully considered pause. "There's hard proof and then there's circumstantial evidence. This footage doesn't qualify as either."

"And what of the hair found at the murder scene?" asked Vigo.

"What of it?" I shrugged. "Thanks to the suspiciously accelerated timeline for this trial, DNA testing isn't even complete yet, so all we know for sure is that the hair is long, straight, and vaguely similar to Lady Dumenyova's. This is the vampire capitol of Europe, not to mention a city of millions. Finding someone with similar hair—even gorgeous hair like hers—can't have been that hard."

"And I suppose the true killer also found a Stonefist capable of taking on the substance of a stone we have never seen and killing the king in a fashion unique to the infamous Stone Lady?"

I felt Lucia's anger spike at the Lady Manassa's sarcastic words, but that question had been a cleverly disguised lifeline. The naga already knew what I'd found at the Bitter End, and she knew I had a much stronger case against the stone fragments than the hair.

Once again, Divya was helping.

"Not exactly," I replied. "If you take away those fragments, all you have is someone being stabbed in the chest and decapitated. It certainly fits the pattern of some of Lady Dumenyova's more public kills, but as you've pointed out, information on those kills is common knowledge. Frankly, anyone in this room could do the same with the right tools and enough strength." I gave that a moment's thought. "Well, except for Dog."

"You're saying I *couldn't* kill the king, asshole?"

"Not unless you tripped him first. His chest would have been barely in reach, and his neck was way too high."

"Oh." Dog shrugged. "Right. Anyway, I was busy getting—"

"I know. A massage from frisky virgins." I shivered at the renewed mental image.

"What about the stone, Mr. Smith?"

Until that point, Denarius had been silent. In fact, I wasn't sure if he was technically allowed to ask questions given that he didn't have a vote. On the other hand, it was a question I badly wanted to answer.

"Contrary to what the Lady Manassa believes, the stone you found *does* occur naturally in the world. Just not this world. If you showed the fragments to any of your younger generations, I believe they would tell you that it matches the walls of the Bitter End."

"Lord Kala's domain?" Vigo snorted. "So, your defense to this point is that it *might* not be Lady Dumenyova in the video, it *might* not be her hair found at the scene, someone else could *conceivably* have reproduced her killing method, and the stone fragments recovered from the king's body were… what… taken from another realm?"

When he put it that way, my defense did sound kind of iffy. Thank God for camera phones. "That was a sticking point for me too," I admitted. "That's why I went to the Bitter End after visiting the murder scene." I'd technically been fleeing for my life from the Illutu, but that didn't seem worth mentioning. "Just inside the entryway, I found this." I waved my wonderphone in the air.

"A crappy last-generation phone?"

"I beg your pardon?" I choked back my angry retort, reminding myself that the imp was stoned out of his mind and not seeing my wonderphone clearly. "I'm not talking about the phone. I found a wall where fragments had been chipped away. Fragments that were the same size and shape as those found in Tomasso's body."

More or less, anyway.

"Then why are you waving a phone?" Dog wanted to know.

"I would assume he has pictures of the wall in question," said Caine, pulling out his own phone, and rattling off a number in his bone-dry voice. The Lord of Bones' device was a flip phone of the type I hadn't seen in years, but Dog didn't even seem to notice. "By all means, send us your photos."

"I don't have a data plan for Italy. Can you just pass it around?"

"Technology will one day kill us all," muttered Vigo.

"Not if my brothers do it first," shot back Dog.

Denarius came to retrieve my phone, flicking through the photos with a long finger. "The images are dark, but the general shapes appear to match those of the fragments in our possession." He carried the phone to Divya, who took a quick look and passed it on down the chain.

"Fragments that you showed him earlier this week," reasoned Duke Marte. "Who is to say that he did not make these indentations himself after the fact?"

"So, *your* theory is that, after barely escaping from the Illutu with his life, my thrall infiltrated Lord Kala's domain and, using nothing but his own hands, physically chipped away at the wall to retrieve precisely measured fragments, all without attracting the demigod's attention?" Lucia's voice was dripping with scorn.

"It does seem unlikely," said the Lord of Bones. "Poor boy can barely take three steps without falling down."

I frowned. Mockery never featured this prominently in television murder trials. "You don't have to take my word for it." I nodded at my wonderphone, which had just reached Vigo. "If you look at the pictures, you'll see that, as dark as it is, the gold striations are glowing. Lord Borghesi, can you confirm that the same holds true for the fragments in your evidence chamber?"

The Kingmaker's eyes were unreadable as he nodded. "Only two of the recovered pieces have significant striations, but that gold does glow in the darkness."

"And what does this prove?" asked the contessa.

"It proves the stone did not come from Anastasia," I said triumphantly. "She's only taken on that particular form once that I know of, but visibility there was total crap, and a tall, beautiful statue glowing gold would have been pretty hard to miss." I looked from the Council to the woman seated next to me. "If she's cool with it, I'd like to demonstrate that for all of you right now."

The Kingmaker turned to the dais. "While I have no voice in this matter, I believe it would be prudent—"

"Just do it already, vampire," yawned the Horned God.

Denarius waited for the other Council members to nod, and then focused on Anastasia. "When you are ready."

Ana rose to her feet, pushing the chair away from her to keep it from being crushed in the transformation. Her eyes glittered momentarily like copper pennies and then the alabaster-skinned woman was replaced by a statue of glittering obsidian and tightly threaded gold.

Denarius waited a heartbeat after the transformation had completed, and then spread his arms wide. The shadows that perpetually followed the tall manpire billowed out like dark clouds to surround Anastasia. The darkness wasn't absolute—we could still see her silhouette within the nimbus of shadow—but it was clear that, unlike the stone in my pictures, Ana wasn't glowing.

After another long pause, Denarius pulled back his shadows. Anastasia resumed her usual form and I turned back to the Council expectantly.

"It proves nothing," insisted Vigo, "save that Lady Dumenyova can take on that particular form and prevent it from glowing."

"There is also the matter of the signet ring," said the contessa. "Wasn't that found on Lady Dumenyova at the time of her capture?"

"It was," I admitted. "And that's why I told you that story at the beginning. You see, after King Tomasso had reestablished ties with his sister—"

"Something which you have yet to prove occurred," said Vigo.

The duke was seriously getting under my skin. Kind of like the bugs he surrounded himself with. "We have phone records."

"And these records include calls from the king's own phone?"

Lucia's voice in my head fed me the answer. I barely restrained my wince. "From a burner phone."

"So, all you can prove is that someone from Rome called your murderous mistress at some point before the king's death." Vigo's avatar tilted its head in an expression of bemused wonderment… though how he managed to convey that emotion through a bug-built simulacrum was totally beyond me. "I wonder what other explanation there could possibly be for someone in Rome reaching out to her. Oh wait… I know! She was communicating with her own assassin!"

For someone who didn't ever leave his suite, and professed to hate technology, Vigo did an uncanny rendition of my generation's particular blend of disdain and snark. It was disturbing. Maybe *he* had a Twitter account?

"Regardless," I continued, "once the two siblings were speaking again, Tomasso—"

"*King* Tomasso!" snapped the contessa.

"—*King* Tomasso told *Lady* Borghesi that he needed her help in identifying their father's real killer. He sent her his signet ring as proof. When she dispatched Lady Dumenyova to Rome to provide the requested assistance, she sent the ring back with her Secundus. Unfortunately, King Aurelius' true killer found out that King Tomasso was onto them and assassinated him before he could unmask their identity. Lady Dumenyova, being already in the city, was an obvious candidate for framing, particularly given the Council's mistaken beliefs about Aurelius' own murder."

In the words of, well, myself: boom.

Truth bomb delivered.

"That's *it?*" asked Dog.

"I'm sorry?" My rosy glow of satisfaction quickly started to fade.

"When you told us you were going to disprove the evidence gathered against little Lucia's Secundus, I kind of assumed you'd have some proof of your own. All you have are alternate possibilities."

"Indeed," added Vigo, "and we have yet to hear anything even approaching proof regarding Aurelius' murder or this supposed conspirator. You said that the killer was in this room, investigator. So, who is it? Or was that too just a *story?*"

Lucia's voice echoed down our bond. *We cannot afford to appear uncertain, Mr. Smith. Pick a suspect: my uncle or the naga.*

As much as I hated to admit it, she was right. I'd backed myself into a corner, and any hope that the last five hours of debate might convince a councilor would disappear entirely if I didn't identify the killer right there and then. The problem was… while I was now convinced that Divya hadn't done it, I still didn't buy Denarius as the killer either. My mind raced, looking desperately for some way out of the trap I'd dug for myself, but after years of skating by on luck and dubious charm, I suddenly found myself entirely out of options.

I was still paralyzed when something heavy struck the massive doors to the banquet room, but I turned in time to see the second blow blast one of those doors off its hinges and send it ten or more feet through the air. In the hall beyond, I could just barely make out a familiar silhouette, ten or twelve feet high.

It was a clear indicator of how desperate things had become that I was *happy* to see the Illutu.

CHAPTER 51
IN WHICH RETROSPECTIVES WILL HAVE TO WAIT

They say your life flashes before your eyes when you find yourself face-to-face with death. I hadn't found that to be true, really; most of my near-death experiences had featured pain and terror rather than thoughtful introspection. The Illutu's sudden and unexpected appearance was no different—either my life hadn't been exciting enough to prompt an in-depth retrospective, or I just wasn't that sort of dude.

Instead, time seemed to slow, for just a moment. I caught flashes of the room around me, like still frames of reaction: the crowd shrinking away from the blown door, Maria Elena and Sabina bearing identical looks of terror, Juliette's mom reaching into her extremely corporate blazer for an extremely non-corporate dagger, and the unruffled serenity of Ambassador Ti An.

Without even realizing I had moved, I found myself positioned between Ana and the door, protecting the shackled femmepire. Out of the corner of my eye, I saw Lucia mirror my motion.

And then, time resumed its normal progress, and the Illutu knight leapt into the banquet chamber.

No… *leapt* was the wrong word, I realized, as the knight crashed to the floor, trailing blood and viscera along what had previously been a lovely wooden floor. It was more like it had been *thrown.*

Moments later, the monstrous form of the individual who had done the throwing entered the chamber, followed by the Watch who had been guarding that door.

"TWO DAYS!" he roared.

"What the hell is that?" murmured Lucia.

"*That* is your other uncle," I said. "Super-sized and looking none the worse for wear."

None the worse for wear was a bit of an exaggeration. Sergei was in full giant form, leaving a lot of torn and bruised skin on display. His arms, thicker than my not-inconsiderable waist, were heavily caked in layers of gore. I wasn't an expert on giant facial expressions, but he looked pissed. He also looked pretty damn good for a vampire I'd given up for roach food.

"Ambassador Sergei!" demanded Contessa d'Verde. "What is the meaning of this?"

The manpire's pale blue eyes, currently the *only* thing he had in common with his niece—narrowed. He picked up the thoroughly dead Illutu knight by the chitinous scruff of its neck and shook the multi-thousand-pound bug at the Council.

"TWO DAYS!" he roared again. "TWO DAYS I AM SEARCH ROME FOR NEST MOTHER WHO SITS IN SHADOWS LIKE COWARD—"

"He's not talking about you, is he?" I asked Lucia.

"—SENDING BUG SOLDIERS AGAINST VASILY'S MONSTER."

"Never mind. False alarm."

"BUT TRAIL OF BODIES DOES NOT LEAD TO ROME. IT LEADS HERE." Sergei dropped the knight's corpse and folded his arms across his chest, giving both audience and Council a withering glare. "SOMEONE AT PALACE HIRE ILLUTU. THAT ONE WILL TELL ME WHERE NEST MOTHER IS IN HOPES I GRANT THEM MERCY OF THE STEPPES."

"That means he only takes one arm," I explained.

"Do shut up, Mr. Smith," hissed Lucia.

Denarius strode past us to meet Sergei. It was weirdly gratifying having the Kingmaker no longer be the tallest creature in the room. "Ambassador, I share your ire, but you must remember that your ways are not our own. In this kingdom, you must have some measure of proof before making accusations."

"I would say this very trial proves otherwise," said Lucia.

Apparently, only *she* was allowed to make smartass comments.

"When Ilyana leave home for this overwarm dung heap, I do not stop her, Kingmaker. When she die and you and your brother do *nothing*, I accept Vasily's order to not burn city to ground." Sergei was rapidly losing size, returning to his short, vaguely piratical form. "Mistake is now obvious. Allowing enemy who send Illutu to live would also be mistake."

"Damn straight!" I called out encouragingly. "I can't wait to see justice done."

"You are not helping, investigator," growled Denarius.

Sergei glanced past Denarius to the table where Ana, Lucia and I stood. "Smith. You run like rabbit, yes? Is good."

"Glad to see you made it out alive. Sorry about your car."

The manpire shrugged. "Was shit. No big deal."

"Ambassador Sergei," oozed Vigo from behind us, "these charges are undeniably serious, but they do not trump the murder of our king."

I turned back to the Council. Vigo and Minerva were the only two members who had kept their seats through Sergei's entrance—presumably because, in their own ways, neither had anything to fear—but the others were again settling down.

"I think I speak for the Council as a whole," continued Vigo, "in saying that we will be more than happy to entertain your wild and unfounded theories once this trial is over."

The duke was a champion at keeping his eye on the prize. Probably because he had so many damn eyes to look through. Before anyone could second his *let's hurry up and execute these clearly innocent people* plan, I spoke up.

"Actually, I have a suggestion on that front."

"Of course you do," groaned Dog. "How can one human be even more tiresome than an entire room of vampires?"

"Imp," warned Minerva, her voice a steel-bladed whisper, "you were granted a seat on this Council as a courtesy, in deference to your position in the Mad King's court. If you so desire, you may vacate this seat at any time."

The goddess had a truly impressive facility for making even the most innocuous of statements into a clear threat. Once again, I found myself wishing I hadn't pissed her off in our very first meeting.

"I'm good," said the devil. "Just eager for justice and all that."

Minerva turned back to me. "What is your suggestion, investigator?"

"I almost hate to make it, given how smoothly the trial has gone so far, but this *would* be a pretty good time for a general recess. Sergei can present his findings to you all, the rest of us can break for lunch—"

"Lunch was two hours ago, human."

"Exactly my point. We've all been so focused on finding King Tomasso's real killer that none of us thought to take a break to eat."

The Horned God yawned. It was the first time in history that a yawn could be truthfully described as sensual. "He has a point. This session has gone long already as it is."

"We could pass judgement now and call it a day," said Vigo.

"You could," I agreed, "but according to your legal system, I'd then get a shot at convincing the one or two of you who had voted incorrectly, and that… well, that could take all night."

"Or days," muttered Dog.

"Or days," I agreed. "Also—"

It was Vigo's turn to pinch the bridge of his nose… which was all the more bizarre for the fact that his avatar didn't have one. "For the first time in our mutual history," he told Lucia, "I feel the smallest shred of sympathy for you. Murderer and liar though you undoubtedly are, not even you deserved to be saddled with this monkey."

"You were saying, Mr. Smith?" asked Denarius, still positioned between Sergei and the Council.

"I'm pretty sure someone or… multiple someones…" I waved to the crowd that surrounded us and was only now returning to some semblance of normality. "…may have had an accident when the ambassador's guest flew in. Or am I the only one who smells that?"

It is a truth as old as time: when a bus-sized roach crashes the party, someone inevitably ends up pissing themselves.

I was just relieved to discover it wasn't me.

ooo

Lunch was held back in the Tower, which was something of a mixed blessing. Anastasia was freed of her shackles, and therefore able to feed herself without dislocating a shoulder or enrolling in classes as a contortionist, but she was also back under the Tower's influence. When Denarius had re-activated the small anklet that triggered the Tower's magic, I'd watched her shoulders droop and the blood drain slowly from her always pale face.

Our food—some sort of pasta that *still wasn't spaghetti*—helped somewhat, but the mood at the table was undeniably somber. With Sergei's timely, if unexpected, assistance, I'd managed to stall the trial, but the recess we'd been granted was shorter than I'd hoped it would be. By the time we had finished lunch, we were only a few hours away from a vote that seemed destined to go poorly for us.

"I'm sorry," I told both women. "I did what I could, but I'm not a lawyer, and it's really hard to argue a case that we still haven't solved."

"You did your best," decided Lucia, in a rare moment of magnanimity. "However, the time for uncertainty has passed. The Council expects a name, and you must give them one."

"As soon as I do that, the Council will also expect to hear my proof," I reminded her, "which will be hard since we still don't have any."

"I thought you did well, given the time constraints," said Anastasia. "By disproving so much of the evidence against me, you may have helped tilt one of the neutral parties toward a more favorable judgement."

"Maybe I could name Ti An as the suspect," I mused. "Pushing her into a cage match with the Council would buy us some more time."

"Or start a war that leaves my family's ancestral home a smoldering ruin."

"Exactly."

"As desperate plans go, I might actually support it," said Lucia, "were it not for one thing."

"The Goddess Minerva."

The queen nodded at her Secundus. "Ti An is a terror, and quite possibly immortal in her own right, but this is the center of Minerva's dominion. The ambassador will not challenge her here."

"Nor, I think, would Ti An allow herself to so easily be brought to violence," added Anastasia.

I sighed. "Okay, so that's out. Anyone have any better ideas?"

"It is as I already told you, thrall. You must pick a suspect and convince the Council that your accusations have merit."

I could have told her that was freaking impossible, but I didn't see the point. If it hadn't sunk in the first five times, a sixth wasn't going to help.

Lucia turned to Anastasia next. "And in the likely event of Mr. Smith's failure, what do you have in store for us?"

"My queen?"

"Come now, Asya. We have known each other since we were children. You *always* have a fallback plan."

The two femmepires traded smiles that spoke volumes about their long history together and Anastasia nodded. "As I told Mr. Smith, the change in our timetable presents issues. However, if we are unable to win the trial, we must escape, and our only hope of doing so is when we are in transit."

"You mean, when they're funneling us through a hallway populated by like a million guards?"

"Yes, John. If we can break free, I have arranged for a car and a gap in the outer perimeter which would allow us to potentially disappear into Rome itself."

"How did you manage that?" Almost immediately, Lucia waved off her own question. "Your mentor."

"Gaius is doing what he can for us without taking up arms against his other students."

"Leaving us to fight our way free of the entire Crown Watch."

"Not all of them. Despite the Kingmaker's words, there remains a contingent safeguarding the Princess Sabina. In addition, the need to secure our route to and from the courtroom has stretched even the Crown Watch's numbers thin."

Given that our escort had consisted of twelve Watch, and every guard post had consisted of at least four more, we had wildly different definitions of *spread thin*.

"Now that you have seen the path we will take, where do you suggest we try to break free?"

"There is only one viable option, my queen: the Sala dei Re."

That place again. "Why there?"

"It has the longest stretch between intersections, and thus, between guard posts, and would therefore allow us to fight our escort alone. After that, a single guard post would be all that stood between us and our exit from the palace."

"So, twelve guards," said Lucia.

"And your uncle. And then four more Watch at the intersection if we make it that far."

"I see." Lucia chewed on the idea for a little bit. "Can you take them?"

"All of them? No; not even with my arms and legs free. I can account for either the Watch or the Kingmaker, not both."

Sixteen trained killers or an eight-hundred-year-old soldier of shadows. If it had been anyone else proposing this plan, I'd have said they were smoking crack.

Lucia frowned. "Leaving the other for me."

"Your skills are in many ways better suited to single combat, my queen. Can you stop the Kingmaker?"

Lucia paused. I'd never seen her look uncertain before. It was… disconcerting. "I am not certain. Were I at full strength—"

"Wait, why aren't you at full strength?" Hadn't I just fed her my blood like four days ago?

"Because your very existence is a curse," she said acidly.

"As explanations go, that one blows."

"Since waking from my coma last year, I have found accessing my Talent surprisingly difficult, as if the pool is significantly shallower than it should be." Glacial blue eyes cut at me like chilled daggers. "Even as my power replenishes, I can feel a portion of it slipping away, through the channel in my core."

"Our bond."

"Yes."

"But I can barely even summon an icicle. Or a cold breeze. If I have so much of your power…"

"I did not say *you* had the power, Mr. Smith. Despite what your witches have done to us, you remain primarily human."

"Meaning?"

"It is as we discussed, John," interjected Anastasia. "Even with access to my queen's power, you lack the physiology of the People."

"You are a teacup," agreed Lucia, "attempting to hold a small lake. What power you cannot contain spills out and is lost." Her laugh was sharp and bitter. "Your gain represents a fraction of what I lose."

Well, shit.

Lucia turned back to Anastasia. "I will do what can be done."

"That is all any of us can do." Ana's own smile was a cool reflection of the queen's. "It is madness and desperation at this point anyway." She turned to me. "The state of your bond does give us one decided advantage, however."

"What's that?" Lucia and I spoke at the same time, traded glares, and then waited for Ana's reply.

"Instead of one person capable of channeling winter, we have two."

"What Mr. Smith channels is not winter, Secundus," scoffed Lucia. "Say instead, a brisk morning's frost."

"Even so, if he can freeze the links of my shackles, I will be able to break free."

"Uhm…" I began.

"Bah. I can do so far better than he."

"Yes, but of the two of you, only you have any chance against your uncle."

Lucia started to reply, frowned, and then conceded the point. "Very well. Mr. Smith will free you so that you can battle the Watch, and I will move immediately to face down my uncle."

"With luck, it may not come to that," said Ana, though her words lacked their usual confidence. "But if it does, we will at least have a fighting chance."

"There's one problem," I said. "I haven't been able to use Lucia's Talent."

"You drew upon it at the airport, and then again when facing down the guards below," Lucia pointed out.

"Yeah, but that was before…"

"Before?"

I winced. "Before Minerva."

○○○

Lucia was, as predicted, seriously pissed.

"She is a goddess, you mouth-breathing, unwashed, mutant breed of monkey offal! And not just a goddess, but *the* goddess of this city. And not just the goddess of this city, but one of the *six* votes that will decide our fate! And you treated her like a servant, and enraged her in the process, costing us not only her vote, but also your limited utility in our contingency plan?" She turned to Anastasia, blue eyes blazing. "Did you know of this, Lady Dumenyova?"

Anastasia shrugged. "I knew that Mr. Smith had angered Minerva, my queen, though I assumed he had already told you so. I was obviously unaware that she had taken his powers."

"Then how can you be so calm?"

"If anger could change things, I would consider being angry. As it is, I prefer to focus instead on our survival."

"We need four votes, Asya," Lucia said heavily. "Four of six. Of those six, we know that Caine and the Horned God will vote for us, and that Duke Marte and Contessa d'Verde will vote against. Dog is a wild card, but we *cannot win the trial* if Minerva votes against us."

"She still might vote our way," I pointed out weakly. "A goddess of wisdom should be able to put aside her personal feelings and vote based on the evidence."

"You have met three deities, and yet you do not know them at all." Lucia sighed again and turned back to Anastasia. "We will almost certainly need to pursue your escape plan. If my thrall cannot access my Talent, I will need to free you of your shackles."

"And Denarius?"

"I don't know." Lucia shrugged. "We will simply have to hope my uncle is slow to react."

Anastasia turned to me. "What of Ms. Zhukova? Would she be willing to assist us?"

I touched the ring still hanging around my neck. "If she could, I am pretty sure she would… but I haven't seen her since Rome. I think she's recovering from whatever it was that Minerva did to her."

"Perhaps in the future, you will think twice before angering a major deity," muttered Lucia.

"I'll be happy if I even get the opportunity," I said.

"What of the ragamuffin you mentioned?"

"The Rag Lady?" I shook my head. "I think that was a one-time deal. A favor for a favor."

"So we are back to our original plan," mused Anastasia, "hoping that Queen Lucia can free me from my shackles before Denarius intervenes."

"Actually, I might be able to help with that. I don't have Lucia's Talent anymore, but I still have mine."

"How does your gift aid us, Mr. Smith?"

"What? Oh… no, I didn't mean my Jedi-mind-trick protection. I meant my ability to annoy your family."

"A distraction, John?"

"Yeah." I met Anastasia's eyes and it was my turn to shrug. "It's not much, but it might give Lucia the time she needs."

"And put you within arm's reach of the Kingmaker as soon as he realizes what we are doing."

"Once you're both free, I'm pretty sure he'll focus on the bigger threats." I hoped so, anyway. I had no interest in discovering what it felt like to be stabbed by a blade forged from shadow.

"It might work," said Lucia, "and gods know, *might* is the best we can expect if we should lose the trial. However, if Lady Dumenyova is going to battle her way past a dozen Watch…" She eyed her Secundus. "How long has it been since you fed?"

"Not since leaving San Diego, my queen."

"After which, you spent days in prison and then additional days in this Tower where your own power has been sapped." Lucia sighed. "This will not do."

The corner of Anastasia's mouth twisted in the smallest smile I'd seen yet. "The circumstances are admittedly not ideal."

"Indeed, yet we should take what few steps we can to improve them." Lucia waved a golden hand dismissively. "You have my permission to feed from Mr. Smith."

"I beg your pardon?" I don't know who spoke first, Ana or I, as our words blurred into a single question.

"Twelve guards at one time is a stretch, even for you, Asya, to say nothing of the subsequent four. It will be impossible if you are weakened. You need blood if we are to survive this escape plan. I could request that a donor be sent to us here, but my uncle would no doubt question why it was suddenly necessary, and I would prefer not to give the Kingmaker advanced warning of our plans."

"Yet Mr. Smith is your bonded thrall."

I… really didn't like hearing Ana say that, but she was right. The queen had blown up at Juliette for drinking from me, and that had been in a desperate effort to save the entire House.

Lucia shook her head. "It is not so great a concession on my part. Should I indeed grant you both my blessing, I could hardly expect you to refrain from feeding upon him."

Anastasia looked to me, the concern in her depthless jade eyes almost masking an unmistakable hunger. "John?"

"I'm willing if you are," I told her.

"Without the bond to override your own gift, it is likely that there will be pain," she warned.

"If I could bear having Juliette feed on me twice, I can certainly help the woman I love fight our way out of the vampire capitol." I grinned. "God knows, I won't be any use in the actual fight."

"Very well." Ana rose and extended a hand. "Shall we retire to the bedroom then?"

I'd never thought hearing *that* particular phrase from the auburn-haired femmepire would be anything but a dream come true. Sometimes, reality kind of sucked. Nevertheless, I took her hand, and let her pull me to my feet.

As we passed through the bathroom and into the suite's small bedroom, I heard Lucia's voice, raised in sudden anger.

"Wait. Lady Middleton fed on you *twice?!?*"

ooo

Anastasia had me lie down on my back, my head propped up on a pillow. She then took my hand in hers and straightened my arm.

"Shouldn't you be taking blood from my neck instead?" There was a complicated set of rules and regulations regarding what location a vampire drank from.

Ana shook her head. "I am too old for dominance games. Especially now, and especially with you. You will heal faster from a bite at the wrist."

"Oh." I extended my arm again. "Okay then."

"Try to stay calm," she murmured, raising my arm to her lips.

I braced myself for a bite, but Anastasia simply trailed her soft lips across the tender skin of my wrist. Her other hand came up to stroke my cheek, and I felt myself relax into the touch of the woman I loved.

I'd only been bitten by three vampires in my life. Juliette's bite had hurt like hell. Zorana's had been worse, but that was probably because she'd been torturing me at the time. Lucia's bite, by contrast, was the closest thing to sex I'd had in years.

The vampires believed it was the bond that made the difference, but that hypothesis was unproven. I found myself desperately hoping— for more reasons than just the pain—that Ana's bite would mirror her queen's.

The first flash of agony as needle sharp fangs sliced into my flesh dashed those hopes for good.

ooo

Pain has a way of making even a second tick by far more slowly than it should, even as pleasure does just the opposite, but I was pretty sure Ana took significantly less blood than Lucia had on our drive from the airport. Mere moments after the agony began, it lessened to a dull throb, and Anastasia was wrapping a bandage around my wrist.

I blinked up at her. "That wasn't enough blood, was it?"

She finished tying the bandage, her face set in the expressionless mask I was slowly learning to decipher. "It should be sufficient."

"Take more." I fumbled at the bandage with my free hand, but she caught my fingers and squeezed, her other hand reaching up again to brush away the tears from my cheeks.

"If I thought it would make a difference, I would, Mr. Smith," she said gently, "but you have already given enough. If I fall, it will be because of the odds we face, not a lack of blood in my veins." In the dim light of the bedroom, her smile was a sad shadow of its usual glory. "I am sorry for the pain."

"I'm sorry that I'm Lucia's thrall, and not yours."

"And I am sorry that I cannot continue to pretend that I am unable to hear you both," came the queen's voice from the other room, "but time grows short."

I met Ana's gaze, sighed, and let the femmepire pull me to my feet by my uninjured wrist. For a moment, she leaned into me, one strong arm around my waist. I buried my face in the silk of her hair and breathed in the scent of her.

All too soon, the moment was over. I let her go when she pulled away, and we made our way back through the bathroom to Lucia.

○○○

Lucia looked like hell… for a vampire, anyway. She was gorgeous, draped in her usual exquisitely tailored clothing, and wearing more rings than the Mandarin, but her usually golden face was pale and drawn, her eyes tight and pinched.

Given what she'd just played third wheel to, it occurred to me that she might be feeling a moment of genuine remorse.

"My queen," said Anastasia, "are you ill?"

Or she had food poisoning, which was even more terrifying. Anything that could give Lucia indigestion would tear its way right out of my abdomen like the creature from *Alien.*

"It is nothing, Secundus," said Lucia, "though should you have the opportunity to feed upon Mr. Smith in the future, I will endeavor to be as far away as possible."

I gave her my patented blank look of utter confusion, but Ana pieced it together. "Your bond."

"Yes. It seems emotions and thoughts are not the only things that now flow both ways." Pale blue eyes flicked my way. "If it does come to battle, thrall, remove yourself from harm's way at all costs. I cannot afford to be distracted by your pain."

It admittedly took a while, but I finally grasped what the hell she was talking about. "You felt Ana bite me?"

Lucia straightened back to her full, if unimpressive, height. "It is of little matter. As I said, our time is short." She nodded to the table. "Eat something more to regain your strength, investigator. I will not have you fainting in court."

She didn't have to tell me twice. I was over at the table, picking through our leftovers before she'd even finished the sentence. I paused though, fresh bread roll halfway to my lips.

"About that… why are we going back to the courtroom at all? Why don't we bust out on our way there, instead of on the way back?"

"If we should escape now," Lucia reminded me, "we will be fugitives forever, with the full might of the European kingdom devoted to hunting us down." Lucia scowled. "It is preferable to death, but an innocent verdict is more preferable still."

I looked down at my roll and sighed. "Yeah, I'd prefer that too, especially since my whole life is back in San Diego. But…"

"But?" prompted Anastasia.

"I don't see any way we can win this case." Like many truths, this one hurt to say out loud. "We're going to lose. And we don't know what will happen when they find you guilty. They might take Lucia and me straight to the dungeon while they bring you back here. They might even just put us face-down on those crappy high school woodshop stools and take our heads right there in the courtroom."

"Surely not the latter," murmured Lucia. "It would be a waste of good spectacle to kill us so quickly. For the rest, however… your point does have merit. Regrettably." She turned to Anastasia. "Will Gaius be ready if we attempt our escape early?"

"I believe so, my queen. My mentor is nothing if not efficient." Ana's face was conflicted when she turned to me. "Are you certain, John? You have friends and family that you would never be able to see again."

"I know." Kayla and Darlene. Mike and my parents. Juliette. It hurt just to imagine it. "But so do you. What would happen to Teresa and Gustavo?"

"I have made provisions for their care." She paused, her voice momentarily uncertain. "I… took the liberty of doing the same for your parents."

If I lived to be a thousand, I would never deserve this woman. And that made me realize I'd misspoken earlier; *some* of my life was back in San Diego, yeah, but the rest of it was right here, my blood still fresh on her lips.

"Thank you." Words were a poor medium for emotions, but judging by the warm glow in Ana's eyes, she'd gotten at least some of the message.

"We are in agreement then?" asked Lucia.

"We are," confirmed Anastasia.

"Totally." I finished off one roll and took another for the road. "Let's go kick some ass."

A desperate fight against overwhelming odds. A future on the run from implacable enemies. A life isolated from my friends and family. As plans went, this one wasn't awesome. On the other hand, it meant I wouldn't have to stand up in court again wearing skinny pants and no underwear.

So, it all kind of balanced out in the end.

CHAPTER 52

At the base of the Tower, Denarius repeated the laborious process from the morning. Once Anastasia was both shackled in iron and freed from the Tower's spell, he paused and turned to me.

"Investigator."

"Yeah?" The first wild thought that flashed through my head was that the manpire had somehow discovered our escape plans, and that I had an imminent date with a sharp, bladed piece of shadow. Only my incredibly sluggish reaction time kept me from trying to run.

"You have done an admirable job in mounting your defense and raising doubt where previously none existed. For what little it is worth, had I a vote, I might be inclined to once again vote for leniency."

"Hopefully, the rest of the Council feels the same way."

Denarius paused, then visibly altered his reply. "Should they not, I promise you that I will continue to look into the matter after you are gone."

"No doubt that will make our corpses feel ever so much better, Uncle," said Lucia sweetly.

I managed not to roll my eyes at the queen, but it was close. Even if she was right. "I'd prefer to be alive to see justice done, myself, but Sabina should know who her father's true killer was. If I can't give her that, maybe you can."

The Kingmaker's nod was the closest thing to a bow I'd gotten from him yet. Hopefully, Denarius would remember all this after we'd escaped the palace and would devote some of his attention to finding the real killer instead of hunting us down.

"Speaking of justice," added Lucia, "shouldn't you be taking us to the courtroom now?"

"Of course." Denarius turned to the Watch at the Tower door and waved a hand.

This morning, the hall had been thick with guards. This afternoon, there were even more of them.

"I thought you said you'd already deployed the entire Crown Watch?" I asked, feeling the bottom fall out of my stomach. "Where the hell did the rest of these people come from?"

"If the Illutu are truly in the palace, as Ambassador Sergei suggests," said Denarius, "our previous security measures were insufficient. A single guard post could be overwhelmed by a knight or two in an instant. Instead, I have cut the number of posts by half, reinforcing the remaining posts with some of the now-available Watch, while the rest…"

"Are coming with us."

"Indeed. Where an escort of twelve Watch might only give the Illutu pause, an escort of twenty-four should ensure safe passage to the courtroom."

"In Aurelius' day, the Watch would have been used to *hunt down* the Illutu," growled Lucia, "but then *he* knew the value of a strong offense."

Denarius nodded. "That he did, and you can rest assured that, once you are safely ensconced in the courtroom with the Council, the Watch will be doing just that. For this moment, other priorities must take precedence."

I looked from the femmepire queen operating at half-power to the auburn-haired love of my life, freshly fed yet still bound in shackles, to the elder manpire and the twenty-plus Watch that had now arranged themselves around us.

Escape had just gone from difficult to impossible.

As if reaching the same conclusion, Lucia glanced in my direction, and I heard her voice, sharp like splinters of ice, echoing across the bond.

"Win this trial for us, thrall."

ooo

The courtroom was, if anything, more heavily packed than it had been before lunch. Apparently, Sergei's interruption had only added to the sense of spectacle. The manpire was now seated at the front of the crowd with his fellow ambassadors and Princess Sabina, unaware that his hunt had doomed our chances of escape. He raised a battered aluminum flask in my direction in salute.

This time, the Council was already present. As we reached our stools, Minerva rose to her feet.

"I have long believed in taking a light hand in matters of this world, but there are limits to even my patience and forbearance. I will brook no further distractions or interruptions from any of you. Is that clear?"

I wasn't sure who she was talking to, but I nodded and mumbled my agreement with the rest of the crowd. The last thing I needed to do was piss the goddess off even more.

Sergei, I noted, took another swig, and said nothing.

Minerva returned to her seat with a satisfied air. For the hundredth time, I wondered what everyone else was seeing when they looked at the drably attired goddess. Juliette's mom had described Minerva as seven-feet-tall and draped in robes of solid gold, but… did she have wings too? A halo? Fire or feathers for hair? When she stood up, was it to the accompaniment of fireworks, unseen angelic choirs, or the sweetest of electric guitar riffs?

My gift had saved my life on too many occasions to count, but it had its drawbacks.

"Where were we?" asked Dog. The imp had his short legs fully extended and spread wide, thick arms crossed behind his head as he leaned back in his chair. The teenager who'd pushed his wheelbarrow that morning now stood behind him, feeding him what looked distressingly like live minnows.

I climbed back off the stool. "I had just finished disproving the ultimately circumstantial evidence gathered against Lady Dumenyova. With that accomplished, maybe we can work on determining who the real killer was."

Vigo's gaze shifted to my bandaged wrist. "Perhaps lunch and blood loss have clouded your mind, human. I heard very little from you that could be considered more than, at best, an alternate explanation for the evidence we do have."

"I showed you pictures from the Bitter End."

"You did. And if your association with Lord Kala was less widely known, perhaps we would even take those pictures as proof of something other than the demigod offering his assistance."

"When this trial began," added the contessa, a few curls of fiery red hair escaping from under her hood, "you told this Council that you stood ready to reveal King Tomasso's true killer. Now is the time for you to disclose that information, investigator, along with whatever proof you have gathered."

"And that proof had damn well better not take the form of a dozen more mumbling witnesses," grumbled Dog.

"I was planning on working my way up to that part," I hedged.

"Consider your work accomplished," said Vigo, with a sneer I could hear if not see, "and give us the name of your intended patsy."

Well… this had snowballed quickly. I could feel a few hundred pairs of eyes focused on me. As Lucia had told me, the time for uncertainty was over. I needed to name a suspect and figure out some way to survive the consequences.

The problem was, I still didn't know who to name.

As Tomasso's ex, the Lady Manassa had a reasonably good motive for killing Tomasso and the means to do so, but what motive was there for her to kill Aurelius, a century prior? I'd had a hard time believing that she was our killer, even before she'd gone above and beyond on my behalf in the morning trial.

To Lucia's mind, that left only Denarius… and the Kingmaker certainly had the means of killing both his brother and his nephew. What he lacked was a motive. And why would the real killer have bothered to offer me even limited moral support the way Denarius so recently had?

Lucia was right; those two *were* the closest things to suspects we had, but something told me that was due more to my failings as an investigator than to any guilt on their respective parts.

"Investigator, we are waiting…"

My heart told me the Lady Manassa could not be involved. My head told me to accuse Denarius. And not just the voice in my head that belonged to Lucia, but the portion of my brain that was mine and mine alone. It might at least buy us a little bit of breathing room, might even provide another chance for Anastasia to read the room and see if the real killer reacted.

But I'd never been all that great at cold-blooded rationality, and I couldn't bring myself to accuse someone I believed was innocent.

"I'm still working on identifying the real killer," I said instead. "With the Council's permission, I'd like a few days to follow up on the leads I've accrued so far."

"You have nothing?" As Divya spoke, the snake coiled about her arm raised its head and hissed.

"I have pieces. With enough time, I'm pretty sure I can—"

"Tomasso's body has begun its decomposition," said Minerva. "By the laws of the king's own People, the trial must occur here and now."

"But maybe—"

"If the investigator has nothing more to add," said Vigo, "I call for an immediate ruling."

"Seconded," agreed Dog, accepting another wriggling fish from his attendant. "Finally."

"You may be seated, Mr. Smith," said Denarius, his deep voice empty of emotion.

I dropped back onto my stool, Lucia's pale blue death stare a mere echo of the recriminations reaching me through our bond.

○○○

Yet again, the lack of ceremony surprised me. As soon as the Council had agreed to issue their judgement, Vigo's avatar was out of its seat and speaking.

"A century ago, Lucia Borghesi murdered her father, yet we chose leniency and exiled her instead of executing her as the crime demanded. Last week, that decision came back to haunt us. The evidence in King Tomasso's death is undeniable, yet her investigator— a thrall who has as much to lose with a guilty verdict as the woman herself—wants us to believe in some elaborate conspiracy instead. I see no conspiracy. I see only a creature who has always wanted more than she could have, sending her handmaiden to murder indiscriminately in pursuit of her own ambitions. I vote guilty."

Big shock there. I shuffled the papers about on the table in front of me, forcibly restraining the urge to flip Duke Marte the bird.

Next to rise was Contessa d'Verde, tall and shapely in green. "Unlike the esteemed Duke Marte, I am an individual of few words. Investigator Smith wishes us to believe that both kings' deaths were the work of some shadowy conspirator, but he has failed to deliver any proof of this fact, let alone the name of the mastermind involved. I will not begrudge him his desire to desperately grasp at straws, but the time for doing so is over. I vote guilty."

Those were the two guilty verdicts we'd expected, so I didn't really sweat either vote. In the end, with Caine and the Horned God voting for us, the swing votes would reside with Dog and Minerva.

The Lord of Bones was the next to stand, cane dangling loosely from one skeletal hand. His voice was even dryer than usual as he let his sunken gaze drift across the crowd. "My fellow councilors are, as ever, swayed by emotion, chief among them envy and hatred. This is not the time for emotion, for impassioned speeches, or for heated blood. This is a time for logic and reason. If Lucia had the presence of mind to send her Secundus to kill the king, why did she then risk her own life to come provide a defense? One action shows calculation, the other foolish sentiment. Pair that discrepancy with Mr. Smith's work in discrediting the evidence the Kingmaker has been able to muster, and I say too little of this adds up. I vote innocent."

Dog didn't bother rising. "Tomasso was a dumbass."

Both the contessa and the Lady Manassa were on their feet in an instant, but Dog talked over their objections.

"Lucia is hotter than a firecracker in your shorts, but she's a dumbass too. How is it that I can be stoned out of my skull and still be less of a moron than this kingdom's last two rulers?"

"Imp," grated Minerva, "what is your vote?"

"Oh, right. Not guilty." Dog flashed Lucia a wild, fish-filled smile. "How do ya like me now, sweet cheeks?"

And just like that, the vote was tied two to two. I didn't know why Dog had voted the way he did, and I didn't really care. All that mattered is that he had given us a chance.

The last of our allies rose to his feet, giving the audience another look at his finely sculpted abs and the small tree he'd somehow stuffed down his pants.

"I believe I know young Lucia better than anyone on this dais today, in both a literal and biblical sense. I have watched her blossom from child to woman, navigating hardship along the way with remarkable deftness. There are few mortals I admire and enjoy more." The incubus lazily shifted his gaze from Lucia to me. "But there is a debt owed for the Hound's fall. I vote guilty."

On the other side of Anastasia, Lucia went still, the bond reverberating with a sense of shock that swiftly gave way to icy rage.

"And there we have it," declared Vigo. "Three guilty votes out of a possible six makes a majority unattainable for the defense." Eyes constructed from tiny carapaces blinked obscenely in Lucia's direction. "We will finally see justice served."

"The trial is not over yet, Duke Marte."

"Is it not, Caine? All that remains is simply a matter of tedious procedure."

Unlike Lucia, I wasn't so shocked by the Horned God's betrayal that I missed the opening Caine had given us.

"As I understand it, once all of the votes are announced, I'm supposed to get a chance to change your minds."

"As I said, simply a matter of tedious procedure, human. Why not count the farce as over and done with?"

Denarius stirred. "Because the law requires otherwise, Vigo."

"Give it a rest, Kingmaker. This time, not even you can help your niece evade punishment for her misdeeds."

"I serve the law." Denarius was on his feet now as well, his great height putting his own head at the same level as the councilor's despite the lack of a dais beneath him. "The law *will* be followed."

As the two manpires glared at one another, the Lady Manassa rose to her feet.

"Lady Manassa, you have something to say?" asked Minerva.

"Yes." Divya's voice was clear and cold, the snake about her arm holding perfectly still. "I believe Duke Marte is operating under a singular misconception."

"And what would that be?"

"That there will be only six votes cast today."

Minerva paused. "You have maintained your neutrality from the day you first joined this Council, lady. Are we to understand that you now choose to involve yourself in the political process?"

"As a sitting member of the Council, it is my right." Divya looked to Vigo and Denarius. "Gentlemen?"

Duke Marte's avatar offered a courtly bow that his real body could never have managed. "By all means, lady. Speak as you wish."

"Thank you." Divya turned toward us, her gaze touching briefly on Lucia before coming to rest on me. "As the human investigator has made public, King Tomasso and I were lovers. All dreams must end, even that one, yet I honor the memory of the man who wore the crown. He was young, saddled with a role he never anticipated, and struggling with the responsibilities of his position, but he never shirked his duty. Tomasso was a caring father and a terrible painter, and I will miss him dearly."

The naga turned back to the council. "I have watched many kings die. Few deserved to be avenged. Even fewer deserved true justice. My Tomasso deserves both, and I will spend every moment of every day watching his murderer slowly die. I will treasure each twitch and involuntary spasm of agony as little more than the just reward that killer is due. Yet I do not believe Lady Dumenyova murdered King Tomasso. I will reserve my vengeance for the one truly responsible. I vote not guilty."

She returned to her chair, ignoring the comforting hand her daughter placed on her shoulder.

"The count is three votes a piece," intoned Denarius, "with one left to be counted. Exalted One?"

Minerva was silent for a long time. "As ancient as the Lady Manassa is, I am older. As much as the Lord of Bones has seen, I have seen more. I have witnessed the end of gods, of my own family, at the hands of those with a burning need for destruction. Wisdom is neither passion nor bloodless logic. It is the ability to analyze and to empathize, and yet make decisions untainted by either extreme."

In her own way, I was finding Minerva just as unintelligible as Bill, but it at least *sounded* like we had a chance.

"Two kings have reigned since I gave leave for the court to move to my city," continued the goddess, "and both kings now lie dead. Two murders, and the same vampire accused of each. Either Lucia Borghesi is the victim of a byzantine plot that would do ancient Rome proud, or she is a murderer of family who had the unmitigated gall to return to the scene of her crime."

"Your judgement, Exalted One?" asked Vigo carefully.

Minerva shook her head. "Wisdom is also knowing when to speak and when to remain silent. I remove myself from this vote."

This time, she opted not to use the door. The wall behind her trembled, as if it were something living, and then split wide to reveal the ruined skyline of Olympus, broken buildings dwarfed by the silent, shackled Fenris Wolf. The goddess turned without a word and stepped through the yawning portal. Moments later, the wall was whole again.

Three votes to three votes, with a single abstention, in a trial where the tie went to the accuser.

We had lost.

○○○

I was still in hurried and hushed discussions with Lucia and Anastasia when I was called upon to speak again. I met two pairs of eyes—one frigid enough to make Antarctica seem balmy, the other cool and green like polished jade—and rose to my feet. Once again, the crowd quieted around us.

"Before I begin, I'd like to thank those of you who were willing to put aside your prejudices or emotions to consider the facts." I nodded to the Lady Manassa, Dog, and the Lord of Bones. "While I've been given a chance to convince your fellow Council members to change their votes, your votes are what make this more than empty procedure."

Lucia had suggested that part, after reminding me that *everyone* had a chance to change their votes, and we didn't want to lose the three we'd already gotten. Unfortunately, neither she nor Anastasia had provided much advice on how to get that necessary fourth vote.

I turned to the contessa first, stepping around our shoddily crafted table to approach the dais.

"Contessa d'Verde, you said you were a woman of few words, but I hope you'll permit me some of my own." I waited for her nod, and then continued. "In a lot of ways, you were right to dismiss my earlier arguments. I *haven't* identified King Tomasso's true killer yet. What's more, it's entirely conceivable that the similarities in the events surrounding both kings' murders are purely coincidental, and that this conspiracy I have outlined is little more than the product of my imagination."

"This is even worse than his opening statement," said Dog.

I ignored the imp. "All of that may be true. But I've had less than a week to investigate the king's murder, and in that time, I *have* disproven the evidence pointing as Lady Dumenyova. You were right to doubt a conspiracy that I am currently unable to substantiate. Shouldn't that same doubt apply to Lady Dumenyova's completely unproven role in the king's death?"

Within the cowl of her hood, the contessa's face was every bit as beautiful as I'd expected it to be, though her expression was slightly sour, as if she'd just bitten into something bitter. She shook her head, fiery red curls bouncing with the motion.

"You make a fair point, investigator, but it asks me to ignore all that has come before this moment, what both this woman and her cold-blooded mistress are known to have done, in favor of believing that King Tomasso put aside a century of enmity and invited a known murderess to his city in secret." There was no mercy in the femmepire's gaze. "I will not change my vote for such flimsy explanations."

Well, shit. I nodded, doing my best to pretend that she hadn't been my first and best hope at getting out of this mess alive, and turned to Duke Marte. Before I could even speak, the insect avatar was shaking its head.

"As amusing as your convoluted and ineffectual attempts at persuasion might be, I will not change my mind, monkey. Save your breath for the gallows."

I frowned. "Gallows?"

"Dear gods, do they teach you Americans nothing in this day and age? A gallows is—"

"I know what a gallows is," I interrupted, "but I thought we were being decapitated, not hanged."

"*They* will be decapitated," he informed me. "As a mere human, you will swing. With any luck, your fat monkey neck will refrain from snapping, allowing us the pleasure of watching you strangle."

"My fat monkey neck will be—" My words trailed off as I realized I once again didn't have a comeback. "Like you're one to talk," I finally managed.

Vigo gave that retort the attention it deserved, his avatar opening its chitinous and multi-limbed mouth in a theatrical yawn.

And just like that, there was only one. I walked past Vigo and Dog to stand before the Horned God. The incubus watched me come with a smug grin, rock-hard, insanely sculpted abs glistening with what was probably a combination of gross demony sweat and abyssal pheromones. At least the demon's betrayal had cut through some of Lucia's lust; the last thing I wanted to do was address him with the queen's libido running amok in my brain. This was hard enough with the dude's oversized crotch resting basically at eye level.

"Unlike the good duke," he told me, crimson eyes sparkling, "I am giddy with anticipation of your bumbling attempts at persuasion. Where would you like to begin, little investigator?"

I shrugged. "I could go back over the information I've already laid out. I could remind you that Lady Dumenyova is more than a *known murderess*; she is an assassin of legendary repute, and therefore unlikely to both leave behind evidence of her own involvement and be caught unawares by Lord Borghesi's men. But you already know all of that. What's more, you've made it pretty clear that you don't care either way."

"I'm shocked by your baseless assertion," he proclaimed, his voice mocking. "A murder has been committed. Someone must be punished!"

I rolled my eyes and lowered my voice—for all the good that it would do in a chamber more than half full of vampires. "You said it yourself: this isn't about King Tomasso. This is about the Hound of Tartarus."

"Yes. It is." There was no sparkle to those crimson eyes now. "Unthinking brute though he is, there must be consequences for those who take up arms against my kind."

I thought about explaining that the Hound had been used as a pawn of Nepenthe's coven, and that by banishing him back to Tartarus, I'd been doing the dude a solid, but something told me the Horned God already knew the circumstances of his fellow demon's summoning and didn't particularly care.

"If he was the aggrieved party, then shouldn't he be the one to mete out punishment?" *Aggrieved party?* Jesus. One trial and I was already talking like a lawyer. "As you also said, he'll make it back to this world eventually."

"He will, but that could take decades," said the incubus, "and think how far the tale of your actions might spread in that time. It would not do to allow you to serve as inspiration to others."

Unless there was some secret website chronicling my adventures—and even with the existence of *Vita Unica*, that seemed unlikely—I didn't see myself ever being an inspiration for anyone, but saying so seemed equally unlikely to convince the demon. I hid a wince and switched gears yet again. If plans A and B were a bust, it was time for Plan C.

Unfortunately, Plan C kind of sucked.

"So, you need to make an example of me."

"Precisely." His needle-sharp teeth gleamed, and I suppressed an involuntary shudder. Either size really *did* matter, or Lucia had truly bizarre tastes in sexual partners.

"Why don't we work out a deal then?"

"Oh, this is even better than I had hoped. What sort of deal did you have in mind, human?"

"Change your vote," I said. "Let Lady Dumenyova and Lady Borghesi walk free."

The demon sighed. "I spoke too soon. How predictable and dull. Tell me, human, what would I get out of this fool's deal if all of you go free?"

"I didn't say we would all walk away. I said they would." I swallowed past the lump in my throat. "As the Hound's one-time killer, I would submit myself to you for punishment."

"John—" began Anastasia, her rich voice strained.

"All I need do is stay silent, and you die anyway," argued the demon.

"True, but there's nothing particularly memorable about a hanging, is there? Hangings happen all the time." I assumed. "When's the last time a human kicked a demon's ass?"

The Horned God lost his smile. "And your point?"

"If you want to make sure nobody follows in my footsteps, my death has to be an event. When someone thinks about striking back at your kind, their first thought should be *'Oh, hells no! Remember what they did to that Smith guy?'*"

"Hell is *my* domain, idiot," said Dog, "not his."

I kept my eyes fixed on the incubus. For the first time, he seemed truly contemplative.

"You present a surprisingly compelling argument," he finally admitted, "and one that I might accept were it not for two things. First, that in doing so, I would have permitted you some measure of victory even in your moment of defeat." He shrugged. "That alone is of minor significance, given the breadth of agony I would inflict as a result."

"Then why not—"

"The second thing you fail to realize is that pain comes in many flavors. Of these, physical pain is the least likely to resonate through time and history. Emotional pain? Spiritual pain? These teach lessons to the masses." He nodded past me. "As implausible as it initially seemed, you care deeply for Lady Dumenyova. I want you to watch her die. I want you to witness her execution knowing that she perished because of your failure. That is the sort of agony the world will remember: tread softly against my kind or you will watch all that you love and cherish be destroyed."

The courtroom was so still I could hear my own heart thumping madly away in my chest.

"Please, dude. They don't deserve this."

"This is vengeance for a past misdeed, Mr. Smith, and sometimes, vengeance demands sacrifice."

○○○

I returned to my stool, shoulders slumped in defeat, the incubus' words still resonating in my head. Vengeance. Anastasia was going to die because we had dared defend ourselves against a four-armed demonic monstrosity, because I had used Lucia's Talent to save both our lives. The unfairness of it all made me want to vomit. Or… maybe that was the thought of watching Ana die. Or even the thought of my own death, for that matter, whether it came from hanging or Lucia's execution.

"Are you finished with your counter-argument, Mr. Smith?" asked Denarius, the faintest shred of sympathy audible in his voice.

I found myself looking at the crowd around us. Despite my arguments, despite everything I had done to disprove the accusations against Anastasia, I saw more anger and hate than genuine consideration. Sabina seemed at least moderately conflicted. Deeper in the crowd, well apart from her friend, Maria Elena seemed downright horrified. But the remainder…

I frowned. Standing almost unseen in the crowd's heart was a small figure, wrapped in rags as dark as any Ringwraith's. Those around her seemed unaware of her presence, yet a small space had opened around her nonetheless; it was that space that had caught my eye.

The Rag Lady met my eyes, her own expression impossible to read. When she saw she had my attention, she held up one hand, index and middle finger spread wide.

Was she giving me the peace sign? *Seriously?*

As if she had heard my thoughts—and whatever she was, I wasn't convinced she couldn't—the Rag Lady frowned and pointed those two fingers to her own eyes. After a moment's pause, she then extended the hand, fingers still spread, and pointed to the Council.

"Mr. Smith?" asked Denarius for what was now the third time. "If you have nothing else to say then these proceedings must, by law, come to an end..."

"One second, D," I told him absently, puzzling through the Rag Lady's charades. Two fingers to the eyes meant *I see*, but... see what? With a mental shrug, I turned to the Council and examined them yet again.

I didn't see anything I hadn't seen already; the Lady Manassa, large eyes soft with a sadness that didn't otherwise show in her expression, Aasha behind her, looking suitably uncertain, Contessa d'Verde, tall and shapely in her green robe and gown, Vigo's bug body that bore no resemblance to his normal form, Dog and his retainer, and the Horned God. What was the Rag Lady telling me to look—

Wait.

"Mr. Smith?" asked Ana, her voice soft as a breeze. "What are you looking at?"

"If I'm right... someone who shouldn't be here," I told her, just as softly. I glanced down at the book that had been missing from Tomasso's shelf, one chronicling the years after Aurelius came to power in Rome: the birth of his children and the death—one fast, one slow— of his two concubines. "Lord Borghesi? Could I ask a favor?"

Denarius was at my side before I even saw him move, giving me serious doubts as to whether our escape plan could ever have worked. "What is it, Mr. Smith?"

Mindful of the sharp ears around us, I wrote down my request on a scrap of notepaper and handed it to the elder manpire. A frown nestled easily in Denarius' dark features, but he nodded. "I will see it brought here, though I do not understand your purpose in seeking it."

"If I'm right," I said, repeating myself, "it's the proof I need."

"I will return shortly," said Denarius, stepping into the shadows and disappearing from sight.

"On second thought," decided Dog, "this *is* worth staying up for. Thanks for the entertainment, ugly."

"I live to serve," I told him absently, tabbing through the pages I'd brought to trial until I found Ana's list of vampires, living and dead, whose Talents would have given them the means to kill both kings and incapacitate Anastasia herself.

Halfway down the list, in the dead column, I found the name I'd been looking for.

"As delaying tactics go," said Vigo, his voice heavy with sarcasm, "this one will be short-lived. Perhaps you should have sent Dog here to fetch your meaningless item, rather than someone who can walk through shadows."

"Are you saying I'm slow?" asked Dog.

"I'm saying that even in your wheelbarrow, it would take you an hour to traverse this palace's halls."

Before Dog could reply, Denarius was back.

ooo

Everyone in the room—Lucia and Anastasia included—craned their necks to look at the framed painting Denarius had retrieved. I'd seen that portrait once before, in a small study that Maria Elena and I had stopped in so that I could call Juliette. Aurelius was every bit as intimidating as I remembered, and Lucia and Tomasso every bit as cute yet standoffish, but it was Tomasso's mother that I looked to. A beautiful woman painted unflatteringly, with fire-red hair and a sour expression.

I looked from the painting to the book to the list that held a particular name upon it and turned back to the council.

"Tell me, my lady, how did you escape the Tower, and what happened to the real Contessa d'Verde?"

CHAPTER 53

Lucia's voice was the first to break through the sudden tumult. "Mr. Smith, what are you saying?"

I pointed to the painting, and then to the red-haired contessa. Even given the artistic liberties taken by the painter, the resemblance was unmistakable. "I'm saying Tomasso's mother escaped the Tower, killed Aurelius, pinned it on you, and then killed her own son when he found out she was still alive. And that she's sitting right over there."

Vigo's sigh was accompanied by the whirring of a few hundred wings. "Even on someone I despise, I must admit this level of desperation is not a pretty sight."

I frowned. Vigo wasn't the only Council member looking at me like I'd cracked. "Am I seriously the only one who sees…?"

"What do you see, Mr. Smith?" asked Anastasia, her voice carrying through the room.

I pointed again at the painting. "Her. Up there in the contessa's seat, draped in green."

Anastasia's sharp eyes turned upon the contessa, but she shook her head. "The woman I see has golden hair, skin the color of moonlight, and hazel eyes."

Which was kind of poetic, but also confusing.

"He's gone loony," agreed Dog. "Happens to the best of us. By which I mean the worst."

"Mr. Smith has a gift," said Lucia. "While you are all aware of the way it protects him from compulsion, I tell you now that it similarly shields him from powers that would fog his mind."

"Like illusions, for example," I added helpfully, thinking of the tired old Minerva that nobody saw but me.

"How fortuitous," said the contessa, speaking for the first time. "When all hope is lost and execution has become inevitable, suddenly this human develops the ability to detect the hidden killer who has been sitting before him for days. All the better that it be one of those who dared to vote against he and his mistress."

"Quite," agreed Vigo. "This trial has passed far beyond the boundary of even acceptable farce."

"Has it?" Caine tapped a bony finger against the skull that topped his cane. "It seems to me that we are only now approaching the truth."

The Lady Manassa's voice was quiet, but it cut through the room's noise like a knife. "Is there any way for us to share your vision, Mr. Smith?"

I looked for the Rag Lady, but she was gone, the crowd thick where there had previously been only space. "I… don't think so."

"Mr. Smith's gift is unique," said Anastasia, "yet there are other means by which we might corroborate his assertion."

"And what would you suggest?" asked the Horned God.

The gaze Anastasia turned upon the incubus made Lucia at her most frigid seem almost tropical, but she answered his question, her words full of steel.

"Contessa Adelina Davili d'Verde is a Firestarter. Tomasso's mother, the late Jehane de la Vallee was not. Let the contessa call fire if she wishes to disprove Mr. Smith's claim."

Next to the incubus, Dog shrugged heavy shoulders. "Seems straightforward enough to me."

I watched the fake contessa's eyes dart back and forth and wondered if anyone could see the motion but me. "I am not a trained animal, here to perform for the amusement of the court."

Vigo's avatar frowned. "It is a small matter, Adelina. One flame and we can proceed with the execution."

Denarius said nothing, but that great blade was in his hands and dripping shadow onto the floor. His dark eyes fixed upon the hooded contessa as if his will alone could pierce her mask.

"One flame is more than this creature has in her," said Lucia in sudden triumph, "for as my thrall has told you, this is not Adelina. Jehane de la Vallee, I name you murderer and kin slayer. For your actions, I will see you buried in that Tower of yours, never again to emerge!"

At the mention of the Tower, Jehane stiffened, and she shot to her feet. "Never again, failed queen! You and all who you love will die!" Her body collapsed inward upon itself, dress and cloak falling to the floor in a pile of garments.

"What was that woman's Talent?" hissed Lucia at me.

I held up the list. "Some sort of gaseous form."

Vigo was pawing through the fallen clothing. "She is not here—"

Before he could complete the sentence, his avatar began to crumble. Bugs fell out of the air by the hundreds, dying *en masse*, as a billowing cloud of noxious green surged upward and through the duke's form.

"Poisonous gas," I corrected.

ooo

As the other councilors dove for safety, Denarius' eyes darted from Lucia at our table to a terrified Sabina, only now starting to rise from her seat. The look he sent me was best described as apologetic, and then he was gone, reappearing in front of the princess and taking her to safety.

Even as they flickered away, the poison cloud surged toward us. Lucia was off her stool and running for the door, but Anastasia was a good deal slower, hampered by shackles.

"Do you breathe in stone form?" I asked her.

Without even pausing to answer, she transformed.

"Stay here and safe until Denarius can release you," I told her, racing after Lucia who, in outright defiance of both her short stride and skyscraper-high heels, was already halfway to the door. A quick glance showed the Jehane-cloud pursuing us, leaving nothing but corpses in its wake.

I caught Lucia at the doors, where the press of bodies was slowing everyone down. With difficulty, the queen forced her way through and then spun to face the banquet hall we had just exited. People were still streaming out in a mass of terrified limbs, but behind them, Tomasso's mother was closing in fast.

Lucia raised one hand, and I felt her Talent surge through our bond in a way I wouldn't have been able to even a week earlier. Instantly, the open door was filled with several feet of ice, choking the passageway.

It also entombed everyone who had been passing through the door, not to mention imprisoned the large number of people who had yet to escape the trial, but neither terrible fact stopped the queen from turning to me with a satisfied smirk.

"And that is that."

"I beg your pardon?"

She waved a golden hand. "Trapped as she is, she will soon tire and return to form, and when she does, Lady Dumenyova will end her."

"Lucia, even if her gas *can't* make it through your ice—" And I wasn't sure of that, given that my last science class had been high school physics. "—I highly doubt the whole room is airtight!"

The femmepire frowned, but before she could reply, screams started from down the hall, where a now-familiar cloud of gas was already billowing forth. "It appears you are correct."

"You think?" I raced down the hall away from the poison gas. "Any ideas?"

Lucia paused for just a moment to remove her heels, and then was running easily beside me. "If the contessa had truly been the contessa, ice would have been sufficient."

"If she had been the contessa, then we wouldn't even be in this mess," I argued, already feeling my lungs start to burn when another thought hit me. To save my breath, I sent my next words down the bond. *Actually, I have an idea. Can you get us to the evidence chamber?*

A room with no exits? If you wish to commit suicide, Mr. Smith, we need not run halfway across the palace to do so. Despite her reply, Lucia took the next right, breaking away from the crowd who had somehow not realized that sticking near us was a potentially fatal plan.

We made it three hallways before my legs, still sore and tired from the terrifying flight through Rome, started to turn to rubber. "How much farther?" I gasped.

"Two… maybe three minutes," came the reply. "My family believes in the grandeur of scale."

Trust Lucia Borghesi, in the middle of running for our lives, to have the breath to boast about her family's penchant for excessiveness. I'd have had something appropriately cutting to say, if I hadn't been gasping for air and filled with the growing realization that I had very little chance of outrunning our pursuit the entire way there.

As if to prove my point, Lucia started to pull ahead, heels still held in one hand. I reached deep inside of me for a fresh burst of energy but there was absolutely nothing there.

Then I remembered Ana's words about what the witches had done to me. I reached again, but this time, I reached through the bond.

Ten paces ahead of me now, Lucia stumbled slightly, as if struck. She shook it off a moment later and continued down the corridor, but now I was right behind her, fresh energy pouring through me, bringing strength to my legs and oxygen to my lungs.

As fast as we ran, the fake contessa was almost as swift. We reached the evidence vault with only a few hundred feet to spare, that literal breathing room courtesy of Lucia's penchant for occasionally filling the hall behind us with sheets of ice.

"We are here now, Mr. Smith," growled Lucia, watching as Jehane slowly filtered through the second to last of her barriers. "What was this plan of yours?"

"Inside," I told her. I took hold of the door to the evidence chamber, spun its wheel to an unlocked position and tried to pull. Nothing happened, and I remembered that it had taken two vampires to move it the first time. "Oh crap."

"Out of the way, thrall." Lucia shouldered me aside, wrapped both of her hands around the handle, and *pulled.* The door swung open slowly, inch by agonizing inch, and we ducked inside.

And now we imprison ourselves within? Well-reasoned, thrall.

For once, there was no scorn in her mental voice, but I was already shaking my head. *That would just leave her free to kill other people... or escape.* I motioned to the interior of the evidence room. *Can you segment this room into ice rooms? Leaving a corner near the door free for us?*

If you have not taken too much power from me already, then yes... but for what purpose? That woman has already demonstrated an ability to penetrate my ice. She will do so again and find us.

Not if we have the proper distraction. I was digging through Denarius' evidence boxes. It took longer than I'd hoped, but I found what I was looking for: photos from the crime scene and the autopsy.

I scattered these across the floor, facing the vault door, as Lucia filled the room with ice. As soon as I rejoined her, she created the last barrier that walled away our small nook.

And now?

Jehane enters the room, comes face to face with the grim reality of what she did to her own son, and is hopefully overcome with grief for just long enough that she doesn't notice you melting this wall, I tapped the icy barrier that impeded our closest path to the door, *and us escaping. Then, more ice to slow her down, and we close the door, trapping her in a room that I'm told is completely airtight.*

As plans go, this one hinges on far too many assumptions for my taste. Sweat dampened Lucia's forehead, and her voice came in short gasps. *Such as my ability to continue to summon ice.*

You could try to sweet talk her into letting you live instead.

Lucia's answering mental laugh was short and sharp. *I think not. Yet there is one piece of the plan that remains unclear to me.*

Yes? That meant she was way ahead of me, which seemed unfair given that it had been my plan.

How are we to know when she has entered the evidence room, and moved a sufficient distance from the door?

That was a *really* good question. Hell, for all I knew, clouds of poisonous gas used something other than sight to navigate, which meant the photos I'd spread as distraction might be every bit as useless as the ice maze Lucia had built.

Shit. Well... provided she's in the room and not between us and the door—

We can at least make the attempt. Lucia's mental voice went silent for a moment. When it resumed, it held something approaching humor. *If we are to die now, Mr. Smith, I must tell you truly; you have been a thrall of positively horrific proportions.*

Before I could reply, she dissolved the ice wall that led to the exit.

○○○

Jehane *was* in the room. Even better, the sentient cloud of gas had traveled far deeper than we had. Best of all, it was paused inside one of the icy chambers, hovering over the pictures I had laid down.

Holy shit. My plans *never* worked! Between this and Ana kissing me, it was like I was a whole new John Smith.

As if she'd heard me or—more likely—seen us, the cloud suddenly shifted in our direction, seeping through the barrier between us.

"More ice!" I shouted, running for the door, but Lucia was, for once, already doing the right thing. Two additional walls sprouted in Jehane's path, and then the queen and I were both out in the hall. We turned and, with my somewhat questionable help, the vault door swung shut with a solid boom. I spun the wheel, and waited, hoping that Denarius at least was not the sort to idly boast.

Thirty seconds later, we were still alive, and there was no sign of the poisonous gas. Thirty seconds after that, and the Kingmaker himself was suddenly in the hall beside us.

"A step too slow as ever, Uncle."

"You trapped her in the evidence room?" Denarius nodded slowly. "An airtight room to imprison a woman who can take gaseous form. Ingenious."

"I have my moments," agreed the queen.

"So it would seem."

"Will it hold her?" I asked, ignoring the casual way Lucia had taken credit for my plan.

"Momentarily, yes. A Winddancer from the Giordano house in Milan is being flown to the palace as we speak, at which point, we will be prepared to take Jehane into custody once more. She has much to explain and even more to answer for, not the least of which are the many deaths she caused tonight."

"But Sabina's okay?"

"She is, Mr. Smith." Denarius regarded us both evenly for a long moment. "I left her with Gaius, who had been wandering the exterior grounds for reasons that I cannot fathom."

Lucia's voice was sweet and innocent in a way nobody who knew her would ever believe possible. "Perhaps he simply tired of these stuffy halls?"

Or perhaps he'd been working his end of our escape plan, as promised. Thank God *that* was no longer necessary.

Denarius nodded. "It is possible. You will both be relieved to hear that Lady Dumenyova is also well. So too are my fellow members of the Council, though Duke Marte suffered a brief shock when his avatar was destroyed."

Confirmation of Anastasia's survival made me giddy with sudden relief. Vigo's continued life was considerably less thrilling.

"And what now, Uncle? With the true killer revealed, do you perhaps have something to say to me?"

"There are still many questions that need answering," warned the manpire, "chief among them how this woman escaped the Tower, not to mention killed both my brother and his son."

"The second answer's pretty obvious, given the mess she made of everyone between us and her." The Tower, on the other hand… that was still a mystery. She wouldn't have been able to escape the Tower without removing the anklet, and she couldn't have done that while the Tower inhibited her power.

"True enough." To his credit, Denarius didn't hesitate. He turned to Lucia and bowed. "Lady Borghesi, for the ills you have suffered due to false accusations, I offer this formal apol—"

"Bide a moment," interrupted Lucia. "So grandiose an apology deserves witnesses. And accompaniment. The Council, perhaps?"

I rolled my eyes, took two shaky steps away, and then, as my body finally flushed away its adrenaline, noisily vomited into a nearby flower vase.

"Yes," agreed Denarius, after a moment of pained silence, "a move to the council chambers suddenly seems an excellent idea."

CHAPTER 54

It wasn't as quick as all that, of course. We had to wait for a contingent of Crown Watch to show up to make certain nobody opened the door to the evidence room in our absence. A servant also came by to remove the offending flower vase, much to my embarrassment and the vampires' obvious relief. Eventually, however, Denarius led us back to the Council.

Instead of returning to the makeshift courtroom—which was, at this point, a makeshift morgue and triage center—we proceeded down a different hall until we reached the small waiting room I remembered from our first night in Rome. This time, there was no prolonged wait to test our patience; we passed straight through the double doors into the official Council chamber.

The Council was all present, save for Minerva (and the fake contessa, of course), each member seated in their usual spots. Dog even seemed to be sober this time. Beyond that, the room was empty except for a scattering of Watch and Anastasia, who was—

"Why is my Secundus still in chains?" demanded Lucia.

"Because this matter is not yet resolved." Vigo's new avatar was a clone of the old in appearance but lacked the same easy coordination;

even as he spoke, one half of his fabricated face stayed still. It was almost as disconcerting as his words.

"What do you mean it isn't resolved?" I frowned. "Did you *not* see me unmask the killer like forty minutes ago? The killer you've been sitting next to in ignorance for the past what… hundred years?"

"If not more," confirmed Lucia. "That woman reportedly died more than one hundred and forty years ago. It seems reasonable to assume she has spent the entirety of that time pretending to be Contessa d'Verde."

"I am well aware of what we all saw," said Vigo smoothly, "but it is one thing to prove that Jehane de la Vallee faked her own death and took the place of one of the Council. It is quite another to prove that she was responsible for King Tomasso's murder."

"Are you kidding me?"

Ana shifted, the motion accompanied by the dull ringing of her shackles. "There is a small matter you are overlooking, Duke Marte."

On the dais, the Lady Manassa nodded suddenly. "Yes, I do believe there is."

"Is it my turn to nod and pretend to know what everyone's talking about?" asked Dog.

"With the contessa removed, and Minerva abstaining," continued Anastasia, "the Council no longer has the votes to convict us."

"Indeed," said Lucia, taking up the thread. "Three votes in favor of Lady Dumenyova's innocence, versus two opposed."

The Horned God shook his head and offered a brilliant smile. "That would be four in favor, actually. With this new information before us, I cannot in good conscience vote to see these innocent and valiant people executed."

"Save your vote, demon," hissed Lucia. "We do not need it."

Which was, of course, why the incubus had changed it in the first place.

"Does anyone else wish to change their vote at this time?" Denarius looked to each Council member, but there were no takers. "So be it. In the matter of King Tomasso's death, this Council finds Lady Dumenyova innocent."

And just like that, we had won.

ooo

Even as Denarius was releasing Anastasia from her shackles, Lucia turned to again address the Council. "With that business taken care of, I believe it is well past time to revisit the matter of my banishment."

"Oh, you do, do you?" asked Dog.

"I did not kill my brother Tomasso and have now proven so to the satisfaction of this Council. With the new information that has come to light, you should now also recognize that I did not kill my father either. *That woman* was responsible for both actions, and for attempting to frame me each time."

"That has not been proven—" began Denarius.

"Nor was my guilt!" Lucia's heels, back on her feet instead of in her hand, clattered loudly as she approached the dais. "With Jehane de la Vallee captured once more, the truth of these events will soon be undeniable. My crown was stripped from me on false pretenses. It is time for that great injustice to be corrected."

I don't know whether it was intuition, familiarity, or the note of triumph blazing across our bond, but something told me that *this* had been Lucia's plan all along. As she'd said back in San Diego, saving Anastasia was but one of her goals.

I couldn't help but be impressed.

The Council, on the other hand, didn't share my admiration.

"Yet again, your ambition outpaces reality, Lady Borghesi," said Vigo. "Upon your banishment, the line of succession fell to your brother. With *his* death, it now falls to the princess Sabina."

"That banishment may very well be lifted," said the Lady Manassa, "should the interrogation of Lady de la Vallee support your innocence. However, I must agree with my fellow Council member. There are no provisions for reinstating a noble to the throne."

"Do not lecture *me* on the rules of succession," said Lucia. "I know the law, but this situation is unprecedented in our history. Surely it is—"

"A matter for the Council to debate," said Denarius. "And we will do so in the days to come."

On the surface, Lucia looked perfectly composed. Regal, even. But beneath that? It seemed she had finally encountered something that pissed her off more than me.

ooo

In the movies, once the last manacle had fallen to the floor, Anastasia would have jumped into my arms to the accompaniment of orchestral music, showering kisses down on me as I swung her about in the air.

Reality had never lived up to my Hollywood fantasies, but when she was finally free, the femmepire caught my attention, and the look in her eyes made all the rest of that stuff utterly superfluous.

"You did it, John."

"*We* did it," I corrected her. "You, me, Maria Elena, the Rag Lady... even Lucia, I suppose."

"*Queen* Lucia," she corrected gently, "yet the lion's share of this victory is yours."

"The question that I cannot help but ask," added Lucia, joining us as the Council broke up into smaller conversations, "is why you allowed it to go so far?"

"I'm sorry?"

"You met the Council on Monday night. By your own recollection, you saw the painting the subsequent day. Yet it wasn't until the eleventh hour of the trial that you made the connection between the two?"

"Eleventh hour?" The trial hadn't really lasted that long, had it?

"It's an expression, you fool."

"My queen…" As ever, Ana played the peacemaker between us.

"I didn't get a great look at the fake contessa during our initial swearing-in process, because of the hood. But even then…" It was my turn to frown.

"Even then?"

"I could swear that she looked different. Blonde hair instead of red. More like the woman Ana described."

"Are you suggesting that Jehane replaced the contessa only in the past week?"

"I don't think so. It's more like I wasn't seeing as clearly when I first arrived."

"Jet lag, perhaps," sniffed Lucia. "I know how susceptible your species can be to such trifles."

"Maybe." Or maybe it was something else. In my memory, I felt the Rag Lady reaching up to tap my forehead with three fingers. What *had* she done to me? "Anyway, it's just one of a bunch of unanswered questions."

"How Jehane escaped the Tower?" asked Anastasia.

"Or replaced the contessa so easily," added Lucia.

"Sure, although I was thinking more about King Tomasso's murder," I said. "How did she know Anastasia was coming to town? Or that Tomasso had found information that she was still alive and had killed Aurelius? What happened to the guards at Tomasso's townhouse?

How did she take stone chips from Kala's domain without the demigod knowing?"

"And where are the Illutu?" added Anastasia.

"With luck, investigator," said Denarius, coming over to join us, "we will learn those answers and more during the interrogation. For now, however, there is someone else who wishes to speak with you." He stepped aside, exposing the young femmepire in his wake.

"Maria Elena?"

Her eyes—gray today and wide with nervous excitement—darted from Lucia to Anastasia and then back to me, as she dropped into a deep curtsey. Her high-necked dress was also gray, and the first color I'd seen on her that wasn't flattering. "Mr. Smith, Princess Sabina asks for a moment of your time."

ooo

"Any idea what Sabina wants?" I asked, trailing Maria Elena through the halls.

"Gaius just said she wanted to meet with you. I assume it's about the case. Maybe she wants to see what else you found?"

"So, you and she are cool again?"

"We're… working on it. You finding the real murderer will help, I think. Although the fact that it was her long-dead grandmother is just plain weird."

"A lot of things here in Rome are weird. Thank you for helping Anastasia find a copy of the missing book."

"You're welcome." She frowned as we walked. "The stories all describe Lady Dumenyova as some kind of monster, but… she isn't really, is she?"

"No more than the rest of us, and considerably less than most," I said. "She's the best person I've ever met."

"Huh. Anyway, finding the book was a small enough thing, even if it did mean I had to visit the library."

"Your sacrifice is appreciated." I grinned. "Between the book and the painting, you were as big a part of solving this case as anyone."

"I'd feel better about that if I hadn't almost cost you the case too." She scowled. "I cannot *believe* Niccolo told the Kingmaker!"

"We asked him to ignore his duty as a lieutenant of the Crown Watch," I pointed out magnanimously. "I'd feel differently if I was scheduled to swing from a rope, but since everything turned out okay… maybe go easy on him?"

"Not until he grovels mercilessly," she growled.

"Well, obviously."

"Maybe I can put him to work as my personal servant for a day," she mused, her voice suddenly lightening. "Dress him in a bowtie and G-string. Maybe a cute little cape too."

And just like that, I was done with the conversation. And possibly *every* conversation ever. Thankfully, we had reached Sabina's suite.

Maria Elena opened the heavy door, and the two of us stepped into the foyer, even as some small thought nibbled insistently at my brain.

"Sabina? I'm here with John Smith, as requested!"

There was no reply but silence.

"That's weird," said the femmepire, taking me deeper into the suite. "Where the heck did she go?"

"And for that matter, where are her guards?" I added, as my brain finally caught up with the moment. "And the minotaur?"

"All excellent questions," said a bland, almost forgettable voice.

I spun to find Maria Elena in a boneless heap on the ground. Standing above her, looking every bit as unprepossessing as he had on our initial meeting, was Gaius himself.

And then the manpire moved, and I was done for.

CHAPTER 55

IN WHICH HINDSIGHT'S A KILLER

I woke to the sound of low voices and the realization that I was, yet again, a prisoner, arms bound tightly behind me, shoulders already aching from the awkward position. I'd been dumped face down, and my cheek was pressed flat against a cold and rough stone floor. With my legs also bound, it took a solid minute of panicked writhing to get to a sitting position.

It did little to improve my view. Wherever I was, it was dark.

I reached for the knot in my brain that was Lucia, but the incessant pounding in my head made concentration impossible, and the bond kept slipping away. If I was lucky, the femmepire queen had already learned of my capture, and was even now tracking me down.

The dull murmur of voices stopped, and a door to my right swung open just enough to admit a small, nondescript figure. Either the light was improving, or my eyes were finally adjusting. Either way, I recognized Gaius immediately.

"You're the piece I was missing." My voice was dry and hoarse. "The explanation for all the discrepancies I kept running into."

"I suppose I am." Gaius' voice was mild and empty of emotion.

"Whatever Jehane is paying you, it's not enough."

"I beg your pardon?"

"Between the two of you, you've killed two kings, at least one contessa, half a dozen nobles, and I don't even want to guess how many of the Crown Watch. I'm just saying… you'd better be getting an island out of this, dude."

"Trust a human to make it about money."

"Are you saying it's *not?*" I shook my head. "Why the hell are you doing this? Isn't a Secundus supposed to be loyal?"

"I would not expect a creature such as you to understand," said Gaius. "Nor have I brought you here to seek absolution."

That was a bummer, as I'd been totally willing to give fake absolution if it would get me back to Anastasia alive. "Why kidnap me? All you've done is expose your role in this mess. If I were you, I'd be running like hell, not sitting around waiting for the Kingmaker to cut me down."

"The Kingmaker." For the first time, some faint trace of emotion entered the manpire's voice. "I was old when he and his swaggering fool of a brother were first presented to the court of the Mad King. Without my aid, their rebellion would have ended in ignominy and death. I do not fear Denarius Borghesi."

Which either made him a lunatic or a badass.

"So, you helped them overthrow the Mad King and move the court to Rome, only to then turn around and murder Aurelius?"

"As I told you once already, I was gone from Rome when Aurelius died."

"Right. You just freed Jehane from the Tower and then stood aside while she gassed your Primus." I frowned. Unless Aurelius and Denarius were both morons, Gaius must have been loyal at some point. So, what had changed? What would convince a decorated Secundus to turn against his sworn liege?

Unbidden, my mind turned to Anastasia, and realization set in.

"You love her, don't you? Jehane, I mean."

"From the moment I met her, when she was first summoned to Rome to be Aurelius' consort," said Gaius. "I could not let her waste away in the Tower at the king's whim."

If seven years as a private investigator hadn't already taught me that love sometimes manifested in horrible ways, Xavier's failed coup, Davis' attempted Infection, and this double-regicide would definitely have brought the lesson home.

"So, she kills Aurelius, Lucia gets blamed for it, and the two of you gain a hundred years of worry-free couples time." I puzzled through the timeline. "Except then Tomasso started digging into his father's death."

"Yes."

"And he told you about it?"

"As we have established, I was one of the few who could *not* have been responsible for Aurelius' murder."

I closed my eyes. Poor, unlucky Tomasso. "And you turned around and told Jehane."

"Only after the king had opted to join forces with his exiled sister. If we needed to leave Rome, I wanted her prepared." He shrugged, his voice flat once more. "She decided instead to reveal her identity to her son."

"She met him at his flat in Rome?" That explained the image of the tall woman on Denarius' security footage.

"She did. In the end, his reaction was… not what she had hoped for. She had little choice but to kill him."

"Keep telling yourself that," I muttered. "And the missing guards?"

"I disposed of them when I arrived to clean up her mess and plant evidence at the scene. With Lady Dumenyova in the city, an anonymous call was all that was necessary to point the Watch in her direction."

"You tossed your former pupil to the wolves."

"It was her decision to return to Rome, not mine."

My head was starting to clear, but my grasp on the bond remained tenuous. Lucia didn't feel any closer.

"And then the Watch caught Anastasia napping. That wasn't a spell, was it? It was Jehane again."

"Hers is a marvelous Talent," agreed Gaius mildly. "When it first manifested, she was able to manage only the poisonous gas, but it is amazing what she is able to do now with an understanding of modern chemistry."

"So, she puts Lady Dumenyova to sleep and the Watch take Ana into custody. Why leave her alive at all?" Before the manpire could respond, I had the answer. "Because you and Jehane needed to make sure all loose ends were firmly taken care of. You wanted Lucia to come to her death in Rome."

"Well reasoned. I am starting to believe your reputation."

"Your frame job was pretty good," I offered generously.

"It was entirely sloppy, but I was unprepared for Tomasso's death, and time was tight." Gaius shrugged. "I hoped it would still prove sufficient."

"Where did you get the hair you planted at the scene?"

"From a woman who no longer needed it."

So, someone out there did have hair almost as beautiful as Anastasia's. Or had until Gaius killed her. This dude was a monster. "DNA testing would have proven it wasn't Ana's."

"Once we moved the trial forward, that became irrelevant."

"That was Jehane too?" It didn't take a leap to get from a gas that killed whatever it touched or could put even vampires to sleep to a gas that caused physical putrefaction.

"As I said, a truly marvelous Talent."

I frowned again. "So, the only real question left is how you got the stone fragments out of The Bitter End. And why Jehane's illusion worked even on the People. And how she faked her death in the first place."

"You do not know?" Gaius's smile held no warmth. "Perhaps your reputation was overblown after all."

"This is your chance to gloat about it."

"I think not. Should we both survive this situation, your continued ignorance will be a source of great pleasure for me." Even now, the manpire sounded like he was reading the phone book. I found myself wondering what Jehane could have seen in him.

Then I remembered that she, too, was a nutcase, and stopped trying to make sense of her life choices.

"Maybe you're not afraid of Denarius, but I think you're overestimating your chances of fighting off the entire Council. Not to mention the Crown Watch."

"Such a conflict would be difficult to survive," he said agreeably, "which is why I do not plan to fight at all."

"You're surrendering?"

"I am proposing an exchange of hostages."

I couldn't quite hold back my laugh. "If you think the Council—or even Lucia—cares enough about me to agree…"

"You?" Gaius waved a hand dismissively. "Of course not." He nodded to the far corner, where a shape huddled in the shadows. "However, the Council will care a great deal about what happens to Princess Sabina."

Well, shit.

ooo

It wasn't until its screen had flickered to life that I realized Gaius had pulled out his phone. He took a few careful shots of me—I sucked in my gut, in case these would be the last images anyone ever saw of me—and then several more of Princess Sabina. I was still blinking away the aftereffects of the flash when I heard the distinctive chime of an email being sent.

"And now they know you are both in my care."

"You're pretty good with technology for an old dude."

"Unlike the Council, I spend much of my time abroad. I cannot afford to stagnate." His phone rang, and he held up one finger. "You will pardon me while I answer this."

I was damn certain I wasn't going to pardon him for anything… ever… but it wasn't like I could stop him from answering his phone. I just nodded.

"Denarius. Prompt as always. As you can see, they are unharmed. They will remain so, provided you meet my demands."

I couldn't hear the Kingmaker's reply, but Gaius' answering laugh was short and patently false. "I am the only one in position to make demands. Or would you like to have yet another family member die on your watch? Will they call you Queenslayer now?" The false humor dropped from his voice like it had never been present at all. "Lucia will bring Lady de la Vallee to the king's resting place. If I see anyone but those two, Mr. Smith and the princess will both die. When Jehane arrives, I will leave Mr. Smith in Lucia's care. Sabina, however, will remain my hostage until we have safely left Rome. Once we are free of the city, I will send the princess back to you, unharmed." His voice sharpened. "You have thirty minutes. Spend them wisely."

"They're not idiots," I told him once he had tucked his phone away. "They know you're not really going to let us go."

"And why would I not?" Gaius seemed honestly perplexed. "Once I have what I want, leaving you alive costs me nothing."

"That's your big plan? The two of you on the run for the next few centuries?"

"It was a life your mistress was considering not so long ago." Gaius shrugged. "The Council's reach is not what it was once, and there are forces at work of which they remain wholly ignorant. We will find safety."

The small manpire turned to the nearby door and knocked. A short time later, the door swung open, and someone new stepped into the room. He could have almost passed for one of the Watch, but after my near-death experiences at the airport and in Rome, I recognized the plain, generic features of an Illutu drone. The creature stood at attention, unmoving even as the door swung shut again.

"Go and wait for Lucia Borghesi to arrive," Gaius instructed. "If she and Jehane de la Vallee come alone, escort them back here. Otherwise, die bravely."

The Illutu nodded silently and stepped past the traitorous Secundus to open a door in the far wall, revealing a narrow tunnel lit by flickering torches.

"You're hiding us in the catacombs?"

"That I am, Mr. Smith. Pray to whatever gods you worship that your stay here is not permanent."

ooo

Shortly after the drone's departure, Gaius disappeared back into the other room, and the low murmur of conversation started again.

"Who do you think he's talking to?" I still couldn't see Sabina very clearly, but her voice and irritated tone were instantly recognizable.

"Can't you tell?" I murmured back at a far lower volume.

"Would I have asked if I could? Until I quench the Thirst, I'm barely better than human, remember?"

I rolled my eyes, and prayed that Summer, at least, wouldn't grow up to be a brat... before remembering that Summer wasn't in San

Diego anymore, and I would likely never know what or who she grew up to be.

"Given the drone that walked out of here five minutes ago, I'm guessing voice number two belongs to the Illutu nest mother."

"That ugly pirate ambassador was right? They're *in* the palace?"

"Until they've fulfilled their contract, anyway."

"Gross." Beneath the tone of bored teenage nonchalance, there was a rising tide of audible panic. "I'm going to die surrounded by bugs."

"It could be worse."

"My father is dead, my grandmother was responsible, and my trainer was complicit in everything. How could this be worse?"

"We could be naked."

Sabina's laugh was at least half sob. "Is that supposed to make me feel better?"

I shrugged. It made *me* feel better. "You've got to take your victories where you can."

"Fitting words for our tombstones."

"It's all going to work out," I told her. "Trust in your great-uncle. And your aunt, I suppose."

"You suppose?"

"I don't think she likes you very much, to be honest. But Denarius is definitely not going to let you die."

"You're not worried at all?"

"This is far from the worst situation I've blundered into," I admitted, "and somehow, I keep surviving. Besides, whatever Gaius says, whatever precautions he's taken, I know one thing for a fact."

"What's that?"

"Anastasia is coming."

I sure as hell hoped so anyway. I'd recovered enough to reach out to Lucia, but our mental conversation had been terse and unhelpful, consisting primarily of me feeding her what little information I had on our surroundings, and her telling me both that the catacombs made locating me difficult and that my shrill voice in her brain made everything else damn near impossible.

"You truly do care for her, just like 'Lena said."

"Yeah."

"Thrall to my aunt and in love with her Secundus." This time, the princess' laugh lacked that sharp edge of hysteria. "I see what you mean about blundering into bad situations." Her voice quieted. "What do we do?"

"Just keep your head down and try not to piss Gaius off."

"Excellent advice," said Gaius, coming back through the door. The manpire now had a long blade on one hip and a dagger on the other. "And given none too soon. Lucia is even now on her way."

I frowned. How the hell did he know that? "Do you have cameras and monitors set up back there or something?"

"Why do you think each cadre of Illutu is referred to as a hive, Mr. Smith?"

"Because they're roaches?" I shrugged. "I'd have gone with motel, myself, but I guess I can see why they went with a different option."

"Motel?"

"You know... roach motel?" In the ensuing silence, it quickly became clear that Gaius did *not* know. So much for not stagnating. My jokes were wasted on the very, very, very old.

"They are called a hive, because they are a single consciousness. What one sees, all see."

"So, you know Lucia is coming because..."

"Because the drone has already met her at the king's rest and verified that she and Jehane are alone. Even now, it is escorting them here."

I hid a frown. That didn't sound like the Lucia I knew at all. But when the hallway door swung inward, there she was.

CHAPTER 56

Lucia walked into the room like she still owned it, followed by the hooded figure that was Jehane de la Vallee. Last of all was the drone, its face impassive and expressionless. Somehow, knowing that it shared one brain with its mother, fellow drones, and the hulking knights Sergei had been hunting down, just made it that much creepier.

"I am here, traitor," announced Lucia. "Against my better judgement and with very little left in the way of patience."

Okay; *that* sounded like the Lucia I knew.

"I give you this one chance," she continued, "in honor of what you once meant to Lady Dumenyova. Hand over my thrall and my niece, and I will give you Lady de la Vallee." She nodded to the woman behind her, lovely face twisting in contempt.

"That was not the deal," said Gaius.

"It is the only bargain you will have from me today, murderer."

"And a poor bargain at that, child."

Lucia drew herself up to her full, unimpressive height. "You refuse, then?"

"I do." Gaius' smile was as colorless as his voice. "And would have done so, even had the woman behind you indeed been Lady de la Vallee, and not the pupil I trained for almost three centuries."

After a momentary pause, the figure in green lowered her hood, confirming Gaius' suspicions. Anastasia's face was hard, her jade eyes cold like the precious stone they usually resembled only in color. She swept aside her cloak to reveal the weapon at her side.

I blinked. The light still wasn't great in our room, but that didn't look like a sword. In fact, it kind of looked like the Lord of Bones' creepy cane.

"Three centuries of friendship turned to ash because of your actions, Gaius. What happened to your speeches on duty? On responsibility?"

"A man's greatest responsibility is to himself."

"Yet betrayal is a sword that cuts both victim and wielder."

"Poetry, Anastasia? I would not expect such pretty words from a woman who once waded through gore so thick her legs were stained from the knees down."

Anastasia's eyes flashed, but her voice was firm. "Death is rarely pretty, and never clean, even when couched in the euphemisms you favor."

"We burned your clothing, child, because the blood and smell would never come out. The blood of the House you *extinguished* on your mistress' orders, and you think to reproach *me?*"

"I am not the girl you knew, Gaius. Time teaches restraint if not wisdom. Whatever my past, I held true to my oaths. A pity you cannot say the same."

"A pity that you—" Gaius stopped suddenly, and his voice turned wry. "Perhaps time teaches wisdom as well as restraint. No student of mine would have thought to fool me with a hood and cloak.

Nor would any student of mine bother with debate when action was required."

I blinked. Were the shadows by Sabina getting darker?

"And yet here I am," insisted Anastasia, drawing all eyes back to her as she stepped past Lucia, voice ringing. "Here to demand answers from one I thought of as a father. You owe me that much at least!"

The shadows around Sabina solidified into the shape of an absurdly tall manpire in deepest black, bending over the princess to gather her into his arms.

"I owe you nothing," said Gaius, "and this distraction—"

I frowned. Denarius wasn't bending down; he was falling forward. It wasn't until he hit the floor with an audible thud that I saw the blade in his back.

"—will not avail you," finished Gaius, stepping out from behind the Kingmaker's fallen form.

Which was impossible… given that he was *also* standing in the middle of the room, facing down Lucia and Anastasia.

"What the hell…?"

The second Gaius was identical in every way to the first, save for the fact that his sword was unsheathed and sticking out of the Kingmaker's back. He offered me a swift, colorless smile, and then shivered once and stepped to the side, leaving behind a vague image of himself which solidified into a third Gaius. This one's blades were sheathed, but the smile on its face matched that of the other manpires.

"They said you didn't have a Talent," I complained.

"They were wrong." Each individual word came from a different mouth. "And you will pay the cost of their mistake."

ooo

A lot of things happened at once, while I sat there, unable to do anything but watch. As Lucia spun to dispose of the drone that had escorted them in, the hallway door swung open, disgorging a veritable sea of black-clad Watch. The inner door didn't so much open as blow outward. Seven drones charged at the incoming Watch, pushing them back into the hallway. As the melee was joined, I heard more than saw the bus-sized Illutu knights charging our Watch reinforcements from neighboring halls.

Anastasia stepped forward to meet the first Gaius, and a visibly wounded Denarius surged to his feet—blade still sticking from his back like some sort of badly placed tail—to attack the second. The smaller man was faster, perfectly balanced, and impossibly precise, but with his sword still stuck in the Kingmaker's back, he had only a dagger to defend himself with. The great shadow blade that came into Denarius' hand gave the taller man the advantage in size and reach.

But the third Gaius… he stepped right past the dueling manpires, closing in on the defenseless form of Princess Sabina.

"This is your fault, Borghesi," he called over one shoulder. "Her death is upon your heads."

"Gaius!" I yelled.

"Bide a moment, human. I will deal with you soon enough."

"Think for a second, you idiot!" Past Gaius, past even Sabina, I saw something that gave me the first stirrings of hope, a head of curly dark hair and two eyes as black as pitch. I met those unblinking eyes from across the room and redirected them to the bound princess lying nearby, praying that my notoriously weak nonverbal communication skills would for once be enough. "Sabina is the only blood Jehane has left. Do you think she'll want you back after you kill her granddaughter?"

Even in the midst of pitched battle, Gaius took a moment to consider my question. Then his sword was out of its sheath and whipping toward the undefended princess like some sort of sharp-fanged adder. "I believe she will."

That lightning-swift sword plunged through Sabina's body to strike the stone wall beyond, its blade still curiously free of blood. The princess looked down at her own unharmed body in shock, and then over at the White Lady who had grasped her shoulder.

"Get her out of here, V!"

The ghost met my eyes again and nodded reluctantly. She and the princess phased into the floor.

"It is over, Gaius," called Lucia, voice rising above the din of battle. "Your leverage has fled, and with it all hope. End this madness and I will see to it that your cell at least neighbors that of my stepmother."

"Soon, you will all be dead, the Crown Watch savaged beyond repair," replied the third Gaius, turning away from the space the princess had so recently inhabited to join his dagger-wielding clone against Denarius. "I will walk the palace without fear and free Jehane myself."

To that point, the Kingmaker had been winning. When the other Gaius joined the fray, however, the tides of battle didn't so much turn as completely invert. Denarius brought his great sword about to deflect both of the newcomer's strikes, but the dagger-wielding Gaius darted in to bury his weapon in the tall manpire's hamstring. When he ducked back to avoid the Kingmaker's return swing, he left the dagger behind, but pulled his sword free from the elder Borghesi's back. Suddenly, Denarius faced two swords instead of just one.

Valentina's head poked up through the floor a few feet to my right, turning until she caught sight of me. She reached out to me with one spectral hand, but I stopped her, nodding again to the battle occurring around us. Lucia had joined Anastasia against the first Gaius, and the two femmepires were holding their own though the battlefield was curiously absent of the queen's usual wintry conjurations. Denarius, on the other hand, was mere moments from death. Once he fell, I had no illusions that even Ana would be able to prevail against three copies of her former mentor. "Can you help them, V?"

Valentina brushed dark strands of hair out of her eyes and gave me a mournful shake of her head. She was, I suddenly realized, little more than a shadow between me and the floor, like a window barely tinted. She looked even weaker than she had in Rome.

"Never mind," I said. "Get me out of here and we'll bring back help." Where we would find that help and how we would fetch it in time were two questions I couldn't answer just then. We'd find a way.

Valentina nodded and reached out again to me. I braced for the cold of her touch and the slightly unpleasant sensation of passing through the veil between our world and the realm of the ghosts.

There was nothing. I looked down to see that Valentina's hand had passed through me without effect and continued to do so as she tried to take hold of my hand. She threw back her head and screamed her wordless cry, but even that was muted, unaccompanied by the slightest gust of spectral wind.

"It's okay." I swallowed past the lump in my throat and dredged up a smile. "You've already done so much. More than enough, really. Can you go back to Sabina, and stay with her until help arrives? Please?"

There was nothing approaching an answering smile in the White Lady's expression, but she nodded just the same. She darted forward to lay an unfelt kiss in the vicinity of my cheek, and then swiftly disappeared.

I was going to have to save myself this time.

ooo

Though it felt like hours had passed, little had changed in the tableau around me. Ana and Lucia were still holding their own—although the queen sported a fresh gash down one golden arm—and Denarius was still desperately trying to stave off his own death.

I didn't know what I could do to help them, but I sure as hell wasn't doing any good trussed up like a pig. I reached toward the bond, trying to remember how it had felt to draw upon Lucia's speed in our desperate flight to the evidence room. This time, instead of speed, I reached for strength, the strength to tear free from the heavy ropes keeping me bound.

A brief rush of power poured into me, and I poured all my energy into pulling my arms apart.

The rope didn't even budge.

A sharp cry to my left, accompanied by searing agony across the bond, reminded me, far too late, of Lucia's words on what happened to her when I pulled on her power.

The queen was down, clutching at the hilt of the dagger that had suddenly sprouted from her stomach. Gaius pivoted smoothly back to face Anastasia, bringing his sword into a guard position, but his former pupil was already blurring forward to smash a stone fist into the manpire's midsection.

It was the sort of strike she'd used to perforate Xavier, but Gaius was in motion before the thrust, and the blow merely clipped his side, knocking him to the floor instead of blasting through his chest. Fury sparked in the femmepire's jade eyes, and then she tossed her cane across the room toward me and transformed fully into the living statue I'd seen only a few times before.

The cane landed no more than three feet away, but tied up as I was, it might as well have been a mile. I started trying to inch my way over.

Across the room, a visibly weakened Denarius lost the grip on his shadow blade, barely blinking as the weapon winked out of existence. The second Gaius—or the third… with all of them now wielding only swords, it was impossible to tell them apart—drove his sword into the Kingmaker's chest with a triumphant shout.

Out of the corner of my eye, I saw the cane tremble, as if touched by an unseen hand, but I couldn't tear my eyes away from the last moments of Denarius Borghesi.

The manpire dropped to his knees, dark face ashen. He reached one long arm up to wrap a hand around the bicep of the man who had killed him. Then, darkness leaked from the Kingmaker's eyes, and he threw himself backward like a diver hurling himself into water. As if to solidify that metaphor, a wave of shadows surged up from the floor to envelop first Denarius, then the sword that had killed him, and then Gaius' hand on that sword. Tendrils of purest black surged toward the suddenly struggling former Secundus.

As fast as those shadow tentacles were, the third Gaius was even faster. His blade flickered out, darting through the shadows to strike at the clasped arms of both Denarius and the other Gaius, slicing through both limbs like they were paper instead of flesh and bone. Suddenly free, if one-armed, the second Gaius threw himself away from the Kingmaker's trap.

Denarius fell into shadow and silence alone.

I dropped my eyes in despair… just in time to see the female figure that formed the shaft of the Lord of Bones' cane sprout dozens of bony legs. That hideous vision scuttled my way like some sort of grotesque centipede.

Leaving his siblings or clones or… whatever the hell they really were… to fend for themselves, the one uninjured Gaius turned toward me with death in his eyes. The cane had disappeared somewhere behind me, but I could feel the fanged skull atop that cane gnawing at my wrists… my wrists and the ropes that bound them.

Any other time, I'd have had some serious complaints to offer on the manner of my rescue. At that moment, the only one that mattered was that it was far too slow. My hands were still securely bound when Gaius reached me. His sword, stained with the golden blood of the Kingmaker, licked out almost lazily.

Once again, my life failed to flash before my eyes. I was left to watch the dripping blade creep ever closer. I had all the time in the world to anticipate its impact, as my mind screamed commands that my body refused to answer.

I had all the time in the world to see the hand and arm of living stone that reached in from the side to knock that sword thrust aside.

And then time resumed its normal course, and Anastasia fell across me like a ton of bricks. She had thrown herself across the room to save me… but sprawled out as she was, she was left defenseless against the Gaius already rising back to his feet, and the two clones still unaccounted for.

No… the *one* still unaccounted for. Behind her, and to the left, the one-armed Gaius reversed his dagger, and brought it down, pommel-first, towards Anastasia.

I'd seen swords glance off of the femmepire's stone form, seen her catch a sword blade in one hand and emerge unscathed, but something told me the hammer-like blow, delivered with all the force of an ancient vampire, would prove far more deadly. The blade plunged down so quickly that I couldn't even see it.

I definitely saw the golden hand that stopped it cold though.

Bloody and angry, Lucia pulled the manpire's arm up and away from Anastasia. Arctic eyes flashed and her hand tightened about Gaius' wrist. Even over the pounding blood in my ears, I could hear the manpire's bone shatter. The queen tugged him to his feet and threw him bodily across the room.

Anastasia had always told me Lucia was stronger than she was… I just hadn't known she meant physically.

Another sharp flare of pain came across the bond and it was Lucia's turn to stagger, her golden face going pale, her eyes wide. The first Gaius, the one Anastasia had initially knocked aside, was behind her, the tip of his own blade sprouting between the queen's breasts, just a few inches above the dagger thrust she had already taken.

Before he could twist the blade, Anastasia was back on her feet, knocking him back, then spinning to keep herself between the two remaining Gaiuses. The third, for what little it gained us, remained where Lucia had tossed him in a boneless heap.

The ropes about my hands finally parted, and I pulled free, trying not to look at the damage the blindly gnawing skull had done to my wrists, as I turned to the ropes at my feet. When they were free, I picked up the horrifying transformer cane and turned to offer Ana whatever help I could.

Neither she nor her opponents had done more than shift their positions in the time it had taken to free myself. Each Gaius clutched a sword, while Anastasia was barehanded. As I watched, one Gaius stepped to the side, but Anastasia rotated smoothly to keep both manpires in her sight and her body between them and us.

I didn't know a lot about fighting, but I recognized a shitty defensive position when I saw one. I looked to the hallway door, but there was no sign of either the Watch or the Illutu that had driven them back.

"You're going to force me to kill you, aren't you, my dear?" Again, each alternating word came from a different mouth, though the Gaius that had fallen to the floor remained silent.

"No." Where the manpire's voice was almost conversational, there was something dark and violent in Anastasia's voice, a fury that stole all the beauty from the voice I had so often described as cheesecake and chocolate.

"You're going to step aside then?"

"No." Anastasia rolled her neck and despite her stone form, I could hear the small bones crack and pop. "I am going to kill you." She spared a glance for the other Gaius, circling warily to her left. "Every last one of you."

ooo

If I lived to be a hundred—and frankly, even living long enough to attend Mike's wedding seemed unlikely—I didn't think I would ever see something so beautiful and terrifying as Anastasia's battle with Gaius.

Despite their differences in height, they were like twisted reflections of one another; the same speed, the same power, the same exhilarating blend of precision, foresight, and skill. The two Gaiuses moved smoothly in tandem to implement attack patterns that would have been impossible for a single individual… or even well-trained partners, but Anastasia shredded those patterns, accepting blows that glanced off of her stone form as she worked to land a blow of her own.

God, she was beautiful.

She was also losing.

"She's dying," I murmured.

"Yes," agreed Lucia, in a voice barely above a whisper.

"Then *do* something!"

"I have been trying." Lucia looked horrific, her face pale, her eyes sunken and bloodshot, her own blood staining her clothes golden. "After this morning, I have nothing left."

"You're still the strongest person in here," I argued.

"A tree is only as strong as its base, Mr. Smith."

"Meaning?" This was a horrible time for Lucia to discover philosophy.

"Meaning I cannot feel my legs. The sword nicked my spine."

Given time and blood, she would heal from even that, but time wasn't something we had. "Then I guess it's my turn."

As last words went, those kind of sucked. I hefted the cane in my hands like a baseball bat and charged at the nearest Gaius.

I didn't see him move. I didn't even feel him hit me, but I found myself back on the floor next to Lucia, something sharp digging into my ribs, each breath a struggle to come by.

Ribs, decided the part of my brain that had—barely—gotten me through high school biology. *Cracked, if not broken.*

The ring of steel against stone continued to fill the chamber. Ana was on her feet but slowing. I couldn't even make it to my knees, but I stretched one hand out toward the three combatants, whispered a silent prayer to whatever deities might be listening, and called for winter.

Nothing happened.

We were all going to die because I'd dared to ask directions from a goddess.

One of the two Gaiuses slid under a blow from Anastasia and drove the pommel of his blade into the back of her knee. There was no blood, but she staggered and almost fell, that leg clearly unable to support her.

A hand, feverishly hot even through my torn shirt, clasped my shoulder, sending waves of agony through that side of my body. Legs or no legs, Lucia had crawled to my side. "Do you trust me, Mr. Smith?"

"Hell no."

"Try, this once. I need you to open yourself to the bond."

"What?!?"

In stone form, Anastasia's eyes were granite, like the rest of her, but I felt the weight of her gaze from across the room.

"Just do it, you mongrel!" hissed Lucia.

I didn't know what the hell she was talking about, but I focused on the knot that was Lucia in my brain. After almost a week of close contact and dream sharing, any mental walls I'd painstakingly erected were long since gone… so what was she asking me to do?

"Hurry, or she dies."

My gaze turned inward, I felt more than saw Ana drop to both knees, her stone form rippling back into pale, vulnerable skin. The two Gaiuses raised their swords in eerie synchronicity.

I stopped looking for walls. I stopped looking for anything at all, and tore at the fabric of the bond itself.

The swords began their downward arc.

The knot in my brain that was Lucia unraveled, and her will rushed through me, into my body, and then back out again through the hand on my shoulder, like we had formed some sort of living circuit.

Lucia's raised hand joined mine.

White light filled the room.

○○○

When I could see again, Lucia and I were sprawled out on an ice-covered floor. The room was filled with crystalline thorn hedges, reaching out from the floor, the walls, and the ceiling, forming a forest of icy constructs.

Gaius—all three of him—hung several feet in the air, his bodies torn and riddled with thorns. Anastasia was sprawled out below him, unconscious, but alive.

"And thus is my family avenged," murmured Lucia, in a voice as bleak and empty as a killing frost.

"It is so like a Borghesi to gloat before the battle's end." I didn't know how he was still alive, or even which one he had been, but one of Gaius' bodies opened bloodshot eyes and turned them on us. Even now, as a makeshift planter for ice thorns, there was something disturbingly nondescript about him.

"Asya and Sabina live and you are dying. You and *that woman* will be buried on separate sides of this city and forgotten. You are undone, Gaius."

A howl of sheer rage, high-pitched, utterly alien, and shattering in its intensity sounded from the interior door, and the manpire somehow found it in himself to smile.

"It would seem the Illutu nest mother disagrees."

Ana was down. Denarius was gone. Lucia and I were barely conscious, and even with the queen flooding freely through my mind, the loop of power that had surged through us was absent.

I really hadn't wanted to die to a bunch of roaches.

The howl swelled even further. I didn't have the strength to imagine what sort of horror the Illutu was birthing. Whatever it was would be ugly and deadly.

The howl faded into silence.

The interior door opened.

That pained smile disappeared from Gaius' battered face.

Sergei limped into the room. In his hands was the head of a plain-featured young woman, nondescript except for bulging, multi-faceted eyes. Insect eyes. The edges of her neck were torn, and a length of spinal column dangled toward the floor.

Sergei's one eye met mine, and the pirate vampire smiled.

"Hunt is over, yes?"

CHAPTER 57

IN WHICH SPAGHETTI IS FINALLY ATTAINED

"Anyway, a bunch of us are heading into the city to celebrate and… hey, are you even listening?"

"What?" My wandering mind snapped back to the present and I gave Maria Elena an apologetic look. "Sorry. The last two days have been…" I frowned as her words caught up to me. "What are you celebrating?"

"Being alive!" The femmepire's eyes, a deep blue that matched her conservative, high-necked dress, lacked their usual sparkle. "A lot of people aren't."

That was putting it mildly. It had been roughly thirty hours since the desperate battle in the catacombs and the casualty count was still rising. Which just made the idea of heading out to party that much more ghoulish.

"I've been to three funerals today," Maria Elena explained tiredly. "Tomorrow there will be even more, and I can't even imagine what the next few weeks will be like. Is it so wrong to take a night to dance and drink and find happiness in our survival?"

"No… not at all," I said. "I think we could all do with some recovery time."

"Great! So, you'll come?"

"Me?"

"Yeah! The Bitter End is closed, for some reason, but Rome has plenty of other places to party, and Niccolo knows the best of them."

"Niccolo? You've forgiven him already?"

"If the Lord of Bones hadn't summoned our dead from the catacombs to help fight off the Illutu…" Maria Elena shivered. "The entire Crown Watch might have perished. Instead, we both survived, the bad guys lost, and Lord Borghesi gave Niccolo the night off. As far as I'm concerned, we're starting fresh."

I was still coming to grips with the discovery that Denarius had survived his bidirectional impaling. It was no wonder that decapitation was so damn popular with the People. While the Kingmaker was a long way from being fully healed, he had wasted little time in reasserting his control over what was left of palace security.

"So, what do you think, John? Want to come with us? Sabina is buying the beer."

"Sabina is sixteen! How is she going to…?" I frowned. "What's the drinking age in Italy, anyway?"

"What's a drinking age?"

My high school years would have been so much easier if I'd been a vampire. To say nothing of my dating life.

"I'm afraid that Mr. Smith has other plans tonight, Ms. Giordano."

I glanced over my shoulder as Anastasia made her way down the hall toward us. "I do?"

A day of rest and large quantities of blood had erased the femmepire's physical wounds, and her jade eyes danced as they met mine. "I suppose that is up to you."

"If you say I do, then I do," I decided. When in doubt, agreeing with the centuries-old assassin I loved seemed like the smart approach. "Did Lucia send you?"

Even before Ana shook her head, I knew the answer to that. In fact, I knew exactly where the former queen was, what she was doing, and who she was talking to. It was damn near impossible *not* to know, now that our bond was wide open instead of relegated to a tiny piece of my brain.

As if in response to my thoughts, I felt Lucia's own mind sharpen and turn toward me. This was going to take a lot of getting used to.

"She will be speaking with the Council tonight," said Anastasia. "In the meantime, you and I have dinner plans."

Maria Elena was watching the entire exchange with poorly disguised delight.

"Dinner?"

"Yes, John." Ana's voice was buttery smooth. "May I suggest you wear your suit?"

When she looked at me like that, saying no was pretty much an impossibility, but this once, I didn't have any choice. "My suit kind of got destroyed yesterday."

"*That* suit most certainly did," she agreed, "but if you check the closet in your suite, I think you will find it multiplied before its death."

Across the open bond, I felt Lucia's smirk.

ooo

I don't know when or how the queen had managed it, but my new suit fit me like it had been made for me. Technically, it probably *had* been made for me, although the idea of some tailor working away on a suit while the palace was almost destroyed from within was…

Well, I guess it was kind of funny. Kingdoms rose and fell, but fashion lived on.

At Maria Elena's helpful—and persistent—urging, I paired a silvery-gray dress shirt with the darker jacket and pants, then slipped on a pair of pale gray socks and the shiny new leather shoes that had appeared with the suit.

I put my well-heeled foot down at the suggestion of a tie, however. Having to go commando—yet again—was bad enough without a scrap of silk trying to choke me to death.

"How do I look?" I finally asked, having given up on styling my hair.

Maria Elena eyed me up and down and smiled. "Like the human who helped bring justice to Rome. Do you have any idea when you'll be heading back to San Diego?"

"That's part of what Lucia is meeting with the Council about, I think." What was left of the Council. Or… *most* of what was left of the Council. After the battle with Gaius, Jehane had been moved into the Tower to await the Council's punishment, and Lady Manassa had taken up position at the top of the long flight of stairs, just outside the prison's inner door. When I'd gone to speak with Divya, I'd found her seated there, telling Jehane stories of the son she had murdered. From all accounts, she was still there and still talking, her voice even and her words relentless.

The Lady Manassa was hard-freaking-core.

"Rome will be quieter without you and your mistress."

"That's a good thing, isn't it? Quiet?"

Maria Elena colored. "Yeah, I guess it kind of is. No offense."

"If you and Sabina ever get bored with your life of Italian luxury, I know a great place in San Diego to get fish tacos. I'd be happy to show you around town. Until then… stay in touch?"

"I'm on Instagram, Twitter, and Snapchat," she reminded me, "and you're following me on all three through the accounts I made for you. Staying in touch is *not* going to be a problem."

That felt a little bit like a threat.

○○○

The name of the restaurant was unpronounceable. The prices were astronomical. The spaghetti was… well, I'm pretty sure it was really, really good. But thinking back on that night, I don't remember the food. I don't remember the long, comfortable car ride into the city or even whether the night was hot or cold.

All I remember is Anastasia, seated across from me.

"You are quiet tonight, John."

"Just taking it all in, I think." I reached for my wine glass and barely avoided knocking it over. "And maybe a little bit nervous."

"Over the past week, you have argued an impossible case in court, imprisoned a sentient cloud of poisonous gas, and helped destroy my former mentor and an entire nest of the Illutu, yet *now* you're nervous?"

"I didn't do any of that alone… and I was nervous or terrified pretty much the whole time," I pointed out. "And this is different."

"Is it?" Ana's smile was breathtaking. "This is hardly our first meal together."

Which was true, but also not. This was our first dinner out since the whole matter of the blessing had been raised, and that seemed to be a very big difference. My heart had been racing from the moment Anastasia showed up at my suite door.

As presentable as I may have looked in my suit, the auburn-haired Secundus put my skinny-panted splendor to shame, sheathed in a deep green dress that flattered her long, elegant lines. A pale green shawl was draped over her shoulders to hide a plunging neckline and her silken hair was pinned up in an arrangement that appeared simple but probably wasn't. She looked every inch the heart-stopping woman who had saved me from crab assassins years earlier.

And yet… there was so much more to her than what my twenty-five-year-old self had seen. The power and control inherent in her graceful movements. The careful consideration that went into every spoken word. And most of all, the maelstrom of emotions—old anger, fresh grief, and something undefinable—swimming in her marvelous eyes.

"I'm sorry, Ana. About how it all turned out. I know—"

She shook her head. "For one night, Mr. Smith, let us put aside talk of such things. Let us just be two people out for a quiet dinner in one of the world's great cities." Her lips curved back again into that devastating smile. "It is a tale as old as time, I'm told."

"That…"

"Yes?" A delicate eyebrow arched.

"That's from *Beauty and the Beast.*"

"I am aware."

"I didn't realize you'd ever seen any Disney movies."

"Until several months ago, I had not."

"What changed?"

Her smile widened. "Someone informed me that you were prone to singing such songs in the shower. It seemed fair that I should at least know the words."

I was going to have words with Juliette.

○○○

Dessert was just as good as dinner, and equally impossible to remember. After signing away a small fortune to cover both meal and tip, Anastasia glanced up at me from across the table.

If I didn't know better, I'd have said she was… uncertain.

"John, I wanted to thank you for saving my life. Again."

"Considering you saved mine in the process…" I grinned briefly, but my next words were serious and heartfelt. "I'm starting to think that saving each other is what we do."

"It need not be the only thing we do."

"I'm sorry?" Yet again, I was the height of intelligent discourse.

"I have secured a hotel room two blocks away. If you don't feel the need to return to the palace tonight..." The pain and grief had left her eyes, leaving behind that undefinable other emotion and something I recognized as hunger. "...we could instead spend the night in the city."

I swallowed past the sudden lump in my throat, as my already racing heart threatened to burst right out of its chest. My voice tried—but failed—to match the femmepire's casual tone. "I think I've seen enough of the palace for one week. Are you sure...?"

Anastasia rose to her feet, the three-inch heels making her even taller than normal, and extended a hand to me. "I am certain. Come with me, Mr. Smith."

"Yes, ma'am."

ooo

If I'd been nervous for dinner, I was one step from terrified during our walk to the hotel. As I'd told Juliette—repeatedly, and with angry emphasis—I *wasn't* a virgin, but... six years of abstinence was like forty-something in dog years and Anastasia was entirely unlike any other woman I'd ever dated.

Which was probably a good thing, since those other relationships had ended in fiery wreckage.

The tension ratcheted even higher when we slipped into the elevator. Anastasia selected the floor and then turned to look at me. "John... relax. I am not going to bite."

From a vampire, that statement had two meanings, but neither one helped settle my nerves. "I'm sorry. It's been a while. A really, really, really long while."

"If you would prefer to wait...?"

"No!" I blushed and forced my voice back down to reasonable decibel levels. "No, thank you. Just give my nerves a second to settle."

"Perhaps I can be of assistance with that." She crossed the elevator, slid one hand around the back of my head, and brought my mouth down to hers.

For a woman who could turn into living stone, I was always shocked by how soft Anastasia's lips were. I kissed her back, hesitantly at first, and then harder as our mouths spread and her tongue tangled with mine.

Dimly, I felt the impact of my back against the elevator wall. Ana's strong arms pinned me there as she kissed me with a single-minded thoroughness that was as intoxicating as it was overwhelming.

Even when we came up for air, she stayed pressed against me, eyes peering up through long, dark eyelashes. "How are those nerves doing now, Mr. Smith?"

"I barely have enough blood in my brain to manage breathing," I told her honestly. "Nervousness is way beyond me at this point."

She pressed tighter against me, letting me feel every inch of her long, lovely body, and moved in for another kiss, when the elevator dinged.

"To be continued very, very soon." Anastasia peeled away, my hand in hers, and led me into the hall.

I shuffled awkwardly past the open-mouthed stares of the family of five that had been waiting for the elevator. Thankfully, there wasn't enough blood left above my waist for blushes either.

ooo

Before our hotel room door had finished closing, Anastasia and I were kissing again, my hands stroking the small of her back as hers worked to divest me of jacket and shirt. She tossed the shirt aside, then hesitated.

"If you need to take this more slowly…?" I offered, trying to guess at the source of her sudden hesitation.

"What? No." She tugged at her hair and it spilled down in auburn waves about her shoulders. "But before this goes any further…"

"Yes?"

She tapped the ring around my neck. "Lady Zhukova?"

Valentina materialized in our luxurious hotel room in her standard, old-fashioned nightgown. Still mostly transparent from the effort of manifesting in Minerva's city, she had nonetheless assured me that she was on her way to recovering from whatever the goddess had done to her. With a careful hand, she tugged aside her curls and looked questioningly at Anastasia.

A silent message passed between the two ladies. Valentina turned from the beautiful femmepire to my partially clad self, and a black-gummed smile spread across her small face. She floated over to me to brush a spectral kiss across my cheek, and then faded and was gone from view.

"Should I even ask what that was about?"

"I was merely asking your guardian for permission," said Anastasia, returning her attention to my pants.

"Permission?"

"And privacy for the night."

I was wrong: blushes weren't entirely beyond me yet.

It took us quite a while to get there, but I was eventually able to return the favor and relieve Anastasia of her clothes: that gorgeous dress, the matching heels, and the scraps of fabric that had so briefly served as lingerie. When she was finally naked, it was my turn to step away.

"John?"

"Just… let me enjoy this for a moment." Moonlight streamed through the suite's open curtains, joining the dim lighting to paint her long, lean body in peaks and shadowed valleys. Her eyes glowed in the half-darkness, both the jade of her iris and the ring of gold that circled her pupils. "You're so beautiful."

"Under your gaze, I almost feel it." Something mischievous sparked in her voice. "But if you are not back over here by the count of two, I forswear all responsibility for what occurs."

One part of my brain really wanted to find out exactly *what* that meant, but the rest of me was wisely already moving back into the femmepire's arms.

We moved to the bed, where the moderate difference in our heights ceased to be any kind of inconvenience at all. She rolled me onto my back, swung one long, sculpted leg across to straddle me, and then rose up like an angel looking down from heaven.

"I love you," I told her.

"Show me," she replied.

So, I did.

OOO

Five minutes later, I pulled myself back together enough to feel embarrassed. "That wasn't... I'm usually... uhm... I'm sorry."

Anastasia was nestled up against me. "It is okay, John. As you said, it had been a while. Between that and your rib injury..."

"Right. My ribs." Gaius had cracked them in the fight, but whatever weird symbiosis I now shared with Lucia meant they were already well on their way to being healed. The shortness of breath I'd been experiencing minutes earlier had nothing at all to do with my injury. "I don't suppose you managed to...?"

"I did not." The femmepire dropped a kiss on my lips and smiled. "But that is okay."

"How is it okay?" From where I was lying, it was anything but.

"Because you are a human man in your twenties." A cool hand slid down my chest, past my abdomen, to curl about my dude parts, where my body's immediate response made it clear that—earlier misfires be damned—it remained ready and willing for further engagements. "And it will be better the second time."

She was right.

CHAPTER 58

IN WHICH THE WORLD SOMEHOW KEEPS SPINNING

Between rounds two and three, a long and glorious night of sleep, and the morning shower that somehow, impossibly gave rise to round four, it was noon by the time Anastasia and I made it downstairs to the hotel restaurant for an early lunch.

Lucia was waiting.

The queen's polished appearance was a far cry from the clothes we had hurriedly thrown on and the ongoing natural disaster of my hair. Glacial blue eyes rolled skyward, and she gestured to the two free seats at her table.

If I'd been paying any attention to the bond, I'd have known Lucia was near, but I'd had slightly more important—and vastly more enjoyable—things on my mind. Luckily, not even the queen's unexpected appearance was enough to ruin my morning. I gave her a wide smile as Anastasia and I took our seats.

Lucia looked to Anastasia. "It was satisfactory then?"

"It was. Mr. Smith shows… significant potential," replied Ana with a smile of her own.

Lucia gave me a puzzled once-over. "I will have to take your word for it."

"Aren't you going to ask *me* if it was satisfactory?"

Lucia rolled her eyes a second time. "You are human and male. Of course it was."

"Honestly, *satisfactory* is kind of underselling it—"

Lucia's golden hand waved me to silence. "I do not wish to hear any more of it. Nor do I need to, given that our bizarre mutation of a bond is wide open, and you know absolutely *nothing* about shielding."

I frowned. What the hell did that—oh. "You mean…?"

"Yes." Lucia shuddered, mouth curling downward in momentary displeasure. A mix of revulsion, distaste, and—weirdly enough—melancholy echoed through the bond. "I am all too aware of how you felt through the *entirety* of your activities last night. *And* this morning." She shuddered again. "My mind may never be clean again."

"Now you know how I felt after your dream with the incubus," I muttered.

"Yes. The incubus." Ice entered Lucia's tone.

Anastasia raised an eyebrow and some of the relaxation faded from her body. "Has there been word?"

"The Horned God is occupied elsewhere, but I am told he will return to Rome eventually," said Lucia. She shrugged and visibly forced herself to relax. "Such matters will take care of themselves, no doubt. We are gathered here for other reasons."

Reasons that apparently included grading my bedroom performance. Thank God I'd made a better showing of things after that initial disaster.

"Am I correct in assuming that this *arrangement* between the two of you will continue?" asked Lucia.

Anastasia and I glanced at each other and nodded.

"All the better then that I have made this decision."

"My queen?" I watched emotions chase themselves across Anastasia's lovely face as she puzzled through the other femmepire's words. "You're staying?"

"Wait… what?" I looked to Lucia for confirmation.

"I am. Our exile has been lifted."

"And your forced abdication?"

"Stands." Lucia's lush lips thinned with the anger that surged across our bond. "However, with the pretend-contessa's exposure and imminent death, there is an opening on the Council. Moreover, my niece cannot be confirmed to rule until she has fed, and even once she has done so, there are those on the Council who feel she will need a century or two of seasoning first."

Again, Anastasia deduced where Lucia was going with this.

"A regency?"

"Yes. I am the only individual left in Rome who was trained to rule. I will serve as regent until Sabina is ready to assume control."

"And you're okay with that?" I asked. "Her taking the crown?"

"I will be." Lucia could no doubt *feel* my own disbelief, but the eyes that met mine were introspective. "It is enough to have the world know that I was not responsible for my father's death. Besides," she added with an ice-sharp smile, "I will be queen in all but name for at least the next century. And much can happen in that time. Which brings me to the two of you."

Oh shit. If Lucia was staying in Rome, then Anastasia…

"Lady Anastasia Dumenyova," said Lucia, her voice quiet yet suddenly ringing with authority, "I relieve you of your duties as my Secundus for a period not to exceed one century in length."

"My queen?"

"Go and live your life, Asya, with my blessing. Love your human… somewhere far, far away from me so I am not kept awake by his pleasure. When Mr. Smith is dust, as all humans must eventually become, I will be awaiting your return."

I didn't really love this talk of me turning to dust, to be honest.

"And what will you do for a Secundus in my absence?" Anastasia's words were guarded, her expression indecipherable.

"My uncle has agreed to serve in your stead." A rare, wry smile broke onto Lucia's face. "Though it is anyone's guess how well he will take instruction."

"Ana, if you want to stay…"

The former Secundus' eyes were uncertain as they met mine. "Yes, Mr. Smith?"

"Then we'll stay."

"It is not that simple…" She paused. "*We?*"

"Yeah. I suck at languages, but give me long enough, and I'm sure I'll be able to learn Italian."

"You would leave behind your friends and family? The agency?"

"Nobody's saying they couldn't visit from time to time. As for the agency, Juliette and our newly hired receptionist will be fine without me." The idea of leaving everything I knew was terrifying, but it wasn't like I hadn't already made that same decision back when we'd considered being on the run for the rest of our lives. "Maybe Rome could use another P.I.?"

Anastasia brushed her fingertips down my cheek in a lightning-fast maneuver that I barely felt, let alone saw. She turned to Lucia.

"One century, your majesty. I accept."

Lucia nodded, as if she had expected nothing less. And given that she had a four-century history with the other woman, maybe that was true. "If you would not mind procuring breakfast for us, there are things I must say to my thrall."

Anastasia rose from her chair to head for the tables laden with food. Only when she was on the far side of the noisy room did Lucia turn back to me.

"Treat her well, Mr. Smith. I gave her a century, but there is nothing to prevent her from returning sooner should you prove unsatisfactory."

"I'll do whatever I can to keep her happy."

"Do better than that," she hissed, "or they will find pieces of you scattered across the floor of two oceans."

"If you didn't think I was capable of making her happy, you wouldn't have let her go."

"I let her go because you were right." Lucia shook her head. "To stand between her and her love is to lose her forever. Only time will tell whether *you* are worthy of that sacrifice."

"Well, thank you anyway. And I'm sure we'll come back and visit at least a few times before I become dust."

"Before you do, you will have learned to shield even during the moment of release… or the two of you will have separate chambers for your visit!"

CHAPTER 59

The next morning found Anastasia and me back at Fiumicino Airport. In addition to Angel's hipster satchel and Juliette's garment bag, I now had a brand-new suitcase, stuffed with the wardrobe Lucia had gifted me. Anastasia, by contrast, had only a single roll-on suitcase to go along with the obscenely expensive purse hanging from her opposite shoulder.

"Did your goodbyes go okay this morning?" I asked as we waited in the security line.

"I had far fewer of them than you, Mr. Smith." Despite the words, her eyes danced. "When did you find time to befriend half the palace?"

"I think most of them were just happy I was leaving." I grinned. I'd gotten hugs from Maria Elena, Sabina, all three nagas, and Sergei himself, along with—decidedly reluctant—smiles from Niccolo and Yovanna and what I had elected to interpret as *respectful* nods from Denarius and Caine. "If you weren't saying goodbye, where *did* you disappear to?"

"I was renewing acquaintances with an old rival." Anastasia's smile was brilliant as she passed a business card over to me.

I looked down at it. Any hopes that my mutated bond would allow me to read Italian were quickly dashed. "What is it?"

"The name, number, and address of the tailor who created Dulcinea's dress," she said, smile deepening. "The next time I am in Rome, I will meet with him to see how he can top this dress of scarves you liked so much."

Best. Girlfriend. Ever.

○○○

We were at the gate when my loaner phone rang.

"This is John."

"You mean you're not dead yet, little bird?"

"Juliette!" I beamed. "It's great to hear from you!"

"It… is?" I could hear her confusion even over the phone. "What time is it in Rome? Are you drunk?"

I traded glances with Ana. "It's mid-afternoon. I'm just happy."

"I guess your case is going well?"

"It's over, actually. Everything worked out—with a few bumps along the way and a ton of things I still have questions about. Regardless, Ana and I are boarding the plane in about forty minutes."

"Oh."

Something about that single syllable gave me pause.

"Is everything okay? You didn't decide to expand the agency even further without discussing it?"

"What? No. The contractors haven't even torn down the wall between offices yet."

"It's not my bed, is it?"

"Your bed is fine."

"The Corolla?"

"It's not your stupid car!"

Stupid car? That seemed uncalled for. "What's going on? Are you having issues closing the Superchargers case?"

"No, that's definitely closed."

"Really? You got proof that Rihanna Mariah Kardashian was cheating on Chief Tomlinson?"

"Actually, no," Juliette admitted. "It turns out you were right… she wasn't having an affair at all."

"That's fantastic!" Maybe it was all the recent sex coloring my perspective, but it felt like everything was turning up roses.

"Not so much, actually."

"It's not?" I frowned, slowly putting the pieces together for myself. "Wait… if she wasn't sleeping with the Chief's top advisors, then why was she meeting with them?"

There was nothing but silence on the line.

"Oh crap. She was planning a coup, wasn't she?"

"Got it in one, partner. With the backing of her former tribe."

"Jesus. What the hell is it with coups lately? From now on, whenever we investigate non-humans, we're going to *start* with the assumption of a coup and eliminate that possibility first." I sighed. "How did Chief Tomlinson take the news?"

"Uhm."

"You haven't told him yet?" I frowned again. "I know I said you should wait until you had solid evidence, but this is one of those times when it's better to be quick than thorough."

"I know that! In fact, I had Angel set up an appointment with the chief for last night."

"But…?"

"But they kicked off the coup yesterday afternoon."

The bottom fell out of my stomach. "Chief Tomlinson…?"

"Turns out he's every bit as ugly in death as he was in life."

Next to me, Anastasia was as concerned as I was. "Was the coup successful, Lady Middleton?"

"Only partly, Anastasia. They got the chief, but the loyal members of his tribe managed to drive the conspirators away."

"So, you're telling me that our client was killed by an unsuccessful coup which we found evidence of too late to warn him," I summarized with a sigh. That wasn't going to do the agency's reputation any good. "Well, that sucks, but it sounds like you did everything you could."

"You're damn right I did." Juliette cleared her throat. "There's one other thing though."

"If you tell me someone actually *did* steal the Corolla, I'm going to hang up," I threatened.

"I already told you that your car was fine! I'm still talking about the goblin tribes."

"Oh." I frowned for a moment. Chief Tomlinson had died, but the coup had failed. So, what… I opened my eyes wide and shook my head, as if the gesture could do anything to change reality. "Please don't tell me—"

"Yep. As of about an hour ago, the two tribes declared war."

Well, shit.

EPILOGUE

Almost a month after our departure, word came that the Horned God's corpse had been found just outside of Venice. There was no evidence of who had killed him, nor witnesses to suggest why.

A week later, Anastasia returned to San Diego.

AUTHOR'S NOTE

The Italian Screwjob is probably the longest book I'll ever write, but it didn't start out that way. Somehow, as I wrote it, and rewrote it, and rewrote it again, it just kept growing, not unlike a certain manpire from the Steppes. Over years of editing, I've made as many cuts as I could, but eventually reached a point where I just didn't want to chop it down further.

And so, here we are… John's first trip to Europe, his first murder mystery, his first (and second, third, fourth, etc.) time with Anastasia, and his very first taste of the greater supernatural world.

We will see a lot of the characters introduced in this book again, but the next book, *A Dead Man's Favor,* will be set back in San Diego, as a certain zombie prince gives John a job, the goblin war threatens to spill out into the open, the mess that is Lucia's former House continues to spawn new problems, and John and Anastasia investigate the coincidences, conspiracies, and mysteries that have started to pile up over the course of the last four books. It's all building to something, I promise.

In the meantime, if you're looking for something a little darker to read, please check out my post-apocalyptic superhero trilogy, *The Murder of Crows*, which starts with *See These Bones.* While the trilogy itself is complete, a stand-alone novel featuring one of that series' standout characters will be coming soon.

Finally, if you enjoyed *The Italian Screwjob* and the continuing adventures of one thoroughly ridiculous P.I. and mediator, please consider leaving a review! As an indie author, I depend heavily on word of mouth and the feedback and support of readers like you.

Thank you!

ABOUT THE AUTHOR

Chris began life as a gleam in someone's eye, but birth and childhood were quick to follow. He's been fortunate enough to live in Spain, Germany, and all over the United States of America, and is busy planning a tour of the distilleries of Scotland.

A graduate of the Johns Hopkins University's Writing Seminars program, he put that degree to ill use for twenty years as a software engineer but has finally circled back around to the idea of writing for a living.

Chris currently lives in Nevada with his angelic wife and ever-expanding whisky collection and occasionally ventures outside to peer upwards, mutter to himself about 'day stars', and then scurry back into the house.

The Italian Screwjob is his seventh novel and the fourth book in *The Many Travails of John Smith*. Chris frequently shares updates on his author website at https://christullbane.com.

www.ingramcontent.com/pod-product-compliance
Lightning Source LLC
Chambersburg PA
CBHW060721190726
48285CB00001B/10